T0388662

Stravinsky and the Musical Body:
Creative Process and Meaning

Specvlvm Mvsicae

Edendum Curavit
Roberto Illiano

Volume XLV

Publications of the Centro Studi Opera Omnia Luigi Boccherini
Pubblicazioni del Centro Studi Opera Omnia Luigi Boccherini
Publications du Centro Studi Opera Omnia Luigi Boccherini
Veröffentlichungen des Centro Studi Opera Omnia Luigi Boccherini
Publicaciones del Centro Studi Opera Omnia Luigi Boccherini
Lucca

Stravinsky and the Musical Body

Creative Process and Meaning

Massimiliano Locanto

BREPOLS

TURNHOUT

MMXXI

The present volume has been published with the generous support of the

UNIVERSITÀ DEGLI STUDI DI SALERNO

(Dipartimento di Scienze del Patrimonio Culturale – DISPAC)

FONDATION
IGOR STRAVINSKY

www.fondation-igor-stravinsky.org

THE ROBERT CRAFT IGOR STRAVINSKY FOUNDATION

© BREPOLS 2021

All rights reserved. No part of this publication may be reproduced,
stored in a retrieval system, or transmitted, in any form or by any means,
electronic, mechanical, photocopying, recording, or otherwise, without
the prior permission of the publisher.

D/2021/0095/348

ISBN 978-2-503-59778-2

Printed in Italy

Contents

FOREWORD   ix

Acknowledgements   xii

Notes on Musical Examples,

    Abbreviations and Conventions   xiii

CHAPTER ONE

In Search of the Musical Body   1

    Part I: Body, Voice, and Music in Stravinsky's Theatre

        Premise: Stravinsky's Bodily Topics   1

        The Emergence of an Anti-Realistic Vision of the Body   4

        Against *Logos*   12

    Part II: Analytic Issues

        Music Analysis, Meaning, and Embodiment:

            The Problem of 'Formalist' Analysis   23

        Music Gestures as Energetic Continuities   26

        An Example: *Variations for Orchestra*   29

        Source for the Choreo-Musical Analysis: Some Issues   43

        The Firebird between Tradition and 'Reconstruction'   50

        A Collaboration Reconsidered   58

CHAPTER TWO

Representing the Body in *The Firebird*   63

    A Collaborative Project   63

    Excursus: Composing Music in the 'Old' Ballet   82

Composing Music for a 'New' Ballet   89

A 'New' Collaborative Method   97

Words, Gestures, Movements   105

Movements, Actions, Processions   116

'Improvising' Ballet Music   125

'Improvising' with Leitmotifs   144

Opposite Characters, Opposite Bodies   172

Conclusion: After *The Firebird*   191

CHAPTER THREE

«Il ne faut pas mépriser les doigts»:

Composing with Hands, Composing with Intervals   195

  Part I: Composing with Hands

        The 'Musical Idea' and the 'Composer's Mind'   195

        The Body and the Hands: A Theoretical Framework   199

        From Keyboard to Paper: Improvisation and Composition   205

        Piano vs Orchestra?   215

        Ways of the Hand, Keys, Steps   219

        Symmetries over the Keyboard:

                From Rimsky-Korsakov to Stravinsky   226

        A '*Danse*' of the Hands   238

  Part II: Composing with Intervals

        'Change of Life'   252

        What Is a Motif?   256

        From Steps to Rows   263

        From Motifs to Rows   269

        From Rows to Motifs   276

        Movements... over the Keyboard   285

        Conclusion: Theory and Practice   295

CHAPTER FOUR

Supernatural Beings, Human Bodies:

The Flood as an Anti-Realistic Television Opera   299

    Intellectuals and Mass Culture   300

    A Collective Work   305

    Between Theatre and Television: The Problem of 'Realism'   318

    Different Styles, Different Bodies   327

    From Heaven to Earth   345

BIBLIOGRAPHY   365

INDEX OF NAMES   393

FOREWORD

THE IDEA THAT THE BODY and embodiment play an essential role in music has recently stimulated a wide range of new musicological approaches. Music, in fact, can be seen as something that is both created and experienced through the body. It can also 'represent' or 'stand for' a vision of the body, and this is probably one of the most basic reasons why music is so 'meaningful' for us, since meaning itself is grounded in the body, as many cognitive scientists and linguists would nowadays maintain. Moreover, if we think of the body as a cultural construct, music can contribute to its 'construction' in the same way as other artistic practices in which the body is more obviously involved, such as dance, acting, or theatrical costumes. Some might even argue that music influences the very bodies of those who create or perform it, or at least modifies their perception of their own corporeality.

This book attempts to apply these insights to the music of one of the most 'bodily' composers of all time: Igor Stravinsky[1]. In keeping with the idea of a two-way relationship between music and body (whereby the former is created through the latter, but the latter can be 'constructed' by the former) the term « Musical Body » contained in my title can be read in two senses: a vision of the body which is created, evoked, and 'meant' by Stravinsky's music; and as the bodily dimension of Stravinsky's musical creativity (how he composed the music through his body). For this reason, I have added the subtitle « Creative Process and Meaning ».

An anti-realistic view of the performer's body — two-dimensional, flattened, angular, puppet-like (as in *Petrushka*) — had important consequences for Stravinsky's music: it affected the stylistic and formal aspects of his work. Its discontinuous formal conception, made of static blocks sharply and abruptly juxtaposed, appears as the equivalent of the broken and angular movements of a performing body. There is a two-way relationship between Stravinsky's music and this anti-naturalistic vision of the bodily attributes: the music has interjected this vision into its own structures, but at the same time the music itself contributes to creating a corporeal dimension which is partly real (i.e. corresponding to the concrete

---

[1]. My approach and the title of my book may recall Elizabeth Le Guin's well known book on Luigi Boccherini (LE GUIN 2006). However, beside some obvious analogies and our common interest in the body as a source of music knowledge, Le Guin's 'carnal' approach and object of interest are quite different from mine. They are essentially aimed at the music Boccherini wrote for his own performance as a concert artist.

physicality of the staged bodies) and partly virtual (i.e. created by the music alone in the mind of the listener). Ultimately, it evokes a bodily quality even when no visible body is present, as in purely instrumental music.

Each of Stravinsky's works, one could say, represents, constructs, or evokes a different vision of the body, and each, therefore, would deserve a detailed and in-depth discussion. While for some works such as *Petrushka* and, above all, the *Rite of Spring*, there is already a considerable amount of literature that deals with this topic, other works remain less (or little) addressed from this point of view[2]. In this book, the focus is directed at two works: *The Firebird* and *The Flood*. Of course, much has been written and said on Fokine's choreography for *The Firebird*, and on its relationship with Stravinsky's ballet score. However, the focus of previous studies has rarely been on how Stravinsky's music represents the staged bodies. This is probably because of *The Firebird*'s evident ties to nineteenth-century ballet music, which prevent this score from having such modernist features as those of *Petrushka* and *Rite of Spring*. This led scholars to underestimate excessively its importance in the evolution of Stravinsky's musical language. As for *The Flood*, it is a very little-known and little-studied work, and not only from the point of view of the subject of this book.

Nonetheless, these are two interesting works from my point of view, for two reasons: in *The Firebird* the foundations of what was to become Stravinsky's typical approach to the representation of the body were laid, and this will be the fundamental thesis of Chapter two. Secondly, the large space devoted to *The Firebird* in this book (Part II of Chapter One also dwells largely on this ballet) reflects my conviction that this work was much more important for the development of Stravinsky's music than has been usually recognized. *The Flood*, for its part, summarizes and epitomizes many typical ways in which Stravinsky's music constructs different, even contrasting, types of bodies.

Overall, therefore, the second and fourths chapters address the way in which music contributes to constructing a culturally-situated idea of the body: male or female, eastern or western, graceful or grotesque, beautiful or ugly, human or divine, tangible or intangible; and even a visible or invisible body. However, how music represents and constructs the body is just one of the two main topics in this book: the second is how the body contributes to the creation of the music. The third chapter deals with the role of the body — or more precisely the role of the hands and fingers, given that Stravinsky usually composed at the piano — in Stravinsky's creative process. Several sections of Chapter Two are also dedicated to this topic, describing the 'improvisational' technique employed in *The Firebird*, in which Stravinsky's bodily approach to the piano plays a fundamental role.

---

[2]. On the *Rite of Spring* see for example the essays contained in the first part ('Dancing *Le Sacre* Across a Century') of Neff – Carr – Horlacher 2017. See also Levitz 2004.

The order of the four chapters roughly reflects the chronology of the compositions examined. Chapter Three is divided into two parts, of which the first is dedicated principally to *The Rite of Spring*, and the second part addresses the last serial compositions. Chapter Four is devoted to Stravinsky's final composition for the stage — speaking in a broad sense as *The Flood* was originally conceived for the television stage. Chapter One, on the other hand, serves as a general introduction to the theme of the book, introducing the reader to some issues concerning Stravinsky's music in general. I titled this chapter 'In Search of the Musical Body', and this 'research' is aimed in two directions: historically, in the cultural roots of Stravinsky's theatre; and, analytically, within his scores. The chapter is thus divided into two parts according to these two distinct approaches: the first concerns the way in which the theatrical experience favoured the development of a propensity towards an anti-realist mode of representation of the body, and a tendency (that I have defined as anti-logocentric) to divorcing verbal language from bodily (and musical) expression. The second part deals with some general issues concerning the analysis of the works in which music and dance interact: firstly, how to analyse the relationship between music and bodily movement; secondly, the problem of the sources of a choreo-musical spectacle; and thirdly, the collaboration between choreographer and composer. In the last two parts *The Firebird* is considered as a case study. In this way the end of Chapter One serves as an introduction to the following chapter, entirely devoted to this ballet.

I avoided starting this book with a theoretical discussion on embodied cognition, which is nonetheless an important aspect underlying my discourse, particularly with regard to the creative process. Even so, I have addressed the question several times throughout the book, especially in the first part of the third chapter. The approach of many sections of the book is essentially a historical-musicological one. Some sections, nonetheless, go deeper into a close reading of the score. Even in these instances, however, analyses invite readers to go 'beyond' the musical text, and to grasp the bodily meanings associated with musical forms and structures. In so doing, they suggest overcoming such rigid dichotomies as formalist/contextualist, or historical/analytical.

The structure and concept of this book is the result of reflections (and sometimes of second thoughts) on what I have been writing on Stravinsky's music over the years. Some sections of the book draw their substance from earlier essays of mine in which the bodily aspects were mainly addressed only in a marginal way. Over time, I realized that the central issue towards which all my reflections converged was, in fact, the body. Therefore, I have reconsidered my former ideas in the light of this new insight and, as a result, the original essays have often been entirely rethought and rewritten.

Massimiliano Locanto

Acknowledgements

The present volume has been possible with the assistance of the Dipartimento di Scienze del Patrimonio Culturale – DISPAC of the Università degli Studi di Salerno, the Foundation Igor Stravinsky (Geneva) and The Robert Craft Igor Stravinsky Foundation. My initial thanks, therefore, go to Luca Cerchiai (Head of DISPAC), Marie Iellatchitch-Stravinsky and to the Board of the RCIS Foundation.

I would like to thank the friends and colleagues with whom, over the years, I had many exchanges of ideas: Valérie Dufour, Tatiana Baranova Monighetti, Gianmario Borio, Maureen Carr, Susanne Franco, Graham Griffiths, Stephanie Jordan, Michela Niccolai, Susanna Pasticci, Patrizia Veroli, and Gianfranco Vinay.

I gratefully acknowledge the Paul Sacher Stiftung (Basel) — in particular Heidy Zimmermann — for giving me permission to publish transcriptions and reproductions of documents held in the Stravinsky Collection; the Pierpont Morgan Library — especially Kaitlyn Krieg — for providing me with a digital copy of Stravinsky's autograph short-score of *The Firebird*; Boosey & Hawkes Music Publishers Ltd. for giving me permission to reproduce some musical excerpts from *The Flood*, *Requiem Canticles* and *Movements*; Joysanne Sidimus for kindly providing me some pictures from her private archive.

Many thanks are also due to John Moore and David Force, for their assistance with some revisions of the English text.

A special thanks to the Centro Studi Opera Omnia Luigi Boccherini's staff: Roberto Illiano, general editor of the 'Speculum Musicae' series, Massimiliano Sala and Fulvia Morabito for their ready acceptance of the idea of this book, and for their work on the editing and layout of the volume... but especially for patiently waiting for my final manuscript for five long years!

Finally, a very special thanks to my wife Federica and my son Giulio, my best supporters.

Foreword

Note on Musical Examples, Abbreviations and Conventions

• References to rehearsal numbers of scores in the main text and in the examples are within square brackets. For instance: «[3]» = rehearsal number 3 of the score.

A number preceded by '+' or '−' after a rehearsal number indicates the bars after or before that rehearsal number. For instance:

[3] − 2 : indicates two bars before rehearsal number 3 of the score;

[3] + 2 : indicates two bars after rehearsal number 3 of the score.

• Instrumental and scoring abbreviations are given according to Boosey & Hawkes conventions (<https://www.boosey.com/downloads/BH_StandardAbbreviations_New.pdf>).

• The classification and pitch numbering of the octatonic collections used in this book are the same as in Van den Toorn 1983 (see also Van den Toorn 1987 and Van den Toorn – McGinness 2012): each of the three octatonic collections (Labelled I, II, and III)[3] is organized as Model A (beginning with semitone, ascending) and Model B (beginning with tone, descending):

Model A (ascending)

Intervals:		1		2		1		2		1		2		1	
Collection I	*e*		*f*		*g*		*a♭*		*b♭*		*b*		*c♯*		*d*
Collection II	*f*		*f♯*		*g♯*		*a*		*b*		*c*		*d*		*e♭*
Collection III	*f♯*		*g*		*a*		*b♭*		*c*		*d♭*		*e♭*		*e*
Pitch numbering (= no. of semitones):	0		1		3		4		6		7		9		10

Model B (descending)

Intervals:		2		1		2		1		2		1		2	
Collection I	*e*		*d*		*c♯*		*b*		*b♭*		*a♭*		*g*		*f*
Collection II	*f*		*e♭*		*d*		*c*		*b*		*a*		*g♯*		*f♯*
Collection III	*f♯*		*e*		*e♭*		*d♭*		*c*		*b♭*		*a*		*g*
Pitch numbering (= no. of semitones):	0		2		3		5		6		8		9		11

---

3. If the overall pitch content is considered, only three different octatonic collections exist.

Chapter One

In Search of the Musical Body

Part 1: Body, Voice, and Music in Stravinsky's Theatre[1]

Premise: Stravinsky's Bodily Topics

In Stravinsky's music the body is implied in different ways and on different levels. His musical forms often 'mean', so to speak, a cultural construction of the body, This statement may seem paradoxical for a composer who went down in the history of music for his 'formalist' aesthetic claim that «music is, by its very nature, essentially powerless to express anything at all, whether a feeling, an attitude of mind, a psychological mood, a phenomenon of nature, etc.»[2]. Such statements have created a distorted image of Stravinsky as a composer radically disinterested in the expressive potential of music. However, besides the well-known fact that Stravinsky's aesthetic convictions, formulated under the influence of other thinkers and ghost-writers, correspond only to a limited extent to the actual characteristics of his music, it is evident that even Stravinsky's famous statement did not intend to deny the expressive nature of music, but rather to distance the composer from the romantic vision of music as a vehicle for the Subject's self-expression.

In fact, in recent years, Stravinsky's compositions have been increasingly considered in terms of the meanings conveyed by music. This orientation can even be seen among many scholars inclined to an analytical approach. Joseph Straus, for example, devoted an entire chapter of his monograph on Stravinsky's serial music to what he calls «expressive» or «symbolic associations»[3]. Drawing on the topic theory of music as defined by the studies of the music of the Classical period by Leonard Ratner, Kofi Agawu and Robert Hatten, Straus compiled a

---

[1].   A shorter version of this section has been published as Locanto 2021a.

[2].   *Autobiography*, p. 53.

[3].   Straus 2001, pp. 183-248.

complete list of meaningful topics that recur in Stravinsky's music[4]. Many of them can be also described as particular ways of 'meaning' a vision of the body. For example: the conclusion through the gradual increase of the rhythmic values, the progressive lengthening of the ostinato, or the fragmentation of the main melodic ideas — as happens for example in the last measures of *Les Noces*, *Apollon musagète*, *Symphony in C*, *Requiem Canticles*, and many other (mostly neoclassical) works — is described by Straus as a way to represent «Ecstatic transcendence; opening out into the infinite; a time beyond time»[5]. However, this musical topic has strong bodily connotations, as it is based on the analogical correspondence between the structures of music and those of some lived processes that lead to a progressive dilation of the perception of time. In this sense it seems to represent a sublimated, ecstatic and aethereal vision *of the body*: an 'incorporeal body', so to speak, living outside time. This bodily connotation is typical of many works from the neoclassical period. Similarly, just to consider another musical topic described by Straus, the use of the continuous repetition of two notes (or two chords) on an oscillatory-pendular rhythm, as can be seen, for example, in the opening music of *Œdipus Rex*, or in the angelic *Te Deum* of *The Flood*, described by Straus as a means for «somber muteness in the face of death», was a typical way for Stravinsky to represent a «rhythmically regulated» body (we will see shortly the origin of this idea in the theatre of the early twentieth century), characterized by a laconic, essential and «ritual» gestural expressiveness[6]. This association is based on the analogy with a structure of the perception of our body as located in the temporal dimension: the continuous repetition of a bodily movement at regular intervals of time. In Chapter 4 of this book we will see many topical associations of this kind, which are typical of an 'ecstatic' and 'immaterial' representation of the divine figures of *The Flood*.

Other topics described by Straus refer to stylistic-musical types: canonical writing, contrapuntal or imitative styles, homophony, etc. The 'expressive associations' of these styles are clearly based on the meaning that they have traditionally assumed in Western musical culture[7]. Their bodily connotation becomes evident when they are placed by Stravinsky within a specific musical context. In many serial compositions, for example, homophonic writing becomes a topical musical gesture to express a 'self-possessed' and composed body, moving with solemn calm. The prototype of this association is undoubtedly the instrumental choir placed at the end of *Symphonies of Wind Instruments*.

Other topical associations described by Straus are conventional ways of representing the characters or the dramatic situations in some theatrical-musical traditions. The association

---

[4]. See Straus' Table 5.1 (*ibidem*). The studies on musical topics I am referring to are Ratner 1980, Agawu 1991; Hatten 1994.
[5]. Straus 2001, p. 187.
[6]. *Ibidem*, pp. 228-237
[7]. *Ibidem*, pp. 214-221.

of octatonic and chromatic harmonies with the sphere of the magical, the supernatural, the artificial, and the evil, as opposed to the diatonic sounds associated with the human, natural, real, benign, etc. is a well-known feature of 19th-century Russian opera, which Stravinsky inherited and reinterpreted in various ways in his theatrical music[8]. However, in Chapters Two and Four of this book we will see how this venerable theatrical convention is used by Stravinsky to construct different visions of the performing bodies: occidental *vs.* oriental, natural *vs.* artificial, human *vs.* superhuman, corporeal *vs.* incorporeal, etc.

Clearly enough all these 'bodily topics' do not apply only to Stravinsky's music for theatre and dance, but to all his compositions, even those in which the music is not associated with visible performing bodies on stage. Nonetheless, from the point of view of their genesis within the evolution of Stravinsky's musical language, we can say that they derive ultimately from Stravinsky's theatrical experiences, especially with ballet. This idea is by no means new: scholars have long noticed how the most typical formal and stylistic features of Stravinsky's music began as a response to theatrical needs. Jann Pasler, for example, demonstrated that many features that later became typical of Stravinsky's modernist musical language were born, in his first two ballets, as a way to find a musical equivalent to certain dramaturgical situations[9]. Stravinsky's characteristic block-form — the juxtaposition of distinct musical blocks within a discontinuous form — was associated, according to Palser, with the rapid succession on the stage of contrasting characters and elements without a clear underlying developing narrative structure. The opening scene of the St. Petersburg fair in *Petrushka* is emblematic: each character or group of characters on stage — the revellers, the organ player, the farmer with the bear, the magician with the puppets, etc. — is associated with different melodic material, which is used each time in a more or less complete way. Consider, for example, the musical material associated with the revelers: a first fragment of only three bars appears in the bass at no. [2] of the score; a larger fragment, of eight bars, is at no. [3], still in the bass; finally the whole theme is presented by the whole orchestra at n. [5]. The association of this melody with the revellers is confirmed by its return to no. [20], concomitant with the indication of the return to the stage of this group of characters. In this way, alternating various fragments with a different temporal duration, Stravinsky generated a form characterized by a type of global 'rhythm', according to a logic that in many ways resembles that of cinematographic editing.

However, in such interpretations the emphasis has been usually placed on 'dramatic' or 'scenic' needs, rather than on performing bodies in themselves. What we should better understand, instead, is how the musical materials and their formal features represent some aspect of the staged bodies and contribute to the construct of their corporeality.

---

[8]. STRAUS 2001, pp. 221-228.
[9]. PASLER 1986, pp. 51-81.

3

To better understand the many aspects of Stravinsky's musical language, therefore, one should focus on his particular vision of the performing body, as it was shaped by his theatrical experience. From this point of view, two fundamental elements can be recognized:

- a tendency towards the vision of the body strongly connoted in an anti-realist sense;
- the tendency to dissociate (rather than merge in an 'illusionistic' way) the expressiveness of the body from other expressive modes (verbal language, music).

In the following pages, therefore, I will try to show how both these trends arose in the context of Stravinsky's musical theatre, also based on other theatrical experiences and models of the early twentieth century.

The Emergence of an Anti-Realist Vision of the Body

The first 'anti-realist' aspect of Stravinsky's treatment of the body can be seen in the unconventional way in which bodily expressiveness is associated with (or dissociated from) the other means of expression in his theatrical works: music and spoken (or sung) text. The ever-changing ways in which music, words and bodily gestures interact in Stravinsky's works for the stage is probably what most contributes to making each of them appear *sui generis*. It is as if Stravinsky was always looking for new ways of combining and amalgamating these components. This also raises certain theoretical questions: first, apart from to the too general and indistinct definition of 'musical theatre', to which genre do Stravinsky's stage works, leaving aside those clearly classifiable as ballets, belong? Secondly, what were the models for such an array of wildly contrasting theatrical experiments? As for the first question, terms such as 'semi-operatic', 'quasi-operatic' and the like have been frequently used. However, such definitions are not terribly accurate. In addition to being rather vague, they do not reflect the great variety of Stravinsky's formal solutions. Works like *Historie du soldat* or *Renard* are quite distinct from any existing operatic or semi-operatic genre. Stravinsky himself sometimes used traditional genre labels, such as opera, oratorio, *mélodrame* and the like. However, these labels can hardly be conceived as true definitions of genre, applicable to entire groups of works. Their function was only to highlight any analogy with the forms or conventions of some music theatrical genre(s?) of the past. For example, the label 'opera-oratorio' in *Œdipus Rex* tells us that in this work the particular use of the soloists and the choir, and the minimizing of acting and theatrical gesture, recalls in part the conventions of a nineteenth-century Italian opera and in part those of a baroque Oratorio. Furthermore, to take another example, the label *mélodrame* tells us that the use of a speaking — not singing — voice and also of pantomime for the title-character of *Perséphone* recall the conventions of the late eighteenth- and early nineteenth-century French and German *mélodrames* (Engl. 'melodramas'), a genre where a spoken recitation, and sometimes pantomime, were alternated with and accompanied by commenting instrumental music.

Clearly enough, therefore, Stravinsky's theatrical output, if considered in its entirety, is hardly conceivable on the basis of a shared, consolidated and stable system of genres, but rather on an aesthetic principle, according to which the meaningful components of the spectacle (music, words and gestures) are conceived as independent components which can be combined in different ways, which is to say as dissociable and — for this same reason — as variously combinable components. We can therefore think of Stravinsky's stage works (including ballet) as a *continuum* of different solutions; on the one hand those in which music, singing and acting are combined and used according to the conventions of traditional opera (*The Rake's Progress* and *Mavra*), while on the other 'pure' (traditional, classical) ballet, where singing is not involved, and in between these there is a variety of different combinations of music, dance, singing and acting.

In addition to reconfiguring the ways in which the various artistic means are combined, Stravinsky's theatre is based on a redefinition of their hierarchical relationships. The importance traditionally attached to the various artistic components in the production of meaning is modified and, in some ways, subverted: the expressive function of the word regresses in favour of the bodily expression and, more in general, the visual components of the spectacle.

From the point of view of the history of culture, these features of Stravinsky's theatre are in keeping with a general tendency to overcome the naturalist/realistic theatrical model, which was quite widespread in European theatre at the beginning of the twentieth century. We can cite in this context several experiments by authors and theatre practitioners from all over Europe, such as Gordon Craig, Adolphe Appia, Georg Fuchs, Vsevolod Meyerhold, Jacques Copeau, Luigi Pirandello and many others. Albeit in different ways and at different times, they all reacted against the naturalism and realism that had so far dominated their respective national theatrical cultures, by conceiving of various «devices for keeping reality at a distance», as Georg Kaiser — who also wrote the libretto of Weill's first opera, *Der Protagonist* (first staged in 1926) — once described his own plays. Actually, the modernist critique of representational realism had characterized all forms of artistic expression — not only theatre — from the early decades of the century. Painting and literature itself were equally affected. In their search for anti-realistic theatrical models, many authors turned to folk, pre-literary, and non-Western sources: *commedia dell'arte*, mystery plays, fairground entertainments, popular festivals, circus, cabaret, Japanese theatre, and so forth[10]. Some of these authors, like Meyerhold and Copeau, also engaged through their writings in the debates over the potential and place of popular theatre[11]. As for Stravinsky, popular and 'rough' forms of spectacle were to remain a central and recurring feature of his music from *Petrushka* to *The Flood*[12]. We can find a similar interest in *commedia*

---

[10]. See Cross 2003, for the definition of «rough theatre».

[11]. See Milling – Ley 2000, pp. 55-58.

[12]. Cross 2003, p. 139, adopts the category of 'rough theatre', derived from Peter Brook's reflection.

dell'arte in Busoni, Francesco Malipiero and many other Italian and French composers of the inter-war period.

However, beyond this very basic anti-realistic common ground, the motivations, modalities, and the models for the rejection of realism were very different in each of the above-mentioned authors. Craig and Appia's experiments, for example, rejected a representational approach in favour of a vision of stage design as visual symbolism expressing the inner qualities and the atmosphere of the play by means of abstract structures made of figures, colours, textures and lights. In so doing, however, they were trying to realize Wagner's ideal of *Wort-Ton-Drama* by unifying the visual elements of his theatre with the poetic and musical. As such, their anti-naturalism came from a typically Wagnerian vision of art and theatre as a transcendent and mystic realm. This is not true of Meyerhold and Copeau's anti-realism, which emerged from an 'immanent' approach to the stage, conceived as a self-referential world with symbolic rules and expressive strategies of its own. Meyerhold referred to these rules as 'the basic laws of theatricality' and the 'primordial elements of theatre', and related them to the actor's skills: movement, pantomime and mask[13]. It is precisely in the context of this anti-realistic theatrical tradition — aimed at rediscovering an autonomous theatrical language by turning to the most fundamental source of theatricality: the actor's body — that we can put Stravinsky's theatrical music.

Stravinsky's anti-naturalist vision of the performing body was due largely to the influence of Diaghilev's artistic and literary symbolist entourage, which had already long embarked on the anti-realistic crusade when the composer entered the company. As early as 1902, Diaghilev's journal *Mir Iskusstva* (The World of Art) had hosted a long article by Valéry Bryusov, with the self-revelatory title *The Unnecessary Truth*. Written from a typically symbolist perspective, Bryusov's article criticized the naturalist methods of Stanislavsky's Moscow Art Theatre, and was recognised as one of the first formulations of the battle of the 'New Theatre' against stage naturalism. Significantly, in 1905 Bryusov would enter the 'literary bureau' charged with the planning of the repertory of Meyerhold's Theatre Studio.

Among Diaghilev's associates, the most decisive impulse for the composer's anti-naturalist tendencies came from the painter and designer Alexandre Benois, whose ideas about opera, ballet and theatre had, in turn, been stimulated by the experimental theatrical productions of Meyerhold[14]. However, there is some evidence that Stravinsky himself had already become aware of a new anti-realistic theatrical mentality from the very beginning of his association with Diaghilev's Ballets Russes. In 1911 he most probably came across the writings of the German stage director and theatrical reformer Georg Fuchs (1868-1949). In a letter to Andrey Rimsky-Korsakov (the elder son of Nikolay) of that year he highly recommended his friend to read the Russian translation of an article by Fuchs entitled *Tanets* (Dance), and all evidence suggests he

---

13. See for example BRAUN – PITCHES 2016, p. 152.
14. WALSH 1999, p. 170.

ILL. 1. Frontispiece of Georg Fuchs' *Die Schaubühne der Zukunft* (Das Theater. Eine Sammlung von Monographien, ed. by Carl Hagemann, 15).

had also came across Fuchs' major publications such as *Die Schaubühne der Zukunft* (1905: ILL. 1), and *Die Revolution des Theaters* (1909), that may easily have formed part of his father's library[15]. The echo of Fuchs' anti-realistic production at the Munich Artists' Theatre, and his theoretical writings exerted a decisive influence over the Russian theatrical and musical world. Diaghilev himself met Fuchs during the Ballets Russes' tour in Munich in April 1911 and drew inspiration from him regarding some stage solutions for the famous 1912 production of *L'Après-midi d'un faune* at

---

[15]. FUCHS 1905; FUCHS 1909. The letter to Andrey Rimsky-Korsakov is in DYACHKOVA 1973, pp. 463-464 and VARUNTS 1997, pp. 300-301. Fuchs' article *Tanets* was published in a volume entitled *Fial' Strastey* (St. Petersburg, Venok, 1910, pp. 59-96). See WALSH 1999, p. 590, n. 11. Walsh could not trace the German original of the article. For a brief account of the vicissitudes of Fyodor Stravinsky's library see e.g. BARANOVA MONIGHETTI 2013, pp. 61-63.

the Théâtre du Châtelet[16]. Fuchs' *Die Schaubühne der Zukunft* proved to hold great sway over Meyerhold, as the extent of quotations from Fuchs' book in his writings clearly shows[17].

Fuch's writings were an important source for the rediscovery of the body in Russian early twentieth-century theatre. In so doing they also gave an important impulse to new, anti-realistic forms of theatre which downplayed the role of language and of the imitation of nature in favour of more immediate and fundamental sources of theatricality, such as the physicality of the actors' bodies. Fuchs drew attention to what he considered one of the most important means of dramatic expression: the rhythmical movement of the human body in space. According to him, the actor's art had its origins in dance, and the extensive use of expressive movements of the body were exactly what differentiated acting from mere imitation of reality and everyday life:

> An agony is imposed on the artist when he is bound by inarticulate rules to the narrowed, useful movements of everyday life. Even the speaker can barely master the urge for a freer symbolism in the gestures. For the actor, this urge is the bearer of all creativity. Remember that the actor's art has taken its origin from dancing. The expressive means of dance are also the natural means of the actor, and they differ from those of dance only in the amount of expressiveness. The closer to the rhythmically bound games of the parts in the dance, the better the actor will create, even though he should never quite become a dancer. The means of expression employed in the dance are equally the natural means of expression for the actor, the difference being merely one of range[18].

Given these premises, Fuchs called for the creation of a new culture and aesthetics of the body involving physical posture, gesture and language on which a social and racial identity could be imposed, thus counter-balancing a drive to the barbarization of the body in modern society. This was, for Fuchs, an indispensable prerequisite for the establishment of a genuine dramatic art. As a model for this bodily culture, Fuchs takes not only the choreo-musical practice of ancient Greece but also of Japanese theatrical tradition. He mentioned the theatre of Otojirō Kawakami (1864-1911) and his wife Sada Yacco, whose company had become famous

---

[16]. See SCHEIJEN 2009, p. 241. BELLOW 2016, p. 52, and fn. 124.

[17]. See BRAUN 1988, p. 48.

[18]. «Eine Qual wird dem Künstler aufgebürdet, wenn man ihn durch unkünstlerische Vorschriften an die eingeengten, nützlichen Bewegungen des Alltags kettet. Kann doch schon der Redner den Drang nach einer freieren Symbolik in den Geberden kaum bemeistern. Für den Schauspieler gar ist dieser Drang der Träger alles Schaffens. Erinnert euch, dass die Kunst des Schauspielers ihre Herkunft genommen hat vom Tanze. Die Ausdrucksmittel des Tanzes sind auch die natürlichen Mittel des Schauspielers, und sie unterscheiden sich von denen des Tanzes nur durch erweiterte Ausdrucksfähigkeit. Je näher dem rhythmisch gebundenen Spiele der Glieder im Tanze, um so Vollkommeneres wird der Schauspieler schaffen, wenn er auch niemals dabei ganz zum Tänzer werden soll». FUCHS 1905, p. 66. My translation.

in the West in the early twentieth century. Fuchs' interest in Japanese theatre depended on the importance that the rhythmically coordinated movements of the body played in it. In this kind of theatre, Fuchs maintained, there was no part that was not directed towards the enhancement of the overall rhythmical scheme, and this alone was able to reflect the dramatic content. The colour composition of the costumes and the setting had to accomplish the general 'rhythm', so to speak, which was created by the poses, the groupings and the movement of the actors:

> The art of a Kawakami and a Sada Yacco, which so wonderfully seized us, is unthinkable without the popular convention of race in matters of physical and linguistic education to expressive form. The Japanese actor does not cry, does not rave, it is hardly ever spoken aloud on the scene, there is hardly anything that goes beyond the good sound of the most distinguished society, yet the Japanese stage attains dramatic accents of an intensity of which we have no idea — purely by stylistic means. Whatever happens on the scene, whether it be the deepest unfolding of the fate of destiny, be it the most terrible thing that breaks our hearts, be it the most exuberant boastfulness and the most insolent grotesque, the bonds of dance rhythms are always preserved, just as the Japanese artist always keeps the regularity of the surface in woodcut[19].

The awareness of Fuchs' anti-realistic productions at the Munich Artist's Theatre and the reading of *Die Schaubühne der Zukunft* were instrumental in Meyerhold's rejection of all vestiges of realism and in his interest in the use of the body in theatre. Fuchs' writings drew Meyerhold's attention to Oriental theatre as a source of inspiration in the use of rhythmical bodily movements — Meyerhold also took as a paradigm the style of Sada Yacco.

Meyerhold's theatre was just one of the many Russian early twentieth-century theatrical experiences that drew fresh attention to the performer's bodily gestures and movements. One may mention, for example, Aleksandr Tairov's Moscow Chamber Theatre founded in 1914. Starting from experimentation on pantomime, Tairov had focused his attention on the body of the interpreter and on his emotional gesture to which he entirely entrusted the task of shaping the scenic dimension[20]. However, Meyerhold's theatrical productions were undoubtedly the

---

[19].   «Die Kunst eines Kawakami und einer Sada Yacco, die uns so wunderbar ergriff, ist undenkbar ohne die volkstümliche Konvention der Rasse in Dingen der körperlichen und sprachlichen Erziehung zur ausdrucksvollen Form. — Der japanische Schauspieler schreit nicht, tobt nicht, es wird kaum jemals laut gesprochen auf der Szene, es geschieht kaum etwas, was über den guten Ton der vornehmsten Gesellschaft hinausgeht, und dennoch erreicht die japanische Bühne dramatische Akzente von einer Intensität, von der wir gar keine Ahnung haben — rein durch stilistische Mittel. Was auch immer geschehen mag auf der Szene, sei es, daß uns das Walten des Schicksals im Tiefsten enthüllt wird, sei es das Furchtbarste, das uns im Innersten zerbricht, sei es tollste Ausgelassenheit und frechste Groteske: immer doch bleiben die Bindungen der Tanzrhythmik gewahrt, gerade so wie der japanische Künstler im Holzschnitt immer die Gesetzmäßigkeit der Fläche innehält». *Ibidem*, pp. 72-73. My translation.

[20].   On Tairov see Egidio 2005.

closest model to Stravinsky's theatre[21]. For Meyerhold, as for Stravinsky, the movements and gestures of the actors should not represent the mood or psychological state of the character. This is a very important premise to understand in Stravinsky's musical aesthetic as well. Movement for Meyerhold meant first and foremost rhythm, as in dance. In keeping with Fuchs' ideas, Meyerhold called for a static staging, unmarked by great differences of emotional and dramatic intensity, but rather by a uniform, regular flow, devoid of dramatic and expressive peaks. The movements of the bodies had to be limited to the essential, be rhythmically punctuated, and separated by large pauses and silences. All these features could be applied to Stravinsky's music as well. In the same way as Meyerhold (and Fuchs) conceived the actors' bodily movements as 'rhythmically regulated' movement that did not reflect either the dynamics, the processes and the inner psychological evolution of the characters, or the development of the narrated story, Stravinsky's static, non-developmental and strongly rhythmic musical materials are likewise imbued with meanings that do not represent the inner psychological development of the characters, but rather their way of moving and bodily expressiveness.

Fuchs' writings probably influenced Stravinsky in a direct way, not only through the mediation of other men of theatre. In the above-mentioned letter to Andrey Rimsky-Korsakov, he told his friend «I shall not rest until you have read this article and given me your opinion in writing with your signature attached, confirmed by the local police»[22]. In any case, in keeping with Fuchs' ideas about theatre originating in dance, Stravinsky, and more in general Diaghilev's artistic circle, gave pre-eminence to ballet over opera, and introduced ballet elements in operatic productions. After his first successful operatic enterprise in Paris with *Boris Godunov* (1908), *Ivan le terrible* (1909), *Rousslan et Ludmila* (first act only, 1909), and *Judith* (1909), Diaghilev had staged no new operas until 1914, when the completed version of *Khovanschina*, Rimsky-Korsakov's *Le Coq d'or* and Stravinsky's *Le Rossignol* were performed. The latter, however, clearly reflected the new anti-operatic stance that Diaghilev and his associates had now taken. Stravinsky himself had already stated in 1911 that ballet meant for him «more than any opera performance whatever»[23]; and in an interview for the *Peterburgskaya gazeta* on 27 September 1912 he stated: «In general, opera does not attract me at all. What interests me is choreographic drama, the only form in which I see any movement forward, without guessing at what the future may bring».

Even when Stravinsky first ventured on operatic terrain, with his completion of the three-act version of *Le Rossignol*, dance and mime were given a place of absolute prominence. Fuchs' advocacy of a theatre based on rhythmical movement was very close in spirit to what Stravinsky and Benois accomplished in 1914 for this opera. The idea of introducing into the operatic genre conventions and expressive modalities that were typical of ballet had already found expression

---

[21].   On the analogies between Stravinsky's and Meyerhold see especially WALSH 1993, pp. 18-19.

[22].   Quoted in WALSH 1999, p. 171.

[23].   VARUNTS 1997, pp. 290-294.

in Benois' 1914 staging of Rimsky-Korsakov's *Le Coq d'or*. Here Benois suggested having each role split into two: an unseen singer off-stage (in the pit or in the wings) and a dancer miming the actions onstage. In the end it was decided that the singers should be placed on a scaffold on either side of the stage. In this way mime and dance were set in the foreground and the opera resembled a sort of ballet with singing. The role of the Fisherman was sung from the orchestral pit and mimed onstage. The role of the Chinese Emperor was also almost purely choreographic. As for the *Nightingale*, it was decided that only a little figure of a bird had to be put on the stage, while its voice was entrusted to a coloratura soprano singing offstage.

In keeping with the Russian-Symbolist reception of Wagner, Fuchs also called for a kind of theatre conceived as a ritual in which performers and spectators — the stage and the auditorium — were not opposed to each other, but rather involved in a common experience. To this end he imagined a performing space where the audience could be in the closest possible proximity to the stage. The proscenium had to be wide rather than deep and divided into three superimposed levels joined by steps, the lowest of which, located in front of the proscenium opening, extended in a shallow arc into the auditorium. The middle stage was used only in the case of crowd scenes or to facilitate rapid scene changes. Alternatively, a painted backdrop was laid behind the rear stage, but without creating any illusion of perspective, merely as a flat background, against which the performers moving on the narrow space of the forestage stood like figures in a bas-relief.

Flattened stage perspectives and constrained bodily movements of the performers were a distinctive hallmark of new Russian theatre. A number of theoretical discussions about the new staging methods had begun appearing from the early years of the century. In 1900 *Mir iskusstva* had published Maurice Maeterlinck's essay on 'Contemporary Drama'. In 1909 the review *Apollon* hosted Georg Fuchs' theory of the 'Relief Stage'; and Fuchs' article 'Theatre of the Twentieth Century' had appeared in the 1911 issue of *Ezhegodnik*. Fuchs' anti-naturalist vision of the staging space was probably the common ground on which moved, independently from each other, both Meyrhold's theatre and Diaghilev's enterprise. Even if Meyrhold's tendencies changed widely over the years (and from 1907 he often abandoned the two-dimensionality by exploiting the stage in all its depth and by using light as an expressive element), debating the issue of the inherent contradiction between the two-dimensionality of the scenic backcloth and the three-dimensionality of the actor's body always remained a central concern for him. While the realistic stage design of the Duke of Meinigen's troupe had provided the model for Stanislavsky's Art Theatre, Meyerhold's staging of Maeterlinck's *Death of Tintagiles* at the Theatre Studio in 1905 was probably the first of several Russian experiments with flattened stage perspectives.

According to Tim Scholl, the Russian experimentations with flattened perspectives and foreshortened stages stimulated a radical rethinking of the modality of dance[24]. While in

---

[24]. Scholl 1994, p. 54-56.

the old ballet the décor addressed only the periphery of the stage, thus leaving as much space as possible for dancing, Léon Bakst's narrow sets designed for Diaghilev's spectacles greatly limited the type of movement that could be performed by the soloists and the *corps*. It also affected the movement vocabulary of the choreographers, and in particular of Nijinsky, whose choreographies challenged not only the academic movement vocabulary but also the traditional modalities of using the stage space. These tendencies culminated in 1912 with the exaggerated 'flatness' and bas-relief character of Léon Bakst's design for the famous 1912 production of *L'Après-midi d'un faune* with Nijinsky's static profile poses and angular, stylised movements.

The propensity towards flattened representation of space and bodies has multiple origins in the theatrical traditions. Among them, Tim Scholl recalls the *tableaux vivants* that were often included in and never entirely absent from the ballet[25]. Nijnsky's flattened and angular movements were also not without precedents in Russian Ballets of the nineteenth century[26]. Some scholars also suggested that Bakst's two-dimensional staging for the *Faune* was «a way to solve the problem of recreating in three-dimensional space the rhythms of the flat, painted figures found on the sides of Greek vases»[27]. An important role was undoubtedly played by Fuchs' writings and experiments. Bakst probably also found a model in Max Littmann's design for the 'relief stage' of Fuchs' Munich Artists' Theatre, a narrow proscenium 26 feet deep[28].

The two-dimensional, anti-naturalistic and flattened view of the stage and of the performer's body had important consequences for Stravinsky's theatre, where it affected both the conception of the performer's body, and the stylistic and formal aspects of music. Much of the ideas expressed by Fuchs in the passages quoted above could refer to Stravinsky's theatrical music. The idea that bodily movements had to be limited to the essential and to be 'rhythmically regulated' was decisive in providing Stravinsky's work with a ritualistic and anti-realistic vision of the body, which he translated into the static, discontinuous non-developmental character of his music.

AGAINST *LOGOS*

Another distinctive aspect of Stravinsky's anti-realist vision of the performing body was its tendency to downplay the role of the sung (or spoken) word. The overcoming of the realistic theatrical model based on the dramatic text was another trait that Stravinsky's stage works

---

[25]. *Ibidem.* Scholl recalls the 'living picture' of Apollo which ended the *Sleeping Beauty* and the one that opened Fokine's *Animated Gobelins*.

[26]. SCHOLL 1994, p. 56, mentions Petipa's reference to the two-dimensional sculptural style of Egyptian art in the choreography for the *Daughter of the Pharaoh* (1862); and remembers that Fokine claimed to have used profile poses for his choreography for the three *Egyptian Girls in Eunice* (1907) and then again in *Une Nuit d'Egypte* (1908).

[27]. See MAYER 1977, p. 139.

[28]. See BRAUN 1998, p. 90.

shared with many other early twentieth-century theatrical experiments. More in general, the dissatisfaction with language as a means of representing reality had characterized many other artistic (and not only theatrical) trends in literature and the visual arts in the early years of the twentieth century. In the domain of opera, we can place in this context many works by Italian composers such as Alfredo Casella and Francesco Malipiero, who clearly stigmatized the tyranny of the word by turning their attention from the libretto to ballet and pantomime, and to the relationship between music and visual arts.

In this respect too, Fuchs' writings exerted a decisive influence on Russian theatrical culture. Fuchs considered the text «nothing but the musical score from which the re-creative, performing intellects must extract the true embodiment of the work»[29]. He condemned the whole classical tradition of «literary theatre», advocating a new approach to the stage in which a pre-eminent role was given to music, dance and bodily movements. Meyerhold was among those who best assimilated Fuchs' lesson. Both his practice and his theoretical writings of the St. Petersburg years clearly show that, although he hardly ever worked without a text, he did not always find the latter of primary importance. In his notes on his staging of Block's *Balaganchik*, he maintained that «words in the theatre are only embellishments of the design of movement» and «[...] so to speak, the mere overtones of the action». His interest in the visual and bodily aspect of theatrical acting came from a rejection of the actor's performing of the dramatic text as an «educated reader»[30]. The actor and his craft became the very focus of his attention, to the point of subordinating the very role of the dramatic text and the work of the dramatist to them.

A «deep-seated anti-literary prejudice» (as Richard Taruskin called it) was shared by Stravinsky and many other Ballets Russes insiders[31]. Diaghilev's revivals of Russian nationalist operas by the Mighty Kuchka in the early Parisian *Saisons russes*, and especially his *Boris Godunov* of 1908, had focused increasing attention on the visual and bodily elements of opera, rather than on its literary (verbal) component. The same can be said of his early ballet productions, in which the visual aspects clearly prevailed over the ballet's *argument*. Diaghilev clearly summarized the idea in a 1910 interview. «The essence and secret of our ballet» he maintained

> [...] lies in the fact that we have renounced ideas in favour of an elemental spontaneity. We wished to find an art through which all complexity of life [...] could be expressed apart from words and ideas — not rationally, but elementally, graphically, self-evidently[32].

---

[29]. FUCHS 1905, p. 105.

[30]. Meyerhold's essay on *The Fairground Booth*, appeared together with his earlier theatrical writings in 1913 under the title *O Teatre* (On the Theatre).

[31]. TARUSKIN 1996, p. 1072.

[32]. DIAGHILEV, Sergey. 'Yeshcho o baletnïk itogakhi', in: *Utro Rossiii*, 24 August 1910, quoted in TARUSKIN 1996, p. 1072.

The crucial anti-logocentric (and anti-realistic) impulse, however, came to Stravinsky from Benois. Their correspondence surrounding the 1914 staging of *Le Rossignol* shows that the main target of their critique was not so much Wagner's music-drama (as one would expect from the well-known anti-Wagnerian feelings Stravinsky would later express) as a romantic operatic tradition which relied heavily on the literary component (the libretto). In this tradition the meanings conveyed by the words were typically expressed by means of hackneyed and trite musical, vocal and mimic clichés, whose conventional character was all the more evident the greater they were charged with pathos. St. Petersburg's theatrical culture even had a noun for this pejorative model of opera: *Vampuka*, from the title of a fortunate one-act opera by Vladimir Ehrenberg parodying, among others, Verdi's *Aida* and Meyerbeer's *L'Africaine*[33]. What Stravinsky and Benois most disapproved of in operas *à la Vampuka* was their claim to «naturalness» and «realism» which, in point of fact, ended up as something most clumsy and far from reality: a sort of 'unwilling un-naturalness', so to speak, against which Stravinsky set a self-conscious, self-evident, anti-naturalist conventionality. In the above-mentioned interview for the *Peterburgskaya gazeta* of September 1912, he clearly stated: «Opera is falsehood pretending to be truth, while I need falsehood that pretends to falsehood. Opera is a battle against nature»[34].

In addition to being the first stage work (apart from ballets) that placed the expressive body in the foreground, *Le Rossignol* was the first of many works by Stravinsky that «do violence to language»[35]. In reviewing, in July 1913, the original libretto by Stepan Mitusov, the composer reduced it dramatically in terms of length and verbal redundancy. The role of the Chinese Emperor, in particular, became almost purely choreographic.

Stravinsky's rejection of a realistic-naturalist literary model of theatre led above all to his rejection of the traditional operatic figure of the singer-actor who, in an attempt to create an illusion of reality, gathered in himself a triple level of signification: gestures, words (text) and music (singing). This redundancy of expressive means was probably for Stravinsky at the heart of all degeneration and excess of the traditional opera, and eventually led to grotesquely emphatic results — *à la Vampuka*. Quite simply, singers had to avoid — or had to be prevented from — acting as if they were realistically expressing the meanings and feelings conveyed by the dramatic *text*. Stravinsky would never let the other non-linguistic signs (bodily and vocal gestures) simply duplicate or corroborate the content of the words. «Music», he said, «can be married to gesture or to words — not to both without bigamy. That is why the artistic basis of opera is wrong and why Wagner sounds at his best in concert-room»[36].

---

[33]. As noticed in *ibidem*. p. 1071.

[34]. 'Teatral', 'U kompozitora I. F. Stravinskogo', in: *Peterbugskaya gazeta*, 27 September 1912, quoted in TARUSKIN 1996, p. 982.

[35]. See ALBRIGHT 1989, p. 28.

[36]. *The Daily Mail*, 13 February 1912.

The first strategy that Stravinsky and Benois devised to prevent the identification of the actor-singer with his role was the separation of his traditional duties within different people figures: an actor, who is reduced to a mime without voice; and a singer who does not act but merely performs his part as in concert form. In this respect, Benois' aforementioned 1914 staging of *Le Coq d'or* and *Le Rossignol* undoubtedly provided a fundamental precedent. After that experience, Stravinsky would repeatedly make use of Benois' splitting strategy in his theatrical works up to *The Flood*. However, it can also be said that his vision of this theatrical device rapidly developed in a quite different direction from Benois'. The difference probably stemmed from their different stance on Wagnerian *Wort-Ton-Drama*. Of course, they both had been strongly influenced by Wagner, as was all early twentieth-century Russian theatrical and musical symbolist culture. Wagner's influence on Stravinsky was overt in *The Firebird* and lasted at least until *The Rite of Spring*. However, Benois believed that by means of his split-roles strategy he had realized «[...] the union of the arts Wagner dreamed about». In his view, the division of the roles between singers and mimes/dancers was a sort of 'reduplication' of the artistic means, aimed at creating a complete fusion between them, in the sense of Wagner's *Gesamtkunstwerk*. He also viewed the genre of ballet as «the most consistent and complete» incarnation of Wagner's ideal. Indeed, it was precisely in a Wagnerian sense that he described *Petrushka* — for which he provided the décors and the costumes — as «a great complete work of art»[37]. Conversely, Stravinsky began to raise doubts about the theoretical validity of Wagnerian music-drama — not only of opera — as early as 1912, as we have already seen in his statement in the 1912 interview. Unlike Benois, he soon turned towards a vision which emphasized the juxtaposition, rather than fusion, of the artistic means, or even their *separation*. This modernist re-reading of Benois' practice would prove far reaching for Stravinsky's theatrical experiments, as well as for his very musical aesthetics.

Stravinsky's dissociating approach had important theoretical consequences. First, the separation of the components traditionally gathered together in the figure of the singer-actor allowed for their different 'recombination' on an ideal plane, in the mind of the spectator. This was clearly noted already by the first Russian critics who reviewed *Le Coq d'or*. According to Nikolai Minsky, for example,

> [...] no doubt this time the inspirers of the Ballets Russes have hit upon a new form of theatrical art, one that has a huge future. It is neither ballet illustrated by music nor opera flavored with ballet, but a union of two hitherto separate art forms: a union that takes place not on the stage, but in the viewer's soul[38].

---

[37].   Benois quoted in Taruskin 1996, p. 661.

[38].   'Soyedineniye iskusstv: pis'mo iz Parizha', in: *Utro Rossii*, 24 May 1914: quoted in Taruskin 1996, p. 1071.

Secondly, while in the early theatrical works with the split roles, such as *Renard*, this strategy was clearly associated with a kind of showy spectacle whose playful dimension was totally devoid of any psychological implications, in the following works disassociation assumed a new 'psychological' dimension, no longer in the sense of the description of the interiority of the characters, but in the sense of the dynamics of the spectator's unconscious. Such a psychoanalytic dimension is especially evident in Stravinsky's stage works of the neoclassical period. *Œdipus Rex* and *Orpheus* are paradigmatic works in this respect.

Thirdly, in Stravinsky's hands the splitting strategy, in addition to preventing the 'pleonastic' of words, music and acting body from being perceived as an unwanted stylistic fault, became an anti-dramatic and 'alienating' effect aimed at highlighting, instead of concealing, the artificial character of the union of music, words and gestures. Finally, and most importantly, this strategy, initially applied to singing and acting, was gradually extended to other aspect of the theatrical spectacle, thus creating a series of disassociations on different levels. The first of them concerned the association of the voice (as characterized by texture, gender, and register) and the performing bodies. While in *Le Rossignol* the voices, albeit separated from the bodies of the mimes or dancers on the stage, were still identifiable with them thanks to the register, extension texture and gender, in the 'Burlesque for the stage with singing and music' *Renard* (*Baika*, 1915-1916), a one-to-one identification was no longer possible. None of the four male voices of the score can be unequivocally associated with any of the four animal-characters miming on stage. Although sometimes an association seems to delineate itself, it is denied immediately thereafter, especially when the four soloists begin to sing altogether, as a polyphonic group, thus assuming the function of a sort of chorus commenting on the *fabula*. In the «Choreographed Scenes with Music and Voices» *Les Noces* (*Svadebka*, 1914-1921, first staged in 1923), individual roles «do not exist [...], but only [...] voices that impersonate now one type of character and now another»[39]. In no sense can the singers be thought of as *dramatis personae*, if for no other reason that the libretto is not a dramatic text but rather a collection of popular wedding lyrics. In the «ballet with singing» *Pulcinella* (1919-1920) there is no fixed assignment of voices to stage characters either. The solo vocal pieces that are among the heterogeneous Pergolesian and pseudo-Pergolesian materials of which the score is composed are not associated with specific characters on stage — in the score they only bear nameless vocal registers (soprano, tenor and bass) and they also lack, with very few exceptions (the opening serenade and the final trio), any clear connection with the *argument* and the action of the ballet.

Unlike these works, where the sung text has no totally linear narrative or dramatic structure, and the 'story' is made intelligible more by the visual aspects than by the sung text itself, in *Histoire du soldat* (1918), «To be read, played, and danced» — as the title page of the work proclaims — the story is made clear and linear enough by the libretto alone. This

---

[39]. *EXPOSITIONS AND DEVELOPMENTS*, p. 115.

unusual literary basis notwithstanding, the work features an even more radical disassociation of the artistic means. The story is told by a Reader and enacted by a dancer and two mimes, who also converse with each other. From the very beginning of their collaboration, Stravinsky and Charles-Ferdinand Ramuz, who wrote the French libretto, agreed that the music should be independent of the text and that it would be possible to perform the work without words, as a concert suite. The musicians, the Reader and the mimes are placed on the same plane on stage. This also allows the Reader to step beyond his narrating role and enter the action at a certain point in the story (the card game), to support the Soldier in his battle against Evil. Stravinsky acknowledged Pirandello's influence in this regard — admittedly not very plausibly, since in 1918 the meta-theatrical phase of Pirandello's production was still to come — while some commentators have perceived an analogy with Brecht's *Verfremdungseffekt*[40]. More convincingly Richard Taruskin has drawn attention to Meyerhold's 1914 staging of Carlo Gozzi's *The Love for Three Oranges*, where similar devices are employed[41].

Another kind of dissociating strategy was adopted in *Perséphone* (1933-1934). Stravinsky described the work as «a masque or dance-pantomime coordinated with a sung and spoken text»[42]. The words of the eponymous role are entrusted to a speaker coordinated with the music, in the form of *mélodrame* (see above), while the story is also being told and commented upon by a chorus and a tenor (Eumolpus). Unlike André Gide, who wanted stage action to occur in between vocal numbers, Stravinsky was firmly convinced that singing, speaking and miming/dancing should occur simultaneously, but split between different performers: «The mime [of Perséphone] should not speak and the speaker should not mime [...] The resulting separation of text and movement would mean that the staging could be worked out entirely in choreographic terms»[43].

One might ask why such dissociating strategies were pursued by Stravinsky with such consistency and at so many different levels in his theatrical production. Benois' initial example is not enough to fully explain the reason why the idea of the separation of the artistic components assumed so central a role in Stravinsky's later stage works. A possible answer has to do with the fundamental stylistic aspect of Stravinsky's music which is the main topic of this book: despite his statements about the autonomy and the 'absolute' nature of music — let alone his famous assertion that «music is essentially powerless to express anything at all» — Stravinsky's compositions are always strongly imbued with *implicit* visual and bodily connotations. In all probability, this is simply because many of its most essential and typical stylistic hallmarks, such as fragmentation, abrupt juxtapositions of musical blocks, and extensive use of ostinati,

---

[40]. *Ibidem*, p. 91.

[41]. Taruskin 1996, p. 1298, fn. 74.

[42]. *Dialogues and a Diary*, p. 36.

[43]. *Ibidem*.

were first experimented in Stravinsky's ballet scores for Diaghilev, in the form of expedients to create a musical equivalent to the bodily movements, the visual aspects and the events on stage. Later, they remained as the distinctive elements of Stravinsky's vocabulary of musical gestures, also independent of any explicit and direct association with movements and images. Given this intrinsic capacity of the signification of the music alone, Stravinsky's tendency to dissociate it from the other expressive means conveying meaning can easily be interpreted as the result of a concern with redundancy: words and bodily gestures, if totally fused with such a gestural and 'meaningful' music, risked creating a sort of pleonasm, a tautology (in the sense of grammar): too many signs being used to express the same signified idea. Gianfranco Vinay, to whom I owe this idea, has summarised the problem in rather similar and very clear terms:

> Stravinsky's musical style, which was developed in the ballet world, maintained mimic, symbolic, structural and functional relations with gestures and choreographic movements, could not, at the same time, be directly related to words, but only to an indirect way, with retractions to weaken or conceal bigamy[44].

Another fundamental strategy Stravinsky used to avoid the pleonastic union of music, words and gestures consisted of a radical removal of the meaning itself of language — the component which, given his anti-literary cultural background, represented the greatest concern for him. According to Richard Taruskin, «It was precisely the dissociation of sound from meaning (present to some degree in all poetry, as it were by definition) that provided Stravinsky with a reassuring validation and a powerful weapon in his avowed campaign [...] of finally dismantling the *Gesamtkunstwerk*»[45].

In almost all of the above-mentioned Stravinkyian stage works, the dissociating strategies go hand in hand with a tendency to reduce verbal expression to the bare minimum and/or to undermine its meaningfulness. As we have seen, the completion of *Le Rossignol* was the first case in which Stravinsky did «violence to language»[46]. In the following works, Stravinsky adopted a number of strategies aimed at undermining or destroying the semantic character of words. One of them was to use texts containing onomatopoeic sounds, nonsense words, or plays of words based on the sound of phonemes (alliterations, assonances, fortuitous rhymes), as occurs in *Renard*. On many occasions Stravinsky's music gives the impression of using words more for their sound properties than for their meaning. This tendency is all the more evident in Stravinsky's settings

---

44. «Le style stravinskien, mis au point dans le milieu du ballet, en entretenant des rapports mimiques, symboliques, structurels et fonctionnels avec les gestes et les mouvements chorégraphiques, ne pouvait pas, en même temps, se lier directement aux mots, mais seulement d'une façon indirecte, avec des escamotages pour affaiblir, masquer ou cacher la bigamie». VINAY 1993, p. 93. See also VINAY 1987, pp. 141-143.
45. TARUSKIN 1996, p. 1207.
46. ALBRIGHT 1989, p. 28.

of Russian popular songs but, as Daniel Albright rightly noticed, Stravinsky «seemed to regard all texts (once incorporated into a musical composition) as nonsense»[47]. Another way to put aside the meaning of words consisted of merely another kind of «disassociation», that between the stresses of musical rhythm and the accentuation of prosodic rhythm in poetry and spoken language. A paradigmatic example in this respect is *Perséphone*, in which Stravinsky practically disregarded André Gide's poetic rhythm, thus attracting the writer's strong disapproval[48]. However, in *Œdipus Rex* and *The Rake's Progress* one can also find many transgressions of obvious prosodic rules of Latin and the English language. Wystan Auden and Chester Kallman were surprised by what seemed to them an improper scansion of the words of their libretto for *The Rake's Progress*, and proposed some revisions aimed at restoring a proper form. In *Œdipus Rex*, not only do the musical accents contradict the normal accentuation of Latin words, but a single word is repeated several times in sequence, each time with different accentuation, due to metric displacement and changing musical rhythm. Shifting accent on repeated words is a typical feature of many Russian folk songs: a well-known example is the third stanza of the song *Akh vï, seni, moï seni*, whose melody was quoted in *Petrushka*, where all three syllables of the words 'pa mostú' (along the bridge), repeated three times within a single verse, receive musical accent.

Stravinsky's own explanation for his disregard of the correct accentuation of words was that he preferred to manipulate texts at the level of syllables instead of words, because «words, far from helping, constitute for the musician a burdensome intermediary. All I want [...] is syllables, fine strong syllables»[49]. However, Taruskin has shown that the origins of Stravinsky's prosodic transgressions lie in his musical settings of Russian folk lyrics during his early Swiss years. Many years later, Stravinsky himself stated that «One important characteristic of Russian popular verse is that the accent of spoken verse is ignored when the verse is sung. The recognition of the musical possibilities inherent in this fact was one of the most rejoicing discoveries of my life»[50]. Taruskin has also shown that this was a reaction, on Stravinsky's part, to a typically 'realistic' nineteenth century Russian musical tradition based on the dogma that vocal music had to faithfully reflect the prosody, the rhythm, the phrasing and the punctuation of the underlying literary text. In any case, it is important to understand that Stravinsky's disregard for prosody was just another way to make the words of his theatrical texts — like those of his folk songs — appear as a constituent part of the music itself, more than a bearer of meaning.

Putting the language into the background was just another way, for Stravinsky, to make the bodily expressiveness emerge on the foreground. This would seem to be contradicted by a

---

[47]. *Ibidem*, p. 29.

[48]. *SSC I-III*, vol. III, p. 478. On Stravinsky's rhythmic treatment of Gide's text see Carr 2002, pp. 153-199; Vinay 2007, pp. 843-857; Levitz 2012, pp. 140-145.

[49]. 'M. Igor Strawinsky nous parole de «Perséphone»', in: *Excelsior*, 29 [April 1934].

[50]. *Expositions and Developments*, p. 121.

striking and well-known feature of Stravinsky's theatre: after Le Rossignol, in stage works such as *Renard*, *Pulcinella*, and *Les Noces*, which adopted the solutions of the split role, a radical solution was adopted: pit singing, in which the singers' bodies were concealed, removed from the stage, and put within the orchestra[51]. In other works, such as *Œdipus Rex*, a different solution to obtain the same result was to conceal only that part of the actor-singer's body which, in theatrical traditions, is usually charged with the expression of the emotions and meanings conveyed by the words, namely the face and the mouth. The crystallized expression of the mask neutralizes and prevents the possibility of a realistic performance of the text on the part of the actor-singer. This strategy is still at work in the *The Flood*, Stravinsky's last 'stage' work (in this case a TV stage), in which one cannot see either singing or speaking bodies. In the score, singing is allowed only to supernatural characters (God, the Angels, Satan/Lucifer). In the movie, the voice of God, conveyed by a duet of basses with musical accompaniment, is associated with various abstract images obtained with electronic television effects. Lucifer/Satan's role is split between a 'high, slightly pederastic tenor' — the only truly operatic voice in *The Flood* — and a dancer. The Angels are represented by paintings in the style of Russian icons, placed on a kind of iconostasis. Holes made in the paintings at face height allow us to glimpse the eyes of the singers standing behind, but not their mouths. Terrestrial characters, who express themselves in *Sprechgesang* or with spoken words upon a musical accompaniment, are embodied by masked mimes. Finally, the Narrator's body is, obviously, never seen, since his voice is a voice-over; an off-camera commentary placed on an extra-diegetic level. In Chapter Four we will see how this corresponds to the representation of different types of corporeality and incorporeality.

It is important to stress that in all Stravinsky's theatrical works the obstructive attitude towards the singers' bodies — or the singers' faces — was not so much a concern with their bodily expressiveness but with the singers' tendency to 'realistically' express the meanings conveyed by the dramatic text. It was, in other words, a concern with the 'illusory device' of the singer-actor and with the sung words as a bearer of meanings, not with the singer's body *per se*. On the contrary, it could be said that the centrality of the body, entirely subsumed within the substance and the character of the music, is confirmed, rather than contradicted, by the very fact of hiding the physical body of the performers. The body, as an aesthetic category, is so central to Stravinsky's music that the sight of it can — and sometimes has to — be avoided, as it would be a pleonastic mean, since the very meaning of Stravinsky's music *is* body.

In fact, in many other stage works based on the split singer-mime strategy, Stravinsky did not conceal the singers' bodies but on the contrary placed them in a position clearly visible to the public, sometimes together with the instrumentalists. Already in Benois' staging for the 1914 *The Golden Cockerel*, the singers were placed in evidence on scaffolds on both sides of

---

[51].   André Schaeffner called this strategy «les chanteurs dans la fosse». SCHAEFFNER 1924.

the stage. The fact that Benois' first idea was to have them hidden in the pit (or in the wings) confirms the inter-changeability of the two solutions.

In any case, whether visible or not, the singers were always prevented by Stravinsky from acting in a realistic manner by expressively singing the dramatic text. In the *The Golden Cockerel*, the singers, albeit visible to the public, were supposed to sing in a hieratic, choir-like and non-dramatic fashion. What is more, in the only two instances where Stravinsky adopted the normal convention of opera, in which visible singers are supposed both to sing and to act, he found a way to avoid their identification with their dramatic role, or at least to prevent the audience from perceiving such an identification. In the one-act 'comic opera' *Mavra* (1921-2), this is achieved by means of parodic devices: the operatic conventions of eighteenth-century *opera buffa* — the presence of arias, duets and ensembles, and the use of a *bel canto* style — are not passively adopted but rather self-consciously 'quoted'. Both music and the libretto bring into play a variety of parodic strategies that undermine dramatic coherence. The Russian libretto by Boris Kochno is based on a poem by Pushkin (*The Little House in Kolomna*) which is the parody (in the sense of its inter-textual practices) of a poem by Lord Byron (*Beppo*), which satirizes in its turn many literary conventions familiar to Byron's readers. In the same way, Stravinsky's music parodies the conventions of the Russo-Italian operatic tradition and of the eighteenth-century *opera buffa*, which, itself was largely based on the parody of the convention of *opera seria*. All this makes the 'pleonastic' union of singing and acting in the single person of the actor-singer appear as an essential aspect of the general parody, and not as an illusionistic-realistic effort at identification in a *dramatis persona*. Both *Mavra* and *The Rake's Progress* are operas only «in quotation marks». For this reason, the use of gestures and singing on the actor-singer's part no longer present themselves as elements endowed with dramatic meaning, and start to look like stereotyped iconic representations, whose tautological and self-reflexive character, far from constituting an undesired effect (as in *Vampuka*-like operas) becomes the very subject matter of the spectacle. In *The Rake's Progress*, this iconic nature is made even more evident by the fact that the libretto is based on William Hogarth's series of engravings with the same title, thus making the characters appear as stylized and iconic representations of themselves.

On other occasions, Stravinsky put the singers in the same space as a visible orchestra. In this way he clearly showed that he considered the singer's body — when properly prevented from acting in a realistic-dramatic way — as a powerful resource of musical expressiveness to be exploited. The first time he put an instrumental ensemble in the foreground was in the 1918 staging of the *Historie du soldat* at the Théâtre Municipal of Lausanne, in which the septet of instruments was put on stage, playing alongside the mimes, the dancer and the Reader. Stravinsky's comment on this idea in his autobiography is one of his best-known statements about the importance he attached to the gestures of the performers for the understanding of music:

[A] consideration which made this idea particularly attractive to me was the interest afforded to the spectator by being able to see these instrumentalists each playing his own part in the ensemble. I have always had a horror of listening to music with my eyes shut, with nothing for them to do. The sight of the gestures and movements of the various parts of the body producing the music is fundamentally necessary if it is to be grasped in all its fullness. All music created or composed demands some exteriorization for the perception of the listener. In other words, it must have an intermediary, an executant. That being an essential condition, without which music cannot wholly reach us, why wish to ignore it, or try to do so. Why shut the eyes to this fact which is inherent in the very nature of musical art? Obviously, one frequently prefers to turn away one's eyes, or even close them, when the superfluity of the player's gesticulations prevents the concentration of one's faculties of hearing. But if the player's movements are evoked solely by the exigencies of the music, and do not tend to make an impression on the listener by extramusical devices, why not follow with the eye such movements as those of the drummer, the violinist, or the trombonist, which facilitate one's auditory perceptions? As a matter of fact, those who maintain that they only enjoy music to the full with their eyes shut do not hear better than when they have them open, but the absence of visual distractions enables them to abandon themselves to the reveries induced by the lullaby of its sounds, and that is really what they prefer to the music itself[52].

Stravinsky's statement is somehow at odds with the formalist aesthetics he had been embracing in his writings in the inter-war period, largely the result of the influence of the French intellectual climate and of his various ghost-writers. Of course, in many respects his description of the musical performance is a typically formalist one: he reduces the performance to a mere 'exteriorization', for use by the listener, of the composer's idea, and the performer to a mere 'intermediary and executant' between the author and his public. And his distinction between gestures motivated by 'purely musical exigencies' and gestures aimed at creating 'extramusical' impressions relies on the basic formalist assumption according to which it is possible to clearly separate the 'purely' musical domain from the extramusical one[53]. However, the idea that the body is able to express music 'in all its fullness' implies a contradiction, and introduces a critical element into an otherwise monolithically formalist aesthetic.

---

[52]. *AUTOBIOGRAPHY*, p. 115.

[53]. For a criticism of the formalist approach in the description of musical performance see especially COOK 2013.

In Search of the Musical Body

Part ii: Analytic Issues[54]

Music Analysis, Meaning, and Embodiment:
The Problem of 'Formalist' Analysis

In the previous section we dealt with the origins of Stravinsky's vision of the body in his engagement with theatre and dance. However, once raised in theatrical realm, this view was thoroughly embedded into the structures, techniques and style of all of Stravinsky's music, not just that for theatre and dance. How can, therefore, we recognize these bodily hallmarks in the characteristics of the music alone, even when no performing body is associated with it?

This question brings us to the problem of musical analysis and its relationship with hermeneutic interpretation, with which I will deal in this section. The main question will be whether a close reading of the musical text (in the widest sense of the term) can tell us something useful about the way music represents and implies the body. We may consider too how this is done: with what methodology and relying on which medium.

Music analysis has hardly been fully engaged with this issue. Of course, in some respects one may say that many concepts, terms, and strategies of music analysis itself — not only of music — are influenced by our experience of the body as located in space and time. Consider, for example, terms like ascent, descent, passing note, interruption, voice 'leading', etc.: they all contain some implied reference to the proprioception (the sense of self-movement — which also implies time) of the body in the surrounding space. This depends much on how music theories conceptualize music according to bodily schemata and images[55]. Though, in addition to implying this bodily dimension in an 'unconscious' way in our analytical categories, we should also be able to explicitly and consciously recognize and describe the bodily dimensions of music. Unfortunately, however, although embodiment has emerged as a central issue in twenty-first-century arts and humanities — including some areas of musicology engaged with cultural studies — the body has rarely been considered within close analyses of music.

The main reason for this has probably been the fact that musical analysis is usually considered as an approach involved only with the *formal and structural* aspects of music, while the body dimension has much more to do with the *meanings* attributed to the music (by those who produce it or by those who listen to it); and it is not so easy to find a criterion that allows us to associate the meanings with the formal and structural aspects of music in a plausible and 'objective' way. This is also because different individuals can associate different meanings to the same musical aspects. This brings us back to the old and long debated question of the alleged 'formalism' of music analysis, first posed by what was once the so-called 'new' musicology of

---

[54]. Some parts and examples of this section are drawn from my article Locanto 2018.

[55]. See Chapter Three on this and Zbikowski 2011.

the mid 1980s, which emerged in the United States in the wake of Joseph Kerman's famous book *Contemplating Music*[56]. The allegation depended ultimately on two assumptions: firstly that music analysis is concerned only with the music as notated in the score, and not with the music as performed and experienced as a meaningful construct; and secondly that it conceives of the structure of music as something which can be mentally represented in visual-spatial terms and «optimally represented in notation», not as something experienced in the concrete temporal dimension[57]. However, the main target of this criticism was probably a well-defined set of methodologies — such as Schenkerism, or the set-theoretical approach of Allen Forte — that have long formed the bulk of the discipline in the English-speaking world, both methods that share a sharp focus on 'structure'. In this respect, one may simply observe that if we consider all its different traditions (including continental ones), music analysis is a much more variegated activity, one that conceives of musical structure in very different ways. More importantly, the allegation of 'formalism' fails to address a central issue, which concerns the relation between analysis, structure and meaning: the only way one could reasonably argue that a certain analytical approach is 'formalist' would be to assume that it highlights structural properties that are really 'meaningless', whatever sense the word 'meaning' may assume in reference to music. This judgment, however, if addressed to the discipline of music analysis in general — not only to some specific approaches — may lead us to the untenable conclusion that musical meanings, insofar as they cannot be related to any analytically demonstrable structure, are purely conventional associations. On the contrary, we can say that the meanings ascribed to music are socially and culturally negotiated but, at the same time, not totally arbitrary and conventional, since as they are determined, to some extent, by the structural aspects of music[58]. The question, therefore, is: how can so many different meanings be associated with just one musical structure?

Many scholars have tried to answer this question. Their answers, however, usually relied on a vision of the musical structure as something univocal — albeit open to a multiplicity of approaches. The process of producing meaning, thus, has been conceived as a process moving from a given structure towards many possible meanings. On the contrary, we should try to conceive of musical structure as a set of relationships that can be differently reconfigured in the concrete, time related experience, according to different subjective ways of meaning attribution. This suggestion roughly corresponds to Nicholas Cook's proposal to think of musical structure as a material object with many different formal attributes which can be variously selected and put into relationship according to different modalities of meaning association[59]. In my opinion,

---

[56]. KERMAN 1985; see also KERMAN 1980.
[57]. COOK 2013, p. 17.
[58]. COOK 2001, pp. 174-177.
[59]. *Ibidem.*

Cook's idea should also lead us to overcome any overly rigid dichotomy between form and content and to imagine the former as something that cannot be entirely established as totally independent of the latter. It should also rule out any rigid binary opposition between «structural listening» and (various types of) associative (non-structural) listening, as well as the opposition, between 'structural' and 'rhetorical' performance styles[60]. Against these dichotomies, I maintain that there are different ways of listening, analyzing, and performing a piece of music, each claiming its own legitimate view of the musical structure as a meaningful construct.

My proposal, thus, is to look at the performer's body as an interpreter of the structure of music. Each performing body (each dancer, each choreographer, each actors-singer, etc.) may interpret the same music in very different ways, which reflect a different perception and rearrangement of some formal and structural features of music. The performers' choices — except when they are entirely and deliberately 'arbitrary' with respect to music, as happens in those choreographies that aim precisely to emphasize a total autonomy of dance from music — usually reflect an embodied response to *some* formal and structural features of music. Considering music analysis from this perspective is a way to avoid another ideological assumption of the 'formalist' approach to music: the notion of 'the music itself'. As Nicholas Reyland and Rebecca Thumpston rightly noticed, «if music is an "it" with a "self" then it "must represent — indeed embody — aspects of its creators" most distinctive trait: embodied consciousness»[61]. One may only add that, in addition to its creator's 'embodied consciousness', music also stimulates an embodied response on the part of its performers, interpreters (including musicologists themselves), and listeners.

A musicological discipline that lends itself very well to this approach is choreomusicology. I believe that its usefulness depends exactly on its ability to demonstrate that the way individuals perform, dance or choreograph a piece of music reflects the selection, on their part, of *some* structural property of music that they perceive as 'meaningful'[62]. These properties do not simply correspond to the formal elements of music represented by notation; nevertheless, they can be grasped by means of an appropriate hermeneutic-oriented analysis of the musical text. Yet, even in the context of choreomusicology, essays based on a close scrutiny of the musical text remain relatively rare. To some extent, this is a consequence of the newest and more promising methodological developments in the discipline. In recent times, in fact, dance and music have been increasingly considered in terms of the overall result of their dynamic interaction rather than as static and distinct component media. As a consequence,

---

[60]. See Cook 2013.

[61]. Reyland – Thumpston 2018, p. 1.

[62]. Locanto 2018. Choreomusicology itself can be seen as one of the many developments in musicology which reaffirmed the validity and usefulness of music analysis, after it had been heavily questioned in the wake of the paradigm shift undergone by the whole discipline of musicology in the 1980s and 90s — the so-called new musicology. See Jordan 2011, pp. 43-45.

the emphasis on analysis of scores has given way, as Jordan has pointed out, to a strong focus «on matters of perception and performance»[63]. Again, this embarrassment over music analysis is due to the persistence of the prejudices against it as a 'formalist' approach[64]. Among the most notable exceptions we can find Stephanie Jordan's studies, produced over the last 20 years. As a matter of fact, the role of music analysis has always been recognized in Jordan's choreomusicological essays[65].

Music Gestures as Energetic Continuities

A theoretical framework that lends itself well to the approach I am advocating is provided by the concept of 'musical gesture', which has attracted ever-greater attention in musicology in the last two decades[66], even though each scholar's conception of the idea is different and it has not yet received a generally accepted definition. The most systematic attempt came from Robert Hatten, whose theory is grounded on a generalized definition of the communicative human movement (gesture) as an «energetic shaping through time» that is «meaningful» or «significant», i.e. able to carry some meaning[67]. In Hatten's view, musical gestures are «synthetic gestalts with emergent meaning» which can be either conveyed through sound or imagined in purely mental terms[68]. Hatten maintains that musical gestures, albeit perceived and conceived as purely aural and mental entities, can be nevertheless be conceived as «gestures», even apart from the direct visual access to the bodily actions ('gestures' in a more strict sense) that generate them. In this sense his definition may be considered as an essentially metaphorical one[69]. More in general, one may argue that the notion of musical gesture, as thematised in recent musicological literature, is a «metaphor», in the sense of the cognitive theory of metaphor originated from the work of Lakoff and Johnson[70]. A cognitive metaphor is not a mere linguistic-rhetoric expression, as it is in literature and literary criticism, but a process through which we conceptualise a domain of experience (the target domain) in terms of another domain (the

---

63. Jordan 2011, p. 45.

64. Some scholars have made more or less explicit claims about the uselessness of music analysis for the study of music-dance interaction. According to Brown 2012, pp. 184-185, for example, a close reading of the musical text is not useful insofar as music analysis is typically concerned with aspects that are not relevant to our experience of music or to «what we hear naturally». This is just another way of saying that music analysis is a 'formalist' exercise.

65. See especially Jordan 2000, pp. 65-102.

66. See for example Godøy – Leman 2010, Gritten – King 2006; Gritten – King 2011, Zbikowski 2011. Unfortunately, so far it has rarely been applied in choreomusical research. Minors 2012 is one of the few applications in the field of choreomusicology.

67. Hatten 2004, pp. 93-95, 102, 109, 114. See also Hatten 2003.

68. Hatten 2004, pp. 94.

69. See Jensenius et al. 2010. in Godøy – Leman 2010, p. 18.

70. Lakoff – Johnson 1980. I will return to Lakoff and Johnson's metaphor theory in Chapter Three.

source domain): «a cross-domain mapping in the conceptual system»[71]. Put in this way, music gestures and bodily gestures, albeit obviously different from an ontological point of view — if only because the former involve sound, and the latter do not — are nevertheless closely linked from the point of view of their conceptualization[72]. In this light, the concept of musical gesture should be set in the context of the integration, 'blending' or networking of different conceptual domains[73]. However, Hatten's theory seems to imply a closer relation between musical gestures and physical actions, one that is based on intermodal perception[74]. According to Hatten, our tendency to conceive music in terms of gestures relies on «the interaction and intermodality of a range of human perceptual and motor systems [that] synthesise the energetic motion through time into significant events»[75]. Thanks to intermodal synthesis musical gestures can be «inferred from a musical performance, even when we do not have visual access to the motions of the performers»[76]. This view seems to be consistent with the role that neurosciences give mirror neurons in the intermodal perception mechanisms, and with the embodied theories of cognition of the human mind, which, by radically rejecting the traditional body-mind dichotomy, assume that high level mental constructs are never separable from sensory perception and motor activity. Body and bodily experience do not limit themselves to give information and inputs to the mind, inasmuch as they shape cognition, and are an essential constituent part of the cognitive system. In a radical 'embodied' perspective, therefore, one may assume that musical gestures, albeit purely aural, are closely related not only with sound-producing bodily gestures, but with expressive body motions in general.

Whatever one's opinion may be regarding the metaphorical-cognitive or intermodal-perceptive ground of the concept of 'musical gesture', my interest in it is due to its usefulness as an analytical tool for choreomusicology. Thanks to this concept we can see how individuals dance or choreograph a piece of music in such ways that denote a tendency *on their part* to think of music as if it were a sequence of physical gestures with precise dynamic shapes and formal attributes that convey meanings. We must distinguish between our tendency, as scholars, to speak of music in terms of 'gestures' — which may also be a rhetorical strategy, or the inevitable consequence of the fundamentally metaphoric nature of our ordinary conceptual system — and our description of the way individuals seem to perceive the music in terms of bodily movements — no matter how metaphorically-cognitively grounded their attitude may be — and to reflect this bodily perception in their expressive-artistic choices. My descriptions in bodily terms of the

---

[71]. LAKOFF 1993, p. 203.

[72]. ZBIKOWSKI 2011, p. 92.

[73]. As proposed by MINORS 2012.

[74]. «Intermodality is a more useful underlying generalisation than the 'metaphors' that Johnson and Lakoff attribute to any cross-domain mapping». HATTEN 2004, p. 101.

[75]. HATTEN 2003, p. 80.

[76]. HATTEN 2004, p. 94.

musical gesture found in the first measures of *Variations* (see below, next section), for example, is an essentially metaphorical one; but it has also been suggested to me by Balanchine's and Farrell's choreography, which clearly denote a perception, on their part, of these musical figures as they were aural equivalent of significant bodily movements.

Another interesting aspect of Hatten's theory is the importance it gives to the perception of continuities and discontinuities in the structure of music. According to Hatten, «when gestures encompass more than one musical event [...], they provide a nuanced continuity that binds together otherwise separate elements into a continuous whole». For Hatten continuity does not depend on continuously sounding (as in *legato*): even a discontinuous sequence of notes (e.g. as separated by rests) may nonetheless be linked «by a continuous thread of intentional and significant movement»[77]. Gestures may also be hierarchically organised so that smaller gestures can be comprised in larger ones, thus creating a sense of continuity on a different, higher level, encompassing otherwise separate musical gestures. These considerations lend themselves very well to be applied to Stravinsky's music, in which the use of continuity/discontinuity is a determining feature of block form.

Finally, Hatten's theory legitimizes a text-based but non-formalist analytic approach. While still relying securely on the score, his hermeneutical strategy 'goes beyond' it, so to speak. According to Hatten, in fact, musical gestures *transcend* music notation insomuch as they address aspects of time shaping «which practical notational systems cannot adequately convey [...]»[78]. At the same time, he maintains that musical gesture can be *inferred from* the reading of musical notation — as well as from the hearing of a performance — «given knowledge of the relevant musical style and culture»[79]. This ability to 'transcend' the musical text depends on the fact that the concept of 'musical gesture' itself cannot be simply conceived in terms of the various aspect or parameters of music that are represented by notation: pitch, rhythm, meter melody, harmony, dynamic, and so on. Nor is a 'musical gesture' the 'sum' of all these aspects represented by music notation: it is rather the overall result of all the musical features perceived altogether in a synthetic way in the concrete musical experience. Unfortunately, one of the greatest limitations of the theoretical framework for the study of music-dance interaction, as it had been laid down by many thinkers, musicologists, musicians and choreographers since the beginning of the twentieth century, was their reliance on the formal aspects of music as represented by notation. These authors tried to determine the aspects that music shares with dance — and which can therefore be considered as a common ground for comparison between the two arts — by focusing on the basic categories with which we usually conceptualise and represent (through notation) the music. For example, Paul Hodgins, whose book of 1992 has

---

[77]. *Ibidem.*

[78]. *Ibidem*, p. 93.

[79]. *Ibidem*, p. 94.

often been regarded as a landmark for choreomusicology, listed six «intrinsic» categories — such as rhythmic (accent and meter in both music and dance), dynamic («volume of musical gesture *vs.* size of choreographic gesture»), structural (motive/figure; phrase/period in both arts) and so on — and three «extrinsic» categories (associations of both music and dance to an «external» element, like an archetypal character or theme, the emotions or psychology of a character, the elements or events of the plot)[80]. Even apart from the fact that Hodgins' «intrinsic» categories reflect more our cognitive attitude to cross-domain mapping than the 'intrinsic' characteristics of music and dance in themselves (notice that many concepts and terms which are usually regarded as pertinent to dance and bodily motion are drawn from the domain of sound, and *vice versa*), this approach has the disadvantage of focusing excessive attention on the separate aspects of music, rather than on the overall shapes and gestalts that result from their dynamic interaction. Such categorizations are based on a rigid form/content dichotomy. According to Hodgins, intrinsic relationships are granted by purely formal aspects of music and dance that do not bear any meaning in themselves, while extrinsic relationships are purely conventional associations created by an external element which superimpose some meaning on both music and dance from outside[81]. This theoretical framework is indebted to a formalist (the term being understood this time in the sense of a precise, historically determined aesthetics) tradition of thought which has its roots in the debates about musical form and musical meaning of the late nineteenth and early twentieth centuries. Not by chance, Hodgins' categorisation (his 'intrinsic categories') was foreshadowed by those formulated between the 1910s and 1920s by Émile Jaques-Dalcroze and by Ruth St. Denis and Ted Shawn (the Denishawn «principles of music visualisation»), who were influenced in many respects by that aesthetics.

An Example: *Variations for Orchestra*

I shall try now to illustrate my above thoughts using as an example a composition which was not originally conceived for dance but was later choreographed[82]. Indeed, many of Stravinsky's compositions originally conceived as purely concert pieces were subsequently choreographed. Several compositions of the serial period, such as *Movements*, *Monumentum pro Gesualdo*, and *Requiem Canticles* — all choreographed by George Balanchine — belong to this category. The example I have chosen is *Variations for Orchestra*, officially recorded as

---

[80]. Hodgins 1992, pp. 26-27 for the complete list. Other lists, more or less similar to Hodgins', had been produced by Elisabeth Sawyer and Katherine Teck. See Damsholt 2018, Damsholt 1999, pp. 82-90 for a more exhaustive account.

[81]. Hodgins 1992, p. 25.

[82]. On the Balanchine-Stravinsky artistic and personal relationship see Joseph 2000; Joseph 2011, pp. 102-196; Jordan 2000, pp. 107-109; Jordan 2007, ,pp. 158-236. For a list of basic typologies of music-dance relationships see Schröder 2018, pp. 141-142.

Balanchine's last choreography, which was created, with a significant creative contribution by Suzanne Farrell, on the occasion of the Stravinsky Centennial Celebration of 1982. This was the second choreography for Stravinsky's *Variations Aldous Huxley in Memoriam*, a composition for orchestra of 1963-1964, first performed in concert in 1965 (hereafter I will use the shortened title *Variations* for both Stravinsky's composition and Balanchine's two ballet versions). In the 1966 version, which premiered on 31 March at the New York State Theater, the music was performed three times, each time with a different choreography: a corps of twelve girls; six men; and a *solo* by Suzanne Farrell. The 1982 version, by contrast, was conceived as an entirely soloistic dance piece for Farrell and was largely based on Balanchine's and Farrell's recall of the 1966 *solo* section — according to Farrell, it began and ended in the same way[83]. The following analysis is based on the videotaping of the premiere at the New York State Theater on 2 July 1982[84].

In the following analysis I will show that the way in which Balanchine and Farrell assembled the various sequences of dance steps reflects the general sense of motion energetic continuity created by various interacting musical aspects. Of course, neither the choreographer nor the dancer accomplished this result thanks to a preliminary 'analysis' of the score. Their musical competence, after all, was very different. Balanchine's high-level of musical training is well known. He was a good musician and a good pianist, and was used to playing, transcribing, and analysing the most complex scores[85]. Farrell's musical knowledge, on the contrary, mainly came from her practice as a dancer. Yet, despite their different musical backgrounds, they both approached the music of *Variations* in a way that denotes a sort of 'structural consciousness', thanks to their ability to bodily respond in a highly sensitive way to the formal features of music. In Farrell's own words,

> [...] a dancer who tries to analyse the music, to interpret every note physically, to accentuate the obvious climaxes, will bypass what music is really about. It is a definition of time, and that can only be spontaneous. Moving with music is not an intellectual feat. It is an emotional, physical, sensual response to a given moment of time[86].

---

[83]. FARRELL 1990, pp. 149-150. See also TAPER 1984, p. 384.

[84]. *Balanchine Celebrates Stravinsky*, Producer: Judy Kinberg. Director: Emile Ardolino. First TV broadcast on 14 February 1983 on PBS in the 'Great Performances/Dance in America' program series. Copy at NYPL, Performing Arts Research Collections – Dance, MGZIC 9-558.

[85]. The first page of his short score of *Variations* (Harvard Theatre Collection, Houghton Library. Series III. Music scores. 2227) is reproduced in JOSEPH 2002, p. 299, where it is erroneously attributed to Stravinsky's hand. Many thanks to Elia Andrea Corazza for the insight.

[86]. FARRELL 1990, p. 152.

As a choreographed piece, *Variations* differs in many ways from other, more celebrated and better-known, creations of the Stravinsky-Balanchine artistic binomial. As a purely musical score, it belongs to a group of late serial compositions by Stravinsky which share a rather different sensibility for time from the chronometric, static and repetitive one Stravinsky had favoured until then. Due to the high complexity of the overall rhythm of the polyphonic structure, the background pulse often becomes imperceptible in these pieces. The structuring function of metre is also greatly attenuated — it is no mere chance that Stravinsky's last scores often adopt the *Mensurstrich* graphic convention. The only moment in *Variations* where the pulse is totally clear is in the three-part fugato at bb. 101-117 (section no. 9)[87]. In fact, as we shall see, this section corresponds to a different type of vision of the body. Secondly, in these late compositions, the musical materials are shorter and more essential than the static musical 'blocks' of Stravinsky's previous scores. The typical Stravinskyan ostinatos almost completely disappear here, making room for small musical figures which follow each other in rapid sequence. Of course, not all of these small figures can be considered as 'musical gestures', and some sections, in particular the three-part fugato and the 12-part polyphonic refrains at sections nos. 2, 4, and 10, are much less 'gestural' in this respect than others. Nevertheless, many musical figures of the other sections are characterised by a distinctive bodily evocativeness, which becomes ever more recognisable and charged with bodily meaning as they continuously reappear throughout the course of the composition. To fully account for all their modifications in terms of motivic variation (in the sense of the traditional categories of musical form) would take many pages and to no purpose, because the transformations are too radical and affect too many musical aspects. On the contrary, if we think of these figures as musical gestures — instead of 'motifs' — we can see that some constant dynamic shapes appear. In the first and last sections (bb. 1- 22; and 130-141: Ex. 1 and 2) of the score, for example, we can recognise at least four different recurrent musical gestures (in my analysis in Ex. 1 and 2 they are shown with the letters in brackets in the second line below the staves: notice how the gestures are transformed, sometimes also by suppressing some of their parts) which can be 'metaphorically' — in Lakoff and Johnson's sense — described as follows:

a. a rapid and short succession of two chords, with the second chord sounding like the sudden stop of the rapid harmonic movement leading to it, thus evoking a short and rapid bodily movement, brusquely ending in a motionless position: a jump-and-landing, a rise-and-drop, etc.;

b. a homophonic passage of three chords on a regular rhythm, like a calm and steadily paced walk;

---

[87]. The composition is divided into eleven sections: see Phillips 1984 for an exhaustive description.

c. a slower-faster-slower rapid melodic figuration, usually ending with a triplet and reaching a melodic apex (downwards or upwards); it may recall a bodily movement in three phases: run-up, rushing and slowing down again;

d. a short descending melodic figure of three-five notes, moving in great leaps, like a rapid and sudden 'fall'.

Ex. 1: Igor Stravinsky, George Balanchine: *Variations for Orchestra*, bb. 1-22. Analysis.

Ex. 2: Igor Stravinsky, George Balanchine: *Variations for Orchestra*, bb. 130-141. Analysis.

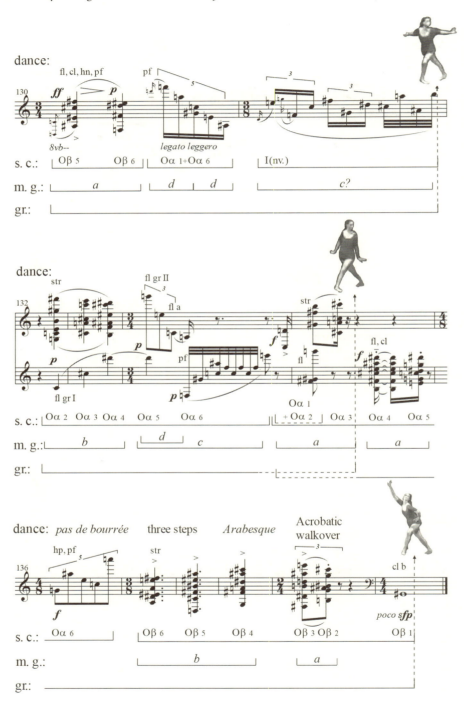

These small gestures are fused into larger 'energetic continuities' (according to the Hatten definition). Many musical gestures in *Variations* are characterised by a particular dynamic shape, which creates a momentary sense of linear process. This is often obtained by means of gradual processes, such as the progressive thinning or thickening of the rhythmic impulses (as at the beginning of gesture *c* at bb. 7-8), or the progressively ascending or descending melodic contours (as in the upper part of gesture *b* at bb. 2-4), which makes it possible, if only for a while, to predict to some extent how the music will develop[88]. The exact ending point of these processes, however, is not predictable, particularly as regards the harmony, due to the almost total absence of centricity and tonal attraction in pitch structure. In Jonathan Kramer's terms, their linearity is of a non-goal directed type[89]. Now, non-goal-directed processes are *open* ones; as such, they do not really *conclude*, they simply *end*. This prompts Stravinsky to adopt two opposed solutions: firstly, to emphasise the sense of interruption and discontinuity between the gestures, by brusquely interrupting their dynamic flow (for example by rests, or with the prolongation of the last note); and secondly to merge each gesture into the other, by creating, in some way, a sense of continuity. Often, however, the situation is more blurred; according to the different musical aspects we focus on, the gestures may seem both separated and merged into larger continuities. All this creates a sense of openness of the musical structure, which can be read in slightly — but also significantly — different ways according to the various subjective responses.

Choreography, like music, is constructed through an assembling of various dance steps, drawn from the vocabulary of classical ballet, and of various bodily gestures drawn in part from the repertory of traditional ballet mime, and in part from a more generic, conventional, and stereotyped repertory of bodily — and facial — signals, as used in both everyday life and in various theatrical traditions. They may signify, say, surprise, supplication, sleep, and so on. Like the musical gestures, these bodily gestures are, in turn, lodged in larger choreographic phrases. To give a sense of their conclusion, Balanchine sometimes makes use of ending positions (mostly in 4th position) that recalls the conventional signals of punctuation belonging to classical ballet (see my silhouettes in Exs. 1-2). Sometimes the arms or the hands also perform some gestures which conventionally signify 'end' or 'stop'. Farrell, however, often performs the concluding signals in an off-balanced and unstable position so as to give the sense of a movement that is not totally interrupted (a 'half stop'), and to make the phrases appear as if merged one into another. Dancing in off-balanced positions had been recognised as one of Farrell's trademarks ever since she achieved star status in Balanchine's company[90]. In *Variations*, off-balance is technically exploited

---

[88]. I am conceiving linearity in Kramer's sense as the product of «implications that arise from earlier events of the piece». KRAMER 1988, p. 20.

[89]. *Ibidem*.

[90]. «Some parts of the music were more specific than others and took on certain sounds or rhythms that could be identified and these became anchors and signposts for me to be finished with one movement and get myself to the back corner for the next». FARRELL 1990, pp. 107-109.

ILL. 2: George Balanchine, *Variations for Orchestra* (1982): Farrell's movements in section 4 (bb. 47-58).

to disrupt the static of many articulating and ending points. This creates the same gradation between discontinuity and continuity as in the musical counterpart. Given the general lack of a reliable rhythmic-metric basis, the principal footholds for adapting the choreographic phrases are the dynamically salient points of the single musical gestures comprised within the larger units[91]. Farrell intuitively recognised the articulating function of these gesturally emphatic points[92].

---

[91]. These may be conceived as Hatten's «nuclear points of emphasis. HATTEN 2004, p. 101.
[92]. FARRELL 1990, pp. 149-150.

Some sections also lack any dynamically salient point — not only a regular pulse — that might serve as a reference point for dance. This is the case of the three 12-part polyphonic *refrains*, where the irrational rhythm of each part, the extremely dense polyphonic intertwining, the low dynamics (**pp**) and the homogeneous timbre make the whole section appear as a unique, jumbled, magmatic and never-ending flux. In the absence of any reference point for dance, Balanchine and Farrell decided to choreograph these sections as a sequence of bodily gestures merged within a single, continuous, very long and very slow bodily movement, to be executed with no counting at all, as in a movie played back at a slower rate[93]. In the second refrain (bb. 47-58), for example, the whole trunk, legs, head and both arms move in a wavelike fashion so as to give the impression of a person moving slowly in a fluid (Ill. 2).

In the other sections, where the nuclear points of emphasis of the various musical gestures are clearly hearable, Balanchine's attention does not usually focus on each of them separately, but rather on the musical energetic continuities that result from their grouping in larger structures. Mere 'visualisation' of a single musical gesture is not the rule[94]. Sometimes, however, the dance also deliberately and playfully lingers on a small musical figure, by mimicking it with some bodily movements, characterised by a somehow similar dynamic shape (sometimes recalling my previous metaphorical description: the jump, the rise-and drop, the walk, the run, the fall, etc.). This happens, for example, at bb. 7-8, where the increasingly frequent repetition of the $g\sharp_4$, with which musical gesture *c* starts, is visualised by Farrell's index fingers repeatedly pointing at something in front of her with a similar increasing rapidity. To quote just another example, towards the end of the piece, at b. 139, Farrell seems to literally 'walk' on musical gesture *b* (the one I have metaphorically described as 'a calm and steadily-paced walk') thus preparing to exit the stage in this manner. Gesture *a* is perhaps the most frequently visualised, by means of dynamically analogous bodily movements (jump-and-landing, rise-and-drop, and so on). See for example section 6 (bb. 72-85), where this gesture is entrusted three times to the orchestral chords that frame the two phrases of the trombones. This is a very common musical figure in Stravinsky's music: we will meet it again in Chapter Two and Four, in *The Firebird* and in *The Flood* respectively. Balanchine focused his attention on this gesture in several choreographies based on Stravinsky's late compositions. In *Movements for Piano and Orchestra*, for example, the three fermatas of the piano solo at bb. 42-42b and the threefold cadence at b (42c) could be interpreted as instances of this recurrent musical gesture. Stephanie Jordan has clearly shown how Balanchine choreographed this passage as a short woman's solo — which was originally conceived for Diana Adams, but in the end was danced by Suzanne Farrell, due to Adam's

---

[93]. Balanchine and Farrell jokingly described these sections a « a mess ». *Ibidem*, p 150.

[94]. On the concept of music visualization in dance see JORDAN 2000, pp. 74-75.

pregnancy — by providing each musical gesture *a* with a corresponding rise-and-drop bodily gesture, which works as the ending point of the previous sequence of steps[95].

Let us now turn to the music. There are many musical aspects that contribute to the grouping of the musical gestures into larger continuities. However, what is important to note is that the grouping structure is different depending on which of these aspects is considered more significant. In Ex. 1 and Ex. 2 the groups are shown by the large brackets in the third line below the staves. The dashed horizontal segments signal different grouping alternatives. In the first section, the sequence of gestures at bb. 1-5 (*a - a - b - a -* sustained chord) may be considered as a single unit since a sense of continuity between the three elements is produced by textural (polyphonic-homophonic) homogeneity. From b. 6 onwards, in fact, the texture changes from polyphonic-homophonic to purely melodic writing. We must also consider that between the twofold gesture a at b. 1 and gesture b at b. 2, there is no sense of interruption, as this would be produced by a sufficiently long pause. Moreover, the whole group is almost literally recapitulated in the last seven bars of the score (Ex. 2); the only difference being the interpolated block of piano and harp at bar 136:

bb.	musical gestures		
1-5	*a – a –*	*b – a –*	[prolonged chord]
135-141	*a – a –* [interp.] *–*	*b – a –*	[prolonged note]

Nevertheless, one may also perceive a different grouping, one which also includes the following musical gesture *c* at b. 6, thus forming a unit a - a - b - a - c. At the end of b. 5 there is no totally clear sense of interruption: the final prolonged chord of the horns is suddenly merged with the beginning of gesture *c* in the next bar. In comparison to this 'half stop', the long rest at b. 7, which follows the melodic apex $d_\sharp$ at the end of b. 6, sounds like a clear full-stop, after which, with the repeated $g_\sharp$ of the flutes and piano, a rather different section (particularly in terms of timbre and texture) seems to start. There are also other formal attributes of music that could make one perceive bb. 1-6 as a unit: the orchestration outlines an antiphonal exchange between the timbre of the brasses and that of the strings (variously combined with harp, flutes and piano); and the dynamics also outline an arch form: *f – p marc. – ff*:

---

[95]. JORDAN 2007, pp. 212-213. Jordan based her analysis on the annotation of the piano rehearsal score for the New York City Ballet 1963 performance, the sequences of steps concluded by the rise-and-drop gesture are annotated as «D[iana]'s steps».

bb.	musical gestures	instruments	articulating points	dynamics
1	*a*	br (+ pf)	none	*f*
1	*a*	str (+fl, hp)	none	***p marc.***
2-5	*b – a –* [prol. chord]	Br	half stop	***p marc.***
6	c	str (+ hp, pf)	full stop	***ff***

The listener, in the end, is left with a sense of uncertainty about the first ending point encountered starting from b. 1: is it already the prolonged chord at b. 5? Or only the final *d♯* at b. 6? A similar ambivalence can be perceived in the last section, at b. 135. Here the function and position of the musical gesture *a* on the downbeat of b. 135 — with the last semiquaver upbeat at b. 134 sounding like an appoggiatura — is twofold: it starts the recapitulation of bb. 1-5 at bb. 135-141, as seen above, but at the same time, due to timbral homogeneity and temporal proximity (being closer to the previous gesture *d/c* than to the following gesture *a*), it also seems to conclude the previous unit, which starts at b. 132. The orchestration again creates an arch form — it begins with gesture *b* of the strings, is momentarily interrupted by gesture *d/c* of piano and flutes (b. 134) and then comes back to the strings on the final gesture *a*:

bb.	musical gestures	instruments
132	*b*	str
[134	*d/c*	pf + fl]
135 (downbeat)	*A*	str

In the end, there are at least two possible groupings:
1. 132-134 /135 (134 upbeat)-141
2. 132-135 (downbeat) /135 (upbeat)-141

Harmony provides an important contribution to the articulation of the musical structure. The pitch content of both sections is drawn from four serial charts based respectively on the Original 12-tone row of the piece (O), its Retrograde form (R); its first half (or hexachord: O*α*); and its second half (O*β*) (Ex. 3).

These arrays are constructed with an interval-rotation technique developed by Stravinsky from *Movements* on, based on a similar procedure employed by Ernst Krenek[96]. We do not need to deal here with the properties of these serial charts: I will discuss them in more detail in Chapter Three. For the time being it will suffice to understand that Stravinsky conceived and used them to create a process of continuous harmonic transformation, thus contributing to a sense of linearity and continuity in time. This is evident from Stravinsky's way of using these matrixes: he usually exploits a complete unfolding of *all* the lines of six notes (or twelve,

---

[96]. On these arrays see for example Straus 2011, pp. 26-32, 64-70, 149-164.

Ex. 3: Igor Stravinsky, *Variations Aldous Huxley in Memoriam* Serial arrays for bb. 1-22 and 130-141.

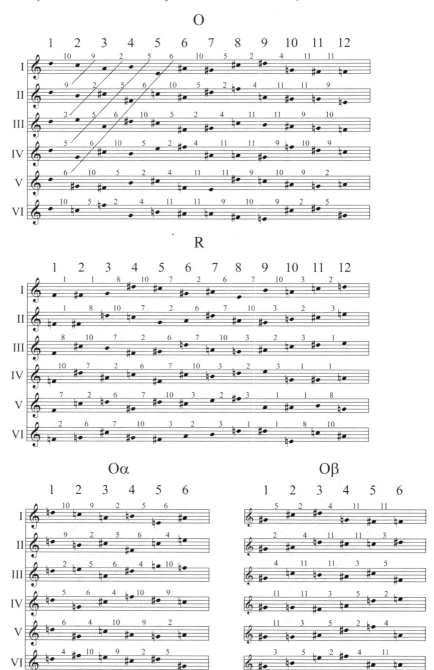

if the matrix is constructed on the complete 12-tone row instead of its two halves), or *all* the columns (which Stravinsky called 'verticals') of an array, and in progressive order, and entrusted them to just as many successive melodic fragments or successive harmonies. To understand how this may contribute to creating a sense of linearity and continuity, we must consider that, as a consequence of the particular construction of these matrices[97], the overall pitch content in each horizontal line is different from the others, even though the overall intervallic content remains the same. Similarly, each vertical column contains a different group of pitches; but when they are used altogether, one after the other, they result in a harmonic progression in which each polyphonic part — which is usually scattered by Stravinsky among various instrumental or vocal parts — feature the same sequence of intervals, which just starts each time from a different point of the sequence, like a canon (see the diagonal lines in Ex. 3). Therefore, a complete unfolding of lines or verticals results in a continuous harmonic transformation within a fixed intervallic framework. It is difficult to say what this aspect alone may produce in the listener — notice, however, that this is rather similar to what happens in a tonal progression, in which harmony changes but the voice leading always repeats the same intervallic patterns — but when we look at music in its entirety (not only with regard to harmony), we see that a complete unfolding of serial lines or verticals usually corresponds to larger energetic continuities (larger *gestalts*) created by several musical aspects, such as timbre, texture, dynamics, form, time proximity, etc. Consider, for example, the first and last sections of (nos. 1 and 11 respectively). A complete series of 12 verticals from row chart R ends at b. 5, exactly in correspondence with the 'half-stop' of the first grouping hypothesis we have already formulated according to texture, timbre, time proximity and form. Then, the remaining passage is entirely entrusted to lines 6 to 1 of row chart O. In the last section, the two series of verticals of Oα and Oβ articulate the passage in two phrases, which correspond to the first grouping hypothesis formulated above (132-134/135-141) on the basis of similar formal considerations, since bb. 1-5 (bb. 135-141 are a varied recapitulation of the first five bars of the score):

Section 1

bb.	musical gestures	serial construction
1-5	a – a – b – a – [prolonged chord]	R: verticals from 1 to 12
6-20	c – c-c; d – d – d; c (;) c – d; c - d	O: lines from VI to I*

<small>*. Line II is repeated twice, the 1st time in retrograde form. Line III is in retrograde form.</small>

---

[97]. A given tone row (either a 12-tone row or a hexachord) is put on the first line of the array. Then, every consecutive line begins with the same note as the first line, and features the same intervals, but in rotated order: line 2 begins with the second interval of line 1; line 3 with the third interval of line 1 (second interval of line 2) and so on, until the last note is reached. Complete 12-tone rows would produce a 12x12 matrix. In this case, however, both 12-tone rows and hexachords are rotated six times in all, thus producing 12x6 (O and R) and 6x6 (Oα and Oβ) arrays. In Ex. 3 intervals are shown in terms of ascending semitones by the superscript numbers above the staves. The diagonal lines show their rotation.

Section 11

bb.	musical gestures	serial construction**
130-131	*a – d-d – (c?)*	Oβ vert. 5; Oβ vert. 6;
		Oα vert. 1+6; Row I(nv)
132-134	*b – d/c*	Oα verticals from 2 to 6
135 (134 upbeat)-141	*a - a – b – a* [prolonged note]	Oα verticals from 1 to 6
		Oβ verticals from 6 to 1

¨. Symbols O, R Oα, Oβ refer to the four matrixes of Ex 3; Roman numerals (I-VI) to their lines; Arabic numeral (1-6 or 1-12) to their columns.

The correspondence between serial construction and other musical aspects clearly shows that serial structure is coordinated with these attributes in order to create a dynamic shape of the bodily energy unfolding in time. However, there still remain some ambiguities — as we have seen before —, since not all the musical aspects concur to determine the same articulating points of these energetic shapes. This allows for different bodily interpretations of the musical structure. The articulation of sections 1 and 11 implied by Balanchine's and Farrell's choreography corresponds to the way they perceived and interpreted the musical structure in a bodily on *this* occasion. The first two musical gestures *a* at b. 1 correspond respectively to Farrell's preparatory running step, entering the stage from right, and a *grand jeté*. This leads, with no interruption, to a series of steps on the slow homophonic passage (musical gesture *b*) ending with a *grand développé à la seconde*. The first clear signal of punctuation is a stop in *croisé*, right leg *plié* and left stretched behind, with left arm pointing forward, in correspondence to the sustained chord at b. 5. However, Farrell's position is off-balanced and unstable (a half-stop) — her trunk seems to fall forward (see my silhouettes in Ex. 1) — and so she has to move immediately, going on to a series of steps in 2nd position on the heels, which ends once again in in *croisé*, right leg *plié* and left stretched behind, but this time in a more balanced and stable way, with high arm and index finger pointing upwards vertically: a clear full stop. Hence the sequence of bodily movements is articulated in the same way as the music: all the musical gestures from b. 1 to b. 5 are given an uninterrupted choreographic phrase, which looks like (and acts as) the theatrical gesture of a character suddenly entering the stage and then stopping in an expressive posture. Both dance and music, moreover, leave us with a sense of uncertainty over the exact point where this theatrical gesture ends (the first half stop at b. 5, or the following stop at b. 6?). In the recapitulation of the last section, we have a similar situation. The first clear sign of punctuation in the music is at the end of musical gesture *c*, at b. 131, which is followed by a long rest. Here Farrell stands for a while in *croisé* with both arms horizontally opened. Then a new choreographic phrase starts, which ends with a rapid turn with her outstretched arms rapidly whirling on the musical gesture *d/c* of piano and flutes at b. 134, and then a little jump ending in a wide 4th position *croisé*, arms down, on the musical gesture *a* on the downbeat of b. 135. The articulating point is clear enough. After this, Farrell, moves on pointe, and starts a new phrase, which lasts for the remaining five bars. Her movements here look like a progressive move towards 'an elsewhere'. During the piano and harp gesture *c*, her arms perform an expressive gesture, as if to push through, on a *pas de bourrée*. Then, three slow steps (like a walk), the last ending with an *arabesque*, on the three homophonic chords of musical gesture *b*; an acrobatic cartwheel on the last *a* figure and, on the last note of the piece, the same gesture of the arm pointing upwards as in the first section, but this time pointing to the exit in the opposite corner of the stage. With her other arm somehow *à la danse de caractère*, Farrell finally exits running from the scene. Farrell's sequences of gestures, therefore, articulate both the first and the last section in two distinct parts. The precise point of articulation between the two parts corresponds to that implied by the music. However, as we have seen, not all the aspects of the music suggest the same articulating points. Pitch (serial) structure, for example, corresponds to the articulation into choreographic phrases only in the first section. In the last section, on the contrary, the choreography reinforces the sensation that the musical gesture *d/c* of piano and flutes at b. 134 and the following musical gesture *a* of the orchestra on the downbeat of b. 135 are a unique, continuous whirling movement, ending with a brusque stop; and that gesture *a* is the end of this energetic continuity, not the beginning of a new one. This choice corresponds to one of the possible groupings of the musical gestures, as suggested by timbre and musical form — as we have seen before — instead of pitch structure.

To sum up: in *Variations* the choreography seems to imply that Balanchine and Farrell perceived both the single musical gestures and their groupings within larger structures as energetic continuities, that is as meaningful bodily gestures. Sometimes their choreography lingers on a little musical figure, by simply visualising it; more often, however, it focuses on larger musical unities, translating them into sweeping bodily movements. The long, uninterrupted sound flux of the 12-part refrains is given the meaning of a slow and wavelike motion of the body. The first bars of the score and their varied recapitulation at the end are respectively associated with the theatrical gesture of the dancer rapidly entering the stage and suddenly stopping in an emphatic pose (the *position* with arm pointing upwards at b. 6), and of his/her final exit from the scene with a calm walk and a final run. These gestures are associated with precise musical unities, which share with them the same kind of energetic shape.

Sources for the Choreo-Musical Analysis: Some Issues

In the above discussion, as well as in Chapters Two and Four of this book, my observations on the relationship between music and dance rely on an analysis of some specific versions or performances of the choreography. In all these cases — as usual in any detailed musical-chorographical analysis — the sources of these performances are some video recordings of the spectacle. Choreography alone can be — and has always been — transmitted in many other ways and by many types of sources: verbal descriptions, visual sources (draft, paintings, photos, etc), choreographic notations such as labanotation, etc. Dancers and ballet masters themselves are an important 'source', thanks to their embodied memories. More generally memory — both individual and collective — acts as an embodied archive in the preservation, transmission, and reception of choreographies[98]. Yet, the more we look for a close description of the relationship between dance and music, the more a detailed and exhaustive description or recording of the performance is needed. In this sense those technologies, such as film or video recording, that allow the registration of moving images may seem the best we can hope for. Unfortunately, these kind of sources pose as many problem as they solve[99]. First, a video production can never be a 'neutral' representation of a live performance, but rather a mediated translation of it, based on the features, limitations, codes, and conventions of the medium itself. Film or TV direction, video editing, and post-production editing superimpose a filter between us and the original performance, which in the end is entirely 'translated' into the terms of the technological medium. Secondly, video recordings, as well as photos, reflects the *gaze* of the individual(s) that produced them; and this, too, is hardly a 'neutral' gaze. So, whenever relying on films or videos a choreo-musical analysis should try to get behind this technological and cultural filter and to imagine how the live stage performance may have looked like to *our* eyes. Secondly, the most obvious, but also more important problem posed by video recordings, is that each recording represents just *one* performance. Even in the case of a strongly consolidated tradition, in which all the features and details of choreography are stable and clearly defined, each performance inevitably gives rise to different results and different meanings. This is quite evident when different dancers interpret the same choreography; but even a single dancer can considerably change her/his own way of interpreting the same choreography from time to time — or over the years. The same should be said even of the music, despite the widespread — but unfounded — belief that its reliance on written text (the score) prevents it from significant change in performance. Each musical performance of a single musical text can be — and usually is — to some extent different from another, even when the same music performers are involved.

Given these issues, only two approaches are possible: the first is to deliberately choose just one of the various existing interpretations of a choreography, bearing in mind that this corresponds to just one of its innumerable possible forms. This is what I have done when relying on the TV broadcast of February 1983 for my analysis of *Variations* in the previous pages. My choice was in keeping with my idea of showing how *this* performance corresponds to a particular and unique bodily response, among the many possible ones allowed by the ambiguities of musical structure. Similarly, my study of the visual aspects of *The Flood* in Chapter Four will be

---

[98]. For an overview see FRANCO – NORDERA 2008, pp. xvii-xxxv.
[99]. See JORDAN 2000, pp. 101-102.

based on the video recording of the first (and last) TV broadcast of 14 June 1962, and in this case the choice is motivated by the particular vicissitudes of this TV opera, as we will see. More in general, focusing on a single performance is the best-suited approach to a close reading that tries to show how music and dance interact in creating meaning. The meanings of a work, like a ballet, in which different artistic means are combined, does not simply correspond to the sum of the meanings associated to each artistic components, but is indeed the 'emergent meaning' of their interaction. This process is strongly dynamic: each different performance — not only each different choreography of a musical score — can convey quite different bodily responses to the music — that is, different meaning associations[100]. In this perspective, even focusing on the 'first performance' should be considered as just one of the many possible choices[101].

The other possible approach is to access and compare the largest possible number of recordings of different performances and interpretations — different 'versions' — of the same choreography. In my study of *The Firebird* in Chapter Two, different interpretations will be sometimes compared to show how they reflect different views of the body that are implicit in music. Either way, my focus will be on Fokine's overall concept of his 1910 choreography. I will not rely on a single performance — be it a 'reconstructed', 'restored, or tradition-based one. Rather I will try to highlight Fokine's (and Stravinsky's) idea of the ballet. This choice will be in in keeping with the overall historical-cultural aspects — rather than analytical, as in my previous analysis of *Variations* — of my discourse. From a historical perspective, in fact, the meanings which the authors associate to their work also reflects the ideas, beliefs and ideologies not only of the authors, but of an entire age and society.

But how can we get an accurate idea of what Fokine's original choreography looked like? There are many visual sources for the *décor* of the 1910 version of the ballet. Golovin and Bakst's designs of the set and the costumes are held in various museums and collections, and many of them can be easily seen in printed books and on the Internet. Several backstage photographs show us the characters of the ballet in their typical poses and with their original costumes, most famously among which are those with Tamara Karsavina as the Firebird and Michail Fokine or Adolph Bolm as Prince Ivan, in their *pas de deux*. However, these static, posed images cannot fully convey the meanings produced by the bodily movements of the original choreography. We can get a better idea by looking at those (recorded or live) performances that seem to have best preserved Fokine's concept, thanks to the continuities between ballet companies and the

[100]. See for example my discussion of the various interpretations of the *Pas de deux* of *The Firebird* in Chapter Two.

[101]. See Jordan 2007, pp. 131-132. A list of the original choreographies on Stravinsky's scores has been compiled by Stephanie Jordan and Larraine Nicholas and is available as an online database (*Stravinsky the Global Dancer*) at <http://urweb.roehampton.ac.uk/stravinsky/index.asp>, accessed on January 2022; the database listed 119 original choreographies of *The Firebird* (including those based on one of the three concert suites) between 1910 and 2012.

embodied memories of the dancers. In this case, however, we must also ask ourselves to what extent these performances correspond to the 1910 original and whether they still convey the same bodily meanings as they did to the 1910 audience.

My main source for the choreographic component, indeed, will be Fokine's memoirs, along with many other documental and visual sources. Fokine's memoirs too, of course, present plenty of issues of their own. The circumstances and motivations behind their genesis raise several questions about their reliability[102]. They represent the culmination of the choreographer's career-long effort to present himself as one of the most important twentieth-century ballet reformers. Fokine strived to appear as an original innovator, in particular where Isadora Duncan's influence on him could be presumed. In fact, he was able to see — and was impressed by — Duncan early in his career, and his works from around 1910 clearly exhibit her influence. This is also recognizable in some 'natural' connotations of the *The Firebird*'s characters, as we will see. In spite of this, Fokine's memories never mention Duncan's name in this respect. That said, Fokine's recollections are still an important source of information concerning the meanings and the view of the body surrounding *The Firebird*. They can give us useful insights into the way the choreographer tried to express certain meanings and bodily qualities which the music too strives to convey with its own means.

It is important to notice that by «Fokine's (and Stravinsky's) general concept of the ballet» I do not mean the 'original' choreography, as represented, for example, by the version of the ballet's premiere. This notion of 'original' is problematic in many respects. First, we cannot assume that the form in which the spectacle was first staged — nor any other version in the following reprises — entirely corresponds to the authors' intentions. In the case of *The Firebird*, in particular, this was not the case, as we will see shortly. Secondly, we cannot say that the choreographer's intentions are the only ones that matter. Choreographies are often the result of a long series of transformations and processes that take place over the time, even as the result of artistic choices of individuals other than the choreographer that were canonized in the tradition. While these issue are very similar to those that have been long debated in the context of philological studies, a third question concerns more specifically the subject of this book: if the meanings (and the bodily meanings in particular) of a choreo-musical creation are our main object of interest, we should be aware that focusing our attention solely on an allegedly 'original' choreography corresponds to considering just one of various meanings that have been historically associated to that music. The meaning of an artwork, in fact, is not necessarily the same as that which its author(s) intended, but rather that emerging among its various audiences.

---

[102]. Fokine's memoirs were completed and published posthumously in 1961 by his son Vitale. In 1962 a Russian edition was issued (FOKINE 1962). This often diverges from the English edition (FOKINE 1961), while the German edition (FOKINE 1974) is more faithful to the Russian. However, in the passage I will quote, the content is essentially the same.

This is precisely the case with *The Firebird*. As I said before, from time to time I will resort to specific performances of the ballet, as preserved in films and video productions created since the early 1950s, but only to show how differently they interpret certain aspects of the choreography, thus resulting in different meanings and bodily connotations. The main problem with these sources — in addition to those highlighted above — is that we cannot entirely ascertain which elements of the 1913 elements of the spectacle they preserve. The tradition of choreographies, which is largely based on the embodied memories of dancers and choreographers, often undergoes radical changes, or it weakens to the point of being completely interrupted. In the last case the attempts to get back to the lost original choreography are usually labelled as 'reconstructions'; but even within an otherwise 'uninterrupted' tradition — like that of *The Firebird* — there are continuous back-and-forth movements on the part of artists who try to 'restore' some elements that that they consider as more 'original' but have been lost over time. So, it is often difficult to draw a clear line between tradition and reconstruction.

All my previous discussion means that I am not so interested in a reconstructed 'original' spectacle, as in the meanings that were originally attached to music and dance. In the last three decades, on the contrary, much attention has been given to the question of reconstruction, which came to the fore after Millicent Hodson and Kenneth Archer's famous reconstruction of Nijinsky's original choreography and of Roerich's décors of *The Rite of Spring*, staged in 1987 by the Joffrey Ballet[103]. The story of this reconstruction has been recounted several times in numerous books, articles and documentaries, but we will recall it briefly as it provides the opportunity to discuss the relationship between music and dance that Stravinsky expressed in his writings.

It can be said that the first impulse for the revival of Nijinsky's 'original' choreography — which was staged eight times during the 1913 season and then disappeared from the repertoire and was ultimately supplanted by Massine's 1920 new choreography — came from Stravinsky himself in the late 1960s. Before that date, his judgments on Nijinsky's choreography had been wavering to say the least. After praising it as «incomparable» a few months after the Paris premiere, he released a much more negative judgment in an interview for the journal *Comœdia* on the occasion of the ballet's restaging with the new choreography by Massine[104]. While still praising the «plastic beauty» of the 1913 choreography, he maintained that Nijinsky, unlike Massine, had missed the purely «architectural» and not «anecdotal» nature of his music, thus filling his choreography with a lot of useless descriptive and narrative elements. This 'error' went hand in hand, according to Stravinsky, with another fault of Nijinsky's: unlike Massine's

---

[103].   HODSON 1996.

[104].   GEORGES-MICHEL, M. 'Les Deux *Sacre du Printemps*', in: *Comœdia*, 11 December 1920, repr. in LESURE 1980, p. 53. As For Stravinsky's more positive assessment of Nijinsky's choreography after the 1913 premiere, see STRAVINSKY – CRAFT 1978, pp. 509-514.

choreography, which was made of [choreographical] phrases conceived according to a principle of «free connection between music and dance» it was entirely «subjected to the tyranny of the bar». In other words: the articulation of the dance steps into phrases simply corresponded to the metric structure of the music. Then, in the 1935 *Autobiography* he entirely condemned Nijinsky — who in the meantime had definitively disappeared from the scene and had been diagnosed with schizophrenia in 1919 — for his «ignorance of the most elementary notions of music» that led him to conceive his choreography as a «very labored and barren effort rather than a plastic realization flowing simply and naturally from what the music demanded», thus showing «his complete inability to accept and assimilate those revolutionary ideas which Diaghileff had made his creed»[105]. This, basically, remained Stravinsky's official verdict on Nijinsky's *Rite* until the early 1960s. In *Memories and Commentaries* he still maintained that Nijinsky had wrongly emphasized «the musical beat and pattern in constant co-ordination', thus reducing the dance 'to a rhythmic duplication and imitation of the music»[106]. The basis for this way of reasoning was again Stravinsky's vision of music and dance as autonomous but 'dialoguing' discourses: since music does not aim at illustrating or describing anything, even dance should not 'duplicate', so to speak, music through a slavish reproduction of the metric structures of music; rather, it should be placed in a dialectical relationship with music, as in in a two-part counterpoint.

However, Stravinsky's negative assessment of Nijinsky's choreography — but not its underlying ideological standpoint — changed radically when, in 1967, Stravinsky had the opportunity to reconsider some choreographic notes of his own that were added to a printed copy of the four-hand piano reduction that had served — according to Stravinsky — in the preparation of Nijinsky's choreography[107]. In the light of this rediscovery, Stravinsky seemed to realize for the first time that Nijinsky's choreography was not then so slavishly based on musical meters, but it too moved, like Massine's praised choreography, according to the principle of 'counterpoint' between music and dance. Stravinsky's statements aroused further curiosity about Nijinsky's choreography: after years in which musicology had dealt exclusively with his score, almost completely forgetting that it was born as ballet music, the rediscovery of the *Sacre* as music linked to dance thus began.

---

[105]. *AUTOBIOGRAPHY*, pp. 40-42.

[106]. *MEMORIES AND COMMENTARIES*, pp. 37-42.

[107]. The annotations were then added by Stravinsky as an appendix to the Boosey & Hawkes facsimile of his notebook of musical sketches for the *Sacre*, later published in 1969. STRAVINSKY 1969, Appendix III, pp. 35-43. The annotated score is now at the Paul Sacher Foundation, Igor Stravinsky Collection. A page of it is reproduced in STRAVINSKY – CRAFT 1978, p. 79. The score was first given by Stravinsky to Misia Sert the day after the Paris premiere. Afterwards, it came back to Diaghilev shortly before the 1920 restaging with Massine's choreography. Later, it came for some time into the possession of the dancer Anton Dolin. Finally, it was sold at a Sotheby's auction, and then returned to the composer.

Millicent Hodson and Kenneth Archer's reconstruction marked a decisive moment in this process. Hodson found a second important musical source for the reconstruction of the choreography: some handwritten annotations to another printed copy of the four-hand piano reduction in the hand of Marie Rambert, who at the time was assigned by Diaghilev as Nijinsky's assistant in the creation of the choreography, thanks to her knowledge of the theories of Émile Jaques-Dalcroze. To these sources, Hodson added several other verbal and visual evidence, such as the memoirs of Bronislava Nijinska, a huge number of criticisms, reviews and memoirs of the ballet premiere, a few backstage photos, four pastels and about seventy pencil drawings made live by Valentine Gross-Hugo. Based on these sources, Hodson was able to reconstruct several sections of the choreography. The rest was substantially deduced from these latter thanks to conjecture. Hodson, for example, hypothesized that the bodily posture of the Chosen One, which according to Bronislava Nijinska (whose recall, however, was most likely fallacious) was the first aspect of the ballet to be conceived by her brother, was applied to many other parts and groups of characters in the ballet. I do not have the space here to discuss the many methodological and philological issues raised by Hodson 'reconstruction'. I can only mention that it has been criticized several times and with valid arguments. Stephanie Jordan, for example, argued quite convincingly that Stravinsky's choreographic annotations in the four-hand piano reduction may not be related to Nijinsky's original version, but rather to Massine's 1920 version[108]. But even apart from these philological issues, much more fundamental methodological and conceptual questions remain. Patrizia Veroli has levelled a deeper criticism of the ideological structure itself that supported Hodson's reconstructive operation, showing how it was conditioned by the American artistic culture of the Seventies, in which Hodson was trained[109].

Nonetheless, the reconstruction of Hodson's *Le Sacre* has given rise to a series of reconstructions of iconic ballets of the first half of the twentieth century. Most of them were made by Hodson herself, who recovered other famous 'lost' ballets such as Nijinsky's *Jeux* (1996) and *Till Eulenspiegel* (1994)[110]. A methodologically groundbreaking reconstruction of Nijinsky's *L'Après-midi d'un Faune* was made in 1989 by Ann Hutchinson Guest and Claudia Jeschke, based on a score of the ballet notated by Nijinsky himself by mean of a personal system derived from Stepanov's dance notation[111]. Hutchinson Guest and Jeschke's study, was very different from that of Hodson in both overall methodology and philological approach. Finally, in 2014 a new 'reconstructed' version of the *Sacre* was created by Dominique Brun on the basis of methodological assumptions very different from those of Hodson[112].

---

[108]. JORDAN 2013, pp. 101-102.

[109]. VEROLI 2014, pp. 52-56. See also ACOCELLA 2001.

[110]. HODSON 2008.

[111]. The score has been translated into labanotation in HUTCHINSON GUEST – JESCHKE 2010.

[112]. See Veroli's discussion of Brun's reconstruction in VEROLI 2014, pp. 56-62.

The bulk of these studies aimed at reconstructing 'lost' choreographies has undoubtedly contributed much to our knowledge of the relationship between music and dance in early twentieth-century ballets. However, they have somehow overshadowed the no less important problems posed by those ballets which have been apparently much better preserved through an uninterrupted performance tradition and which, therefore, do not require a 'reconstruction' based on documentary sources. Even these ballets though raise complex question about the concept of 'original' in the tradition of choreography. This is also the case with *The Firebird*: a detailed account of its performance history will help to highlight these questions[113].

The Firebird between Tradition and 'Reconstruction'

The Firebird is one of the relatively few ballets produced by Diaghilev's Ballets Russes that has enjoyed an uninterrupted performance tradition[114]. Along with a handful of other works by Fokine (*Les Sylphides*, *Scheherazade*, *Petrushka*, and *Le Spectre de la Rose*) and a few others by Vaslav Nijinsky and Léonide Massine, it belongs to the group of ballets that remained stable in the Ballets Russes repertory, surviving the collapse of the company after the death of the impresario in 1929 and entering the repertory of the post-Diaghilev enterprises, such as Colonel Wassily de Basil and René Blum's Ballets Russes de Monte Carlo[115]. This was probably the most 'ideologically faithful' company to Diaghilev's traditions, thanks also to the presence in the troupe of the long-time Ballet Russes *régisseur* Serge Grigoriev.

In Stravinsky's motherland things worked out differently. A five-year (then further prolonged) agreement gave Diaghilev's company exclusive rights over the ballet. This prevented

---

[113].   In Chapter Two I will only deal with some of the most important productions based on Fokine's choreography. I will not consider productions based on the ballet suites, nor those with original choreography by other authors. For the latter see the *Stravinsky the Global Dancer* database.

[114].   The ballet was staged on 25 June 1910 at the Paris Opéra within Diaghilev's second *Saison russe*. The orchestra was conducted by Gabriel Pierné (1863-1937). The title role was danced by Tamara Karsavina (alternating with Lydia Lopokova in the following performances), Ivan Tsarevich by Fokine, the Tsarevna by Vera Fokina (wife of Mikhail Fokine), and Kastchei by Aleksey Bulgakov alternating.

[115].   The company was founded in 1931 by Colonel de Basil and René Blum with the financial help of Serge Denham. Léonide Massine was initially involved in the company as choreographer, along with George Balanchine who, however, was fired by de Basil after only one year. In 1934, after de Basil's break with Blum, the company was renamed Ballets Russes de Colonel W. de Basil. The name Covent Garden Russian Ballet was the result of a lawsuit by Massine, who left his role as choreographer in 1937 to join Blum in the Ballet Russe de Monte Carlo in 1938 (notice the singular form, which differentiates this company from de Basil and Blum's 1931 company). The final name of de Basil's company, Original Ballet Russe, was adopted in 1939, and was retained until the company's winding up, in 1951. On de Basil's Ballets Russes see Sorley Walker 1982. A more detailed synthesis of the various names, headquarters and locations of the post-Diaghilev companies can be found in García-Márquez 1990, pp. xvi-xvii ('Lineage of the Ballets Russes Companies').

the Russian Imperial Theatres from staging *The Firebird* for many years[116]. The first Russian ballet production in Russia (as well as the first new choreography of the ballet since Fokine) was created, in a modernist style, by Fedor Lopukhov in 1921 at the Mariinsky Theatre[117]. Afterwards, *The Firebird* disappeared from Russian-Soviet theatres.

During the 1930s, Fokine restaged *The Firebird* many times outside his motherland, which he had left in 1918. In 1931 he promoted and supervised a reprise at the Colón Theatre in Buenos Aires — a theatre with close links to European ballet traditions — with new scenery by Ivan Bilibin. Then, in 1934, he again revived the ballet in London with de Basil's company, using the original 1910 costumes and sets. In fact, in 1922 the original scenery by Golovin had been destroyed by damp, and in 1926 Diaghilev had the ballet redesigned by Natalia Goncharova[118]. In 1936-1937, another restaging by de Basil's troupe was held in Melbourne, under Fokine's supervision[119]. After Fokine's death in 1942, and after World War II, *The Firebird* entered the group of canonized works that continued to be performed on a regular basis by the most important national dance companies in the West, such as the Ballet Theatre (today's American Ballet Theatre), Sadler's Wells Ballet (later the Royal Ballet), and the New York City Ballet. In 1945 a new choreography by Adolph Bolm, based on Stravinsky's 1945 suite, was created for the (American) Ballet theatre[120]. Despite Marc Chagall's sets, which would become world-famous, and Alicia Markova's acclaimed interpretation of the title role, Bolm's choreography did not enjoy great fortune. Balanchine's 1949 choreography for the New York City Ballet, with Marie Tallchief as the Firebird and the same sets by Chagall as Bolm's 1945 version, was more successful, and contributed much to the fortune of *The Firebird* in the United States. This setting, however, was also based on the 1945 concert suite, and, of course, Balanchine's new choreography, like Bolm's, was different from Fokine's — although Balanchine introduced many overt references to Fokine's original steps[121]. The original version of the full ballet entered the repertory of the (American) Ballet Theatre only in the late 1970s. Since then the company has staged many other Fokine-based productions of *The Firebird*.

However, it was above all the Royal Ballet that inherited Fokine's legacy, thanks to the company's founder Ninette de Valois — who was part of Diaghilev's troupe from 1923 to 1927 — and to other important figures that had had prominent roles in the Ballets Russes,

---

[116]. This also happened with *Petrushka*, but in the case of *The Firebird* the exclusivity agreements with Diaghilev were extended further. See *SSC I-III*, vol. II, pp. 213, 225-226.

[117]. Souritz 1990, pp. 263-266. See also Jordan 2007, pp. 126-127.

[118]. Beaumont 1937, p. 584.

[119]. In 1937 Fokine had joined de Basil's company as resident choreographer .

[120]. Bolm had danced the role of Prince Ivan in Diaghilev's company since 1911. During the 1930s he had settled in California. In 1940 he had staged another version based on the 1919 concert suite with his own company at the Hollywood Bowl, Los Angeles, where he was resident choreographer.

[121]. Jordan 2007, p. 135. Jordan's analysis of Balanchine's 1949 version is based on a 1951 film source.

ILL. 3. Tamara Karsavina coaching Margot Fonteyn in *The Firebird*, restaged by the Royal Ballet in 1954 (Harvard University, Houghton Library, htc_ms_thr-412_2_63_to_76_METS).

in particular Tamara Karsavina, who had moved to England in 1917. An important role was played by the *régisseur* and ballet master Grigoriev and his wife Lubov Tchernicheva, who had danced in the Ballets Russes from 1911 to 1929, and had been ballet mistress of Diaghilev's company's in its final years. During the 1950s and early 1960s they produced and rehearsed several Fokine revivals for Sadler's Wells/Royal Ballet — *Les Sylphides* (1955), *Petrushka* (1957), the *Polovtsian Dances from Prince Igor* (1965), and *Scheherazade* (1956, for the London Festival Ballet) — including what was to became probably the most celebrated *Firebird* of the second half of the twentieth century, that with Margot Fonteyn as the Firebird and Michael Somes as Tsarevich Ivan, first staged on 23 August 1954 at the Empire Theatre of Edinburgh. For the occasion, Natalia Goncharova revived her 1926 designs, and Tamara Karsavina in person coached Fonteyn and Somes (ILL. 3)[122]. This performance was later made into a successful 1959

---

[122].   The other principal dancers were Svetlana Beriosova as Tzarevna and Frederick Ashton as Kashchey. See also SCHOUVALOFF – BOROVSKY 1982, p. 47.

film, and it is usually considered one of the most convincing interpretations of Fokine's original choreography[123]. Through Grigoriev-Tchernicheva's 1954 restaging, Fokine's legacy has passed down to younger generations of famous Royal Ballet dancers such as Monica Mason, who took over the role of the Firebird in 1978, and Leanne Benjamin. Today, their performances can be seen in various video recordings. That with Leanne Benjamin (Firebird), Jonathan Cope (Ivan) and David Drew (Kashchey), produced for the BBC in 2001 and then released on DVD, is probably the one that comes closest to the 1910 original[124].

Despite having enjoyed such an uninterrupted performance tradition, however, Fokine's *Firebird* changed considerably over the years. It probably began its transformation from its first appearance, even when it was still under the author's supervision. Fokine was able to continue exerting control over his works only in the few years — until 1912 and then again for a while in 1914 — in which he stayed in Diaghilev's company[125]. Subsequently, when his creations passed from his hands, he could not prevent unpredictable changes being made. In his memoirs, he gave a detailed account of the various betrayals and 'wrong interpretations' that he could see in Diaghilev's productions during the 1920s, on which he commented[126]:

> If I were to enumerate only a small part of the changes introduced by Diaghilev, it would probably sound like a bitter complaint. But it is not to complain, not as an accusation against anyone, that I am writing this. Indeed, I would like the reader, the public, and the performers to know what remained in the ballet in accordance with my intentions, and what was introduced in complete disregard of my wishes. I feel that the following will be clearly understood as my desire to renounce responsibility for the senseless distortions that have taken place in my absence and without my consent[127].

Fokine's stance towards the modifications introduced by the dancers in his spectacles resembles in some ways that which Stravinsky would later assume towards the interpreters of his music: they both demanded the utmost fidelity to their prescriptions. What Fokine believed should be kept unchanged was not the form the of the ballet at its premiere, but the concept he had had originally in mind. In his memoirs he repeatedly stated that when practical circumstances prevented him from fulfilling his aspirations in the first performances, in subsequent productions he tried to rectify what had not succeeded before[128]. More generally,

---

[123]. *The Firebird*, The Royal Ballet, dir. Paul Czinner, Hollywood (CA), Bel Canto/Paramount Home Video, ©1959. In this version, however, a number of short passages (but with important leitmotifs) of the score are deleted.

[124]. *The Firebird and Les Noces*, Heathfield, East Sussex, BBC – [Netherlands], Opus Arte, ©2001.

[125]. In 1912 Fokine left Diaghilev's company, only to return for a while two years later.

[126]. FOKINE 1961, pp. 174-176.

[127]. *Ibidem*, p. 74.

[128]. See FOKINE – ARROWSMITH 2014.

he always vouched for the 'authenticity' of his own restaging[129]. As for *The Firebird*, Fokine lamented how even the original 1910 production had fallen short of his intentions in many respects. After very few performances, in fact, some of the elaborate theatrical devices were soon found to be unnecessary and were dropped from subsequent performances, in order also to create a more efficient and easily transportable spectacle[130]. In his memories, Fokine also described a number of alterations introduced in the few performances of the ballet that he could attend during the 1920s. His complaints were clearly motivated by a realistic theatrical conception: he condemned all those alterations in the scenery or the costumes that made the plot and the actions onstage meaningless. Just to quote a few examples, he complained about the lack of any fence surrounding the garden, without which Ivan's efforts to force the gate seemed unmotivated, and about the elimination of the rise behind the garden, from which the princesses would have to come down, fully illuminated, as from a mountain path, thus appearing like angels descending from heaven[131]. Fokine also maintained that in his later revivals of *The Firebird* he tried to represent the ballet in a more faithful form compared to his original plan[132]. However, such statements should be considered with caution. They were more of an ideological stance; Fokine himself presumably had to make many adaptations contrary to his 'original' plans when reviving his ballets[133].

In any case, neither Fokine's efforts to restore his 'original vision', nor the diaspora of former members of the Ballets Russes present among companies such as Sadler's Wells/The Royal Ballet, could prevent The *Firebird*'s choreography from undergoing many subtle but significant changes during its long memory-based history. Marcia Siegel recalls, for example, Alexandra Danilova's account of her own interpretation of the ballet's title role in de Basil's revival of 1934. She had already danced this role in both Fokine's and Lopukhov's productions. When dancing it again in the de Basil company, she had to recognize that « [...] there were a lot of blank spots in my role, because no one exactly remembered Fokine's choreography. So I used

---

[129].   About *Les Sylphides*, for example, Fokine claimed that «I have never changed anything in this ballet». And of *Carnaval* «I have never changed a single movement in it». FOKINE 1961, pp. 134, 137.

[130].   According to *ibidem* (p. 170), in the 1910 production there were at least four such shortcomings: the elimination of the two Horseman (of Day and of Night) due to the impossibility of using real horses on stage; the failure to change the scenery in the final coronation; the abandoning of the use of machines to lift Karsavina into the air in the scenes where the Firebird fights; the giving up of the dance in the final scene. I will comment on some of these changes later on.

[131].   Fokine commented at length on a number of other modifications and shortcomings of this kind that were described by him in respect to Diaghilev's 1921 restaging at the Théâtre de la Gaîté in Paris. *Ibidem*, pp. 173-175.

[132].   *Ibidem*, pp. 174-176.

[133].   Fokine's own account of his 1931 restaging of *The Firebird* in Buenos Aires is telling on this regard: «In some details it came out even better than at Diaghileff's. However, the sets were far from being as good as those of Golovin. The production in some details was new (many things I have forgotten after eighteen years), many things were better than in the first version». *Ibidem*.

to mix the two versions [Fokine and Lopukhov's], adding some Lopukhov steps here and there, and they blended very well. No one seemed to notice»[134].

In the early 1990s, as a result also of the new historicity that pervaded both the scientific literature on ballet and performance practice — a tendency to which Millicent Hodson and Kenneth Archer's reconstruction of *The Rite of Spring* in 1987 gave decisive impulse — a new 'reconstructed' version of *The Firebird* appeared on the scene, no longer based on performance tradition and embodied memories, but on source-based inquiry. This was undertaken by Fokine's granddaughter Isabelle, who received her grandfather's own materials — notes, film footage of early films' rehearsals, choreographic scores and many other sources — from her father Vitale, the son of Michail. In the early 1990s she began restoring the ballets in association with the ballet star Andris Liepa (the son of the famous Bolshoi Ballet dancer Maris Liepa). This led to a number of Fokine revivals with the Kirov (Mariinsky) Ballet both in Russia — where many of Fokine's works had been long unseen (or never seen before), and only very few of them had remained in the Mariinsky repertoire — and abroad. Fokine-Liepa's *Firebird* first went on stage, along with a reconstructed *Scheherazade*, on 26 May 1994 at the Mariinsky Theatre, with a reconstructed set and costumes based on Golovin and Bakst's original designs[135]. In this version, the ballet was performed and video recorded on many occasions. A film version was also realized in 1997 and released on DVD a few years later[136].

At an undisclosed date in the early 2000s, Isabelle Fokine founded the Fokine Estate-Archive to be the custodian of the Michail Fokine Collection[137]. Since its establishment, any new performance of *The Firebird* — as well as of many other Fokine ballets — had to obtain its permission, due to copyright constraints[138]. As a consequence, very few new productions have

---

[134].   Alexandra Danilova quoted in Siegel 2018, p. 235.

[135].   The sets and costumes were reconstructed by Anna and Anatoly Nezhny. Andris Liepa danced the role of Ivan Tsarevich.

[136].   *Return of the Firebird*, Moscow, Universal Music Russia – London, Decca Music Group, ©2002, with Nina Ananiashvili (Firebird), Andris Liepa (Ivan Tsarevich) Ekaterina Liepa (Tsarevna). A widespread video recording of the Fokine-Liepa reconstructed version is contained in the film *The Kirov Celebrates Nijinsky* (section: *The Firebird*), directed by Ross MacGibbon, West Long Branch (NJ), Kultur, ©2002 (DVD), which was recorded live at the Théâtre du Châtelet in Paris in 1999, with Diana Vishneva (Firebird), Andrei G. Yakovlev (Ivan Tsarevich), Yana Serebriakova (Tsarevna), Vladimir Ponomare (Kashchey) (reprinted London, Digital Classics Distribution, ©2013).

[137].   See the Estate-Archive's official website at <http://www.michelfokine.com/>, accessed on January 2022: «The remit of the F[okine] E[state] A[rchive] is to preserve his ballets and artistic philosophy. Its purpose is to educate and inspire future generations. The FEA is run by Fokine's direct heirs and Trustees'. The Archive consists of '[Fokine's own] memoirs, diaries, paintings, sculpture, set and costume designs, sketches, costumes, audio recordings, artifacts, posters, photographs, scores, orchestrations, dance-notations, rare books, manuscripts, press clippings, programmes, contracts, correspondence, personal mementoes, and archival film footage».

[138].   According to the Fokine Estate-Archive website (see previous footnote), «Michel Fokine registered his ballets for copyright in Paris. The change to US law in 1978 and the Copyright Extension Act, mean that Fokine

appeared in recent years, and the Fokine-Liepa reconstructed version is now the most performed and most readily available in video recordings and on the web.

Determining just how reliable and 'authentic' is Fokine-Liepa's reconstructed Firebird, and, more generally, addressing the methodological problems — and ideological implications — underlying the concept of authenticity in dance reconstructions falls outside my scope, not least because only someone with full access to the sources used in such reconstructions could say whether they were correctly used (unfortunately, the Fokine Estate-Archive does not make its inventory available for individual researchers). What is interesting in view of a comparison between dance and music, indeed, is not whether, or to what extent, the formal aspects of the choreography were faithfully transmitted or plausibly 'reconstructed', but rather whether and to what extent they still carry the same embodied meanings as the 1910 original. From this point of view, we can only say that, in dance, the construction of meaning is largely up to the interpreters and performers, even in the case where the formal aspects of choreography have been 'faithfully' preserved or reconstructed. Whatever the continuity or changes in the tradition of the choreography, it is the performers who make sense of the steps, by giving them a specific bodily connotation. In the next chapter we will see, for example, how decisive the dancers' choices in the case of Ivan and the Firebird's pas de deux are, where different interpretations lead to very different meanings of the whole piece. Is it more a seduction or a capture scene? And is the Firebird a pleading woman or a seductive one? The answer — as far as choreography is concerned — lies largely in the performers' hands. Filmed performances of The Firebird can demonstrate the series of interpretative and stylistic changes and the modifications imposed by the various interpreters on the 'original' choreography. These modifications, although subtle, can result in important changes of meaning, and in different representations and constructions of the body. This can also happen — and usually does — to those dancers who had access to the 'authorized' Fokine repertory. What Fokine himself, in the end, was particularly attentive to and worried about was not so much the exactness of the dance steps as the overall style, the expressiveness and the meaning associated with the bodily movements[139]. In his memoirs he wrote about the 1937 restaging in Melbourne:

---

works are still under copyright. The expiration date in the US is 31 December 2047. It is therefore necessary to secure rights from the FEA prior to planning any public performance [...] Please note, and for the avoidance of doubt: Any "versions" of Fokine's works are still subject to the copyright, due to the fact that a version (of a copyrighted work) is by its nature, a derivative of the copyright. Therefore, the legal status of a "version" is the same as the original work and carries the same restrictions». There has been much criticism of Isabelle Fokine's license policy. According to Marcia Siegel, the Estate-Archive has «prevented the public from judging for itself whether a given production is convincing or misguided». SIEGEL 2018, p. 235. GARAFOLA 2011, p. 45, observes that «herself the sole guardian of her grandfather's artistic legacy, has had a disastrous effect on his ballets: they are now seldom danced».

[139].   According to Fokine's biographer (BEAUMONT 1937, pp. 574-575), when Fokine could no longer exert his control the dancers 'distorted' the original meanings of the movements by adding their own connotations.

What can I say about the choreography [of *The Firebird*]? Did it survive from 1914, when I worked for the last time with the Diaghilev company, until 1937, when I joined that organization's successor [Colonel de Basil's Original Ballets Russes]? To my absolute amazement, and notwithstanding that there were no members of the original production in the new company, and in spite of the fact that everything was transferred without any written directions from one generation of dancers to another, by word of mouth — or, to be more exact, from feet to feet — I recognized all my steps. Only the groupings had disintegrated, and the climax seemed to be entirely different. I could be amazed, but not overjoyed. Everything seemed to have lost its former force, characteristics and expressiveness, and its former consistency. [...] No one smiled. Generally speaking, the smile had left the ballet. I believe the reason for this was the weariness of the dancers with daily performances, and the repetition of the very same ballets over a period of several years. I believe that this is the result of a unique theory by which everything spirited is displaced by mechanical soullessness, and by which puppet-like movements are preferred to the movement created by sincere feelings. [...] when I made fiery addresses [...] about the necessity of having the face express what the body does, the artists seemed to understand me. Later they told me confidentially that, in former years [...] just the opposite had been required of them. An expensive face was considered to be old-fashioned, for mechanization, lifelessness and automatization were what was required. [...] I spoke about the meaning of [the infernal] dance and its purposes in the ballet. The artists listened to my speech sympathetically and made an effort both at the rehearsal and at the performance, but the results were not too great[140].

Can we, therefore, 'reconstruct' the dramatic sense and the embodied meanings in the same way as they were expressed by the original performers and perceived by the original audience? What makes this task even more difficult is an unbridgeable aesthetic and cultural gap between today's performers and audience and those of the early twentieth century. Fokine's aesthetics was largely founded on principles of dramatic coherence, expressivity and realism which for today's performers and ballet-goers are no longer high priorities. Decades of modern abstract ballets have generated the idea of a dichotomy between 'expressive' and 'pure' dance. For today's dancers the kind of realistic and naturalistic expressiveness which was still a vital component of the ballet's aesthetics at the beginning of the twentieth century would be rather difficult to understand; ballet dancers are usually celebrated more for their technical skills than for dramatic and expressive qualities[141]. Ironically enough, Stravinsky was among those who most contributed to generating this gap.

---

[140]. FOKINE 1961, p. 175.

[141]. See SIEGEL 2018, p. 238. This problem is also recognised by Isabelle Fokine: «I also think we're in a period of ballet history where modern abstract ballet has created a generation of dancers for whom naturalism can be difficult». FOKINE – ARROWSMITH 2014.

A COLLABORATION RECONSIDERED

A final question to be addressed concerns the practical circumstances of the creation of a choreo-musical work. Any consideration about the way in which music represents a vision of the body or, *vice versa*, how dance translates some aspects of music into bodily expression, cannot ignore how music and dance were put together, and therefore also the modalities of collaboration between composers, musicians, dancers and choreographers. Was the music composed to a pre-established choreography? Or was it the latter that was created to the music? And in the latter case was it music written ad hoc for that particular choreography or pre-existing music?

From this point of view too, the case of *The Firebird* is worth reconsidering. Stravinsky scholars have so far assumed that Stravinsky, on his debut as a composer for the ballet, composed the music of *The Firebird* based on a choreography which had already been defined by Fokine, according to a well-established system of work organization in the tradition of nineteenth-century ballet. Secondly, the evolution of the personal relationship between Stravinsky and Fokine seems to suggest that after an initial 'submission' to the choreographer in *The Firebird*, Stravinsky gained autonomy in subsequent ballets. The sudden and obvious changes that Stravinsky's theatrical and musical aesthetics underwent after *The Firebird* seem to correspond to the way he, just as quickly, turned his back on the choreographer. Fokine's aesthetic was tied to a realistic theatrical aesthetic that was soon to be rejected by Stravinsky. In a way, Stravinsky had already started questioning Fokine's ideas from the very beginning of their collaboration to *The Firebird*; and shortly after the ballet's premiere, he started complaining about Fokine's artistic methods and his ideas in general. In a letter to his mother of March 1912, he described the choreographer as «an exhausted artist, one who travelled his road quickly, and who writes himself out with each new work [...], and all of them are immeasurably inferior and weaker». He went on to claim that Fokine had «not even dreamed» of the new forms which had then to be created. «At the beginning of his career», he said, «he appeared to be extraordinarily progressive, but the more I knew of his work, the more I saw of him, the more clearly I understood that in essence he was not new at all»[142]. Stravinsky's later judgments of Fokine's choreography for *The Firebird* were equally negative. It «always seemed to me to be complicated and overburdened with plastic detail», he maintained, and «the artists felt, and still feel even now, great difficulty in coordinating their steps and gestures with the music», thus leading to «an unpleasant discordance between the movements of the dance and the imperative demands that the measure of the music imposed»[143]. Even more trenchant was Stravinsky's verdict in *Memoires and commentaries*:

---

[142]. STRAVINSKY – CRAFT 1978, p. 30.
[143]. *AUTOBIOGRAPHY*, p. 30.

> I didn't really like the dance movement of either ballet. The female dancers
> in the Firebird, the Princesses, were insipidly sweet, while the male dancers were the
> ne plus ultra of brute masculinity: in the Kastchei scene, they sat on the floor kicking
> their legs in an incredibly stupid manner. I prefer Balanchine's choreography for the
> 1945 version of the Firebird suite to the whole Fokine ballet[144].

Fokine, for his part, was no less critical of Stravinsky's music. He claimed not to like or understand Stravinsky's score for *Petrushka*, and while collaborating on this ballet, the two artists continuously disagreed over many details[145]. All this also corresponded to Diaghilev's gradual disenchantment with Fokine, which culminated in the latter's abandonment of the Ballets Russes in 1912[146].

All these circumstances have led scholars to greatly underestimate the importance of Stravinsky's first collaboration with Fokine. Their work on *The Firebird* has been usually considered, in truth, a sort of 'non-collaboration', so to speak. According to Richard Taruskin, Stravinsky's role in the creation of the ballet was limited to fulfilling the choreographer's requirements. «The "close collaboration" of which [Fokine] writes in his memoirs», he maintains, «had in reality been a dictatorship», and there was no room for «a "collaboration" *on the story or the steps*»[147]. Altogether, this has also led many scholars to underestimate the importance of *The Firebird* in Stravinsky's artistic evolution, and to recognize the only innovative aspect of the ballet score in terms of its apparently less conventional features, (in respect to the convention of classical ballet) such as the innovative leitmotif construction of the mimic scenes.

One of my purposes in the following chapter of this book, on the contrary, is to reconsider the importance of Stravinsky's artistic collaboration with Fokine, and to show that *The Firebird*, while remaining hardly comparable with *Petrushka* and the *Rite of Spring*, also displays many innovative aspects, particularly with regard to the modalities of collaboration. I will show that Stravinsky's role was subordinate to Fokine's above all, although not exclusively, with respect to the choice of the libretto and of the overall scenario. As for the way in which music and dance steps were created and combined, things were quite different: the idea that Stravinsky limited himself to fit the music to a largely pre-established sequence of dance steps, as was the case in nineteenth-century ballet, is incompatible with both the formal features of his score and Fokine's aesthetic premises. In short, I believe that Stravinsky and Fokine's working methods

---

[144]. *Memoires and Commentaries*, p. 33.

[145]. Fokine 1961, p. 162.

[146]. Buckle 1979, p. 182. According to Buckle, Diaghilev had «sensed in Fokine the beginning of decay and he wanted to get rid of him» due also to Fokine's «pig-headedness, conceit and limited vision».

[147]. Taruskin 1996, pp. 584-585. My italics. Elsewhere (pp. 584-585) Taruskin argues that Stravinsky and Fokine's working methods resemble more those of «the beginning of nineteenth-century theatrical ballet, [in] the days of Noverre and Didelot than those of Petipa with Tchaikovsky or Glazunov».

were more 'collaborative' than was generally acknowledged. Even Fokine's importance in the evolution of Stravinsky's musical style and aesthetics should not be underestimated. Although a much more decisive influence in the innovative aspects of Stravinsky's aesthetic came from his collaboration with Benois in 1914, Fokine provided Stravinsky with a first and important drive towards a less 'realistic' and less 'literary' way of expression.

But how can we ascertain how 'collaborative' any interaction between a choreographer and a composer was? In the case of *The Firebird*, we can get much information from the recollections of various individuals — including those of the choreographer and the composer themselves — but we must consider that their reliability is quite limited. They are often influenced by personal opinions and relationships between individuals — and those between Stravinsky and Fokine were never friendly, and not only for artistic reasons. Even when they depend on sincere artistic beliefs and aesthetic visions, these too can change a great deal, and sometimes very quickly. Stravinsky's negative judgments on the choreography of *The Firebird*, although formulated shortly after the 1910 premiere, reflect a later stage in the evolution of his theatrical aesthetics, which does not correspond to his convictions in 1910. In his memoirs, in fact, Fokine stated that «in 1910 [Stravinsky] was of a different opinion» about the choreography, and that the negative assessment, quoted above, expressed twenty-six years later in the composer's autobiography, was «formed from impressions of performances which for many years have been presented without my supervision». In these corrupted performances, Fokine maintained, «the dancers [...] counted so loud [the bars] that I could hear them from my seat, but they were still not in time with the music»; and he emphatically stated that «such was not the situation while I was connected with the company»[148]. Something similar to Stravinsky's change of mind about Fokine's choreography also happened with Nijinsky's 1913 choreography for the *Rite of Spring*.

Stravinsky's musical sketches would have been another important source of information about his collaboration with Fokine. Unfortunately, no extensive set of musical sketches for the original ballet version of *The Firebird* have survived. This circumstance is particularly unfortunate, especially when compared to the situation with other ballet scores, such as *The Rite of Spring*, for which we have a considerable amount of holograph documentation. Nonetheless, in Chapter Two we will see that some insights can be gained from other musical sources than sketches, such as Stravinsky's autographical piano reduction used in rehearsals. Furthermore, I will argue that the lack of sketches from the first phase of the creative process depends not only on the loss of the sources, but also on Stravinsky's particular creative modalities, based on a particular pianistic improvisational technique.

Many other clues to Stravinsky's creative interaction with Fokine can be drawn from a comparison between the formal aspects of the *The Firebird* and those of classical ballet. In the tradition of the ballet-pantomime, to which in fact *The Firebird* belongs, the collaborative

---

[148]. FOKINE 1961, p. 168.

methods between the ballet master and the composer were closely related to — and relied upon — the formal conventions of the genre. Although these conventions were largely preserved in *The Firebird*, they were implemented in unusual ways, and in part even ignored — if only in terms of the concentration of the dramaturgical time. Therefore, Stravinsky and Fokine's work organization also had to be less 'conventional'. Comparing the formal characteristics of *The Firebird* with those of nineteenth-century ballet-pantomime will be another aim of Chapter One.

Unlike the choreographic component, however, on which there is a huge literature with pedagogical, critical and historical intentions, the formal aspect of nineteenth-century ballet music still lacks a thorough investigation. Apart from some seminal, but now dated, works, such as Roland Wiley's book on Tchaikovsky's ballets, and more recent investigations such as Marian Smith's study of the ballet music in the age of *Giselle*, little attention has been paid to the formal aspects and the compositional techniques of ballet music. Moreover, we still lack a clear historical view paralleling the developments in ballet music with those of operatic, and above all, instrumental music. This is particularly unfortunate since the ballet composers — even those who specialized exclusively in this genre — usually had a background in the forms and techniques of 'pure' instrumental music. Many of the difficulties in understanding the innovations introduced by Stravinsky in *The Firebird* are due precisely to the lack of adequate terms of comparison with the technical features of ballet music in the Romantic era. Obviously enough, filling this gap would go far beyond the possibilities offered by my scope here. In Chapter Two, therefore, I will limit myself to recalling some essential features of ballet music in the nineteenth century. As a starting point, I will consider the musical conventions in French ballet around 1830-1840 which, in turn, provided the late eighteenth-century Russian Imperial ballet with many of its typical features. This comparison will show that in *The Firebird*, the formal conventions on which the collaborative routine between choreographers and composers had been based for over a century are partially preserved and partially superseded. Stravinsky devised a complex balance between the traditional phraseological regularity of classical ballet music and various irregular and asymmetric features. For this reason, the methods of collaboration could also no longer be entirely based on traditional nineteenth-century routines. After the break which occurred with *Petrushka* and, above all, with the *Rite of Spring*, in which almost every formal convention of classical dance seems to be completely replaced, two new ways of coordinating dance and music were possible: either the dance had to be completely adapted to the irregularities and asymmetries of music, by following its phraseology in a slavish way; or the dance had to be freed more resolutely from the music to develop its autonomous structure, albeit coordinated in some way with that of music. The first approach was the one that, according to Stravinsky, Nijinsky followed in the original choreography of the *Rite of Spring*. The second was to lead to Stravinsky's idea of a 'counterpoint' between the two arts.

CHAPTER TWO

REPRESENTING THE BODY IN *THE FIREBIRD*

It was interesting to watch him at the piano. His body seemed to vibrate with his own rhythm; punctuating staccatos with his head, he made the pattern of his music forcibly clear to me, more so than the counting of bars would have done.
(KARSAVINA 1948, p. 8.)

A COLLABORATIVE PROJECT

To understand how closely Stravinsky's music for *The Firebird* is related to bodily expression, we could start by asking ourselves a few questions. How were music and dance created and coordinated? Which came first, the music or the choreography? What were Stravinsky and Fokine's collaborative methods? Some evidence in this respect can be drawn from the accounts of the two artists and of other individuals involved in the production of the spectacle. Much, however, can be inferred from the study of the the genesis of the ballet and of the existing musical sources[1]. Therefore, I will first summarize the events surrounding the creation of the ballet.

---

[1]. A description of the existing musical sources for *The Firebird* can be found in Louis Cyr's study included in the facsimile of the 'Geneva' manuscript full score (STRAVINSKY 1985) and in Herbert Schneider's Preface to the critical edition (STRAVINSKY 1996, p. vii). A reliable and updated study is STESHKO 2000. A partial catalogue of the manuscripts and (annotated) printed scores of *The Firebird* in the Stravinsky library, now at the Paul Sacher Foundation in Basel, is in JANS – HANDSCHIN 1989. This catalogue does not include the materials belonging to the Robert Craft Collection, which were acquired by the PSS after 1989. The list included in SHEPARD 1984 — which was completed in 1983, shortly before the Stravinsky library left New York, where it had been temporarily sited, for Basel — is also largely incomplete. A more complete, but unpublished, inventory, including Robert Craft's materials, is available on site at the Paul Sacher Stiftung. For the visual sources of the ballet (Golovin's stage designs, printed photographs of the original costumes, Bakst and Golovine's sketches and designs) see Herbert Schneider's preface in STRAVINSKY 1996, p. vii, fn. 26 and 27, available at <gallica.bnf.fr>, accessed on November 2021.

The Firebird was a truly collaborative project from its very initial conception[2]. According to Alexandre Benois, the libretto was sketched out by a group of artists of Diaghilev's entourage, including himself, Fokine, Aleksandr Golovin and the painter Dmitry Stelletsky. Some *litterateurs* also made their contribution, including the writer Aleksey Remizov, who inspired many folk-like aspects of the spectacle. The décors and costumes were designed by Golovin, except for the costumes of the Firebird, of Ivan Tsarevich, and of the Tsarevna, which were designed by Léon Bakst. The libretto mixed various themes and characters from different Russian fairy-tales by Aleksandr Afanasyev and others sources, above all the famous *Tale of Ivan-Tsarevich, the Firebird, and the Grey Wolf* published by Afanasyev in 1863 in the seventh volume of his anthology *Narodnïye russkiye skazki (Russian Folk Tales)*[3].

The central idea around which the project was developed was that the ballet should be 'authentically' and 'integrally' (in the sense of an involvement of all artistic means) Russian, a sort of neo-nationalist *Gesamtkunstwerk*[4]. This 'Russianness', of course, was to a large extent a mythical Russianness invented ad hoc for the Parisian public, in the wake of the neo-nationalist orientations widespread in St. Petersburg in the early twentieth century. A 'Russian myth for export', to use Taruskin's illuminating formula.

---

[2]. The title page of the libretto for the premiere reads: «L'OISEAU DE FEU (première audition) CONTE DANSÉ EN UN TABLEAU de M. Fokine / Musique de I. Stravinsky / Scenes et danses composées et reglées par M. Fokine / Décor d'après maquette de Golovine / peint par MM. Sapounow et Charbey / Costumes de Golovine: Costumes de Mme Karsavina et Fokina par L. Bakst /éxecutés par M. Caffi./ L'Oiseau de feu: Mme Karsavina / Ivan Tsarévitch: MM. Fokine / Kostchéi l'immortel: [Aleksey] Boulkakov / La belle Tsarévna: Mme Fokina / [etc]». PR. OFF. 1910, p. 23bis. The orchestra was conducted by Gabriel Pierné (1863-1937).

[3]. For the literary source of the libretto see TARUSKIN 1996, pp. 555-574; FLAMM 2013, pp. 23-26. The program, as printed in the libretto of the premiere, was very short and slightly different from the final form of the story line: «Ivan Tsarévitch voit un jour un oiseau merveilleux, tout d'or et de flammes; il le poursuit sans pouvoir s'en emparer, et ne réussit qu'à lui arracher une de ses plumes scintillantes. Sa poursuite l'a mené jusque dans les domaines de Kachtcheï l'Immortel, le redoutable demi-dieu qui veut s'emparer de lui et le changer en pierre, ainsi qu'il le fit déjà avec maints preux chevaliers. Mais les filles de Kachtcheï et les treize princesses, ses captives, intercèdent et s'efforcent de sauver Ivan Tsarévitch. Survient l'Oiseau de feu, qui dissipe les enchantements. Le château de Kachtcheï disparaît, et les jeunes filles, les princesses, Ivan Tsarévitch et les chevaliers délivrés s'emparent des précieuses pommes d'or de son jardin». PR. OFF. 1910, p. 39.

[4]. «A true Russian (or perhaps Slavonic) mythology». BENOIS 1910, quoted in TARUSKIN 1996, p. 555. See also BENOIS 1941, p. 304: «I had expressed the wish that the ballet should make use of really Russian — or Slav — mythology [...] The working out of these elements [of the libretto] was undertaken by a sort of conference in which Tcherepnin, Fokine, the painters Steletzky, Golovine, and I took part. Our excellent writer Remizov, who was not only a great crank but a great lover of all things Russian, was carried away with our idea». Also the *régisseur* Grigoriev maintained that the libretto was the result of a collective work (GRIGORIEV 2009, p. 28). See on this WALSH 1999, p. 134 and fn. 31; TARUSKIN 1996, pp. 569-570. Fokine, on the contrary, always credited himself alone with the initial concept of the ballet. See for example FOKINE 1961, p. 159, where the choreographer entirely neglects the other collaborators mentioned by Benois.

It was with *The Firebird* that Diaghilev first understood that if his ballets were to continue to impress the Parisian audience, he had to improve their musical component by commissioning an original score by a skilled composer. All previous Fokine ballets of the 1909 and 1910 *Saisons russes* had been based on some pre-existing music. *Le Pavillon d'Armide*, staged in the first *Saisons russes* of 1909, had been originally composed by Nikolay Tcherepnin (1873-1945) for an unrealized scenario by Alexandre Benois[5]. *Les Sylphides* and *Cléopâtre*, both staged in June 1909, had been set respectively to music by Chopin and by Anton Arensky (1861-1906)[6]. *Carnaval*, premiered by Diaghilev's company in Berlin in May 1910, was set to Robert Schumann's piano suite of the same name, as orchestrated by Rimsky-Korsakov, Glazunov, Tcherepnin and Anatoly Lyadov (1855-1914).

Diaghilev's idea of commissioning the music of *The Firebird* from Stravinsky was largely a matter of chance[7]. Stravinsky had already received two small commissions from the impresario (the orchestration of some sections of *Les Sylphides*, for the 1909 Ballet Russes Parisian season; and that of Grieg's *Kobold*, which was used in the ballet *Les Orientales*, in the same 1910 season as *The Firebird*), but at that time was still an almost unknown young musician, while Diaghilev's first idea was to resort to a well-established composer of his entourage. The task had been initially entrusted to Nikolay Tcherepnin who was by then closely associated with Diaghilev's enterprise[8]. Tcherepnin began to work on the ballet score, but for reasons which remain unclear he abandoned it early on. Diaghilev then resorted to Lyadov, who was well known for his musical treatment of Russian fairy-tale and mythological themes in a typically neo-nationalist style. However, due probably to Lyadov's delay, the offer was soon rescinded.

---

[5]. Tcherepnin's score was performed as a concert suite on 13 December 1903 (see Taruskin 1996, pp. 543). Fokine then adapted his choreography, largely based on Benois' original scenario, to Tcherepnin's concert suite, thus creating a first version of the ballet, under the title *The Tapestry that Came to Life* («Ozhivlyonniy gobelen»), staged in St. Petersburg on 15 April 1907.

[6]. *Cléopâtre* had been performed in Russia as *Egyptian Nights*. For his 1909 reprise, Diaghilev replaced the original score by Anton Arensky with some musical fragments by Arensky himself, and others by Sergey Taneyev, Rimsky-Korsakov, Glazunov, Musorgsky and Tcherepnin. *Les Sylphides* originated from a 1892 concert suite by Glazunov entitled *Chopiniana*, then choreographed by Fokine in 1907 for the Mariinsky theatre. A second version was later staged with almost all of Glazunov's music replaced by new music by Maurice Keller. For the 1909 premiere of the Ballets Russes in Paris, Diaghilev commissioned a new orchestration of Keller's music from Lyadov, Taneyev, Tcherepnin and Stravinsky himself, who was entrusted with the orchestration of the opening and closing numbers of the score (Chopin's *Nocturne*, Op. 32, No. 2 and *Grand Valse brillante*, Op. 18).

[7]. On the circumstances surrounding Stravinsky's appointment and his first encounter with Diaghilev see the detailed account in Steshko 2000, pp. 36-41. See also Taruskin 1996, pp. 576-583; Walsh 1999, pp. 132-133.

[8]. Tcherepnin conducted the entire first *Saison russe*, and then conducted again for Diaghilev on multiple occasions. He belonged to the group of artists who had conceived the initial project for *The Firebird*. His sketches for the introduction of the ballet ended up in an orchestral sketch entitled *Le Royaume enchanté* (*Začarovannoe carstvo*, Op. 39, 1910).

Perhaps Diaghilev also thought of Aleksandr Glazunov (1865-1936), at the time one of the most prominent and well-established St. Petersburg composers. His fame as a ballet-music composer was principally associated with his ballets *Raymonda* (1898), and *Les Saisons* (1900) which marked the culmination of his collaboration with Marius Petipa, then in the last years of his career[9]. In the end, due to various circumstances, the task passed to Stravinsky, at the time twenty-seven years old. Presumably he was appointed by Diaghilev in December 1909, although Stravinsky would maintain that he had already begun to compose more than a month before, in early November, when he was in Lyubensk, in a *dacha* of the Rimsky-Korsakov family[10]. According to his recollection, the music he composed there was the beginning of the *Introduction*, up to bar 7[11].

Unfortunately, no extensive set of musical sketches from the earliest stages of the compositional process have survived, apart from a bifolio (four pages) with some early annotations, dating probably to Stravinsky's stay in Lyubensk or shortly thereafter[12]. The music contained in it, however, does not correspond to the *Introduction*, nor to any other piece of the final score[13]. Together with the bifolio, however, there is a loose leaf with the title of the

---

[9]. Glazunov, along with Therepnin and Lyadov, was among the composers who had contributed orchestrations to *Les Sylphides*. On Glazunov's ballets see LETELLIER 2012. Glazunov, who was appointed professor (and then director) at St. Petersburg Conservatory in 1899, had no official roles at the Imperial Theatres but was much involved in St. Petersburg theatrical life. He was a close friend of Riccardo Drigo (1846-1930), who had been director of music, *répétiteur*, and *chef d'orchestre* at the Mariinsky Theatre since 1886. Before Drigo, his post (which until 1886 had consisted of an official appointment as resident composer) had been held by Ludwig Minkus (1827-1890) and Cesare Pugni (1802-1870).

[10]. «I had already begun to think about *The Firebird* when I returned to St. Petersburg from Ustilug in the fall of 1909 though I was not certain of the commission (which, in fact, did not come until December, more than a month after I had begun to compose); I remember the day Diaghilev telephoned me to say go ahead, and I recall his surprise when I said that I had already started. Early in November I moved from St. Petersburg to a *dacha* belonging to the Rimsky-Korsakov family». *EXPOSITIONS AND DEVELOPMENTS*, pp. 127-128. The version of the events in the *AUTOBIOGRAPHY* is vaguer about the date he began the composition: «By the end of the summer the orchestration of the first act [of *The Nightingale*] was finished, and, on returning to town, I meant to go on with the rest. But a telegram then arrived to upset all my plans. Diaghileff, who had just reached St. Petersburg, asked me to write the music for *L'Oiseau de Feu* for the Ru ssian Ballet season at the Paris Opera house». *AUTOBIOGRAPHY*, p. 25.

[11]. «[...] I went there [to Lyubensk] for a vacation [...] but instead began to work on *The Firebird*. *The Introduction* up to the bassoon-and-clarinet figure at bar seven was composed in the country, as were notations for later parts». *EXPOSITIONS AND DEVELOPMENTS*, pp. 127-128.

[12]. Paul Sacher Foundation in Basel (Stravinsky Collection). Reproduced in *SSC I-III*, vol. II, p. 223; SAVENKO 1995, p. 32.

[13]. Only some vague resemblance can be seen with the *Jeu des princesses avec les pommes d'or (Scherzo)*, the *Supplications de l'Oiseau de feu* and the *Carillon féerique*, as shown by TARUSKIN 1996, p. 580, fn. 60. The unrecognized sketches are discussed in CARR 1993, SAVENKO 1995 (with a facsimile reproduction of pp. 1-3 of

ballet in Stravinsky's hand («L'oiseau de Feu. Ballet Fantastique en 1 acte avec apothéose, de M. Fokine»; ILL. 1) and the following annotations by Fokine[14]:

1) First Horseman
2) Flight of the Firebird
3) Entrance of the princesses
4) Musical number – alarm: [below] second Horseman
5) Musical number with bells
6) Musical number after the general dance
7) Darkness [crossed out] [left margin] 7) Release of the Firebird
8) Light [crossed out]

The dating of this source deserves a few words. In the Stravinsky Collection of the Paul Sacher Foundation in Basel, both the bifolio and the loose title page are filed in the same folder This circumstance has led many scholars to believe that they both belong to the Lyubensk period[15]. However, apart from being collected together, they do not bear any other relationship, and we do not know whether they were assembled by Stravinsky or by someone else, such as a librarian[16]. Louis Cyr has suggested, quite plausibly, that the title page originally belonged to the manuscript piano short score now held at the Pierpont Morgan library, to which I will return shortly[17]. If Cyr's hypothesis is correct, this page may have been drafted between the end of December 1909 and the beginning of 1910. In any case, even if it does not go back to Stravinsky's stay in Lyubensk, it is quite evident that it belongs to an early stage of the creative process (from

the *bifolium*) and TARUSKIN 1996, pp. 580-583 (with a transcription). See also STESHKO 2000, pp. 144-150. A number of sketches for the 1919 suite (17 leaves, plus 20 more pages of annotations contained in the so-called «Sketchbook I») are now in the Paul Sacher Stiftung, in Basel (Stravinsky Collection), along with some drafts of the 1911 and 1945 suites (also in the Robert Craft Collection at the Paul Sacher Stiftung). However, these sources do not give any information about the 1909-1910 gestation of the music for the full ballet. In the end The 'Lyubensk bifolio' is the only surviving autograph sketch for the 1910 full ballet score of *The Firebird*.

14. Both Savenko and Taruskin had verified the handwriting as Fokine's. Transcription: 1) I-ый Всадникъ / 2) Полет жар-птицы / 3) Выход царевен / 4) Муз. номер, тревога [below] Второй всадникъ / 5) Муз. номер съ колоколами /6) Муз. номер общего [пляса] [?] 7) темень / 8) свет 7) Выпуск Жар-птицы.

15. So did TARUSKIN 1996, p. 580, SAVENKO 1995 and WALSH 1999, p. 133 and FLAMM 2013, pp. 29-30. Of a different opinion are STESHKO 2000, pp. 144-150 and Cyr, in STRAVINSKY 1985.

16. In the folders of the Stravinsky Collection at the Paul Sacher Stiftung, the sketches are usually ordered according to their correspondence to the definitive score, not according to the chronology of the creative process — which, of course, is difficult to ascertain.

17. See Cyr's study in STRAVINSKY 1985, pp. 230-231. In fact, as far as I can see from the reproductions, the type of paper and the number of staves in the title page are the same as those of the Morgan Library manuscript. It remains unclear why the title page was detached from the piano score, and how the rest of the score found its way to the Morgan library.

ILL. 1: Fokine's notes for The Firebird on Stravinsky's title page of *The Firebird*. Paul Sacher Stiftung, Igor Stravinsky Collection. By kind permission. Title page of the so-called 'Lyubensk sketches', but more likely the original first page of Stravinsky's holograph piano short score at the Morgan Library.

here on, I will continue to refer to it as the 'Lyubensk' — in quotation marks — title page), as is also shown by certain discrepancies between the musical numbers annotated by Fokine and the final form of the scenario. According to Christoph Flamm, the list exactly follows the plot originally devised by Fokine, in which Ivan Tzaevich was supposed to defeat Kashchey not by breaking the egg containing the evil magician's soul but by playing a magic *gusli*, an idea clearly derived from Rimsky-Korsakov's opera *Sadko*, where the legendary title character enchanted the Kingdom of the Sea with his instrument[18]. This interpretation explains both the lack of some musical numbers such as the *Berceuse* and the presence of the number *Release of the Firebird*, since in this version of the plot it is Ivan himself who releases all the imprisoned characters with his instrument. In this case, the *danse générale* (no. 6 in Fokine's list) corresponds to the *Danse infernale*[19]; and the 'musical number – alarm' (no. 4) (or maybe the following 'Musical number with bells' (no. 5) refers to the music for the *Carillon féerique – Apparition des monstres-gardiens de Kastchei et capture d'Ivan-Tsarévitch*[20]. In support of Flamm's thesis there is also the lack of certain dance numbers, such as the Khorovod of the princesses, which had to be added at a further stage, when Stravinsky had started working on the music.

The 'Lyubensk' title page also shows that at this early stage Fokine was still uncertain as to what form the finale should take. One of his main concerns was the symbolic representation of the triumph of good over evil by means of a transition from darkness to light. His first idea was probably to provide two specific ballet numbers for darkness and light respectively (nos. 7 and 8 of his list). In the end he abandoned this plan (notice that entries nos. 7 and 8 in his annotations are deleted; eventually, in the definitive form of the plot no. 7 became the *Berceuse*) in favour of a final change of backdrop. In the end, however, Diaghilev did not order the creation of the backdrop which was supposed to represent «the kingdom of light» — Golovine probably did not even design it — so that at the premiere the happy ending took place with the same backdrop that served for the whole ballet from its very beginning in the darkness[21]. The effect of a transition from darkness to light, however, was obtained with a change of lighting[22].

Clearly enough, the listed pieces in the 'Lyubensk' title page do not represent the complete structure of the ballet, but only some musical numbers that Fokine would have liked to see set to music first. A sort of assignment, in other words, by the choreographer for the composer.

In the first months of 1910 Stravinsky wrote the piano short score, which was finished on 3 April (21 March O.S.), as shown by the final date in his holograph, now held at the Morgan Library[23]. Immediately after this manuscript was finished, the rehearsals with the

---

[18].   According to FOKINE 1961, p. 159, Benois persuaded him to substitute the *gusli* with the famous Firebird's feather.

[19].   SAVENKO 1995 believes that the term 'general dance' here refers to the traditional divertissement-like finale which was later rejected by Stravinsky (see below). However see FLAMM 2013, p. 174.

[20].   TARUSKIN 1996, p. 583, limits himself to noticing that the list does not match the order of the final scenario and does not recognize its correspondence to the original 'gusli' version of the plot.

[21].   FOKINE 1961, pp. 169-170.

[22].   The dramaturgical use of lightning was an important aspect of the *The Firebird*, and more in general of Diaghilev's spectacles. On this aspect see JACKSON 1991.

[23].   «*Zhar-Ptitsa skazka-balet v Dvukh kartinakh perelozheniye dlya f-piano v 2 ruki avtora rukopis / L'Oiseau de Feu conte dansé en 2 tableaux / Réduction pour piano à 2 mains par / L'Auteur. Manuscrit*», Pierpont Morgan

ILL. 2: Stravinsky sitting at the piano, with Fokine (standing) and Tamara Karsavina at rehearsals of *The Firebird*, 1910. St. Petersburg, 1910 (repr. in *COMŒDIA* 1910, p. 26; *COLLECTION* 1922, p. 43).

choreographer and the dancers began in the Catherine Hall on the Yekaterininsky Canal in St. Petersburg, where Diaghilev's company had moved a year before from the previous location at the Hermitage Theatre (ILL. 2). The preparations lasted until Diaghilev's company left Russia for Berlin and Paris at the end of May[24]. Stravinsky in person served as *répétiteur* (rehearsing musician) at the piano. At this stage the Morgan manuscript was the only score he could use[25]. During the rehearsals Stravinsky also worked to the orchestration. The manuscript full score

Library, Robert Owen Lehman Collection, holograph piano score, signed and dated at end, «21 March [3 April N.S.] 1910. S[t.]p[etersbur]g». See STESHKO 2000, pp. 15-155. A second title page is dated 6 December 1918 at Morges, and bears a dedication to V. V. Iuzhin and dated «6 December 1918, Morges», but this is clearly a later addition, since the manuscript is dated 21 March (3 April N.S.) 1910. If Cyr's hypothesis is correct (CYR 1985, p. 130), the original title page of this manuscript is that usually associated with the Lyubensk sketches (ILL. 1), which was probably detached from the piano score in 1918, when it was replaced by the new title page and the second title page dated 6 December 1918. The date of 21 March (3 April N.S.) is confirmed by Stravinsky's account: «I returned to St. Petersburg in December and remained there until March, when the composition [of the piano score] was finished». *EXPOSITIONS AND DEVELOPMENTS*, p. 28. This was most likely the manuscript from which the first Jurgenson edition of the piano reduction was drawn in 1911.

[24]. See WALSH 1999, pp. 139-140. On the location of the rehearsals see also BENOIS 1941, pp. 281-282.

[25]. Not the published piano score — as erroneously stated by JOSEPH 1982, p. 330 — which had not yet been printed. See STESHKO 2000, pp. 154, 164-165.

was almost finished by mid-April, when it was sent to Diaghilev who had, by then, moved to Paris with the whole company[26].

When the first performance of *The Firebird* finally took place on 25 June 1910, neither the piano reduction nor the ballet full score had yet been published. The piano reduction was issued in the first months of 1911 by the Russian publisher P. Jurgenson[27]. The full score followed shortly after[28].

An annotated copy of the printed piano reduction, held at the Morgan Library, contains many corrections and annotations in Stravinsky's hand, along with some piano fingerings, and performance indications[29]. The signs cannot date back to the rehearsal period, simply because the score had not yet been published at that stage. It was most likely that it was the Morgan

---

[26]. « The [manuscript] orchestral score was ready a month later [the end of the piano short score], and the complete music was mailed to Paris by mid-April. (The score is dated May 18th [1910], but by that time I was merely retouching details.) ». Expositions and Developments, p. 28. Two different manuscripts of the full score were prepared. The first, dated 18 May 1909 (as correctly stated by Stravinsky himself), was later sold to the collector Jean Bartholoni, and then donated to the library of the Geneva Conservatory, where it is now held. In Stravinsky 1985 it was reproduced in facsimile. However, this is a holograph fair copy, almost identical to the first published score (Jurgenson, Moscow, 1911, plate number 34920), and gives little or no information about the creative history of Stravinsky's score, as clearly demonstrated by Taruskin 1985. It was never used for performance. Shortly thereafter, another manuscript full score in an unidentified hand — Joseph's hypothesis of it being Stravinsky's first wife Catherine has proved unfounded (Joseph 1982, p. 330): see also Steshko 2000, p. 159 — was prepared (dated « Mar.-May 1910 »). It was this manuscript which was used for performance by the Diaghilev company and for many years. They are now held, along with 61 (out of the original 76) mixed manuscripts and printed orchestral parts, at the Pierpont Morgan Library (Mary Flagler Cary Collection).

[27]. Moscow, 1911, plate no. 34903-34919. As Steshko 2000, p. 163, has observed, there have been two different versions of this print. The first was done in Moscow in 1911. The second appeared in 1918 in « Moscow & Leipzig » by « Jurgenson/Forberg » (according to the title page), with the same plate numbers, but with some revisions. Stravinsky and Fokine's annotated copies (see below, fn. 29 and 41) belongs to the early Jurgenson/Moscow edition. According to Robert Craft the first edition appeared in July 1911, but Steshko 2000, p. 165, believes that the publication date was sooner.

[28]. Plate number No. 34920. A set of corrected (by Stravinsky) first proofs of the score, now held at the Paus Sacher Stiftung (Stravinsky Collection) are stamped « First corrected 16 March 1911 ». See Stravinsky 1996, p. viii) Steshko 2002, pp. 165-166 for further details.

[29]. Igor Stravinsky, *Zhar-Ptitsa skazka-balet v Dvukh kartinakh*, Moskow, Jurgenson, 1911, plate number 34903-34919, with annotations and revisions in the composer's hand. Pierpont Morgan Library, Robert Owen Lehman Collection. Among the various revisions, this copy features some interesting changes of metre, in particular in the concluding passage at [208]. Joseph 1983, p. 330, erroneously believed that this score was used in the rehearsals in St. Petersburg. According to Joseph, Stravinsky's piano fingerings « seem to have been engendered in an effort to facilitate his own performance of the reduction at rehearsals of the original production of the ballet » (*ibidem*). On the contrary, Louis Cyr (Stravinsky 1985, p. 193) has demonstrated that the fingerings were added by Stravinsky for the 1924 piano roll recordings. Cyr's hypothesis is confirmed by the fact that some Roman numerals added to many pages of the piano score correspond to the numbering of the piano rolls.

holograph piano short score that was used for the rehearsals. In this sense, it fulfilled the same function as the so-called *violon répétiteurs* used in rehearsals in nineteenth-century ballet practice[30]. A few words on the features of these kinds of sources will be helpful in clarifying the nature and function of Stravinsky's manuscript.

Nineteenth-century *répétiteurs* usually contained the melodic part set against a simple and sketchy harmony, so that it would be possible for a violin (or a pair of violins) to perform all the structural parts of the music — since nineteenth-century ballet music was largely monodic in texture — during rehearsals. They also contained many choreographic and stage indications, and for this reason they are a key source for our knowledge of the role of music in ballet-pantomime. Some *répétituers* may have been drafted in the very early stages of the creative process. Fedor Lopukhov maintained that they were usually prepared before the full score, which was drawn from them — not *vice versa*[31]. According to Stephanie Jordan, this statement makes little sense, since the other way round was the normal procedure[32]. From Tchaikovsky's letters and dated manuscripts, for example, we can ascertain that the *répétiteurs* for his ballets were copied after the full score[33]. However, the possibility that on certain occasions the reverse could happen should not be discounted *a priori*[34]. (in many other nineteenth-century musical symphonic and theatrical genres the full score was normally drawn from a more 'condensed' musical annotation)[35]. In particular, the 'reverse procedure' was necessary when, due to the tight schedule of theatrical programs, the composer (usually a staff composer) had no way of finishing the orchestral score in time for rehearsals. This is precisely the case of the Morgan manuscript; as we have seen, Stravinsky drew the full score from it — and not *vice versa* — while still rehearsing the ballet in St. Petersburg.

On the other hand, unlike the nineteenth-century *répétiteurs*, in which only the main melodic part is fully notated, Stravinsky's manuscript contains all the musical substance of the score. The fact that such a manuscript could be used for ballet rehearsals might seem obvious, but

[30]. The term *répétiteurs* applies to both a rehearsing musician and a rehearsing score. The study of nineteenth-century manuscript *répétiteurs* has had a major impact in recent ballet historiography. See Smith 2000, p. xviii.

[31]. See Lopukhov 2002, p. 58: «Music was written from the outset as individual parts, without there ever being a full score».

[32]. See Jordan in Lopukhov 2002, p. 204, fn. 7. Jordan quotes a personal communication from Roland Wiley in support of her statement.

[33]. This happened for *Swan Lake* and *The Sleeping Beauty*.

[34]. Wiley 1985, p. 4, also admitted that «the procedure of reducing an orchestral score to accommodating performing forces available at rehearsal occasionally worked in reverse, when the composer would have to orchestrate a ballet from a *répétiteur*».

[35]. In the case of Italian opera, whose music was usually monodic in texture like ballet music, the orchestration was usually preceded by a sketch with just the vocal parts, some annotations of the bass and of a few other instrumental interventions. In Italian operatic tradition this was called *partitura scheletro* ('skeleton score').

it is a significant aspect that sheds light on the difference between Stravinsky's music and that of eighteenth-century ballet. By Fokine's time, the use of violin accompaniment in rehearsals had long since gone out of use and the piano score was normally used for rehearsals[36]. The texture of ballet music had become much more complex than the simple monodic music of the mid-nineteenth century, and therefore a simple violin (or even a pair of violins) no longer lent itself well to making the music sufficiently similar to what the dancers would then hear from the full orchestra. Harmony had become a much more distinctive aspect of the music. *The Firebird*, in fact, is almost entirely 'harmonic' in conception and sometimes a genuine melody is absent. Thus, reducing it to a melodic part with a few sketched harmonies would have contravened «the rule that really mattered for ballet at that time» that is, «that all of the composer's work must sound exactly the same when played by a full orchestra as it would in rehearsal», as Lopukhov put it[37]. What was needed was a piano score that contained as many details as possible of the full score. This is precisely what the Morgan manuscript looks like: more than a 'piano score' — or a 'piano reduction', a term that would be a misnomer in this case, since it was written before the full score —, it looks like a true short score written down with as many staves as needed to contain all the structural parts (note the extra staves in Ex. 1a)[38]. Composing a preliminary piano short score with some indication about orchestration (many sketched-in instrumental ideas occur throughout the manuscript) and then orchestrating it in the full score was the normal working method for Stravinsky since his first orchestral compositions[39]. More in general, short scores (It. *particella*; Germ. *Particell*) were normally used by many other nineteenth- and twentieth century composers as part of their standard working method. On the other hand, unlike other works, such as *The Rite of Spring*, for which we have the holographs of both the short score and of the piano four-hand version (as well as some fragments of manuscripts of the two- or four hand-versions), for the *Firebird* we only have the Morgan manuscript, so we do not know if this was the only

---

[36]. See Lopukhov 2002, pp. 57-58, 67. Neither were more complete forms of trio-*répétiteurs*, scored for two violins and piano (see *ibidem*) any longer in use. However, according to Roland Wiley (personal communication to Stephanie Jordan, quoted *ibidem*, p. 204, fn. 7), even two-violin *répétiteurs* for Fokine's repertory survive. According to Lopukhov (*ibidem*, p. 67), «before starting working on any production of a ballet, Fokine played the music countless times on the piano».

[37]. According to Lopukhov (*ibidem*, p. 57).

[38]. Although the title page of the manuscripts reads «Réduction pour piano à 2 mains par L'auteur. Manuscrit», the term 'piano reduction' was just a common and conventional term for this kind of score, and should not be understood in the strict sense of a piano score actually drawn from an existing full score. Joseph 1982, p. 129, also considers the term 'piano reduction' to be a misnomer.

[39]. Although many scholars have described this writing process, little reference is made to sketches in the pre-*Sacre* works. Craft 1984, p. 297, has argued that Stravinsky had acquired that habit (Craft uses the term 'piano reduction') precisely in *The Firebird*, but it probably dates back to Stravinsky's earliest orchestral compositions.

preliminary score he wrote, thus serving as both a short score in the compositional process and a *répétiteur* in rehearsals, or if there was another short score that had been lost[40].

Secondly, unlike the nineteenth-century *violon répétiteurs*, the Morgan manuscript does not contain any indication about choreography and mime. Some annotation of this type, in Fokine's hand, can only be found in another copy of the Jurgenson edition of the piano reduction, which is held in the Morgan Library as well. However, these annotations can necessarily bear no trace of the collaboration between Stravinsky and Fokine that took place during rehearsals, since at that stage no printed piano score was yet available[41].

Despite all these differences, there is an aspect of Stravinsky's manuscript that is typical of many nineteenth-century *répétiteurs*: along with many annotations concerning the musical performance — tempo changes, interpretative signs, and suggested piano fingerings — it also contains a number of modifications — erasures, cross-reference marks and insertions — that were most likely introduced during rehearsals, in order to better adapt the music to the choreography[42]. Significantly, the changes usually affect 8-bar or 16-bar groups, containing a complete musical phrase. Stravinsky, for example, had crossed out the first eight measures of the initial Adagio section of the *pas de deux* Ivan-Firebird (*Supplications de l'Oiseau de feu*) at [29] section. In this shortened form the whole passage was only half as long as in the published version; the piece began at [31] with the second, varied statement, of the chromatic and melismatic theme representing the Firebird's supplications, which lasts eight more bars. This kind of modification involving entire eight-bar phrases are quite typical of the modification

40. The (incomplete) short score of *The Rite of Spring* is at the Paul Sacher Stiftung in Basel (Paul Sacher Collection). Unfortunately, unlike the holograph full-score and the manuscript of the piano four-hands version, both published in 2013 by Boosey and Hawkes, it has not yet been published in facsimile. Some pages are reproduced in DANUSER – ZIMMERMANN 2013, pp. 407-412. On the various piano versions of *The Rite of Spring* see Felix Meyer's preface in STRAVINSKY 2013A.

41. Igor Stravinsky, *Zhar-Ptitsa skazka-balet v Dvukh kartinakh*, Moscow, Jurgenson, 1911, plate number 34903-34919 with annotations in Russian on pp. 18-23, possibly in the hand of Fokine (according to Louis Cyr, in STRAVINSKY 1985, p. 192), Pierpont Morgan Library, Mary Flagler Cary Collection (Cary catalogue, no. 201). Fokine's annotations — which still await a thorough examination — are an important source in understanding his ideas about the staging of *The Firiberd*. Charles Joseph missed this important source in his description of Stravinsky's manuscripts in the Pierpont Morgan Library (JOSEPH 1982). The editors of the Geneva facsimile of the autograph full score (STRAVINSKY 1985) erroneously listed this score as a later printing than the original Jurgenson first edition (Moscow/Leipzig 1911-1918), but the score is, in fact, the original 1911 Russian printing (Jurgenson/Moscow only). In a source chart the editors also listed this source score under the heading «holograph drafts», but the source is actually printed. See STESHKO 2000, p. 137.

42. These changes have been studied by JOSEPH 1982, pp. 330-334, and JOSEPH 1983, pp. 260-270, who also reproduced in facsimile some passages affected by the modifications. Here I will add a few considerations to those made by Joseph.

required by the ballet master, when the choreography contains more choreographic phrases (*enchainements*) than the music. In this case the modification did not find its way into the final version: in the Jurgenson 1911 printed piano reduction and orchestral scores, the eight bars were preserved, even in a more texturally-dense version than the original one, featuring a more elaborate left hand, with octave doublings. Clearly, when the eight bars were restored, Fokine had to lengthen the choreographic phrases. Hence this case gives us a first glimpse of the feedback between the composer and the choreographer to which I shall return later[43].

Some displacements in the Morgan manuscripts involve blocks of music that contain leitmotivic statements. One of these cases concerns Kashchey's leitmotif (K). This characteristic figure was most likely conceived by Stravinsky not as a true leitmotif associated with Kashchey but as the music that accompanies the magician's mime gestures at [110], during his dialogue with Ivan (as we will see in more detail later). Later, Stravinsky decided also to use this motif in other points of the ballet, even before Kashchey's first apparition at 110. In the definitive version of the score we find it also at the very beginning of the ballet, in the *Jardin enchanté* at 4 mm before [2]; and at [46] immediately before the *Apparition des treize princesses enchantées* ([48])[44]. However, the six-measure statement at [46] was originally placed in the Morgan manuscript at a different point, immediately before the *Apparition de l'Oiseau de feu, poursuivi par Ivan-Tsarévitch* at [3]. All this suggests that Stravinsky used motif K as a sort of movable patch to prolong or shorten the end of a mimed scene. Perhaps the statement of the motif at 4 mm. before [2] is also the result of a similar cut-and-paste that was done in the first sketches, before the Morgan manuscript was written. In any case, these patches were not inappropriate from a musical dramaturgical point of view. Although none of the statements of the motif beforehand [110] are associated with the visible presence of Kashchey on the stage (since he will only appear at [110]), all of them work well as an ominous harbinger of the still unseen figure of the evil magician[45]. The statement at [46], in particular, in both its definitive and original position before [3], suggests the invisible but menacing presence of Kashchey just before the apparition of a benign element (the Firebird, the princesses).

These types of changes usually involve the mimed sections of the ballet, in which the music fulfils an important narrative function, but on occasion, the displaced blocks also occurs within a dance number. This is the case of Exs. 2a-b, where the affected passage is the *Danse*

---

[43].   As observed also by CRAFT 1984, p. 236. Craft also maintains that «these Firebird repairs [were] probably made during the St. Petersburg rehearsals of the ballet».

[44].   The statement at [46] is reproduced in my Ex. 14b and will be discussed in more detail later.

[45].   In the synopsis published with the 1928 Aeolian piano roll (STRAVINSKY 1928), the statement of the motif at 4 mm before [2] is labelled «In the darkness Kashchey looks for victims».

Ex. 1a: *The Firebird*, Stravinsky's holograph piano short score (Pierpont Morgan Library). Fragment of the *Infernal dance* (at [103]) originally included in the *Carillon féerique* ([163]-[169]) after [168].

Displaced block (to the *Carillon féerique)*

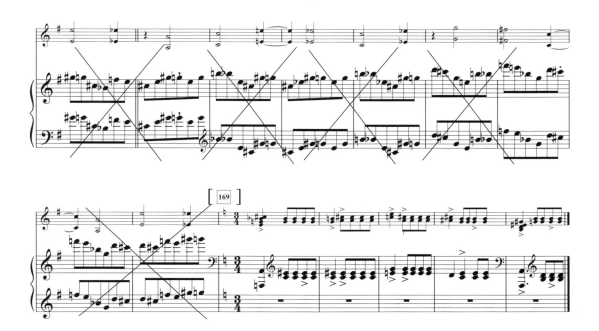

infernale. Ex. 1a reproduces the whole passage between [163] and [169], as originally annotated in Stravinsky's manuscript. The sixteen erased measures in 3/4 metre (see the holograph erasures), between [168] and [169] (according to the numbers of the printed score) were later moved to the middle of the *Carillon féerique – Apparition des monstres-gardiens de Kastchei et capture d'Ivan-Tsarévitch*, where they were also rebarred as 6/4, thus becoming the eight bars at number [103] of the printed edition. Ex. 1b shows the whole music for the *Carillon féerique* in the final version of the Jurgenson piano score, with the interpolated eight bars enclosed in boxes[46]. This is an astonishingly subtle and consistent modification from a musical point of view: the displaced measures contain a two-part canon based on the leitmotif (M) associated with Kashchey's monster servants. Quite surprisingly, the displaced block works perfectly in both contexts from a harmonic and a narrative point of view, since both the *Carillon féerique* and that particular point of the *Danse infernale* are based on the reiterated use of the monsters' distinctive leitmotif, as we will see later.

In the end, although Stravinsky's modifications were largely aimed at satisfying the demands of the choreography in terms of phrase lengths, they also correspond to a narrative-musical logic and are highly consistent with the intrinsic features of music.

---

46. In Stravinsky's holograph, the eight bars are notated on a loose sheet taped into the binding of the manuscript, but their insertion in the *Carillon féerique* is signaled by a remark in Russian (meaning «insert»). See the facsimile reproductions in Joseph 1982, pp. 331-333.

Ex. 1b: *The Firebird*, [98]-[105]: *Carillon féerique – Apparition des monstres-gardiens de Kastchei et capture d'Ivan.* Piano reduction (Jurgenson 34903-34919) with the interpolated section (boxed measures) from the *Danse infernale de tous les sujets de Kastchei -* [163]-[169] (see Ex. 1a).

Rebarred (Morgan ms)

Interpolation (from the *Danse infernale*)

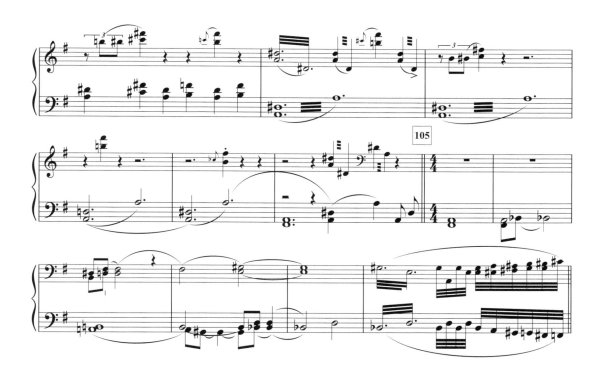

In summary, judging from the existing evidence it appears that Stravinsky's role was quite limited as far as the definition of the ballet scenario is concerned: Fokine's 'assignments' in the 'Lyubensk' title page, along with the chronological succession of the events, show that the composer had to comply with a largely pre-established plan[47]. In his memoirs, Stravinsky claimed to have contributed to the definition of the overall structure the ballet[48]; but his statement is questionable as he was hired as a composer only in late 1909, while the scenario was already complete at the latest by November 1909[49]. While in the ballets from *Petrushka* onwards he would always play a central role even in the early stages of the creation of the libretto, on his debut as a composer of ballet music — and still a relatively unknown young composer — he had to comply with a largely pre-established libretto.

This led many scholars — in particular Richard Taruskin — to believe that the music itself was also created under Fokine's direct and strict supervision, according to a well-established hierarchical work organization in nineteenth-century ballet, in which not only the

---

[47].   His only contribution in this respect probably consisted of the final scene of the ballet, as we will see later.

[48].   «Fokine is usually credited as the librettist of 'The Firebird', but I remember that all of us, and especially Bakst, who was Diaghilev's principal adviser, contributed ideas to the plan of the scenario». *EXPOSITIONS AND DEVELOPMENTS*, p. 129.

[49].   As WALSH 1999, pp. 132-133, convincingly argues.

type and number of the musical pieces, but also their formal features were determined by the ballet master, who had devised in advance the choreography[50]. On closer inspection, however, it appears that such a working method is inconsistent with many aspects of *The Firebird*. Of course, Stravinsky's modifications to his manuscript short score reflect almost exclusively a process of adapting the music to the choreography (although we have also seen that some changes also reflect a more collaborative process)[51]; but this is simply because the reverse process — that of adapting the choreography to the music — could not be recorded on the musical score (and it is a process that usually does not leave any written trace). Hence we cannot exclude that such a process also took place only on the basis of the written musical sources.

To better understand how 'collaboratively' *The Firebird* was created, we must turn out attention from written sources to the historical context and to the stylistic features of music. The possibility that Stravinsky limited himself to providing the score for an entirely pre-established choreography would rely on the persistence of well-established stylistic formal conventions, which in *The Firebird* are in part preserved, in part overcome. To comply entirely with them would have been contrary to Fokine's most basic aesthetic premises. A better knowledge of these convention will allows us to understand that *The Firebird* required a more synergic collaboration.

Excursus: Composing Music in the 'Old' Ballet

In the French ballet tradition of the Paris Opéra, any new ballet took shape from a preliminary libretto commissioned by the theatrical direction. In this phase, the story line was established along with the atmosphere, the character and the exact position of the dramatic pantomimes, of the dance numbers and of the large-scales danced scenes (*divertissements*)[52]. Next, the choreography was devised in all its parts by the ballet master. This was largely done in the foyer or on the stage. It was only at this point that a staff musician started to provide the music accompaniment to the choreography. This had be done in a very short time. Usually a resident composer was simply told to write the music for a certain number and type of dance numbers and dramatic pantomimes. He could accomplish this task even without ever seeing

---

[50]. According to Taruskin 1996, pp. 584-585, Fokine and Stravinsky's working methods resemble more those of «the beginning of nineteenth-century theatrical ballet, [in] the days of Noverre and Didelot» than those of Petipa with Tchaikovsky or Glazunov; and «The 'close collaboration' of which [Fokine] writes in his memoirs [...] had in reality been a dictatorship», and there was no room for «a 'collaboration' on the story or the steps» (*ibidem*, pp. 584-585).

[51]. According to Joseph 1983, p. 255, they «may well have exceeded Stravinsky's control and simply could have been dictated by Fokine and others», as Joseph argues.

[52]. This also roughly corresponds to the standard nineteenth-century procedure in the creation process of operas.

the choreography, only on the basis of the choreographer's indications in terms of number of bars per phrase, and of his knowledge and mastery of the formal and stylistic conventions of the various dance genres. If the result of this 'first attempt' proved unsatisfactory — in particular if the length of the musical phrases did not match the length of the choreographic phrases — the composer was asked to lengthen or shorten the music, by cutting or adding entire groups of measures. In the worst case, an entire piece of music was dropped and replaced with an already existing one[53]. Many nineteenth-century accounts clearly reflect these working methods. According to an 1834 reviewer, for example, there was

> [...] no task more painful and thankless than that necessarily imposed on the composer of ballet music. When he has finished, they make him start all over again. He is pleased with one passage, of which he has carefully established the musical conduct and development; then the ballet master arrives and says he must cut it, elongate it, cut out a phrase or even the whole passage. Then at the rehearsals the dancers ask for another instrumentation: someone asks for trombones, others for a bass drum where the composer had used, maybe, some flutes with a pizzicato accompaniment. The poor composer!... when the musician is a distinguished artist [...], one must truly feel sorry that he has found himself placed in such a frightful position[54].

The often-quoted testimony of the composer Alphonse Duvernoy, of 1903, shows that at the Paris Opéra these methods remained standard throughout the second part of the nineteenth century:

> Once the plan of the piece and the dances were arranged, the musician was called in. The ballet-master indicated the rhythms he had laid down, the steps he had arranged, the number of bars which each variation must contain — in short, the music was arranged to fit the dances. And the musician docilely improvised, so to speak, and often in the ballet-master's room, everything that was asked of him[55].

This hierarchical labour organization was also the norm in the Russian Imperial Theatres tradition, where it continued even when the music was commissioned to first-rate composers, such as Tchaikovsky. Clearly, Tchaikovsky's music was different from that of ballet composers such as Cesare Pugni, Ludwig Minkus and Riccardo Drigo in many respects: in addition to

---

[53]. See for example LOPUKHOV's (2002, pp. 54-55) suggestive description of the process.

[54]. *La Gazette musicale de Paris*, 21 September 1834, quoted in SMITH 2000, p. 4.

[55]. *L'Art du théâtre*, January 1903, p. 14, quoted and translated by GUEST 1980, p. 11. See also TARUSKIN 1966, p. 585; SMITH 2000, p. 5. Duvernoy worked as a composer at the Paris Opéra toward the end of the nineteenth century, but in this quotation he was speaking of a ballet master who preceded him in this role.

a magnificent orchestration, it introduced into ballet music what Roland Wiley called 'the symphonic element': a sense of the musical architecture defined by cadential articulation and tonal organization together with the idea that musical form grows out of the musical ideas (themes and motifs) themselves[56]. Nonetheless, while corresponding to higher aesthetic standards of composition, even Tchaikovsky's ballet scores remained within the coordinates dictated by the dance steps. We know that Petipa gave Tchaikovsky detailed written instructions for the music of the *Sleeping Beauty* and the *Nutcracker*, and that Tchaikovsky did not hesitate to comply with these instructions[57]. Petipa established the precise metre, tempo character and number of bars of each number of the ballet. He was also allowed to make any alteration to the ballet scores he deemed necessary, also without the composer's consent[58]. Alina Bryullova's recollection of Tchaikovsky's feelings about his first encounter with ballet music is very telling:

> When Pyotr Il'yich wrote his first ballet, Swan Lake, he set to work completely unaware of the techniques of ballet writing [in which] the composer was completely at the mercy of the choreographer. The latter decides how many measures should be in each pas; also rhythm, tempo, and everything else is strictly determined in advance. "[H]aving dived into the water without knowing the ford [Tchaikovsky said], I began to compose as if I were writing an opera or a symphony, and it turned out that not a single dancer or ballerina could dance to my music: all the musical numbers were too long, no one could have held them entirely. For example, you have to stand on pointe, and I wrote an andante beat"[59].

These working methods relied on the existence of a well-established set of conventions that regulated both the music and the choreography. The most basic of them was the differentiation into two types of music: one for the dance numbers and one for the dramatic pantomimes. The style of the first type of music is undoubtedly one of the best-known aspects of the romantic ballet. Its essential feature was the regular four-bar phrasing, almost invariably based on the basic classical theme forms, such as the eight-bar 'period' (4 measures of antecedent ending with a half cadence + 4 measures of consequent ending with an authentic cadence on the tonic) or

---

[56]. WILEY 1984, p. 693.

[57]. See Petipa's instructions for the *Sleeping Beauty* and the *Nutcracker* in WILEY 1985, pp. 354-359; 371-376.

[58]. He and his collaborator Lev Ivanov, for example, felt free to rearrange Tchaikovsky's music for the 1895 version of *Swan Lake*.

[59]. BRYULLOVA 1980, p. 113 (my translation). Bryullova's reminiscences of Tchaikovsky are also included in English translation in BROWN 1993. Alina Bryullova (1849-1932, born Alina Ivanovna Meyer) was the wife of Vladimir Aleksandrovich Bryullov (1846-1918), the manager of the Russian National Museum. From a previus marriage to the agriculturist Herman Konradi (1833-1882), she had had a deaf-mute son, Nikolay Konradi (1833-1882), to whom Tchaikovsky's brother Modest became tutor in 1876. Her recollections, written in 1929, date from her first meetings with Tchaikovsky in the 1870s until his death in 1893.

the eight-bar 'sentence' (4 measures of presentation + 4 measures of continuation, with final cadence on the tonic or the dominant)[60]. These basic structures were normally incorporated into larger theme forms such as the small ternary (a|b|a), the small binary (a|b), or the 'rounded binary' form (a|ba') — each letter corresponding to an eight-bar group, sometimes repeated — thus giving rise to longer compound themes, typically of 16 or 32 bars. These, in turn, were put together within larger formal schemas, such as the large ternary form (A|B|A) — each letter corresponding to a compound 16- or 32-measure theme, according to the formal conventions of the various genres of dance: marches, waltzes, polkas, final *gallops*, etc. Thus an entire piece was made up of such tight-knit theme types, sometimes repeated, also in *soli-tutti* schemes. Short connecting passages between the main sections, and a few preparatory measures on the dominant chord, provided the necessary accessory elements. As a rule, each main section of the overall form remained within a single key, with no changes of tempo and metre[61]. Developing passages and, more in general, developmental composition techniques, were avoided. As for style, simple monodic textures were very common. The main melodic part — sometimes entrusted to an *obbligato* instrument, such as a violin — was usually accompanied by simple chords of the strings, bowed or plucked (*pizzicato*).

The style of the second type of music (that for dramatic pantomimes) is much less familiar to us than that of the dance numbers. To understand the fundamental dramatic motivations underlying this kind of music, we must recall that in the mimed scenes, in the absence of sung or spoken words, the dancer-actors mimicked their actions, their feelings, their thoughts and also their 'untold words', so to speak, by means of a conventional body-gestural code. However, the latter would have been insufficient for the purpose without the aid of the music, which made up for the lack of a verbal (literary) component with its own 'narrative' means. The musical component was thus entrusted with a task similar to that of a 'storyteller': it had to 'tell in sound' what happened and what was 'silently told' on stage. The most basic formal aspects that responded to this need were tonality and time organization: the changes in key, metre and tempo represented the inner dynamics of the narrative. As a consequence, the music of the mimed scenes tended to be much less tonally and metrically stable than that for the danced numbers; there were continuous key and metre changes from phrase to phrase. Even within a single phrase, modulations or harmonic sequences were very frequent.

Until the end of the nineteenth century, the classical theme-types, such as 4+4 periods or sentences, were often used even in the narrative music for the mimed scenes, and not only for the

---

[60].   My terminology of classical forms is based on Caplin 1998 (for quick reference see Caplin's 'Glossary of terms' at pp. 253-258). However, I am using here the term 'phrase' in a very generic sense, and not in Caplin's strict sense of « four-measure unit, often [...] containing two ideas ».

[61].   This corresponds to the distinction between tight-knit and loose formal organization, to which I will return to shortly. See also *ibidem*, pp. 17-18. The two terms correspond to (and originated with) Schoenberg and Erwin Ratz's distinction between, respectively, *fest* and *locker* formal organization.

dance numbers. However, they were embedded within a different kind of formal organization. Music for a dance piece was, as a rule, *entirely* made up of eight-bar theme-types, only *repeated* and assembled in a larger formal scheme. Therefore even its overall organization was of a 'tight knit' (*fest*) type for it was harmonically and tonally stable, had an entirely symmetrical grouping structure, and was based on a limited quantity of melodic-motivic material. The music for the mimic scenes, on the contrary, tended to be much 'looser' (*locker*) and was almost entirely through-composed (*durchkomponiert*), with no repetitions. Typically, the music for an entire mimed scene was made up of a sequence of short segments with a different key, tempo, metre, and motivic material. Even within each segment, modulations were frequent. Classical eight-bar theme types were usually modified by means of repetitions of sub-segments, thus producing unconventional and asymmetrical non-thematic groupings. Many sections were entirely made up of loose sequences of several four-bar groups, occasionally in harmonic sequences. Recitative-like sections, sustained dominant-chords, and short modulating passages often punctuated the structure. Symmetrical eight-bar theme types were used as well, especially when the symmetry between two halves served to mirror some similarly structured stage events, such as back-and-forth stage movements, or question/answer dialogue lines. However, such symmetric episodes were just one of the various elements used in a through-composed musical patchwork.

The two different types of music also implied two different ways of coordinating music and choreography[62]. However, in both case the composers was able to provide the music on the basis of a few indications from the choreographer. In the case of the danced numbers, they had to provide some music whose metre, tempo and bar groupings matched the metre, tempo and length of the choreographic phrases (*enchaînements*) previously devised by the choreographer. This procedure was facilitated by the composer's mastery of the ballet conventions, meaning that a knowledge of the phrasing structure, of the larger formal scheme (large ternary, binary, etc.), and of the tempo and metre associated with the various dance genres allowed him to know in advance how many musical phrases, how many numbers of measures per phrase, and which overall musical form he had to provide. Sometimes he was even required to prepare several regular eight-bar groups which could be omitted or repeated according to the needs of the choreography. The music for a large *danse général*, for example, could be quickly assembled by combining an opening sixteen-bar theme, a number (depending on how much music was needed for the choreography) of further eight-bar groups, and a final *coda*. This 'modular' construction made the music easily and quickly adaptable to a largely pre-established sequence of *enchaînements*[63].

---

[62].   They were also consistently differentiated in the scores, where the danced segments were usually marked with terms such as *danse, pas, ballet*, or *divertissement*, while the dramatic music immediately following the danced numbers was usually labelled *après la danse*.

[63].   Many sections of Cesare Pugni's music for *La Fille du pharaon* (1862), for example, were actually composed, *ex post facto*, as an accompaniment to a number of dance *enchaînements* that Petipa had already established. See EDGECOMBE 2006, p. 40.

In the second type of music, that for the dramatic pantomimes, the composer was not so much bound by the structure of the choreography in terms of number of bars as by the dramatic content of the storyline. He was usually asked by the choreographer only to use a specific tempo, metre and character. However, he had also to take into account the overall duration of the movements of the mimes on stage, which sometimes were expressed by the choreographer in terms of number of bars as well. The most important function of the music in these scenes, however, was a narrative one with the music having to depict the actions, the feelings and sometimes the 'silent words' of the characters. In the Paris Opéra tradition before 1850, a series of techniques were used to this end, including the use of descriptive music, recitative-like passages, and reference to musical topics (such as fanfares, horn-calls, *musette*, *pastorale*, ethnic music, and so on)[64]. Frequently musical materials were borrowed from other compositions. After 1850, many of these techniques fell from public favour. Borrowings, in particular, became rare after the mid-nineteenth century, when they started being viewed with suspicion by critics. Many other musical 'narrative' techniques, however, continued to be used. One such important technique was the use of recurring themes (often, although not very accurately, referred to as 'leitmotifs' in the literature on ballet). Halévy's *Manon Lescaut*, of 1830, was probably the earliest ballet in which this technique was used as a narrative device. Recurring themes were often associated with the reminiscences of characters in a state of semi-consciousness or suffering from some mental disorder. Many nineteenth-century writers and critics used the term 'recalling motifs' (Germ. *Erinnerungsmotif*) with regard to both operas and ballets of their time. In *Giselle*, recurring themes and motifs were associated with some characters of the story, and they also corresponded to 'choreographic leitmotifs' (recurring step combinations) created by Jules Perrot and Jean Coralli. In the ballet repertory of the age of *Giselle*, recurring themes occurred as frequently as in the operas of the authors that are usually considered as the forerunners of Wagner's 'mature' leitmotivic technique, such as Cherubini, Méhul, Spohr, Weber, Marschner or Meyerbeer[65]. They also continued to be used in later ballets; in *La Bayadère* (1877), for example, Ludwig Minkus associated a specific motif with each of the main protagonists of the story, and used a recurring theme to represent musically the notion of tragic love[66].

The main difference between the balletic use of recurring themes/motifs and the truly Wagnerian leitmotifs is that the latter were used in a much more pervasive and systematic way, and had a more fundamental structural function, thanks to the continuous melodic, harmonic, and rhythmic variations to which they were subjected. In this way they also allowed

---

[64]. SMITH 2000, pp. 8-9. I use the term 'topics' in the sense of the topic theories of music developed by authors such as Leonard Ratner, Kofi Agawu, Raymond Monelle, and Robert Hatten.

[65]. *Ibidem*, p. 13.

[66]. See LETELLIER 2008, p. 183.

for accumulative meaning association; with each varied re-statement of a motif something new was added to its previous meanings However, neither did ballet composers who made use of recurring melodies limit themselves to repeating these materials in an unvaried form, but also modified them in subtle ways. Marian Smith, for example, describes the manifold transformations that a motif first heard in the *pas de deux* of the Harvest Festival in Act 1 of *Giselle*, undergoes throughout the ballet. Minkus too subjected the recurring motifs to subtle variations that corresponded to the developments of the story. Although this does not help much in demonstrating an analogy with Wagner's leitmotivic technique, it clearly shows that recurring musical ideas were one of the many devices at the ballet composer's disposal, and that they «proved valuable within a textless dramatic music to which the audience regularly turned for help in following the story»[67].

An important aspect of these musical narrative techniques, which has not yet received much attention, concerns their function in the creative process. Recurring themes and motifs, quotations of well-known melodies and borrowings were 'ready-to-use' musical materials. The composers had only to adapt them to the overall length of the choreographic phrases (in the dance numbers) or to the harmonic progressions (in the mimed scenes). For a skilled musician, such an operation was simple enough to perform both in written composition and on the instrument. This brings us back to Duvernoy's statement, quoted above, that «the musician docilely improvised, so to speak, and often in the ballet-master's room, everything that was asked of him»[68]. Improvising during rehearsals allowed the composer to make the music immediately correspond to the length of the choreographic phrases, thus avoiding having to lengthen or shorten any musical phrases later, when dance and music were finally put together. The results of his improvisations, of course, were suddenly set down and fixed in writing, in order to be also further organized and, finally, fully orchestrated.

The improvisational element of nineteenth-century ballet music is worthy of attention. Unfortunately — but obviously enough — no written record of this improvisational practice can, by definition, be found. Some traces might be glimpsed in certain features which the *répétiteurs* used in rehearsals; but Stravinsky's manuscript piano short score — which, as we have seen, already reflects a high degree of written formalization — bears no traces of his improvisation technique. However, later in this chapter, we will see that Stravinsky's technique can be inferred from the analysis of the score. We will see that it is of a 'pianistic' kind, very different from that which was — presumably — used by nineteenth-century violinist-composers. Nonetheless, a continuity with older practices can be discerned in some basic principles, such as the use of simple recurring motifs as ready-made materials.

---

[67]. SMITH 2000, p. 14.

[68]. See above, fn. 55.

REPRESENTING THE BODY IN *THE FIREBIRD*

COMPOSING MUSIC FOR A 'NEW' BALLET

We have seen that nineteenth-century ballet composer were bound by a rigid code of conventions, on which both music and choreography relied. But it was precisely these conventions that made it possible for the composers to adapt the music to a largely pre-established choreography. These working methods underwent an upheaval in the second half of the nineteenth century, when the use of the conventions ended up as an ossified musical idiom, made of generic and stereotyped formulas. According to Roland Wiley, this was precisely «[...] the problem that Tchaikovsky had to face», when turning to ballet music, since «under Pugni and Minkus [this genre] had frozen in the stylistic clichés of the 1830s and 1840s». Such stereotyped music often lacked any consistency with the subject matter, the dramatic content, the character and the style of the represented story[69].

A first drive towards a less conventional and more dramatically coherent ballet music had already been made by Ivan Vsevolozhsky. The influencial intendant of the Imperial Theatres had done away with the position of staff musician (the Imperial Ballet Composer) and had started commissioning new scores to first-rate composers such as Tchaikovsky. His efforts to create the conditions for a more organic collaboration between the artists was an important premise to the new intellectual climate in which Diaghilev's ideal of a spectacle gradually took shape. Not by chance, Alexandre Benois, to whom we owe much of the idea of making the 'old' ballet the privileged genre of a new art form, credited Vsevolozhsky with having conceived the ballet as a unitary and coherent artwork, thus providing Diaghilev with a model for his role as impresario[70].

The same problem as the music, however, was already affecting the choreography itself. The conventional dance forms and standardized step combinations of classical ballet could no longer correspond to the dramaturgical requirements that the ballet had to meet in the new intellectual climate. This was the most fundamental motivation behind the idea of a 'new' ballet that Fokine began advocating in 1907[71]. By that date the adjective 'new' was circulating in

[69]. See WILEY 1985. Fedor Lopukhov summed up the issue with a curious but instructive anecdote about some «bookshelves» from which the composers took «ready-made pieces of music marches, waltzes, and variations that could be placed on the relevant shelf in the expectation that sooner or later they would be needed. And inevitably they would be needed since, in accordance with the contract, two new ballets had to be written every year». LOPUKHOV 2002, pp. 55-56.

[70]. See TARUSKIN 2010, pp. 148-151.

[71]. Fokine displayed his ideas on the new ballet in a group of writings published between 1907 and 1916. These are a text enclosed with the scenario of the ballet *Daphnis et Chloé*, a letter to the *Times* of London (FOKINE 1914), and an article in the Russian periodical *Argus* of 1916. The notes to *Daphnis et Chloé* were long believed to date back to 1904, but most likely they are of 1907 or later, as KRASOVSKAYA 1971 has suggested. The date of 1904 was supported by Fokine's biographer Cyril Beaumont and, implicitly, by Fokine himself (BEAUMONT 1935).

Russian intellectual circles, where it was used to refer to the new 'stylized' (symbolist) Russian theatre[72]. But 'new' was also a widely-used term to refer to the ballet productions of those choreographers who in those years were renewing the structure and choreographic conventions of the Russian ballet, which had changed very little since the mid-nineteenth century. Among these there were Fokine himself in St. Petersburg and Aleksandr Gorsky in Moscow. According to Fokine, the 'new' ballet no longer needed to favour conventions over expressive and dramatic needs. In each ballet, the specific stylistic characterization had to supersede the conventions of the genre. The first three of his famous 'five principles', as illustrated in the open letter to the editor of the London *Times* of 6 July 1914, were closely related to this basic aesthetic premise:

> Not to form combinations of ready-made and established dance-steps, but to create in each case a new form corresponding to the subject [...] The second rule is that dancing and mimetic gesture have no meaning in a ballet unless they serve as an expression of its dramatic action, and they must not be used as mere divertissement or entertainment, having no connection with the scheme of the whole ballet. The third rule is that the new ballet admits the use of conventional gesture only where it is required by the style of the ballet, and in all other cases endeavors to replace gestures of the hands by mimetic of the whole body. Man can be and should be expressive from head to foot[73].

Fokine recognized that an excessively conventional character affected both the choreography and the music of the 'old' ballet. He understood that if the music was to raise this genre to new dramatic heights, it «should not consist of waltzes, polkas and final *gallops* — indispensable in the old ballet — but must express the story of the ballet, and, primarily, its emotional content»[74]. Karsavina credited him with the idea that music was «[...] not the mere accompaniment of a rhythmic step, but an organic part of a dance»; and that «the quality of choreographic inspiration is determined by the quality of the music»[75]. Even before collaborating with Stravinsky on *The Firebird*, he was looking for a less conventional (and more

---

According to Beaumont, the text was annexed, as explanatory notes, to the scenario for the first *Daphnis et Chloë* project, which Fokine sent to the director of the Imperial Theatres, Teljakovskij, in 1904. However, no copies of such a scenario with notes survive in the archives of the Imperial Theatres. The only two copies, kept in private archives, can be dated a little earlier than 1912 (when *Acis and Galatea* was performed by Diaghilev's company). Probably, therefore, Fokine (and Beaumont) backdated the notes to the scenario to 1904 to demonstrate that the ideas contained in it were formulated before Isadora Duncan's first Russian *tournée* in 1904, thus denying Duncan's influence over the «Greek» elements in *Acis and Galatea*, created in 1905.

[72]. In particular after the publication in 1908 of the book *Teatr: Kniga o novom teatre* (Theatre: a Book about the New Theatre).

[73]. FOKINE 1914, pp. 260-261. See also BEAUMONT 1935, pp. 146-147.

[74]. FOKINE 1961, p. 72.

[75]. KARSAVINA 1961, p. 169.

'symphonic') kind of music than could meet his dramatic needs. In 1906 he had turned to Anton Rubinstein's (1829-1894) score for the ballet *The Vine* (1892). Tamara Karsavina, who danced in Fokine's 1906 production of the ballet, clearly recognized that Rubinstein's music was «certainly different from the favourite type of ballet music, a string of obvious tunes squared up in 32 or 64 bars to fit an amount of steps considered the limit of a dancer's endurance»[76]. Another opportunity to escape the conventions of traditional ballet music was offered to Fokine by the Diaghilevian formula of the ballet based on pre-existing (and often non-ballet) music, which he experienced in *Le Pavillon d'Armide*, *Les Sylphide*, *Cléopâtre* and *Carnaval*. However, it was above all in Stravinsky's new score for *The Firebird* that he was able to find a full realization of his ballet music ideal. A closer look at many aspects of *The Firebird* will make it clear that its classification as a 'new ballet' — in Fokine's terms — would be questionable in some respects. Nonetheless, *The Firebird* was the first ballet in which Fokine's ideas were, at least in part, realized in both the choreography and the musical score. His ideals of dramatic coherence, expressiveness, 'naturalness', and verisimilitude, although soon to be abandoned by Stravinsky in favour of a markedly anti-realistic and anti-naturalistic theatrical aesthetics, were still largely accepted on this occasion.

It is important to recognize that Fokine endeavored to avoid the 'conventionality' of classical ballet without entirely abandoning its 'conventions', for he only made them more suitable for its dramaturgical and expressive purposes. Similarly, he did not reject the forms and conventions of classical ballet music, but only on condition that they were made capable of expressing each time — in each ballet — the same specific meanings conveyed by the other components of the spectacle (choreography, costumes and décor). In the music of *The Firebird* this principle was applied even in the dances that seem more conventional and traditional, such as the *Scherzo* (*Jeu des princesses avec les pommes d'or*) ([55]), or the *Khorovd*. (*Ronde des princesses*) ([75]). Both pieces feature a quite traditional, even conventional form, but their style and character is totally in keeping with the atmosphere and dramatic situation of the ballet's story line.

Let us consider in particular the Khorovod. The piece is based on two main themes, the first of which was drawn from Rimsky-Korsakov's 1877 collection *100 Russian Folk Songs* (song no. 79)[77]. Rimsky-Korsakov's six-bar tune (Ex. 2a: in the example the melody is transposed from A major to B major to match the tonality of Stravinsky's theme) is made of two parts (A and B); in the first part, a two-bar phrase (labelled *a*) is stated twice, with the first statement time ending with a half-cadence (*z*), and the second with an authentic cadence. The phrase is

---

[76]. *Ibidem*.

[77]. This melody had already been used by Rimsky-Korsakov in his *Sinfonietta on Russian Themes*, Op. 31 of 1887. According to Stravinsky (*Memories and Commentaries*, p. 98), also the second theme, which follows at [77] was a folk melody, but he was not able to remember the anthology from which it was drawn.

made of three melodic cells, labelled *w*, *x* e *y*, with *w* serving as an opening (intonation) formula, and *x* – *y* as continuation formulas. The two-bar phrase *b* is quite similar to phrase *a* (see *w*, *x* and *y*) but it is set against a dominant harmony, and ends with a half cadence, after which all of part A can be repeated. Stravinsky modifies this binary-circular structure by expanding it from six to eight bars (four two-bar phrases, see numbers 1-4 in Ex. 2b). The first statement of phrase *a* (oboe 1) is the same as in Rimsky-Korsakov, while the second statement is transposed to the sixth degree of the scale, and omits cell *y* (the final cadence formula *z* is also expanded so as to fill the two-bar group). Then, before phrase *b*, Stravinsky introduced a third statement of phrase *a* (violoncello), this time in a metrically displaced variant: cell *w* is set in anacrusis (instead of the downbeat) at the end of the fourth measure, and is shortened from ♫♩ to ♫♫, so that the following cells (*x*, *y*, and *z*) are shifted backwards by two crotchets (half measure). (Note also the cell *w'* on the upbeat at the end of the sixth bar, which serves to lengthen the third sentence, metrically displaced, and to connect it to the fourth.) The last two measures, entrusted to the bassoon solo, are identical to Rimsky-Korsakov's phrase *b*, except for the harmonization of the last note *c♯*, which is turned from the dominant of B major into the root of a C♯ minor chord, serving as the sixth degree of the new tonality (E major) of the following theme at [77].

An even more radical transformation concerns the original monodic writing of Rimsky-Korsakov's tune. The first part of Stravinsky' theme is entirely monodic, with only a simple harmonic accompaniment of harps and strings. In the following four measures, however, the oboe's note *f* is sustained as a pedal, around which two polyphonic lines unfold; in addition to that of the cello and bassoon just discussed, another voice, entrusted to the clarinet in A, performs a new combination of the basic cells: *w'*, *x*, *w*, *z*, and finally *w*. According to Richard Taruskin, this polyphonic treatment of the tune was strongly reminiscent of the *podgolosok* ('sub-voice', 'under-voice', 'supporting voice') technique of the improvised polyphony in Russian folk singing[78]. There were, in fact, different types of *podgoloski* techniques, involving heterophony, simple descant polyphony, or more elaborate forms in which the 'sub-voices' were more independent of the main voice, but all types featured some form of elaboration of the principal voice, which usually started alone, with the 'under-voices' joining immediately thereafter, as in Stravinsky's Khorovod[79]. The use sustained tones (see the *f♯* of the oboe 1-2) against which the other arts unfold, are also a typical trait of the *podgoloski*. What is interesting from our point of view is that all these modifications entirely conceal the underlying symmetric and tight-knit formal conception of the original model. The metrical displacement of phrase

---

[78]. See TARUSKIN 1996, p. 627. On this technique see for example PROKHOROV 2002, pp. 79-82. The *podgoloski* were used in all Russian folk songs genres, but they were a distinguishing trait of the genre of the *protyazhnaya* (protracted songs), to which I will return later when discussing Ivan's theme.

[79]. According to SWAN 1973, p. 25, a typical *podgolosok* would start «[...] with a solo intonation», after which, «the ensemble of singers would without any warning split into parts, each of which was also a self-sufficient melody not too divergent from the one that could conceivably be termed "principal"».

a, the almost-imitative polyphonic writing — drawing the listener's attention to the imitative entries at non-symmetrical points of the theme (at bar 5 and 6) —, the modifications of the phrases and of the melodic cells, and the recombination of the cells *w'*, *x*, *w*, *z*, in the clarinet part —also altering the functions (intonation, continuation) of the melodic cells — prevent any impression of symmetry and regularity.

In a few words, despite its eight-bar length, which lends itself well to choreography, the Khorovod's theme sounds anything but conventionally structured in terms of traditional ballet music. It is much more like a lyrical flow, with a natural, popular, almost rhapsodic character. All this was in keeping with Fokine's idea that coherence and appropriacy of style was more important than adherence to formal conventions. Such a natural-sounding Khorovod was entirely appropriate to the ballet action fitting a neo-nationalist representation of a folk-like round dance of Russian women. The choice will appear even more suitable when we consider that, as Taruskin noticed, the original text to which Rimsky-Korsakov's melody was set was a wedding song with a specific ritual function, and its text was about « a fine youth » who « went walking [...] around the garden, around the vineyard green », which is precisely Ivan's situation in the enchanted garden with the princesses[80]. Perhaps, had the ballet been addressed to a Russian and not a Parisian audience, and had Korsakov's melody been sufficiently known in his homeland, one could intriguingly think of these 'unsung words' as a sort of early-nineteenth-century '*air-parlants*'.

Ex. 2a: RIMSKY-KORSAKOV 1877, no. 79; melody of the song; transposed from A major to B major.

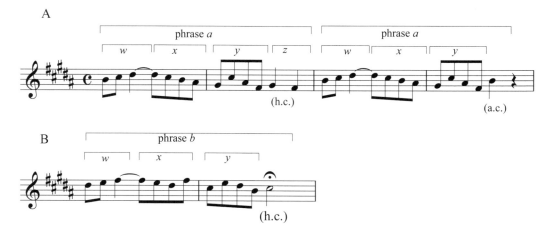

---

80. TARUSKIN 1996, p. 627. Taruskin explains that the song was to be sung during the *devichnik*, the wedding ritual at which the bride's maids of honour plait her hair (the same ritual as in the opening tableau of Stravinsky's *Les Noces*).

Ex. 2b: *The Firebird*: *Khorovod*, (*Ronde des princesses*), [75]. Melody and analysis (compare with Ex. 2a).

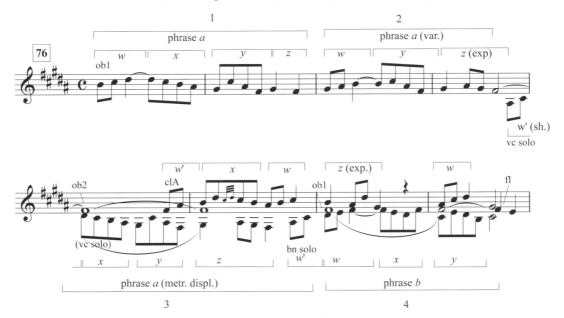

Fokine's revision of the conventions of the 'old' ballet invested even the basic distinction between dance numbers and dramatic pantomimes. In keeping with his idea of a more holistic use of the body, he claimed that both dance and mime should possess a specific expressive quality which harmonized with each other and with the general epoch setting and style of the story represented. This resulted in a weakening of the difference between the two expressive codes, in favour of a greater dramatic and stylistic continuity. A more unitary dramatic conception, moreover, was well suited to the short, mostly one-act, kind of ballet promoted by Diaghilev, which implied a much more concentrated and coherent dramatic time in respect to that of the traditional multi-act nineteenth-century ballet.

In a sense, this concept of dramatic continuity corresponded to an 'anti-operatic' tendency, since it marked a departure from the basically operatic model — the distinction between recitative and aria — underlying the traditional ballet-pantomime, as the young Sergei Eisenstein would clearly recognize in 1919:

> The enchanting impression I got from his [Fokine's] ballets (and I have seen the most significant ones!) does not diminish, not even in comparison with the Sleeping Beauty or The Useless Precaution. I believe that the reason lies in the purely theatrical, as well as choreographic, component of Fokine's art: in the fact that he has eliminated the difference between 'pantomime' and 'danced divertissement'. In his works there are no embellishments or logical — or of other kind — digressions, which, being disconnected from the whole, could offend the 'unity of action'. [...]

> The ballet was still in the situation of Italian opera: an aria until the next aria!
> Therefore I believe that the merit of Fokine, if not in 'ballet' at least in 'theatre-
> dance' [...] consisted of the creation of a unitary and accomplished action starting
> from fragments of pantomime and individual 'dance numbers'[81].

According to Tim Scholl, Fokine's anti-operatic tendency can be ascribed to the influence of Wagner's *Musikdrama*. Scholl notes that Fokine's prescription that the conclusion of each dance should not be such as to invite an applause — which would interrupt the dramatic flow — was also ultimately «a Wagnerian notion popularized in Russia by Stanislavsky's Moscow Art Theatre»[82]. In keeping with Fokine's ideas, Stravinsky managed to blend the features of the two types of music, thus making room for a more continuous music-dramatic conception[83]. Usually the music of a danced number is connected with the surrounding symphonic discourse by avoiding a clear-cut final cadence. Even when the music of a dance number is distinct enough from the surrounding music — this is the case, for example, of the dance of *The Firebird* — other aspects, such as orchestration or tempo contribute to attenuating the gap. A more subtle continuity is created by the use of shared musical material. In the mimed scenes of the ballet, in fact, Stravinsky devised an entirely through-composed orchestral accompaniment in which a number of leitmotifs recur, thus representing the events of the story line. I will refer to them by the following capital letters (the right column of TABLE 1 shows at a glance how these leitmotifs support all the music of the score except for the dance numbers):

---

[81]. Text of an untitled fragment dated 27.05.19 (my translation) belonging to a group of short writings on the theatre of the years 1919-1920, now held at the Russian State Archive of Literature and Arts. Edited in EISENSTEIN 2000. Italian translation in EISENSTEIN 2004, pp. 93-96. In this text Eisenstein was commenting on André Levinson's critique of Fokine's ballet.

[82]. See SCHOLL 1994, p. 48.

[83]. In light of Fokine and Stravinsky's unitary approach, TARUSKIN's 1996, p. 587, statement that in this ballet «miming [...] alternates with dance in a manner exactly analogous to the interplay of operatic recitative and aria», and that this makes *The Firebird* «the most operatic of ballets», a ballet aspiring «to the condition of opera», makes little sense. In nineteenth-century ballet-pantomime the stylistic distinction between the music for dance and that for mime was as clear as in *The Firebird*, if not more so; this aspect was precisely what made many nineteenth-century commentators perceive an analogy between ballet and opera, since it reproduced the distinction between recitatives and lyrical movements (arias, duets, *concertati*, etc.). In this (as well as in many other) respects, the strongly 'operatic' nature of nineteenth-century ballet has been amply demonstrated by SMITH 2000. Taruskin's statement probably refects Stravinsky's famous assertion that the music of *The Firebird* was «as literal as opera» (*EXPOSITIONS AND DEVELOPMENTS*, p. 128), but we will see that Stravinsky was referring to a specific aspect of the music (its story-telling and speech-like character) that was a distinctive feature of all nineteenth- century ballets. Also from this point of view we can only say that *The Firebird* was as «operatic» as any other ballet.

F(irebird)	=	Firebird's leitmotif
K(ashchey)	=	Kashchey's leitmotif
M(onsters)	=	Monster's leitmotif
P(rincesses)	=	Princesses' leitmotif
I(van)	=	Ivan's theme

TABLE 1: *THE FIREBIRD*: SECTIONS AND LEITMOTIFS

Sections. In bold = dance numbers; In italics = mimed scenes	Leitmotifs (see Exs. 12-17)
1. *Introduction*	
Tableau I	
Le jardin enchanté de Kastchei – [1]	K
Apparition de l'Oiseau de feu, poursuivi par Ivan-Tsarévitch – [3]	F - I
Danse del l'Oiseau de feu – [14]	
Capture de l'Oiseau de feu par Ivan-Tsarévitch – 1 bar after [22]	F
Supplications de l'Oiseau de feu [pas de deux Ivan-Firebird] – [29]	
[The feather, Firebird's Escape. Ivan remains alone in the garden] – [41]	F - I - K - P
Apparition des treize princesses enchantées – [48]	P
Cadenza – [52]	
Jeu des princesses avec les pommes d'or (Scherzo) – [55]	
Brusque apparition d'Ivan-Tsarévitch – [71]	I
Corovod (ronde) des princesses - [76]	
Lever du jour – [89]	P [92] - I [96]
Ivan-Tsarévitch pénètre dans le Palais de Kastchei – [97]	P
Carillon féerique - Apparition des monstres-gardiens de Kastchei et capture d'Ivan-Tsarévitch – [98]	M
Arrivée de Kastchei l'immortel – [107]	K
Dialogue de Kastchei avec Ivan-Tsarévitch – [110]	K - I
Intercession des princesses – [115]	P
Apparition de l'Oiseau de feu – [119]	F
Danse de la suite de Kastchei enchantée par l'Oiseau de feu – [126]	F - M (d. bass part at 129])
Danse infernale de tous les sujets de Kastchei – [133]	F - M
Berceuse (l'Oiseau de Feu) – [183]	F
Réveil de Kastchei – [188]	
Mort de Kastchei – [193]	
Profonds ténèbres – 2 after [193]	
Tableau II	
19. Disparition du palais et des sortilèges de Kachtchéï, animation des chevaliers pétrifiés, allégresse générale [197] – [209]	F [202], [209]

Some of these motifs are used not only in pantomimes but also in dance numbers, thus creating a continuity between the two kinds of music. This applies in particular to the short chromatic four-note motif associated with the Firebird, which can be found in almost every piece associated with the magic Bird. In addition to all the music accompanying the Bird's mimes, it appears throughout in the *Berceuse* and in the melodic lines of the *pas de deux* (see below, Ex. 13g), where its presence creates a motivic continuity with both the preceding *Capture de l'Oiseau de feu par Ivan-Tsarévitch* and the following mime scene at [41], in which the Bird's release is represented.

Clear evidence of the continuity between the two types of music is provided by Stravinsky's block displacements in the Morgan Manuscript, as discussed before. We have seen that the canon of the *Carillon féerique* was originally contained in the *Danse infernale*, were it worked no less well, since that part of the dance is based on the same motivic material (motif M) of which the *Carillon* scene is also made. This clearly shows that the two pieces have quite similar formal features.

Shared motivic-thematic materials, along with many other formal, harmonic and timbral continuities, create an almost complete fusion between the *Danse infernale* and the previous two scenes, *Apparition de l'Oiseau de feu* and *Danse de la suite de Kastchei enchantée par l'Oiseau de feu*. The end of the *Apparition* is indistinguishable from the beginning of the following number at [126] due to the continuous presence, in between the two pieces, of a chromatic *perpetuum mobile* in semiquavers (based on motif F as well). The *Danse de la suite de Kastchei*, in turn, leads directly to the *Danse infernale* at [133]: both pieces are made of a regular stream of 8 bars and both make use of Motif F and M, thus resembling more the two parts of the same music for an ensemble dance than two distinct pieces. The *Danse infernale* is a long symphonic piece made of a succession of different sections, in each of which a different motivic/thematic material is employed. In the first 32 bars (4 x 8) the famous bassoon syncopated theme (in part derived from motif M; see Ex. 15a) is exposed. In the subsequent two sections (mostly of 16 bars) motif F and the opening theme alternates in the various sections, along with other motivic materials. In the choreography, each section with a new theme/motif is given by the Firebird to a different group of characters, who are thus forced to dance[84]. In the end, the whole section of the score from the last part of the *Apparition* at [128] to the end of the Infernal dance and the beginning of the following *Berceuse* at [183] emerge as a coherent musical choreographic and musical entity.

A 'New' Collaborative Method

Consistent with his critique of the 'old' formal convention, Fokine also understood that the old system of 'collaboration', in which the choreographer indicated only the number of

---

[84]. «The Bird of Fire gives each group of demons a theme to which she forces them to dance again and again, and then she gives another group a different theme and so forth. Stravinsky was very well pleased with this plan which is accurately expressed in his music». Beaumont 1981, p. 53.

bars and a few other musical details to the composer, could no longer work. As the formal conventions that allowed for that working organization faded away, new ways of coordinating music and choreography had to be found. His fifth 'rule', in fact, reads:

> The new ballet, refusing to be the slave either of music or of scenic decoration [...] allows a perfect freedom both to the scenic artist and to the musicians. In contradistinction to the older ballet, it does not demand 'ballet music' of the composer as an accompaniment to dancing. It accepts music of every kind, provided only that it is good and expressive [...][85].

Fokine's statement that the new ballet «allows a perfect freedom [...] to the musicians» does not mean that he was advocating a less collaborative working method between composers and ballet masters (in a sense, quite the contrary is true), let alone a radical separation of music and dance as it would be more radically practiced in modern dance. His main concern was the subordination of dance and music to a system of rules and conventions that did not correspond to the needs of dramatic coherence. These could be satisfied, in his view, by using different types of music — also traditional, provided only that it was in keeping with the style and the historical setting of the ballet — and different creative methods:

> There can be different systems of creating a ballet. I had varied experiences in choreographing a ballet to music written long before and not for a ballet or even for the theatre. In these circumstances I got hints from the program notes which I found for the music. As with *Les Préludes* and *Carnaval*. At other times I fitted the story to purely abstract music, such as Tchaikovsky's Sixth Symphony, Rimsky-Korsakov's *Capriccio Espagnole*. Then again I adapted to the music a story other than the one the composer originally had in mind, as was the case with *Scherazade*. And then there were times when I choreographed ballets having no plot at all, as *Les Sylphides* and *Les Elfes*. Sometimes I would give the composer a fully developed libretto and wait for him completely to finish the music to suit my story, as in the case of *Daphnis and Chloë* by Maurice Ravel. And another time I would receive a ballet with a complete scenario. In such a case, in addition to composing the dances, I had to devise the details of the scenes, trying to find the dramatic representation of each music phrase. *Petrouchka* is an example of this[86].

While admitting different types of music and different working methods, Fokine understood that in the absence of the old hierarchical work organization the best way of obtaining a close match between music and dance was a close collaboration between the ballet masters and the composer:

---

[85]. FOKINE 1914, pp. 260-261. See also BEAUMONT 1935, pp. 146-147.
[86]. FOKINE 1961, pp. 161.

All these are entirely different approaches to the creation of a ballet and I have no intention of singling out one in particular for recommendation. I also do not mean to suggest that a ballet must be choreographed precisely, as was done in our work with Stravinsky on *The Firebird*. But I can state that the most absorbing system of creating a ballet is that of close collaboration between the choreographer and the composer, when the two artists work out the content of each musical moment together. For this, full co-operation is essential and conditions must exist whereby one can be inspired by the other[87].

Co-operation was precisely the creative method of *The Firebird*. «I have staged many ballets since *The Firebird*», he maintained, «but never again, either with Stravinsky or any other composer, did I work so closely as on this occasion»[88]. But in which way, exactly, did Fokine and Stravinsky 'collaborate' in *The Firebird*? What did their method consist of?

Stravinsky's statements on this point are quite contradictory. On some occasions he seems to allude to a rather old-fashioned method, based on the priority of the dance over music and on the measures of the phrases:

> To speak of my own collaboration with Fokine means nothing more than to say that we studied the libretto together, episode by episode, until I knew the exact measurements required of the music. In spite of his wearying homiletics, repeated at each meeting, on the role of music as accompaniment to dance, Fokine taught me much, and I have worked with choreographers in the same way ever since. I like exact requirements[89].

On other occasions, however, he seems to put it the other way round:

> Throughout the winter [of 1909] I worked strenuously at my ballet; and that brought me into constant touch with Diaghileff and his collaborators. Fokine created the choreography of *L'Oiseau de Feu* section by section, as the music was handed to him. I attended every rehearsal with the company [...][90].

Fokine, for his part, gave an interesting account, according to which he did not wait for a finished score, nor did he give Stravinsky precise indications about the choreography in terms

---

[87]. *Ibidem*, pp. 161-162.
[88]. *Ibidem*. This admission is all the more telling given that Fokine always tended to over-emphasize his role as creator of the ballet, also with respect to the composer. In *Memories and Commentaries* (p. 35) Stravinsky maintained that Fokine always complained about royalty matters connected with *The Firebird*, and always continued to refer to the ballet score as «the 'musical accompaniment' to his 'choreographic poem'».
[89]. *Expositions and Developments*, p. 129.
[90]. *Autobiography*, p. 42.

of number of bars. Rather, he showed the dance steps and mimes to the composer, so that he could directly improvise the appropriate music, while also reacting, in his turn, to the music thus arising:

> Stravinsky visited me with his first sketches and basic idea, he played them for me and I demonstrated the scenes to him. At my request, he broke up his national themes into two short phrases corresponding to the separate moments of a scene, and separate gestures and poses. I remember how he brought me a beautiful Russian melody for the entrance of Tsarevich Ivan. I suggested not presenting the complete melody all at once, but just a hint of it, by means of separate notes, at the moments when Ivan appears at the wall, when he observes the wonders of the enchanted garden, and when he leaps over the wall. Stravinsky played, and I interpreted the role of the Tsarevich, the piano substituting for the wall. I climbed over it, jumped down from it, and crawled, fear-struck, looking around my living room. Stravinsky, watching, accompanied me with patches of the Tsarevich melodies, playing mysterious tremolos as background to depict the garden of the sinister Immortal Kotschei. Later on I played the role of the Tsarevna (Princess) and hesitantly took the golden apple from the hands of the imaginary Tsarevich. Then I became Kotschei, his evil entourage — and so on[91].

According to Cyril Beaumont this was the basic working method that give rise to almost all the music for the mimed scenes:

> In a similar manner [to Ivan's theme], he explained the incidents of the shaking of the golden apple tree, the entrance of Kotschei and his followers, the scene where Ivan Tseravich seeks the egg containing the enchanter's soul, the death of Kotschei, and so forth. He expressed his ideas in pantomime, then Stravinsky devised appropriate themes, and the two collaborators discussed them in detail from the choreographic and musical view-points... The dances for the Bird of Fire were likewise the result of this close collaboration[92].

It is hard to say what value these accounts might have[93]. As Stephen Walsh notes, «we cannot be sure that the music Stravinsky wrote down was what he had improvised for Fokine»[94]. What is interesting, however, is not *what* but *how* the music and dance steps (or mime) were created. In my opinion, Fokine's account deserves much more attention than it has received so far. The 'method' described in it may have provided an effective solution to the problem I have

---

[91]. FOKINE 1961, p. 161.
[92]. BEAUMONT 1981, p. 53.
[93]. See TARUSKIN 1996, p. 584; WALSH 1999, p. 135.
[94]. WALSH 1999, p. 135.

highlighted in the previous pages. Fokine did not give Stravinsky his indications in the form of number of bars per phrase, nor did he give them in the form of *written* instructions. Rather, he showed the composer the dance steps and the mime directly *from his body*. In this way, he could get several results at once:

1) by directly showing the composer the body movements, he immediately let him understand which character the music should have and what meanings it should convey;

2) by asking the composer to 'improvise' on his movements, he allowed him to immediately find the right lengths of the musical materials;

3) by interacting in real time with the composer, he could establish continuous communication with him, so that even the dance could be modeled, to a certain extent, on the music, following any asymmetries and irregularities of its form.

There are many other accounts that hint at a close — though sometimes difficult and troubled — collaboration and continuous mutual interaction between Fokine and Stravinsky during the creation and rehearsals of the ballet. Tamara Karsavina maintained that they «[...] worked over a score and appealed to Diaghileff in every collision over the tempi»[95]. According to the *régisseur* Grigoriev, Stravinsky's percussive piano performance during the rehearsals «was invigorating to watch» and «certainly inspired Fokine in his work [...]»; and «the extraordinary music [of Stravinsky] led Fokine to the invention of original steps, which the dancers could not but enjoy and be amused at»[96].

Even more than these accounts, it is the formal features of the music that suggest a closer collaboration than in the 'old ballet'. Although, as a rule, four-bar grouping is preserved, on many occasions the music features an unconventional, and also asymmetric, structure that could hardly have arisen from the choreography. This also applies to the most 'conventional' dance numbers of the ballet. Although they are largely based on conventional formal schemes and symmetrical bar groupings, various features aim at concealing or disrupting the regularities of the form: frequent syncopations, intricate rhythms, shifting accents, complex orchestration, and sometimes even asymmetric phrases can be found[97]. Let us consider, for example, the *Danse del l'Oiseau de feu* at [14], a dance number that has been related to the traditional *'allegro pizzicato'* of classical ballet[98]. Firstly, the piece does not have a sufficiently clear melody for what gives it

---

[95].   KARSAVINA 1961, p. 213.

[96].   GRIGORIEV 2009, p. 32.

[97].   This is not to deny that many dance numbers of *The Firebird* are «highly, if conventionally, structured», as TARUSKIN 1996, p. 614, observes nor that they clearly belong «to the styles of [their] time» as Stravinsky himself stated. *EXPOSITIONS AND DEVELOPMENTS*, p. 131. Admittedly, many of their characteristics are specific reflections of specific models. However, as Taruskin himself has shown, these models are not so much balletic as operatic, in particular with regards to style and harmonic language; and this is *per se* a rather 'unconventional' feature for a ballet score.

[98].   TARUSKIN 1996. See also Smirnov, quoted *ibidem*.

its structure is harmony, which is almost entirely based on progressions of French sixths. The various instrumental parts are limited to filling the underlying harmonies with arpeggios, chromatic scales, short figures or short motifs (some of which are related to the Firebird motif which we will discuss later). All this makes it rather difficult to grasp the musical structure with which the dance steps have to be coordinated. Secondly, groupings 0 are not always based on module 4; and even when they are, rhythm systematically contravenes, through syncopations and crossed rhythms, the regular downbeats. The whole movement's grouping structure is as follows:

A ([14]): eight-bar theme: 2 x 4
B ([15]-[17]): 13-bars contrasting section: = 5 + 8 (3 x 2 + 2)
A¹ ([18]): expanded recapitulation of A: (2 x 4) + (2 x 2)
Coda ([19-20]): 9 bars: 5 + 4

Part A appears as a rather conventional eight-bar 'theme' (although in this case, in the absence of a true melody, the term sounds inappropriate), with a four-bar phrase repeated twice on two French sixths a minor third apart: *g - b - c♯ - e♯* and *b♭ - d - e - g♯* [99]. The few notes that do not belong to the French sixth form a whole tone collection, while the sum of the two French sixth results in an octatonic collection. In the first part of each 4-bars group the French sixth is first spelled as a seventh chord (with roots on *c♯* and *e* respectively), and then as a proper French sixth (with roots on *g* and *b♭* respectively). The added notes creating the whole-tone collections are obtained as the ninth of the implied root [100]. However, although the structure is regularly based on the classic four-bar module, the downbeats — and therefore the metric structure of the theme — is anything but clear when listening. The only parts whose rhythm clearly corresponds to the compound time signature 6/8 are the inner accompanying parts of the violin I and II (*divisi*) in the first two bars, whose repeated quaver chords move up a semitone in the uppermost part of every dotted crotchet beat. Much more immediately apparent is the *pizzicati* cello part, which is heavily syncopated and offbeat, according to the following pattern:

6/8:

At bar 3 the regular pattern of quavers in violin I-II (now coordinated with the semiquaver groups of the viola) changes into three chords in hemiola (on the first, third and fifth beat of a

[99].   The *g♯* and *b* in the bass part at b. 1 an 5 of the 1911 Jurgenson piano reduction are wrong and should be corrected respectively in *g* and *b♭* (as in the full score)

[100].   TARUSKIN 1996, p. 616, identified the model of this harmonic procedure in a passage marked *Allegro volando* of Scriabin's *Poème de l'extase*.

6/8 measure). In this way, the rhythm of the violin I-II and viola parts complements the cello part in the following way:

vln I-II, vla: 6/8:

vlc: 6/8:

Moreover, the above scheme provides only the essential rhythmic skeleton of the four-bar group: in many instrumental parts (in particular in the wind parts) each quaver is further subdivided into duplets, triplets and quadruplets.

In addition to the intricate rhythm, the structure is complicated by the use of irregular and asymmetrical bar groupings. The B section, of 13 measures, is not divisible into two four-bar groups: it is made of two asymmetrical phrases of 5 and 8 measures respectively. The first phrase is based on the triple repetition in sequence, each time a semitone higher, of a one-bar harmonic idea — an arpeggiation based on a French sixth, first reordered as a seventh chord. However, two interpolated bars are added after the first and third repetition of the sequence, thus transforming the 3 x 1 structure into a five-bar group 1 [+1] +1 + 1 [+1]. The recapitulation A¹ at [18] (A¹) is four bars longer than A, because after the two statements of the four-bar phrase, two more statements of the first half of the same phrase are added, with each of the four statements on a different French sixth, according to a sequence of ascending minor thirds ($f_\flat$ - g - $b_\flat$ - $d_\flat$). Also the Coda, which resumes the material of the B section, is asymmetrical too, since the first part is of 5 measures, as in B.

Such unconventional formal features also made it difficult for the dancers to coordinate the dance phrases with the music during rehearsals. They couldn't easily find the usual «string of obvious tunes squared up in 32 or 64 bars»[101]. According to Karsavina, Stravinsky tried to circumvent the problem by stressing the music accents on the piano, so as to make the musical phrases as clear as possible. But even more helpful than the sound of the instrument was the sight of Stravinsky's performing body: his gestures allowed the dancers to 'bodily understand' the overall grouping structure of the music, even without counting the number of bars:

> [...] how difficult it had been at first to assimilate Stravinsky's music. He was kind and patient with my shortcomings. Often he came early to the theatre before a rehearsal began in order to play for me over and over again some specially difficult passage. I felt grateful, not only for the help he gave me but for the manner in which he gave it. For there was no impatience in him with my slow understanding; no condescension of a master of his craft towards the slender equipment of my musical education. It was interesting to watch him at the piano. His body seemed

---

[101].   Karsavina 1961, p. 169.

to vibrate with his own rhythm; punctuating staccatos with his head, he made the
pattern of his music forcibly clear to me, more so than the counting of bars would
have done[102].

A similar account was provided by the *régisseur* Grigoriev, according to whom as soon as
Fokine began rehearsing the ballet, the dancers...

> [...] were all too obviously dismayed at the absence of melody in the music and
> its unlikeness to what they were used to dancing to at the Mariinsky. Some of
> them indeed declared that it did not sound like music at all. Stravinsky was usually
> present to indicate the tempo and rhythms. Now and again he would play over
> passages himself and, according to some of the dancers, "demolish the piano". He
> was particularly exacting about the rhythms and used to hammer them out with
> considerable violence, humming loudly and scarcely caring whether he struck the
> right notes[103].

The dress rehearsals were also performed on the piano, so that it was only at the first
performance that the dancers had the opportunity to listen to the music with the full orchestra.
This created fresh difficulties; no longer helped by the percussive sound of the piano and by
Stravinsky's performing body, the dancers found it again very difficult to coordinate their
movements with the music. According to Grigoriev, the rehearsal on the stage, as well as the
two dress rehearsals, were «absolutely vital on account of the complicated set and lighting and,
above all, of the music, which sounded quite different when played by the orchestra from what
it had sounded like when played on a piano»[104].

This brings us back to Fedor Lopukhov's *caveat* «[...] all of the composer's work must
sound exactly the same when played by a full orchestra as it would in rehearsal»[105]. Although
Stravinsky's piano short score was similar in structure to the final score, the sumptuous, brilliant
orchestration still made it very different.

The unconventional formal features of the music and its complex orchestration
even created problems for the musicians conducted by Gabriel Pierné. As Grigoriev recalls,
Stravinsky «endeavoured to explain the music» to the musicians «but energetically though
[they] attacked it, they found it no less bewildering than the dancers»[106].

---

[102]. KARSAVINA 1948, p. 8. My emphasis.

[103]. GRIGORIEV 2009, p. 32.

[104]. *Ibidem*, p. 37.

[105]. LOPUKHOV 2002 (p. 57).

[106]. GRIGORIEV 2009, p. 37. See also Stravinsky's letter of 19 June (2 July, N.S.) in VARUNTS 1997, pp. 224-226
(quoted in WALSH 1999, p. 584, fn. 6; Eng. transl. in STRAVINSKY 1969), in which the composers tells Roerich
that the musicians found the score so difficult that they needed no less than nine rehearsals to learn it.

In conclusion, the unconventional features of Stravinsky's music made at the very least undesirable, if not impossible, a mechanical adaptation of the music to a pre-established and conventional sequence of dance steps, and continuous interaction between him and Fokine highly likely. Their 'new' methods were deeply rooted in the use of the body as a source of knowledge. The sight of Fokine's dancing body provided Stravinsky with an immediate understanding of the choreography. In turn, Stravinsky's piano performance and the sight of his performing body allowed Fokine and the dancers to understand how to face the 'unconventional' features of his music. In the end, this 'new' method was based on a more direct interaction between the bodies, as Fokine's famous 1931 account of the creation of the Dying Swan (1905) for Anna Pavlova also shows:

> It was almost an improvisation. I danced in front of her [Pavlova], she directly behind me. Then she danced and I walked alongside her, curving her arms and correcting details of poses[107].

Words, Gestures, Movements

The relationship between music and mime is an important — but almost entirely neglected — aspect of *The Firebird*. Its study could shed further light on Stravinsky's evolution from a purely 'mimetic' and descriptive to a more subtle and indirect representation of the bodily movements[108]. The mimed sections of the ballet are the most interesting ones from the point of view of both the compositional techniques and the musical narrative strategies[109]. A deeper knowledge of the kinds of gestures to which Stravinsky's music was linked in the mimed scenes, therefore, would be worthwhile. A number of obstacles, unfortunately, present themselves in this respect. First of all, due to the lack of sufficiently reliable visual sources for the 1910 production, we cannot be sure whether recent performances still preserve Fokine's original use of gestures. Secondly, we have very little information about the traditional gestural code used in St. Petersburg before Fokine's 'reform'; and, although Fokine, at least in his statements, largely rejected this code in favour of a different kind of bodily expression, we will see that something of it still remained in *The Firebird*. Nonetheless, a number of comments can be made on the basis of certain constant elements in the various Fokine-based performances at our disposal.

---

107. Interview with Fokine, in: *Dance Magazine*, August 1931, n. p.

108. On this relationship in nineteenth-century opera see Smart 2004.

109. According to Taruskin 1996, p. 588, these sections «[...] contain practically the only music of interest in the score, surely the only music that gives any inkling of the Stravinsky to come».

Ballet mime was a fairly consolidated practice in Russia, where it owed much to the Italian tradition — in which the use of mime was of great importance — and to Cecchetti's teaching. Throughout the nineteenth century, it had become a sort of conventional code of body signs, largely made up of movements of the arms, the hands and the fingers, and of stereotyped facial expressions[110]. These signs had a true 'vocabulary' and 'grammar' of their own, which allowed them to stand for words and dialogues[111].

Fokine's general approach to mime broke with this practice. According to his third 'rule', the new ballet could admit the use of conventional hand gesture only where it was required by the style of the ballet, while in all other cases it had to « replace gestures of the hands by mimetic of the whole body », because the body « can be and should be expressive from head to foot »[112]. In this way, Fokine also endeavoured to make mime, like dance, more suited to a more 'natural' and less conventional expressiveness. His ideas reflect in part realist theatrical aesthetics, in part the growing sensitivity in twentieth-century theatre towards holistic bodily expression.

In discussing his use of gestures in *The Firebird*, Fokine showed an essential manner of distinguishing between the 'old' and the 'new' mime:

> The Tsarevich did not say, as was customary in ballet tradition, "I have come here". Instead, he just entered. The princesses did not say, "We are having a good time". Instead, they had a good time, in reality. King Kostchei did not state: 'I will

---

[110]. Thorough research on ballet mime has been rarely undertaken. On theatre mime in Italy and its evolution into ballet mime, see POESIO 1993. Unfortunately, the vocabulary of nineteenth-century mime was never codified in the same way as that of the formal dances, so we have very few sources for it. A few conventional gestures, aimed at providing the dance sequences with a specific narrative or metaphorical meaning, were included in some sets of training *enchaînements*. A few of these sequences are still performed and taught today. They give us a very useful insight into the quality and features of the old gestures. On the use of gestures in the Cecchetti method, see BENNET – POESIO 2000. Dance historians usually credit Jean-Georges Noverre and Gasparo Angiolini with the introduction of mime into *ballet d'action*. Their theories were later incorporated in Salvatore Viganò's reflection on the *coreodrama*. However, these authors relied on a theatrical mime tradition which had developed during in the eighteenth century from the acting techniques of the Italian Commedia dell'Arte. In the nineteenth-century ballet mime evolved above everywhere else in Italy. From there, mime was made universally known by itinerant theatrical troupes and by the many Italian dancers who toured and worked abroad, thus becoming the standard gestural vocabulary used in ballet across Europe. However, ballet mime always remained an Italian specialty. The genre of the Italian *ballo* always gave more importance to mime than French 'technical' dancing. At the Imperial Ballet School in St. Petersburg, Enrico Cecchetti coached generations of Russian dancers in the use of the traditional Italian conventional gestures. Cecchetti himself had always been famous for creating and interpreting fortunate roles belonging to the *caractère* or grotesque type (one of the three main styles of male dances in the early nineteenth-century classification, along with the noble and the semi-serious), in which the use of expressive gestures was particularly important.

[111]. On the vocabulary of mime in general see LAWSON 1957, pp. 83-115.

[112]. See above, fn. 73.

destroy thee; instead, he attempted to turn Tsarevich into stone. The fairest princess and the Tsarevich did not use sign language to express their love. But from their positions and looks, from their longing for each other, from the very fact that Ivan wrenched at the gates in order to follow her, and from her tearful pleading with him in trying to save him from King Kotschei — from all this one could conclude and feel their mutual love. In short, no one had to explain anything to anyone else or to the audience; everything was expressed by action and dances. [In footnote:] Reading the story of this ballet I have often come upon such phrases as «the Princess tells... the sad story of her abduction» [...]; «During the games and the cordial conversation the girls do not notice». «Ivan explains that he is a prince who has become separated from his companions» [...]. I am obliged to make a correction. The authors of these books give an incorrect impression of my ballet and the method by which the story is told. I use storytelling but not narration. There is no conversation in The Firebird. Ivan explains nothing. This is a vital difference between the old and the new ballet[113].

Fokine seems to allude to a theoretical distinction between two different types of mime, the first of which is based on language imitation, while the second draws more directly from body expression, without any linguistic intermediation. His rejection of the first type relies on the idea that gestures should not represent actions, feelings and concepts as if they were expressed through verbal language. This also accounts for the much shorter length, in respect to nineteenth-century ballets, of his libretti, and the drastic reduction of the dialogues in them. In a sense, Fokine's ideas also recall those expressed a century and half earlier by Jean-Georges Noverre, whose *Lettres sur la danse et sur les ballets* of 1760 is often credited with the fundamental ideas and definitions of *ballet d'action*. One of Noverre's fundamental tenets was that dance could be made more meaningful than words themselves if the body was freed from the constraints of conventions.

In order to understand in which sense 'old' ballet mime 'relied on language', we must recall that, as senseless as this statement may seem — since ballet is, as a rule, a genre in which the use of language is entirely avoided in favour of bodily expression — nineteenth-century ballet-pantomime depended heavily on a literary basis. The libretto could sometimes contain explicit 'words' in the form of dialogues and speech in the first person. Other times, the latter could be implicit in the story itself. In any case, these 'words', though never spoken or sung aloud on stage, determined many aspects of mime as well as music. This was just one of the many important analogies between ballet and opera[114]. Traditionally, the conventional hand signs

---

[113]. FOKINE 1961, pp. 168-169. My emphasis. According to Fokine himself, the authors of the sentences he quoted were from books by André Levinson and Cyril W. Beaumont.

[114]. On this issue see SMITH 2000, pp. 97-114. The problem of the relationships with language and the reliance on the (written) word of the libretti had always been a central issue from the very founding of the genre of *ballet d'action* in the eighteenth century.

and facial expressions of ballet mime had to remain not only for feelings and emotions, but also for the concepts, the ideas, and sometimes the specific words of the libretto. A general distaste for this kind of speech-like pantomime had already begun to affect the French audience in the years of the July Monarchy[115]. Merely by way of example, this is how an eighteenth-century critic reviewed a performance of *La Gipsy* in 1839:

> [...] in this booklet you can read: "Stenio says to the Bohemians: «I have strong arms; I am young, courageous; would you like me to join you?» Someone asks, «But who are you? Who are you?» «An unfortunate fugitive, without money without refuge, without hope». «Thus he may enter among us»". You may have noticed the expressions... «Stenio SAYS», etc. Well, Stenio, instead of SAYING, rotates his two arms like a windmill in a frightening manner, and then he socks the first Bohemian in the eye. Literal translation: «I have strong arms». Then he caresses the backs of his legs in a friendly manner, as if he feels an itch; he... pinches his waist, he rubs his chin, he lightly curls his forelock... Translation: «I am young». Then he draws his sword, if he has one, and frightens two or three small children posted near the wings... Translation: «I am courageous». Then he strikes a haughty pose in the manner of Caesar... Translation: «Would you like me to join you?»[116].

The kind of speech-like gestures ridiculed in this comment was precisely the one Fokine was referring to in his previous quotation. Fokine's aversion to the speech-like gestures, however, had quite different motivations to these nineteenth-century complaints; it was in tune with the general trend in early twentieth-century theatre — and arts in general — to minimize the role of language by depriving it of its traditional role as the most important bearer of meaning and, instead, elevate the importance of other components of the spectacle and of other means of expression (bodily, visual, and musical).

In much the same way as conventional gestures in mime, ballet music was traditionally supposed to compensate for the absence of sung or spoken words. In a sense, it had to provide a lot of 'unspoken verbal cues' to the audience, even more than mime itself did. This role of ballet music was largely recognized by many nineteenth-century critics, commentators and theorists. In 1873, for example, Gustave Chouquet, wrote that «Noverre [...] created the *ballet d'action* and made a certain type of musical drama out of it, since instrumental music in it took the place *of the word* and of singing»[117]. According to Carlo Blasis, music supplemented and clarified «all

---

[115]. See *ibidem*, pp. 116-123. Smith quotes many authors who complain about the obscurity and failure of mime when it tried in vain to convey too many complicated details, concepts and words of the libretto.

[116]. *La France Musicale*, 3 February 1839, quoted in SMITH 2000, p. 119.

[117]. «A l'Opera [...] ce fut Noverre qui créa le ballet d'action et en fit un drame musical d'un genre particulier, puisque la symphonie instrumentale y tient lieu de la parole et du chant» (Gustave Chouquet, *Histoire de la Musique Dramatique*, 1870, quoted in SMITH 2000, p. 5, fn. 14, my italics).

the mental movements which the dancer or mime artist cannot convey in gestures and the play of the physiognomy». Clearly enough, by 'mental movements' Blasis also meant 'words'[118]. In the first decades of the nineteenth-century, many techniques had been devised to this end, such as the *airs parlants* — melodic quotations of well-known operatic melodies whose origina, here unsung words, could be easily recalled by the audience, thus enhancing the narrative function of music, and creating a certain dramaturgic effect — or else recitative-like instrumental passages that sometimes matched the words written in the score or libretto. Frequently, ballets were parodies of comic operas, whose libretti (and whose words) were well-known to the audience. After the 1830s, all these ploys went out of fashion, but to some extent nineteenth-century ballet always remained a *musique parlante* ('speaking music'), although in a less evident and direct way[119]. Composers continued to be tasked with rendering the dialogues of the libretti with their music. Sometimes it was the musical form that provided an equivalent for words, as for example when certain question/answer dialogue lines were represented respectively by the antecedent and consequent of an eight-bar musical period.

Fokine maintained that in *The Firebird* he had «completely excluded the stereotyped hand pantomime and ballet gesticulation for the development of the plot on stage»[120]. However, despite his peremptory statement, many old-fashioned speech-like gestures can be found in both the pantomimes. As far as one can see in many performances — whether they are reconstructed, such as that of Isabelle Fokine, or relying on the memory-based tradition, such as those of the Royal Ballet — there are several points in which the characters resort to conventional hand gestures to express their 'inner words' or dialogues with each other.

Similarly, in Stravinsky's music there still remain a mixture of styles, including some instances of a sort of *musique parlant*, in which the gesticulations of the mimes and the speech-like character of the music go hand in hand. When, many years later, Stravinsky would 'apologize' for the fact that «The Firebird [...] like all story ballets, [...] demanded descriptive music of a kind I did not want to write», and that it was «as literal as an opera», he was commenting precisely on this aspect of the ballet[121]. His preoccupation was above all with a kind of 'descriptiveness'

---

[118]. *Tantsy voobshche, baletnye znamenitosti i natsional'nye tantsy* [Dances in General, Ballet Celebrities, and National Dances], Moscow, Lazarevsk, 1864, p. 46, transated and quoted by WILEY 1985, p. 5. See also SMITH 2000, p. 5.

[119]. In 1824 Auguste Baron stated that ballet music was «[...] plus accentuée, *plus parlante*, plus expressive que la musique d'opéra, car elle n'est pas destinée seulement à accompagner et à rehausser les paroles du poète, mais à être elle-même le poème tout entier». Auguste Baron, *Lettres et entretiens sur la Danse*, Paris, Dondey-Dupré Père et Fils, 1824, quoted in SMITH 2000, p. 5, fn. 11, my italics.

[120]. FOKINE 1961, p. 168.

[121]. «The Firebird did not attract me as a subject. Like all story ballets it demanded descriptive music of a kind I did not want to write. [In footnote:] See, for example, the dialogue of Kastchei and Ivan Tsarevich (No. 110) where the music is as literal as an opera». *EXPOSITIONS AND DEVELOPMENTS*, p. 128.

which implies language imitation, and his rejection of this style is symptomatic of his (later) anti-literary stance, on which was also depended his distaste for a kind opera in which the music endeavoured to express the meaning of words of the libretto[122]. In this respect, however, the music of *The Firebird* was no more 'descriptive' than any other ballet, since nineteenth-century ballet-pantomime relied even more heavily on a literary conception.

One might argue that the 'mixed' mime style of *The Firebird*. was not incongruent with Fokine's aesthetic premises, since it corresponded to his idea that also more conventional and 'old' styles could be adopted if they fitted the character, the general atmosphere and the genre of the represented story. In fact, in *the Firebird*, the variety of styles reflects the differentiation between two main expressive styles (natural *vs* magic-grotesque), which I will deal with later; speech-like hand gestures and descriptive music occur almost exclusively within the magic-grotesque sphere of the ballet.

The clearest example in which Stravinsky's music is in tune with the mime's old-fashioned hand gesticulations occurs in the long scene of the 'dialogue' between Kashchey and Ivan at [107]-[118]. The original libretto of the 1910 premiere is decidedly laconic here: there are no dialogues at all and all that is said is that Kashchey, «[...] the fearsome demigod [...] wants to take him [Ivan] and turn him into stone, as he already did with many valiant knights. But [...] the thirteen princesses, his captives, interceded and tried to save Ivan Tsarevich»[123]. However, the mime contains many more 'words' than the libretto itself. The scene begins at [107], where Kashchey appears in the background and then comes up close to Ivan, who has been imprisoned by the monsters-guardians. At [110]: Kashchey 'speaks' to Ivan; his hand gestures, as invariably performed in all the most important productions, and their meaning are as follows:

	Gesture	*meaning ('words')*
1)	finger repeatedly pointing at Ivan	«you»
2)	finger pointing down	«why are you here?»
(*1 and 2 repeated twice*)		
3)	beckoning sign	«come here!»

After Ivan's reply (at [111]) and the princesses' supplications to spare Ivan's life, the scene ended with Kashchey laughing at their request [116] and trying to turn Ivan into stone [117],

---

[122]. His omission of the 'recitative' scenes of the ballet — in particular those with the 'dialogues' — from his three concert suites also went in the direction of concealing the original 'literary' and 'operatic' component of the ballet. All three concert suites omit almost all of the music for the pantomimes. In MEMORIES AND COMMENTARIES, p. 30, Stravinsky described the original ballet score as «too long and patchy». In EXPOSITIONS AND DEVELOPMENTS, p. 132, he said: «My feelings towards [*The Firebird*] are purely those of a critic — though, to be honest, I was criticizing it even when I was composing it [...] I have already criticized The Firebird twice, however, in my revised versions of 1919 and 1945».

[123]. See above, fn. 3.

Ex. 3a: *The Firebird* [110]-[118]: *Dialogue de Kastchei avec Ivan-Tsarévitch.*

* As in David Drew's performance (Royal Ballet, The Royal Opera House, Covent Garden, 2001).

before the Tsarevitch extracted the Firebird's magic feather [118]. The mimicry with which Kashchey's 'silent words' were 'pronounced' was that associated to the figures of the old man and the evil wizard, as can still be seen in today's performances. No doubt, in addition to using the hands, Aleksey Bulgakov's mime [ILL. 3] made use of the whole body, according to the grotesque Italian tradition imported into St. Petersburg via Enrico Cecchetti's teaching[124].

Ex. 3a shows how these gestures are translated into music. The melody of motif K slavishly accompanies the hand gestures — each repeated note corresponds to a movement of the hand: four eighth notes are repeated and then followed by four accented semiquavers descending chromatically and ending brusquely on the following downbeat a major third lower. The rhythm, the accents, the restricted range and the sudden interruptions seem to imitate the inflection and the rhythm of human speech. Even the use of low-register wind instruments (horns and muted trombones) seems to imitate a basso voice (the most appropriate vocal range for such a character). All this recalls, strikingly, much nineteenth-century *musique parlante*. Marian

---

[124]. See BUCHANAN 2017. After the 1910 premiere Cecchetti interpreted the role of Kaschkey on some occasions. In some photos he is portrayed with the same costume as Bulgakov (ILL. 3). One of these is reproduced in Buchanan's essay.

Smith's description of technique, as used by nineteenth-century French ballet composers, could be applied equally well to Kashchey's music: «[...] a sort of music [*parlante*] [that] imitated the inflections of the human voice by employing the wide tessitura of spoken French, sometimes breaking the flow with rests». Ex. 3b quotes an example from Smith's book reproducing an example of *musique parlante* in Filippo Taglioni-Adolphe Adam's *La Fille du Danube* (1836), where the analogy with Kashchey's music is self-evident. Most likely, it was only after composing this *musique parlante* that Stravinsky decided to use it as a leitmotif representing the figure of Kashchey *tout court*, not only his 'words'.

Ex. 3b: From SMITH 2000, p. 111 (Ex. 4.7): *musique parlante* in Filippo Taglioni – Adolphe Adam's *La Fille du Danube* (1836).

Ex. 3c: *The Firebird* [116]: *Dialogue de Kastchei avec Ivan-Tsarévitch*: musical imitation of Kashchey's laugh (see also Ex. 11a and 17f).

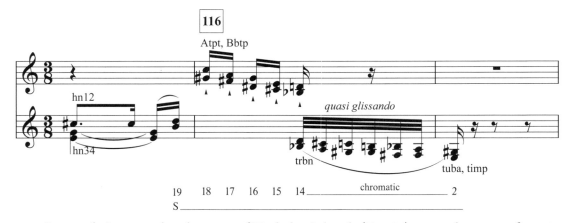

Stravinsky's musical realization of Kashchey's laugh (Ex. 3c) is another case of *musique parlante* (or perhaps we should say 'laughing music' in this case). The descending melodic

Ill. 3: Right, photograph of Aleksey Bulgakov as Kashchey in *The Firebird*, costume designed by Léon Bakst (photo August Bert, repr. in Svetlov 1911, p. 48bis). Left side: Bulgakov and Bolm (Ivan Tsarevich) in the same production (photo by August Bert).

profile — based on a sequence of six alternating major/minor thirds to be discussed later — the *staccatissimo* accents on the semiquavers of the two trumpets, followed by the *quasi glissando* of the trombones, and by the final peremptory arrival of the tuba and timpani, imitate as faithfully as possible Kahchey's laughter.

Such grotesque scenes were not the only ones in which old-fashioned hand gestures and descriptive music were used. Another possible case can be seen, for example, in a scene in which no grotesque, old or evil characters are involved, but the noble, young, moral and socially elevated figure of Ivan. This happens at [96], at the end of the *Ivan-Tsarévitch pénètre dans le Palais de Kastchei* scene, just before the *Carillon féerique*. In the story, the Prince decides to enter Kashchey's palace, so the mime has to make the audience understand that he had made this important decision. According to Fokine's memories, he devised the mime without resorting to any hand gesticulation. While commenting on the 1937 restaging of the Ballet with Colonel de Basil's Original Ballets Russes, he said:

As for the pantomime, it remained in its original state, as I had produced it. That is to say that no one had added, during my absence, any of the old-fashioned ballet gesticulations or stereotyped storytelling movements, with one exception (I must mention this, so that future performers may not think that «Fokine staged it so»): Ivan Tsarevich (the part was played by Léonide Massine), before hacking at the gates, addresses himself to the audience and says, gesticulating, "I have an idea! He points to himself, places his index finger on his forehead and then points the finger up to the sky. This gesture is identical with and done in precisely the same manner as that of Pierrot in my "Carnaval". There the thought is about catching the Butterfly; here, to break open the gates. Of course, I never staged this in "The Firebird". The gesture is appropriate for Pierrot: addressing oneself directly to the audience is a typical characteristic of Commedia dell'Arte. The index finger to the forehead fits Pierrot very well. In the role of the Tsarevich, however, matters are quite different. He does not converse with the audience; for him the audience does not exist. There is no similarity between "The Firebird" and "Carnaval". They are totally different in style, temperament, and everything else. Such injections and graftings from one of my ballets to another endanger them greatly[125].

We do not know how reliable this account is. One cannot rule out the possibility that in later years Fokine tried to purge his 1910 original of every element that could be seen as old-fashioned or incoherent with the general style of the ballet. In any case, recent Fokine-based performances display a variety of approaches and solutions. In the Royal Ballet tradition one can usually see the mime performing some stereotyped hand gesticulation (also turning eyes to the audience) of a kind akin to the ones Fokine dealt with in his previous quotation. Ill. 4 shows Jonathan Cope in one of these typical gestures: he points his index finger first to himself and then upwards. This means that he has had a sudden illumination. Performances based on Isabelle Fokine's reconstruction conversely avoid this use of hand gestures in favour of a more realistic solution — Ivan's decision is simply represented by the fact that he suddenly begins to move. In Fokine's terms, he does not say «I have an idea»: he simply starts doing what he has decided to do.

Ex. 4: *The Firebird*, music accompanying Ivan's gestures at 1 bar before [97]. (See also Ex. 17e.)

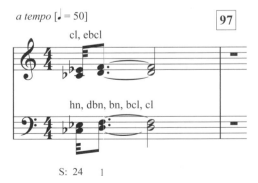

---

125. FOKINE 1961, p. 178.

ILL. 4: Jonathan Cope as Ivan Tzarevich in *The Firebird* (Royal Ballet, The Royal Opera House, Covent Garden, 2001, Heathfield, East Sussex, BBC - [Netherlands], Opus Arte, ©2001).

What is quite clear, however, is that Stravinsky's music at this point contains a musical gesture that, while clearly fulfilling a narrative function, is of a slightly different kind to Kashchey's *musique parlante*. This is shown in Ex. 4. It is a very short and simple musical figure. The harmony, again, is based on the usual alternating major/minor thirds (see Ex. 17e for the harmonic structure of the previous passage). More than harmony, however, what is significant is the overall *gestalt*, a very rapid succession of two chords, with the second one higher than the first and sounding as the sudden stop (see the prolonged sounds of the second dyad) of the harmonic flow. The effectiveness of this little musical gesture lies in the way it 'describes' — corresponds to — a bodily (and embodied) dynamics, a sudden change in the dynamic state of the body, from stasis to movement, or vice-versa.

Such two-note (or two-chord) gestures would become a sort of little *topos* of Stravinsky's style. Not by chance, when choreographed by Balanchine, will they usually take on the form of a sudden bodily movement brusquely interrupted or, vice-versa, abruptly starting: a jump-and-landing, a rise-and-drop, etc.[126] But also independently of any 'visualization' they will preserve a strongly gestural character and bodily connotation. We can say that these kinds of associations rely in part on some formal analogies between the temporal dynamics of music and those of — seen or unseen — bodily movements, and in part on a pre-existing set of cultural conventions in which the association was initially established. In this respect, Stravinsky's use of the two-chord musical gesture in *The Firebird* still corresponds to the first stage of the process, in which the music is still associated with a visible bodily gesture. Interestingly enough,

---

[126]. We have already seen this musical gesture in Chapter One, while discussing *Variations*.

however, in this case the bodily gesture also reflected an 'idea' — an inner, non-visible change of mental condition — so that we might argue that Stravinsky's musical gesture reflects both the visible bodily gesture on stage and an implicit — unseen, embodied — dynamic. This is probably why at this point of the ballet this little musical gesture music tells us that 'something suddenly changed' in the dramatic development of the story line, also independently from the kind of bodily gesture actually performed on stage. If so, this small example provides us with an anticipation of Stravinsky's typical style, in which musical gestures are capable of conveying embodied meanings, even in the absence of a visible bodily counterpart.

MOVEMENTS, ACTIONS, PROCESSIONS

The Firebird contains many examples where the music conveys the meanings of the story line in a highly effective way. In these cases too the meaning association relies in part on an analogy between an embodied dynamic and some formal features of the music, in part on conventional (topic) associations. To better illustrate the concept, I will consider two cases: the musical representation of the two Horsemen[127] and that of the coronation procession, with which the ballet ends.

As can be seen in the previously discussed 'Lyubensk' title page (ILL. 1), Fokine had the idea of representing the transition from night to day by the appearance of two horsemen, the first black and the second white[128]. The black rider was supposed to appear a few bars after the curtain rises on Kashchey's enchanted garden immersed in darkness. The appearance of the white horseman was planned in the 'daybreak' scene. Fokine drew the idea from the Russian fairy tale *Vasilisa Prekrasnaya* (*Vasilisa the Fair*), where the protagonist, on the way to the house of Baba Yaga, meets three horsemen — the first dressed in white and on a white horse, the second in red and on a red horse, and the third all in black and riding a black horse — whose appearance corresponds to daybreak, sunset, and night respectively. In addition to the mythological and archetypical meaning that these symbols had in the folkloric sources, the use of the two knights were meant above all to be spectacular since they were supposed to ride real horses on stage[129]. Unfortunately, due to inevitable challenges in managing the animals, the idea

---

[127]. To my knowledge, FLAMM 2013, pp. 60-61, was the first scholar to focus attention on these short but significant — with a view to *The Firebird*'s 'descriptivism' — musical passages.

[128]. According to Stravinsky's — erroneous — recollections (*EXPOSITIONS AND DEVELOPMENTS*, p. 130) there were two processions of several horses (not just two horses), and this was actually Diaghilev's idea. FOKINE 1961, pp. 171, on the contrary, maintained that there were just two horseman riding on two «beautiful stallions».

[129]. These semantics of colours and this archetypical meaning of the horse image was widespread in Slavic and Euroasian folklore and literature, where they not only symbolized the main moments of the daily path of the sun, but also embodied certain deeper mythological values (the white horse was a symbol of beauty and purity, and in

proved impractical and was abandoned after a few performances — or maybe after the dress rehearsal[130].

Nonetheless, Fokine was quite fond of his idea; in his 1931 restaging of *The Firebird* in Buenos Aires he had the two knights painted by Ivan Bilibin on glass projected on the backdrop[131]. In any case, he wanted Stravinsky to compose some music to represent the two riders, as is clearly shown by the entries in his list on the 'Lyubensk' title page[132]. Stravinsky did, in fact, provide the music for the entrance of the two horses, in the form of short motifs embedded within a larger musical narration. They can be found respectively in *Le jardin enchanté de Kastchei* at [2], a few bars after the curtain rises, and in the *Lever de jour*, at [89][133]. The music for the first knight (Ex. 5a), like much of the music of the mimic scenes relating to the area of magic is based on a series of alternating minor and major chords. However, in this case the characteristic element associated with the figure of the horse is given by rhythm and timbre, rather than harmony. While the parts for violins, violas and cellos — in tremolo — continue to play the ostinato with which the entire score begins, which is based on a composed ternary rhythm, the part of double basses (divided) and double bassoons performs a figure of dyads on a duplet (binary) rhythm. This contrasting rhythm, which opposes and disrupts the

---

some cultural contexts also of death; the black horse personified a certain disturbing essence of world harmony; and the red horse, antithetical to both white and black ones, represented sun, fire, war and new life). Fokine only discarded the red horse from Afanasyev's tale and from these mythological semiotics. Thus in his own symbolism, as well as in Slavic folklore, the two horses did not represent, *per se*, good and evil, but only day (light) and night (darkness). However, in *The Firebird* the latter was in turn associated with good and evil so that even the two knights end up taking on this moral connotation.

[130]. According to FOKINE 1961, p. 171, they were employed only «at the general rehearsal — or it may have been at the opening performance» (*ibidem*). KARSAVINA 1961, p. 214, recalled that «the symbolic horsemen of day and night gave much worry to the committee while discussing the Fire Bird. "Impossible to let horses stamp all over the stage, pull the scenery to pieces. The apparition will be grotesque – let us fake it". "No", said Benois, "let the rider pass slowly along the proscenium. The symbolism will be evident when not underlined". Eventually it was done following Benois' suggestion and stood for a moment of stirring beauty». Also according LIEVEN 1973, p. 108, «[...] in the end the horsemen had to go on foot, pacing slowly across the stage».

[131]. In her reconstructions of the ballet, Isabelle Fokine tried to incorporate this effect.

[132]. Notice, however, that the words «Второй всадникъ» [Second horseman] seem a later addition in Fokine's hand.

[133]. In *EXPOSITIONS AND DEVELOPMENTS*, p. 130, Stravinsky remembered the point where the black horse entered the stage: «[...] in step with, to be exact, the last six quavers of bar eight». Stravinsky was counting the bars from the rising of the curtain at [1]. Therefore his «bar 8» corresponds to bar 27 ([2]) of the published score (see Ex. 5a). Flamm's assertion that Stravinsky's recollection was erroneous (FLAMM 1913, pp. 60-61) is based on the incorrect assumption that Stravinsky meant bar 8 from the beginning of the score. In the copy of the printed piano reduction which Fokine employed during rehearsals, now at the Pierpont Morgan Library, the entrance of the black horse is signalled at [2] with the words «vsadnik vypuskayu» (release of the horse). See Cyr in STRAVINSKY 1985, p. 216.

Ex. 5a: *The Firebird*, 1 after [1]: music for the first horseman (Horseman of the night).

ternary rhythm of the ostinato for the first time from the beginning of the score, together with the use of the lowest register, immediately attracts attention, evoking the regular, slowly paced, and dark sound of the black horse's hoof beats slowly passing through Kashchey's magic garden at nightfall. Christoph Flamm noticed that the model for this type of association was provided for Stravinsky by the representation of the oxcart in *Bydło (Cattle)*, the fourth movement of Musorgsky's *Pictures at an Exhibition* (Ex. 5b): the heavy (*sempre pesante*, in the 1886 Rimsky-Korsakov edition) reiterated left-hand low-register bichords, with which Musorgsky had depicted the oxcart rumbling down the road, strongly resembles Stravinsky's representation of the passing black horse.

For the music accompanying the white horseman at [89] (Ex. 5c), Stravinsky resorted to a very simple yet highly evocative musical gesture: a motif of two notes a tritone apart, each with acciaccatura. This figure was a sort of onomatopoeic representation of the galloping horse (one need only think of such onomatopoeic sounds as «clippity clop» or «tlot tlot», etc.). For Prince Lieven (see fn. 130) this was truly «'equestrian' music [...], very appropriate with the suggestion of the mysterious stamping of hoofs», and so he was very sorry that «there was great difficulty in staging the passing of the two horsemen [...] by the footlights». What is interesting about its use, however, is the temporal dynamics of musical events. Although the harmony is entirely based on the same whole-tone collection, it seems to 'move' from an initial static condition to a more dynamic one: the first five bars are static on the French-sixth chord formed by the *b-d♯* and the *f-a* of the clarinets (doubled by harp), with the *a-d♯* of the tritone motif as a link between the two other parts. In the following measures the French sixth is

Ex. 5b: M. Mussorgsky, *Pictures at an Exhibition - Bydło (Cattle)*, bb. 1-10.

Ex. 5c: *The Firebird*, [89]: music for the second horseman (Horseman of the day).

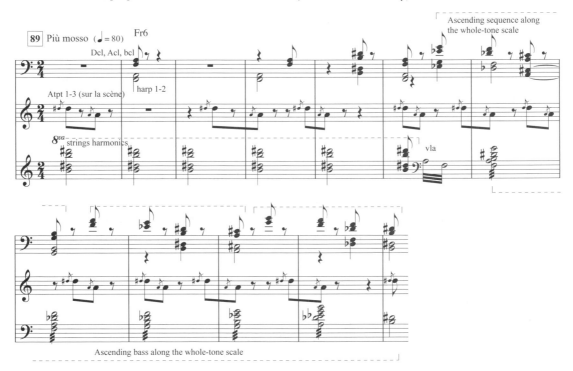

turned into a complete whole tone collection articulated in a sequence-like form: the bass part of the string chords ascends stepwise along the whole-tone scale; in the clarinet part a stepwise ascending sequence of a three-major third model unfolds. In each chord, two of the three parts

119

feature a French sixth, while the third part provides the notes lacking to complete the whole-tone collection. The impression that something starts 'moving on' is reinforced by the overall rhythm: the motif itself becomes increasingly short (from three quavers to two quavers) while the major-third dyads in the clarinets and the harp, which punctuate the motif, become closer and closer. The dynamics also move from *piano* to *mezzoforte*. To suggest the idea of something moving on the stage, Stravinsky also resorted to the spatialization of the music: the tritone motif is repeated several times, entrusted respectively to trumpets 3, 2, and 1 on stage; it then moves on to trumpet 1 in the orchestra, and finally it comes back to the trumpets on stage. Overall, the combination of these formal, temporal and spatial aspects create a close correspondence between the 'movement' of the music and the horse moving on stage[134].

Interestingly, once the two riders were eliminated, this 'equestrian' music caused some embarrassment from the dramatic standpoint. Sometimes it was entirely omitted from the performance. The orchestral parts that served for the 1910 season contain many deletions precisely on this issue, while in the copy of the printed piano reduction which served Fokine in rehearsals, the opening of the curtain is postponed to [3], so as to entirely avoid the problem of what to put on stage in place of the black horseman[135]. In any case, once the black rider was removed from the scene, Stravinsky's music, although no longer directly associated with elements of the scene, retained its strongly gestural and evocative character. In the end, the story of the two 'removed horses' is symptomatic of how the gestural character of Stravinsky's music originated in the representation of a 'removed body'.

My second example — the final *Apothéose* — shows a more subtle and complex kind of association involving a different kind of musical gesture, one concerning musical form on a broader scale. Despite this difference, however, in this case too the possibility of meaning association relies on a combination of topic aspects and formal analogies between the movement of music and that of bodies on the stage.

The final scene of the ballet was to depict the wedding of the Tsarevich and the Princess. To this end, according to Fokine's memoirs, a danced *divertissement* was originally devised but Stravinsky feared that this solution «would [...] resemble other ballets, which usually ended in weddings and dances», and asked Fokine to replace the dance with a «mimed procession»[136].

---

134. As noted by FLAMM 2013, pp. 61-62.

135. As noted in *ibidem*, p. 61.

136. «[...] yielding to the wish of Igor Stravinsky, I agreed to substitute a coronation for the gay processional dances with which I had wanted to end the ballet. [...] Stravinsky was of the opinion that it would otherwise resemble other ballets, which usually ended in weddings and dances». FOKINE 1961, pp. 159, 171. According to Fokine (*ibidem*, p. 171), the finale was «the only place in the ballet on which we disagreed». TARUSKIN 1996, p. 586, argues that the decision was not a concession by the choreographer to Stravinsky, but a decision taken within the Diaghilev directorate. Among the ballets ending with a general wedding dance, one can mention Petipa-Glazunov's *Raymonda*, or the famous *The Little Humpbacked Horse* (1866), by Cesare Pugni and Arthur

Fokine then created the scene as a sort of mimed procession with no dancing, in which two groups of characters (the twelve knights and the twelve Princess) and two individuals (Ivan and the Tsarevna) perform coordinated movements in rows on the stage, with rhythmic and solemnly-paced stepping. The procession ends when the two groups align themselves in a final tableau-like figure, with the Tsarevich and the Tsarevna in a prominent position (Ill. 5)[137].

Fokine argued that Stravinsky's request to avoid the *danced divertissment* was aimed at concentrating the final scene on «a specific musical effect», instead of on dance[138]. We do not know what he meant by these words, but we can assume that he was referring to the famous homophonic passage at [203][139]. More than the much-discussed — in the music-analytical literature — asymmetric rhythm, the aspect of this music that seems to match Fokine's procession most is the overall rhythmic and temporal dynamic of the piece[140]. In the music, in fact, something similar to the coordinated processional movements of the characters on stage takes place. The whole piece is based on the variation of another melody drawn from Rimsky-Korsakov's 1877 collection (song no. 21: *U vorot sosna raskachalasya*: *The Pine-Tree Swings by the Gate*), another typical Khorovod tune (Ex. 6a)[141]. Notice that the eight-bar melody is made of two identical phrases of 4 bars, while each phrase, in turn, can be divided into two half-phrases (labelled 'a' and 'b'). Starting from figure [203], where the first exposition is entrusted to the horn (*piano dolce and cantabile*) on a *Lento maestoso* time, Stravinsky repeatedly states the theme in the melodic part, each time with a different harmonic and contrapuntal accompaniment, according to the «changing background» technique (an ostinato-like variation technique, in which a melody was repeated several times, each time with a different harmonization) which was well established in Russian tradition from Glinka's famous *Kamarinskaya*. After three repetitions of the whole melody (six repetitions of the basic four-bar phrase), and after a brief, final return of the Firebird's motif ([202]), at rehearsal [203] Stravinsky modified the tune, now harmonized in strictly homophonic style, by flattening out the different values of its notes in a 7/4 even-crotchet rhythm (Ex. 6b). Richard Taruskin noticed that this apparently original effect was also suggested by the frequent use of hymns in asymmetrical meters in Rimsky-

---

Saint-Léon, one of the most frequent targets of the criticism by the Russian progressive artists. This latter ended with a *grand divertissement* within which a series of national dances was performed.

[137]. In his memoirs, Fokine recalls that for the premiere there were not enough costumes for all the twenty-four characters, so Diaghilev had to resort to the costumes from his previous *Boris Godounov* production (Fokine 1961, p. 172).

[138]. *Ibidem*, p. 171.

[139]. On the *Apothéose* see, for example, Flamm 2013, pp. 55-56; Taruskin 1996, pp. 632-637.

[140]. Of course, along with these original and innovative aspects, there are many derivative and conventional elements in this piece. Taruskin 1996, p. 636, noticed many analogies with the final chorus of Rimsky-Korsakov's opera *Snegurochka*, of 1881.

[141]. Rimsky-Korsakov 1877, p. 46.

Ex. 6a: N. Rimsky-Korsakov, *U vorot sosna raskachalasya* (RIMSKY-KORSAKOV 1877, no. 21).

Korsakov's operas. Nonetheless, Stravinsky's technique still contains some original elements. First of all, notice that in order to fill an entire 7/4 measure, the phrase labelled 'a' in Ex. 6b is metrically shifted forward, so as to begin with an upbeat — emphasized by the eight-note acciaccaturas. Secondly, the two phrases 'a' and 'b' are treated as two independent elements of six and seven quarter notes respectively. This allows Stravinsky to recombine them into new sequences, creating three segments of different length, of which the second is also transposed a semitone up from *b* to *c*:

First segment [203], on *b*:	a - b - a - b
Second segment [204-205], on *c*:	a - a - a - b - b - a
Third segment [206-208], on *b*:	a - b - a - b - b - b

In this way, the upbeat of phrase 'a', with its orchestral acciaccaturas, occurs at irregular and unpredictable intervals of time. Even more intriguing is the relation between the upper and lower parts. In the first two segments, the bass is totally static, first on a pedal point on the tonic *b* for four 7/4 measures; and then on a still longer dominant pedal point (for five measures, plus a measure on the third degree of the scale). In the third and last segments, on the contrary, it starts moving more and more frequently: the dominant $f\sharp$ and the tonic *b* are repeated into progressively shortening segments of 11, 6, 8, 6, 4, 2, 2, 2 and 1 quarters respectively. This creates a particular time dynamic as the two layers undergo two opposite process: the repeating patterns in the bass part are progressively shortened, while the note values in the upper parts are lengthened (*Doppio valore... poco a poco allargando*). The process is complete when the dominant $f\sharp$ in the bass finally matches the $c\sharp$ in the upper part, thus creating a dominant (incomplete) chord, after which, at [209], the entire orchestra states the tonic *b* in unison.

Ex. 6b: *The Firebird*, [203]: Finale.

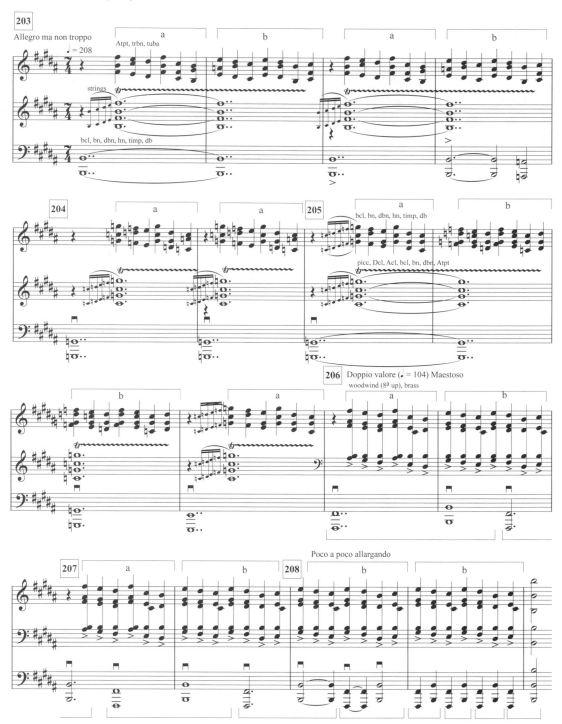

ILL. 5: *The Firebird*, Finale. Théâtre du Châtelet, Paris 1999 (London, Digital Classics Distr., ©2013).

This dynamic of musical events corresponds to the gradual achievement of the ending point of the two rows of 12 characters (12 princes, 12 princesses) in the walking procession on stage. During the scene, the two rows move in regularly paced steps performing various coordinated movements in stage space: they cross each other, repeatedly swap positions and move into two distinct (male/female) rows or into couples. When they finally reach their ending point, this forming the final 'coronation' figure, the musical process of the two musical layers also ends (ILL. 5). Much of the meaningful association between music and stage movements depends on their formal analogies: they are both characterized by repetitive (patterned) and regularly paced movements (even quarter note rhythm / regular steps). What really matters is not that the steps are precisely coordinated to the rhythm, but the general temporal dynamics of the process. Topical aspects also play an important role: the music has many features (monophonic style, regular rhythm, diatonicism, solemn character, *Maestoso* being the indication in the score) in part with fanfare music and in part with choral hymn music. Not by chance Taruskin noticed a particularly close analogy with the finale of Rimsky-Korsakov's *Snegurochka*, where a strophic hymn to Yarilo is set on a 11/4 meter[142]. These topical references are all in keeping with the ritual and processional character of what takes place on stage.

As Stephen Walsh rightly noticed, the choice of a procession instead of a general dance, « [...] already suggests [Stravinsky's] feeling for the ritual aspects of dance drama »[143]. This was, in effect, the first time in which an ostinato-like technique was associated with a processional, ritual element. In this case we could also say with a 'liturgy', since the coronation was conceived to a large extent as a sort of Christian liturgy. According to Fokine, in the original — although not entirely realized, since Golovine's backdrop for the second tableau could not be produced — conception of the spectacle, « The evil kingdom vanishes. Instead, in its place,

---

142. TARUSKIN 1996, p. 636.
143. WALSH 1999, p. 134.

arises a *Christian city*. And the castle turns *into a cathedral*»[144]. Various type of ostinato would be used by Stravinsky throughout his *oeuvre*, often in a similar ritual, conclusive position, and often independently of a direct visual association.

Ironically enough, this music, to which *The Firebird* owes much of its fame and success — also in concert halls — was one of the most dissatisfying parts of the ballet score for Fokine[145]. He would have preferred a final group of dances: «I pictured the transition into dance», he maintained «and the dances themselves, differently from what Stravinsky saw in the old ballets». He also feared that «the ceremonial scene of walking people, after so much action, would be an anticlimax». Nonetheless, Stravinsky's 'anticlimax' resulted in one of the clearest foretastes of the Stravinsky to come.

'IMPROVISING' BALLET MUSIC

We have seen that Stravinsky composed the music for *The Firebird* in a very short time; the piano short score was finished in just over four months, from November-December 1909 to the beginning of April 1910. Such a circumstance was hardly unprecedented in the history of ballet music. We have also seen that providing the music in a brief time frame was a routine task for many nineteenth-century ballet composers, and *ex tempore* creative methods may probably account for the abundant presence of many ready-made musical materials in their score. In *The Firebird*, Stravinsky resorted to a particular 'improvisation' technique to compose the whole music for the mimed scenes of the ballet. I use the term 'improvisation' in quote marks, in a sense that will be clarified in the following chapter of this book. It is essentially a preliminary exploration on the piano in order to immediately (quickly) find the materials to be elaborated in the following compositional (written) process[146]. The peculiarity of the 'improvisation' technique of *The Firebird*, with respect to those used in Stravinsky's later compositions, is that it is based on the systematic use of chord sequences and progressions, a trait which can be traced back to Rimsky-Korsakov's compositional habits. Stravinsky would never resort again to such 'mechanical' harmonic procedures as those he used in *The Firebird*. Nonetheless, the most basic conceptual premise underlying these procedures continued to characterize his creative methods until the end of his life[147].

---

144. FOKINE 1961, p. 165. My italics.

145. *Ibidem*, pp. 171-172. Fokine's preoccupation with the Finale depended above all on the lack of costumes for the scene: («there were not enough people to walk around anyway, since the costumes for the final scene had not been made in sufficient numbers»).

146. See *infra*, Chapter Three.

147. As we will see in Chapter Three, 'improvisation' still plays an important role in Stravinsky's serial compositions.

In a sense, the starting point of Stravinsky's 'improvisation' technique had been illustrated by Stravinsky himself — most probably with the help of the English music critic Edwin Evans — in the introductory notes to a set of AudioGraphic rolls for the Duo-Art Pianola, produced by the Aeolian Company in 1928[148]. Stravinsky's explanation provided the basis for countless analytical studies of the score[149]. However, none of these studies fully recognized the essentially procedural (improvisational) nature of the 'system'. Rather, they focused on its leitmotivic function, encouraged in this sense by Stravinsky himself, as we shall see later. This is reflected in their methodological approach, which is usually 'analytical', that is to say concerned with the finished score, not with the compositional — even less improvisational — process that led to it[150].

Stravinsky's own description of his harmonic technique was as follows:

> It is made up of alternating major and minor thirds, like this [see Ex. 7a]: A minor third is always followed by a major third, and vice versa. Likewise, the melodic intervals that form these thirds consist of an ascending augmented fourth and a descending minor second, alternately in the upper and the lower part[151].

---

[148]. STRAVINSKY 1928 (see the bibliography for a more detailed description and the catalogue number of the rolls). On Stravinsky's involvement with the Pianola see LAWSON 1986, MCFARLAND 2011, CARR 2014, p 121. On Edwin Evan's role in the making of the notes for the AudioGraphic roll see MCFARLAND 2011. A French typescript of the notes for both *The Firebird* and *Petrushka*, dated London 1927, is now in the Stravinsky Collection at the Paul Sacher Stiftung. This was consulted by TARUSKIN 1996 and MCFARLAND 2014. In the following pages, I will always quote from the French typescript as quoted also in TARUSKIN 1996, pp. 587, 589, 596, 616, 664. I give the original French text in the footnotes and my English translation in the main text.

[149]. Among the first, see CARR 1993; MCFARLAND 1994; TARUSKIN 1996, pp. 589-560. In Carr's study — probably the first to draw attention to the close harmonic relations between the leitmotifs and the 'let-harmony' — the analysis of the *Carillon féerique* is based on a typical set-theoretical approach. I am infinitely grateful to Prof. Carr for providing me with a copy of her article, which greatly inspired me, notwithstanding my different approach. My choice of the letimotif's letters is modelled on Carr's study.

[150]. McFarland's study (MCFARLAND 1994), for example, is clearly conceived as a pure analysis of the score. In Taruskin's discussion of *The Firebird* (TARUSKIN 1996), in keeping with that of the author's general methodological orientation, the emphasis is admittedly more on the compositional procedures than on 'analysis', but the improvisational and keyboard-based nature of these procedures is not taken into account. Both McFarland and Taruskin recognized that the music for the mimed sections of *The Firebird* is almost entirely made of a combination of dyads from the scale of alternating thirds. However, they did not recognize the keyboard-based criterion underlying the very choice of the dyads (my sequences dS1 and dS2). TARUSKIN 1996, p. 591, for example, recognizes that in the passage at [88] (*Mort de Kastchei*) «two ladders a tritone apart are unfolded concurrently, to give an expended four-part harmony of alternating French sixths [...] and diminished sevenths [...]». This description corresponds to my sequence dS1 (Ex. 9a), but misses an essential point, which is that these kinds of four-part sequences were not an occasional invention at this point of the score, but one of the most important constructs on which Stravinsky's 'improvisation' technique relies.

[151]. «Elle se compose de tierces majeurs et mineurs alternées, comme ceci [...] Toujours une tierce mineure est suivie d'une tierce majeure, et vice-versa. De même les intervalles mélodiques qui forment ces tierces consistent en

Ex. 7a: Illustration of the alternating major and minor thirds according to Stravinsky 1928.

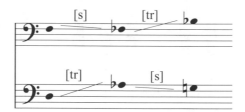

The 'alternating major and minor thirds' (for the sake of brevity I will often call them simply 'alternating thirds') are reproduced in Ex. 7a: In Stravinsky's contrapuntal (linear) explanation, they are obtained by means of a repetitive crossing voice-leading pattern: first, the lower note (*d*) of the starting minor third (*d* - *f*) moves up a tritone to *a♭* [*g♯*], while the higher note (*f*) moves down a semitone to *f♭* [*e*], thus creating a voice crossing. The resulting major third *f♭* - *a♭* [*e* - *g♯*] is then subjected to the same voice leading pattern but in the opposite (reverse) way: the lower part moves down a semitone, while the higher part moves up a tritone, thus producing a minor third (*g* - *b♭*).

Ex. 7b: The resulting dyads.

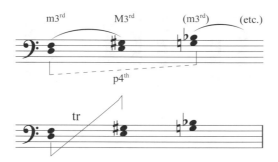

The same sequence of dyads, however, can be described and conceived in purely harmonic terms; one could simply say that it is a sequence of minor and major thirds (Ex. 7b) whose roots are alternately a whole tone and a minor third apart, so that each pair of thirds is a perfect fourth apart from the other (Ex. 7c). So why did Stravinsky resort to such an intricate explanation that it involves counterpoint and voice crossing? The reason is clear when we try to play the sequence on the piano; to play the sequence correctly, one just has to keep two 'rules' in mind — the following dyad will always be of the opposite type to the previous one (major instead of minor, and *vice versa*) and will always have as its lower note *the key immediately below* the higher one in the previous dyad. Stravinsky's 'contrapuntal' explanation, therefore, is just the translation

une quarte augmentée qui monte et une seconde mineure qui descend, alternativement à la partie supérieure et à l'inférieure». Stravinsky 1927, pp. 6-7.

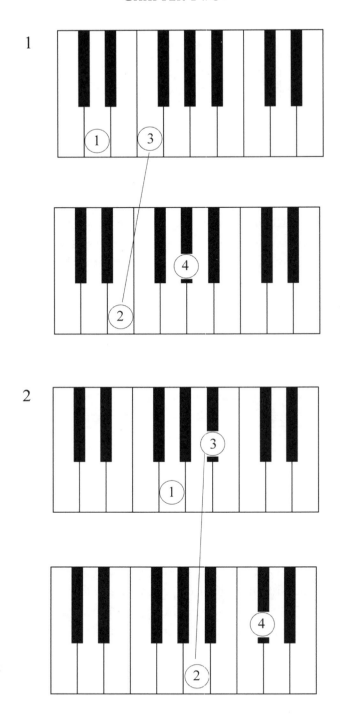

ILL. 6: Stravinsky's alternating major/minor thirds as a keyboard-based procedure.

Ex. 7c: A chain of alternating major/minor thirds.

into music theoretical terms of this keyboard-based procedure: the semitone to which he draws attention (fingered 3-2 and 4-1 alternately: see the connecting lines in Ill. 6), simply corresponds to one of the two 'rules' that allow for the correct performance of the sequence. Note too how the sequence corresponds to a repetitive fingering pattern: the first dyad (minor third) will always be fingered as 1-3 (right hand), and the second dyad (major third) as 4-5, after which the thumb passage will be needed and the same fingering will be repeated (Ill. 6).

By continuously repeating this pattern on the piano, a complete sequence — up to the return of the initial dyad six octaves higher — of 12 pairs of (minor/major) thirds (24 dyads) takes shape in the musical examples, it will be abbreviated as sequence S[152]. Assuming dyad *d - f* (on which the opening ostinato of the score is based: see Ex. 12a) the sequence appears as in Ex. 7d[153].

Ex. 7d: Sequence S: a complete sequence of 12 pairs of alternating minor /major thirds: Below the staff: numbering of the dyads.

---

[152]. I prefer to use the term 'sequence' instead of 'scale' (or ladder) as in Taruskin, McFarland and others, since this is not a 'scale' in the proper sense, in that it is not an ordered succession of pitches, but rather a sequence of couples of bichords repeated at regular intervals (of perfect fourths). Moreover, it does not span a single octave, but several octaves — in this sense it could, at best, be considered a 'non-octave-repeating scale'.

[153]. McFarland 1994 assumes as dyad no. 0 the $g_\flat$ - $c_\flat$ (=$f_\sharp$ - b) minor third in the trombone part at b. 5 of the *Introduction*. This is, in fact, the first apparition of the alternating thirds in their vertical form. However, also the opening ostinato of the cellos at b. 1 is based on a linearization of the 'magical thirds' starting from *d - f* (see below, Ex. 12b). Taruskin 1996, therefore, assumed this dyad as no. 0. Notice that Taruskin and McFarland's dyads no. 0 are a tritone apart from each other. This is because the trombone part at b. 5 and the cello ostinato are combined according to the scale which I will refer to as dS1, in which two parallel sequences S a tritone apart are layered. In the following examples of this chapter I will always refer to Taruskin's numbering (*d - f* = dyad 0).

Many scholars have observed that Stravinsky borrowed the model for his alternating thirds from Rimsky-Korsakov's opera *Kashchey the Deathless* (*Kashchey bessmertnïy*), of 1902, where the use of a similar harmonic device was associated with the title character[154]. In Rimsky-Korsakov's model (Ex. 8a), the minor and major thirds were not regularly alternated: within each pair, the order changed: major third-minor third/minor third-major third/major third-minor third, and so on. In this way a sequence of six thirds fits a single octatonic collection, and at the seventh dyad the sequence ends by reaching the starting note at the upper octave. Note also that Rimsky-Korsakov's sequence is conceived in purely harmonic terms, with no underlying contrapuntal structure, such as that provided in Stravinsky's AudioGraphic notes. In Stravinsky's pattern of alternating thirds, on the contrary, the octave is reached only after a complete cycle of 24 dyads (12 minor third/major-third pairs), and only three consecutive dyads, starting from a minor third dyad, can be referred to a single octatonic collections (Ex. 8b). In other words, every minor third dyad begins a succession of three dyads contained within an octatonic collection, but the third dyad is also contained in a different octatonic collection, thus serving as a pivot between the two collections (Ex. 8c). In this way, while the overall pitch content of a fragment of three dyads is octatonic, the whole sequence of dyads is entirely chromatic.

Ex. 8a: Alternating major-minor thirds within an octatonic collection in Rimsky-Korsakov, *Kashchey the Deathless*.

Ex. 8b: Partial correspondence between the Octatonic collection and sequence S.

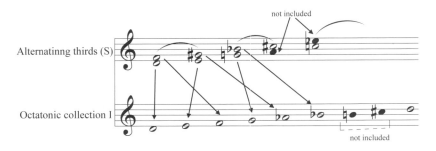

---

[154]. See TARUSKIN 1996, pp. 590-591. See also VAN DEN TOORN 1983, MCFARLAND 1994.

Ex. 8c: continuous overlapping of the three octatonic collections within sequence S.

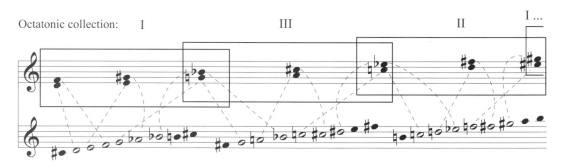

Sequence S is just the starting point of Stravinsky's 'improvisation' technique. The next step is the creation of four-note chords. To this end, two sequences S have to be played on a different transposition level by the two hands (Ex. 9a) — this is also like stating that the two sequences do not start from the same dyad. In this way, a sequence of four-note chords takes shape, in which the type of chords depends on the transposition interval. Stravinsky uses two basic 'double sequences': in the first (dS1), two sequences S are a tritone apart from each other (as shown by the arrow in the example) so that a regular alternation of diminished-seventh and French-sixths chords takes shape. In the second (dS2), two sequences S are at a distance of a major third, but one of them is shifted forward by one step (see the arrows in the example) so as to match a minor third on the left hand with a major third on the right hand, and *vice versa*, thus producing alternating half-diminished sevenths (hd7) and dominant sevenths (D7) chords.

The two double sequences dS1 and dS2, although both generated by alternate thirds (S) and thus chromatic overall, sound quite different, especially when single pairs of chords are extrapolated; the dominant sevenths/semi-diminished sevenths of dS2 sound much more 'diatonic' than the French sixths/half diminished sevenths of dS2, also because the French sixth is a subset of the whole-tone collection. We will see that Stravinsky exploits this difference to give different characterizations.

In addition to dS1 and dS2, other ways of layering two sequences S would have been possible. Limiting ourselves to those that produce common-practice chords, the last staff of Ex. 9a shows some possible forms. In the first form, the dyads are a tritone apart as in dS1, but they are shifted so as to produce alternating major and minor triads. In the second form, the dyads are a minor seventh apart, so as to produce dominant ninth chords (with omitted fifth) every two dyads. In the third form, the dyads are a minor sixth apart, thus creating an augmented triad every two dyads. Stravinsky, however, never uses such sequences to create entire chord progressions, as he does with dS1 and dS2. This is probably because they contain unwanted (excessively dissonant or uncommon) chords and/or voice-leading issues. The sequence with alternating major and minor triads, for example, systematically produces consecutive perfect

Ex. 9a: Double sequences of alternating major and minor thirds (dS) producing various types of four-note chords.

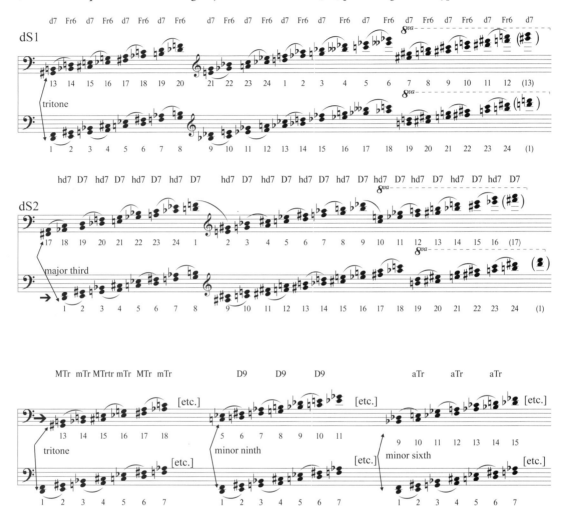

fifths; the sequence with the incomplete dominant ninths also contains half-diminished ninth chords; and in the third sequence, the augmented triads alternate with major/minor triads (four-note chords containing both a major and a minor third). Stravinsky often pairs dyads so as to produce an augmented triad or a dominant ninth, but he uses these chords individually, in isolation — see for example the augmented triad in Ex. 11a, at [112] or the dominant minor ninth in Ex. 17e, at the end of [96]—, and not within a larger sequence of chords. The augmented triad and the incomplete dominant ninth, in particular, are often used in view of their whole-tone content. Ex. 9b shows that if the (omitted) perfect fifth of a dominant ninth is raised a semitone higher, a five-note whole-tone cluster takes shape. Four of the five notes, in turn, correspond to a French sixth (also contained in dS1), which in turn can be read as a subset of both the whole-tone and the octatonic collection. Note also that the French sixth —

Ex. 9b: Other combinations of major/minor-third dyads producing whole-tone chords.

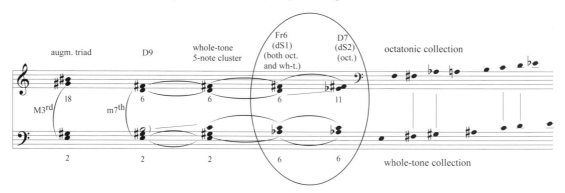

probably the most used chord in *The Firebird* — can be changed into a dominant ninth simply by raising by a semitone one note, since the two chords have three of the four notes in common the whole-tone collections (see encircled chords). We will see some occasions where this feature is used by Stravinsky to shift from dS1 to dS2 (or *vice versa*).

Ex. 9c illustrates an important feature of dS1 that Stravinsky exploits extensively to enrich his harmonic vocabulary. If the dyads forming a diminished seventh-French sixth pair are swapped as in a chiasmus (e.g. chords 1/13 and 2/14 become 1/14 and 2/13), two major triads at tritone distance (as in the famous «Petrushka chord») result. If the same procedure is applied to the same chords, but in reverse order (i.e. French sixth-diminished seventh), two minor triads are obtained at a tritone distance. If the two procedures are applied to the entire dS1 sequence, two sequences of major and minor triads are obtained respectively, the roots of which are alternately a tritone and a semitone apart from each other, as illustrated in Ex. 9c. The crossed arrows in the first and third systems show the dyad exchanges in dS1 producing the 'swapped' sequences in the systems immediately below (second and fourth systems). In these latter, the zigzag dashed lines indicate the path of the fundamentals of the triads at alternating tritone-semitone distance.

Although all this may appear 'theoretical' and 'abstract', in reality the chiasmus is only a consequence of the extremely creative (but no less logical and rigorous) way in which Stravinsky uses sequence dS1 on the keyboard. We will see, in fact, that the 'swapped' forms can be obtained simply by disposing the dyads in a 'syncopated' manner between the two hands. (in Ex. 11c we will see in more detail how Stravinsky systematically uses the procedure in the *Introduction* of the ballet). Stravinsky's very empirical (keyboard-based) *modus operandi* looks, inevitably, 'abstract' only when, for the sake of explanation, it must be translated into theoretical terms.

Altogether, the fundamental sequence S and the two double sequences dS1 and dS2 (and their 'swapped' forms) provide the most basic harmonic vocabulary of Stravinsky's 'improvisation' technique. Almost all the harmonic structure of the mimed scenes of the ballet can be obtained thanks to these. This can be seen immediately by the fact that the most frequent

Ex. 9c: Dyad exchanges in dS1 producing two sequences of major triads and minor triads a tritone apart.

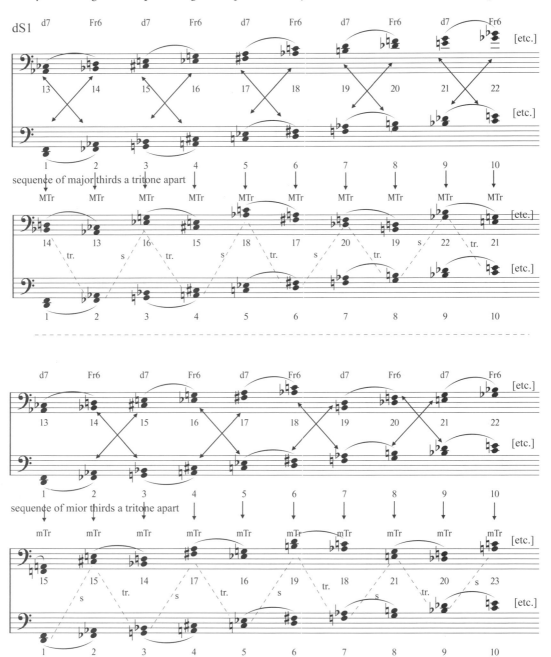

and characteristic harmonies of these sections, meaning dominant sevenths, diminished sevenths, and French sixths, are all included in dS1 and dS2. Of course, they all belong to the common vocabulary of late nineteenth-century harmony; but in the mime scenes of

The Firebird they are never treated as common-practice chords — the norms for resolving dissonances are systematically neglected, as are the tonal functions — and they usually follow one another in the same order and form as in dS1 or dS2.

Dominant sevenths, diminished sevenths and French sixths, along with major and minor triads and augmented triads, also correspond to the various types of triads and four-note chords included in the octatonic collection, as shown in Ex. 10a. However, in *The Firebird*, they do not work entirely according to an octatonic (nor whole-tone) logic. In fact, in the same way as a sequence of alternating thirds (see again Ex. 8c), the four-note chords of dS1 and dS2 (Ex. 10b) also contain a different octatonic collection every two dyads; more precisely, in dS1 the third chord of a sequence of three can refer to two different octatonic collections (as in S), while in dS2, due to the shifting of the two sequences S, only two consecutive chords can be found within a single octatonic collection, with the third chord belonging to a different collection (with no pivot).

Ex. 10a: Various types of triads and four-note chords contained within an octatonic collection.

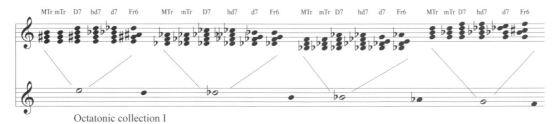

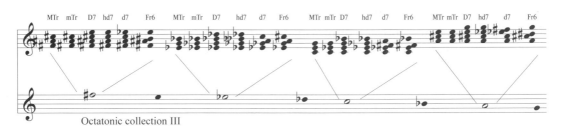

Ex. 10b: Continuous overlapping (dS1) and alternation (dS2) of the three octatonic collections within the double sequences of alternating thirds (compare with Ex. 8c and 9a).

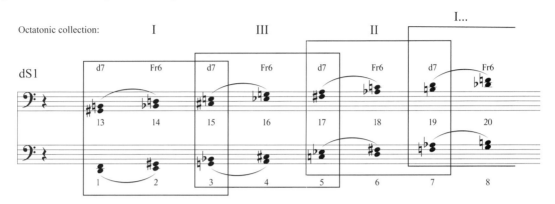

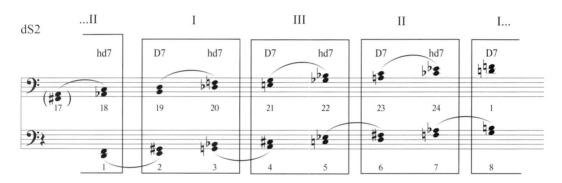

Ex. 11a-c show the harmonic structure of three scenes of the ballet in which Stravinsky made a particularly extensive and systematic use of the harmonies derived from S and/or dS1 and dS2. In these examples — as in all the other examples of this chapter — I will refer to the numbering of the dyads of Ex. 7d (for example: 1/13 - 2/14 corresponds to the two four-note chords *d - f - a♭ - b* and *e - g♯ - b♭ - d* contained in dS1). The dyads are *not* indicated in the exact octave register of the score; my choice of the registers only aims to show in the clearest manner the concatenation of the dyads (as in examples 7d and 9a). In the examples, as well as in my discussion, I will also use the common-practice chord names, *but these names should be understood in quotes, since they do not imply any tonal function or voice-leading rule, and do not account for the enharmonic spelling*, which often does not correspond to the correct tonal spelling or position (for example: 'diminished seventh' will be used for *d - f - a♭ - b*; but also for *d - f - g♯ - b*; 'French sixth' will be used for *b♭ - d - e - g♯*, also if spelled *e - g♯ - b♭ - d* or inverted as *e - a♭ - b♭ - d*).

Ex. 11a summarises the whole scene of the confrontation between Kashchey and Ivan. From a dramatic point of view, it is articulated as follows:

1. [107]: Kashchey appears and draws close to Ivan, who has been imprisoned by the monsters-guardians

2. [110]: Kashchey 'speaks' to Ivan, asking him why he is in his kingdom and what he is doing there. He orders Ivan to draw closer to him.

3. [111] Ivan replies calmly, faces Kashchey, and finally spits at him.

4. [112] Ivan tries to escape

5. [113] The monsters immobilize Ivan again

6. [114] At Kashchey's command, the monsters drag Ivan around him

7. [115] The princesses beg Kashchey to spare Ivan's life

8. [116] Kashchey laughs at the princesses' pity for Ivan, and orders them to turn away from him.

9. [117]: Kashchey tries three times to turn Ivan into stone

10. [118] After Kashchey's third attempt, Ivan extracts the Firebird's magic feather.

Ex. 11a: *The Firebird*, [108]-[118]: *Arrivée de Kastchei l'immortel – Dialogue de Kastchei avec Ivan-Tsarévitch – Intercession des princesses*: harmonic structure of the whole scene.

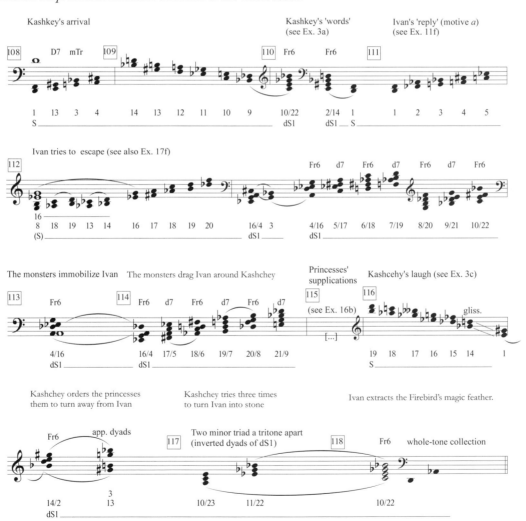

At Kashchey's arrival at [108] sequence S starts from the dyad *d - f*. After dyads 1-4, at [109] the sequence is interrupted and resumed in descending form from dyad 14 to 9. The following dialogue between Kashkey and Ivan at [110] is based on two French sixth chords extrapolated from dS1 (10/22 and 2/14). Ivan's reply at [111] takes up again the sequence S from d - f, this time with Ivan's leitmotif set against it. Between the chords of dS1 and the sequence of dyads of S there is a continuity, as shown by my ligatures in the example: dyad 9, with which the descending sequence ends at [109], is contiguous to dyad 10 contained in the sixth French dyad 10/22 at [110]; in the same way, dyad 2 contained in the French sixth 2/14 continues in dyad 1, which starts a new sequence S at [111]. This method of chaining the various segments of the sequences is systematically used by Stravinsky, as shown from the ligatures in my examples.

At [112], where Ivan attempts to escape, an unusual, for this score, combination of dyads is realized: while dyad 16 (*e♭ - g*) is held as a pedal, dyads 18-19 and 13-14 form a very dissonant succession of four-note chords with it. This is one of the very rare points of the mimed scenes in which Stravinsky extrapolates single dyads and recombines them to obtain harmonies and chord progressions different from those of S, dS1 and dS2. However, the strongly dissonant character is in keeping with the dramatic situation — at this point Ivan, after trying to escape in vain, is struggling with Kashchey's monsters.

In the following part of [112], in the scene in which Ivan is tossed around by the monsters (up to [114]) a long chain of chords from sequence dS1 is used. At [115] the sequence is interrupted by the princesses' supplications on motif P, which I will deal with in detail later (Ex. 16b). For the time suffice it to say that this passage is based on dS2. Kashchey's following answer, with his 'laugh' has already been considered before (Ex. 3c); it simply corresponds to a descending succession of dyads from S. The final part of [116] in which Kashchey chases away the princesses, is based on the sixth French 14/2: each of the two dyads is elaborated with an 'appoggiatura', consisting of the two contiguous dyads, but in opposite motion: dyad 14 moves down to 13 and dyad 2 moves up to 3. Finally, Kashchey's attempts to turn Ivan into stone are based on a French-sixth/diminished-seventh pair 10/22 - 11/23 from dS1, but with the 'swapped' form 10/23 and 11/22 producing minor triads a tritone apart (as clarified in Ex. 9c). Finally the French sixth 10-22, accompanied by the two notes (*d* and *a♭*) needed to complete the whole-tone scale signals Ivan's final resolution to use the magic bird's feather.

Ex. 11b illustrates the harmonic structure of the scene of the ballet in which Kashchey is finally killed by Ivan by breaking the egg that contains his soul. Kashkey's awakening (as well as his arrival in the scene noted above) is initiated by a short succession of alternating dyads from S ending on dyad 13 (*f - a♭*) — also transformed into a major triad *f - a - c* and a minor triad *f - a♭ - c* - to which a long sequence of chords from dS1 is connected by a common dyad (13). When Ivan finds Kashchey's egg, a succession of four chords of dS1 is superimposed on a pedal on *b♭*, thus creating a more complex harmony, which revolves around a dominant ninth

Ex. 11b: *The Firebird*, [188]-[196]: *Réveil de Kastchei – Mort de Kastchei.* – Tableau II *Disparition du palais et des sortilèges de Kachtcheï.* Harmonic structure.

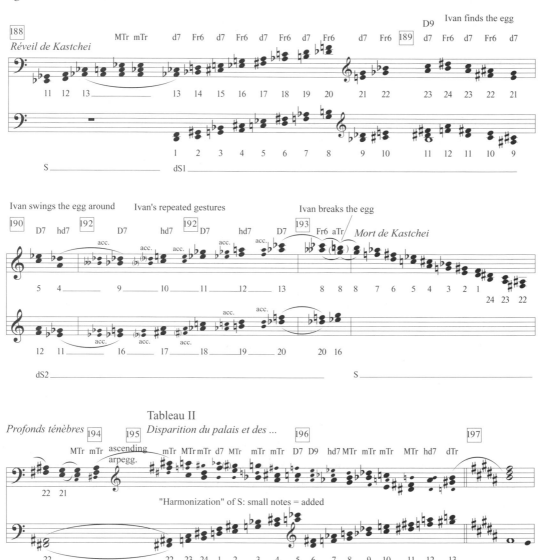

chord. Then, at [190], two segments of dS2, respectively of two and five chords unfolds — again connected with two common notes. In the second segment, each chord form dS2 is preceded by a peremptory acciaccatura, on the same notes, of the orchestra. The statements of the chords are increasingly close. All this corresponds, in the scene, to the repeated gestures of Ivan who rotates the egg more and more rapidly, before finally throwing it to make it break. Here again we note how the temporal dynamics of the music 'mimics' the dynamics of (bodily) movements on stage.

The breaking of the egg is represented by the transformation of the last French sixth (20/8) of dS2 into an augmented triad — by means of the semitone shift of one of the two dyads — from which a long descending sequence (from 8 to 1 and then down to 21) of dyads of S follows. The dyads are entrusted to solo instruments who divide them into a leaping rhythm of triplets and between different octave registers. The strongly mimetic character of the music is entirely self-evident: the precipitous descent of the dyads perfectly evoke the image of the magician who collapses. At [194], the penultimate dyad of S (n- 22), $f_\sharp$ - $a_\sharp$ is used as a pedal and transformed, with the addition of the $d_\sharp$, into a minor triad. To represent the 'deep darkness' of the ballet story line, Stravinsky devised an ascending orchestral arpeggiation of all the muted strings *divisi*, gradually spanning from the $f_\sharp$ 3 of the viola to the $f_\sharp$ 6 of the violin 1. The construction and the atmosphere of the passage have an unmistakably Wagnerian character. Finally, the gradual passage from darkness to light in [195] — and to the second Tableau — is constructed again on sequence S. When the arpeggiated $d_\sharp$ - $f_\sharp$ - $a_\sharp$ triad has reached its highest point, in the lover strings parts a long ascending chain of 16 dyads (divided into two strokes, 8 + 8) of S starts from dyad $f_\sharp$ - $a_\sharp$, while the other parts harmonize each dyad in a different way by adding a third, and in some cases a fourth, different note (smaller notes in the example). The upper parts gradually move downwards, in contrary motion to the ascending S. The resulting chords are a mixture of minor triads, major triads, and various types of seventh and dominant ninth chords. Finally, at [197], the last diminished triad, $g_\flat$ - b - d, is transformed into the tonic of the B major, on which the final *Apothéose* is set.

While the final transition from darkness to light is the most complex harmonization, in terms of variety of chords, of the entire score, the *Introduction* (Ex. 11c) is no doubt the most ingenious and 'systematic'. The famous ostinato of cellos and double basses (Ex. 12a), with which the score begins (bb. 1-4), is based on dyads nos. 1 and 2 of S[155]. It simply consists of the linearization, in melodic form, of the notes of the dyads, with the addition of two passing notes (marked with '+' in the example,) as explained by Stravinsky himself in his notes in the Duo-Art AudioGraphic roll:

---

[155]. According to McFarland it is the opening ostinato that generates both the alternating major/minor thirds and the structural interval of tritone. McFarland 1994, p. 207, maintains that Stravinsky's comments in the AudioGraphic piano roll «[...] fail to point out the derivation of supernatural music from either of these two leitmotifs. Because the supernatural music can be traced back to the string ostinato, this opening figure serves as the chromatic *Grundgestalt* of the ballet». This interpretation relies on the fact that in the ballet score the opening ostinato is the first thing to appear, while the alternating thirds only make their first appearance five measure later. As I see it, on the contrary, the ostinato is just one of the many forms that can be obtained by 'improvising' on the alternating thirds. The fact that it precedes, in the score, the first statement of the alternate thirds in their 'pure' (vertical) version is not significant, precisely because the alternate thirds are just a technical procedure, not a musical material (like a theme or a motif) whose position in the piece reflects its formal function.

REPRESENTING THE BODY IN *THE FIREBIRD*

At the beginning we are in the enchanted garden of Kashchei. Thus, here are the thirds, first in the form of groups of three notes, the third of which is a passing note, and then taking the form of a straightforward game of thirds, of this kind [see Ex. 12a][156].

Ex. 11c: *The Firebird*, *Introduction*, mm 1-20. Harmonic structure.

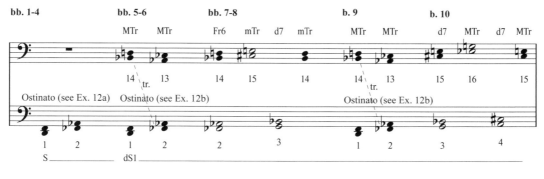

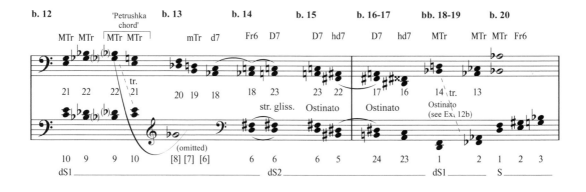

---

[156]. «Au commencement nous nous trouvons dans le jardin enchanté de Kastchei. Voici donc les tierces, d'abord en forme de groupes de trois notes, dont la troisième est une note de passage, et prenant ensuite la forme d'un franc jeu de tierce de l'espèce [...]». STRAVINSKY 1927, p. 8.

141

At bb. 5-6 the ostinato is set against a two-part accompaniment of the trombones (Ex. 12b) according to the first two chords dS1 (nn. 1/13 and 2/14). In realizing the counterpoint between the two parts, however, Stravinsky inverted the order of the dyads, according to the 'swapped' form of the sequence, thus obtaining two major triads (2/13 and 1/14) a tritone apart, as discussed above (Ex. 9c).

Then, at bb. 7-8, a new musical material, made of a four-part passage of syncopated and dotted semiquavers, appears. This is based on the 'swapped' form of dS1 producing minor triads a tritone apart. Clearly, the reversal of the pairs is not the result of a 'theoretical' choice by Stravinsky, but the consequence of his 'improvisation' technique, in which the two hands independently perform the two sequences 'out of phase'. In this way each dyad enters into a contrapuntal relationship with both the others, as in the fourth-species (syncopated) counterpoint:

	Fr6	mTr	d7	mTr
Right hand	14	15	15	14
Left hand	2	2	3	3

The cello-trombone ostinato and the syncopated semiquavers figurations are the two basic materials of which the entire Introduction is composed. They alternate with each other in a manner that, apart from the strong harmonic continuity, can be considered as a typical Stravinskyan block-form. Thus at b. 9, in fact, a short fragment of the opening ostinato returns, and then at [10] the syncopated figurations start again, as at b. 7-8, but on the following chords (3/15 and 4/16) of dS1, producing two major triads (3/16 and 4/15) a tritone apart. This brings us to the astonishing passage at b. 11 in which the syncopation device is systematically exploited on an entire segment of seven chords (from 5/17 to 9/21) of dS1. This time the syncopated contrapuntal relationships between the dyads are such as to create all the possible forms of chords (French sixth, diminished seventh, minor triad, major triad):

	M	d7	M	Fr6	m	d7	M	Fr6	M	d7	M	Fr6	M	d7	m	
Right hand	17	17	17	18	19	19	19	20	21	21	21	22	21	21	21	etc.
Left hand	4	5	6	6	6	7	8	8	8	9	10	10	10	9	8	etc.

Notice that in this way the major/minor triads are never consecutive (they are always separated by a diminished seventh or a French sixth). At the end of b. 12, however, couples 9/21 and 10/22 are reversed as 9/22 and 10/21, thus producing two major thirds a tritone apart, the typical sonority of the 'Petrushka chord'. Once reached, chord 10/22, dS1 is turned backward toward 6/18 (at b. 13 only the upper dyads of 8/20, 7/19 and 6/18 are used, while in the other parts a $g\flat$ is held as a pedal tone, thus creating a minor triad and a diminished seventh) until, at b. 14, the 6/18 French-sixth chord is changed into a dominant seventh chord 6/23 merely by raising up one of the four notes, thus moving smoothly from dS1 to dS2 (as illustrated before, in Ex. 9b). The dominant seventh thus obtained is entrusted to the natural-harmonic string glissando, one of the most characteristic and celebrated aspects — along with the trombone glissando — of the orchestration of the score, on which Stravinsky himself drew attention[157]. At b. 16-17, then, the opening ostinato is stated by the flutes on chords the 6/23 and 5/22 of dS2, and then by the oboes at bb. 18-19 on chords 24/17 (linked to 5/22 by two common tones; see ligatures) and 23/16 of dS2. Immediately after, at bb. 18-19 the ostinato, now in the strings, moves back to its initial form on dS1. In this way, put side by side, the three statements of the ostinato display quite different characters (more 'diatonic' when set to dS2), according to the changing harmonic background. Finally, the whole Introduction ends with the return of dyad 1-3 of S.

In summary, my description clearly shows how Stravinsky's 'improvisational' technique consisted of the use of a small number of harmonic sequences (S and dS1-dS2) whose segments are used to give harmonic substance to quite large passages of music. Stravinsky moves on these successions of chords in an upward and downward direction, with a freedom that clearly denotes an initial *ex tempore* invention on the piano. Even in moving from one segment to another, he usually adopts criteria, such as common or adjacent dyads/notes, that denote a 'tactile' approach based on the instrument.

The utility of the various sequences should be understood form the point of view of the piano performance. Although the simultaneous performance of two sequences S at the piano is anything but easy and immediate, the task is facilitated by the fact that, when superimposed, the two sequences create common-practice chord types, which can be easily handled on the keyboard. These chords are like 'ready-to-use' objects whose correct positioning is easy to remember: two chords of the same type will be always at a distance of a perfect fourth (as shown in Ex. 7d and 7e), while two chords of different types (e.g. a diminished seventh and a French sixth, as in dS1) will always be a whole tone or a minor third apart. In this way, attention focuses on the harmonies, more than on the single dyads that compose them or on voice leading (this shows once more that Stravinsky's improvisational technique is essentially harmonic, not contrapuntal, in nature, as his explanation in the AudioGraphic roll would suggest), and the whole sequence becomes a useful referential scheme for improvisation.

---

157. «The orchestral body of The Firebird was wastefully large but I was more proud of some of the orchestration than of the music itself. The horn and trombone glissandi produced the biggest sensation with the audience, but this effect, at least with the trombone, did not originate with me. Rimsky had used trombone slides, I think in Mlada. [...] For me the most striking effect in *The Firebird* was the natural-harmonic string glissando near the beginning [...] I was delighted to have discovered this, and I remember my excitement in demonstrating it to Rimsky's violinist and cellist son». *EXPOSITIONS AND DEVELOPMENTS*, pp. 131-132.

CHAPTER TWO

'IMPROVISING' WITH LEITMOTIFS

Stravinsky's systematic use of leitmotifs is another aspect that is closely related to his 'improvisation' technique. As we have seen, for the mimed scenes of the ballet, Stravinsky devised an entirely through-composed orchestral accompaniment in which a number of leitmotifs recur. According to Taruskin, this use of leitmotifs was «of an unprecedented sort» for ballet[158]. However, it was hardly 'unprecedented' in traditional ballet-pantomime but was just one of the many musical 'narrative' devices in the hands of composers from the age of *Giselle*, as we have seen before. What *was* unprecedented, was the *way* in which leitmotifs were used. In fact, there is a close relationship between the leitmotifs and Stravinsky's creative procedures on the piano.

We can get an idea of this relationship by comparing Stravinsky's use of the leitmotifs with that of Wagner. First, in *The Firebird* the leitmotifs contribute to musical structure in a quite different way: they are very short and rather simple — sometimes only a few notes drawn from a single chord — and they are often used as little melodic cells in repetitive sequences, a feature that recalls to an extent the baroque *fortspinnung* technique, in which large musical phrases were constituted from the repetition of short motifs set against changing chord progressions and sequences. While such a feature can sometimes be found in Wagner, in Stravinsky, the motifs are usually set to quite mechanical and predictable harmonic sequences, mostly based on S, dS1, dS2, or on the whole-tone scale. In Wagner, on the contrary, the harmonic transformations of the motifs are anything but schematic and mechanical: they obey transformations at the level of tonal organization which parallel the dramatic developments of the characters and events.

All this suggests that *The Firebird*'s leitmotifs themselves are nothing more than building blocks for Stravinsky's 'improvisation'. Many of them are simple linearization or arpeggiations of chords included in the basic sequences; other motifs, although of an entirely different (diatonic) origin, are often set against such chord progressions, thus assuming their harmonic form. Let us see then in more detail how the various leitmotivs relate to Stravinsky's technique.

The first 'motif' encountered in the score is the ostinato of the cellos and double-basses (Ex. 12a-b). Some commentators, in fact, consider it as a 'leitmotif', but it is not a leitmotif in the strict sense of the term, as it is not clearly associated with any character or aspect of the drama. Its association with the enchanted garden and the presence of the evil magician is rather vague and generic. In the mimed scenes of *The Firebird* there are many other motifs which, while being very characteristic and playing an important function in both the narrative

---

[158]. TARUSKIN 1996, p. 587. According to Taruskin (*ibidem*), «as Fokine had sought, through his novel 'choreodrama', to transcend ballet, so Stravinsky relied for these mime sections on the techniques of the old Wagnerian 'music drama' that had, a couple of generations back, aimed to transcend opera» (*ibidem*). However, we have seen that leitmotif-like technique were also used in many nineteenth-century ballets.

Ex. 12a: *The Firebird*: relationship between the opening ostinato (*Introduction*, bb. 1-3) and the alternating thirds.

Ex. 12b: *The Firebird*, bb. 5-7. Alternating thirds and opening ostinato in counterpoint.

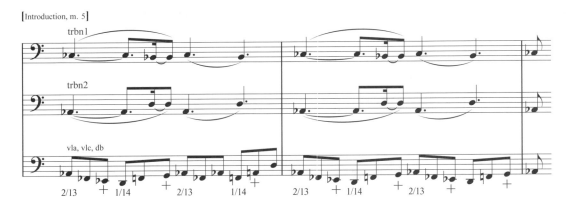

and the musical structure, do not have a true leitmotivic function, since they do not reappear throughout the ballet, and are not clearly associated with a specific character or situation of the story. Many of them are based on the tritone interval. This is the case, for example, of the motif of the Horseman of the day at [89] discussed earlier; or the motif encountered twice in the opening scene of the *Jardin enchanté*, first in the French horn I, at the very beginning of the scene ([1]), and then in the English horn toward the end (two bars before [3]) (Ex. 12c).

Ex. 12c: *The Firebird*, [3] - 2: recurring tritone-figure in the French horn part.

Clearly, such motifs say little about Stravinsky's creative method as they are simply short elaborations of the tritone interval. On the contrary, the little motif associated with the title role (motif F: three chromatic notes followed by a major third leap) is undoubtedly one of the most relevant from this point of view. After its first appearance at figure [3] in the scene *Apparition de l'Oiseau de feu, poursuivi par Ivan-Tsarévitch*, it is used pervasively throughout the entire score, including in the dance numbers for the title role, such as the *Berceuse* and the *pas de deux*. However, unlike these dance numbers, where its presence is just an elaboration of the foreground level of the piece, in the mimed scenes motif F is used in such a continuous, repetitive and systematic way that we are led to reconsider its constructive function in the light of Stravinsky's improvisational methods. Even before its being a 'leitmotif', in fact, it is a true building block used to generate long melodic chromatic lines. The 'improvisational' function of the motif is already evident from its origin in the mechanism of the alternating thirds: this motif can be obtained by the triton spanning a couple of alternating thirds, as shown in Ex. 13a, first two staves. The formal analogy is particularly evident when the inverse form of

Ex. 13a: The Firebird's leitmotif (F): derivation form the alternating thirds and variants.

the motif labelled as F ↓ is compared with the opening ostinato (first stave, on the right). The difference between the alternating thirds and motif F lies above all in their different uses on the keyboard; while the alternating thirds are used to crate *chord* progressions F is used to generate *melodic* lines.

In order to obtain a greater variety of melodies from motif F, Stravinsky has it undergo all the possible symmetric transformations — inversion, and retrogrades: see the forms labelled F, F ← (retrograde), F ↓ (inversion) and F ↓ ← (retrograde inversion) in Ex. 13a — and then combines them in various configurations. In spite of appearances, these manipulations have nothing to do with 'abstract thinking', let alone a sort of 'proto-serial' technique[159]. Mirror-writing was just a distinctive trait of Rimsky-Korsakov's — and more in general of St. Petersburg — harmonic language based on the exploration of symmetrical octave partitions such as the whole-tone scale[160]. Rimsky-Korsakov used it extensively in his fantastic and fairy-tale operas in order to characterize magical (or otherwise non-human) animal figures, such as the mechanical bird of the *Golden Cockerel*. Stravinsky had already brought mirror-technique to a peak of invention in the *Scherzo fantastique* and in the *Fireworks*. In the case of *The Firebird*, the use of motif F and mirror writing was just another 'improvisation' device in Stravinsky's hand. The motif is made up of three chromatic notes followed by a major third leap, but if its second note is treated as a passing tone (see the notes labelled with '+' in Ex. 13a), it turns out to be nothing more than a fragment of whole-tone scale which, given the perfect symmetry of this scale, can be easily played in reverse or in retrograde motion on the keyboard for one has only to reverse the order of the two components (the major third leap and the three chromatic notes) and/or the direction (ascending or descending) of the intervals. The improvisator's skill consists in matching the 'real' notes of the motif with those of the referential whole-tone scale.

Staves 3-6 of Ex. 13a show some 'leitmotivic variants' obtained by combining various 'serial' forms of motif F. The form of the third stave, with F and F ↓ in sequence produce a characteristic wavy chromatic line, particularly suitable for representing the bird's flight, which is used in the *Apparition de l'Oiseau de feu, poursuivi par Ivan-Tsarévitch*, at [3] (Ex. 13b): consider in particular the passage at [4]), and at [8]. Ex. 13c shows the piano reduction of the passage, which can be created by repeatedly playing the motif in three-parts parallel motion on the augmented triad on *b♭*, according to the symmetric (whole-tone) partitioning of the octave in three major thirds (*b♭ - d - f♯ - b♭*). Stravinsky elaborated this simple structure in many ways: the right hand starts with the full three-part repeated motif; a measure later, the left hand does

---

[159]. The later Stravinsky would allude to some 'serial tendencies' of these procedure: «When some poor Ph.D. candidate is obliged to sift my early works for their 'serial tendencies', this sort of thing will, I suppose, rate as an *Ur-example*». EXPOSITIONS AND DEVELOPMENTS, p. 133. But this was just another by-product of his late interests in serialism conceived as an essentially 'intevallic' technique. See also LOCANTO 2009.

[160]. See TARUSKIN 1996, pp. 596-599.

Ex. 13b: *The Firebird*, [3]-[4]; *Apparition de l'Oiseau de feu, poursuivi par Ivan-Tsarévitch.*

Ex. 13c: *The Firebird*, [8], reduction: musical representation of the Firebird's 'flight' in the *Apparition de l'Oiseau de feu poursuivi par Ivan-Tsarévitch*.

the same but progressively introducing the three parallel parts. The simplicity of the procedure is only concealed in the score by the complexity and opulence of the orchestration. Ex. 13d shows the same passage in the full score: the 'right-hand' triadic lines are entrusted to the woodwinds, while the 'left-hand' part, which gradually thickens harmonically, is given to the strings. In the score, all this is further complicated by the orchestral doublings. The sparkling orchestration, with woodwinds and strings in the high register, contributes significantly to suggesting the image of a magic lightness.

Ex. 13a, fourth staff, shows how the 'Flight' motif is turned into what I call the 'capture' motif: the magic bird's imprisonment in Ivan's harms at n. [27] (just a few measures before the *pas de deux*) is represented by Stravinsky by transforming the chromatic 'flight' motif (F + F ↓) into a French-sixth (whole tone) chord $b_\flat$ - d - e - $g_\sharp$ (spelled as d - e - $b_\flat$ - $a_\flat$). The chromatic passing tones (labelled with '+' in the left-hand part of the stave) are omitted from the chord (on the right). In this way, by turning the melodic flow of the motif into the stasis of the chord — melody into harmony, chromatism into whole-tone collection — Stravinsky represents in a very simple but also very effective way, the interrupted flight of the imprisoned bird. The musical representation is made even more telling when, at [27], the rapid figurations of the clarinets in *a* and *d*, featuring the 'flight' motif, are finally interrupted by the reappearance of the French-sixth chord, entrusted to the horns, violins and violas, and immediately after two more isolated statements of cell F ↓ only from the 'flight' motif, alternate with the 'capture' motif. It is as if the music strives to represent the bird's repeated attempts (the repeated F ↓ of clarinet) to free himself from Ivan's embrace (the French-sixth chords) (Ex. 13e).

Another leitmotivic form is what I called the 'Firebird's glide' (Ex. 13a, fifth and sixth staves). It takes the form of a long melodic descent, thus evoking a gliding plane. It has two

Ex. 13d: *The Firebird*, [8], musical representation of the Firebird's capture by Ivan.

variants: in the first (fifth staff) F ↓ is repeated in descending sequence, with a whole-tone between each statement of the motif, so as to form the whole tone scale (if chromatic passing

Ex. 13e: *The Firebird*, [27]: musical representation of the Firebird's 'flight' in the *Apparition de l'Oiseau de feu*.

notes are discarded); in the second variant (sixth staff) the restatements of F ↓ are imbricated, thus forming again a whole-tone scale, but in a more dense version, with more chromatic passing tones. These forms appear in three moments of the ballet story, when the Firebird descends from the sky or starts again to fly: at [5], when the Firebird first lands in the enchanted garden;

at [44], immediately after her release by Ivan; and at [28], immediately after her capture. Here, the motif takes on a strongly gestural character, which evokes the bird's surrender to Ivan, who brings the magic animal from the sky back to earth: the 'glide' motif is entrusted only to the viola (*arco con sordina*), while the horns feature the 'capture' motif. Tempo (*poco a poco rallentando*), dynamic (*diminuendo*), and expression (*dolce*) indications make the viola seem to embody the 'voice' of the captured bird, as it sadly descends from the sky (see Ex. 13e, last stave).

In addition to serving as a building block with which a series of leitmotivic variants can be constructed, motif F also provides the reference structure for the 'improvisation' of certain passages of the score. This is the case of the recurring *coloratura* figuration that follows the tritone motif discussed above of the horns and English horns in the *Jardin enchanté*, first at [1]), in the celesta part, and then two bars before [3], in the celesta and harp parts. Ex. 13f shows how it can be obtained by playing melodically, one after the other, the four vertical dyads of a two-part counterpoint with two motifs F a major third (or minor sixth) apart, in contrary motion (F and F ↓) (see circled notes numbered 1-4), and by adding two more notes as octave doubling (marked with '+'). Ex. 13g also shows how motif F is embedded within the main melodic line of the *Berceuse* and the *pas de deux*. Clearly enough in this case the use of the motif is above all a chromatic elaboration of the melodic line.

Ex. 13f: *The Firebird*, *Coloratura* figuration of the celesta at [1] + 1, and its derivation from motif F.

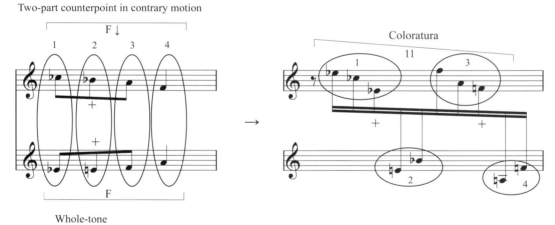

Finally Ex. 13a, last two staves, shows two more instances of motif F in a symbolically relevant form for the neo-nationalist project of the libretto (as we will see later). The first is in the final *Apothéose* at [202], where forms F and F ↓ onwards are imbricated so as to create a wavy melodic line made of three-note descending-ascending groups. The line, staring on *b*, is imitated a major third below on *g*, then in contrary motion (= F ↓ and F) an octave lower (*b*) and finally at a major third above the inversion (*e♭*), which is according to the symmetric (whole-tone) partitioning of the octave in three major thirds (*b - g - e♭ - b*). The second instance is the final reappearance on the last cadence of the whole score: on a pedal point on the tonic *b* motif s F

Ex. 13g: *The Firebird*, motif F in the main melody of the *pas de deux* and the *Berceuse*.

and F ↓ imbricated are performed on three major chords in first inversion in parallel motion. This is the first time in the whole score in which the notes of the motif are harmonized with diatonic chords.

Kashchey's motif K is of an entirely different type. Although its chromaticism bears some resemblance to motif F (and therefore to the opening ostinato) it is not used as a building block in the same manner as the Bird's motif. Unlike the latter, which can assume a variety of rhythmic forms and orchestral colours, rhythm and instrumentation are essential and distinctive aspects of its physiognomy. It is always entrusted to low-register wind instruments (bassoons at 4 before [2] and [46]; horns and trombones at [110]), which this is due to its origins in Kashchey's 'voice' in the dialogue with Ivan at 110, as discussed before.

Ex. 14a: *The Firebird*, 4 before [2]: Kashchey's motif and its derivation from dS2.

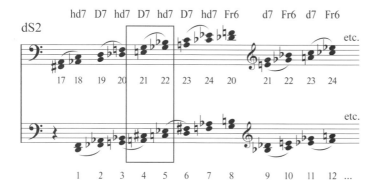

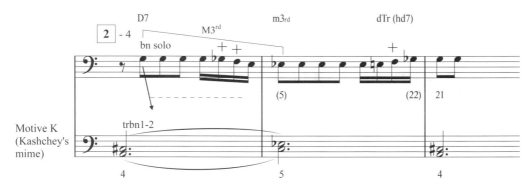

Nonetheless, motif K is also related to Stravinsky's 'improvisational' technique. Apart from [110], where it fulfils its (original) 'speech-like' function, in the other two statements it is used as an ostinato: the descending profile of [110] is turned into a continuously descending-ascending chromatic line moving within a major third. This allows Stravinsky to set it against the sequences of alternating thirds. Thus, at 4 before [2], it is paired with a trombone ostinato based on dyads 4-5, with which it produces respectively a dominant seventh and a minor third, according to sequence dS2, as shown in Ex. 14a. At [46], in the mimed scene that follows the *pas de deux* (Ex. 14b), it is entrusted to the bassoon, while woodwinds, strings, xylophone and celesta move through various segments of S (dyads 4-10; 24-16; 11-12). Simultaneously, the

Ex. 14b: *The Firebird*, [46]. Use of motif K as ostinato against an unfolding sequence of thirds from S.

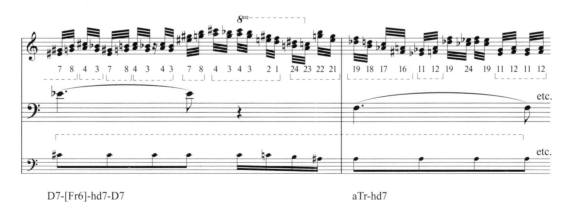

English horn and trombones perform alternately six notes drawn from a two-part counterpoint in which the parts move chromatically — thus recalling motif F — in contrary motion (as can be seen in Ex. 13f). From the harmonic encounters between the three layers, a variety of typical harmonies contained in dS1-and dS2 take place (see the symbols in the example)[161].

---

161.   We have seen that in the Morgan holograph piano score the whole passage was originally placed before [3].

The motif associated with Kashchey's monster servants (motif M: Ex. 15a) is used extensively in the *Carillon féerique – Apparition des monstres-gardiens de Kastchei et capture d'Ivan-Tsarévitch* and in the following *Danse infernale*. Its melodic profile is based on a diminished-seventh chord, as derived from dS1. Like the Firebird's motif, it works as a building block that can be subjected to various transformations. In this case, the modifications are not retrograde and mirror inversion, but simple chord inversions. The motif is obtained by linearizing the notes of a diminished seventh chord, with an added appoggiatura before the last note. Stravinsky uses several variants, depending on which of the four notes (root, third, fifth, seventh or octave doubling) of the diminished seventh are used: 1 - 5 - 8; 1 - 3 - 5; 1 - 5 - 7; 1 - 5 - 10 (third + octave), etc. while in Ex. 15a the three most used forms are represented in the columns of the central table. Given the complete symmetry of the diminished seventh chord, each variant can in turn have four inversions (represented in the lines of the same table), depending on the note chosen as root. An extended version of the variant 1 - 5 - 7 on $d\sharp$, with two preparing added notes (f and $f\sharp$), is introduced at [103]. This gives rise to the famous syncopated subject of the *Danse infernale* at [133] (Ex. 15a, last two staves), and to the imitative section at 101, in the *Apparition des monstres-gardiens* (Ex. 15b). Here, after a few bars in which the different forms of the motif on $d\#$ are repeatedly started against a sustained diminished seventh chord on the same root, a strict two-part canon starts in which each part is entirely made of inversions of the variant 1 - 5 - 7 of motif M. Then at 103 another 'canonic' episode begins, this time using the extended six-note form (the same as the theme of the *Danse infernale*) of the motif, and with the lower part moving in quavers and the upper part in syncopated half-notes, as a sort of prolation (mensuration) canon. Each part is entirely made of the unending repetition of motif M (extended form), each time in a different (higher) inversion. This sixteen-measures canonic passage is precisely the displaced block we have discussed in Ex. 1a-b.

The complexity of this passage is only apparent: this kind of 'canon' (the quotation marks are mandatory) is about as far from a *tour de force* in the technique of (written) counterpoint as one can imagine. The 'polyphonic parts' in fact, are simple sequential repetitions of various forms of the same motif, which all derive from the same chord. In this sense there is no melody (and therefore no polyphony and counterpoint) at all, as Stravinsky himself admitted:

> Does the Firebird contain more real musical invention than I am able (or willing) to see? I would this were the case [...] but the few scraps of counterpoint to be found in it — in the Kastchei scene, for example — are derived from chord notes, and this is not real counterpoint (though it is Wagner's idea of counterpoint in Die Meistersinger, I might add)[162].

---

162. *EXPOSITIONS AND DEVELOPMENTS*, p. 132.

Ex. 15a: The monsters' leitmotif (P): derivation and variants.

Ex. 15b: *The Firebird*, [101]: use of motif P in the *Carillon féerique – Apparition des monstres-gardiens de Kastchei et capture d'Ivan-Tsarévitch.*

To some extent, Stravinsky's 'polyphonic writing' can be compared to Wagner's or Richard Strauss' *Scheinpolyphonie* (false, or apparent polyphony) — also hinted at by Stravinsky himself in the above quotation — in which the continuous combination and interweaving of motifs and themes based on triads or four-note chords create a dense texture which is not really generated by counterpoint and linear thinking, as would be the case with the Brahms-Schoenberg tradition, for example. If compared to *Scheinpolyphonie*, however, Stravinsky's 'counterpoint' is even simpler and more 'false': the polyphonic parts are much more repetitive — being mostly made up of sequential repetitions of a single motif — harmonically static and, most importantly, reducible to a more simple texture — mostly a two-part texture as in the case we have just seen — which can be managed by the two hands on the keyboard.

However, while not 'real counterpoint', Stravinsky's technique was perfectly suited for the essential purposes of a ballet composer, as discussed above in this chapter, which is to quickly compose the music and to make the music fulfil a narrative function. From the first point of view, the continuous repetition of motifs according to a pre-established chord progression is an operation which, once the appropriate technique has been acquired, can be performed almost extemporaneously on the keyboard. As for the narrative function, the example we have just seen is among the most eloquent; by repeating the M motif each time in an inversion with the highest fundamental, Stravinsky gives the music a character that is both immobilizing (since the harmony is completely static) and developing (due to the progressively ascending melodic lines). This, together with the use of ever-closer 'polyphonic' imitations (the 'prolation canon'), creates a temporal-musical dynamic that fits with the precipitous crowding of the scene by Kashchey's monsters imprisoning Ivan.

The motif of the princesses (motif P) is a simple chord arpeggiation. As can be seen in the upper part of Ex. 16a, it is obtained by changing into an ascending-descending arpeggio a couple of dominant seventh — half-diminished-seventh chords of dS2. The lower part of the same example shows the motif's use in the *Apparition des treize princesses enchantées*: at [48] the motif is based on couple 16/9 - 15/8; then, at [49] it is based on a segment of two couples: 20/13 -21/14 and 24/17-1/18) are used. The string introduction at [48] is one of the few examples in which Stravinsky frees himself from the use of the sequences of alternating thirds: however, also in this case the procedure is of a quite similar (keyboard-based) kind: against a pedal note on $d\flat$ of the horns, three chords containing this note (a dominant seventh $e\flat$ - g - $b\flat$ - $d\flat$ and two major triads $b\flat\flat$ - $d\flat$ - $f\flat$ (= a - $c\sharp$ - e) and $d\flat$ - f - a) move in various inversions.

In a quite similar way to motif M, motif P also undergoes a 'false' polyphonic-imitative treatment. This can be seen at [115] in the *Intercession des princesses* (Ex. 16b) and at [92] in the *Lever du jour* (Ex. 16c). In the *Intercession*, the three-part imitation is based on couples 18/11 - 19/12 of dS2, with each part simply stating motif P; then a more dense, four-part imitation follows on the following chord (20/13) of dS2 , but this time only the first part (with the ascending arpeggio) of motif P is used. The thickening of the texture and the ever closer and

Ex. 16a: *The Firebird*, [48]-[49]: motif P: its derivation and use.

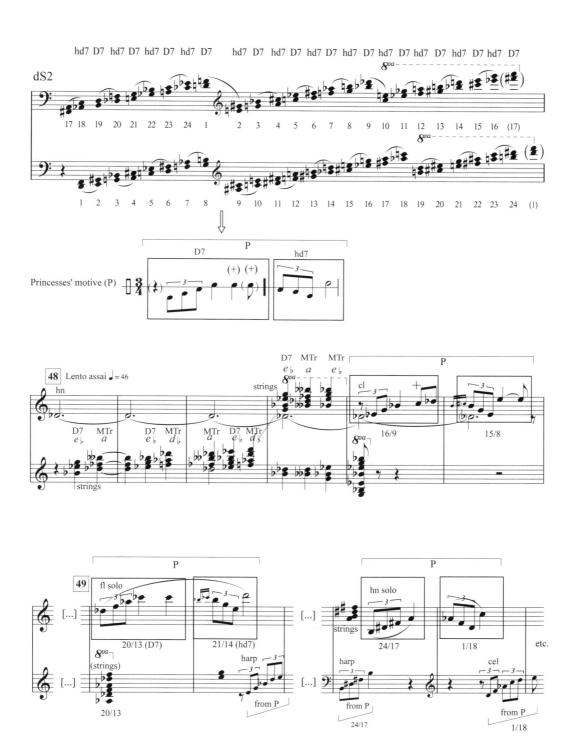

Ex. 16b: *The Firebird*, [115]: *Intercession des princesses*: four-part canon on motif P in sequence on dS2 (see also Ex. 11a).

shorter repetitions of motif P seems to mimic the insistent pleas of the princesses. The music is halfway between an old-fashioned *musique parlante* and Stravinsky's mature 'gestural' style. In the *Lever du jour*, a quite similar temporal dynamic is used to represent the hasty 'dialogue' between Ivan and the Princess before the latter's departure. This time there are two polyphonic parts in a strict canon. The whole episode unfolds on a segment of six pairs of chords from dS2 (see the upper part of the example), from 6/23 to 18/11. Once again, despite the apparent 'polyphony', the music is just a sequence of arpeggiated chords from dS2, just entrusted to both

Ex. 16c: *The Firebird*, [92]-[95]: *Lever du jour*: two-part canon on motif P on a sequence of six D7-hd7 pairs from dS2.

hands and shifted in a canon-like way. What makes this music, otherwise quite mechanical, expressive (almost *parlante*) is the variegated use of the two parts (the first, with the dominant seventh, or the second with the semi-diminished seventh) of motif P: When just one of them is used, an intensification of the entries of the motif results. At the culminating moment, on the sixth couple of chords of dS2, the canon is broken and the shortening of the fragments of P reaches its peak, thus representing the hasty conclusion of the dialogue.

Finally, let us turn to the music associated with the most important character in the ballet, Prince Ivan. He is the only character for which an entire recurring theme, instead of a simple motif, is used. However, this theme is rarely used in its entirety. Usually, Stravinsky just focuses on one of its parts, and treats it as a leitmotif. This seems quite in keeping with Fokine and Beaumont's description quoted above, according to which Stravinsky did not use the theme in its entirety but broke it into smaller motif corresponding to various moments of the plot and mimed actions of the Prince[163]. If we look at the way the Russian theme is used in various moments of the ballet, we can see that it is perfectly compatible with Fokine's description. Apart from its full statement at [71], only some fragments of the theme are used in the other points of the ballet. Furthermore, the theme itself has a rather rhapsodic and fragmentary character, even in its complete form. In much the same way as in the Khorovod melody, it is based on a symmetric formal model which, however, is made irregular through interpolations and by lengthening or shortening the constituent parts.

The complete form of the theme (Ex. 17a) appears in the French horn solo at [71]-[74], in the scene *Brusque apparition d'Ivan-Tsarévitch*. This is the crucial moment of Prince Ivan's first meeting with the Tsarevna, just before the *Khorovod* of princesses. Here the theme is based on a diatonic scale of G minor. According to Richard Taruskin, the model for Ivan's theme was provided by a tenor aria in the first act of Rimsky-Korsakov's opera *The Maid of Pskov* (*Pskovityanka*, 1873), which shows many formal aspects typical of the Russian *protyazhnaya* folk-song style[164]. The *protyazhnaya*, was a type of slow, melismatic lyrical folk song which in the mid-nineteenth century came to be seen as a paradigm for all Russian folksong, or even as the essence of Russian creativity and the 'Russian soul' itself. Overall, it is appears as a small ternary form A-B-A' (exposition – contrasting middle – compressed recapitulation), with each of the three parts divided into two phrases, the first of which ends on a middle cadence on the third or the seventh degree of the scale ($b\flat$ and f), while the second phrase always ends on the tonic g. Each phrase is made of a restricted number of motifs (lower case letters in the first line above the staves): motif w and x in A and A'; and motif y and z in B. The cadential function is mostly performed by motif w in an expanded form — of 2 bars instead of 1.

The symmetry of the theme, however, is disrupted in many ways: part A is of 6 + 3 bars, instead of the regular 4 + 4. The asymmetry is obtained by interpolating two silent bars

---

163.   Fokine 1961, p. 161. Beaumont 1981, p. 53. See above.

164.   Taruskin 1996, p. 606. In this aria the character of Michail Tuča (tenor) entered the scene in almost the same way as Ivan in the *Firebird*. Rimsky-Korsakov's *The Maid of Pskov* had been revived in Paris in the Russian season of 1909 with the title of *Ivan le Terrible*.

Ex. 17a: *The Firebird*, [71] + 2. Ivan's theme.

Ex. 17b: *The Firebird*, [12] incomplete statement of Ivan's theme before the *Dance of the Firebird*.

[see square brackets] after the first occurrence of motif *w*. If these measures are discarded, the underlying four-bar regular structure becomes evident. Another interpolation occurs between the six-bar (3 + 3) contrasting middle (B) and the following recapitulation (A'), where the theme is interrupted by a four-bar counterpoint of the solo A clarinet I ending with a cadence on *b♭*, while the main melody of the horn lingers on two prolonged notes — something that strongly recalls the *podgoloski*-like polyphony of the Khorovod. The recapitulation resumes the second phrase of A only, but in a different version of 6 bars — again obtained from 4 bars, by adding an empty bar and by repeating the final cadence. The motivic construction, too, contributes to asymmetry, since the motifs (in particular motif *w*) often recur in shortened or prolonged shapes. All this gives the theme a fragmented and irregular physiognomy. Ultimately, what is most evident are the single individual parts — the individual motifs — more than the global structure of the theme. This allowed Stravinsky to more easily take up Fokine's suggestion to use just one of the parts of the theme whenever Ivan's character must be evoked, without resorting each time to the whole melody.

It is interesting to see how the various fragments of the theme are modified and harmonized in the other points of the ballet, according to the dramatic situation, as true leitmotifs. At [12], immediately before the *Dance of the Firebird*, the first phrase of part A and the second phrase of part B are entrusted to the oboe. Here the melody is simply harmonized in the tonality of *b* minor, with the string tremolo chords moving on a dominant pedal on F♯ (Ex. 17b). Much more harmonically complex is the use of motif *w* in the French horn solo at no. [6] of the

Ex. 17c: *The Firebird*, [6] use of motif *w* from Ivan's theme in the *Apparition de l'Oiseau de feu, poursuivi par Ivan-Tsarévitch*.

score — *Apparition de l'Oiseau de feu, poursuivi par Ivan-Tsarévitch* — immediately before the magic bird enters the enchanted garden (Ex. 17c). This is the first apparition of a motif from Ivan's theme in the whole ballet score. Stravinsky superimposes several statements of *w* (in various modified forms) on a sequence of dyads from S, thus obtaining an alternation of diatonic (triadic) and octatonic moments (see the harmonic analysis below the lines in the musical example). In the first three bars, the motif *w* (entrusted to the horns) is presented in

Ex. 17d: *The Firebird*, [45] -1: use of motif *w* from Ivan's theme after the end of the *pas de deux*.

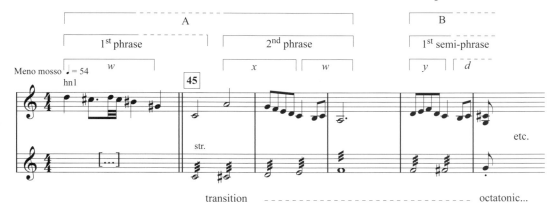

a melodic form that outlines a triad of *b* minor (the notes indicated with + in the example are non-harmonic tones), whose notes *d* and *f♯* are also in the tremolo of the violas. In the following bars these two notes are understood as dyads n. 6 of sequence S, of which dyads no. 5 and 6, belonging to the octatonic collection II, are given to the wind parts. In the meantime the horn part, with motif *w*, dwells on note *g♯*, which belongs to the same octatonic collection. Immediately after, the dyad 4, on which the viola tremolo again lingers, forms a new major triad on *f♯*, with Ivan's horn motif, which now takes the form of this triad. An entirely octatonic progression follows, in which the combination of motif *w* and the alternating thirds, now entrusted to the violins' quaver figurations, produce the octatonic collections III (dyads nos. 3-4-5) and II (dyads 5-6-7). In short, Stravinsky exploited the property of sequence S according to which at every two dyads of the scale a new octatonic collection starts (with the third dyad as a pivot, as shown in Ex. 8c), to obtain a continuous unfolding of octatonic collections; he then adapted motif *w*, so as to alternately fit the octatonic scales and create a major triad in between one collection and another. The result is a sort of developing and 'modulating' passage, in which the transformation of motif *w* takes on a clear story-telling character. Something similar, but simpler, happens in the solo horn at [45], at the end of the *pas de deux of Ivan with the Firebird*, in the scene were Ivan remains again alone in the castle of Kashchey (whose leitmotif, in fact, appears immediately afterwards) (Ex. 17d). Here the entire part A and the beginning of part B of the theme are played against the ascending chromatic line of strings tremolo, which gradually leads the harmony from the tonality of A minor to the following octatonic passage with Kashchey's motif K (see again Ex. 14b).

The use of fragments of Ivan's theme in the scene *Ivan-Tsarévitch pénètre dans le Palais de Kastchei* at [95]-[96] deserve special attention (Ex. 17e). Here Stravinsky creates a true musical narrative, which represents the changing mood of the Prince before his final decision — with the gesture of the 'idea', which we have extensively discussed — to enter the enchanted palace, by alternating motif *w* and a five-note motif that can be considered as a variant of the first

Ex. 17e: *The Firebird*, [95]-[96]: use of two motifs from Ivan's theme in the scene *Ivan-Tsarévitch pénètre dans le Palais de Kastchei.*

sentence of part B (with motifs y and z backwards: see *z' - y'*) of Ivan's theme. In the first three bars, two statements of this motivic form are set to a succession of dominant-seventh / half diminished chords drawn from segment 14/7 - 17/10 of dS2. Then at [96] motif *w* is harmonized on a couple of 'swapped' chords of dS1 (12/23 and 11/24), producing two major triads (on *f* and *b* respectively) a tritone apart, in the same way, therefore, as in the opening double-bass-trombone ostinato representing the enchanted garden (Ex. 12b). Next a third statement of the motif *z' - y'* follows on the following 'swapped' chord of dS1 (14/1). Finally, the last four bars are based on an ingenious harmonic procedure: dyad 14 of dS1 is alternately paired with dyad 13, thus producing a dominant minor ninth chord ($b\flat$ - d - ($[f]$ - $a\flat$ - $c\flat$)), and with dyad 2, as in the normal form of dS2, producing a French sixth chord ($b\flat$ - d - e - $a\flat$). On these two chords a two-part imitative episode unfolds, with motif *w* set alternately on the two notes ($c\flat$ and *e*) that turn the dominant minor ninth into a French sixth. The motif is set to this complex harmony by interpreting some of its notes as appoggiaturas or neighbor tones (see letters *a* and *n* in the musical example). In this case, unlike the 'false' polyphonic episodes on motifs M and P (see above), we have a 'true' and complex counterpoint, in which the vertical encounters of the parts are fairly obvious. This is one of the most sophisticated moments of the whole score in both harmonic and contrapuntal terms: the fragments *w* of Ivan's theme are systematically set against a long sequence of chords drawn from dS1 and dS2.

The last occasion on which a fragment from Ivan's theme is used (Ex. 17f) is when the Tsarevich's 'replies' to Kashchey's beckoning signs at [111], in the previously discussed *Dialogue de Kastchei avec Ivan-Tsarévitch*. Here a sequence of three statements of motif *w* a perfect fourth apart is set against a continuous unfolding of dyads belonging to segment 1-5 of S. From the vertical encounters of the notes of the motif and that of the alternating thirds in the lower part, a variety of common-practice chords (major and minor triads, dominant and half-diminished sevenths) takes shape. The end of this episode at [112], where Ivan attempts to escape, has been already discussed in Ex. 11a: note only how dyad 16 ($e\flat$ - *g*) is held as a pedal against dyads 18-19 and 13-14.

The last examples clearly show how even Ivan's theme, although diatonic in its original form (a [71]), repeatedly assumes the harmonic form of alternate thirds. Despite Ivan being the absolute protagonist in these scenes, the music is as chromatic as any of Kashchey's scenes. This brings us to a final consideration: all the motifs considered thus far are used, in one way or another, according to sequences S, dS1 and dS2; in some cases they are a simple linearization of chords taken from these sequences while in other cases (as in Ivan's), although having a different origin, they are adapted to their harmonies. In these cases, adaptation can usually be achieved by playing on the piano the underlying harmonies of the basic sequences with one hand, while finding the harmonically correct form of the motifs with the other. The only example, among all those considered, where this approach is inadequate, requiring a more complex written elaboration, is probably the counterpoint to the last measures of [95] (Ex. 17e).

Ex. 17f: *The Firebird*, [111] – 2: use of motif *w* in Ivan's 'reply' to Kashhky in the *Dialogue de Kastchei avec Ivan-Tsarévitch* (see also Ex. 11a).

OPPOSITE CHARACTERS, OPPOSITE BODIES

In *The Firebird*, the musical characterization relies on a well-established convention in Russian operatic tradition: human characters are associated with diatonicism, and supernatural (magic) with chromaticism. The association of non-diatonic harmonies with magical, supernatural or marvelous characters and situations had been an operatic cliché since Glinka's *Ruslan and Ljudmila* of 1842. Rimsky-Korsakov had resorted very often to it in the 'fantastic' sections of his operas, where magical characters or situations were involved. His use of various types of chromatic harmonic constructs based on the symmetrical partitioning of the octave, like the whole-tone scale or the octatonic scale — whose resources he began to explore more and more systematically in the early 1890s —was decisive for Stravinsky's musical treatment of the magical sphere.

However, in the *Firebird* this old convention works itself out in a more specific and complex way. Different interpretations have been made, but none is entirely satisfactory. The first was famously provided by Stravinsky himself in his notes for the AudioGraphic rolls. The composer maintained that in *The Firebird* all the magic characters and elements of the ballet story are characterized by a 'leit-harmony' — a harmony fulfilling the same role as a leitmotif — which simply consists in the mechanism of the alternating thirds[165]:

> When I composed The Firebird I had not yet completely broken with all the procedures involved in the [Wagnerian] Music Drama. For example, I was still quite sensitive to the system of musical characterization of the various characters, and dramatic situations. And these systems resulted in the introduction [in The Firebird] of some procedures of the type called leit-music. Thus in The Firebird everything related to the evil genius, Kashchey, everything that belongs to his kingdom, the enchanted garden, the ogres and monsters of all kinds that are his subjects, and in general all that is magical or mysterious, marvelous or supernatural, is characterized musically by what one could call a Leit-harmony. It is made up of alternating major and minor thirds [...][166].

Stravinsky traced back to his 'leit-harmony' both the music for Kashchey and his retinue as well as the Firebird's motif F. «These intervals [of semitone and tritone]», he maintained, «serve, in turn, to create the basis for the benevolent, but still magic, apparition of the

---

[165]. According to TARUSKIN 1996, p. 598, the term (in its Russian form: *leyt-garmoniya*) was first used by Rimsky-Korsakov in a 1905 essay on his opera *Snegurochka*.

[166]. «Quand j'ai composé l'Oiseau de Feu je n'avais pas encore complètement rompu avec tout ce que comportait comme procédé la drame musicale. Par exemple je restais encore assez sensible au système des caractéristiques musicales des différents personnages, ou des différents situations dramatiques. Et ces systèmes se traduisait par l'introduction de quelques procédés de ce qu'on appelle la leit-musique. Ainsi dans l'Oiseau de Feu, tout ce qui a rapport au mauvais génie, Kastchei, tout ce qui appartient à son royaume, le jardin enchanté, les ogres et les monstres de toutes sortes qui sont ses sujets, et en général tout ce qui est magique ou mystérieux, merveilleux ou surnaturel, est caractérisé musicalement par ce qu'on pourrait appeler une leit-harmonie. Elle se compose de tierces majeurs at mineurs alternées, comme ceci [...]». STRAVINSKY 1927, pp. 6-7. The description followed with the illustration of the alternating thirds quoted above.

Firebird»[167]. In fact, the intervals of a semitone and the tritone are contained in both a pair of alternating thirds and in motif F, as we have seen in Ex. 13a. The same line of argument was later developed by Edwin Evans in his 1933 book on *The Firebird* and *Petrushka*. Evans recognized that in *The Firebird* the 'magical' sphere «is of two kinds: evil and beneficent. Kastechï is an ogre and the Firebird is a good fairy, but neither is human»[168]. Therefore, in his view, there still remained a close link between the two types of music, consisting of the tritone interval. Stravinsky simply differentiated, he argued, the two sides of the magic by means of two different uses of this interval, as contained in 'harmonic' form in the alternating thirds (Kashchey and monsters) and in a purely melodic form (Firebird). The resulting schema, thus, is as follows:

Human characters = diatonic

Kashchey, monsters: harmonic form
↗
Magic sphere = alternating thirds ('leit-harmony')
↘
Firebird: melodic form

However, Stravinsky's and Evans' explanations are not entirely consistent. Despite their strongly formal (intervallic) resemblance, the Firebird's leitmotif F and the alternating thirds, when put into concrete music, sound anything but similar (apart from a very generic chromatic character). Motif F is usually set to an entirely whole-tone (and mirror-writing) harmony, which bears little resemblance to that, more conspicuously octatonic, derived from the major/minor thirds. How, then, can something that is so different function as a recognizable characterizing element of the whole 'magical sphere', to which both the Firebird and the world of Kashchey belong?

As I see it, the problem with the Stravinsky-Evans explanation consists of the equation «alternating thirds = 'leit-harmony'», which creates confusion between two distinct levels: the compositional technique and the musical dramatic characterization. The 'alternating thirds' are not, *per se*, a musical characterization of the magic sphere of the ballet but first and foremost a technical-compositional (and 'improvisational') device (this is also why I preferred not to call them a 'Leit-harmony'). The intervallic resemblance highlighted by Stravinsky and Evans, while providing very useful insights into Stravinsky' *technique*, seems to be of much lesser consequence for the concrete music characterization[169].

---

[167].   «Ces intervalles servent à leur tour pour former la base de l'apparition bienveillante, mais toujours magique, de l'oiseau [...]». STRAVINSKY 1927, p. 7.

[168].   EVANS 1933, p. 9, fns.

[169].   The striking resemblance between Stravinsky's comments in the AudioGraphic rolls and Evans' book, suggests that the whole line of argument did not originate with Stravinsky only, but more likely with both he and Evans, who may have served as something more than a simple translator of Stravinsky's French text, and may indeed

In the 1980s and 1990s, Stravinsky's comments on the AudioGraphic rolls served as the starting point for several analyses, based on set-theoretical approaches or on the then-new octatonic theory, fully developed and systematized by Pieter van den Toorn. These studies gave a rather different picture of the harmonic characterization of *The Firebird* from Stravinsky and Evans[170]. McFarland's essay, in particular, showed that while the Firebird's music is strongly whole-tone, that of Kashchey and the monsters tends towards octatonicism[171]. The resulting scheme is therefore as follows:

Human characters = diatonic

  Kashchey, monsters: 'alternating thirds' = octatonic
  ↗
Magic characters
 ↘
  Firebird : tritone = whole-tone

However, this interpretation too holds some inconsistencies. First, it could also be questioned in its own (analytical) terms. We have seen, in fact (Ex. 8c, and 10b), that both sequence S and the double sequences dS1 and dS2 contain a different octatonic collection every two dyads/chords (more precisely, in S and dS1 the third chord of a sequence of three can be referred to two different octatonic collections, while in dS2, only two consecutive chords belong to a single octatonic collection). Therefore, had Stravinsky conceived these sequences as a means to generate octatonic scales, he would have limited himself to selecting pairs, or at most three consecutive dyads/chords. This is precisely what McFarland argues, in fact, but my examples in the previous pages have clearly demonstrated the contrary[172]. Although Stravinsky sometimes rests on only two-three dyads/chords (for example in the opening ostinato from b. 8) he much more often uses longer segments of the sequences, thus moving continuously and erratically from one octatonic collection to another. This clearly shows that his reference point is not the

---

have largely ghost-written the AudioGraphic notes. See McFarland 2011, p. 106. McFarland argues that the French typescript in the Paul Sacher Foundation (Stravinsky 1927) was not the original from which the English version was later translated, but a French translation of the original English text, which was provided first by Evans himself. McFarland 2011 quotes in this regard a letter from Robert Lyon to Stravinsky of 29 March 1925 which clearly shows that at least in that case the original was written in English and then translated into French «so that the composer could read it before giving his approval».

[170]. Forte 1986, in particular, gave an entirely incongruent picture not only with regards Stravinsky and Evans' explanation, but also with the traditional chromatic/diatonic division between supernatural and mortal characters. See McFarland's discussion of Forte's article: McFarland 1994, pp. 206-207.

[171]. See McFarland's 1994.

[172]. See *ibidem*, p. 211.

octatonic scale *per se*. The fact that S, dS1 and dS2 produce momentary octatonic contexts is just a consequence, not the motivation for their use. Moreover, there are some instances in which even the music of the monsters sounds more whole-tone than octatonic, in particular when French-sixth chords are used, since this chord is included in both dS1 (and therefore in the octatonic collection) and the whole-tone collection (see Ex. 9b).

Apart from these music-analytical remarks, however, the most serious problem — one which has been clearly recognized by McFarland himself — is that the alternating thirds — and the resulting octatonicism — are not only used for the characters of the magical sphere, but for humans as well. This is not to deny, of course, that in *The Firebird* the traditional (Russian) characterization that associated the human characters to diatonicism play a fundamental characterizing role, for this association is still at work, but much more — if not exclusively — in the dance numbers than in the mimed scenes. The only truly and entirely diatonic pieces are dances such as the *Khorovod* of the princesses or the final coronation. In the mimed scenes, on the contrary, the non-diatonic harmony of the alternating thirds is pervasive, including when human beings are involved. We have seen that the princesses' motif (P) was entirely worked out from a pair of dominant-seventh — semi-diminished chords contained in the double sequence of alternating thirds in dS2. Ivan's theme, of course, is fully diatonic and Russian-popular in character, but only in its formally complete statement at [71], to which one may probably add [12]. In all its other appearances, on the contrary, it is closely embedded within the chromatic context of the alternating thirds. We have seen that the scene *Ivan-Tsarévitch pénètre dans le Palais de Kastchei* at [95]-[96] is the clearest example. This music, in which Ivan is the absolute protagonist, is as 'chromatic' as any of Kashchey's scenes. It also uses the same 'swapped' form of dS1, producing major triads a tritone apart, as the opening double-bass-trombone ostinato representing the enchanted garden. Even his gesture of the 'idea' at 1 - [97] (Ex. 4) simply consisted of a pair of alternating thirds. More in general, if we look back to all the musical examples in this chapter, we will find that alternating thirds and/or whole tone harmonies are used in almost every mimed scene, both for supernatural and for human characters — as well as for a number of characters that, in a sense, probably belong to both spheres, such as the two horsemen (Ex. 5a and 5c).

In short, the more we look closely to the music of the mimed scenes and learn about it, the more we realize that, in one way or another, the harmony of the alternating thirds affects a great deal of the music in this part of the ballet. What does this mean in terms of 'characterization' (or 'leit-harmony')? Some may argue that this reflects (or 'represents') the fact that in the mimed scenes the human beings also find themselves, in a sense, in a 'magic condition' or in a magic environment. This perhaps could be said — as some scholars have — of the Princesses, who in the plot of the libretto are under Kashchey's spell. But what about the many fragments of Ivan's theme set against the harmony of the alternating thirds? Is Ivan under the influence of the evil magician as well? One may, perhaps, assume that the ubiquitous presence of the alternating thirds simply 'represents' the fact that the whole story line of the mimed scenes — including the action of the humans — moves within Kashchey's enchanted kingdom. McFarland's solution to the problem was that, due to the necessity of coordinating music with mimed action, in the music for the pantomimes Stravinsky «did not have the freedom allowed him in the dance scenes», thus using systematically the «leit-harmony» (the alternating thirds) for the latter, while liberating himself «from this [harmonic] formula» in the dance scenes, as McFarland recognizes[173]; but this simply means admitting that the alternating thirds are not a matter musical characterization (a 'leit-harmony', in Stravinsky's or whatever sense) but rather a procedure with which Stravinsky created (at the piano) the harmonic structure of *all* the mimed sections of the ballet. What is important about them is not so much what they *represent* but how *they work*.

Another problem — closely related to this confusion — with all the interpretations mentioned thus far is that they rely exclusively on harmony, while my point is that harmony, in addition to being conceived more as a procedure than as a formal characteristic of music, should be regarded as just one of the many aspects that contribute to the representation of the staged body and to the production of meanings. In this sense, summarizing various observations made in this chapter, we can say that the human sphere is characterized by:

1. diatonic collections articulated in modal, folk-like scales;
2. monodic texture;
3. vocal, often *cantabile* style;
4. popular in character.

Kashchey' sphere is associated with:

1. alternating thirds used in their simplest (vertical) form;
2. purely harmonic textures, with no true melodic parts;
3. instrumental writing;
4. gloomy orchestration, with low-register wind instruments (bassoons, horns, trumpets, muted trombones, etc.).

The typical features of the magic Firebird's music, on the contrary, are:

1. strongly chromatic melodic motifs, but within a whole-tone harmony;
2. mirror-writing (symmetrical partitioning of the octave);
3. polyphonic/heterophonic texture;
4. instrumental-melismatic style;
5. brilliant orchestration, with woodwinds and strings in the high register.

---

[173]. *Ibidem*, p. 215.

Finally, in all previous interpretations based on the — misleading — notion of 'leit-harmony', what harmony is supposed to 'represent' is not the characters as physically represented on stage by the dancers' bodies and their costumes, but rather the characters as 'literary' described in the libretto. This is a crucial difference and from which many consequences ensue. In Stravinsky and Evan's account, for example, what distinguishes the Firebird from Kashchey's monsters within the magic sphere is the fact that the in the story the first is benign towards Ivan, while the monsters are his evil enemies[174]. This distinction rests entirely on a literary basis. As I see it, on the contrary, what most characterizes the Firebird in respect to the other supernatural characters of the ballet is precisely her staged body, as theatrically constructed by dance, music and costumes. Her grace and beauty are the exact opposite of the monsters' grotesque ugliness and clumsiness. She is a wonderful creature; she looks and moves as a light and agile body, while the monsters have to appear ugly, awkward and heavy. She belongs to the wonderful type of magic characterization while the monsters belong to the *grotesque* side.

In keeping with the anti-literary theatrical aesthetics embraced by Stravinsky, Benois and, more in general, Diaghilev's artistic circle, thus, we should turn our attention not so much to the libretto as to the stage. We should ask ourselves how music, dance and costumes represent these bodies, and what are the cultural premises and ideologies behind this construction. Seen in this light, the previous threefold schema could be rewritten as the following:

Human bodies: *natural, simple, expressive, Orthodox, moral*

Monsters: (magical-grotesque)*: ugly, heavy, clumsy, masculine, Oriental (threatening)*
↗
Magic bodies:
↘
Firebird (magical-marvellous): *beautiful, light, agile, feminine, Oriental (seductive)*

A key factor in the creation of this system of opposite bodies was no doubt Orientalism: the different types of bodies corresponded to a large extent to the distinction between an imaginary Orient and an idea of Russianness. In this sense *The Firebird* lies in the wake of an old tradition of Russian opera, stretching from Glinka to the early twentieth century, and implying the complex question of Russian national identity, its relations with Western culture and its representation as an entity partly connected to Europe and partly to Asia[175]. In the

---

[174]. Incidentally, this was a deliberate deviation of the libretto from its fairy tale sources, in which the Firebird was usually a beautiful and marvellous, but also indifferent, if not perhaps even dangerous, creature, a kind of chimera, and Ivan's ally was another magical animal: the grey wolf.

[175]. For an overview, see the chapter entitled 'Orientalism' in Maes 2002, pp. 80-83. Russian musical Orientalism — as well as Russian Orientalism in the arts in general — was historically linked to the expansionist

Ill. 7: Aleksandr Golovin. Design for the backdrop of *The Firebird* (Tretyjakov Gallery, Moscow).

ballet, various visual aspects contribute to the association between the magical sphere and the Islamic East. According to Fokine, «in the ornamental arms of the bird, as in the movements of Kostchei's servants, *there was an Oriental element*»; and in Golovine's scenery «the garden was like a *Persian* carpet interwoven with the most fantastic vegetation»[176]. The profiles of the mosque domes in the backdrop for the first Tableau looks Islamic, as can be seen from Golovine's set design held at the Tretyakov Gallery in Moscow (Ill. 7). In the visual dimension of the spectacle, the Oriental characterization also concerned the Firebird: the costumes designed by Bakst are clearly oriental in taste, amalgamating heavy plumage, jewels and ornaments referring

---

politics of the Russian Empire towards the Middle East and Central Asia. Clearly enough, in this context the term 'Orientalism' is used in the sense of Edward Said's famous book (Said 1978).

[176]. *Ibidem*, pp. 168, 166. My italics. The importance of décor was clearly recognized by the first critical reception of the spectacle. See Dufour – Niccolai 2020.

179

ILL. 8: Léon Bakst. Sketch for the costume of the Firebird, signed 1910 (private collection).

to a generically Islamic world characterized through an Orientalist prism (ILL. 8)[177]. These clothes contributed significantly to the construction of the Firebird's as an 'Eastern body'[178].

The music for the title role was also 'Oriental', according to a long tradition of Orientalist Russian music, in which 'Eastern' style was a combination of various musical components: non-diatonic scales (chromatic, pentatonic, whole-tone, with a lowered second degree, altered, etc.) and particular rhythmical, melodic and timbral aspects. The melismatic figurations of Scheherazade's theme in the famous symphonic suite by Rimsky-Korsakov, or the arabesques of the clarinets in the *Introduction* to *The Golden Cockerel* are among the best-known examples of this style, made of swirls of rapid and repeated notes alternated with longer ones, all set to a typically woodwind idiom. In *The Firebird* this style appears in the central *Allegretto* of the *pas de deux* role, a passage that Taruskin calls «'Oriental' in the particular nineteenth-century Russian sense of that word»[179]. The long melismas of this section are typical of the «Arabian» and «Central Asian» style of Russian Orientalist music. They contain a typical combination of chromaticism, melismatic style and symmetrical construction, with the melodic line moving within the span of a tritone, and are made of continuous mirror inversions, like those of the motif F we have seen in the mimed scenes.

In comparison to the *pas de deux*, the other music for the Firebird sounds less 'Oriental(ist)'. The pervasive presence of leitmotif F, however, although not 'Oriental' in the same sense of the *pas the deux*, gives an Eastern character also to the other pieces, such as the *Berceuse*. Orientalist hallmarks of motif F are, of course, its chromaticism, but also the symmetrical transformations to which it is subjected, which recalls Rimsky-Korsakov's treatment of the vocal part of the Queen of Shemakha — a character clearly connected to Islamic culture — in the second act of *The Golden Cockerel*.

Sally Banes has drawn attention to the fact that in the *Firebird*, the *pas de deux* is not danced by Ivan with her beloved Princess, but rather with the Firebird. She omits to say that Ivan and the Princess also have their love moment at the end of the *Khorovd*, and although this is not a conventional *pas de deux* between two lovers — it is just a fairly short mime — it is nonetheless a dramatically intense point. Nonetheless, Banes' interpretation deserves attention for according to her, the duet was not so much devised by Fokine as the representation of the Bird's plea to be released or as a struggle between her and Ivan (as implied by the story of the libretto) but as a concealed seduction scene. The poses taken by the dancers, Banes maintains, show that the supplication of the Bird is also a seduction, and that Ivan, in holding and balancing

---

[177]. DAVIS 2010, pp. 79-84 compares this costume to that worn by Karsavina in the role of the Firebird in *Le Festin* of 1909.

[178]. See Davis' overall description of the costumes (*ibidem*).

[179]. According to the comments in the 1929 AudioGraphic Aeolian piano roll (STRAVINSKY 1928), at this point Firebird tries to persuade Ivan-Zarevič «with visions of the fantastic Orient» (quoted in TARUSKIN 1996, p. 624).

ILL. 9: Photograph of Michel Fokine as Prince Ivan and Tamara Karsavina as the Firebird in *The Firebird*, 1910. Photo by August Bert (repr. in *COLLECTION* 1922, p. 49).

the Bird, is caught by her charm. (ILLS. 9-10)[180]. This interpretation could be questioned, since much of the meaning of the male-female relationship in this, as in all other *pas de deux*, depends on the performance of the various dancers, and to a large extent also on the subjective points of view of the scholars. Marcia Siegel's interpretation, for example, is entirely at odds with Banes', while being based on the same performance — the famous 1959 film production with Margot Fonteyn and Michael Somes[181]. Siegel argues that the main task of the dancers in this piece is precisely to make it look different from a conventional love duet, and that although the vocabulary of steps used by Fokine is not so different from that of many traditional *pas de deux*,

---

[180].   BANES 1998, p. 97.

[181].   See *ibidem* p. 248, fn. 6. SIEGEL 2018, pp. 237-238. Siegel considers this performance faithful to Fokine's original idea, which was handed down by Karsavina to Fonteyn.

ILL. 10: Photograph of Michel Fokine as Prince Ivan and Tamara Karsavina as the Firebird in *The Firebird*, Photo by August Bert. Retrieved from the Library of Congress, <https://www.loc.gov/item/ihas.200156311/>, accessed on November 2021.

a correct performance of the original steps would show that the two dancers are *not* engaged in a seduction scene. Siegel's interpretation seems to fit many recent performances, such as that by Leanne Benjamin and Jonathan Cope in the 2001 production of the Royal Ballet, in which Benjamin inserts dramatic gestures that indicate a struggle — not a seduction — with Ivan: extreme backbends, movement of the shoulders that imitate the Bird's effort to shrug away from the Prince's hands, frightened facial expressions, etc.

It is very difficult to judge from the various performances whether in Fokine's original idea the Bird's body in the *pas de deux* was to look more like a frightened creature or like a seductive woman. It is also difficult to say what the first interpretation of the title role looked like. We know that Tamara Karsavina was not Diaghilev's first choice. The impresario had initially approached

Anna Pavlova, but she withdrew, opting for a season performing in London[182]. Pavlova and Karsavina's bodies and ways of dancing were quite different, in a sense even opposite. According to Stravinsky, Pavlova, had a «slim angular figure», while Karsavina, had a «gentle feminine charm» that would also have been well suited «for the part of the captive princess»[183]. Perhaps the Bird in *pas de deux* would have been much more like a frightened animal than a seductive woman, had the role been danced by Pavlova. Moreover, in the first season Karsavina shared the role with Lydia Lopokova, who interpreted it in a very different way, as Benois vividly recalled:

> The impression of the 'flying fairy' as created by Karsavina had something of an Eastern languor. How perfect she was in her moments of suffering, when she endeavored to free herself from Ivan's imprisoning hands! Lopokova's interpretation was more lively, nervous — even, perhaps, childish. One was a flaming phoenix, the other a delicate humming bird, but both performed with faultless accuracy the complicated choreographic design composed by the 'merciless' Fokine — a design as difficult as it was original[184].

Nonetheless, Banes' interpretation of the *pas de deux* as a 'seduction dance' is in keeping, if not with the way in which the role was performed by the various dancers, at least with the basic cultural and ideological premises behind the original conception of the spectacle. What is important to note is that the Firebird's role was given to a dancer that was *both* female *and* Oriental. It was not entirely granted that the Bird had to look 'Oriental'. Nor was it entirely obvious that it should be given to a female dancer. According to Richard Buckle, after Pavlova's withdrawal at the beginning of February 1910, Nijinsky begged Diaghilev to be allowed to dance it, and when the impresario replied that it was for a female dancer on points, Nijinsky insisted that he too could dance very well on toes[185]. In Diaghilev's company, similar reversals of roles were not impossible, in both directions (an originally female role danced by a man and vice-versa). For example, in 1909 Diaghilev had inserted in the ballet *Le Festin* a reversed gender

---

[182]. See BUCKLE 1979, p. 161. According to Stravinsky (*MEMORIES AND COMMENTAIRES*, p. 32), Pavlolva disliked Stravinky's music (she had had occasion to hear the *Scherzo fantastique* and *Fireworks*) which she considered «decadent». According to WHITE 1997, p. 28, after hearing the music of *The Firebird*, Pavlova said: «I shall never dance to such nonsense».

[183]. «The casting was not what I had intended. Pavlova, with her slim angular figure, had seemed to me infinitely better suited to the rôle of the fairy bird than Karsavina, with her gentle feminine charm, for whom I had intended the part of the captive princess. Though circumstances had decided otherwise than I had planned, I had no cause for complaint, since Karsavina's rendering of the bird's part was perfect, and that beautiful and gracious artist had a brilliant success in it». *AUTOBIOGRAPHY*, p. 45.

[184]. BENOIS 1941, pp. 307-308.

[185]. See BUCKLE 1979, p. 162. Nijinsky, in fact, used to performed exercises *sur les pointes*. Buckle credits a conversation with Boris Kochno (who reportedly heard the tale from Diaghilev) as the source of this quarrel between Diaghilev and Nijinsky about the Firebird's role.

version — entitled *L'Oiseau de feu* (*The Firebird*), precisely like the 1910 ballet — of the *pas de deux* of the Bluebird and of Princess Florine from the third act of *Sleeping Beauty*. In his version the two roles, originally (in Petipa's 1890 version) performed by Enrico Cecchetti and Varvara Nikitina, were danced conversely by Karsavina and Nijinsky[186].

Even less obvious is the Firebird's characterization as an 'Oriental' creature. One could speculate as to why the Firebird was endowed with such 'Eastern' characters in both music and costumes. According to Taruskin, this fact owes much to the model provided by an unattempted Firebird opera by Balakirev. Taruskin also argues that the creators of the ballet were influenced by a theory, widespread in the mid-nineteenth century, according to which the basis of many elements of Russian folk tales, including the figure of the Firebird, had come to Europe from Persia or India[187]. However, the question is not so much why the Firebird was represented as an Eastern 'creature', but why it was represented as a Eastern *woman*, and why this characterization is evident above all in the music of the *pas de deux*.

Clearly, both things have much to do with a typical trait of Russian Orientalism, which represented the 'East' as a seductive and lascivious woman. As is well known, this vision was part of a wider cultural construction expressing ideals of racial superiority[188], with the West depicted as rational, moral and civilized, with the East as irrational, instinctive, sensual and barbaric. Russia, of course, was identified with the former, which was typically associated with male features, considered as active and moral by nature, while the latter was associated with feminine features, which is to say, irrational, passive, sensual and sometimes immoral[189]. A similar misogynistic vision was expressed in many nineteenth Russian operas, as well as in programs and subjects of many symphonic compositions such as Rimsky-Korsakov's *Antar* or Balakirev's *Thamar*. Through the identification of the East with a seductive woman, nineteenth-century Russian Orientalism represented the Other and at the same time attributed to it aspects that would have been taboo in Russian society.

---

[186].   The 1909 *Oiseau de feu* was then staged again in 1911 in London, with the title *L'Oiseau d'or*, with Nijinsky and Pavlova (instead of Karsavina). Later it was repeatedly staged in isolated form (not included in *Le festin*), with various titles such as *L'Oiseau et le Prince* or *Aurore et le Prince*. Se Veroli – Vinay 2013, vol. ii, p. 347, fn. 13.

[187].   Taruskin 1996, pp. 622-624. Some Oriental suggestion was also *in nuce* in the description of the Firebird in *The Tale of Tsarevich Ivan, the Firebird and the Gray Wolf*, which served as the main source in the construction of the plot of the ballet: «her feathers are golden, and her eyes are like *Oriental* crystal». Since many translations (in different languages) omit the term «Oriental» (восточный) I give here the text of the tale in the version based on Afanasyev's 1863 edition, published in St. Petersburg in 1901 with illustrations by Ivan Bilibin (Afanasyev, *Skazka ob Ivane-tsareviche, Zhar-ptitse i o serom volke*, St. Petersburg, Ekspeditsiya zagotovleniya gosudarstvennykh bumag, 1901, p. 1), which was most likely the edition Fokine used: «Povadilas' k tsaryu Vyslavu v sad letat' zhar-ptitsa; na ney per'ya zolotyye, a glaza vostochnomu khrustalyu podobny».

[188].   Russian Orientalism was historically linked to the expansionist politics which set Russia against Britain for dominance in the Middle East and Central Asia. It peaked with expansion to the East under Alexander ii.

[189].   On the exotic-feminine association in Western musical culture see especially Austern 1998.

The fact that *The Firebird* was not created for a Russian public but for the Parisian *Saisons* only reinforced these stereotypes. With the reception of Russian music in France, Russian music Orientalism gave rise to a sort of 'second-order' Orientalism. The French public, in the presence of these Oriental themes, saw in them the true face of the Russians, the authentic 'Slavic soul'. In the eyes of the French, Russia itself was part of a barbaric, mysterious, lascivious, sensual 'Orient'. They attributed to the Russians what the Russians attributed to their own East. For both, the 'Eastern' woman indeed represented what they could not identify with, but also that sensual, exotic and erotic element to which they were attracted. Diaghilev's productions from 1909, which reformulated many of the works of the Mighty Five, were fundamental to the French reception of Russian musical Orientalism. The theme of the woman as lascivious, Oriental, immoral, irrational, and sometimes fatal, but in any case strongly seductive, constituted the subject of more than one ballet in the early *Saisons russes Cléopâtre*, *Thamar* and *Tragédie de Salomé* staged the quintessence of the exotic-erotic-Asian features, that the French public loved to associate with the Slavs. If we look at the list of the most successful spectacles in the first two *Saisons russes* of Diaghilev's company, we are struck by the number of works in which the eroticism emanated by female-oriental figures played a central role: the «Polovetsian Act» from *Prince Igor*, the 'Apparition of Cleopatra' in Rimsky-Korsakov's opera-ballet *Mlada*; the Dances of the Persian Slave Girls in Musorgsky's *Khovanshchina*; the Arabian Dance from Glinka's *Ruslan and Lyudmila*, included in Fokine's *Le Festin*; Rimsky-Korsakov's *Sheherazade*, choreographed by Fokine.

Of course, *The Firebird*'s most fundamental subject was not so much the exotic-erotic seduction as the neo-nationalist representation of the 'authentic' Russian spirit in the shape of Ivan Tsarevich and of the Tsarevna, and in this respect this ballet was quite different from others in which the erotic theme was more obvious and more central. Moreover, there are other aspects in the dance, the music and the ballet story line that clearly contradict the vision of the Firebird as a seductive Oriental woman, making her appear, rather, as a primordial element of nature, with whose alliance (or from whose domination) the system of power on which Russian civilization is founded draws its strength and legitimacy. The final return of the Firebird's motif F at [202], immediately before the final coronation procession, and its use in a triadic (diatonic) harmonization in the final cadence of the ballet, symbolizes the natural and primitive force that legitimizes the re-established the power of the tzarist monarchy. However, the coexistence of two different sides to the Firebird is incongruent only in a 'literary' perspective. A coherent characterization, as we would expect from a literary text, was not the most important thing in Diaghilev's spectacles, where the focus was first and foremost on the meanings conveyed by the dancing bodies. In this sense, it did not really matter if different bodily connotations co-existed in the same spectacle or even in the same character. Taruskin maintains that *The Firebird* too was created, at least in part, to supply a new infusion «of semi-Asiatic exotica-cum-erotica, the sexual lure that underpinned Diaghilev's incredible success»[190]. The best — perhaps the only — point of the ballet's scenario in which such exotic-erotic element could be introduced was precisely the *pas de deux*. This is most likely why Stravinsky adopted the 'Oriental' melismatic style precisely in this dance; and it would come as no surprise if, as Banes argues, Fokine's choreography of the *pas de deux* also emphasized the seductive characterization.

The Firebird's body provided the term of comparison by which that of the other characters was constructed. While she embodies the fantastic, marvellous and fascinating side of the Orient, Kashchey's enchanted kingdom clearly represents its threatening — for Western culture — and barbaric side. To characterize such opposite bodies, Fokine resorted to two contrasting dance styles which were «vastly different both in character and technique». The dances of the Firebird were devised on toe and with a large use of jumps. This style was «highly technical but without *entrechats*, *battements*, *rondes de jambs* and, of course, without a turnout and without any *preparations*», while arms «would now open up like wings, now hug the torso and head, in complete contradiction to all ballet arms-positions». In Fokine's representation of the Firebird's marvellous body, the idea of lightness and 'flight' is essential. Different artifices were devised to actually raise Karsavina in the air, but were then abandoned in favour of the series of *grands jetés* with which the dancer makes her first appearance on stage at [4] in the *Apparition de l'Oiseau de feu, poursuivi par Ivan-Tsarévitch*[191]. All this is particularly evident in the *pas de deux*, in which dance has a highly technical character and there is a massive use of *pointe* technique, but with an unconventional use of the limbs, in part reminiscent of Fokine's 1905 *Dying Swan* for Anna Pavlova, but with an entirely different connotation.

In opposition to the beauty, the lightness and agility of the female body of the Firebird stand the grotesque bodies of Kaschey's kingdom. This consisted of an incredibly large and variegated group of different monsters and creatures. According to the official program of the original production, they were divided into several groups: «Kikimoras [...] Suite de Kostchéi [...] Indiennes [...] Les Bolibochki [...] Femmes de Kostchéi [...] Les monstres à deux têtes» (Kikimoras, Kashchey's retinue, Indian women, Bolibochki, Kashchey's women, two-headed monsters)[192]. The costumes and the body movements of these monsters — as well as other aspects of the décor based on Russian folklore — were devised on the basis of the suggestions offered by Aleksey Remizov, the renowned novelist and fabulist, who was part of the circle of artists that contributed to the initial conception of the ballet[193]. Some of these monsters, like

---

[190].   Taruskin 1992, p. 279.

[191].   See Fokine 1961, pp. 170, 163-164. See also Benois 1941, pp. 305-306.

[192].   Quoted from the original libretto. The information of the official program is also quoted, in an abbreviated form, on the title page (French version) of the 1911 Jurgenson printed full score (plate number 34920): «Suite de Kastchéi, Les Kikimoras, Les Bolibochki, Les monstres à deux têtes, etc.».

[193].   See above, fn. 4. See also Lieven, 1973, pp. 106-107. On Remizov's role in *The Firebird* and his involvement in the Eurasiansit movement of the 1920s see Taruskin 1996, pp. 571-574.

ILL. 11: Photograph of the 'Bolibochki' in the 1910 production of *The Firebird*. Photo by August Bert. (repr. in SVETLOV 1911, p. 44bis).

the Kikimora — a female spirit that resides in houses, usually depicted as an evil and ominous being — were authentic figures of folklore or of Slavic mythology, while others were entirely Remizov's invention[194]. Each group had its own costumes but we do not know if also their movements were differentiated in character. Fokine gave a general description of all their dance styles:

> The evil kingdom included movements that were at times grotesque, angular
> and ugly, and at times comical. The monsters crawled on all fours and leaped like
> frogs. Sitting and lying on the ground they stuck the palms of their hands out like

---

[194]. «Had the horrible Bolebochki and all the vile goblins and creeping things that Remizov so mysteriously told us about really existed in the imagination of the people? Perhaps he improvised them then and there, but in any case Fokine had believed in the fiction of the poet and all the horrors that crawled out on the stage, twirling and jumping, evoked a feeling of genuine repulsion, even when the artists were in their working dresses». BENOIS 1941, pp. 305-306.

fins now from under the elbows, now from under the ears, tying their arms into knots, rolling from side to side, jumping in squat positions, and so forth. In short they did everything which twenty years later appeared under the label of "modern dance", but which, at the time, seemed to express most adequately nightmarish horror and hideousness. Simultaneously I used virtuoso leaps and spins[195].

Regardless of the monsters' gender — as represented by the costumes — their dance style had to correspond to a grotesque deformation of the male body. Their «brute masculinity» — as Stravinsky called it — had to stand in opposition to both the 'femininity' of the Firebird and the 'gentle virility' of Ivan[196].

If we look at the music in the light of this description, we can see that Fokine's dance characterization of the monsters' dance style is clearly in keeping with the ungainly mechanics of the monsters' obsessive repetitions of motif P within the 'false polyphony' (the canonic episode) of the *Carillon féeerique*. An important reason for the use of such an unconventional and 'unaesthetic' music style is the representation of a grotesque (male) body. There is also a more subtle analogy concerning the poetics of the two arts. In Fokine's view, as also his final allusion to the *virtuoso* technique in the above quotation shows, all of these dance styles — that of the Firebird, that of the monsters, and even the princesses' barefoot dancing — could be obtained through different uses of the academic technique, if the latter were understood in a non-crystallized and non-conventional way. For Fokine, in fact, technique should never be pursued as an end in itself, but only as expressive means[197]. The clear distinction between technique and style, on which this assumption relies, strongly resembles my distinction between the technical (procedural) function of harmony and musical style (and musical characterization); a single harmonic technique, like that used in *The Firebird* (the use of alternating thirds in sequences or double sequences) allows for different musical styles and characters.

The Firebird's body also provides the term of comparison for the construction of the other female characters, the twelve princesses and the Tsarevna. The dance style devised by Fokine for the princesses was the exact opposite of that of the Firebird. While the latter was highly technical — however expressive and unconventional — and entirely *en pointe*, «the princesses danced barefoot with natural, graceful, soft movements and some accent of the

---

[195].　Fokine 1961, p. 167.

[196].　*Memories and commentaires*, p. 33.

[197].　As a side note, this brought Fokine much criticism from both the most radical innovators, who saw him as a conservative still tied to academic dance, and those who would preserve dance in an even 'purer' condition. According to André Levinson — one of the most strenuous defenders of classical ballet and Fokine's fiercest critic — Fokine had «sacrificed the forms of abstract movement for expression, pure dance for pantomime». Quot. in Acocella – Garafola 1991, p. 64.

Russian Folk dance»[198]. Clearly enough, such a dance style, so tilted towards the expression of naturalness and simplicity, was inspired by Isadora Duncan. The long, simple, white clothes of the princesses express this Duncanesque vision of the 'natural' body.

The Tsarevna does not receive specific characterization, distinct from that of the other princesses — she is simply represented as one of the twelve young girls. She does not even have a specific motif in the 'recitatives' for her leitmotif is that of the other princesses (P). The musical piece in which she identifies most is the Khorovod, danced with other women like the previous *Scherzo*. The popular origin of the Khorovod's first tune and its original link to a folk wedding song reinforce the idea of a popular 'naturalness'. All these elements contribute to making her body appear as closely linked, by a natural bond, to the collective body of the society to which she belongs, and as the ideal body of a Russian bride. Her final emergence and distinction from the group of princesses takes on a symbolic meaning which legitimizes the Tzarist power, and contributes to making her an ideal of racial superiority over the 'Oriental' woman. In this light, the Firebird's 'seductiveness' became that of «a discreet and mighty concubine that makes possible the Russian empire»[199].

The contrast between the lasciviousness of the Oriental woman and the purity of the Russian princesses is well represented by the musical characters of their leitmotifs. motif P is as far from that of the Firebird as one can imagine: F is entirely instrumental in character and is used as a building block and to create rather hypnotic chromatic-symmetrical figurations; motif P has a more lyrical and almost *parlante* character. Although originating from dS2, it sounds much less chromatic than expected. When compared to the Firebird's strong chromatism, entirely made of self-inverting semitones and tritones, its melodic form, emphasizing the initial dominant seventh, sounds almost tonal, not only diatonic[200].

Finally, the last 'body' to be described is that of Ivan, in which the idea of Russianness was resumed. It was supposed to have all the male features — strength, morality, rationality, virility, aptitude for action — that were associated with the Eastern world by the Orientalist perspective, in opposition to the idea of an irrational, passive, sensual and lascivious 'Eastern body'[201]. Fokine's interpretation of the role no doubt endeavoured to provide Ivan with all these 'virile' features.

In contrast to the exotic-oriental characterization of the Firebird and the Eastern-Islamic character of Kashchey's entourage, the diatonicism and popular character lie in particular in two numbers: the Khorovod and the final *Apothéose*) and become the mark of an «authentically Russian spirit». The fact that the model of Ivan's melody was an aria from Rimsky-Korsakov's

---

[198]. FOKINE 1961, p. 167.
[199]. BANES 1998, p. 100.
[200]. TARUSKIN 1996, p. 602.
[201]. See also FLAMM 2013, pp. 58-59.

The Maid of Pskov (*Pskovityanka*, 1873) which presented the character and formal features of the *protyazhnaya* — as Taruskin noticed — is noteworthy in this respect; this was a kind of melismatic song that had been considered by Balakirev as the highest form of Russian folk musical expression[202]. Yet the melodies of the Khorovod of the princesses and of the final *Apothéose* are based on Russian folk songs that Rimsky-Korsakov had included in his collection of 1876[203].

Diatonicism, modal structure, polyphonic (heterophonic) writing, melodic-vocal style and popular ancestry become not only references to the 'natural' dimension, but also to display the markings of a vision of Russian national identity. All the visual and musical aspects characterizing the human characters imply the representation of the Romanov dynasty in its autocratic ideological, nationalist and religious-orthodox aspects, in opposition to everything that identifies the Eastern-Islamic world. A central aspect to this ideological construction of Russian national identity was the component of religious faith. Stravinsky maintained that in *The Firebird* Prince Ivan is finally able to overcome Kashchey only «because he yielded to pity, a wholly Christian notion which dominates the imagination and the ideas of Russian people»; and that pity and faith are the most important reasons why in Russian legends «characters that are simple, naive, sometimes even frankly stupid, devoid of all malice» can be victorious «over characters that are clever, artful, complex, cruel and powerful»[204]. From the dissolution of the Kashchey kingdom, from the liberation of the petrified knights, from their meeting with the princesses and from the marriage of Zarevich to Zarevna, in the final scene, a new political order emerges, which is based on the Christian Orthodox faith: «The evil kingdom vanishes. Instead, in its place, arises a *Cristian city*. And the castle turns *into a cathedral*»[205]. The last reappearance of the Firebird's motif at [209], now for the first time harmonized with diatonic major triads, symbolizes the final reunion of the 'natural dimension' with the Christian faith as the foundation of tsarist power.

CONCLUSION: AFTER *THE FIREBIRD*

Several conclusions emerge from the above discussion. First, Stravinsky's creative methods were profoundly rooted in his physical interaction of his body with the musical instrument. Secondly, the harmonic constructs used by Stravinsky should be understood as a technical-

---

[202].   TARUSKIN 1996, p. 606. In this aria the character of Michail Tuča (tenor) entered the scene in almost the same way as Ivan in *The Firebird*.

[203].   *Ibidem*, pp. 624 e 631-636.

[204].   Stravinsky's statement was reported by EVANS 1933, p. 6.

[205].   FOKINE 1961, p. 165. My italics.

compositional procedure and not as a characterizing element in itself. Third, harmony is just one of the many aspects that contribute to characterization. Fourth, what music contributes to characterization or representation is not so much the characters as conceived in literary terms (by the libretto), but a vision of their staged bodies, as expressed also by the other artistic means (dance, mime and costumes).

After *The Firebird*, with *Petrushka*, and *The Rite of Spring*, Stravinsky would take new paths as regards theatrical conception and the relationship between dance and music. In his following ballet scores for Diaghilev, he would move more and more resolutely away from the old speech-like descriptiveness that still informs some scenes of *The Firebird*, and from Fokine's still 'realistic' aesthetics. The naturalistic descriptiveness that still typifies many aspects of *The Firebird*'s theatrical conception would give way gradually to a convinced anti-naturalistic stance. The most decisive influence in this respect came from his collaboration with Alexandre Benois, which pushed him toward new theatrical approaches. In the meantime, Stravinsky would also move more determinedly away from the conventions and the collaborative methods of classical ballet. While *The Firebird* was still largely a ballet in which the music had 'to serve dance' — as was the norm in the tradition of classical ballet — *Petrushka* marked an important change in this respect: with this ballet, Stravinsky not only «made music not to serve dance, but to control it», as famously stated by Lincoln Kirstein, but also created a new way of relating music and dance — given that much music that ended up in *Petrushka*'s score was not originally conceived as ballet music[206].

After *The Firebird*, Stravinsky would also embrace a new, discontinuous conception of the musical form that in his first ballet still seems largely absent. In the *Petrushka*, and above all with *The Rite of Spring*, almost every formal convention of classical dance music seems to be overcome. In this new scenario, therefore, two new ways of coordinating dance and music would be possible. Either the dance had to be adapted to the irregularities and asymmetries of music, by following its phraseology in a fairly slavish manner, or the dance had to be freed more resolutely from music to develop its autonomous structures, albeit in some way coordinated with that of the music. The first path will be the one that, according to Stravinsky, Nijinsky would follow in the original choreography of the *Rite of Spring*. The second would lead to Stravinsky's idea of a 'counterpoint' between the two arts.

Nonetheless, despite all these differences, many important anticipations of the following ballet and of the Stravinsky to come can be seen in *The Firebird*. Firstly, Fokine's ideas probably provided Stravinsky with a first drive towards an anti-literary — and anti-logocentric — theatrical aesthetics. The discontinuous conception of the musical form is also foreshadowed in some way in the block displacements of which we have some evidence in the Morgan manuscript. As for the use of conventions, we have seen that though still relying to a good extent on the

---

206. KIRSTEIN 1970, p. 194.

formal conventions of classical ballet music, Stravinsky was able to overcome them in many ways. In the more 'traditional' — in respect to the mimed scenes — dance numbers he also devised a complex balance between the traditional phraseological regularity of classical ballet music and various irregular and asymmetric features. In this way, *The Firebird* also questioned the basis on which the collaboration routine between choreographers and composers had lain for over a century. Stravinsky and Fokine's collaborative methods relied on the new importance acquired by the visible body as a source of knowledge and a bearer of meaning.

Finally, a continuity between *The Firebird* and Stravinsky's later ballets can be seen in the way the music contributes to the production of meanings and to the construction of the staged body. While still featuring many mimetic and descriptive uses of the music, *The Firebird* contains many anticipations of Stravinsky's strongly 'gestural' style, in which music is finally at one remove from the immediate presence of the body on stage, but is still able to convey a variety of implicit bodily meanings. In the end, behind the various vicissitudes and aspects surrounding *The Firebird*, we can see the new role that the body had assumed in a moment in history when age-long artistic conventions were going into crisis.

Chapter Three

«Il ne faut pas mépriser les doigts»: Composing with Hands, Composing with Intervals

Part i: Composing with Hands
The 'Musical Idea' and the 'Composer's Mind'

In 1926, Henry Cowell wrote a short article for *The American Journal of Psychology*, in which he tried to describe his own 'process of musical creation'. «A popular misconception», he maintained,

> [...] is that in order to be inspired a composition must have been improvised or played on the instrument for which it was written, and that when a composer writes music at his desk, without recourse to his instrument, he does so by means of some cut-and-dried formula or purely intellectual process. [...] The misconception is doubtless caused by a lack of appreciation of the fact that the most perfect instrument in the world is *the composer's mind*. Every conceivable tone-quality and beauty of nuance, every harmony and disharmony, or any number of simultaneous melodies can be heard at will by the trained composer; he can hear not only the sound of any instrument or combination of instruments, but also an almost infinite number of sounds which cannot as yet be produced on any instrument.

Then, after describing the long process of self-training that, since childhood, had led him to develop his unique skills as a composer (his — alleged — ability to entirely create and control all the aspects of music in his mind alone) he concluded:

> I shall never forget the disappointment I experienced when I first wrote down a composition and played it. Could it be that this rather uninteresting collection of sounds was the same as the theme that sounded so glorious in my mind? I rehearsed it all carefully; yes, it was the same harmony and melody, but most of the indescribable flowing richness had been lost by the imperfect playing of it on the imperfect instrument which all instruments are[1].

---

[1]. Cowell 1926, pp. 234-236.

It may sound paradoxical that these words came from one of the most 'physically' engaged composers in experiments with musical instruments: the composer, by the way, who went down in history as the inventor of 'elbow music' — the piano clusters played with the arms. What is striking about his account is not the idea that any aspect of music, even the most complex ones like timbre, can be managed entirely in the mind — under certain circumstances, this could also be done — but the total disavowal of the physical and bodily dimension of music in the process of acquisition of the musical skills. «The sounds which [he] produced», maintained a commentator reporting Cowell's narration in 1932, «were heard first in his own brain and [...] the effects he produced on the piano were but the necessitous inventions which he had to create to produce those sounds [...] First he heard the clusters of sounds; then he invented the medium for their expression»[2]. This is the exact opposite of what today's cognitive theories would suggest, since they consider the gradual formation of concepts, language, and more generally of human thought, as the consequence of bodily processes and of the interaction of the body with the environment. As a matter of fact, despite Cowell statements, we know that the unusual characteristics of his musical language arose in large part from his close involvement with uncommon instruments — especially those he played as a child — and, perhaps, even from some limitations of his body[3].

I quoted Cowell's words just to show how much prone to a disembodied vision of the 'composer's mind' was the musical culture of the early twentieth century. The mind-body dualism, of course, has been deeply rooted in Western culture since its very beginning, and an incorporeal notion of 'musical thought' was a common trait of many early twentieth-century modernisms, including the so-called 'ultra-modernism' to which Cowell is usually ascribed.

It might also sound paradoxical, thus, that Stravinsky, who was no less 'modernist', and whose writings are notoriously filled with misleading — if not entirely false — statements about himself and other composers, had offered such a more realistic and truthful view about the role of musical instruments in his creative process. «When I became his [Rimsky-Korsakov's] pupil», he recalled in the *Autobiography*,

> [...] I asked him whether I was right in always composing at the piano. «Some compose at the piano», he replied, "and some without a piano. As for you, you will compose at the piano". As a matter of fact, I do compose at the piano, and I do

---

[2]. HENLEY 1932, p. 10.

[3]. See for example HICKS 1993, pp. 431-433. Cowell's first instrument, found in his home when he was about four years old, was an out-of-tune zither, an instrument that could produce a cluster of adjacent pitches with a single stroke. His first compositional experiments were carried out, according to some testimony «on an old, decrepit piano». EWEN 1936, p. 53. Since his infancy, Cowell suffered of juvenile chorea, a disease whose symptoms include an uncontrollable clenching of the hands that makes the sufferer continuously clench their fists — just as in the performance of piano clusters.

not regret it. I go further; I think it is a thousand times better to compose in direct contact with the physical medium of sound than to work in the abstract medium produced by one's imagination[4].

Stravinsky always considered the movements of the fingers on the keyboard as one of the most important sources of his 'musical ideas'. While dwelling on the genesis of his *Piano-Rag-Music* (1919) he said:

> [...] I finished a piano piece I had begun some time before with Artur Rubinstein and his strong, agile, clever fingers in mind. I dedicated this *Piano Rag Music* to him. I was inspired by the same ideas, and my aim was the same, as in Ragtime, but in this case, I stressed the percussion possibilities of the piano. What fascinated me most of all in the work was that the different rhythmic episodes were dictated by the fingers themselves. My own fingers seemed to enjoy it so much that I began to practice the piece; not that I wanted to play it in public — my pianistic repertoire even today is too limited to fill a recital program — but simply for my personal satisfaction. *Fingers are not to be despised: they are great inspirers, and, in contact with a musical instrument, often give birth to subconscious ideas which might otherwise never come to life*[5].

The last part of this quotation seems to translate into simple terms the most basic idea of today's scientific theories of embodied cognition: the body is an essential part of our cognitive system; and musical ideas, in the same way as concepts and emotions, do not arise in an abstract and disembodied 'mind' but from the interaction between the central nervous system the body, and the objects and cultural artifacts (such as musical instruments) that we build and use. Stravinsky's special sensibility for the physical elements of music seems a perfect match to these theories. In the 1957 NBC television documentary *A Conversation with Igor Stravinsky*, while discussing with Robert Craft in his Hollywood studio, he said:

> We have to *touch* the music, not only to hear it, because touching it makes you feel the *vibrations* of the music. It is a very important thing. When you think about the Beethoven's case. You remember, when Beethoven was absolutely deaf, he took a stick in his mouth, like this pencil and he played the music touching the stand [in the video Stravinsky mimes the gesture of touching the piano stand with

---

[4]. *Autobiography*, p. 5.

[5]. *Ibidem*, p. 82. My emphasis. The words «a musical instrument» in the English edition were translated from the original French «matière sonore». The whole passage reads as follows: «Il ne faut pas mépriser les doigts; ils sont de grands inspirateurs et, au contact avec la matière sonore, éveillent souvent en vous des idées subconscientes qui, autrement, ne se seraient peut-être pas révélées». Original French edition: *Chroniques de ma vie. 1*, Paris, Denoël et Steele, 1935, p. 178. However, it is evident that the 'sound matter' Stravinsky alluded to here were the musical instruments.

the pencil in his mouth] to have the vibrations, because he needed to enjoy the vibrations, otherwise the music was an abstract matter for him[6].

Of course, also Stravinsky's statements must be handled with a certain amount of suspicion. It is well known that they were formulated under the influence of other thinkers and with the help of ghostwriters, and that they often conceal ideological standpoints and self-promotional purposes. This is especially true of his conversation books with Robert Craft. It is difficult to say how useful they are for our understanding of events, facts and circumstances dating back more than half a century before they were published. Even the words from the 1935 *Chroniques* quoted above should be read in the light of Stravinsky's antiromantic stance which led him to demystify any 'abstract' vision of the musical creativity in favour of the technical, practical and material aspects of art[7]. Nonetheless, it can be said that Stravinsky's statements concerning the most 'material' aspects of his own creative process are those that most often turn out to be truthful and reliable. They often find a confirmation in the study of the sketches and of other testimonies of the creative process. This is precisely the case of the two aspects on which I will focus in this chapter: the central role of the piano and the use of intervals as a building material for the composition.

It could be argued that composing at the piano was anything but an unusual practice in the first part of the twentieth century, and that many, perhaps even most, other composers of the time habitually composed in this way: one might wonder, thus, why so much attention should be paid to this aspect in Stravinsky in particular. However, scholars have shown that there is a close relationship between the formal and stylistic characteristics of Stravinsky's music and his use of the piano in the compositional process. The most important effort in this regard has been made by Graham Griffiths in his groundbreaking book *Stravinsky's Piano: Genesis of a Musical Language*, which I will often comment on in this chapter[8]. Confirmation of the central role of the piano in Stravinsky's creative process also came from musical philology. In the preface to the facsimile of the manuscript that served as a model for the first printed edition of the four-hand piano version of the *Sacre du Printemps*, the editor, Felix Meyer, summarizes: «The piano version [...] directly transmits something of Stravinsky's initial musical ideas invented the piano», since «[...] for Stravinsky, the piano was far more than an expedient that allowed him to make his compositional ideas audible and subject to inspection»[9].

---

[6]. From the documentary *A Conversation with Igor Stravinsky*, directed by Robert D. Graff, NBC, 1957. My transcription.

[7]. See for example Stravinsky's discussion of the concept of 'inspiration' in the POETICS, pp. 50-51.

[8]. GRIFFITHS 2013. See also GRIFFITHS 2005. Charles Joseph was the first to systematically explore the topic in his Ph.D. Dissertation (JOSEPH 1974, from which the 1983 book largely draws), thanks also to his acquaintance with Stravinsky's son Soulima, who was among his piano teachers. See the chapter of the 1983 book, titled 'The piano as Stravinsky's compositional «fulcrum»'). Other illuminating observations on the role of the piano in Stravinsky' creative process can be found in ANDRIESSEN – SCHÖNBERGER 1983, pp. 145-149.

[9]. Preface to STRAVINSKY 2013a, p. 33.

The focus of this chapter, however, will not be on Stravinsky's relationship with the piano in general, nor on the role of this instrument in the evolution of his musical style. On these aspects we can still rely on Griffiths' exhaustive book. Rather, I will try to describe some basic aspects of Stravinsky's harmonic procedures — his use of common-practice chords within symmetrical collections (in works of the Russian period) and of intervallic motifs (in serial compositions) from the perspective of embodied cognitive processes. To begin, however, I will recall some basic concepts of embodied cognition, to provide a theoretic framework for my reflection.

The Body and the Hands: A Theoretical Framework

The scientific debate on the role of the body in musical cognitive processes has drawn heavily from the studies on embodied cognition that have developed in various disciplinary areas[10]. Cognitive sciences have shown that human thought does not live in a 'separate' and 'abstract' dimension which is represented through symbolic systems such as writing and language, but is closely related to the body, the environment, and the physical media. The body is not conceived as an intermediary between two distinct dimensions (that of the mind and that of the physical or real world), but as an integral and essential part of a cognitive process and cognitive system. This 'radical' incorporated approach stands in open contrast with the computational, representational, modular visions that conceive the human mind as a sort of huge set of dedicated computers, which receive inputs from the external physical dimension, thus processing their symbolic representations[11].

Many experiences that have contributed to the definition of the 'embodied' theoretical approach came from the fields of philosophy of mind, psychology, and cognitive sciences, as well as from fundamental discoveries of neuroscience, which have shown how bodily experiences, movement and emotions can directly affect knowledge[12]. In the analytic philosophical tradition,

---

[10]. For an overview on embodied cognition see Shapiro 2011; Chemero 2004 (especially, chapter II, pp. 17-44). In musicology, the area of 'embodied music cognition' has undergone extensive development in past two decades years. In addition to Marc Leman's essay (Leman 2007) which I will focus on shortly, see above all Cox 2016; Reyland – Thumpston 2018. See also the chapter titled 'Embodied Cognition' in Kozak 2020. Just to quote a few other titles (of articles) see Schmidt 2011; Gillan 2013; Sedlmeier – Weigelt – Walther 2011; Bowman 2004.

[11]. A term often associated with 'embodied cognition' is 'grounded cognition' (Barsalou 2008, pp. 617-645), but the two approaches differ, since grounded cognition, while assuming that that the content of any mental representation is grounded on corporeality, still relies on a representational view of the mind. See for example Golonka – Wilson 2013.

[12]. See for example Damasio 1994; Damasio 1999; Damasio 2010; Jeannerod 2002; Jeannerod 2006.

language and meaning have been typically conceived according to a dualist (mind-body) viewpoint: concepts and meanings are described as 'abstract' formal and structural properties. In contrast, cognitive linguistics emphasizes the central role of the body (including the brain) in shaping our thought. Meaning is not conceived in 'purely' linguistic terms, since language itself is the outcome of various bodily (sensory, motor, and affective) processes. The bodily processes affect in many ways the syntax, the semantics, and the pragmatics of human language through image schemata, body-oriented grammatical constructions, and conceptual metaphors. A decisive contribution in this sense came from the approach based on cognitive metaphor first taken by George Lakoff and Mark Johnson in 1980 in their famous book *Metaphors We Live By* (1980)[13]. They showed that cognitive metaphors are basic, pervasive cognitive structures through which we 'understand' (conceptualize) a 'target' domain, in terms of a source, by 'mapping' the latter onto the former (just to take a couple of examples from the musical sphere: we think and speak of the timbre of the sounds in terms of colours of visual objects; and Italians such as myself call the sound frequency [pitch] '*altezza*' [height]). Then, in his book *The Body in Mind* of 1987, Johnson tried to find an ultimate foundation for this 'cross-domain mapping' in the idea that the creation of concepts in the source (not in the target) domain is based, ultimately, in our body[14]. The continuous repetition of bodily experiences and behaviours based on the same dynamic pattern gives rise to what Johnson calls 'image schemata': dynamic structures that recurs within different experiences, perception and activities thus working as an abstract structure that connects all of them, thus providing the basis for the creation of all types of metaphorical cross-mappings and cross-relationships. Conceptual metaphor, cross-domain mapping and image schemata have proved very effective to explain how we conceptualize the musical phenomena (for example, how we conceptualize pitch by metaphorical associations between frequencies and high/low positions in space, according to the 'verticality' schema). The work of the musicologist Lawrence Zbikowski has made an important contribution to the application of the theories of cognitive metaphor in the theoretical-musical field[15].

From a philosophical point of view, a fundamental point of departure was the phenomenological perspective of Merleau-Ponty. In his *Phenomenology of Perception* of 1945, the French philosopher argued that the essence of perception is not an abstract notion of 'conscience', because all 'consciousness' is 'consciousness of something' and the very place of consciousness is the body itself[16]. In this sense, a key concept is that of 'intentionality', which Merleau-Ponty derived from Husserl: the attitude of consciousness to 'direct' its acts towards the objects. The term intentional had already been used in this sense in the context of medieval

---

13. LAKOFF – JOHNSON 1980.
14. JOHNSON 1987.
15. See ZBIKOWSKY 2002. See also COX 2016.
16. MERLEAU-PONTY 2012.

scholasticism but had been reintroduced into contemporary thought by Franz Brentano. In this philosophical tradition, being aware of something and tending (intentionality) towards it, are conceived as the essential and distinctive traits of all cognitive phenomena. Merleau-Ponty accepts this aspect of Husserl's and Brentano's definition; however, while Husserl's intentionality is still conceived in relation to a transcendental 'I' (the intentionality of our judgments and our voluntary decisions, as Merleau-Ponty defines it), and therefore takes place on a conscious level, the intentionality defined by Merleau-Ponty as 'operative intentionality' (*intentionnalité opérante*) precedes and is essentially independent of a conscious reflection. A central role in this idea is played by the concept of 'body scheme', which the French philosopher takes up from Paul Schilder's psychology studies: the movement of the body as pre-reflective, independent motility preceding conscious reflection. The body and its movement are by their very nature 'intentional' (i.e. goal-directed). We can therefore speak of a 'motor intentionality' of the body.

More recent cognitive studies tend to relate this intentionality to a biological substratum, in which it arises, ultimately, from the adaptation mechanisms of the organism to the environment. In this way a continuity between the biological level and the level of conscious intentionality is postulated[17]. Many scholars today tend to include in an integrated cognitive 'system' not only the entire body but also the environment and cultural artefacts. The philosopher Mark Rowlands, for example, in addition to rejecting the Cartesian vision of the mind as a circumscribed and monadic entity, proposes a radically 'externalist' and 'ecological' model of the cognitive processes, in which objects placed entirely outside our body — and we can also think of musical instruments — as well as aspects of the environment that surrounds us, are considered as components of the cognitive processes[18].

The most fundamental premise of these theories consists in overcoming any dualistic ontology (of Cartesian ancestry) that postulates a clear-cut separation between body and mind. Dualism is deeply rooted in Western culture and sometimes resurfaces even in those discourses that are presumed to recognize the cognitive role of the body. Often, for example, we tend to think that the body is not distinct from thought because it constitutes an essential 'intermediary' between it and the 'external reality'; or that the body is a tool of our 'thought', or that the instruments (including musical ones) we use are 'extensions' of our 'mind', etc. Such statements would seem to underlie an embodied point of view; on the contrary, they all hide a dualistic prejudice. This can be seen even in some scientific discourses involved with embodied musical cognition such as, for example, Marc Leman's book *Embodied Music Cognition and Mediation Technology*[19]. Leman's premise is that «neuroscience has provided compelling arguments

---

17. For a synthesis of this view see MENARY 2013, pp. 349-367: 350-352.
18. See ROWLANDS 2006, ROWLANDS 1999.
19. LEMAN 2007. See for example the review of Leman's book in MENIN – SCHIAVIO 2013.

that the Cartesian division between mind and matter can no longer be maintained and that a disembodied mind as such does not exist»[20]. At the same time, Leman states that the purpose of his research is to explain how the gap between music considered as codified physical energy (the way in which we tend to consider music from the perspective of modern digital media) and music as an action-oriented system of values — human content, emotions, meanings and interpretations — can be bridged. His theory is based on the idea that musical communication is based on a relationship between the mental experience of music and sound energy (matter). Within this mind / matter dialectic, the human body is seen as an intermediary that transfers physical energy to the level of the mind, which in turn transforms it into meanings and emotions. According to Leman, moreover, it is possible to observe and describe the reverse path, that is, how the human body, through movement, translates these mental contents into an energetic form[21]. Although Leman's idea that the meanings associated by the human mind with musical experience are not 'abstract' but action-oriented — are typical of the 'embodied' point of view, there is still a contradiction in his argument: since body and matter should not be considered as distinct entities, how can (and why should) the body bridge the gap between them, acting as an 'intermediary'? Leman's approach seems to contradict his own anti-dualistic premise. Even his use of the term 'mental representations', denounces a typically representational view of the mind. In fact, Leman conceives musical instruments — both traditional (acoustic) and electronic and digital ones — essentially as mediators between the physical-energetic dimension of musical matter and that of the human mind. On the contrary, a genuinely embodied approach should consider both the body and the instruments as essential elements of an integrated cognitive system, only placed 'outside our head' and 'outside our skin'[22].

What can these theories tell us about the use of the piano in musical composition? If we assume that the cognitive activity is a whole-body process that cannot be reduced to the mind's activity alone, even the process of musical creation cannot be conceived as a purely 'mental' process that is only 'aided' by instruments (such as the piano) and then transferred to paper (or other media). Musical creativity depends on a large extent on what happens in the whole body when interacting with musical instruments and media within a given environment. We should pay particular attention to the role of the hands, which are no doubt one of the most important parts of our body from the cognitive point of view[23]. To this end, some useful insight can be

---

[20]. LEMAN 2007, p. 13.

[21]. *Ibidem*, p. xiii.

[22]. NOE 2009.

[23]. The cognitive role of the body-instrument interaction is a central feature of the 'audio-tactile theory' developed by the musicologist Vincenzo Caporaletti in a series of writings appeared over the last twenty years (see especially CAPORALETTI 2005, CAPORALETTI 2014, and CAPORALETTI 2019). Caporaletti distinguishes different types of musical practices according to the specific cognitive modality involved: music based on oral tradition, music based on writing, and 'audio-tactile' music. In the latter, psycho-bodily factors strongly condition

gained from the reflection on the '*enculturated hand*' developed by the cognitivist Richard Menary[24]. His view seems well suited to our purposes, since he attaches great importance to the objects, systems and processes placed outside our brain (according to the so-called Extended Mind thesis) and to the role of acculturation, teaching and learning in the cognitive processes. I will try to briefly summarize his theory.

Drawing on various scientific disciplines (cognitive sciences, psychology, biology, neuroscience, ecology), Menary starts from the assumption that cognitive systems are integrated systems of interacting parts of various kinds: neural, bodily, and environmental. In this respect, Menary's approach is quite akin to Mark Rowlands', since they both assume that cognitive processes are not located exclusively within the subject's body (within his 'skin') but include the manipulation of external elements. Menary's thesis is that cognitive processes are «cognitive practices [which] can be thought of as bodily manipulations of informational structures in public space»[25]. According to him, during the long process of biological adaptation and of establishment of their 'ecological niche', humans have managed to integrate into their cognitive processes not only environmental structures, but also the structures and artefacts created by themselves as constitutive parts of their cultural practices. These latter had been created and developed according to enormously faster (shorter) time scales than biological evolution. The technology of writing, for example (and we can also think of the various forms of musical notation created over the centuries), has been created only in the most recent phase of human history. Consequently, unlike other environmental elements which have been incorporated both in the cognitive process and in the biological structure of the human species and of his brain, they have not yet caused changes in the brain anatomy. Cognitive skills such as writing, developing symbolic systems, mathematical reasoning, and musical practices, which could not be integrated into the human cognitive system via biological adaptation, are incorporated through normative cultural practices: teaching, learning, exercise. As neuroscience has shown, these practices modify our neuroanatomy, reshaping the cortical circuits with which we are endowed by biological evolution. This allows our brain to engage in these culturally acquired practices, even if its shape had evolved to perform other functions. In fact, although in humans 'neural plasticity' and the ability to develop new cortical functions are extremely high, they still require a large amount of time to develop, and this explains the particularly complex and long — when compared to other species — learning period in children and young adults. The symbolic systems that we have developed to perform various functions appear to us as 'abstract'

---

the cognitive processes. Caporaletti's theories have greatly influenced my reflection. Stravinsky's combination of 'improvisation' at the piano and written composition, as described in this chapter, could be conceived as the presence of an 'audio tactile' component within a writing-oriented creative practice.

[24].   Menary 2013.
[25].   *Ibidem*, p. 353.

structures and 'abstract concepts only because they have been entirely assimilated during our childhood. However, they are the consequence of a repeated interaction between our body and what Menary calls 'inscriptions in public space': manipulations of tangible structures located outside our body (but not extraneous to our cognitive system), from which the brain (not the 'mind') extrapolates some structural information.

A central role in the neural modeling process is played by the body and, particularly, by the hands. They are crucial to the process of 'acculturation' of the brain: they manage, organize, and manipulate physical and tangible objects, from which structural information is acquired. In this way continuous feedback is created between the hands and the brain activity:

> We create, maintain, and manipulate cognitive niches. We do so with our bodies, but primarily with our hands. We group objects together into classes; we store information in easily accessible places to use in future bouts of thinking; we update the information, delete it, reorder it, reformat it — and we do so always with our hands. We write or type, we push or pull; the hand is ever present in our construction of cognitive niches[26].

Another interesting aspect of Menary's theory is the idea that the cultural practices implemented by our body in the public space are 'normative': the acculturation process establishes, in the various contexts, what is the correct or wrong way to carry them out. The socially correct modalities are codified in the form of rules or procedures to be followed in the learning process. Once acquired, however, these practices are no longer activated by the body by referring to those rules: the body (and the hands) begin to move in an 'intentional' way, with no more conscious reference to the 'content' of their movement, nor to the acquired norms that regulate them.

All this sheds new light on many aspects of musical practices and creativity. We can think of the rules of traditional harmony as embodied normative practices, acquired through the study and exercise in part at the keyboard, in part through the technology of music writing. The hands of the musician are musically 'enculturated' hands, in the sense of Menary. The normative aspect of the cognitive system is given by the codified rules of harmony, also as explicated in verbal and written form (in treaties). The keyboard is an integral part of the system: its technical-constructive characteristics and its tuning system — the 7 white / 5 (3 + 2) black layout and the various temperament systems — are not immutable data of nature but reflect the rules underlying a precise cultural practice. They are not, 'external elements', nor an 'extension or a 'medium' of the 'musical mind'. Not nature, in short, but *second nature*.

Menary's idea of considering writing, understood as the physical act of handling the space of the paper and the pen, as an essential element of an integrated cognitive system, suggests considering musical notation as a coordinated and harmonized — rather than antagonistic —

---

[26]. *Ibidem*, p. 358.

element with the use of the piano in the process of music composition. In the following pages I will often emphasize the continuity and interchangeability of roles between writing and the use of the keyboard in composition. This idea also relies on some analogies between the two media. The use of the piano keyboard in music composition displays many obvious differences, but also some important cognitive similarities with musical writing. Unlike notation, the piano is a medium that exposes the performer to a variety of visual, auditory, and tactile cues. If we were to also consider the importance of the perception of vibrations, we should also consider it as a somatosensory, and vibrotactile medium — as Stravinsky himself reminded with his words[27]. Unlike music writing, moreover, a piano does not (usually) allow for the recording of these constructs, since it is essentially intended for real-time music performance. Even a performance on a keyboard, however, could be recorded, not only with electronic technology: Stravinsky's engraving of player-piano rolls is a good example. More importantly, both the keyboard and musical notation have some basic cognitive aspects in common: they are both based on (and encourage a) conceptualization of the sound frequency according to visual spatial-criteria (up/down – left-right)[28]. The keyboard's left-to-right organization corresponds to the low-high cognitive metaphor of the sound frequency on which Western music notation relies (down/left = lower frequencies; up/right = higher frequencies)[29]. In this sense, if conceived as a tool for managing the pitch organization of a piece of music, a piano could be used to 'write' (to 'inscribe', in Menary's sense) with hands on the keyboard, which can somehow work like music writing.

From Keyboard to Paper: Improvisation and Composition

Before trying to apply this theoretical framework to Stravinsky's case, let us briefly reconsider the harmonic procedure used in the mimed sections of *The Firebird* discussed in the previous chapter. We saw that the use of bichord progressions, combined with the two hands in the form of quadriads, is the basis of this technique. In addition to the repetitive fingering pattern we have shown in Ill. 6 of Chapter Two, we can now add that performing the bichord sequences of the Ex. 9a of Chapter Two with both hands is anything but immediate, and requires, indeed, a lot of practice, due to the difficulties encountered in fingering (thumb passage is not always practicable) and because it is not so easy to maintain the correct alternation of major and minor thirds in both hands. However, the task is facilitated by the fact that the hands quickly 'recognize', so to speak, the sum of the bichords as familiar (for an 'enculturated' hand, in Menary's sense) chords, such as the major and minor triads, or the various types of sevenths

---

27. See above, fn 6.

28. I use the term 'conceptualization' in the sense of embodied cognitive theories, as in Zbikowski 2002.

29. On the concept of 'image schemata' and 'cognitive mapping' applied to the musical.theoretical domain see *ibidem*, pp. 65-71.

chords. In this way they start focusing, in an intentional and goal-directed way, on these chords as ready-made objects, and no longer on the single bichords, thus executing the whole sequence correctly. In handling these chords, the hands disregard the system of traditional (tonal) rules within which they were originally assimilated and begin to move 'intentionally', according to new criteria (the use of the symmetric progressions of alternating major and minor thirds). Stravinsky, thus, 'improvised' the harmonic structure of the mimed sections of the ballet on the keyboard, by exploiting techniques and strategies typical of extemporaneous creation.

As these observations on *The Firebird*'s 'improvisation' suggest, recognizing the role of hands in the process of musical creation entails a redefinition of the very concept of 'composition': in Stravinsky's creative process two different components interacted: an 'improvisational' component, carried out directly at the keyboard, and written composition. If we were to refuse this view, we would conclude that the use of the piano was a mere 'substitute' of written composition; or even worse, a mere 'aid' for an activity that could be carried out in the 'composer's mind' alone (as in Cowell's account quoted at the beginning of this chapter). We should conclude, in other words, that the piano was only « an expedient that allowed Stravinsky to make his compositional ideas audible and subject to inspection » — to quote again Meyer's statement quoted before. On the contrary, what makes the piano — and more generally musical instruments and technologies — a useful tool for composition is the possibility that it offers to implement the harmonic structures of music in the temporal dimension; that is, to manage them directly in the performance, rather than in a deferred moment, as in written composition. In a very few words, to *improvise* music.

Although *The Firebird* represents a special case, in which the use of progressions is quite systematic and 'mechanical', an improvisational element was always present, to some extent, in Stravinsky's creative process, from his first musical experiments as a child, up to his latest serial works, as the composer himself acknowledged on several occasions. In the *Autobiography* he recalled that...:

> When I was nine my parents gave me a piano mistress. I very quickly learned to read music, and, as the result of reading, soon had a longing to improvise, a pursuit to which I devoted myself, and which for a long time was my favorite occupation. There cannot have been anything very interesting in these improvisations, because I was frequently reproached for wasting my time in that way instead of practicing properly, but I was definitely of a different opinion, and the reproaches vexed me considerably. Although today I understand and admit the need of this discipline for a child of nine or ten, I must say that my constant work at improvisation was not absolutely fruitless; for, on the one hand, it contributed to my better knowledge of the piano, and, on the other, it sowed the seed of musical ideas[30].

---

30. *AUTOBIOGRAPHY*, p. 5.

A quite similar account can be read in a letter of 1908 containing a sort of brief self-portrait — with no ghost writer, for once, behind it. «I did a large amount of sight-reading», Stravinsky wrote, «which helped my development. The lack of education in theory became an ever-greater obstacle, however, and though I improvised endlessly and enjoyed it immensely, I was unable to write down what I played. I ascribed this to my lack of theoretical knowledge»[31]. Allusions to improvisation continue to appear in Stravinsky's writings until his last books with Robert Craft in the 1959 *Conversations*; in addition to reaffirming the concept, he also alluded to another important aspect, especially for his neoclassicism: the music materials used as the basis for the improvisation could be his own creation but also borrowings from the music of other composers:

> When my main theme has been decided I know on general lines what kind of musical material it will require. I start to look for this material, sometimes playing old masters (to put myself in motion), sometimes starting directly *to improvise* rhythmic units on a provisional row of notes (which can become a final row). I thus form my building material[32].

Improvisation is a central topic in Graham Griffiths' book as well. Griffiths recognizes the central role of piano improvisation as an essential component of Stravinsky's creative process and not as a distinct activity from (written) composition. This is entirely in keeping with Griffiths' approach to Stravinsky's piano as compositional tool. «Stravinsky's piano» he maintains, «was more than a musical instrument for the access it provided to improvisation which, since childhood, had been his preferred stimulus to creativity»[33].

On the other hand, while recognizing improvisation as an essential part of Stravinsky's creativity, we also know that he was very tied to music writing and 'paper'. As a 'composer', in the traditional-classical sense of the word, he systematically used manuscripts, even according to an articulated work organization, which included various typologies of notations corresponding to the various phases of the creative process: sketches, drafts, short scores and full scores. Writing music was as essential an activity for Stravinsky as was playing and improvising:

> Ideas usually occur to me while I am composing, and only very rarely do they present themselves when I am away from my work. I am always disturbed if they come to my ear when my pencil is missing, and I am obliged to keep them in my memory by repeating to myself their intervals and rhythm[34].

---

[31]. Stravinsky's letter to Grigory Timofeyev of 13 March 1908, quoted in Stravinsky – Craft 1978, pp. 21-22.

[32]. *Conversations*, p. 12

[33]. Griffiths 2013, p. 255.

[34]. *Conversations*, p. 13.

Stravinsky's own 'Stravigor' (ILL. 1) — the little dynamo he invented so that he could trace the staves on any type of paper (even blank paper) — shows how essential it was for him to be able to *write* music anywhere and anytime[35]. Many of his musical sketches, especially those for the last serial compositions, are jotted down on notepad sheets, postcards, visiting cards, hotel and restaurant letterheads, and so on.

ILL. 1: Stravinsky's 'Stravigor', the little dynamo he invented so that he could trace the staves on any type of paper.

How to reconcile, then, Stravinsky 'the piano improviser' with Stravinsky the 'pen and paper' composer? In my opinion, much of the problem lies in our tendency to conceive written composition and improvisation as two unreconcilable activities. The origins of this prejudice lie far back in time in musicological and ethnomusicological studies, and ultimately go back to the classical studies on literacy and orality of the mid-twentieth century, such as those by Walter J. Ong and Eric Havelock, and to the Parry/Lord model of oral creation. These studies provided both literary scholars and musicologists/ethnomusicologists with an influential model of non-written creativity. In their 'classic' formulation a strong focus was put on the aspects that differentiate oral and written creations. In the musicological field, an excessively clear-cut distinction was made between written cultures — as was Western art Music in a crucial phase of its history — and oral cultures, such as folk and popular musical traditions. This is quite evident in the field of sketch studies of Western art music composers, whose methodological paradigm was provided by the studies on Beethoven's creative process: they usually imply a vision of the musical creation as a process that takes place entirely on paper. Moreover, the process has been usually conceived as a linear and straightforward path, in which each phase leads to another:

---

35.   The 'Stravigor' — the nickname is a combination of the first and last parts of, respectively, Stravinsky's last and first names — was an evolution of a 5-pointed pen called a *rastrum*, using five rollers instead of five fixed points. Stravinsky invented it around 1911, and his friend Nikolai von Struve tried to obtain a patent for him. Although this never happened, the Stravigor continued to be produced in small quantities. Stravinsky used it from his early compositions (in the *Rite* sketchbook it is used extensively) to the end of his life.

from the sketches to the first drafts; from these latter to more continuous drafts; from larger drafts to a short score, and finally to the full score[36]. What is missing in this vision is the part that cannot be witnessed by the writing, as it is worked out on the musical instruments.

However, more recent studies on oral cultures, while not denying the fundamental conceptual acquisitions of traditional studies in this field, tend to put orality and literacy in a complementary, rather than antagonistic, relationship. They conceive them as two activities that, despite obvious conceptual differences, can often perform similar functions. This is especially evident in those cultures, such as medieval literature, which while systematically using written texts, were still closely linked to oral creative strategies[37]. As for musicology and sketch studies, some scholars are now starting to look at musical sketches from the perspective of improvisation. Nicholas Cook's idea of 'improvisations on paper', for example, is very suitable for our purposes[38]. Cook's approach aims precisely at recognizing an important function for improvisation in the creative process of Western art music, without, however, dismissing in any sense the primary role that music writing had had in the definition and development of this musical culture. Cook invites us to think of music composition as a much more complex process than has been usually assumed; one in which improvisation and written composition alternate and interact in a complex way. While, of course, this cannot be applied in the same way to all composers, I assume that this is the best way to look at Stravinsky's creative process and at his sketches.

In a few words, I'm assuming a perfect symbiosis and complementarity in Stravinsky's creative process between improvisation and written composition. In the improvised part of the process, Stravinsky mostly defined the essential harmonic/contrapuntal structure of his musical ideas, according to some procedures — use of scales and reference collections, progressions, harmonic/contrapuntal models, intervallic motifs, etc. — and started to give these pitch structures some concrete rhythmic shape. At the same time, music writing served him to both fix in a defined form the musical ideas first improvised, and put them in larger sequences, according to his typical formal strategies, such as block juxtaposition — the use of insulated and static textural blocks of music that are abruptly and sharply juxtaposed one after the other without any transition[39].

---

[36].   As Cook 2018, p. 94, note, «composition is represented as a process of developing ideas on paper. Musicologists, too, have traditionally seen composition as a practice that takes place within the domain of writing, and Cooper [...] underlines the linear nature of this conception when he writes that shorter sketches might be regarded as 'sketches for the continuity drafts rather than as direct preparations for the autographs'».

[37].   See, for example, how the two components are included in the medieval concept of 'memory' according to Carruthers 1990. As for musical cultures, just to make an example, the idea of a continuum between composition and improvisation resonates in many essays collected in Cumming – Locanto – Rodin 2017.

[38].   Cook 2018, pp. 85-96.

[39].   Although described — and named — in different ways, block juxtaposition has been widely recognized as a central feature of Stravinsky's conception of musical form. See above all Cone 1962; Kramer 1988, pp. 174-194; Cross 1998, pp. 17-80, Horlacker 2011.

This hypothesis fits well with Stravinsky's most succinct, but also illuminating, description of his own creative process:

> [...] I begin work by relating intervals rhythmically. This exploration of possibilities is always conducted at the piano. Only after I have established my melodic or harmonic relationships do I pass to composition. Composition is a later expansion and organization of material[40].

The improvisational component of the process corresponds to what Stravinsky calls «relating intervals rhythmically [...]» which was «always conducted at the piano»; the written component, that is composition, was usually carried out mostly on the paper and was conceived as «a later expansion and organization» of the materials invented in the previous, improvisational phase.

However, while Stravinsky's statement seems to assume that improvisation and composition simply succeeded each other in the chronology of the creative process (first improvisation, and then composition), a more realistic scenario should imply continuous feedback between the two modalities. We should not think, in other words, of improvisation as just a preliminary phase, which led to an entirely and exclusively written process, but rather as a complementary activity to written composition, with which it continued, to some extent, to interact even in the later stages of the creative process.

There are obvious differences between the kind of 'improvisation' I'm arguing for and improvisation in proper sense (this is the reason why I usually put the term in quote marks). An essential requirement of the improvisational practices, as typically defined by ethnomusicologists, is missing in the 'improvisation on paper': the coincidence between creative act and performance. 'Improvisation on paper' should be understood as just a partial component of the creative process, one aimed at the definition of musical materials to be further elaborated in writing. Given this limited function and non-self-sufficient nature, these materials cannot be considered suitable for — nor are they aimed at — an improvised musical performance. However, they bear some similarities with 'true' improvisation: first, they are generated from the bodily interaction between musician and instrument; secondly, they are worked out according to specific extempore generative techniques.

This view may also help us to better understand many features of Stravinsky's musical sketches that would otherwise be difficult to explain, such as, the multiple variants of single musical ideas which are often found among the various manuscript sources: they may reflect a sort of zigzag, or back-and-forth path between the paper and the instruments, as we will see later in some examples discussed in this chapter. The interaction between improvisation and

---

40.   *CONVERSATIONS*, p. 11. This was part of the conversation between Craft and Stravinsky quoted above.

written composition is also well suited to the appearance, typology, and chronological order of the manuscript source of Stravinsky's creative process, which in its most complete (ideal) form is as follows:

1) Little sketches containing single, short musical ideas[41];

2) Short drafts assembling the previous sketches (often with a montage-like technique);

3) More continuous drafts, assembling several sketches into a coherent whole[42];

4) Short score (fair copy) assembling all previous drafts;

5) Full score.

This succession corresponds to the articulation of Stravinsky's work in successive phases in which the use of the piano and of music writing performed different functions:

1) Rhythmic improvisations on some harmonic (or intervallic) structures: usually at the piano; then registered on paper;

2) Combination of previous ideas in the form of larger musical passages (Short drafts: both at the piano and on the manuscripts;

3) Composition (montage) of larger formal structures: usually on paper, but possibly also checked and reworked at the piano[43];

4) Assembly phase of the various musical ideas in larger musical forms: almost an entirely written process; the piano served only to check the result.

This work organization underlies all of Stravinsky's compositions for which there is enough written evidence, from the earliest compositions to the last serial compositions. However, each work has its own peculiarities. In the case of *The Rite of Spring*, for example, most of the initial ideas, as well as more advanced annotations (continuative drafts) were collected in a quite rational way in the so-called — and well-known — '*Rite* sketchbook'. This is not the most typical situation: more often Stravinsky scattered his early sketches among several loose sheets and/or into notebooks gathering materials belonging to several compositions[44]. However, we will see that even for *The Rite of Spring* some sketches can be found outside the *Rite* sketchbook[45].

---

[41]. In the last serial compositions this may include (or be preceded by) annotations of pitch-class series, twelve-tone rows, and serial charts and arrays.

[42]. This corresponds to what Beethoven scholars call a 'continuity draft': a typology of musical manuscript in which the composer «can be seen fitting together the more fragmentary ideas made earlier into a coherent whole». COOPER 1990, p. 105.

[43]. This part of the process is well exemplified in the composition of the *Symphonies d'instruments à vent*: see SCHERLIESS 1993, pp. 161-185.

[44]. STRAVINSKY 1969. The so-called '*Rite* sketchbook' of *The Rite of Spring* (held at the BnF, Paris) contains various types of annotations: little sketches of isolated musical ideas and more continuous sketches and drafts, sometimes in form of short score.

[45]. See below.

Secondly, although Stravinsky's working method remained substantially unchanged throughout his life, as he changed his 'styles', some differences arose, due to the different formal conception. This is particularly evident in the works of the serial period, in which Stravinsky's habit of cutting out short musical ideas, even of very few bars, from the sheets on which they had been originally written, and then pasting them on larger sheets of paper or cardboard, increased considerably. This procedure was in part a simple way for replacing older, discarded versions of a musical passage; in part the consequence of Stravinsky's block-juxtaposition technique: it allowed him to physically handle the various blocks of music as separate sheets of paper, and to displace them on a visual space according to a certain overall form. To some extent, such a procedure had always been used by Stravinsky, but in his later years it become more and more frequent and systematic.

Just to give a typical example, let us consider the case of the *Interlude* of *Requiem Canticles*. The amount of preparatory material which survives for this piece is uncommonly large: more than twenty small sheets and strips of paper of different sizes, forms and typologies for a piece lasting only 67 bars[46]. Some sketches contain only one or two brief musical phrases, sometimes corresponding to the exposition of the 12 notes (a single row form). They were obtained by cutting into smaller pieces some ideas that Stravinsky had haphazardly recorded on paper from his preliminary piano improvisations, in which he had provided the pitches of various row forms of a twelve-tone series[47], with a specific rhythm and contrapuntal texture. These pages of sketches were later cut out and reduced into smaller scraps, so that some parts could be modified and/or replaced with a new version — mostly a different rhythmic improvisation on the same twelve-tone row. Consequently, we now have a lot of little clippings often containing different versions of the same passage. Their comparison, along with the analysis of the various type of ink and paper, and the autograph dates on some pages, allows, to a good extent, the reconstruction of the chronology of composition[48]. In order to reassemble different variants of the same passage, Stravinsky pasted the clippings close to each other on a sheet of paper. Finally, the last versions of the various musical passages were either pasted onto larger cardboards or directly copied into

---

[46]. They are held at the Paul Sacher Foundation, Igor Stravinsky collection. For a complete inventory and dating of the sketches see LOCANTO 2002, pp. 115-117.

[47]. The whole *Requiem Canticles* is based on two different twelve-tone rows: in each movement either one or the other of the two series is used. The *Interlude* is the only movement of the score which uses both series. The bassoon duet discussed here is based on the series labelled as no. 1 by Stravinsky, as shown by the symbol 'I' put over 'R' in the first clipping of ILL. 2.

[48]. This was done in LOCANTO 2002, pp. 113-117. Thanks to the dates that Stravinsky wrote on many sketches (also confirmed by some testimony in Craft's books) we know that the composition of the *Interlude* took place between the beginning of March and October 17 of 1965, and that it was the first of the nine movement of *Requiem Canticles* to be composed.

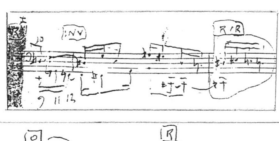

Ill. 2: Igor Stravinsky, two sketches the *Interlude* of *Requiem Canticles*: Above: sketch for bb. 155-158; below: sketch for bb. 152-158. Paul Sacher Foundation, Igor Stravinsky Collection. By kind permission.

a draft of the short score[49]. Although all this may seem a purely paper-oriented process of cut-and paste, the whole procedure was most likely checked at the piano during the whole process. Stravinsky usually put the cardboards over the piano stand, so that they could be played as the clippings were assembled in the right order.

The two clippings reproduced in Ill. 2, for example, contain the contrapuntal structure of the episode for alto flute and two bassoons at bb. 152-158 of the *Interlude* of *Requiem Canticles*. The first clipping (in the upper part of the illustration) contains only the bars from 155 (second half) to 158 (first half). It was worked out by providing the pitches of three row forms (see Stravinsky's autograph serial symbols: R[etrograde], Inv[ersion], and R[etrograde of the] I[nverted] R[etrograde]) with a particular rhythm and a two-part contrapuntal texture[50].

---

49.   Below, I discuss the reworking of one of these ideas, which served as the intervallic model for the definition of one of the two twelve-tone rows used in *Requiem Canticles*.

50.   A clarification is needed with respect to the serial symbols O, R, I and RI employed in the sketches. Normally, Stravinsky does not obtain the fourth basic ordering of the row (RI) by reading the inverse form (I) backwards (as is typical of Schoenberg and his students), but by inverting the retrograde form (R) (on the respective consequences, see for example KRENEK 1940, p. 11). The two forms differ with respect to the level of transposition: the inversion of the retrograde begins on the same pitch as the retrograde; the retrograde of the inversion begins on the last pitch of the inversion. In order to avoid a disparity with the sketches which I have transcribed, I will likewise

ILL. 3: Igor Stravinsky, a page from the short score of the *Interlude* of *Requiem Canticles* (bb. 148-165), including the passage at bb. 155-158 and 152-158 of the sketches reproduced in ILL. 2. Paul Sacher Foundation, Igor Stravinsky Collection. By kind permission.

The sketch bears no instrumental cues and is written as a pure two-part counterpoint with no metre at all, but no doubt it was conceived at the piano having in mind the sound of a duet between two wind instruments. In the final form of the printed score, in fact, the episode is divided into two wind duets: alto flute and bassoon I (first duet, bb. 152-155); and bassoon I and II (second duet, bb. 155-158). In the origin, also the first clipping had to contain the whole episode with the two duets (from b. 152 to 158), which was based on a complete unfolding of the four row forms O, R, I, and RIR. Then, however, Stravinsky decided to modify the beginning and the end of the passage, so he cut out with scissors the first part (from b. 152 to the first half of b. 155, corresponding to the alto flute - bassoon I duet) and the second half of last measure (b. 158, the last part of the bassoon duet). The result of this operation is what can be seen in the first clipping: from the second half of b 155 (with note 9 to note 12 of row R: e - $d_\sharp$ - g - f) to the first half of b. 158 (with notes 1-4 of RIR: $d_\sharp$ - $e_\sharp$ - e - d). This was reused as the music of the bassoon duet in a new version of the whole episode, contained in the second clipping. There are a few rhythmic variants between the two versions, but the contrapuntal substance is the same. The whole passage thus obtained was then included into a larger episode conceived in block-form. ILL. 3 reproduces a page of the short score with the wind duets of bb. 152-158 shown by my square brackets, along with other musical blocks. The two-bar block immediately after the bassoon duet (after the square brackets), for example, is the chordal refrain of flutes, horns, and timpani reappearing several times throughout the *Interlude*. In the end, the final form of the

---

employ the symbol RI to indicate the inversion of the retrograde. The factor of transposition (Tn) is computed in ascending semitones from 0 to 1 1 (taking octave equivalence into account).

piece was the result of a montage of cut-and-past of sketches containing a few measures that had been first found at the piano and randomly recorded on paper. In addition to the earliest stages of the process, however, the piano was, no doubt, also used during the assembly phase.

PIANO VS ORCHESTRA?

One of the most essential precepts of Rimsky-Korsakov's teaching of the orchestration, as epitomized in in his posthumous *Principles of Orchestration*, was that the creation of the orchestral sound should not be conceived as the process of providing musical ideas created with another medium — such as the piano — with some orchestral or instrumental 'colour'. Rimsky-Korsakov insisted that musical ideas should be conceived in proper vocal, instrumental or orchestral terms, since «orchestration is part of the very soul of the work» and «certain tone-colours being inseparable from [a musical work] in the mind of its creator from the hour of its birth»[51]. For him, this precept held true even for those composers, like Stravinsky, who used to rely on the piano from the very early stages of the creative process. The ability to compose at the piano while thinking, at the same time, in orchestral (or other instrumental) terms was an essential skill required by Rimsky-Korsakov's teaching curriculum, as Graham Griffiths has demonstrated[52].

This teaching was deeply assimilated by Stravinsky: thanks to it, the composer's ability to handle the orchestral sound while 'sitting at the piano', so to speak, grew a lot compared to his youthful skills[53]. On closer inspection, in fact, Stravinsky's sketches show that his early musical ideas were conceived since the very beginning according to the sound qualities of a particular instrument or instrumental ensemble, not only because sometimes the early sketches are often accompanied by instrumental cues, but also because their features reflect the range, the expressive qualities, and the technical possibilities of the instruments for which they were intended. Just to make a couple of examples: the music for the *Interlude* contained in the sketches discussed above, in the previous paragraph (ILL. 2), was surely conceived since the beginning in view of the sound of the alto flute and the bassoon, no matter if the sketches bear no instrumental cues (which is provided only in the short score: ILL. 3). The same can be said of the short excerpt from the Sketchbook for *The Rite of Spring* I will discuss shortly (ILL. 6), which contains the original notation of an orchestral *glissando*).

The ability to combine orchestral thinking and use of the piano in creative process also led Stravinsky to develop a unique skill: that of composing scores that sound perfectly both as

---

[51]. RIMSKY-KORSAKOV 1964, p. 2.

[52]. GRIFFITHS 2013, pp. 55-64.

[53]. The topic is discussed at length in *ibidem*, pp. 64-70.

orchestral pieces and as piano pieces. The paradigmatic case is, of course, the *Rite of Spring* (of which we know from Stravinsky's famous account that it was entirely composed at the piano)[54]: Felix Meyer's philological study has shown that the four-hand piano version is very close, both chronologically and conceptually, to the early stages of the creation of the ballet full score[55]. From many testimonies we know that before being definitively realized as an orchestral piece, the *Rite* was performed on various private occasions on the piano, using from time to time the version for two pianos in progress or perhaps a piano version that has been lost[56]. We have evidence of such 'piano previews' from the early months of 1912. Therefore, Felix Meyer rightly concludes that the four-hand piano score should be considered as a different and self-standing 'version' of the piece, rather than a 'reduction', *stricto sensu*, of the orchestral version.

On occasion, the sound of the piano did actually affect Stravinsky's orchestral sound, but this is just another manifestation of his extraordinary skills in creating new, original orchestral sounds. This is certainly the case with such pieces as the *Glorification de l'Élue* and the *Danse sacrale* of *The Rite of Spring*, which, according to Griffiths, «were not only composed at the piano, but, exceptionally, [...] also retained in the composer imagination a perfectly acceptable pianistic identity during their passage from initial spark to final score»[57]. More in general, the dry and percussive sound of the piano and of the energy and physicality of Stravinsky's piano performance style is clearly captured in the long chordal repetitions, in the obstinate rhythms, and in the pounding rhythm that everyone recognizes as essential traits of the music of the *Rite of Spring*. However, this simply shows, even more so, that the piano did not limit nor impair Stravinsky's orchestral thought, providing him, indeed, with an opportunity to give the orchestra an original sound, when compared to that of the late romantic orchestra. The choice itself of such a 'piano sound', was an intentional stylistic and expressive choice, not a side effect of Stravinsky's use of the piano in the creative process.

This said, in view of the main topic of this book, we should also ask ourselves some questions. From a purely cognitive point of view, can we really assume that the use of the piano as an instrument (that is, as a technology) for composition tends to impair 'orchestral thinking'? In what sense can it be more of an obstacle to orchestral writing, than the use of musical notation (or other technologies)?

---

[54].   «Almost the entire *Sacre du Printemps* was written in a tiny room of this house [the Châtelard Hotel in Clarens, Switzerland], in an eighty-feet-by-eight closet, rather, whose only furniture was a small upright piano which I kept muted (I always work at a muted piano), a table, and two chairs». *EXPOSITIONS AND DEVELOPMENTS*, p. 141.

[55].   On the chronology of the compositions of *The Rite of Spring* see the prefaces to the facsimiles edited by Ulrich Mosch and Felix Meyer (STRAVINSKY 2013A; STRAVINSKY 2013B). On the history of the revision of the full score see CYR 1982.

[56].   On these piano 'previews' of *The Rite of Spring* and on their sources see Felix Meyer's introduction to STRAVINSKY 2013A.

[57].   GRIFFITHS 2013, p. 75.

The idea that composing at the keyboard — rather than 'on paper' or entirely 'in mind' — is an activity that hinders the timbral imagination and the quality of the orchestral writing is a quite widespread misconception, not only in the pedagogy of composition — in which it could have, at least, a pedagogical justification — but also among musicologists. To give just one example, even in an excellent essay on the orchestration of the *Rite of Spring*, the author, Thobias Bleek writes:

> Although Stravinsky wrote *Le Sacre* at the piano, as he did all his music, and although this personal muse and workbench left clear traces into score, the surviving documents on the work's genesis prove that it was conceived throughout in orchestral terms[58].

Bleek's observation is entirely correct, but his use of the word 'although' at the beginning of his sentence implies the idea that the use of the piano in musical composition may somehow conflict with a genuine symphonic conception (Stravinsky *did* conceive the *Rite* «throughout in orchestral terms» but not 'despite' his use of the piano. I would even say 'thanks' to it, indeed). This is not, of course, to deny that, under certain circumstances, the use of the piano in composition can really impair timbral imagination and the quality of orchestral writing; nor to deny that something like that really happened to some composers (one could find several cases in the history of music, mostly among second-rate composers). But the idea that composing at the piano *necessarily* tends to limit these skills conceals a misunderstanding about the cognitive functions that musical instruments (and instruments in general) perform in musical creativity. It does not consider the fact that the piano, if conceived as a tool for composition (instead of an instrument for the music-performance), is just a technological medium like any other, such as music notation, the use of midi keyboards, computers, sampling, etc. It can be viewed as technology no more no less than many other technologies[59]. Since we know from the studies of Marshall McLuhan and the Toronto school of communication that technologies modify human thought, the idea that one of such technologies prevents a 'pure' orchestral thinking is untenable, since there is no 'pure' way to think in orchestral terms, but only different tools, technologies and methods with which we can handle an orchestra in order to obtain the desired sound effect. So, one can only find a suitable technology for one's expressive purposes. Composing at the piano was a technology used by many composers in the nineteenth and twentieth centuries: Brahms, Mahler, Ravel, and many others, habitually composed at the piano, and that certainly did not impair their orchestral 'writing'. But even composers who did not use the piano still had to resort to a certain 'technology' to compose orchestral music. Of course, to be easily 'imagined' and therefore properly 'handled', the sound of the orchestra, like any other

---

58. Bleek 2013, p. 83.
59. Goody 1987.

aural, visual or sensorial data, need to be deeply assimilated (embodied) through continuously repeated, direct physical experiences; and this was, probably, the 'secret' of Rimsky-Korsakov's orchestration teaching method, which consisted in familiarizing the student with the sound, the technical features, limitations, and the expressive qualities (in the various octave registers) of the various instruments and ensembles, and in the gradual internalization of the sound of the different categories of instruments (percussions, woodwinds and strings)[60]. Rimsky-Korsakov himself acknowledged the importance of the immediate experience of sound when recalling that he had had the opportunity of «hearing all my works performed by the excellent orchestra of the St Petersburg Opera»[61]. Once entirely assimilated, however, the orchestral sound had to be handled in some way, that is by means of a given 'technology'. Now, in the tradition of Western art music this technology was provided by music writing, which in turn relied on a conceptualization of sound phenomena according to an implicit distinction between 'primary' musical parameters concerning pitch and temporal structure — pitches, intervals, rhythm, metric hierarchies — and 'secondary' parameters like loudness, and timbre. This distinction is embedded not only in traditional music notation and in its underlying music theory, but also in the very organization of the method of composition of Western art music, as used by Rimsky, Stravinsky and many other nineteenth- and twentieth-century composers. In fact, the other important thing to be said about Rimsky-Korsakov's *Principles of Orchestration* is precisely that the art of orchestration was inseparable from the art of counterpoint and harmony. In the preface to the *Principles of Orchestration* , Maximilian Steinberg — Rimsky-Korsakov's student, son-in-law, and editor — noted that in his teaching, Rimsky-Korsakov «repeated the axiom that A good orchestration», he maintained, «means proper handling of parts»[62]. Not by chance, the second chapter of Rimsky-Korsakov's treatise begins with a summary of practical voice leading. As Paul Matthew notes, the emphasis on both orchestral colour and counterpoint, as found in Rimsky-Korsakov's *Principles*, was «[...] the emblematic feature of New German orchestration and its dominating influence on fin-de-siécle composers»[63]. Now, 'handling of parts', means 'handling of primary parameters of pitch and rhythm through musical writing (not in an abstract 'mind', nor directly in performance). Since counterpoint and harmony, as compositional techniques, both relied on the technology of music writing, also orchestration depended, to some extent, on this technology.

The close relationship between orchestration and the evolution of written composition techniques of pitch organization, such as counterpoint and harmony, was clearly recognized by Stravinsky. In the *Conversations*, in a long answer to Craft's question «What is good

---

[60].   RIMSKY-KORSAKOV 1964, pp. 3-4. See GRIFFITHS 2013, p. 57.

[61].   RIMSKY-KORSAKOV 1964, p. 2.

[62].   *Ibidem*, p. x.

[63].   MATTHEWS 2006, p. 117.

instrumentation?» he maintained, first, that this was «when you are unaware that it is instrumentation» — meaning that the word 'instrumentation' itself concealed a wrong vision of an orchestral piece as a 'instrumented piano piece' — but immediately after he added that...

> Many composers still do not realize that our principal instrumental body today, the symphony orchestra, is the creation of harmonic-triadic music. They seem unaware that the growth of the wind instruments from two to three to four to five of a kind parallels a harmonic growth. It is extremely difficult to write polyphonically for this harmonic body, which is why Schoenberg in his polyphonic Variations for Orchestra is obliged to double, treble, and quadruple the lines[64].

Both Rimsky-Korsakov and Stravinsky recognized the importance of the harmonic and contrapuntal organization of music for orchestration. Insomuch as harmony and counterpoint can be viewed as composition techniques based on music notation, we can say that also orchestration relied to some extent on the technology of music writing. Given the affinity and complementarity between this technology and the use of the keyboard as a compositional tool — as we have seen — we can only conclude that the impact of the piano on the orchestral 'writing' was not necessarily greater, nor worse, than that of music notation or any other technology used in music composition.

Ways of the Hand, Keys, Steps

The most important contribution that Charles Joseph and Graham Griffiths' studies gave to our understanding of the role of the piano in Stravinsky's creativity consists, as I see it, is in the importance they attached to the *fingers* — more than to the piano *per se* — as a source of musical ideas. They helped us to ask ourselves a crucial question: how did *the fingers' movements* on the piano provide Stravinsky with musical ideas? Many examples in Griffiths' book demonstrate that in Stravinsky's music some aspects of the piano technique become real compositional materials. An important pianistic-technical aspect considered by Griffiths concerns, for example, piano fingerings: Griffiths noted that several musical ideas of the *Sonata* (1924), for example, correspond to particular fingering patterns of the piano studies of Isidor Philipp, a piano teacher with whom Stravinsky had been studying in Paris in the early 1920s, in view of his first concert tours[65]. Something similar occurs in other piano pieces from the

---

[64]. *Conversations*, p. 27.

[65]. Griffiths 2013, pp. 173-185. See also Griffiths 2005. Philipp's didactic work from which Stravinsky draws is the *Complete School of Technique for the Pianoforte*, Philadelphia, Theodor Presser, 1908. The whole question is reconsidered in Carr 2014, pp. 275-277.

neoclassical period, such the *Capriccio* (1928-1929), in which Stravinsky employed studies, exercises or fingering schemes as if they were musical ideas in themselves, rather than mere technical expedients of the piano performance. The idea that piano fingering patterns may provide Stravinsky with musical ideas for his composition was not entirely new: as early as 1992 Robert Craft had suggested that «to compare the sketch and published score of the [...] *Sonata* is to discover that piano fingerings were a part of the composing process, though Stravinsky might remove them later as a builder does his scaffolding»[66]. A similar idea had been developed by Charles Joseph, who also noted that some passages of the *Capriccio* almost literally take up piano figures from the studies of Op. 337 by Carl Czerny, which also provided various musical material for the *Concerto for piano and wind instruments* (1923-1924)[67]. Joseph also found confirmation of his hypothesis in Stravinsky's annotations on the copy of Czerny's studies held in his personal library at the Paul Sacher Foundation.

However, in the following pages I will follow a different — but complementary — path to that based on piano 'fingering' — in the traditional sense of the word, that is the act of choosing and prescribing which fingers are to be used on each note — as employed by Joseph and Griffiths. I will reconsider the issue more from the point of view of cognitive theory, above all Menary's notion of 'encultured hand'. Put in the simplest way, my idea is that Stravinsky conceptualized his harmonic procedures in part in terms of hand position ('ways of the hands') and in part in terms of distances (steps) between the keys, and that this was the result of his bodily approach to the problem posed by a conflict between the particular (asymmetric) shape of the piano keyboard and the systematic use of harmonic procedures based on the symmetrical division of the octave. In just five words: 'way of the hand' and 'steps'[68]. But to explain this idea, I must briefly recall some well-known historical facts about keyboard instruments and harmony.

The traditional arrangement of the keys in 7 (white, down) + 5 (black, up), was originally conceived with a view to an asymmetric organization of the pitches within the octave, with the black keys standing for unequal (asymmetric) alterations of the notes of the heptaphonic diatonic scale according to various types of tuning: just intonation, Pythagorean tuning, meantone temperaments etc. After the mid-eighteenth century, with the gradual introduction of equal temperament in keyboard and fixed-pitched instruments, the equal temperament of the black keys (each black key standing for both the ascending ♯ and descending ♭ alteration) allowed for the transposition of any chord or scale on every key, but due to the asymmetric arrangement of the keys the hand had to assume different positions and make different

---

[66]. CRAFT 1992, p. 329.

[67]. JOSEPH 2001, p. 80. According to Soulima Stravinsky — with whom Joseph studied piano at the University of Illinois — he and his father had familiarized with Czerny's studies in 1921, when they were in Biarritz. See Soulima Stravinsky's testimony quoted *ibidem*, p. 91.

[68]. I'm borrowing the expression «ways of the hand» from David Sudnow's book (SUDNOW 2001) I will discuss shortly.

movements to reproduce the same chord or the same melody at different transposition levels. These positions and movements, therefore, had to be deeply assimilated (embodied) through practice and exercise. The whole tradition of piano pedagogy can be conceived as a cultural practice aimed at making it possible to reproduce the same structures (scales and chords) regardless of their level of transposition, using each time the position of the hand (chords) and the appropriate fingering (melodies) in an immediate and pre-reflective way. As a way, in other words, to learn the correct 'way of the hand' for each chord and each scale in whatever position on the keyboard.

Between the end of the nineteenth century and the first decades of the twentieth century, the dissolution of tonal harmony led to the affirmation of new modalities of pitch organizations that relied systematically on the symmetric subdivision of the octave. Many composers from all over Europe began to use harmonic procedures based on enharmonic change ($\sharp = \flat$) in a much more systematic way and characterized by symmetrical properties: parallel harmonies, exact inversions of melodies or chords, symmetrical collections such as the whole-tone and octatonic scales, third- or tritone-related chord progressions that divides the octave in equal steps ('false' progressions), and complete circles of intervals (e.g. chords for thirds, fourths or fifths). Authors as different as Berg, Bartók, Schoenberg, Webern, Stravinsky, Scriabin all adopted, albeit in very varied ways, constructive criteria based on symmetry[69]. In Russian and French music between the two centuries harmonic procedures based on parallel voice leading became very widespread — a typical example is movement in parallel fifths. The essential peculiarity of these procedures is the idea of symmetrically transforming the same construct within a symmetric diastematic 'space'. They all imply a vision of harmony no longer based on acoustic criteria, such as the consonance-dissonance opposition, but rather according to a spatial-visual metaphoric conceptualization. This phenomenon was developed for multiple historical-cultural reasons, including the great importance assumed by the concept of symmetry, understood in a mathematical sense (as a transformation that produce an invariance), in the sciences (mathematics, geometry, psychology, studies on perception, *Gestaltpsychologie*, natural sciences), and in the visual arts[70]. In the musical domain, however, a decisive role was played by the cognitive-metaphoric representation of pitches as discrete points in space by means of music notation, and by the definitive consolidation of equal temperament in both musical theory and musical practice[71]. All the above mentioned

---

[69]. In Schoenberg and his pupils, symmetry even assumed a more concealed, but also more fundamental role: it can be seen not only in the inversion (*Umkehrung*) of the twelve-tone row, but also in the internal structuring of the series itself, such as the use of the 'inversional combinatoriality' of the two hexachords. On the inversional balance as an organizing principle in Schoenberg's music there is a huge analytical literature: see for example Lewin 1962; Lewin 1968. See Perle 1991, pp. 98-99 for an overview.

[70]. Bernstein 1993; Locanto 2007.

[71]. Equal temperament was only gradually adopted in the various European countries during the late eighteenth century and the first half of the nineteenth century.

harmonic procedures based on symmetry, in fact, were ultimately based on the possibility of considering the enharmonic notes to be equivalent both acoustically and from the point of view of theory. On the contrary, music theorists of the nineteenth century always considered the natural intervals of the harmonic series as the theoretical basis of harmony[72]; and many theorists and manufacturers proposed keyboard instruments based on natural intervals, with more than 12 keys per octave (such as Arthur von Oettingen's Orthotonophonium, with an Enharmonium in which the octave is divided into 72 or 53 pitches, and with which almost any chord with pure thirds, fourths and fifths can be played)[73]. Let us consider for example the whole-tone scale: if we try to write it with the traditional notation system based on the seven notes and ascending or descending alterations, at a certain point of the scale we will be forced to assume an enharmonic equivalence to close the cycle.

$$c - d - e - f\sharp - g\sharp - a\sharp$$
$$\downarrow$$
$$b\flat - (c)$$

It is no mere coincidence, then, that from the early twentieth century new theories of harmony began to appear that questioned the long positivist theoretical tradition, according to which harmony was based on natural intervals — which do *not* symmetrically divide the octave into equal parts — thus raising the intervals of equal temperament to the level of the theoretical basis of modern harmony, and not only as a necessary compromise between theory and practice — due to the constructive and practical-executive requirements of fixed-intonation instruments. The question was formulated in very clear terms by the French composer and music theorist René Lenormand in 1912: «Will [the composers]» he wondered, «adopt, in theory, the division of the octave into twelve equal semitones, as it in practice exists for instruments with fixed sounds? That will not change the sound of the music but would modify the theory and banish the accidental signs ♯ and ♭»[74]. Many theorists, in fact, also called for a new musical notation — or a reform of traditional notation — that abolished the difference between the two signs of alteration (♯ and ♭).

Returning to the keyboard, an imaginary instrument whose physical layout corresponded to the cognitive structures of the early nineteenth-century 'symmetric' musical practice had to be constructed with twelve keys per octave with identical shape, position, and size. In this way the hand could always assume the same position for the same chord, at any transposition level.

---

[72]. The whole issue is examined in LOCANTO 2007.

[73]. Von Oettingen conceived this instrument in 1870, but the first models were not developed and built until 1914.

[74]. LENORMAND 1915, p. viii.

Let us think of a major triad: in a keyboard such as that represented in the upper part of Ex. 1, it would be played always in the same position, whatever the point of the keyboard at which it is placed, because both the number of steps and the shape of the keys between the three notes are identical. By contrast, on a traditional piano keyboard (below in the same example) the position of the hand changes according to the starting point on which the triad is constructed, since even though the intervals between the notes remains the same (in terms of half steps = semitones), the combination of white/black keys will be different according to the relative position of the chord in respect to the 7 + 5 arrangement of the keyboard.

Ex. 1: Above: transposition of a major triad in a ideal symmetrical keyboard; below: transposition of the same triad in a traditional keyboard.

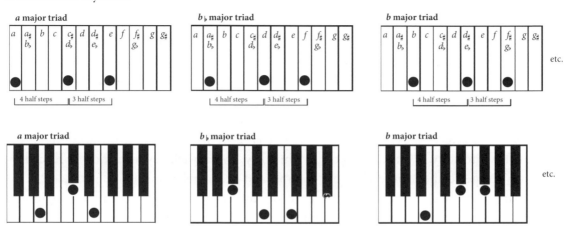

Of course, keyboards such as that imagined in Ex. 1 never came into use (not least because they would make it very difficult to perform any diatonic scale). My example was only a challenging way to show that the symmetric translation of harmonic constructs (harmony or melodies) within the asymmetric space of a traditional keyboard is an operation that, as simple as it may seem, is not so immediate to be performed in improvisation, unless the 'musically encultured hand' has fully mastered the positions of the chords and is thus able to perform it without having to reflect about the operation it is carrying out. There are two basic ways in which this operation can be done: 1) by using some familiar harmonic constructs whose 'ways of the hand' have already been consolidated in a given musical cultural practice; 2) by developing a greater ability in immediately identifying on the keyboard the number of whole steps and half steps to be performed to obtain the desired result, also regardless of the fingering and of the hand position to be adopted.

These two ways correspond precisely to the two above mentioned criteria ('way of the hand' and 'steps'): The first consists of exploiting the ability of an 'encultured hand' to translate at ease some well-assimilated harmonic constructs. In the Russian and neoclassical period these chords are mostly traditional examples made by stacking thirds (to form triads, seventh chords, ninth chords and various kinds of augmented sixth chords) but are also derived from common simple melodic material such as those based on the minor tetrachord. These constructs, in fact, are entirely embodied as 'ways of the hand' which can be reproduced in real-time improvisation on whatever point of the keyboard (mostly according to a referential collection such as the octatonic collection).

This operation, however, is much more difficult when the constructs to be symmetrically translated or inverted are unfamiliar chromatic harmonies and melodies. This may require some different skill than the use of use of well-established 'ways of the hand'. Not surprisingly — given the increasingly widespread use of procedures based on symmetry — some early nineteenth century musicians tried to find a solution to the problem. The one proposed by the German-American music theorist and music teacher Bernhard Ziehn — author of a 1912 treatise entitled *Canonical Studies*, containing a brief theoretical discussion and several musical examples based on the exact symmetrical inversion of intervals — relied precisely on the characteristics of the piano keyboard. His vast experience in piano pedagogy led Ziehn to realize that the exact inversion of intervals around *d* on the keyboard also produces an exact symmetry of keys, and therefore of fingering. As his musical example (ILL. 4) shows, when *d* is the centre of the inversion, a white key will map into another white key; and a black key into another black key. In this way the performer can rely on this «simple and clear» relationship[75].

Apart from these experiments, however, the difficulty created by the increasing use of unfamiliar harmonic constructs and the tendency towards the indistinct use of chromatic tones leads inevitably to the second criterion: the hands start looking for intervallic distances between the pitches in terms of the number of separating white/black keys. This approach increased considerably in Stravinsky's later years, when he gradually abandoned both the use of chords referable to common-practice harmony and his favourite referential collections such as the octatonic scale, in favour of a more direct and immediate method with intervals, or equally, with distances between keys. This criterion partially corresponded to and partially conflicted with serial techniques. The way Stravinsky faced this problem will be the subject of the second part of this chapter.

---

[75]. ZIEHN 1976, p. 23. Actually, the property also applies to the note *a♭*. Ziehn's method can be seen as a modern version (allowing for the inversion of chromatic harmonies and melodies, based on equal temperament) to the *contrarium reversum*, a technique illustrated by a long series of composition treatises, from the Giovanni Maria Bononcini's *Musico prattico* (1673) to the Simon Sechter *Grundsätze der musikalischen Komposition* (1853-1854). Ziehn's theories were anything but solitary speculation. They were greatly admired by influent theorists and musicians, especially Ferruccio Busoni whose *Fantasia contrappuntistica* was strongly influenced by Busoni's theories on symmetrical inversion.

Ueber die symmetrische Umkehrung

Die überwiegende Mehrzahl der hier darge-botenen Canons ist auch in symmetrischerUm-kehrung dargestellt. Diese Umkehrung ist das chromatisch erweiterte Contrarium reversum, das sich nur auf das Ionische und Aeolische bezog, und zwar ohne Beachtung der von jeher zulässigen, chromatischen Beifügungen: im Ioni-schen übermässige Prime, Quarte und Quinte, nebst kleiner Septime; im Aeolischen grosse Terz, Sexte und Septime, nebst kleiner Secunde. (S. „Die Musik", III, 3. Ueber die Kirchentöne.) Die symmetrische Umkehrung dagegen kennt keine Beschränkung.

Als Ausgangspunkt lässt sich irgend ein Ton annehmen; doch nur von *d* aus ergeben sich ein-fache und klare Verhältnisse.

On the Symmetrical Inversion

With but a few exceptions the canons con-tained in this book are also symmetrically inverted. This inversion is the classic Contra-rium reversum chromatically expanded. The symmetrical inversion is much more practica-ble, because it relates to any chromatic altera-tion, while the contrarium reversum was re-stricted to the Ionian and Aeolian modes only, and that without their characteristic addi-tions: augmented Prime, Fourth and Fifth, and small Seventh in the Ionian, and large Third, Sixth and Seventh, and small Second in the Aeolian mode.

Any tone may serve as a center, but from d only we receive relations simple and clear.

ILL. 4: A page from Bernhard Ziehn's 1912 *Canonical studies*, featuring the author's keyboard-oriented system for the symmetric inversion of chords and melodies (see ZIEHN 1976, p. 23).

To conclude this section, the expression 'ways of the hand' was suggested to me by the title (*Ways Of the Hand: The Organization of Improvised Conduct*) of the challenging book by the sociologist and jazz pianist David Sudnow (1978), a book that «speaks to many different constituencies of readers: sociologists, linguists, cognitive scientists, musicologists, teachers, and philosophers»[76]. Sudnow's most basic and original idea was precisely that a study that starts *directly* from the observation of the positions (or 'ways') of the hands over the keyboard would be better suited to the study of jazz improvisation than a theoretical description of the various types of scales and chords. His method relied on the observation of how the body acquires the skills of finding a certain order in the temporally unfolding experience[77]. He gave a detailed

---

[76]. SUDNOW 2001. The quotation is from Hubert Dreyfus' foreword to the 2001 edition.

[77]. Sudnow's approach was strongly influenced by Merleau-Ponty's Phenomenology of Perception: «Sitting at the piano, trying to make sense of what was happening, and studying Merleau-Ponty's discussions of embodiment,

description of how the hands of a jazz pianist acquire the skills to perform an increasingly complex set of functions. His starting point was the substitution of the music-theoretical notion of 'intervals' with the simple distances between the keys, expressed in terms of half steps (the distance from a note to the immediately adjacent higher [on the right] or lower [on the left] one, regardless of its black/white colour) or whole steps (the sum of two half steps):

Ex. 2: From SUDNOW 2001, p. 7: half steps and whole steps on a traditional 7 w + 5 b keyboard.

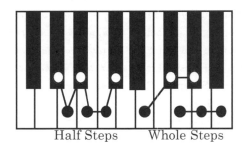

Half Steps   Whole Steps

Then Sudnow described the positions assumed by the hands (in terms of half steps and steps) in various basic harmonic constructs used in jazz improvisation. His description precedes by steps: first scales, then chords, and so on. In this way he showed how, after much experience, the hand finds itself able to use these constructs as ready-to use objects, by assuming the correct 'way' without having to 'think' any more about them, and finally begins to apply these 'ways' within formal schemas and patterns. Although my use of the term 'way of the hand' in the following pages is not entirely in keeping with Sudnow's theory — which is applied to a different object, in which improvisation plays a quite different role than in Stravinsky's 'improvisation on paper' — I will often make reference to this concept.

SYMMETRIES OVER THE KEYBOARD: FROM RIMSKY-KORSAKOV TO STRAVINSKY

Symmetry — arguably the most important principle of Stravinsky's harmonic language — was to a good extent another legacy that he inherited from Rimsky-Korsakov's teaching. The use of harmonies based on the symmetrical division of the octave was a distinctive trait of Rimsky-Korsakov's own harmonic language, especially in his last compositions. Rimsky-Korsakov attached great importance to the study of harmony, even more than counterpoint. Although his teaching of contrapuntal techniques was decisive in making Stravinsky a complete 'Russian musician' — as Griffiths has brilliantly pointed out[78] — it can be said that harmony, rather than counterpoint,

---

I found myself, in his own terms, "not so much encountering a new philosophy as recognizing what [one] had been waiting for". A copy of his Phenomenology always remains close at hand». *Ibidem*, p. 131, fn. 5.

78.   On the importance of the counterpoint in Stravinsky's musical training see GRIFFITHS 2013, pp. 2-12.

was the most distinctive and original component of his compositional thought, musical style and teaching methods. Before his *Uchebnik garmonii* (Manual of Harmony) appeared in 1884-1885, the most influential textbook of harmony in Russia was Tchaikovsky's *Rukovodstvo k prakticheskomu izucheniyu garmonii* (A Guide to the Practical Study of Harmony) of 1871[79]. Rimsky-Korsakov conceived to a large extent his treatise as an attempt to update Tchaikovsky's manual, by modifying some aspects that he considered no longer adequate to the harmony of his time[80]. Both Tchaikovsky's and Rimsky-Korsakov's manuals, however, emphasized the role of harmony over counterpoint. According to Philip Ewell, «Rimsky-Korsakov felt that writings on harmony were at a higher conceptual level than writings on counterpoint, which was simply a subject to be learned in order to enter the world of harmony»[81]. One of the most innovative and original aspects of Rimsky-Korsakov's 1884-1885 manual was precisely the discussion of chord progressions based on the symmetrical subdivision of the octave. An entire section (chapter XIV), entitled 'False Progressions Outside the Limits of a Tonality, and Cyclic Modulations' was dedicated to illustrating various types of symmetrical (non-tonal) harmonic chord sequences ('false [= enharmonic] progressions') in which the bass moves in major thirds, minor thirds, and whole tones[82]. Although by 1884 chord progression of this kind had become quite common in the music of composers from all over Europe, their theoretical discussion was no doubt forward thinking[83]. Ex. 3 reproduces a false major-third progression in the major mode from Rimsky-Korsakov's textbook[84]. Interestingly enough from our point of view, in each of such examples Rimsky-Korsakov wrote the progression first according to the rule of the smoothest voice leading — the

Ex. 3: Rimsky-Korsakov 1884-1885, p. 221: 'False major-third progressions in the major mode' (as reproduced in Ewell 2020, p. 125).

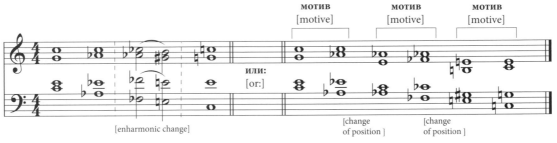

79. Rimsky-Korsakov 1884-1885; Tchaikovsky 1957.

80. See Ewell 2020, p. 123. Carpenter 1988, p. 314.

81. Ewell 2020, p. 124.

82. Rimsky-Korsakov 1884-1885, pp. 225-245. Some pages from this section of the treatise, are reproduced in Taruskin 1996, pp. 304-306. See also Ewell 2020, p. 125. In addition to Ewell and Taruskin this part of Rimsky-Korsakov's textbook has been discussed by a few other musicologists. See Ewell 2020, p. 124, fn. 11 for references.

83. As Ewell 2020, p. 124, notes. Probably due to its excessive modernity the chapter on false progressions was not included in the 1886 edition of Rimsky-Korsakov's book.

84. Rimsky-Korsakov 1960, p. 221.

Ex. 4: Above: Transposition of a dominant seventh chord on the (0 3 6 9) partition of the octave. Below: the same rewritten whit voice-leading (Rimsky Korsakov's 'False minor-third progressions in the major mode').

Dominant sevenths on (0 3 6 9)

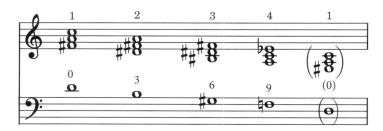

False progression along the cirle of minor thirds

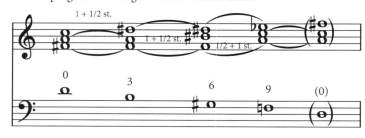

Octatonic cllection, model B (t-s, descending)

one in which each voice performs the shortest possible movement (from a neighbouring tone) — and then as a threefold statement on the symmetrical divisions of the octave — in this case on semitones 0, 4, and 8 starting from the first note of the scale — of the same two-chord model (which he calls 'motif'). The first chord of each motif is the same as the first chord of the previous motif, but in a different (close instead of open) position. In this way, while avoiding consecutive fifths and octaves, Rimsky-Korsakov can repeat three times the same chords on semitones 0, 4, 7 and 10 of the octave — articulation (0 4 7 10). This shows that behinds the 'false progressions' (even when voiced according to the traditional rules of voice leading) there is the idea of a symmetrical translation of the same chord within the space of the 12 equal tempered semitones.

Both aspects have consequences for the movements of the fingers and the 'ways of the hand'. To understand why, let us first consider Ex. 4, which represents a complete cycle of four dominant sevenths whose basses, a minor third apart, divide the twelve semitones into four equal parts, according to the articulation into 0, 3, 6, and 9 semitones from the first note of the scale; this is a 'false progression along the cycle of minor thirds', according to Rimsky-Korsakov's nomenclature. In the upper part of the example the sequence is realized with no voice-leading at all, only as the translation of the same dominant seventh chord on the four levels of the symmetrical partition of the octave. In the lower part, the sequence is rewritten in the form of a 'false' progression'. The performance of the dominant seventh chords in the translation (with no voice-leading) is made easier (for the hand) by the fact that these are traditional (in the common-practice period) chords and can be handled as 'ready-to-use' objects: the classical training in common-practice harmony made the hands embody the correct positions to reproduce these chords on the keyboard starting with any white or black key, despite the asymmetrical 7 + 5 layout. So, an 'enculturated hand' can improvise with these chords even without the brain having to make conscious reference to the codified system of rules, and according to entirely different criteria, such as those based on the division of the octave in equal steps. On the other hand, a chord progression with smooth voice-leading allows a different, but no less 'rational' (for the fingers) criterion: at each chord one of the three upper parts, alternatively, moves up of three half steps (a minor third, but I prefer to count the intervals as distances for the fingers) either in the form of whole step + half step or the reverse.

It is difficult to say whether it is easier for the hand to perform the sequence without voice leading or with voice leading. This, however, is not so important: what my example aims to demonstrate is that the two modalities correspond to two different cognitive approaches: in the first case (without voice leading) what is important is the assimilation of the various positions and movements (the 'way of the hand') that the hand must perform to reproduce the same chord in the various points of the keyboard. In this case the focus is on the whole chords. In the second case (with voice leading), instead, the focus is on the repetitive movements (steps) of the individual fingers. Since these steps are also unequal, depending on where they are placed on the keyboard — three half steps (a minor third) can correspond to the distance between: a black and a white key, a white and a black key, two white keys, and two black keys — the ability to extemporaneously perform the correct sequence distance depends on the ability of the fingers to correctly 'translate' the distance of the minor third each time into the correct combination of keys. The use of similar symmetrical progressions, thus greatly boosts the development of this skill, encouraging the fingers to 'think', so to speak, of the intervals in terms of steps and half steps on the keyboard. The thesis that I will develop in the second part of the chapter, in fact, is that the growing sensitivity to Stravinsky's intervals, culminating in his late serial production, is the consequence of this cognitive process.

Clearly enough, my discussion of Rimsky-Korsakov's chord progressions assumes that, in addition to being studied in theory and written on paper, they were also systematically performed on the keyboard. In fact, Rimsky-Korsakov's teaching method strongly encouraged the study of harmony at the piano. In his overall music-pedagogical approach the use of this instrument was more closely related to the study of harmony than to counterpoint. At the end of each example of the chapter devoted to the 'false progressions' of his manual, there is usually an indication such as «complete the progression» or «elaborate with chromatic passing tones»; and despite some prescriptions that require the student to «write» the progressions in different forms (in the parallel minor key, in the ascending — instead of descending — form, etc.) Rimsky-Korsakov wanted this to be done, most likely, both in writing and on the keyboard. More generally, Rimsky-Korsakov's manual of harmony entrusted playing the piano with a decidedly more important role than many other late-nineteenth century pedagogical approaches, which aimed at providing the student with the ability to compose 'in the mind' (really: in writing) without the potentially 'harmful' aid of the musical instrument. In the preface to the second edition (1886) of the manual — in which the word *'Practical'* was suggestively added to the previous title — Rimsky-Korsakov wrote that: «[…] the student should be able to perform on the piano […] any harmonic succession of chords and progressions, and to prelude in any key»[85]. The Russian musicologist Elmira Fatykhova-Okuneva, drawing on the notebooks that Aleksandr Glazunov used in his harmony classes with Rimsky-Korsakov in 1879-1880, concluded that «a significant part of his lessons was devoted to modulations. Rimsky-Korsakov provided the student with a modulation plan, whose execution was either written out or not fixed on paper (these were likely played on the piano)»[86].

The use of symmetric chord progressions of the type used in Rimsky-Korsakov's music and discussed in his manual had no doubt a decisive impact on the musical language of the young Stravinsky. However, in Stravinsky's music a process that was already enshrined in Rimsky-Korsakov took place much more quickly and radically: the symmetrical chord progressions and the symmetrical partition of the octave led to both the conceptualization and the systematic use of these harmonic procedures as the consequence (not the cause) of the symmetrical scales: in extreme synthesis, the progressions by major thirds and whole tones corresponded to the whole-tone scale; the progressions by minor thirds corresponded to the octatonic scale (see again the bass part in the Exs. 3 and 4).

Octatonicism has been recognized as the most distinctive aspect of Stravinsky's harmonic language (and not only in his early compositions) both by analysts (since Arthur Berger and Pieter van den Toorn's studies) and by those historical musicologists, such as Richard Taruskin, who tends to consider it from the point of view of the history of compositional techniques[87]. It is interesting, then, to reconsider this scale in the perspective of Sudnow's 'ways of the hands' and of his distinction between 'chordal' and 'scalar' way.

We don't know when the octatonic collection began to be considered as a self-standing 'scale', and not, rather, as the consequence of the use of chord progressions based on the symmetrical subdivision of the octave, as was typical of much music of the second half of the nineteenth century. According to Taruskin, the first explicit mention of the term 'tone-semitone

---

[85]. RIMSKY-KORSAKOV 2005, p. 4.
[86]. FATYKHOVA-OKUNEVA 2008.
[87]. VAN DEN TOORN 1983; BERGER 1963.

scale' (*gamma ton-poluton*) in a Russian printed text appeared in a 1900 article by Rimsky-Korsakov's pupil and friend Vasily Iastrebtsev[88]. Yet, it is clear — as Taruskin himself has demonstrated — that its historical origins lie in the late-romantic harmonic practice, in which the progressions of triads and seventh chords along the circle of the major and minor thirds had become quite common, especially in the music of composer-pianists such as Franz Liszt[89]. If so, we can conclude that the octatonic scale has its origins in the tendency to manipulate chords on the keyboard according to a symmetrical logic; that is in a chordal 'way of the hand'.

However, the octatonic collection can also be conceived as a purely linear (scalar) construct, that is as a succession of the finger's steps and half steps. In this respect it is suggestive to note that the first full discussion of this scale outside Russia is contained in a little manual of 1930 by the Italian composer and pianist Vito Frazzi, entitled *Scale alternate. Per pianoforte* (Alternated scales. For piano), and that this is not a book of music theory (a treatise on harmony) but rather a manual devoted to piano pedagogy, as the title itself clearly shows[90]. The last section of the book contains 25 exercises for piano with various kinds of 'alternate scales' (that is, octatonic scales, since they alternate whole tones and semitones) to be played in parallel and contrary motion, in thirds, sixths, double thirds and double sixths, as in ordinary piano training with diatonic heptatonic scales. The fingerings had been provided by the renowned Italian pianist Ernesto Consolo. The first part of the manual also contained a brief theoretical description of the characteristics and properties of the '*scale alternate*'. Here Frazzi stated that modern composers had at their disposal three well-defined 'systems' — the diatonic, the hexatonic and the alternate system — and that it would therefore be interesting to analyze the «most important modern compositions», in order to understand «how the composers have so far applied this [alternate] system and what are its likely developments»[91]. Clearly enough, however, the purpose of Frazzi's manual is not primarily music-analytical or theoretical, and — what is most interesting for us — he seems to conceive the '*scala alternata*' as a harmonic construct deeply rooted in modern piano practice. ILL. 5 shows Ernesto Consolo's ingenious system for representing in the most synthetic way all the possible fingerings for each form of the

---

[88]. TARUSKIN 1996, p. 298. According to Taruskin, around 1900 the term had already been in use for some time in Rimsky-Korsakov's circle: Iastrebtsev's diaries contain clear evidence that in 1900 it had been used for at least five years.

[89]. TARUSKIN 1996, pp. 255-305.

[90]. FRAZZI 1930: see SANGUINETTI 1993. Frazzi studied organ and composition in Parma, and then spent most of his life at the Conservatory of Florence, where he was first appointed in 1912 as professor of supplementary piano, and later (from 1924) of harmony and counterpoint and (from 1926) composition. From 1932 to 1963 he taught at the Accademia Musicale Chigiana in Siena. As a composer, Frazzi was strongly influenced by the music of Ildebrando Pizzetti. However, his compositions also show some individual traits, in particular an extensive use of melodic and harmonic patterns derived from the octatonic scale.

[91]. FRAZZI 1930, pp. 8-9.

scale, also in the typical forms and combinations of the traditional piano pedagogy (in contrary motion, in thirds and double thirds, in sixth and double sixths, in octaves).

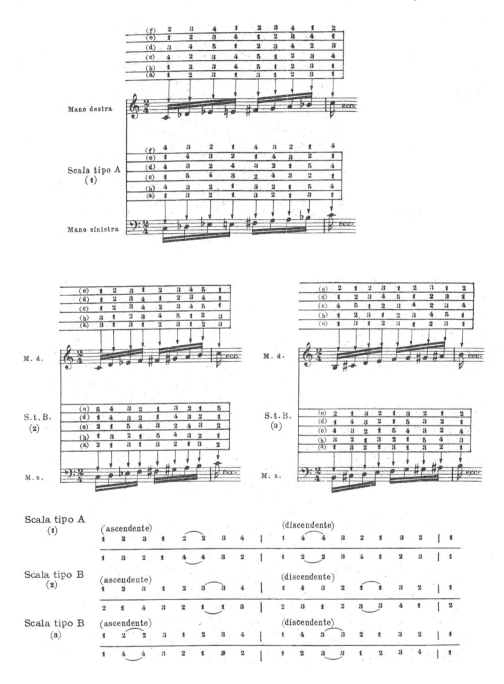

ILL. 5: FRAZZI 1930, p. 11. Ernesto Consolo's fingerings for the octatonic scale.

In addition to the octatonic scale, Stravinsky used extensively, from his earliest compositions, several other types of scales that had become very important in Russian and French music of the time. Some of these, such as the whole-tone scale, are also symmetrical constructs; others, such as modal heptaphonic diatonic scales, are of a non-symmetrical type. A particular category, widely used by Stravinsky both in the Russian and in the neoclassical period, are the diatonic collections obtained by superimposition of perfect fifths/fourths. Consider, just to give a well-known example, the cycle $e_\flat$ - $b_\flat$ - f - c entrusted to the bass part at no. [16] of *Les Augures printaniers* in *The Rite of Spring*, which then expands up to five fifths ($e_\flat$ - $b_\flat$ - f - c - g - d) with the addition of g and d in the wind (trumpets and horn) parts.[92] If considered in scalar form ($b_\flat$ - c - d - $e_\flat$ - f - g - [a]) such harmonies are not symmetrical, as they form portions of the diatonic scales. According to George Perle, this contrast between symmetrical and non-symmetrical elements is the most characteristic feature of the music of the *Rite of Spring*[93]. From the point of view of my approach, Perle's observation could be translated in terms of a dialectic between two different ways of managing harmonic constructs on the keyboard: according to an essentially acoustic logic, in which the acoustical quality of intervals, scales and chords is still more important than the subdivision of the octave into equal parts; and according to geometrical logic, which privileges the symmetrical subdivision of the octave over other (phonic) criteria.

Stravinsky's use of the octatonic scale in *The Rite of Spring* is unique insomuch as it exploits its internal tetrachord structure in an original way: one which allows the simultaneous use of two distinct parts of the scale that present different notes but the same intervallic structure. I suggest that this use, too, can be viewed as a keyboard-oriented practice, as the result of an ideal split of the scale between the two hands according to its intervallic structure. Hereafter, therefore, we should consider the intervals in terms of both semitones and number of 'half steps'. This also applies to the numbers in round brackets representing the symmetric partitions of the octatonic scales, which will always stand both for semitones/half steps. For example:

(0 3 6 9) = number of semitones/half steps starting from the first (lowest or highest, according to model A or model B) note of the octatonic scale.

The most obvious way to perform an octatonic scale is to play it with just one hand with the passage of the thumb (see for example the fingering proposed by Consolo). However, it is intriguing to think that by using both hands one can also *simultaneously* play two of the four identical tetrachords — 0134 or 0235 according to model A or B —, that can be found at the (0 3 6 9) symmetric articulation points of the octave. Let's consider for example Model B

---

[92].   On interval cycles in Stravinsky's music see Antokoletz 1986.
[93].   Perle 1990, p. 83. See also Meyer 2013, p. 18.

(tone-semitone - descending): it can be obtained by playing the two minor tetrachords (tone-semitone-tone = whole step - half step - whole step) of a Dorian scale (D-scale) separated by a tritone (**6** semitones = 6 half steps) instead of a perfect fifth (7 semitones = 7 half steps), thus creating a major seventh (**11** semitones = 11 half steps) — instead of an octave — between the first and last note, as can be seen in Ex. 5.

Ex. 5: Tetrachord structure of the octatonic scale and simultaneous use of the hands.

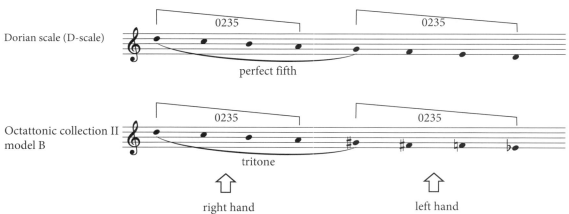

The simultaneous use of diatonic tetrachords and/or chords according to the symmetrical subdivision of the octave into a tritone + perfect fourth, or a perfect fourth + tritone (depending on whether one starts from the highest or lowest note), that is the well-known — to music analysts — (0 5/6 11) articulation, is precisely what, according to Taruskin, distinguishes Stravinsky's original way of using the octatonic scale in *The Rite of Spring*, if compared to Rimsky-Korsakov's 'traditional' way — the progressions of triads and seventh chords along the cycle of the minor thirds[94]. In fact, many popular and folk-like melodies used by Stravinsky in *The Rite* are based on the four notes of a minor tetrachord, and are placed against another tetrachord (or a chord) at a distance of a tritone and/or a major seventh. This can clearly be seen in the original 1913 version for two pianos, whose division of the musical material between the hands of the two pianists often reflects the original conception of the piece[95]. For example, in the *Jeux des cités rivales*, at nos. [64-65]) the tetrachords 0235 are always entrusted at the two hand at the distance of a tritone — articulation (0 5) — or a major seventh — (0 11) interval span (in Ex. 6 the tetrachord *g - f - e - d* (in the upper part of the melody in parallel thirds and *c♯ - b - a♯ - g♯*, a tritone apart, are played at the same time, thus producing, overall, a whole octatonic scale). To sum up: we can think of Stravinsky's

---

[94]. TARUSKIN 1996, pp. 935-941. VAN DEN TOORN 1987, pp. 145-146. VAN DEN TOORN 1983 usually refers to the (0 5 11) articulation.

[95]. STRAVINSKY 2013A.

234

'simultaneous' use of the octatonic scale as the result of a particular way of arranging the notes of the scale on the keyboard, by splitting them between the two hands according to their repetitive intervallic structure.

Ex. 6: Igor Stravinsky, *The Rite of Spring*, original four-hands piano version, *Jeux des cités rivales*, nos. [64-65]. Simultaneous use of tetrachord 0235.

Many typical octatonic situations of *The Rite of Spring* can be described as juxtapositions of two triads/seventh chords entrusted simultaneously to the two hands, which arrange them on the keyboard according to the (0 3 6 9) articulation. In these cases, Stravinsky's four-hand arrangement divides the harmonies — usually in close voicing — between the two hands. The *Jeu du rapt*, to give just one example, is entirely based on the juxtaposition of two dominant sevenths a minor third apart, entrusted to the two hands. This basic idea was reworked in the written phases of the creative process, by rearranging the notes of the two seventh chords

Ex. 7: Igor Stravinsky, *The Rite of Spring*, original four-hands piano version, *Jeu du rapt*, nn. [37-38]. Alternating dominant-seventh chords on articulation (0 3 6 9).

in different ways (in different inversions and positions) from the original improvisational arrangement, which simply entrusted a seventh chord to each hand. Ex. 7 shows the beginning of the piece at no. [37], in the version for piano four-hands. In the opening bars, two seventh chords, on *c* and *e*♭ respectively, rapidly alternate between the two hands of the first pianist on a semiquaver tremolo, while piano 2 provides the third note (the tritone, *f*♯) of the (0 3 6 9) articulation of octatonic collection III. In piano 1, the note *g*, the 5th of the dominant seventh chord on *c*, is shifted from the left hand to the right hand, where it corresponds to the 3rd of the dominant seventh on *e*♭. The latter is arranged in first inversion with the root and the 7th (*e*♭ - *d*♭) in the upper parts. Two bars later, the two pianists reverse their roles: piano 2 performs the seventh-chord tremolo, while piano 1 provides the accompaniment (this time based on a G-major diatonic scale). Then at no. [38], the tremolo is taken up again by piano 1, and the whole idea is repeated, this time on octatonic collection II: the two seventh chords in piano 1 are on $g\sharp$ and b respectively (at a tritone from the c - $e\flat$ of no. [37]) and the accompanying piano 2 provides the notes c - b of the (0 11) articulation of octatonic collection II. Here, the notes of the two dominant seventh chords are rearranged between the two hands of piano 1 in a yet different way: the 3rd (not the 5th) of the dominant seventh chord on $g\sharp$ is shifted from the left hand to the right hand, where it does *not* correspond to any of the notes of the dominant seventh chord on b. The latter is arranged in first inversion with the root and the seventh ($e\flat$ - $d\flat$) in the upper part and omitted 3rd and 5th. In cases like this, the idea of the juxtaposition of dominant seventh chords is not so far from the typical procedures *à la* Rimsky-Korsakov; however, Stravinsky exploits all the various combinational possibilities of the two hands in a unprecedented way. Arthur Berger, in fact, defined the *Jeu du rapt* as a sort of compendium of all the ways in which it is possible to connect two triads/ seventh chords a minor third apart[96].

Stravinsky's original approach to the octatonic scale in *The Rite of Spring* can be generalized in a more basic principle, which simply consists in entrusting to the two hands two identical melodic or harmonic *models* at a certain intervallic distance and then performing some chords or melodies. The juxtaposed constructs are usually quite common (traditional) chords or tetrachord, and this is very important in view of the strategies of an 'enculturated hand'. This basic principle is at work in many well-known and characteristic constructs of Stravinsky's harmonic language. We can think, for example, of the famous '*Petrushka* chord' (Ex. 8), which contains two major triads a tritone apart: what is interesting about their pairing is how the two triads are arpeggiated: the first is in root position; the second is in the first inversion. As trivial as it may seem, both chords are in close position with octave doubling of the lowest note: a very comfortable and natural position for the hand. The only difficulty that the two hands encounter in performing this musical gesture is given by the fact that the two triads overlap one another, thus preventing an easy performance (also the two hands should overlap). However, this situation can be imagined as the result of an ideal two-stage process; in the first stage (improvisation at the keyboard) the two triads are performed one octave apart on the keyboard; in the second (written) stage they are placed in the same octave 'on the paper', thus creating the alternation between consonant (major third) and extremely dissonant (second major second minor) vertical encounters, which is the most salient feature of this musical gesture. In short: we can think of the famous '*Petrushka* chord' as a very simple, but very effective gesture of the two hands reworked thanks to music writing. The fact that Stravinsky had also in mind the characteristic sound of the wind instruments, does not contradict the ultimate tactile origin of its harmonic structure.

---

[96].   Berger 1963, pp. 26-29.

Ex. 8: Igor Stravinsky, *Petrushka*, I, no. [49]. The '*Petrushka* chord' as a keyboard-oriented gesture.

A '*DANSE*' OF THE HANDS

In *The Rite of Spring*, the octatonic scale plays another important role: it works as a symmetrical framework within which harmonies of various types can be placed. The notes that serve as the support base for these constructs are precisely nos. (0), (5/6), and (11) of the scale. We can consider these points as a sort of system of space coordinates based on key-steps (half steps) within which quite common chords — even chords which do not entirely belong to that octatonic scale — can be placed by the two hands. The famous chord of *Les Augures printaniers*, just to cite a well-known example, can be conceived as the juxtaposition of two triads/seventh chords whose roots are placed on the extreme notes (0 11) of the (0 5/6 11) articulation of octatonic collection III, Model B (tone-semitone, descending) starting from e_b (upper note)[97]. The two chords, at their first appearance at p. 3 of the *Rite* sketchbook look this way (Ex. 9)[98].

• **right hand**: dominant seventh, in first inversion (bass = *g*) and close position, on note e_b, note 0 of octatonic collection III, model B.

---

[97].   For an overview of the various analytical interpretations of this famous chord see CHUA 2007, pp. 62-74.
[98].   STRAVINSKY 1969, p. 3.

- **left hand** = major triad in root and close position, with octave doubling, on *e*, note 11 of octatonic collection III, model B.

Ex. 9: The '*Augures* chord': derivation from the octatonic collection.

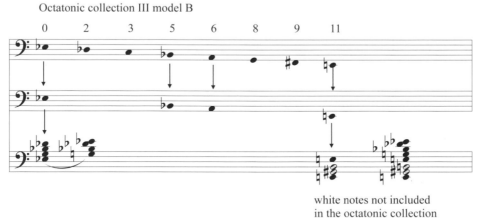

Octatonic collection III model B

white notes not included
in the octatonic collection

Ex. 10: The '*Augures* chord': derivation according to Pieter van den Toorn.

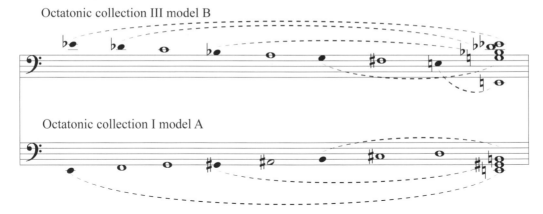

Octatonic collection III model B

Octatonic collection I model A

Note that I am not assuming the simultaneous presence of two different scales — let alone two different tonalities — as some theorists have done. According to Pieter van den Toorn, for example, the *Augures* chord would be better explained as an 'interference' between octatonic collection III model B starting (from the top) from *e♭*, and octatonic collection I model A (semitone-tone) starting (from the bottom) from *e*. (Ex. 10). Van den Toorn, in fact, assumes that all the notes of a musical passage should be related to some reference scale, and if they do not it must be assumed that two different scales are interacting at the same time at that point[99]. In comparison,

---

99. «[...] both G (A) and B of the motto chord are foreign to Collection III, while, excluding the important E, the pitch content of the chord refers equally to Collection I. Hence [...] the chord may smoothly accommodate blocks referring to either Collection III or Collection I». Van den Toorn 1987, p. 178.

my vision seems much more in keeping with Taruskin's 'historical' approach[100]. However, while conceiving the (0 5/6 11) articulation of collection as a framework, thus motivating the use of notes that do not belong to octatonic collection III, Taruskin's explanation does not provide a motivation for the use of traditional chords on these articulating points. On the contrary, this seems quite logical if we think of these chords as the objects of an 'encultured hand', which has so deeply assimilated the vocabulary of tonal harmony that it can easily displace them over the keyboard, even according to a non-tonal syntax.

In *The Rite of Spring*, in addition to working as 'reference points' on which common-practice chords can be placed, the articulation (0 5/6 11) also seems to work as a chord in itself: a sort of 'octatonic triad', so to speak. While not a traditional chord formed by stacking thirds, it is one of the most deeply internalized sounds by Stravinsky, who in his preliminary improvisations must have used it as a ready-to-use object that can be translated everywhere over the keyboard. Taruskin dubbed it the '*Rite* chord'; and in fact, it is the most characteristic sonority of the score[101].

However, the '*Rite* chord' is a 'chord' only in an improper sense. Traditionally, in fact, the concept of chords implies the possibility that the single constituent notes can be doubled and transposed, according to the various positions and inversions. On the contrary, the '*Rite* chord' is always in the same position (0 5/6 11), with the major seventh (eleven half steps) the two extreme notes and the third note in the middle at 5 or 6 semitones (half steps) from the bass. Only from time to time does Stravinsky opt for the form with the (11) and (0) swapped, which we could define as 'open position'. For example: the chord $c\sharp_4$ - $g_3/g\sharp_3$ - c_4 (close position) can become c_3 - $g_3/g\sharp_3$ - $c\sharp_4$. However, even this position can be easily played with one hand since the extension of a minor ninth is not prohibitive. The immovability of these sounds from their fixed positions shows how the so-called '*Rite* chord' is better understood as a 'way of the hand' based on the count of distances in terms of keys (steps) (Ex. 11):

- thumb on key 0;
- index finger on the key at 5/6 half steps from the first key;
- little finger on the key at 11 half steps from the first key (or 6/5 half steps from the index finger).

This characteristic hand gesture is deeply embedded in the *Rite's* music: in some sections, in particular, it can be seen almost everywhere over the staves of the sketches. The *Glorification de l'Élue*, for example, is entirely constructed by repetitions and translations of this 'chord'. In ILL. 6 I have reproduced three fragments of the *Rite* sketchbook containing three musical blocks, labelled *a*, *b*, *c*, from whose montage the entire piece takes shape. The musical materials are annotated in form of a drafted short score with multiple staves and instrumental cues. This

---

[100]. See TARUSKIN 1996, pp. 934-950.
[101]. See *ibidem*, p. 940.

Ex. 11: The '*Rite* chord' as a hand gesture.

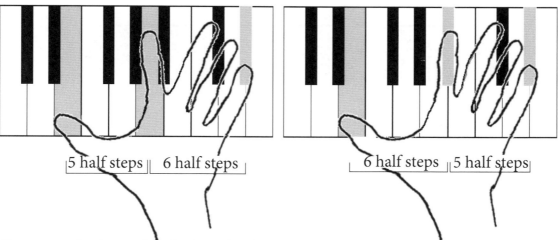

allows us to clearly visualize the '*Rite* chords' on the staves of the short score. If we looked only at the full score, instead, we would get a much less clear insight, since it displays the notes of the chord widely scattered between the various instruments and orchestral doubling. In block *a*, the '*Rite* chord' can be seen of the second staff of the system, where it moves chromatically from $f_{\times 4}$ - $c_{\sharp 4}$ - $g_{\sharp 3}$ (0 6 11) to $f_{\sharp 4}$ - $c_{\sharp 4}$ - $f_{\times 3}$ (0 5 11). Note that, thanks to the possibility of choosing between note (5) and note (6) of the (0 5/6 11) articulation, the central $c_{\sharp}$ is prolonged between the two chords, thus obtaining a parallel movement of major seventh between the extreme parts, and an oblique motion between these latter and the central part. In this way, the index finger remains fixed on $c_{\sharp}$, while the thumb and little finger slide in semitones from $g_{\sharp}$ to $f_{\times}$ and from $f_{\times}$ to $f_{\sharp}$ respectively. Later, however, Stravinsky changed the central note of the first chords from $c_{\sharp}$ to *b*: we will see the reason for this shortly.

In block *b*, a '*Rite* chord' $f_{\times 4}$ - $c_{\sharp 4}$ - $g_{\sharp 3}$ is repeated in syncopated quavers alternating with the *a* in the bass part. In the orchestral version, the repeated chords become the dotted strings (with occasional wind doublings) alternating with the strokes of cellos + double basses + bass drum. Block *b'* is a varied form of block *b* in which the symmetry (0 5/6 11) takes on a descending profile t -t - s ($c_{\sharp 4}$, b_3, a_3, $g_{\sharp 3}$). While in block *b* the four repeated chords are always (0 6 11), in *b'* the first three chords alternate from (0 6 11) and from (0 5 11), and the fourth chord — $f_{\times 4}$ - $b_{\sharp 3}$ - $g_{\sharp 3}$ (0 6 11) — is identical to the first of block *a*. This allows Stravinsky to create connections between block *a* and block *b'* through a common chord, as can be seen in the analysis of Ex. 12, which represent the passage at nos. [109-110], in the version of the sketches (upper system) and of the four-hands piano score of 1913 (lower system). Capital letters *a* and *b'* indicate the two blocks. The entire sequence is *b' - a - b' - a*, but in the second *b'*, the (0 5 1) chords are turned into (0 6 1) and vice versa. In block *c*, the '*Rite* chord' is used in a yet different way. On the first staff of the system, a rapid ascending chromatic line starting from $c_{\sharp}$ is imitated in a three-part canon. The second and third imitating voices enter after 5 and 6 semiquavers

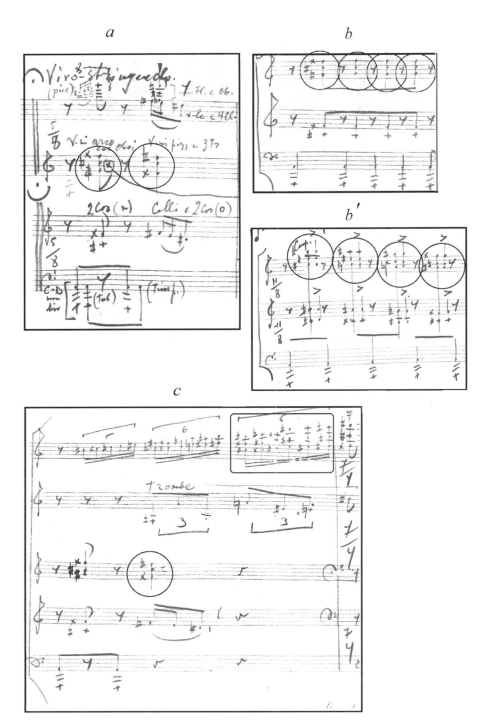

ILL. 6: Igor Stravinsky, *Rite* sketchbook (STRAVINSKY 1969, pp. 67 e 69), sketches for the *Glorification de l'Élue*.

respectively (see the numbers of the irregular groups): since each semiquaver corresponds to a semitone ascent, when the third voice arrives the result is precisely a '*Rite* chord' which continues to ascend chromatically. This 'heterophonic canon', therefore, simply results from the translations of the '*Rite* chord' over the keyboard. While relying on the piano, however, Stravinsky conceived this passage from the very beginning in orchestral terms. The sketches provide detailed instrumental cues for all the three blocks. The rapid chromatic ascent is entrusted to the *glissandi* of the winds at no. [106] (see, in fact, the cue 'trumpets' on the triplets of the glissandi in the sketch). The instrumentation of the whole passage was better defined in the fair copy of the short score[102].

Ex. 12: Igor Stravinsky, *Rite of Spring*, – *Glorification de l'Élue*. [109-110] above: transcription of a detail from the *Rite* sketchbook, p. 69; below: the same passage in the piano four-hand version.

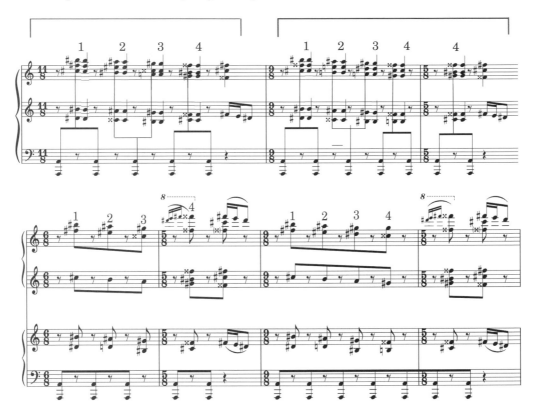

---

[102]. The short score of del *Rite of Spring*, is another important source for our knowledge of Stravinsky's creative process. It is held, along with the manuscript of the version for piano four hands and the autograph full score (STRAVINSKY 2013A; STRAVINSKY 2013B) at Paul Sacher foundation. Unlike these two latter sources, however, the manuscript short score has not yet been published in facsimile. Some pages are reproduced in DANUSER – ZIMMERMANN 2013, pp. 407-412. A page with one of the orchestral *glissandi* of the *Glorification de l'Élue* (reh. no. 117) is reproduced in *Strawinsky. Sein Nachlass, sein Bild*, Basel, Kunstmuseum Basel, 1984, p. 47 and cover.

The study of the sketches shows that the logic followed by Stravinsky's hands is often very simple since it consists of the symmetric translation of a very restricted number of chords. These are usually written in a close position in the staves of the sketches, so that they are immediately visible and easily manageable with just one hand. Comparison of the discarded versions, moreover, suggests a continuous back and forth path between written composition and improvisation on the piano. Let us consider for example the *Danse sacrale*. The *Rite* sketchbook contains many sketches for this piece. However, there is much evidence that this famous source records only the final stage of a long period of experiments and improvisations at the piano. Many other sketches recording earlier stages were most probably written before those gathered in this notebook. A few early sketches, in fact, have survived among Stravinsky's autographs that came into the possession of the Paul Sacher foundation after the composer's death[103]. Significantly, they are often jotted down on small sheets of paper found by chance, such as telegrams and receipts; a clear sign that they were intended to record extempore experiments, rather than a more systematic work of written composition. In some cases, we can even argue that they were written when Stravinsky was away from his piano, not only from his desk. However, such ephemeral annotations mostly contain very simple melodies, or purely rhythmic ideas, which could have been conceived even without the piano.

At least four sketches of the Sacher collection concern the *Dance sacrale*[104]. The first is roughly sketched on the reverse side of a telegram on which Stravinsky wrote: «For the 'Sacrificial Dance' / Rhythm, pitches don't matter»[105]. It contains two short melodies and a third folk-like diatonic melody on the margin. None of the melodies can be identified with certainty in the final score[106]; however, Stravinsky's note «Rhythm, pitches don't matter» clearly show that in this case he was looking for a rhythmic — not melodic/harmonic —idea. In fact, another sketch from the same collection — written on the back side of a receipt from a restaurant — contains a purely rhythmic idea (this time with no melody at all) with Stravinsky's note: «This is the rhythm from which the 'Sacrificial Dance' grew / In spring, during a walk

---

[103]. A detailed study of this collection of sketches is in BARANOVA MONIGHETTI 2014. Some sketches have been reproduced in facsimile or transcription in Baranova Monighetti's essay, as well as in other publications. In particular, the third sketch for the refrain *Danse sacrale* I'm about to discuss here is reproduced in VAN DEN TOORN 1987, p. 33.

[104]. In addition to those I'm about to discuss, there is an important sketch for a transitional progression at no. [161] on which Baranova Monighetti's essay dwells at length. However, it does not concern the refrain of the *Danse sacrale*, on which I will focus my attention; therefore, it will not be discussed here.

[105]. BARANOVA MONIGHETTI 2014, p. 5 (Baranova Monighetti's translation). The following discussion of the sketches for the *Danse sacrale* not included in the *Rite* sketchbook is based on Baranova Monighetti's essay.

[106]. According to *ibidem* (p. 7) some resemblance can be sees between the second melody and no. [171] of the *Danse sacrale*, and between the rhythm of the first annotation and the pulsation of the French horns and percussion at nos. [174-175]. However, Baranova Monighetti also notices some resemblances with other parts of the ballet score, such as the 'Ritual of Abduction', and the 'Ritual Action of the Ancestors'.

Ex. 13: Igor Stravinsky: rhythmic sketch for the *Danse sacrale*. Paul Sacher Stiftung, Igor Stravinsky collection.

with Ravel in 1912 in Monte-Carlo»[107]. The little sketch is transcribed in Ex. 13: it contains a two-layer syncopated polyrhythm, in which the quaver rests in the upper layer outlines a grouping structure of 5 - 4 -3 - 2 quavers[108]. It is difficult to say to which part of the *Danse sacrale* this sketch might correspond[109]. The rhythmic pattern is not literally applied anywhere in the piece. In my opinion, any attempt to find an exact match is in vain since the sketch does not contain the rhythm for a particular passage, but, in a sense, for the entire piece: it is just a rhythmic improvisational pattern, whose essential rules are:

1) the use of a polyrhythm between the upper parts and the bass;

2) the use of a mixed meter based on the numbers 5 (which can become 3 + 2) 4, 3 and 2.

The first 'rule' is applied, as we will see, above all in block *a*, in which the bass (left hand) alternates with the chords of the upper parts, creating a typical polyrhythmic situation. The second 'rule' characterizes the whole refrain, in which various succession of measures of variable amplitude (in terms of units: quavers in the sketches, semiquavers in the score), from two to five, unfold. Based on these two simple 'rules' and of a given harmonic material Stravinsky formulated, no doubt, several different piano improvisations before finding the final one that we can see in the sketchbook. «The dances of the second part [of the *Sacre*]», he maintained, «were composed in the order in which they now appear, and composed very quickly, too, until the *Danse sacrale*, which I could play, but did not, at first, know how to write»[110].

In the *Rite* sketchbook, Stravinsky first annotated (from p. 80) little sketches for the individual blocks of which the *Danse sacrale* is made, and then, in the subsequent pages, combined them into larger drafts[111]. The first section (refrain)[112] of the piece (from no. [142]

---

[107]. *Ibidem.*

[108]. Here, as in the other Basel sketches and in those of the *Rite* sketchbook, the rhythmic unit is the quaver.

[109]. According to BARANOVA MONIGHETTI (2014, pp. 8-9) it corresponds to a passage towards the end of the first refrain (second measure of no. [147]; = measure 25 of the four-hand version: see Ex. 14) whose resemblance with the model was concealed by Stravinsky by «applying his creative methods: he uses rests, omissions of the bass line, other combinatorial interchanges of various structural elements, as well as randomly prolongs certain notes».

[110]. *EXPOSITIONS AND DEVELOPMENTS*, p. 141.

[111]. Sometimes the order is not respected, and we find again individual sketches after an entire section had been drafted (In this cases Stravinsky often puts symbols to connect the various parts). Overall, however, the order of the sketches follows that of the final score.

[112]. The overall form of the *Danse sacrale* can be described as a sort of asymmetric *rondo* in seven parts: A B A[1] C A[2] C[1] A[3] (D) (capital letters stand for sections: section A is the refrain made of the *a*, *b*, and c small blocks).

Ex. 14: Igor Stravinsky, *The Rite of Spring*, *Danse sacrale*, nos. [142-149] version for piano four-hand, with analysis of the block-form.

to [149]) is entirely made of a montage of three very little blocks of music (labelled *a*, *b* and *c* in my examples), which alternate in various sequences. Each block, therefore, is repeated several times throughout each refrain. Ex. 14 shows the entire refrain in the version of the first printed edition for 4-hand piano, with letters indicating the three alternating blocks. In

However, the definition of *rondo* is not entirely appropriate since this form does not correspond to any classical *rondo* model (in five parts: ABACA; or in seven parts: ABACADA). Given the similarities between the various *refrains* the considerations made for the first refrain also applies, to some extent, to the following ones.

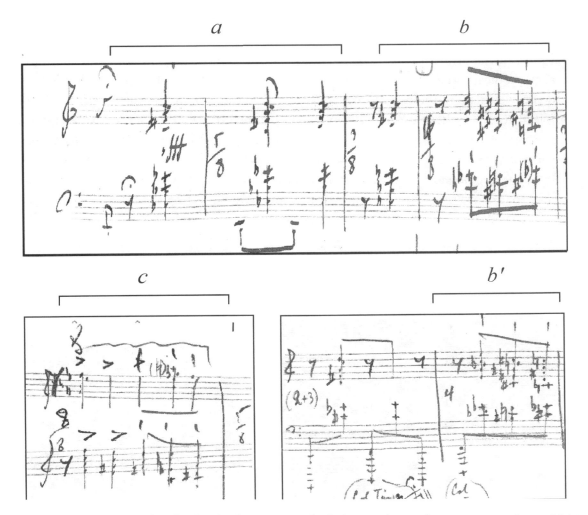

ILL. 7: Igor Stravinsky: Sketches for the *Danse sacrale* of *The Rite of Spring* (STRAVINSKY 1969, pp. 84-85 [excerpts]).

the sketchbook (pp. 80-85), Stravinsky first wrote several versions for each of the three blocks, then he gradually combined them into larger groups of two-three blocks and, finally (p. 86), into a single continuous sketch in the form of a short score on three staves, corresponding to the entire refrain. It is not so easy to understand to which of the various repetitions of the block each version of the sketches refers. In ILL. 7 I have selected just three short excerpts, respectively containing blocks *a* + *b*, block *c*, and block a + a variant of block *b* (labeled *b'* in my example). They are just some of the many variants that can be found in this part of the sketchbook, but they are sufficient for my purposes[113]. Apart from some evident — but not very significant from

---

[113]. Another little sketch, contained in the so-called Sketchbook I, shows blocks *a* + *b* in a very similar form as no. [147]. The harmonic substance of this annotation is almost identical to that of the sketches reproduced in

our point of view — differences, such as the use of a different unit of measurement (quavers instead of semiquavers: compare ILL. 7 and EX. 14), they almost entirely correspond to the final form of the printed score[114]. Nevertheless, even if the sketches do not show substantial or macroscopical variants, they can still give us useful information: if we were using only the full score, we would not notice the logic that generated the harmonies, which is hidden by the complexity of the orchestral doublings and by the complex distribution of the real parts among the various instruments. On the contrary, the notation of the sketches gives us a clear insight into Stravinsky's original organization of the harmonic blocks between the two hands.

Let us see, therefore, how the harmony of three blocks is arranged on the keyboard. Block *a* is made of a chord whose structure is very similar to that of the *Augures* chord — so that many scholars consider it as a variant of the latter: see Ex. 15):

Ex. 15: Derivation of block *a* of the refrain of the *Danse sacrale* from the octatonic collection.

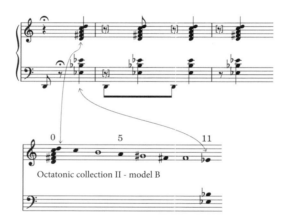

ILL. 7 — it only contains some instrumental cues which found their way into the 1913 autograph but were later abolished in the 1921 revised edition of the full score.

[114]. In the autograph full score (STRAVINSKY 2013B, p. 69) Stravinsky opted for semiquavers (in *EXPOSITIONS AND DEVELOPMENTS*, p. 147, he maintained that this notation better highlighted the musical phrasing). The semiquaver unit was also used in first printed edition of the score, of 1921, and in its revision of 1929. The quavers used in the sketches were restored in the revised version (Boosey and Hawkes) of 1943, and then abandoned again in favor of the semiquavers in the 1947 revision. In both the sketches and the manuscript of the four-hand piano version reproduced in my Ex. 14, as well as in the first printed edition of the orchestral score of 1921, measures are organized according to different (larger) groupings, than in subsequent revision, in which each measure of 5 units were broken down into two measures of 2+3 units. On the layers of revisions in Stravinsky's full score and the history of the revisions see Ulrich Mosch's preface in STRAVINSKY 2013B, and CYR 1982, pp. 89-148. A facsimile reproduction of the opening section of *Danse sacrale* of the 1921 (in the pocket-size of 1922) showing Stravinsky's handwritten re-barring can be seen in BARANOVA MONIGHETTI 2014, p. 135.

• **right hand** = dominant seventh on *d* — note (0) of octatonic collection II, model B, in root position, with octave doubling of the bass, in close position.

• **left hand** = open fifth chord on *e♭* — note (11) of the same octatonic collection as the right hand — with octave doubling of the bass. The chord alternates with *d* — the jumps of the hand recall the left-hand technique in jazz stride — according to the polyrhythmic idea of the sketch discussed before.

The construction of block *b* is entirely based on parallel harmony, but this origin has been somehow concealed by Stravinsky: the first chord is the same as the one that concludes block *a*; the next three chords are constructed in this way:

left hand = three parallel whole-tone bichords moving up and down by half step (semitone):

d♭ - e♭
b♯- d
c♯ - e♭

right hand = two major triads and a dominant seventh a half step (semitone) apart, respectively on *c*, *c#* and *d*:

c - e - g - (c)
c♯ - e♯ - g♯ - (c♯)
d - f♯- a - (d).

The origin of the chords in the parallel movements of the hand is concealed by the choice of different inversions for each chord, respectively first inversion, root position, and third inversion, with octave doubling of the bass:

e - g - c - e
c♯ - e♯ - g♯ - c♯
c - d - f♯- a - c.

In the variant of block *b* labelled as *b'* in ILL. 7, the first two chords of the right hand, which in block *b* were major triads, are turned into dominant sevenths, by adding the seventh note (respectively *b♭* and *b*) to the first two chords, thus obtaining three five-note (including the doubled octave) chords:

e - g - b♭ - c - e
c♯ - e♯ - g♯ - b - c♯
c - d - f♯-a - c

This variant shows that Stravinsky conceived the major triad and the dominant seventh as interchangeable forms in his symmetric progressions. If we were to consider the other variant contained in the sketchbook, as well as in the Sacher collection, we would find many other little variants, but they are of little importance from our point of view because they do not contradict the keyboard-oriented idea which served as Stravinsky's starting point: parallel movements of a triad/dominant seventh in the upper part (right hand); and parallel movements of a whole-tone bichord in the lower part (left hand). The variants do nothing but add or remove the seventh dissonance to the various transposed triads or modify the doubled note (which is sometimes the bass and sometimes the root). This is not to say, of course, that these little variants are *musically* insignificant: on the contrary, they are the very soul of this music, as also shown by the large number of variants produced by Stravinsky, in his search for the best solution. His very method consisted of starting from a quite simple 'idea of the hand' such as parallel harmonies, and then modifying them by making them more and more elaborate and less obvious. Consider, for example the form assumed by block *b* in the version for piano duet: here the right hand is based on the all-dominant-seventh version of *b'*, apart from the last chord, which is now in the simple form of a dominant seventh chord in root position, with no doubling:

e - *g* - *b*♭ - *c* - *e*
c♯ - *e*♯ - *g*♯ - *b* - *c*♯
d - *f*♯ - *a* - *c*

The upper parts of each chord are given to the first player, who splits them between the two hands, while the bass notes of the three chords (*e* - *c*♯ - *d*) are entrusted to the right hand of the second pianist. In this way, they clash with the three whole-tones that in the sketches had been given to the left hand, thus creating a succession of three strongly dissonant trichords (almost a sequence of three-note clusters) in the right hand of player 2

d♭ - *e*♭ - *e*
b♯ - *c*♯ - *d*
c♯ - *d* - *e*♭

Nonetheless, even though much of the result depends on these subtle changes, they do not contradict the essence of Stravinsky's first idea found on the keyboard; they simply rework it.

Finally, let us see block *c*:

• **right hand** = dominant ninth on *e*♭ in first inversion (with omitted seventh):
g - *b*♭ - [*d*] - *e*♭ - *f*

The chord is repeated five times on the rhythm ♩♩♪♪♪; only on the second quaver the two upper notes *g*♭ - *a* are added

• **left hand** = 5 major triads, with octave doubling of the bass, respectively on *f, e, d, a*♭, *b*, all in root position apart from the fourth chord (on *a*♭), which is in first inversion (bass: *c*), so that overall the bass of the five chords produce a fragment of descending diatonic scale: *f* - *e* - *d* - *c* - *b*. This version of the sketches is modified in the four-hand piano version, in which the 5 major triads are built on different roots: *f, b, d, a*♭, *b*, and are alternately in root position and first inversion, so that the basses produce a fragment of an octatonic scale: *f* - *d*♯ - *d* - *c* - *b*.

To sum up: all the chords of block *a*, *b*, and *c*, (i.e. the whole *refrain* of the *Danse sacrale*, since it is entirely made of these three blocks only) are obtained, ultimately, from the translations of major triads/dominant sevenths on the keyboard, that is, in our terms, from the symmetrical translations of a well-known 'way of the hand'. This simple origin is just concealed in the compositional process through a series of modifications.

One might wonder if these variants of the early sketches were also the result of further improvisations on the piano, or if they were elaborated through musical writing. Although I have no answer to this difficult question, my idea is that, given Stravinsky's working method and cognitive propensities, both things are possible. In some cases, this could even be true for the part of the creative process that seems to depend most on the use of writing: the combination of the various musical blocks in an overall form. Of course, when the blocks of material were very large, or even entire formal sections, this operation had to be based on the visual control offered by the notation and the score. This is the case of such pieces as the *Symphonies d'instrument à vent*, which have been often discussed as a paradigmatic example of block form[115]. However, when the materials were very short, as is the case of the *Danse sacrale*, their combination could also be managed by playing on the keyboard. In this case *rhythm* — conceived as the overall rhythm of the piece resulting from many aspects determining its temporal dynamics — could be the most important driving force. The complete sequence of bloc *a*, *b*, and *c* in the first *refrain* is as follows (in square the number of units [quavers]):

a (3) - *a* (5) - *b* (3+4) - *a* (5) - *b* (3+4) - a (3)
c (3+5) *a* (4) - *b* (3+4) - *c* (5)
a (5) - *a* (4) - *b* (3+4) - *a* (3)
------
a (5) - *b* (4) - *a* (2) - *b* (4) - *a* (3) - a (53) - b (4)
c (5) - c (3+4)

A new analysis of the form of this much analysed passage is outside the scope of this chapter (my arrangement of the blocks above, based on the articulatory function of block *c*, only suggests an articulation into two parts, in turn divisible respectively into 3 and 2 phrases)[116]. I limit myself to observing that beyond the formal characteristics that have been revealed by the various analyses, what stands out most from the combination of blocks is its unpredictability, due above all to the lack of any obvious formal symmetry, and the general sense of flow that surpasses the metric. Now, these two aspects are precisely what force us (unpredictability) and

---

115. On the creative process in the *Symphonies* see Scherliess 1993.
116. This roughly corresponds to the famous analysis provided by Pierre Boulez (Boulez 1968, pp. 117-118). For an overview of the various analytical interpretation of the *Danse sacrale* see Buharaja 2018.

help us (flow) in memorizing this sequence *as it is*, despite the lack of any regularity and predictability of the structure (in terms of bar grouping). So that after a few listenings we can easily follow the overall rhythm, which indeed is the unique feature of this piece. It is much the same for the performer as for the listener: despite its apparent complexity and the continually changing meters, the *Danse sacrale* is a piece that can be easily memorized and performed without a score, thanks to the uniqueness of its rhythmic flow. It is a true '*Dance for the hands*'.

To what extent, then, was the block form of this piece the result of (written) composition? Could not this form have been the (written) recording of a (piano) performance, in which Stravinsky extemporaneously combined the three blocks of musical material in the form we all know, maybe after improvising other (never recorded on paper) combinations? The sketches alone will never give a definitive answer to these questions, but no doubt Stravinsky had deeply assimilated the rhythmic and harmonic characteristics of blocks *a*, *b*, and *c*. The hypothesis that he was also able to combine them ex tempore seems entirely plausible to me; it would also explain why, despite innumerable analytical efforts, the formal 'logic' of this music remains so elusive.

PART II: COMPOSING WITH INTERVALS — 'CHANGE OF LIFE'[117]

The examples of the previous paragraphs show that intervals were vital to Stravinsky's piano improvisations. We had clear proof of this since the discussion of the alternating thirds of *The Firebird* in Chapter One; even the combinations of intervals of tritone and perfect fifth in the harmonies of *The Rite of Spring*. The '*Rite* chord' can be understood as a combination of two intervals[118].

Yet, although intervals consistently served as an important aspect of Stravinsky's approach to the keyboard, as long as he continued to use harmonic constructs that were still conceivable as chords in the traditional sense — that is, as superimpositions of notes by thirds, by fifths/fourths, by whole-tones etc. — the chordal 'way of the hand' prevailed on the intervallic criterion. This is particularly evident in the case of chords referable to the vocabulary of the common-practice-period; but the same can even be said of many post-

---

[117]. A preliminary version of this section has been published as LOCANTO 2009. 'Change of Life' is the title of a section of *THEMES AND EPISODES* (p. 23) in which Stravinsky famously described his two 'crisis': the «loss of Russia» and the decision to adopt the serial technique.

[118]. STRAUS 1991 discusses the process of elaboration that a very simple intervallic motif (just a semitone) undergoes throughout the sketches of *The Rake's Progress*. Straus' suggestive formula «the progress of a motif» does not refer to a formal process of thematic-motivic elaboration throughout the score (which is absent), but rather to Stravinsky reworking of the motif in the creative process.

tonal harmonies, such as chords in fourths or fifths, which can be reproduced in real time performance by an 'enculturated hand', in any point of the keyboard and in any position and inversion. This is because they are part of a consolidated cultural practice and the hand 'knows' how to perform them in the various harmonic contexts. Although the use of such chords may seem not so important in many compositions of the Russian or Neoclassical period, we must consider that the final version of the score was usually the result of a process in which the initial harmonic 'improvisations', based on these harmonies, were gradually elaborated in the written component of the creative process, as we have seen in the sketches of the *Rite of Spring*. Secondly, in Stravinsky's compositions before 1951, the use of these chords (and of their intervals) was often associated with — or subordinated to— the use of scales, such as the octatonic and whole-tone scale, or diatonic heptaphonic collections[119]. All this made the intervals a subordinate element — albeit a very important one — to both scales and harmonies

Things changed after 1951, when Stravinsky started abandoning both his privileged chords and his collectional routines. After *Threni*, particularly, the use of octatonic, whole tone and diatonic collections was noticeably reduced in favour of a more markedly chromatic context[120]. Although from time to time he apparently resorted again to these collections (many tetrachords prominently used in compositions of the 1950s belong to the diatonic or octatonic collections), his sketches clearly show that the creative process moved from individual intervals to larger combinations (and not vice versa), thereby producing results which can appear diatonic, octatonic or chromatic. As a consequence, intervals took on greater importance and greater autonomy. As Walter White rightly remarked, «one can be sure that no interval or combination of intervals in the maturity was ever accepted by him without the most careful scrutiny and consideration»[121]. We can also be sure that his 'control' took place for the most part at the keyboard. As the intervals acquired more importance in his creative process, also the 'step-count' of the fingers became more decisive.

It is not mere chance, therefore, that Stravinsky's last writings abound in declarations about the importance of the intervals and of the piano, sometimes also putting the intervals into close relationship with fingers. The first of such statements is found in an interview of December 1952, just in the aftermath of the composition of the *Cantata* (Stravinsky's first composition showing the use of serial techniques): «Always I have been interested in intervals», he said, «Not only horizontally in terms of melody, but also the vertical results that arise from the

---

[119]. On Stravinsky's use of non-diatonic collections other than the octatonic and whole-tone scales see JOHNSON (1987), TYMOCZKO (2002) and VAN DEN TOORN – TYMOCZKO 2003.

[120]. To some extent, however, a diatonic element persisted even in Stravinsky' most chromatic compositions. On this diatonic component see NEIDHÖFER 1999. TARUSKIN 1993 and TARUSKIN 1996, pp. 1648-1673, assumed the persistence, up to the final serial compositions, of a routine based on the use of octatonic collections, but this idea has been questioned (see for example STRAUS 2001, p. 39 and fn. 79).

[121]. WHITE 1979, p. 557.

combinations of intervals. hat, by the way, is what is wrong [...] That by the way is what is wrong with most twelve-tone composers: They are indifferent to the vertical aspect of the music.»[122]. Then, the theme of the piano, the intervals, and the fingers became a recurring *leitmotif* in the conversations with Robert Craft. The first occurrence was in the already mentioned 1957 NBC documentary, just a few lines after the words I had quoted at the beginning of this chapter:

> R.C.: Do your ideas always occur to you at the piano? I. S.: Mostly on the
> piano, mostly when I touch the instrument, I am looking for some distance of my
> fingers which corresponds to intervals and these intervals are really musical ideas[123].

The documentary provided the format for the subsequent Craft-Stravinsky conversation books, in which a series of declarations in the same vein can be found. The piano and the intervals are again the topic in a passage of the *Conversations* of 1959:

> R.C. The musical idea: when do you recognize it as an idea?
> I.S. When something in my nature is satisfied by some aspect of an auditive
> shape. But long before ideas are born, I begin work by relating intervals rhythmically.
> This exploration of possibilities is always conducted at the piano[124].

And a few lines later also the fingers are called upon in a curious narrative which can only be explained as an allusion to the tactile perception of intervals.

> R.C. You often speak of the weight of an interval. What do you mean?
> I.S. I lack words and have no gift for this sort of thing anyway, but perhaps it
> will help if I say that when I compose an interval, I am aware of it as an object (when
> I think about it in that way at all, that is), as something outside me, the contrary of
> an impression. Let me tell you about a dream that came to me while I was composing
> *Threni*. After working late one night I retired to bed still troubled by an interval. I
> dreamed about this interval. It had become an elastic substance stretching exactly
> between the two notes I had composed, but underneath these notes at either end
> was an egg, a large testicular egg. The eggs were gelatinous to the touch (I touched
> them) and warm, and they were protected by nests. I woke up knowing that my
> interval was right. (For those who want more of the dream, it was pink — I often
> dream in color. Also, I was so surprised to see the eggs I immediately understood
> them to be symbols. Still in the dream, I went to my library of dictionaries and

---

[122]. Interview with Jay S. Harrison, in: *New York Herald Tribune*, 21 December 1952 (quoted in TUCKER 1992, vol. II, p. 187).

[123]. Transcription from the documentary *A Conversation with Igor Stravinsky*, directed by Robert D. Graff, NBC, 1957.

[124]. *CONVERSATIONS*, p. 11.

looked up "interval", but found only a confusing explanation which I checked the next morning in reality and found to be the same.)[125].

Thanks to sketch study, it can be said that, overall, Stravinsky and Craft's statements contain something true: Stravinsky *did* begin to «work by relating intervals»; this activity took place at the keyboard; and intervals were conceived and manipulated by him as distances between the keys, not as music-theoretical concepts. This was also confirmed by those who had the opportunity to see the composer at work (at the piano). Nicholas Nabokov claimed to have been impressed by the way Stravinsky «explored the keyboard» in search of particular distances. «I stood behind him» he remembered «and watched the short, nervous fingers scour the keyboard, searching and finding the correct intervals, the widely-spaced chords and the characteristically Stravinskyan broad melodic leaps»[126].

On the other hand, such accounts should be interpreted in the light of the ideological implications and propagandistic purposes of Stravinsky's last writings. His emphasis on the physical dimension of music in his reply to Craft's question about the 'musical idea' contained an implicit criticism to Schonberg's abstract, almost metaphysical, *musikalische Gedanke*. Secondly, a strong emphasis on the intervals was a common trait of many serial composers of the time, who conceived the serial technique as a particular form of interval 'syntax', as Milton Babbitt remarked:

> One of the remarkable things that Stravinsky said, when people felt that he committed a treasonable act by starting to write pieces where you could find a succession of twelve [notes] at the beginning, was "There's nothing to it; I've always composed with intervals". Basically, of course, it was something of a witticism, but what it did show, much more than a witticism, was how profoundly this is an interval kind of syntax and not just a pitch-class syntax — fundamentally and centrally an interval syntax[127].

Finally, the most questionable assertion is precisely that Stravinsky had been «always» interested in intervals» or — as Milton Babbitt put it — he «had always composed with intervals». This emphasis on the 'continuity' is quite understandably aimed at demonstrating that a coherence of method existed from the *Firebird* to his recent (serial) compositions, thus casting a light of 'modernity' on his previous 'styles'. Yet, this statement can be trusted only to a certain extent, for two basic reasons. First, as we have seen, before he adopted the serial technique, the use of intervals was coordinated — or even subordinated — to the use of scales,

[125]. *Ibidem*, p. 14.
[126]. Nabokov 1949, p. 146.
[127]. Babbitt 1987b, p. 20; see also Babbitt 1968, p. 167.

chords and collections. Secondly with the adoption of serial technique a new, different criterion was superimposed to the use of interval (this idea will be the main argument of the rest of this chapter). Thirdly, the way Stravinsky managed the intervals on the keyboard changed tangibly; the difference can be summed up in two basic points:

1) the intervals, free from scales and traditional chords are now combined in small 'motifs';

2) In his last compositions Stravinsky seems to make a different approach to intervals, in which octave equivalence played a more important role.

Both points changed sensibly Stravinsky's approach to the intervals and introduced new possibilities in for both the improvisation on the keyboard and the composition. The description of his interval technique, of course, is all but obvious and can only rely on the information provided by sketches. Let us see both aspects in more detail.

WHAT IS A MOTIF?

Stravinsky never specified exactly what he meant by the expression 'composing with intervals', nor does the study of his sketches offer any definitive answers. This circumstance, too, depends on the fact that a great deal of his work with pitch material took place at the keyboard, in a phase prior to that documented in the earliest sketches. Stravinsky's interval procedures were not codified according to any kind of systematic approach. Therefore, different interpretations have been given. Joseph Straus, for example, formulated on a definition of 'intervallic motif' quite similar — but also with some important difference — to the one I will offer here[128]. For Straus, an intervallic motif results from the combination of a limited number (usually two) of 'atomic' intervals (one of which is generally a tone or semitone). Through the choice of an appropriate transpositional level, these intervals produce some specific pitch-class sets, which are then used as motifs in melodic construction[129]. Straus conceives of motifs in an exclusively melodic sense, as his analyses clearly demonstrate. To my mind, in contrast, Stravinsky's method displaced the notes of his motifs either horizontally — and in any order — or vertically. This is because his 'motifs' are not primarily conceived as melodies (nor harmonies) but as the result of the spatial arrangement of the intervals on the keyboard in terms of steps and half steps. More importantly, for Straus a motif, although initially obtained by a particular combination of elementary intervals, *does* correspond to a set of pitch classes which could be transformed (also by means of serial techniques, that is in retrograde, inverted or reordered form), but would

---

[128].   As an example of the different results to which these two approaches can lead, see fn. 154. Yet another approach is adopted by SMYTH 1997, pp. 21-23, which considers interval types (not interval classes). See also SMYTH 1999 and 2000.

[129].   STRAUS 2001, pp. 82-92, 92-103.

Ex. 16: Igor Stravinsky, *A Sermon, a Narrative, and a Prayer*: subset structure of the original twelve-note row.

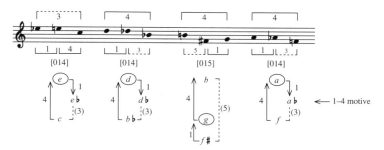

continue nonetheless to belong to *the same set class*[130]. From my point of view, on the other hand, in Stravinsky's late compositions a motif is conceived as the result of the combination of the *individual* intervals on the keyboard. Intervals, in sum, are treated as *individual* entities which can be oriented in different directions (upwards or downwards), thus creating different configurations belonging to *different set classes*.

The consequences of this way of managing the intervals on the keyboard can be observed even in the interval structure of many of Stravinsky's twelve-tone rows. I will use as a brief first example the original twelve-note row of *A Sermon, a Narrative, and a Prayer* (Ex. 16). The series can be subdivided into four distinct trichords, three of which — the first, second and fourth — belong to set class [014]. Segments 2 and 4 are ordered as <0, 1, 4>, while segment 1 is ordered as <1, 0, 4>[131]. From an intervallic point of view, if we consider the intervals apart from their melodic direction (ascending or descending), that is, as unordered pitch-class intervals (interval classes), all three segments contain a segment semitone (interval class [ic] 1), a minor third (ic3) and a major third (ic4)[132]. In consequence, we could describe the three segments as three statements, differently ordered, of the same group of three interval classes, or equally well

---

[130]. I refer to the definition of 'set class' according to musical set theory: see definition in Straus 1990, pp. 26-41.

[131]. Hereafter I will often use set-theoretical (numerical) symbols to refer to ordered and unordered sets. This is only because they provide a useful system of representation of pitch classes and sets. The prime forms of unordered sets (the form of the set class that is most compact to the left and is transposed to begin on 0: see *ibidem*, pp. 41-42) are represented by a sequence of numbers (standing for pitch classes) between square brackets, as in *ibidem*. *Ordered* sets, on the contrary, are represented by a numerical sequence in angle brackets which follows the actual order of the notes. For example: the succession of notes *b♭ - a - c - b* belongs to set class [0123]; considered as an ordered set, however, it will be represented as <1, 0, 3, 2>. Note that neither ordered nor unordered sets should be confused as indication of number of half steps since while these are always numbered starting from the first note (the first key to be played), ordered and unordered sets assume as note 0 the lowest note in the prima form).

[132]. For a definition of 'interval class' see *ibidem*, pp. 6-8. In this study, interval classes are indicated in the orthodox manner by 'ic' followed by an Arabic numeral indicating the interval class measured in semitones. The terms of traditional tonal theory, when used, refer — unless otherwise indicated — to interval classes. For reasons of space, in most of the musical examples the 'ic' is omitted and the intervals are indicated by Arabic numerals alone.

as three statements, differently ordered, of the same pitch set class [014]. So far there is nothing different from either Straus' definition of 'intervallic motif' or serial technique in general. The difference becomes clear if we return to the third segment of the row (see again Ex. 16). This segment does not belong to set class [014] like the others, but rather to set class [015]. Its global intervallic content is also different. However, it shares with the other three segments two out of the three intervals: ic1 and ic4. They are merely arranged in a different way: in the third segment they are joined in the same direction, thereby producing an ic5; in the first, second and fourth segments they are joined in opposed directions, thereby producing an ic3 (Ex. 17). In other words, considered as unordered pc sets, only three of the four segments of the row turn out to belong to the same class; considered, however, as intervallic motifs formed through the combination — in varying directions — of two intervals on the keyboard, they turn out to all be members of the same motif class: the semitone and the major third conjoined, expressed symbolically as 1-4.

Ex. 17: Intervallic motif class 1-4 in the two forms of set class [015] and [014].

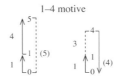

The reader may think that there is an inconsistency in my terminology: since I am using unordered intervals, it may seem senseless to speak of their 'direction' or 'orientation', since an 'unordered interval' is, by definition, the shortest distance between two pitches or pitch classes, without any reference to their order. However, the intervallic motifs which are the focus of my interest always result from the union of two (or more) *conjoined* intervals on the keyboard, for which these terms refer simply to the orientation assumed by the intervals relative to each other according to the pivotal key. Two conjoined intervals united in the same direction produce a third interval corresponding to their sum (such as ic 1 and ic4, which together produce ic5 in Ex. 16); conversely, two conjoined intervals united in opposite directions produce an interval corresponding to their difference (such as ic1 and ic4, which together realise ic3 in Ex. 16). This is represented graphically by the arrows in my examples, in which the pc sets are conventionally arranged in their 'normal form' from lowest to highest[133]. Thus, my use of the terms 'direction' or 'orientation' refers precisely to Stravinsky's spatial-visual approach based on the keyboard's layout.

In addition to this motivic technique, Stravinsky adopted a different approach to the concept of 'distance'. While in his previous compositions the intervals were conceived as

---

[133]. For a definition of 'normal form' see *ibidem*, p. 27.

absolute distances, measurable by the fingers in terms of the number of half steps, now they are also treated as *relative* distances, modifiable through octave equivalence.

To take an example: the chord of a major 7th c_1 - b_1 contained within an octatonic collection, which in terms of half steps is represented by the number 11, always maintains this distance in all its transformations, as we have seen for example with the translations of the (0 5/6 11) '*Rite* chord'. In Stravinsky's last compositions, on the contrary, the octave register of the two pitches can be modified, so that the same intervals can be reduced, by octave equivalence, to b_0 - c_1, thus becoming just one step.

The music theorist will suddenly recognize that this change corresponds to the introduction, in Stravinsky's interval technique, of the concept of 'interval class'. In fact, in my following example intervals will usually be represented as interval classes

This change in Stravinsky's approach to intervals was probably due to his greater acquaintance with serial technique — strongly encouraged by Robert Craft and made possible by the study of the scores of Schoenberg and his pupils, and by direct, close contact with composers like Ernst Krenek and Milton Babbitt, who also adopted or devised serial techniques —[134] in which octave equivalence is usually an implicit and basic criterion. However, this does not mean that Stravinsky changed radically his attitude towards intervals, and that he abandoned his habit of conceiving and managing them as concrete measures (in terms of number of half steps) to adopt a purely 'theoretical' approach: on the contrary his hands and fingers had now to develop a new skill: that of immediately 'thinking of' an intervals in terms of a series (a class) of distances (of steps) over the keyboard: limiting us to those distances that can be reached by a single hand:

1 half step = 11 half steps
2 half steps = 10 half steps
3 half steps = 9 half steps
4 half steps = 8 half steps
5 half steps = 7 half steps

To sum up: Stravinsky's different orientation of the *individual* intervals on the keyboard, radically modifies the physiognomy of the motifs of which these intervals are made, thus making them assume various forms, corresponding to different *set classes*. Conceived in this way, a 'motif' no longer corresponds, in any sense, to a class of unordered pitches. Stravinsky's finger-oriented operations act more on the level of single intervals than on the level of the global configurations within which these single intervals are included. The orientation of the intervals on the keyboard, radically modifies the physiognomy of the *motifs*, which can thereby assume forms corresponding to different *set classes*. In this intervallic language, then, a motif no longer corresponds, in any sense, to a class of unordered pitches.

---

[134].   See STRAUS 2001, pp. 6-38.

Clearly, in defining this type of intervallic syntax as 'motivic', the term 'motif' is being used with some degree of latitude. Stravinsky, in fact, can hardly be thought of as a 'motivic composer', and, in fact, the kind of 'motivic' usage I'm describing is an aspect of his creative process which has little to do with motivic development in the classical sense. In the Austro-German *Formenlehre* tradition a motif is typically conceived as a structural nexus of different aspects, including harmony, rhythm and metre. According to some scholars, the Schoenbergian concept of 'motif' which correlates with the idea of 'developing variation' essentially concerns only the intervallic aspect[135]. However, even in Schoenberg's pedagogical writings the motif is usually conceived as a complex of intervals, rhythm, metrical position, harmony, and so on. In Stravinsky's practice as I am describing, on the contrary, a 'motif' is a simple configuration of intervals first experienced on the visual space of the keyboard and then put into writing: pitch components and rhythm are treated as initially distinct and separate dimensions which can subsequently be related. In Stravinsky's own words: «I begin work by relating intervals rhythmically»[136]. The first annotations of these intervallic motifs in the initial sketches tend to be rhythmically very vague. As these intervallic ideas are brought to a more advanced state, the manuscripts often become increasingly more rhythmically defined.

Despite some apparent similarities, Stravinsky's use of intervallic motifs differs radically from that usually applied to the post-tonal music of Schoenberg, Berg and Webern. For these composers, the concept of motivic elaboration which guaranteed coherence in tonal music was gradually replaced by a constructive principle based on the use of fundamental intervallic constellations which operate at a more basic level. According to Martina Sichardt, this reduction of the various *Gestalten* within a passage to its most elementary intervallic basis — a tendency Schoenberg himself had consciously put into practice in his own analytical formulations — represented a fundamental premise for the elaboration of the twelve-note method[137]. In this respect, it is interesting to note that most of the basic intervallic constellations which form the expressive vocabulary of melodic gestures in Schoenberg's compositions consist merely of the union of two or three intervals — one of which is usually the semitone — disposed in a particular arrangement[138].

An interesting analogy with Stravinsky's practice can nonetheless be glimpsed wherever Schoenberg subjects these basic combinations of intervals to a process of variation. Jack Boss, for example, has demonstrated that the majority of the intervallic motifs in the first of Schoenberg's *Vier Lieder*, Op. 22, could be derived by applying three types of modification to a

---

[135]. See for example DAHLHAUS 1986, p. 283.

[136]. See above, fn 40.

[137]. See SICHARDT 1990, pp. 30-52.

[138]. See for example the motifs identified by *ibidem*, pp. 50-52, in the compositions and fragments dating from the years immediately preceding 1919.

motif formed from the combination of one ic1 and one ic3.[139] Boss considers all of the possible arrangements of these two intervals (that is, <+1, +3>, <+1, -3>, <-1, +3>, <-1, -3>, <+3,+1>, <+3, -1>, <-3, +1> and <-3, -1>) as variants belonging to the same motivic class. Moreover, each of these forms can undergo in its turn three fundamental types of variation, two of which involve octave complementation and pitch reordering. All of this corresponds exactly to my definition of motif class 1-3. However, despite this similarity, a profound discrepancy remains regarding the very concept of motif. Schoenberg's procedures, as described by Boss, «effectively identify motif as an entity which may be subjected to a wide range of transformations while remaining largely recognisable». According to Boss, for example, the third basic category of variation employed by Schoenberg involves the expansion of intervals.[140] In this respect, the Schoenbergian concept of variation implies a decisively greater quantity and variety of forms derivable from a single motif than those which occur in Stravinsky. Still more important is the fact that the Schoenbergian concept of variation implies a broader process, one which involves the entire plan of the musical form. Indeed, in Schoenberg, the variation of a motif cannot be dissociated from the concept, central to the Austro-German tradition, of motivic elaboration, understood as a means of conferring coherence and organic unity on a composition[141]. All of this is foreign to Stravinsky's musical thought, in which the manipulation of intervallic motifs is understood as a procedure for generating primary compositional material capable of being employed as a point of creative departure.

The idea — as developed, for example, through the work of George Perle —[142] that a 'basic cell' or 'referential sonority' can be presented even in a vertical sense could be considered another point of contact between Stravinsky's motivic- intervallic syntax and the post-tonal harmonic language of Schoenberg, Berg and Webern. However, unlike the notion of the Stravinskian intervallic motif, the concept of the basic cell consists of a fixed configuration of intervals and corresponds therefore to a single set class, while this is not true for Stravinsky's 'motifs', as we will see shortly[143]. The most decisive difference, however, concerns the contrasting aesthetic-

---

[139].   See Boss 1992, pp. 125-150.

[140].   Boss 1994, pp. 194-196.

[141].   It is more difficult, especially in twelve-note music, to establish whether (and, if so, to what extent) motivic elaboration, applied in the sense of the Schoenbergian concept of developing variation, also confers a teleological orientation on the musical discourse, as maintained, for example, in Haimo 1997.

[142].   See for example Perle 1991, pp. 9-38, especially Perle's analyses of Schoenberg's Op. 23 No. 1, based on a minor third-semitone cell. Perle (p. 9) conceives the 'cell' as a group of pitches which «may operate as a kind of microcosmic set of fixed intervallic content, statable either as a chord or as a melodic figure or as a combination of both». The difference between this and my definition of 'intervallic motif' is obvious enough.

[143].   The same thing can be said of the 'cells' which, according to different authors (Perle 1955, Treitler 1959 and Antokoletz 1984, pp. 78-137), play a determining role in the music of Béla Bartók. Nonetheless, Bartók' s use of intervallic cells presents some analogies with Stravinsky's practice, especially in the preference for symmetrical aggregates (see for example the cells labelled X, Y and Z in Treitler's analysis). Different theoretical

musical aspects within which a motif unit is taken to function: in the music of Schoenberg, Berg and Webern an intervallic configuration disposed vertically always maintains a motivic character — from which, in fact, the idea of 'chord as motif' arises — even in a dynamic sense. The nature of this element is expressed by the Schoenbergian concept of unrest:

> *What is a motive?* A motive is something that gives rise to motion. *A motion is that change in a state of rest, which turns it into its opposite.* Thus, one can compare a motive with a driving force [...] What causes motion is a *motor*. One must distinguish between *motor* and *motive* [...] *A thing is termed a motive if it is already subject to the effect of a driving force, has already received its impulse, and is on the verge of reacting to it* [...] The *smallest musical event* can become a motive if it is permitted to have an effect; even an individual tone can carry consequences[144].

In Schoenberg's music, the simultaneous presentation of pitches produced by an intervallic configuration can be considered the result of an extreme concentration in time of an event whose essence is decidedly dynamic — tied, that is, to the movement of time. Therefore, while Schoenberg's motivic conception is essentially temporal — the very idea of a suppression of temporality associated with the Schoenbergian 'law' of the unity of musical space implies the concept of time — the Stravinskian approach belongs to a conception we may define as 'spatial' or 'visual': the motif is understood as a configuration of intervals which can be arranged in two dimensions, as in visual space (the keyboard, as well as the diastematic space of the music notation). The 'motif' is conceived more as a 'building material' than as a salient aspect of the musical form; It is used as a compositional (and improvisational) resource; an aspect therefore, which relates more to the compositional process and technique, than to the musical form or musical structure.

It is important to underline once again that the distinctive feature of Stravinsky's 'motivic' technique is not the idea that the note of a motif can be used in any order and horizontally as well as vertically, but the possibility to modify the direction of the individual intervals. In fact, considering the segments of the row as unordered sets corresponds to a constructive logic which, far from being exclusive to Stravinsky, seems deeply rooted in most twelve-note and serial music in general and is certainly very familiar from the published literature on serialism. However, while the idea of globally — regardless of the order — considering the pitches and/or intervals contained in some serial segments, far from being a peculiarity of Stravinsky's technique, is just one of the most basic constructive criteria of twelve-note serialism in general, this criterion corresponds only in part to Stravinsky's approach to intervals.

---

aspects concerning the use of intervallic cells in the music of Bartók are addressed in ANTOKOLETZ 1984, p. 16 fn. 27 and pp. 78-137.

[144]. SCHOENBERG 1995, p. 386; emphases in original.

From Steps to Rows

The manipulation of the orientation — in the sense explained above — is a precious resource in Stravinsky's hands, aimed at creating long musical passages (or twelve-tone rows) out of a restricted number of intervals and 'intervallic motifs' — that is a group of motifs made of the combination of the same intervals[145]. By simply changing, on the keyboard, the direction of the intervals forming a single (or at most two) motivic class(es) he can create twelve-note rows — as in the previous example — as well as smaller or larger successions of pitches to be employed either melodically or harmonically in a musical passage.

To some extent this technique was not new to Stravinsky's serial compositions but had already been used, in much the same way, in the past. An example is the passage from the *Concerto in D* for violin and orchestra (1931) shown in Ex. 18: here the melodic lines of the violin solo and of the woodwinds appear sometimes diatonic, sometimes octatonic, other times clearly chromatic, but the only constant element remains in practice the use of stepwise motions of tones and semitones, in various sequences and directions. The melodic parts contain an uninterrupted chain of tones and semitones (steps and half steps). In the first part of the passage the intervals are orientated both in the same direction oriented than in the opposite direction thus producing chromatism: in just three bars it exploits all the chromatic notes between *b* e *f*; then, in the second part, the intervals are oriented in the same direction, thus producing a fragment of diatonic scale (*e - f♯ - g - a - b - c - d*). Clearly, the overall result, diatonic or chromatic, does not depend on the preliminary choice of a reference collection, but on the way (from the orientation) in which the intervals of tone and semitone have been combined on the keyboard by Stravinsky. The improvisational *style* of the violin in this passage reflects the improvisation *technique* with which this melody had been created on the keyboard.

With the progressive adoption of serialism, during the 1950s, this motivic-intervallic technique was integrated by Stravinsky into the serial technique. All this, however, raised an important issue: while in previous compositions (like the *Concerto in D*) Stravinsky could still employ all twelve pitch classes according to the intervallic logic described so far, with the adoption of serial procedures a new constructive order was imposed that does not work on the level of individual intervals, but rather of pitch-class sets[146]. Intervallic syntax and serial technique operate according to different criteria: while different orientations of the

---

[145]. From here on, the 'intervallic motifs' will be represented by two or more Arabic numerals (corresponding to the interval classes) separated by a dash (-) and ordered, only as a convention, from the smallest to the largest. For example: 1-2 indicates a motivic class which includes the following possible configurations: <+1. +2>, <+1, -2>, <-1, +2>, <-1, -2>, <+2, +1>, <+2, -1>, <-2, +1>, <-2, -1>.

[146]. The discrepancy is also recognised by STRAUS 2001, p. 92, who notes «the basic formal paradox of [Stravinsky's] music, namely the centrifugal tendency of the musical units [intervals] toward isolation and the centripetal tendency of the transpositions and inversions to link them together into larger wholes». Nevertheless,

Ex. 18: Igor Stravinsky. *Concerto in D* for violin and orchestra, I, from 1 to [34] – 1.

in Straus' vision the discrepancy concerns «the very immediate level of structure», that is, the structuring of the motifs and ordered sets used in the composition.

single intervals can produce melodies which belong to different set classes (as we have seen before), neither the retrograde, nor the inversion, nor the retrograde inversion, nor any type of permutation of the order of a particular pc set is capable of generating a different set class. Put simply, intervallic logic tends towards disintegration, serial technique towards unification. From the point of view of musical perception, one could even say that motivic-intervallic syntax attributes to the quality of single intervals an importance superior to the globalising tendency of pc sets. However, this contradiction provided Stravinsky with a stimulus, rather than an obstacle, to composition. And this also allow us to interpret some 'unorthodox' characteristics of Stravinsky's serial technique, which are by now well-known but whose deeper motivations still require further investigation.

The problem of the interaction between intervallic-motivic logic and serial technique became central in the compositions following *Agon*, which were more and more systematically based on the use of ordered series of pitches (tetrachords, hexachords, twelve-note rows, and so on). The composition of *Agon* was crucial in this development. The score was elaborated from the end of 1953 until April 1957, overlapping the composition of *In Memoriam Dylan Thomas* (February-March 1954), of *Canticum sacrum* (June-November 1955) and of the *Choral Variations on "Von Himmel hoch"* by J. S. Bach (December 1955-March 1956), and shows a stratification of serial and non-serial techniques. The first two parts of the ballet, from the opening *Fanfare* to the *Coda* of the first *Pas de trois* (b. 185), were composed in the first phase (October 1953 - February 1954); they are the ones less involved in serial technique: the introductory *Fanfare* (*Pas de quatre*) is not serial at all and shows a marked diatonicism. In the following movements and up to the Coda of the first *Pas de trois* serial materials are mixed with freely composed parts. Starting with the second part of the *Double pas de quatre* (b. 81), however, small non-dodecaphonic series of 5-7 sounds are used, which are subjected to the usual operations of inversion and/or retrogradation and transposition[147]. Susannah Tucker has shown that in this part of the ballet Stravinsky moved from a still 'thematic' conception to a more markedly serial one, viewing the sounds of a thematic fragment as a potential generating series of derived forms. The remaining parts of the ballet incorporate the use of series (of various types) and serial transformation techniques[148]. However, the use of interval motifs can be seen in both the strictly serial and non-serial parts of the ballet.

A clear example is the passage of the first violin (doubled by the cello) at bars 97-102 of the *Triple pas de quatre*, which derives from a dense chain of overlapping 2-1-2 motifs (Ex. 19). The intervallic orientation of the motifs is almost always a zigzag, forming the chromatic set class [0123], but at times (see the circled motifs) the intervals are oriented in the same direction, thus forming the set class [0235]. Something very similar happens in the clarinet melody at

---

[147]. As shown by Tucker 1992, vol. II, pp. 61-73.
[148]. *Ibidem*, pp. 66ff.

bb. 67-68 of the *Double pas de quatre*[149]. Such almost-improvisational passages in the non-serial sections of *Agon* strongly recalls the chromatic chains of the violin part in the *Concerto in D* we have seen before.

Ex. 19: Igor Stravinsky, *Agon*, *Triple pas de quatre*: motivic construction of bars 97-102.

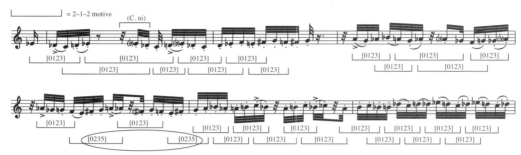

A point of contact between this use of intervallic motifs in a strictly melodic sense, and the serial technique employed in the serial movements can be glimpsed in bars 104-107 of the *Triple pas de quatre*, where the 2-1-2 motif, which first appeared in various forms (see for example its use in the melody of Ex. 19), now becomes fixed in the form of the ordered tetrachord <1, 3, 2, 0>, which from that moment comes to be used as a four-note row from which other row forms can be derived via retrogradation and inversion. The intervallic motifs containing the tone and semitone generate most of the rows (ranging from four to twelve different pitches) used in the following (serial) movement of the ballet. Almost all of them show a very clear and motif-intervallic design, which can be traced back to motivic-intervallic combinations of ic1 and ic2. The notes, however, are often subjected to a reordering[150]. The ordered tetrachord <0, 1, 4, 3>, which appears for the first time in the *Pas de deux* (Ex. 20), for example, can be generated by a 1-2-1 motif, with the intervals oriented in the same direction to form set class [0134], then reordered to the succession <0, 1, 4, 3> in which the whole tone is found between the second and fourth notes and the two semitones on either side. The central position is then occupied by a major third; but this interval should be considered as a 'by-product' of the combination of tones and semitones.

The only essential difference between this technique and that of the *Concerto in D* is that while in the *Concerto* (and more in general in the compositions before the serial turn) Stravinsky limited himself to 'improvising' on a combination of intervals (such as tone-semitone [step-half step]), now the result of his keyboard improvisations is reworked according to a typically serial procedure: the reordering of the elements.

---

[149].   See POUSSEUR 1971, p. 42.

[150].   On the various 12-tone and non-12 tone rows in *Agon* see TUCKER 1992, vol. II, pp. 60-92; POUSSEUR 1971, pp. 27-30, and VAN DEN TOORN 1983, pp. 390-413.

Ex. 20: Motif 1-2-1 in [0134] form, reordered as tetrachord 1-2-1 motif in form the same reordered as <0, 1, 4, 3>.

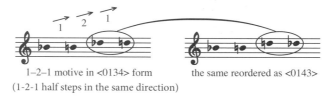

1–2–1 motive in <0134> form   the same reordered as <0143>
(1-2-1 half steps in the same direction)

While the first component (the creation of the chains of intervals) is still linked to the use of the keyboard and to the intervals as 'tactile' elements (as 'steps'), we can assume that the second phase (the reordering of the notes) was an operation based on music writing. In this light, Stravinsky's serial compositions appear as a complex mix of written 'tactile' thought (improvisation). Furthermore — and this is the second innovative aspect introduced by the serial technique — the sequences of sounds obtained from this rearrangement are subjected to the typical serial operations (inversion and retrogradation) and used, in turn, as a starting series for the construction of larger ensembles. Most of the rows (from six to thirteen pitches) employed in the ballet score are obtained by combining different statements of the <0, 1, 4, 3> tetrachord. For example, the serial heptachord g - $a\flat$ - $c\flat$ - $b\flat$ - a - c - $d\flat$ that appears in the *coda* of the *Pas de deux* (bars 495-496) results from the union through a common tone of a tetrachord g - $a\flat$ - $c\flat$ - $b\flat$ and its RI form ($b\flat$ - a - c - d). Then, by combining through a common tone two forms of this heptachord placed a tritone apart (d - $e\flat$ - $g\flat$ - f - e - g - $a\flat$ + $a\flat$ - a - c - b - $b\flat$ - $d\flat$ - d), the thirteen-note row employed in the second section (Adagio) of the *Pas de deux* — a row containing all twelve pitch classes with a single repetition — takes shape. The twelve-note row used in the two final movements of the ballet (*Four Duos* and *Four Trios*) is obtained by joining — through two common tones — the heptachord of the *coda* of the *Pas de deux* with a row of seven notes, obtained by the union (again via a common tone) of the <0, 1, 4, 3> tetrachord with its reordered form <1, 4, 3, 0>[151]. In the end, because of this process of derivation, the original 1-2-1 motif, on which the fundamental <0, 1, 4, 3> is based, becomes a fundamental starting point for the composition of many sections of the work.

Ex. 21: Igor Stravinsky, *Agon*: *Bransle Simple* (opening): motivic construction.

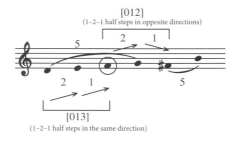

[012]
(1–2–1 half steps in opposite directions)

[013]
(1–2–1 half steps in the same direction)

---

[151]. For a summary see Tucker 1992, vol. ii, pp. 182-242. On Stravinsky's technique of tetrachordal linkage, see Van den Toorn 1983, pp. 409-414.

In *Agon*, even many rows not based on the <0, 1, 4, 3> tetrachord can be traced back to a combination of ic1 and ic2. The first five notes of the hexachord stated in canon at the beginning of the *Bransle Simple* (Ex. 21), for instance, can be seen as two 1-2 motifs united by a common tone: the first motif is in the form [013], with the intervals oriented in the same direction; the second is in the form [012], with the intervals in opposite directions. The only pitch which lies outside the 1-2 pattern is the sixth and last note, *b*. However, between this note and the preceding *f♯* there is the same interval as that between the first (and lowest) note, *d*, and the fourth note, which is the highest note of the two 1-2 motifs. This results in a symmetrical structure, with two ic5s (*d - g* and *b - f♯*) a semitone apart. Just to make another example: the twelve-note row employed in the coda of the first *Pas de trois* (presented for the first time in bars 185-189) is entirely formed from a chain of 1-2 motifs in the two forms [012] and [013] (Ex. 22).

Ex. 22: Igor Stravinsky, *Agon*, Twelve-note row of the *coda* of the first *Pas de trois*: motivic construction.

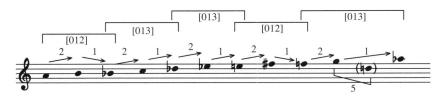

The use of motifs formed by the combination of steps and half steps, far from being an exclusive characteristic of *Agon* alone, is a typical trait of many of Stravinsky's serial compositions. Particularly common are the motifs defined by Joseph Straus as 'twist motifs', formed by the tone and semitone conjoined in opposite directions to form set class [012].[152] These motifs can be identified in many twelve- note rows, from the *Surge, Aquilo* of *Canticum sacrum* to *The Owl and the Pussy-Cat*[153], as well as in several pre-serial compositions. A typical example is the serial melody of *Fanfare for a New Theatre* (Ex. 23): at first glance the row may seem made of four serial forms of the same *ordered* trichords containing a tone and a semitone always in the opposite direction (see the first line in the example). However, on closer inspection, a fifth statement of the same motif can be seen between notes 8-10 (*f - e - f♯*). Moreover, if we consider the other form of motif 1-2, with the intervals in the same direction producing set [013], two more motifs can be seen between notes 3-5 (*b - c♯ - d*) and 5-7 (*d - c - d♯*) (second line of my example)[154].

---

[152].   STRAUS 2001, p. 91.

[153].   See the statistic in *ibidem*, p. 90 n. 13, based on JERS 1986, pp. 33-35. On the use of this motif in The Rake's Progress see CARTER 1997.

[154].   Although STRAUS 2001, p. 90, observes that the semitone and tone often appear united in the same direction to form a set of class [013], in his analyses the two forms [012] and [013] are considered to be distinct motifs, not as two forms of the same intervallic motif, as I am assuming. Consequentially, Straus notes only the presence of five (not seven) motifs in the row of *Fanfare for a New Theatre* (those in the first line of my Ex. 23).

Ex. 23: Igor Stravinsky, *Fanfare for a New Theater* intervallic motifs in the twelve-tone row: first line: ordered motifs with intervals always in the opposite direction; below: 1-2 motifs in both the opposite and the same direction.

From Motifs to Rows

It is important to note that in the aforementioned compositions of the mid 1950s the intervallic motifs are combined into melodic material (they are rarely used to crate harmonies) and that Stravinsky rarely modifies the octave registers of the individual notes. This means that intervals are still rigidly treated as absolute distances between the keys in terms of steps and half steps. With the adoption of the principle of the octave equivalence, Stravinsky's technique became much more flexible.

By comparison with the rows used in *Agon*, the motivic structure of the twelve-note rows employed in the compositions which succeed it chronologically appear to be less well defined. Beginning with *Movements*, Stravinsky seems to have derived many of his twelve-note rows from a reading of a concrete musical idea — most often a brief polyphonic passage previously 'improvised' at the keyboard. This procedure guarantees that the intervallic motifs contained in the initial musical idea are less evident in the related twelve-note row, in which the structural intervals can be found between non-adjacent pitches. This creates a sort of circularity between the two stages into which Stravinsky's creative process can be subdivided: (1) the initial definition of a row of pitches and (2) the transformation of the 'abstract' row into concrete musical contexts. In either of these stages, motivic-intervallic logic can take on a role of greater or lesser importance. In the first stage, the combination of intervals on the keyboard determines the physiognomy of the row. In the second stage, a similar intervallic logic determines the way the rows are transformed into concrete music. In this case, in other words, Stravinsky does not 'improvise' with intervals to create a row, but 'improvises' on the row itself to highlight some intervallic relationships contained between its notes — even non-adjacent ones. Given this circular process, if the motivic-intervallic structure of the row is less evident and more ambiguous, the row more easily allows for different musical realisations which illuminate different aspects of its motivic-intervallic content.

Stravinsky hinted at different cases in which the formulation of a twelve-note row could derive from an initial concrete musical idea. In *Themes and episodes*, for example, he described the twelve-note row of the *Variations for orchestra* (also discussed in Chapter One) as «a

269

succession of notes that came to my mind as a melody»[155]. Even clearer is his description of the composition of *Epitaphium*:

> I began the *Epitaphium* with flute-clarinet duet (which I had originally thought of as a duet for two flutes, and which can be played by two flutes [...]. In the manner I have described in our previous conversations, I heard and composed a melodic-harmonic phrase. I certainly did not (and never do) begin with a purely serial idea, and, in fact, when I began, I did not know, or care, whether all twelve notes would be used. After I had written about half the first phrase I saw its serial pattern, however, and [...] began to work toward that pattern. The constructive problem that first attracted me in the two-part counterpoint of the first phrase was the harmonic one of minor seconds. The flute-clarinet responses are mostly seconds, and so are the harp responses, though the harp part is sometimes complicated by the addition of third, fourth and fifth harmonic voices[156].

In Stravinsky's sketches from *Movements* onwards many other melodic or contrapuntal annotations which served as the model for the formulation of a twelve-tone row can be found, and they often display a clear motivic-intervallic design. This is the case of the two twelve-note rows employed in the *Requiem Canticles*, which Stravinsky explicitly attributed to «some intervallic designs which I expanded into contrapuntal forms»[157]. The original form of this counterpoint can be found among the sketches for the instrumental *Interlude*, which was the first movement, in chronological order, to be composed[158]. One of the very first ideas sketched by Stravinsky is reproduced in Ex. 24[159]. It is formed from the union of two brief contrapuntal phrases based on the two original rows employed in the movement, as indicated by the autograph serial symbols. The two phrases, initially notated separately on two small clippings of paper, were then pasted onto a piece of cardboard (the continuity between the two phrases is indicated by Stravinsky's autograph arrow; the two clippings are oriented as shown in my transcription)[160].

---

[155]. *THEMES AND EPISODES*, p. 60.

[156]. *MEMORIES AND COMMENTARIES*, pp. 99-100 Stravinsky's account finds confirmation in the analysis of the fundamental row of *Epitaphium* and in the way it is transformed into concrete music, as shown by STRAUS 2001, pp. 61- 63, 99-102 and 130-131, and LOCANTO 2002, pp. 125-131.

[157]. See CRAFT 1972, p. 98. In the *Requiem Canticles*, the two different fundamental rows are employed simultaneously only in the *Interlude* and the *Postlude*. The remaining movements employ them alternatively.

[158]. See above my discussion of the collection of sketches for the *Interlude*.

[159]. Stravinsky (*SSC I-III*, vol. II, p. 467), maintained that this sketch was preceded by another, dated March 1965, containing three annotations of row II, in each of which various metrical indications are visible, followed by a brief musical passage (also based on row II) of which there is no trace in the final score. However, there is no proof that this sketch preceded the sketch transcribed in my Ex. 24, and, in any case, it does not contain annotations of row I.

[160]. The second clipping is now detached from the piece of cardboard, on which, however, remain the traces of the adhesive tape which originally held them together. Thanks to these traces we can see that the second

Ex. 24: Igor Stravinsky, sketches for *Requiem Canticles*, Interlude (Paul Sacher Foundation, Igor Stravinsky Collection).

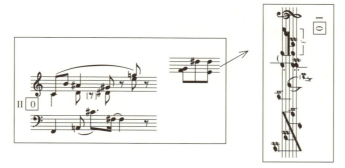

The two phrases correspond respectively to bb. 161-162 and 173-175 of the score, of which the clippings preserve a very rudimentary version. In the following sketches, Stravinsky added new musical material between them, thus creating the whole musical passage at bb. 163-172, and then bars 176-192, thus creating the entire episode for four flutes (bars 161-192), the largest and most important formal section of the piece.

In summary, it seems that the two musical ideas were indeed the point of departure in the composition of the Interlude. If this is so, they may well feature the original 'intervallic designs' to which Stravinsky alluded. In fact, the contrapuntal relations of the two musical phrases illuminate a very clear motivic-intervallic construction, based on the 1-2 and 1-5 motifs (Ex. 25). The triplet in the first crotchet of the second phrase — probably composed first[161] — presents within itself a sort of polyphony: the lower 'part', delineated by the pitches f - g - e placed in the same register, produces a 1-2 motif; the $d\sharp$ of the upper 'part' forms, however, a relation of a semitone with the lower e. By holding these two pitches firm and adding the $f\sharp$, another 1-2 motif is obtained in the second crotchet of the phrase, this time vertically ($d\sharp$ - e - $f\sharp$). Furthermore, the two motifs are a semitone apart from each other (e - f - g and $d\sharp$ - e - $f\sharp$). In the remaining part of the phrase, three overlapping 1-2 motifs, in both [012] and [013] forms, are unfolded horizontally. In the first phrase (reproduced on the left in Ex. 25), the first two vertical simultaneities of three pitches form two motifs of class 1-5 — respectively in the forms [016] and [015] — while the following group of four pitches delineates a cycle of three ic5s ($c\sharp$ - $d\sharp$ - $g\sharp$ - $f\sharp$), divided symmetrically into two ($f\sharp$ - $c\sharp$ in the bass; $g\sharp$ - $d\sharp$ in the upper parts). The last vertical sonority of three pitches ($f\sharp$ - e - g) forms a 1-2 motif which creates a strong link with the following phrase, beginning with the motif f - g - e, another member of the 1-2 motivic class. The link — illustrated also by Stravinsky's cue in the upper right-hand corner of the first sheet of Ex. 24 — is reinforced by the presence of the notes e and g in both of the motifs. The 'intervallic designs' contained in the two ideas thus become quite clear.

---

clipping was pasted in vertical, as shown in my transcription.

[161].   As shown by Stravinsky's numbering of this row as no. 1.

Ex. 25: Motivic analysis of the musical ideas contained in the sketches of Ex. 24.

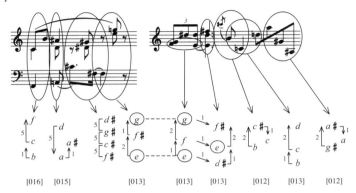

In cases like that of *Epitaphium* and *Requiem canticles* just discussed one might ask which came first, these two musical ideas or the two twelve-note rows — whether, in other words, the rows were obtained from the musical ideas or could instead have been fixed in advance as an abstract sequence of pitches on the basis of which the musical ideas were subsequently elaborated. The fact that the musical ideas contain all twelve notes without repetition does not mean we must prefer the second solution: generally speaking, in fact, we may suppose that Stravinsky initially elaborated his musical ideas following a predominantly motivic-intervallic logic, and although even at this stage — of which, however, hardly any written traces remain — he tended to exploit all twelve notes of the chromatic gamut, that did not prevent him from using some pitches more than once. Only in the final formulation of the idea were the repetitions eliminated until a fundamental twelve-note row was obtained. This is clearly demonstrated by a set of 25 photographs taken in December 1966 by the photographer Arnold Newman in Stravinsky's Hollywood studio and then reproduced in Robert Craft's 1967 volume *Bravo Stravinsky*[162] Newman's photos record step by step the creation of a musical idea — a brief instrumental passage that was to have been employed, according to Craft, as part of «a string passage in the middle section of a symphonic piece», which was never brought to completion[163] — and its successive transformation into a twelve-note row to be used throughout the piece. In this case Stravinsky is portrayed while working out the sketch entirely at the table — not at the piano —

---

[162]. CRAFT 1967, pp. 12-21. STRAUS 2001, pp. 49-52, has first drawn attention on (and analyzed) the music sketched in Newman's photos. The whole photo shoot reproduced in Craft's volume include two large photos at pp. 12-13, in which Stravinsky is about to trace the staves on the blank page with his 'Stravigor'; a series of 24 little photos portraying the progress of Stravinsky's musical sketch at pp. 14-15 and 18-19; a full-page photo at pp. 16-17, with Stravinsky reflecting halfway through his work; and another full-page photo with the clipping of the final twelve-tone note at pp. 20-21. In the following discussion and in Ex. 26, with the numbers 1-25 I refer to the series of 24 photos at pp. 14-15 and 18-19 and to the final photo with the twelve-tone row at pp. 20-21, numbered as 25.

[163]. CRAFT 1967, p. 13.

but we know that this was not his normal habit. In the short introductory text to the photos, Robert Craft wrote:

> During the morning of December 13 [1966], Stravinsky mentioned the «need to put an idea in order» but when the sketch was completed, in about thirty — five minutes, he said that the music he had actually written was something different and that it had not been in his mind as long as an hour before. And he always seems to know exactly when his imagination is at the starting line. Shortly after he had finished, [...] to show what he meant by putting in order, the composer placed three wine glasses in parade formation, then interchanged the first and third, saying «It is a matter of knowing that the notes must be this way and no other». [...] The appearance of instrumental indications (violas and cellos) in this initial stage argues that the springs of his inventions are concrete, and that the scissoring out of a twelve-note series, which is rather the beginning of a formulating then of an abstracting process, does not contradict the claim. The composer's next step was to chart his fields of choice by drawing derivative serial forms. These he attached, like dressmakers' patterns, to the side of the piano writing board, pinning the sketch itself to the center, whence it became the incremental center of the composition. From this point, too, he worked exclusively at the piano; he had not touched the instrument that morning but, as he says, was composing from his inner ear[164].

This story contains some truthful information, including the one that concerns us most at this moment, namely that the series was usually derived by Stravinsky from a concrete musical idea, and not vice versa. Craft's description of working methods — Stravinsky's use of cutting out pieces of paper containing various musical materials, then recombining them in later stages of composition, or keeping them handy as a reference — also matches to the description of Stravinsky's methods that I made in the first part of this chapter. However, although Craft admits that the later stages of the composition were conducted by Stravinsky «exclusively at the piano», he maintains that before putting his idea in writing Stravinsky «had not touched the instrument» and that he composed this idea only «from his inner ear». This may well be true, but Craft's narration seems affected by a typically dualist vision of the mind-body relationship. His use of terms like 'imagination', 'to have in mind' 'inner ear' as well as his assumption that the first 'ideas' of a musical composition (themes, motifs, musical subjects, etc.) may generate exclusively in the composer's 'mind', are symptomatic of a 'disembodied' vision of the creative mind. His words vaguely recall those of Cowell quoted at the beginning of this chapter. Moreover, we cannot exclude that even in this case the idea written down on the paper was first 'improvised' at the keyboard: Newman's photos could only portray a phase of a broader and more complex process that included various stages, even distant in time, which took place

---

164. *Ibidem.*

partly in the writing and partly in the instrument. Craft' need to clarify that Stravinsky «had not touched the instrument that morning» depends precisely on the fact that Stravinsky did usually compose at the piano.

In any case, whether it was previously 'improvised' at the keyboard or directly composed on the paper, Stravinsky's musical idea photographed by Newman, clearly shows the composer's typical motivic-intervallic approach, and that the formulation of the 12-tone row followed — rather than preceded — his initial musical idea. According to Joseph Straus, this idea was based on a tone-semitone motif belonging to set class [013][165]. My interpretation is different: the intervallic motif that guided Stravinsky's choices — as well as his second thoughts — was the semitone-major third (1-4) in its two possible forms, [014] and [015]. In the first stage (Ex. 26a: corresponding to photos 1-10), Stravinsky notates five notes (*b - c - b♭ - d♭ - a*) as a purely abstract succession of pitches, with noteheads only (without rhythmic values). The five pitches can be read as the beginning of an *Allintervallreihe* (a row containing all the intervals). In the next stage (Ex. 26b: photos 11-13), Stravinsky adds two more notes (*b - c*) at the end of the previous five, and introduce a second polyphonic voice with two notes only. Only at this point does he provides the whole idea with a specific rhythmic design. In the third stage (Ex. 26c: photos 14-17) he prolongs the melody with three more notes (*b♭ - g♭ - f*), and replaces the first *c* with an *e♭*, thus avoiding the repetition of *c*. He also adds the indications of the instruments: violas (upper stave) and cellos (lower stave). The choice of *e* throws light on the motivic-intervallic logic which guides the composition of the passage: the first three notes of the viola (*b - e♭ - b♭*) now form a motif of the semitone-major third type (1-4). This motif — in its two forms, [014] and [015] — appears at numerous other points within the passage: in the first five notes of the viola part (twice: *b - e♭ - b♭* and *b♭ - d♭ - a* with *b♭* in common); in the last three notes of the cello (*b♭ - g♭ - f*), grouped together as a triplet; between the first two notes of the viola (*b - e♭*) and the *d* of the cello which follows immediately afterwards (a semitone lower); and finally in the contrapuntal relationship between the *b♭ - d♭* of the viola and the *d* of the cello (see the motivic analysis in Ex. 26d). Note that up to this point Stravinsky was not trying to avoid the repetition of pitches: in stage 2 the initial notes *b* and *c* were repeated at the end of the passage. And in stage three the notes *b* and *b♭* appeared twice. Clearly, he was *not* trying to sketch down a complete (with no repeated notes) 12-tone row, but rather a musical idea with a particular motivic-intervallic shape. Only in the following (fourth) stage (Ex. 26e: photos 18-21) he starts copying all the notes of the passage onto a third staff, to obtain a row, but he suddenly stops (photo 21), since he notices the repetition of *b* and *b♭* and replaces them with *g* and *a♭*, respectively. By making this adjustment, he not only obtains all twelve notes without repetition, but also preserves the

---

[165]. See STRAUS 2001, pp. 49-52. The divergence between my analysis and that of Straus depends, even in this case, on our different conceptions of 'intervallic motif'. In this case, moreover, the difference is accentuated by the fact that in my analysis, as opposed to Straus', the presence of the motif also arises in the vertical dimension.

Ex. 26a-g: Arnold Newman's photos (reproduced in Craft 1967, pp. 14-15 and 18-21).

a) Stage 1 (photos 1-10)

b) Stage 2 (photos 11-13)

c) Stage 3 (photos 14-17)

d) Analysis of stage 3

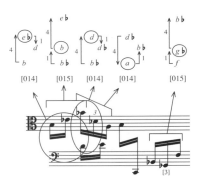

e) Stage 4 (photos 18-21)

f) Analysis of stage 4

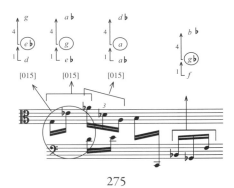

275

g) Final row (photos 22-25)

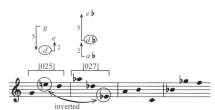

motivic construction of the passage, which remains based on the conspicuous presence of the 1-4 motif, now in the form [015] (Ex. 26f).

The final phase occurs in the Ex. 26g (photos 22-25), in which Stravinsky finally writes down the complete twelve-note row, arranging in succession the notes of the polyphonic passage just composed, and cutting it out with scissors, so that it can be kept at hand on the piano's music stand during the rest of the compositional process. Here a small adjustment in the order of the pitches conceals the original motivic-intervallic shape of the passage while at the same time illuminating a new one. The second and sixth pitches ($e♮$ and $e♭$) are inverted with respect to stage 4 (see the circled notes in the example). Thus, the first two segments of three pitches (g - e - d and $a♭$ - $d♭$ - $e♭$) become two motifs of the class 2-5. Moreover, the four segments of three pitches which form the row delineate a symmetrical structure: the combination of the even-numbered segments forms a partial circle of fifths from $g♭$ to f, while the combination of the odd-numbered segments forms the remaining part of the circle (from c to b) (note also Stravinsky's enharmonic spelling, which reflects the circle of perfect fifths):

1. e - $d♭$ - $a♭$ (segment 2) + $b♭$ - $g♭$ - f (segment 4) = $g♭$ - $d♭$ - $a♭$ - $e♭$ - $b♭$ - f
2. g - d - e (segment 1) + a - b - c (segment 3) = c - g - d - a - e - b.

FROM ROWS TO MOTIFS

At this point let us consider in more detail how Stravinsky's motivic-intervallic approach influences the transformation of an 'abstract' row into concrete musical contexts. Stravinsky uses innumerable musical devices to highlight some interval relationships that would otherwise be hardly recognizable in the linear form of the row, between its adjacent pitches. They concern, for example, the polyphonic writing — the horizontal or vertical arrangement of the notes of the series —, or the musical emphasis of some notes with respect to others. However, even before starting to put the row into music he often deliberately modifies the very physiognomy of the series itself. He does so basically in two ways:

1) by freely reordering the notes of the row, thus highlighting other interval relationships than those immediately visible between the consecutive notes in the linear form of the series in its original ordering;

2) by disintegrating the series into smaller and smaller fragments, down to only two-three notes (a single interval or two conjoined intervals), which are extrapolated from the serial charts and treated individually, as if they were autonomous units.

This last procedure, in particular, has very little 'serial' logic, since one can hardly speak of such logic in the case of successions of only two notes. Clearly, what matters here are the individual intervals, rather than the succession of pitches.

As an example of the first procedure (the reordering of the notes) I will consider a brief musical fragment drawn from the beginning (bars 46-48) of the second of the five *Movements* (Exs. 27 and 28)[166]. The passage is based on the two discrete hexachords (labelled α and β) of the fundamental row used throughout the entire composition (Ex. 27, first and third lines). In the upper part of the sketch transcribed in Ex. 28, Stravinsky wrote the RI (T6) form of hexachord α and the R form of hexachord β (Ex. 27, second and fourth lines) — as indicated also by the autograph labels 'Riv-Inv α' and 'Riv β' (which stand for RI α and R α, respectively.

As my analysis shows, hexachord β can be divided into two trichords belonging to set class [012], which can in turn be related to motif class 1-2. Hexachord a is formed by two trichords of set class [016], which can be related to three different intervallic motifs: 1-6, 1-5 or 5-6. In this case, Stravinsky clearly placed the intervals of a semitone and perfect fifth (motif 1-5) in relief. To this end, a particular permutation of the order of the pitches of hexachord a is carried out: besides placing the pitches in reverse order (from the sixth to the first), he also reversed the order of the first two pitches of each trichord. In this manner the pitches which form ic5 (represented in bold in the schema below) are always adjacent:

$$6 - 5 - 4 / 3 - 2 - 1 \text{ becomes } \mathbf{5 - 6} - 4 / 3 - \mathbf{1 - 2}$$
$$(g - f\sharp - c / d - d\flat - a\flat \text{ becomes } \mathbf{f\sharp - g} - c / d - \mathbf{a\flat - d\flat})$$

The purpose behind this reordering can be appreciated in the musical passage outlined in the sketch transcribed in Ex. 28, immediately below the two hexachords: the pitches which form ic5 are arranged vertically as a perfect fifth; the pitches which form ic1 precede the fifth in a register at the distance of an octave. The two fifths ($c - g / d\flat - a\flat$) are separated by a semitone, thereby producing a symmetrical configuration. All these choices are clearly intended to throw the ic1 and ic5 into relief.

This brief example shows how some operations which alter the physiognomy of the row were intended by Stravinsky to facilitate the transformation of an abstract row in a specific musical passage which highlights some motivic-intervallic characteristics. One such operation is order permutation, as we have just seen.

---

[166]. The dotted minim in the middle of the third line of the sketch shown in Ex. 28 clearly appears to be a b_3 in the sketch. However, this is obviously an error. The understood note is doubtless c_4, as is seen either in the serial hexachord employed in the passage (first line above in the sketch), or in the final score (bar 47, trombone I).

Ex. 27: Igor Stravinsky, *Movements*, II: hexachordal forms employed in the sketch shown in Ex. 28.

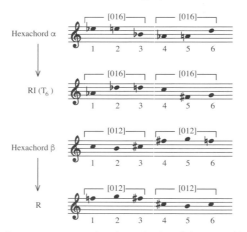

Ex. 28: Igor Stravinsky, sketches for *Movements*, II (see bars 46-48 of the printed score) (Paul Sacher Foundation, Igor Stravinsky Collection).

Stravinsky's second, and more important, device aimed at highlighting some interval relationships within the rows — the disintegration of the series into small fragments of two or three notes —, was probably adopted for the first time in *Threni*. In the *De elegia tertia* (*Sensus spei*) section of the score, for example, a complex fabric of serial segments is used for the tenor melody on '*Eradicationem*' (bars 252-259), as it was shown by Susannah Tucker with the assistance of the sketches. Tucker, however, concluded that Stravinsky's choice of various segments «was determined by no compositional "system"» (p. 251). On the contrary, in my Ph.D. dissertation, I was able to demonstrate that in all of the preliminary versions of the passage, as in the final version, the choice was determined by the desire to create a dense chain of overlapping 1-5 motifs[167].

---

167.   TUCKER 1992, vol. II, p. 251. LOCANTO 2002, pp. 134-137.

Ex. 29: Igor Stravinsky, *Requiem Canticles*, 'Dies irae', bars 81-83, 86 and 97-98: motivic-intervallic construction.
© Copyright 1967 by Boosey & Hawkes Music Publishers Ltd. By kind permission.

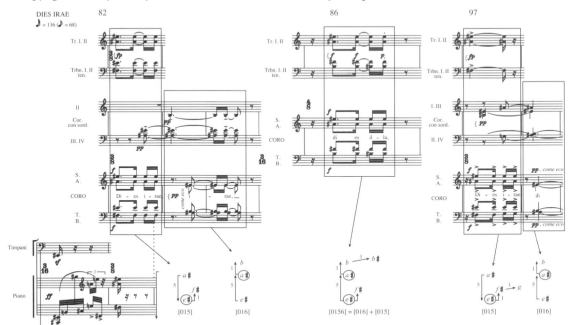

In cases such as *The Elegia tertia*, however the serial fragments selected by Stravinsky are still quite long: mostly they are fragments of four-five sounds extrapolated from the four basic forms of the row. In the following compositions, on the other hand, the fragments get smaller and smaller, down to just the two notes (a single interval) and used in an increasingly sophisticated fashion. A good example is the '*Dies irae*' section of the *Requiem Canticles*. Here, the basic intervals combined into the motifs are ic 5 (perfect fifth/fourth) and ic1 (semitone). Ex. 29 reproduces the three choral statements at the beginning, in the middle and towards the end of the section. Overall, they constitute a formal layer which alternates with other blocks of music, whose features are very different, thus creating a typically Stravinskyan block-form. In my example, the contrasting measures (bb. 84-85, 87-96) are omitted, in order to show the whole formal layer in a continuous (uninterrupted) way — as, in fact, it was composed by Stravinsky before splitting it into three different fragments. The first block (bars 82-83) divides in turn into two parts: in the first part the chorus (doubled by the brass) sings the words 'Dies irae' on a *forte* chord repeated in a dotted rhythm; in the second, the single word 'irae' (chorus and horns *con sordini*) is repeated as an echo to a *piano* chord which bears a certain affinity with the preceding harmony. The second block (bar 86) contains a repetition of the *forte* chord on '*dies illa*', but with no echo response. The third statement (bar 97 onwards) is a recapitulation of the first, although it presents a slight harmonic departure. Thus, the entire layer assumes a type of ABA' form. My analytic symbols (below the score) show the motivic- intervallic construction.

The two chords of the first block (bars 82-83) correspond to the two forms — [015] and [016], according to the direction of the intervals — of the motivic class 1-5. Moreover, the two chords share the pitches $e\sharp$ and $a\sharp$, which form ic5. The impression that the first chord is echoed by the second (*come eco*) therefore derives not only from the presence of two common tones, but also from the intrinsic motivic-intervallic affinity of the two harmonies. The second choral statement (bar 86) opens onto a symmetrical sonority, a member of set class [0156] containing two ic1s and two ic5s. This sonority is obtained through the sum of the two 1-5 motifs appearing in the two chords of the first statement: $e\sharp$ - $f\sharp$ - $a\sharp$ [015] + $e\sharp$ - $a\sharp$ - b [016] = $e\sharp$ - $f\sharp$ - $a\sharp$ - b [0156]. This time the chord is not simply repeated: in the middle of the bar, the lowest voice moves a semitone from b to $b\sharp$, thereby giving rise to a vertical sonority containing an ic1 (f - $f\sharp$) and two conjoined ic5s ($a\sharp$ - $e\sharp$ - $b\sharp$). The recapitulation (bar 97) is almost identical to the first statement, but in the first part (the *forte* chord on 'Dies irae'), the bass moves a semitone from $f\sharp$ to g. In this way, the perfect fifth $a\sharp$ - $e\sharp$ is a constant presence throughout the layer, thus forming a kind tonal axis.

Stravinsky's sketches for this layer of the piece, transcribed in Ex. 30 and 31, bear the traces of his work with ic1 and ic5 at the keyboard and of his attempt to make the result of his work reflect, in some way, the internal characteristics of the twelve-tone series and its various serial transformations. The first sketch reproduces a strip of paper containing an early version of the first block (bb 82-83), preceded by the pre-emptive instrumental gesture which introduces it (bar 81). (Stravinsky's serial symbol «II inv» in Ex. 30 indicates that the passage is based on the inverse form of the second fundamental twelve-note row used in the whole score). Note that in this version the harmony of the choral part includes a move of a semitone from $f\sharp$ to g in the bass voice, a solution which Stravinsky will subsequently adopt for the varied recapitulation (compare Ex. 30 with Ex. 29). The move of a semitone from $f\sharp$ to g in the bass part is also found in the lower system of the sketch reproduced in Ex. 31, which reproduces a sketch containing two different versions — in the upper and lower systems respectively — of the first and the second block (on the words 'Dies irae' and 'dies illa' respectively), worked out as an unbroken layer. In the version of the upper system the $f\sharp$ of the bass part moves by ic5 directly to b — not by ic1 to g — thus anticipating the same note in the following chord. Here, the echo response, which in the final version is used only for the first statement and the recapitulation, is used also for in second block. In the first version of the passage (upper system), the chord of the second block is a series of three conjoined perfect fifths (b - $f\sharp$ - $c\sharp$ - $g\sharp$). In the second version (the lower system) the b is modified to a $b\sharp$. The alteration forms set class [0157], which contains two conjoined ic5s ($f\sharp$ - $c\sharp$ - $g\sharp$) along with an ic1 between $b\sharp$ and $c\sharp$. In the final version, Stravinsky opted for a chord containing two ic1s and two ic5s, as we have already seen. Clearly, all of the variants in the sketches, like the final version, can be interpreted as the registration on the paper of various preliminary attempts (various 'improvisations') to create the whole layer through various combinations of ic1 and ic5 in different directions and configurations.

Ex. 30: Igor Stravinsky, sketches for *Requiem Canticles*, 'Dies irae' (see also bars 81-83 of the printed score) (Paul Sacher Foundation, Igor Stravinsky Collection).

However, Stravinsky also tried to give these preliminary intervallic explorations a sort of 'serial coherence', by relating them to the inner structure of the row. The only serial symbols discernible in the sketches are on the page transcribed in Ex. 31 and refer to the second of the two fundamental twelve-note rows employed in the *Requiem Canticles*, or, more precisely, to the two 'rotational arrays' generated respectively by the first hexachord of series I (Ia) and the first hexachord of series RI (RIa) in Ex. 31, below the sketch. Without going into detail on the various properties of this type of table and the ways of using it, I will briefly describe its construction[168]. The pitches of the original hexachord are first made to rotate systematically from right to the left: the first rotation begins with the second pitch of the original hexachord, while the first pitch moves into the final position; the second rotation begins with the second pitch of the first rotation (the third pitch of the original), and so on for five iterations, after which it returns to the original form. The five rotated forms thus obtained are transposed successively so that they all begin on the same pitch as the original hexachord (in the specific case, *f* for the forms generated by hexachord Ia; *g* for the forms generated by hexachord RIa). In this way, each of the five rotated-transposed forms thus obtained contains the same succession of intervals globally — each time beginning at a different point within the succession — but different pitch classes.

---

168.   On the properties of Stravinsky's serial rotational arrays see especially Spies 1965a, Spies 1965b and Spies 1967; Rogers 1968; Hogan 1982; Van den Toorn 1983, pp. 442-444; Babbitt 1986 and 1987a; Morris 1988; and Straus 2001, pp. 26-33. Stravinsky's first composition to make use of rotational arrays is *Movements* (1958-1959).

Ex. 31: Igor Stravinsky, sketches for *Requiem Canticles*, 'Dies irae' (see bars 81-83, 86 and 97-98 of the printed score) (Paul Sacher Foundation, Igor Stravinsky Collection); (below) rotational arrays of the hexachord a of the inversion (left-hand column) and retrograde inversion (right-hand column) of twelve-note row II, with encircled serial segments employed in the upper sketch (the circles and connecting arrows are not part of Stravinsky's original autograph); (below, on the right:) motif 1-5, in the forms of sets [016] and [015].

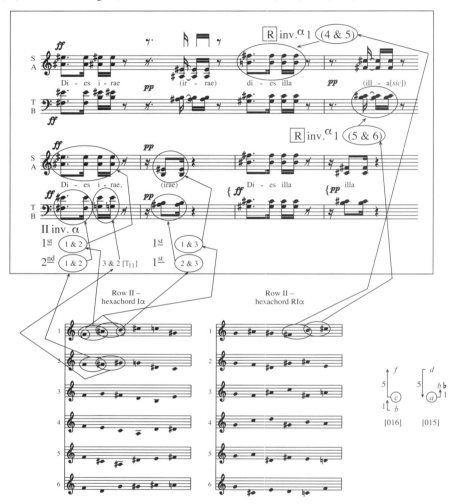

The symbols on the sketches clearly indicate that the chords of the choral part are related by Stravinsky to a combination of dyads freely selected from the two rotational arrays[169]. In general, the dyads derive from segments of two consecutive notes within a line of the tables. In

---

[169]. The serial symbols of the sketch can be deciphered as follows: II = second fundamental row; 'Inv' = inversion (I); 'R inv' = retrograde inversion (RI); 'a' = first hexachord; '1st' = first line of the rotational array; '2nd' = second line of the rotational array (etc.); '1st, 1 & 2' = first and second notes of the first line of the array; '2nd, 1 & 2' = first and second notes of the second line of the array; and so on.

one case, however, they even derive from two non-consecutive notes ('1ˢᵗ, 1 & 3' = the first and third note of the first line). In another case, the dyad derived from the third and second note of the second line ('2ⁿᵈ, 3 & 2' = g♯ - f♯) is transposed up a semitone (or eleven semitones upward: T11), so as to become g - e♯. As can be seen, Stravinsky does not seem to have selected the dyads according to a pre-established criterion or precise order within the table. Rather, it seems that his only intention was to find numerous ic1 and ic5 relations within his serial chart. These intervals, in fact, attain a certain importance within the original form of hexachord a, where they form two motifs of class 1-5, in the forms [016] and [015], respectively (as shown in in the left-hand corner of Ex. 31). Given the structure of the tables, these intervallic motifs also appear in the rotated(-transposed) forms. Clearly enough, by extrapolating only dyadic segments, rather than complete hexachordal units, Stravinsky tried to obtain from his row charts a denser and more cohesive motivic construction than could be achieved using the hexachords in their entirety. Note, for example, that the two 1-5 motifs interlaced to form the symmetrical set [0156] in the second choral statement derive from neither hexachord a nor from its rotated(-transposed) form. This demonstrates that from Stravinsky's point of view serial technique is not essential *per se*, but instead functions only as a means to an end with regard to motivic-intervallic syntax. The use of complete serial forms does not, as a matter of fact, represent a restriction: if necessary, their use can pass into the background in favour of a more immediate and direct engagement with single intervals.

Another good example is provided by the 'Rex tremendae' section of the *Requiem Canticles*. The serial construction of its first bars of the piece is illustrated on the first page of the autograph short score (containing bars 203-208), transcribed in Ex. 32[170]. The symbol 'I Rα' stands for row number I, retrograde form, hexachord α. The circled numbers at the beginning of each choral part in the short score indicate the lines of the rotational arrays of the first hexachord. Only limited portions (three to five notes) of each line are used (shown circled in Ex. 33). The zigzag line traced across the choral parts (note also the effect created by the occasional doubling of pitches in the vocal parts) corresponds to the brass part (trumpet and trombone) elaborated on the lower portion of the page. The autograph symbols indicate that even this line was obtained by the combination of three serial segments drawn from the two rotational arrays of the R hexachords. For example, the symbol 'Rα 5ᵗʰ 3 4 5' stands for retrograde, hexachord α, fifth line of the rotational array, notes 3-4-5. In Ex. 33 the rotational array is represented with the segments used in the brass part indicated within boxes. As can be seen, the first three bars of the

---

[170]. The complete autograph short score comprises four separate pages. Only the page transcribed in Ex. 32 — which, unlike the others, is merely drafted — contains serial symbols. Its content corresponds to the printed score, with the sole exception of the *e* in place of *d* in the third bar of the tenor. The reading *d* is probably incorrect: the *e* of the autograph short score finds confirmation in the serial tables; the reading *e* appears for the first time in the clean copy of the score.

Ex. 32: Igor Stravinsky, first page of the short score for *Requiem Canticles*, 'Rex tremendae' (see bars 203-207 of the printed score) (Paul Sacher Foundation, Igor Stravinsky Collection).

choral part and the brass parts are entirely obtained through a combination of serial segments extrapolated by the arrays[171]. As in the case of the *'Dies irae'*, the segments are selected in an apparently arbitrary manner. Nevertheless, they demonstrate a significant presence of motifs of class 1-2: four of the five segments of three-note segments (Rα 1st 4-6, Rα 4th 4-6, Rα 5th 3-5, Rα 6th 4-6 and Rβ 5th 4-6) directly correspond to this motif class; one of the two segments of five notes (Rα 3rd 2-6) contains two overlapped 1-2 motifs ($d_\sharp$ - $c_\sharp$ - c + c - b - a); and the other (Rα 1st 1-5) begins with a 1-2 motif ($f_\sharp$ - $g_\sharp$ - a). The reason for this arrangement was Stravinsky's desire to create an imitative texture: at regular intervals of a minim the contralto, the trombone, the sopranos and the tenors display motif 1-2; but because this motif can assume two different forms — [012] and [013] — and given that the three pitches can be combined in any order, the imitative responses repeat neither the same melodic profile (as in traditional imitative style) nor the same set class. Motif 1-2 is also repeated three times in the brass part which runs throughout the choral passage. Note also that the initial pitches of each imitative part ($a_\sharp$ - $g_\sharp$ - $d_\sharp$ - $f_\sharp$) gradually take the form of a sequence of perfect fifths ($f_\sharp$ - $c_\sharp$ - $g_\sharp$ - $d_\sharp$ - $a_\sharp$),

---

171. Starting in bar 4, the pitch organisation of the choral part is based on a different serial technique, which involves reading the rotational arrays vertically. On this technique see especially STRAUS 2001, pp. 152-164.

Ex. 33: Igor Stravinsky, *Requiem Canticles*, twelve-note row I: rotational arrays of the hexachords α and β of the retrograde form, with encircled serial segments employed in the sketch of Ex. 32.

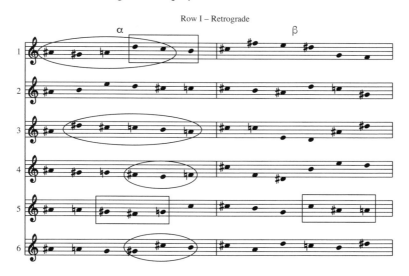

Row I – Retrograde

which is completed in bar 3 with the addition of the pitches $g_\sharp$ and $d_\sharp$ in the bass part. This homogenous motivic design is due largely to the structure of the row itself. Indeed, it should be evident that numerous 1-2 motifs are already contained in row I of the *Requiem Canticles* (as we have seen). Nevertheless, by choosing ad hoc fragments, Stravinsky created an imitative texture which was more coherent than would have been possible had he used complete hexachords.

One might ask in what sense and to what degree such a procedure could be defined as genuinely 'serial'. The fact that the composer had indicated the serial origin of the various segments in the short score demonstrates that he conceived of the row as a reservoir of motivic-intervallic material, and that he understood serial technique as a means of managing this material in a more systematic way than he would have done intuitively, at the keyboard.

MOVEMENTS... OVER THE KEYBOARD

To conclude my series of analyses based on sketches, I will finally turn my attention to the composition that was in many ways the arrival point of Stravinsky's search for a personal serial technique during the 1950s: *Movements* for piano and orchestra, composed in 1958-1959.

The beginning section of the first movement contains a flute episode which is very familiar to Stravinsky scholars, since Stravinsky himself drew attention to its construction, thereby instigating a long series of attempts at analysis:[172]

---

[172]. Analyses of the flute solo can be found in WHITE 1979, p. 612; MÜLLER 1984; BABBITT 1986, p. 255; TUCKER 1992, vol. II, p. 258; RUST 1994, pp. 64-71; STRAUS 2001, pp. 65-68 (based on Rust) and 125-130.

No theorist could determine the spelling of the note order in, for example, the flute solo near the beginning [of *Movements*] simply by knowing the original order [of the 12-tone row], however unique the combinatorial properties of this particular series[173].

Ex. 34 shows the succession of pitches on which the flute episode is based. Actually, it serves as the basis for all the three solo episodes — for, respectively, piano alone, flute solo accompanied by piano and clarinet, and piano accompanied by strings — included in the first section (up to the *prima volta*) of the movement (bars 7-22), not only for the central flute episode recalled by Stravinsky. Much of the difficulty in understanding how it is built depends on the fact that it is not made of sufficiently long row forms, but of a series of short serial fragments, mostly of only three notes which were selected according to Stravinsky's typical intervallic logic, so that describing this passage as 'serial' wouldn't be entirely appropriate. As can be seen from my analytical symbols, the succession conceals a closely woven fabric of overlapping motifs of the semitone-tone (1-2) and semitone-tritone (1-6) types (indicated by square brackets). Depending on the orientation assumed by the two intervals, the first motif (1-2) produces sets of three pitches belonging to set classes [012] and [013]. The second motif (1-6), on the other hand, produces collections belonging to set class [016] regardless of the orientation assumed by the two intervals[174].

Ex. 34: Igor Stravinsky, *Movements*, I: motivic structure of the succession of pitches contained in each of the three solo episodes of bars 7-22.

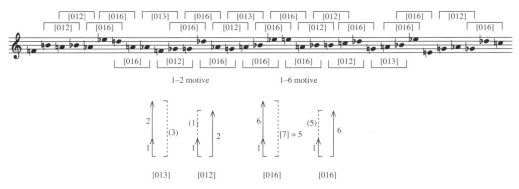

To better understand the relationship between this intervallic construction and Stravinsky's serial technique, it is useful to begin with the subset structure of the two hexachords of the fundamental row (Ex. 35). The first hexachord is formed by two disjunct trichords belonging to set class [016]. In the middle, starting with the third note, one finds a trichord

---

173. *MEMORIES AND COMMENTARIES*, p. 106.

174. Since the tritone divides the octave into two equal parts.

of set class [012]. The second hexachord contains two disjunct trichords of set class [012] and one [016] trichord at its centre, thus complementing the first hexachord. Other interesting properties of the two hexachords emerge when one takes into consideration their rotated forms.

Ex. 35: Igor Stravinsky, *Movements*: subset structure of the fundamental twelve-tone row.

Ex. 36 reproduces one of the rotational arrays employed by Stravinsky for the composition of *Movements*: columns α and β contain the rotated forms of the two hexachords of the original form of the row; columns γ and δ display the rotated- transposed forms. Ex. 37 reveals the subset structure of all these rotated (-transposed) forms. Eight of the twelve hexachords contain within them three trichords belonging to set class [016] or [012]; two hexachords (γ II and γ III) contain four trichords of the same type, which closely overlap with one another. The remaining two hexachords (δ I and δ IV) contain two each. Clearly enough, the internal structure of the two hexachords is such that the rotated forms generate a large number of trichords belonging to set classes [012] and [016]. Now, set [012] can be understood solely as a 1-2 motif with the intervals arranged in opposite directions[175], while set [016] could be associated with three different motifs: 1-5, 1-6 or 5-6. A deeper analysis will clarify which of these intervallic motifs was the object of Stravinsky's interest.

Ex. 36: Igor Stravinsky, *Movements*, sketch showing the rotated (columns α and β) and rotated-transposed (columns γ and δ) forms of the two hexachords of the original twelve-note row (Paul Sacher Foundation, Igor Stravinsky Collection).

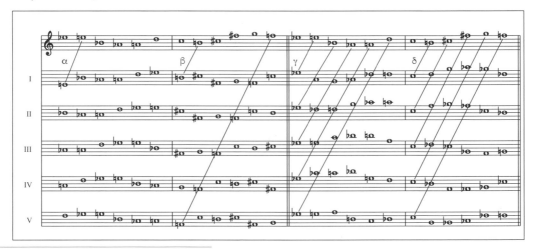

---

[175]. Set class [012] could also be formed by uniting two semitones, but the motifs formed by two different intervals are far more typical of Stravinsky's music.

Ex. 37: Stravinsky, *Movements*: subset structure of the rotated-transposed forms of the two hexachords of the fundamental row.

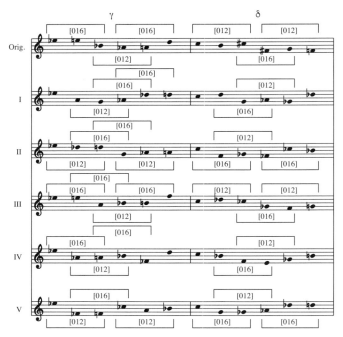

With the aid of the sketches, I have reconstructed the chronology and serial origin of the three episodes which form the entire section, summarised in TABLE 1[176]. As can be seen, all three episodes are based on a combination of serial segments chosen from columns g and d of the rotational array. The serial segments employed for the second episode, the flute solo (bars 13-17), are indicated in the sketch transcribed in Ex. 38; the symbols here refer to the sketch with the rotational array transcribed in Ex. 36 (the Greek letters refer to columns γ and δ of the array and the roman numerals to the lines; the Arabic numeral indicate the selected segments).

---

[176]. The manuscripts (Paul Sacher Foundation, Igor Stravinsky Collection) include (1) the sketch for bars 13-17 transcribed in Ex. 38; (2) the page of sketches with two versions of bars 7-12 transcribed in Ex. 42; (3) a clipping with a preliminary version of bars 18-21, without serial symbols (not reproduced here); (4) a clipping with the definitive version of bars 18-21 and (on the other side) bar 22, without serial symbols (not reproduced here); and (5) the autograph short score, some of the serial symbols from which are transcribed in Ex. 43. Only sketch no. 1 has been cited and discussed numerous times in the musicological literature. One of the first transcriptions appeared in NEIDHOFER 1991 (in the same year Joseph Straus presented this document in a paper at the Annual Meeting of the Society for Music Theory in Cincinnati). Later the document was analysed by TUCKER 1992, vol. I, p. 66 [transcription] and TUCKER 1992, vol. II, p. 258 [commentary]; RUST 1994, pp. 63-64; and STRAUS 2001, p. 67, which finally established the serial construction of the flute solo, without, however, comparing it with either the construction (actually quite similar) of the other two episodes, or with the motivic-intervallic construction to which it is subjected.

TABLE 1: CHRONOLOGY AND SERIAL ORIGIN OF THE THREE EPISODES
IN STRAVINSKY'S *MOVEMENTS*, I, BARS 7-22

EPISODES (IN CHRONOLOGICAL ORDER)	TWELVE-NOTE MATERIAL EMPLOYED
bb. 13-17: second episode (solo for flute I)	Serial segments drawn from columns γ and δ of the rotational array of the hexachords. The entire succession is transposed T4 to *g*. The accompaniment uses complete hexachords
bb. 7-12: first episode (first solo episode for piano)	The same serial segments from the flute solo but transposed T2 (on *f*)
bb. 18-22: third episode (second solo episode for piano)	The same serial segments from the flute solo, not transposed (on *e*♭)

Ex. 38: Igor Stravinsky, sketches for *Movements*, I, bars 13-17 (Paul Sacher Foundation, Igor Stravinsky Collection).

The 34 notes of the flute melody are obtained by combining ten serial segments, freely chosen from the array (Ex. 39). In the final version (Ex. 40), the melody thus obtained was completely transposed a major third higher (T4) to start on *g* instead of *e*♭. In the third episode (bars 18-22; see Ex. 41) the piano and string parts employ the same serial segments as the flute solo, as is suggested by the serial symbols and the indication 'follow the flute solo before (same series)' in the short score; however, it is not transposed (compare Ex. 41 with Ex. 40).

Ex. 39: Columns γ and δ of the array reproduced in Ex. 17 (hexachordal rotated-transposed forms), with encircled serial segments employed in the sketch shown in Ex. 38.

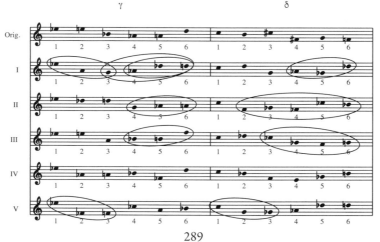

289

Ex. 40: Final version of the flute solo in bars 13-17 showing the serial segments.

Ex. 41: Igor Stravinsky, *Movements*, I, bars 18-22. © 1960 by Hawkes & Sons (London) Ltd. By kind permission.

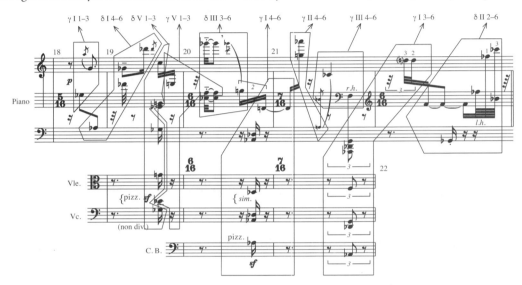

The first episode (bars 7-12; Exs. 42 and 43) is based upon the same succession of serial segments, even if in the final version the resulting correspondence is obscured owing to some errors Stravinsky committed in the preparation phase. On the first two lines on the page transcribed in Ex. 42, up to the pitches *b - c - d♭* before the clefs, the composer had initially outlined a first version of the passage transposed to begin on *g*, in a manner identical to the final version of the episode for flute. Ex. 43 presents this first version together with the related serial symbols derived from his autograph short score. As is evident by comparing Ex. 43 with Ex. 40, Stravinsky obtained the same pitches as the final version of the flute episode by utilising only slightly different serial fragments[177]. Up until this point, therefore, the first piano episode corresponds exactly with the flute solo, with respect to pitch content. At a later point, represented in lines 6-9 of the sketch in Ex. 42, Stravinsky elaborated a second version —

---

[177]. The major discrepancy concerns the first two segments: in the short score of the piano episode they are labelled segment 3-6 of hexachord γ5 and segment 5-6 of hexachord δ1. In the sketch for the flute episode, however, they are labelled segment 1-3 of hexachord γ1 and segment 4-6 of hexachord δ1. However, note that when the two piano segments are transposed by T2 (rather than T4, as in the flute), the resulting pitches are the same as in the flute episode.

Ex. 42: Igor Stravinsky, page of sketches for *Movements*, 1, bars 7-12 (Paul Sacher Foundation, Igor Stravinsky Collection).

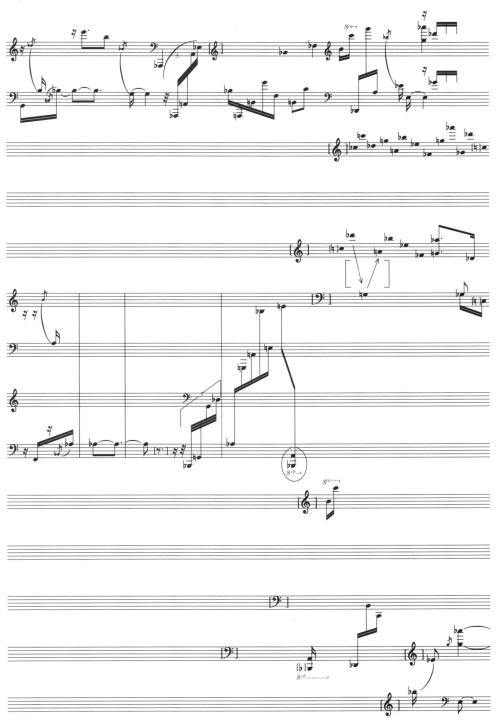

Ex. 43: Igor Stravinsky, *Movements*, I (see bars 7-10 of the printed score). The symbols above the staves represent serial segments drawn from the short score (Paul Sacher Foundation, Igor Stravinsky Collection). Below them is an excerpt (first two staves) from the sketch transcribed in Ex. 21.

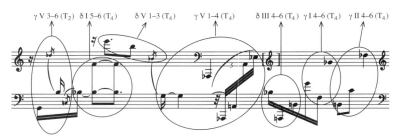

different from the first in both rhythm and the octave registration of some pitches — transposed to begin on *f* instead of *g*. Later, after the clefs (where the elaboration of the first version was interrupted) on lines 1-2 of the same page, Stravinsky completed the episode with the final missing part. Although neither the sketch nor the short score presents serial symbols at this point, it is obvious that the segments employed are the same as those used for the last part of the flute episode (transposed by T2)[178].

To sum up, the second version of the piano passage stretches in part across lines 6-9, up to the dyad *a - b♭* circled in the middle of the ninth line — which corresponds to the pitches *b* and *c* of the preceding version on *g*, as demonstrated by the vertical line drawn across the page — and in part (following Stravinsky's arrow) on lines 1-2, to the right of the treble and bass clef[179]. In setting the entire passage in the short score, however, Stravinsky failed to recopy pitches *b* and *c*, placed on the first line immediately after the treble clef, perhaps mistaking them for a repetition of the *b* and *c* immediately preceding it on the second line — which, however, belonged to the first version on *g*. Thus these two notes do not appear in the final score. By restoring them, one will easily notice that the entire sequence of pitches in the piano's first episode corresponds exactly to that of the flute's solo episode, transposed a whole tone lower[180].

178. In the first version, the serial segments were transposed a major third higher (T4); the second version, on the other hand, was obtained by lowering the first version by a tone (T2). Therefore, in the second version, the serial segments prove to be transposed a whole tone higher (T4 - T2 = T2). The short score does not contain serial symbols for the final part of the passage, formed by the succession of thirteen pitches notated in the final part of the third line of Ex. 42. The same succession of pitches — this time without the initial *c♭* — is transcribed again lower on the page (lines 5-6) but with a different choice of octave register for the single notes and using a rhythm outlined for the final cadence.

179. The *b* that appears as the first note after the treble clef corresponds to the *d♭* of the preceding version, placed immediately before the treble clef. See also the line drawn by Stravinsky. A different version of the final part of the phrase alone (starting with the dyad *b♭ - a* on line 13) is also notated by hand in the lower part of the page (lines 12-14).

180. The error in the printed score has created some difficulties in the analytical literature. See for example RUST 1994, p. 68, where the omission of the notes *b* and *c* prevented the author from recognising the T2 relation

According to Stravinsky's initial intent, then, all three episodes were to be based on the same succession of pitches, transposed onto three different levels: *g*, *f* and *e♭*. It was most likely in this manner that Stravinsky sought to obtain something like a 'tonal' organisation on a broader formal plane[181]. However, considerations of this type are beyond the scope of this study. What is important from my point of view is to observe how the intricate combination of serial segments on which the three episodes are based produces a homogeneous and cohesive motivic-intervallic texture.

To this end, the question which arises is: according to what criterion did Stravinsky select and combine these serial segments? If one takes into consideration the original hexachords from which the segments were extrapolated, it becomes apparent that Stravinsky usually used pivotal pitches: another well-known and widespread procedure in serial music which, however, we can reinterpret in the light of the 'ways of the hand': *a pivotal pitch is just a pivotal finger*. For example, the first segment of three pitches (γ1 1-3) is followed by *a♭*, from the middle of its original hexachord γ1 (see again Ex. 39). The second segment must therefore begin with this pitch. In its turn, the second segment (δ1 4-6), also containing three pitches, is followed, in its original hexachord, by the pitch *c*[182]; thus, the third segment must begin with that pitch. The whole passage consequently unfolds as follows:

$$\gamma\text{I } 1\text{-}4 = \quad e♭ \text{ - } a \text{ - } g \text{ - } (a♭)$$
$$\downarrow$$
$$\delta\text{I } 4\text{-}1 = \quad a♭ \text{ - } g♭ \text{ - } d♭ \text{ - } (c)$$
$$\downarrow$$
$$\delta\text{V } 1\text{-}4 = \quad c \text{ - } g \text{ - } g♭ \text{ - } (e♭)$$

Nevertheless, this criterion can determine only the first pitch of the following segment and not the internal characteristics of that segment (as the serial table shows, there are different segments which also begin with the same pitch). Moreover, the mechanism of pivotal pitches is employed only in a limited number of cases. A fuller rationale nevertheless emerges if the ten serial segments employed across the three episodes are re-examined in relation to the concept of intervallic motif. Given the structure of the hexachords (see again Exs. 34 and 37), these segments are almost all members of set classes [012] and [016], as Ex. 44 demonstrates (the

---

between the last ten notes of the first piano episode and the corresponding notes of the flute solo. Moreover, Rust's analysis omitted the last bar (bar 22) of the second episode for the piano, so that he failed to notice the T8 relation with the flute solo in the last six notes.

[181].   See Boykan 1963, p. 158; Walden 1979; Rust 1994, pp. 62-76; and Straus 2001, pp. 124-128.

[182].   Given the mechanism of rotation on which the serial tables are based, one could say that the pitch 'following' the final pitch of a hexachord is the first.

only exceptions are the two segments indicated by the exclamation marks). All of the four-note segments (nos. 5, 9 and 10) contain overlapping sets [012] and [016], as Ex. 44 indicates.

Ex. 44: Igor Stravinsky, *Movements*, I: serial segments employed in the succession of pitches contained in each of the three solo episodes of bars 7-22.

What is intriguing, however, is the global result obtained from the combination of the segments. Let us return to Ex. 34 and examine all the consecutive three-note groups (bracketed above and below the musical stave) starting from each note of the complete succession of pitches[183]: with the sole exception of seven groups (indicated by the exclamation marks), all of the trichords belong to set class [012], [013] or [016], which, in turn, can be obtained on the keyboard from two motivic-intervallic classes, according to the orientation of the two intervals: set classes [012] and [013] from the tone-semitone motif (1-2); set class [016] from motif 1-6[184]. It is important to note that the [013] form of motif 1-2 *is not* included in the serial hexachord, which contains only the [012] form (see again Exs. 17 and 18). Therefore, the presence of form [013] in Stravinsky's succession of pitches clearly demonstrates that his primary concern was with intervallic motifs, more than with pitch class sets *per se*.

It is evident that the selection and arrangement of the serial segments was done in such a way as to obtain a continuous interlocking of two motivic classes (1-2 and 1-6), 78 generated by handling on the keyboard just three interval classes: ic1, ic2 and ic6. The use of complete serial forms (twelve-note rows or hexachords) would not produce so dense and coherent a fabric: hence the exigency of fragmenting the hexachords into smaller units, which can then be recombined at will.

---

[183]. For the sake of convenience, in Ex. 34 the entire succession of pitches is transposed to F (as in the first piano episode).

[184]. Set class [016] could have been generated by three different motivic- intervallic classes: 1-5, 1-6 or 5-6. Nevertheless, the form [015] of motif 1-5 — obtained by orienting the two conjoined intervals in opposing directions — never appears in the entire succession of pitches, which suffices to exclude it as a possibility. Of the remaining two motifs (5-6 and 1-6), it is more logical and economical to think primarily in terms of motif 1-6 since the entire passage can then be read from the point of view of only three interval classes — ic1, ic2 and ic6 — contained in motifs 1-2 and 1-6.

Conclusion: Theory and Practice

The extensive sketch study that occupied the entire second part of this chapter is intended to highlight some aspects of the creative process that are not directly recorded by the writing materials, as they are related to 'improvisation' on the keyboard. To trace the part of the creative process that took place 'in the hands' of the composer, a complex interpretation and a close reading of the sketches are required. The possibility of this hermeneutic operation implies a vision of improvisation and written composition as two complementary (non-antagonistic) activities. The creative process must be seen as a continuous 'back and forth' interaction between writing and improvisation, paper and keyboard. It is with this in mind that I interpret both the process of formulating the twelve-tone series starting from concrete musical ideas found on the keyboard, and the inverse process of transforming the series into concrete musical objects ('from intervallic motifs to rows' and 'from rows to motifs'). Of course, this operation often requires going into more minute details of the manuscript sources, particularly because an essential part of Stravinsky's creative process was linked precisely to the 'artisanal' chiselling of these details. They are, I would say, the very essence of his music.

The study of the sketches confirms some aspects that have long been well known to Stravinsky's scholars, but which have not received an entirely exhaustive exploration and description. It shows that many typical aspects of Stravinsky's harmonic language depend on his physical approach to the piano keyboard. We should assume that the interaction between body (hands) and instrument had a fundamental cognitive role for his music. To understand how this interaction worked, it is necessary to imagine Stravinsky's use of the keyboard as an 'integrated' cognitive system (in the sense of the embodied cognitive theories of which I wrote at the beginning of this chapter) in which various elements of neural, bodily, and environmental features combine, along with some consolidated cultural practices. As we have seen, two essential elements of this interaction were the physical layout of the keyboard itself and the propensity of early twentieth-century (and not only Stravinsky's) harmony to conceive harmonic constructs according to the symmetrical subdivision of octave. From the interaction between these two elements — or rather from the clash, since we have seen that they underlie two cultural practices that are not entirely compatible — two tendencies took shape which in Stravinsky's music manifest themselves at different times: the tendency to use 'objects' deeply introjected into the practices of the 'cultured hand' — what I have called 'ways of the hand'; and the tendency to conceive harmonic constructs in terms of distances (steps) between the keys, and therefore the keyboard as a tactile 'space'.

The thesis that I have argued in this chapter is precisely that all this strongly developed two types of skills in Stravinsky's practice and that the balance between them has characterized his different styles and periods. Despite Stravinsky's emphasis on the continuity of his creative methods throughout his entire output, these skills characterized his music in different ways over the years. As long as he continued to use referential collections such as the octatonic scale, and harmonic constructs that were still conceivable as chords in the traditional sense, the first of them — the use of 'ways of the hand' — remained prevalent. As these superordinate structural elements became less important, the skill based on the distance between the keys became more decisive.

Examination of the creative process also revealed another important change in Stravinsky's practice that occurred in his last creative phase. The tendency towards 'disintegration' into little motivic intervals resulting from the direct manipulation of single intervals, although not incompatible with serial technique, required an 'adjustment' process, the main compromise of which consisted in the possibility of no longer conceiving the intervals *only* as distances between the keys in terms of 'steps' of the fingers, but also in terms of the principle of octave equivalence. The study of the sketches shows that although Stravinsky continued to conceive his ideas as a combination of 'steps' found at the keyboard (this is very evident in *Agon*'s melodic chains, for example) in the written phase of the creative process he reworked the pitches by modifying their individual octave register.

This corresponded to a 'compromise' between Stravinsky's 'bodily' approach and another cultural practice that around 1950 was widely consolidated in nineteenth-century composition: twelve-tone composition. In other words, one could say that Stravinsky's last works were the result of an encounter between his 'physical' approach to intervals and a 'theory' implicit in the practice of dodecaphonic composition (which in fact presupposed the equivalence octave). We can therefore ask ourselves how much all this was the result of a 'theoretical' reflection by Stravinsky. We know, in fact, that, despite the fact that his portfolio of techniques included all the traditional disciplines of the pedagogy of composition (counterpoint, harmony and orchestration), Stravinsky's approach to composition was always minimally based on theoretical concepts. This was despite the fact that in the early 1950s Stravinsky collected a great deal of information, including theoretical ideas, on dodecaphony thanks to his contact with musicians and scholars who were profound connoisseurs of this subject (Robert Craft and Ernst Krenek in primis).

However, the study of the sketches in the second part of this chapter clearly shows that Stravinsky did not assimilate another essential theoretical aspect implicit in the practice of twelve-tone composition: the idea that a series is an altogether recognizable, albeit modified, *Gestalt*. As my analyses have shown, even in his latest serial compositions Stravinsky often continued to prefer direct engagement with the combination of a few — often very few — intervals to the detriment of the unity of the series. The particular technique adopted by Stravinsky, which allows the modification (inversion) of the individual intervals, ensures that his motifs are not attributable to a single ordered pitch-class sets, but can be transformed into different set classes. This criterion conflicts with the idea of 'series' understood as an ordered succession of both intervals and pitches.

Of course, some aspects of twelve-tone 'theory' are in common with Stravinsky's practice. The idea of considering the pitches and/or the intervals contained in some serial segments globally (i.e. apart from the order of the pitches) *was* one of the basic constructive criteria of many other serial or twelve-tone composers, serial and/or twelve-tone music. Considering the segments of the twelve-tone row as unordered sets was a deeply rooted criterion in the greater part of twelve-tone and serial music, and is certainly very familiar from the literature on serialism. Many of the basic operations that concern the subset structure of the twelve-tone row are based on this logic. In Schoenberg, Berg and Webern, the rows are often organized in such a manner as to contain certain segments within them that, if considered apart from the order of the notes, belong to the same set-class[185]. This principle was essential for establishing various types of formal relationships. According to the internal structure of the row, in fact, some of its subsets can preserve the same global pitch content, even when following the typical transformational operations (transposition, retrograde, inversion). This gives rise to a network of relations among the various forms of the row employed in a composition. Even the basic notion of hexachordal combinatoriality, which plays a fundamental role in Schoenberg's twelve-tone music, is based on the possibility of conceiving the hexachords as unordered collections. In addition to pitch content, the global intervallic content of the serial segments also plays an important role in this type of relationship, from the moment that each segment can be considered either as an unordered set of pitch-classes or as an unordered set of interval-classes. Particular attention to the intervallic content is at the centre of Webern's practice of generating the row from the reiteration of a single basic cell.

However, all these criteria *do not* correspond to Stravinsky's' interval-oriented approach — which in fact has deep roots in the compositional practice of his previous, non-serial, music. None of the above mentioned aspects of twelve-tone composition entirely corresponds to the concept of 'intervallic motif' that I have described in the previous pages. Working with the orientation of *single* intervals, Stravinsky radically modifies the physiognomy of his motifs, which can thereby assume forms corresponding to *different set-classes*. From this point of view, then, an 'intervallic motif' no longer corresponds, in any sense, to a class of unordered pc sets. Stravinsky's operations act, in other words, more on the level of *single intervals* than on the level of the global configurations in which these single intervals are included.

In this sense, Stravinsky's last compositions were not the fruit of a 'theoretical' reflection. Stravinsky's viewpoint on music theory, after all, was always very clear:

---

[185].   To mention only a few examples, one could cite the row of Schoenberg's String Quartet No. 4, in which one can identify four segments of three notes belonging to set-class (015), which assumes a role of particular importance in the first movement of the composition or the row employed in the twelve-tone section of the third movement of Berg's *Lyric Suite* which contains four segments belonging to the class (0126).

R.C. What is theory in musical composition?

I.S. Hindsight. It doesn't exist. There are compositions from which it is deduced. Or, if this isn't quite true, it has a by-product existence that is powerless to create or even to justify. Nevertheless, composition involves a deep intuition of "theory"[186].

These considerations on theory also apply to a more basic aesthetic-musical level. Stravinsky's adoption of serialism relies upon an aesthetic vision which does not attribute to the row the value of a fundamental *Gestalt* for the composition. The same can be said of Stravinsky's motivic-intervallic syntax, at the base of which lies an aesthetic conception foreign to the ideal of organic coherence which characterises the Austro-German tradition. The idea that intervallic configurations should provide a unifying function for the general internal relations which govern an entire composition — a function comparable to that of traditional tonality — is largely alien to Stravinsky's approach, which conceives of the intervallic motifs simply as starting materials for the act of musical construction. His creative process always proceeds from the particular to the general, following an itinerary open to deviations and metamorphoses which are realised through continuous motivic-intervallic re-reading of both the pre-compositional row and its concrete musical correlations. The elementary materials (the intervallic motifs) from which this mode of construction primarily derives evidently leave a mark, a recognisable impression on the final physiognomy of the musical edifice, without, however, assuming a determining role with regard to structural connection. To what degree and at what level this impression is discernible and perceptible is a question which evidently remains open. Whatever the answer, we must not lose sight of the essential significance of working with intervals (and with the hands) that characterised Stravinsky's compositional process.

---

186. *CONVERSATIONS*, pp. 12-13.

SUPERNATURAL BEINGS, HUMAN BODIES:
THE FLOOD AS AN ANTI-REALISTIC TELEVISION OPERA

S TRAVINSKY'S LAST DRAMATIC WORK, the television opera *The Flood* — first telecast on 14 June 1962 by CBS — lends itself well to a final reflection on the meaning of the body in Stravinsky's music. *The Flood* is most typical of Stravinsky's distinctive mixing of music, dance, mime, narration, and of the ritual and epic tendencies of his musical theatre. It exemplifies many of his musical strategies aimed at the dissociation of bodily expressiveness from that of other artistic means and at the construction of different, even contrasting, types of bodies through music. Moreover, as a *television* opera, it stimulates a reflection on the condition of mediatized body and on intermediality in musical theatre. These considerations would be true regardless of any judgment on the artistic value of *The Flood*, both as a TV spectacle and as musical composition. Even from this point of view, however, many elements, including Stravinsky's great commitment to the score, the elaborate musico-dramaturgical organization of the music, and the complex (serial) compositional technique employed, should lead us to consider *The Flood* as one of the most significant works of Stravinsky's later output.

All this notwithstanding, this opera remains an almost unknown — and widely underestimated — work to the public and, to some extent, to scholars as well. This is probably due to the disastrous failure of the television première, after which the work was never telecast again, nor released in video format for commercial use. Nowadays very few copies of the 1962 original production can be found in some US libraries[1]. Another reason could lie in the apparent

---

[1]. My study is based on the copy held at the Jerome Robbins Dance Division of New York Public Library. A few theatrical productions were made over the years: see below note 39. Among them is worthy of mention Balanchine's restaging, with the help of Jacques D'Amboise, as part of the 1982 Stravinsky Festival at Lincoln Center. In 1985 the Dutch Graphic Artist Jaap Drupsteen set the original 1962 audio recording (Columbia Symphony Orchestra and Chorus conducted by Robert Craft: originally distributed in LP format by CBS – SBRG 72063) to an entirely new video, made of electronically-generated video effects and actors lip-syncing the original

'simplicity' of some scenic and musical solutions, which may seem almost naïve and not up to par with the best 'avant-garde' pages of the late Stravinsky[2].

Some renewed interest in the 1962 TV spectacle has been generated by Charles Joseph's important studies of the early 2000s[3]. Thanks to Joseph's research — based on a large quantity of reviews, correspondence, manuscripts, and visual materials held in the Jerome Robbins Dance Division at NYPL and the Paul Sacher Stiftung in Basel — we now know a great deal about the opera's genesis, early reception, and socio-cultural context. Joseph considered *The Flood* as the focus for a reflection on the position of Stravinsky's last works between post-war musical avant-gardes and mass culture. As for the music, its style, and its compositional technique, and, above all, its relationship with the moving images, however, we still need much research and reflection[4]. No study has so far applied a multimedia approach to analysing the spectacle. Analysis of the visual component was mostly limited to very general considerations.

In this chapter, I will focus my attention on the ways in which music, dance and moving images interacts and contribute to the construction of bodily meanings. I will begin by reconsidering some of the sociological and cultural issues, mostly discussed by Joseph, surrounding the genesis of the opera, but in the light of the main topic of this book.

INTELLECTUALS AND MASS CULTURE

Noah and The Flood (this was the title of the original TV production of *The Flood*) was in large part the result of a series of fortuitous circumstances and of the broader cultural climate in which the work grew. Its creation fell in a period in which the American production system was couched to reconcile the demands and expectations of the ever-wider mass media audience and the prerogatives of 'high' art associated with the intellectual elites. By 1962 American television had been trying for several years to bridge the gap between mass and 'highbrow' culture by investing in educational documentaries and programs. Stravinsky himself had been the subject

---

soundtrack. Drupsteen's version (produced by NOS-TV and the Stiftung Muzt, Amsterdam; videotape NVC Arts International) can be seen on Vimeo, <https://vimeo.com/18597173#>, accessed on November 2021.

   [2]. The reasons for the failure of the 1962 TV show are discussed at length in the chapter entitled 'Television and *The Flood*: Anatomy of an «Inglorious Flop»', in JOSEPH 2001, pp. 132-161. Joseph notices that the work was often judged to be «artistically indecisive», «confused in its musico-dramatic action» and marked by a «naivety [that] is almost shocking». *Ibidem*, p. 136.

   [3]. In addition to the above-mentioned chapter of JOSEPH 2001, see the chapter 12 ('Television, *The Flood* and Beyond') of JOSEPH 2002, pp. 277-303. Among more recent studies are DÜBGEN 2012 (the only monograph entirely devoted to *The Flood*) and LOCANTO 2014 (on which this chapter is largely based).

   [4]. About the compositional technique JOSEPH 2001, p. 132, merely observed that Stravinsky's musical autographs show how the musical construction rests on «elaborately structured serial underpinnings». Dübgen's book, on the other hand, never addresses specific aspects of the 1962 video production.

of such TV documentaries: in 1957 Robert Graff, director of the Sextant Company — and the would-be producer of *The Flood* — had directed for NBC *A Conversation with Igor Stravinsky*, the first full-length documentary entirely devoted to the composer[5]. Art music, dance and theatre had become the object of many popular television programs[6]. The genre of television opera — that is, a work expressly commissioned and conceived for television[7] — had experienced a great expansion in England and the United States. Many renowned composers of 'art music' have been engaged to television. According to Jennifer Barnes, television opera «was one of the television industry's earliest attempts to confront the distinction between 'high' and 'popular' culture»[8].

The Flood was designed by the producer Robert Graff precisely in the context of this project aimed at popularizing 'high art'. Many artists involved in the creation of the screenplay, the choreography, and the music, albeit closely linked to the circles of highbrow modernist art, were all well known to the public for this very reason. The dancers included such stars of Balanchine's company as Jacques D'Amboise, Jillana, and Edward Villella, who had been largely popularized by television and film industry. Other individuals, such as the British actor Sebastian Cabot (Ill. 1) — who had been a voice performer in many Disney animated films and a few years later would become the world-renowned gentleman's gentleman of the famous CBS-TV sitcom *Family Affair* — who was chosen for Noah's voice, were closely tied to mass culture.

Moreover, since Stravinsky's score was only 22 minutes long (instead of the fifty minutes or so he was asked for by the producer), thirty-five minutes of 'padding' material had to be added to fill the one-hour special that the producer had promised to both CBS and the sponsor — the break shampoo. Many of the professionals involved in these additions, too, had had a role in popular television productions, or in popular culture. The actor Lawrence Harvey (the narrator's voice of the biblical sections of *The Flood*), (Ill. 2), who had recently come to international prominence thanks to such successful films as *Room at the Top* (1959), introduced

---

5.   The narrative strategies and the title itself (*A Conversation with Igor Stravinsky*) of this documentary anticipated the format of the following Stravinsky-Craft conversation books. A second documentary, simply entitled *Stravinsky*, was produced for CBC in 1965 by Roman Kroitor and Wolf Koenig. It was centered around Stravinsky's journey to Hamburg to record the *Symphony of Psalms*. In the same year, Richard Leacock and Rolf Liebermann filmed *Ein Strawinsky-Portrait* for Norddeutscher Rundfunk Television. Another important film was produced and written by the clarinetist and TV producer David Oppenheim, with the narrating voice of the famous journalist Charles Kuralt, and was broadcast in the CBS News Special Igor Stravinsky of 3 May 1966.

6.   On television and the performing arts in the USA, see ROSE 1986.

7.   On the definition of television opera and its difference from other uses of television to simply broadcast live performances from traditional opera houses ('televised opera', 'telecast opera', 'video opera') see BARNES 2003, pp. 1-3.

8.   *Ibidem*, p. vii.

ILL. 1: The British actor Sebastian Cabot (Noah's voice).

the program with an ambitious anthropological discourse about the meaning of the flood myth (an evident allusion to the looming nuclear threat) in various ancient and tribal societies and in the modern world A large documentary section on both Stravinsky and Balanchine was added at the end of the performance. Finally, Stravinsky in person — a very well-known name of a not-so-well-understood artistic world for the American television audience — introduced himself with a short address and a few shots of him conducting the first measures of the orchestral *Prelude* of the opera. In fact, those like Graff, who were trying to make highbrow art suitable for mass media, were perfectly aware that the television audience was more curious about the 'artists' then interested in the 'art' itself.

Ironically enough, a few years earlier, during the late 1940s and the 1950s American intellectuals' condemnation of mass and popular culture had reached its height. The writings of Clement Greenberg and Dwight Macdonald — whose critique of mass culture was even more trenchant than Adorno's — had become central in the so-called mass culture debate[9]. Until then, Stravinsky had been one of many well-known and influential enemies of popular culture, as shown for example by his attack on film music in a famous article on *The Musical Digest* of September-October 1946[10]. Here Stravinsky had offered a totally negative assessment of film

---

[9]. GORMAN 1996, pp. 158-184; BRODY 1993, pp. 174-179.

[10]. STRAVINSKY 1946. In 1948 the same journal published a rebuttal by the film composer David Raksin, entitled *Hollywood Strikes Back*.

302

ILL. 2: Stravinsky and the Lithuanian-born British actor and film director Lawrence Harwey (the Narrator's voice) during the videotaping of *The Flood* (NYPL, Jerome Robbins Dance Division.).

music, recognizing as its only role that of providing a 'background' to the images, bridging the 'holes', and filling «the emptiness of the screen [...] with more or less pleasant sounds». The target of his critique, was not only (or not so much) film music as such but rather film music as used in mass culture, together with «film people» who had «a primitive and childish concept of music', and whom he «[found] it impossible to talk [to] about music because we [had] no common meeting ground»[11].

However, a quite different attitude toward mass media — especially television — developed among the artists and intellectuals who gravitated around Stravinsky in the 1950s, such as Aldous Huxley, Christopher Isherwood, Lincoln Kirstein, and George Balanchine[12]. Although they considered television as a place not suitable for serious art, they nevertheless recognized its benefits in terms of visibility. This favorable attitude was crucial to direct Stravinsky towards a medium that in previous years he had always ostentatiously denigrated[13]. In 1962 he had been reflecting for some time on the expressive possibilities offered by the television as a medium for divulgating art music, dance, and literature. He also believed that intellectual

---

11. STRAVINSKY 1946, quoted in LOCANTO 2021B, p. 157.
12. JOSPEH 2001, pp. 140-145.
13. *Ibidem.* See for example Joseph's remarks about Isherwood's hopes of being involved in television projects.

elite could take control of mass media. «As for the question of mass media», he maintained, «I can only say that 'the intellectual elite' — if one exists, and I hope it does [...] — is not opposed to mass media, but to those who seek to determine what is suitable for mass media»[14]. Television also raised Stravinsky's hopes of revenge (soon to be disappointed, given the failure of the opera in terms of audience) against the film industry. Although his compositions had often been used in films and he had had innumerable failed negotiations with the world of cinema — some of which gave rise to music that was later reused for other purposes — he never completed an original film score[15]. On other occasions he had already taken on board the idea of a work originally and expressly conceived for television. In 1952 he had evaluated a proposal from the English filmmaker Simon Harcourt-Smith to write music for a film about the *Odyssey*. I will come back to this commission shortly, since it gave Stravinsky the opportunity to start formulating some ideas that were later reused in *The Flood*, and that have some implication on the bodily/unbodied nature of the characters.

As Charles Joseph's studies have demonstrated, Stravinsky's commitment to television was also the result of his personal aspirations to popularity. Unlike many other American and European serial composers of the day, he had not given up all hope that even the most 'advanced' music could be understood by the widest possible audience. He owed most of his fame and his first successes to theatre goers in Paris and throughout Europe, so that the idea of a «total, resolute, and voluntary withdrawal from this public world to one of private performance», as famously set out in a 1951 article by Milton Babbitt, was unacceptable for him[16]. The 'public' was to remain a constant preoccupation throughout his life.

As for *The Flood*, he sincerely believed that its music would go down well with a vast audience, since he had «[...] tried hard to keep The Flood very simple as music», because «it was commissioned for television, after all [...]»[17]. The assumption underlying this statement was that in the audience's perception of the day, 'serial' meant 'difficult', 'obscure' or 'unpleasant'. In an article in Newsweek advertising the TV show one month before its première, the music and dance critic Emily Coleman tried to reassure the public by noting that «the score is in Stravinsky's latest musical style, which uses the so-called 'serial technique', a complex and frequently trying method of composition [...]; *The Flood*, however, is extremely easy to listen to»[18]. Unfortunately, however, neither Stravinsky nor Emily Coleman understood that the

---

14. *DIALOGUES AND A DIARY*, p. 98.

15. LOCANTO 2021B. The only occasion when Stravinsky succeeded in writing the music for a movie was in 1963, with Joseph Strick's film *The Balcony*. However, he did not write an original score but simply adapted some excerpts from his Octet and The Soldier's Tale. Moreover, there is some evidence that the adaptation was made by Robert Craft.

16. BABBITT 2003.

17. *EXPOSITIONS AND DEVELOPMENTS*, p. 127, fn. 1.

18. *Newsweek*, LIX/21 (21 May 1962), p. 53.

problem for the audience would consist more in the overtly modernist style of the staging and costumes and in the modernist-theatrical conception of the spectacle, than in the music itself. Nor did Stravinsky really grasp the difference between the theatre and concert goers and the audience of mass-media, although on occasions he seems to have faced the problem:

> Whether or not the musical idiom is more accessible to a large audience than it would have been if I were composing directly for the stage, I cannot say, but *The Flood* could become the first work in a so-called serial idiom to achieve a degree of lay-listener popularity — a serial "Peter and the Wolf"[19].

Stravinsky's question was relevant, but it was ill-posed: the main problem with the audience's reception was not so much « the musical idiom» *per se*, as it was the overall conception of the spectacle, which made *The Flood* a work difficult to understand, also on a purely visual ground, especially for an audience which was accustomed to such different conventions, codes, and bodily modes of expression such as those of Hollywood cinema. The use of an 'advanced' musical language was, by comparison, a far less relevant problem.

A Collective Work

Just as it had happened for Stravinsky's first work for the stage — *The Firebird* — *The Flood*, too, was an entirely collaborative project. At least five names should be mentioned as co-authors: Robert Craft, George Balanchine, the scenographer Rouben Ter-Arutunian — who designed the costumes and the sets — and the TV director Kirk Browning, and of course Stravinsky. My assumption, then, is that also the theatrical and visual ideas and the vision of the performing body underlying the work's conception should be considered as the expression of the whole visual culture to which these individuals belong. To their names, moreover, we should also add those of other artists such as Dylan Thomas, Thomas S. Eliot, and the English filmmaker Michael Powell, with whom Stravinsky had previously started collaborating on other projects that did not go through, but which nevertheless offered him a first opportunity to imagine some musical, visual and bodily aspects that later found their way in *The Flood*. Michael Powell had reiterated Simon Harcourt-Smith's 1952 invitation to write the music for a film about the *Odyssey*, and on that occasion, he was thinking of the film as « a sort of television masque», for which Stravinsky would write the music and Dylan Thomas the verses. Powell and Stravinsky, then, planned to include « two or three arias, as well as pieces of pure instrumental music and recitations of pure poetry»[20]. The project did not come to fruition, but a central aspect found

---

[19]. *Ibidem.*
[20]. *Conversations*, p. 86.

its way in *The Flood*: the idea of a theatrical form with masked actors (invisible bodies) and allegorical figures (visible bodies representing abstract ideas or concepts), and the mixture of song, music, and dance.

Another central aspect of the *The Flood* was foreshadowed by a second aborted project with Dylan Thomas, this time commissioned by the Boston University in 1953. On that occasion, Thomas proposed a libretto «about the rediscovery of our planet following an atomic misadventure», after which a single man and a single woman, who fortuitously survived the catastrophe — or arrived on Earth from space — would recreate an entirely new world and humanity, including its language. In view of the abstract/physical dichotomy we will see in *The Flood*, it is interesting to notice that this new language would have no *abstractions* as there would be only words for concrete «people and objects»[21].

Clearly enough, both Thomas' project and the definitive subject of *The Flood* established an analogy between the story told in Genesis and what could have happened after the atomic catastrophe; however, while in Thomas' conception it was contemporary times that were read from the point of view of the biblical story, in *The Flood* the opposite is true: the narration of genesis is represented as an allegory of the present condition. The Flood, a symbol of the eternal catastrophe that strikes humanity because of original sin, becomes a metaphor for modern times and for a final, looming catastrophe: the nuclear war. The moralizing foray into the contemporary dimension should not surprise us at all in the years at the height of the Cold War, when on American screens there were already numerous films on the nuclear nightmare; let it suffice to think of *Dr. Strangelove* by Kubrick, of 1964.

Apart from the abovementioned preliminary aborted projects, the story of the genesis of *The Flood* began when, in early 1959, Robert D. Graff, producer of the Sextant television company, invited Stravinsky to compose a work for Columbia Broadcasting Systems (CBS)[22]. Graff suggested Auden as a librettist, but Stravinsky turned to Eliot, who had just received another commission for the libretto of an opera and then proposed to Stravinsky that he compose the score, not without some doubts about his own aptitude as a librettist[23]. Stravinsky, therefore, thought of diverting Eliot's proposal to Graff's television commission, expressing his lack of interest in 'opera' in the traditional sense of the term. On this occasion Stravinsky clearly outlined some of the essential characteristics of what would become *The Flood*: the story of Noah represented in a form that combines dramatic representation and narration — according to the formula already experienced in the *Histoire du soldat* and *Œdipus Rex* — along with dance inserts, all according to the model of a medieval morality play. The piece was also intended to include the choir in addition to the solo singers and orchestra.

---

[21]. *Ibidem*, p. 87.

[22]. Not for NBC, as repeatedly but erroneously stated by Stravinsky himself in his correspondence.

[23]. As shown by Eliot's letter to Stravinsky of 19 March 1959, quoted in JOSEPH 2001, p. 145.

The reference to the genre of morality play shows how Stravinsky was oriented, from the earliest stages of the genesis of the work towards forms traditionally characterized by the allegorical and symbolic sense; in the morality play, widespread in England and France between the fifteenth and sixteenth centuries, the characters represented, more than people in a dramatic sense, personifications of purely moral contents. This has interesting implications for the vision of the performing body: the association of a physical (corporeal) presence on the stage with a figure that is not a *dramatis persona* but a personification (an allegory) creates a contradiction between bodily and disembodied elements typical of Stravinsky's strategy of expressing their corporeality through music while removing, distancing or 'dematerializing'.

their visible bodies. The situation seems quite like what can be seen, for example, in the allegorical prologue of the Baroque operas, in which the representation of allegorical characters (not *dramatis personae*) clashed with the physical presence of the body and the strongly corporeality of the voice of the singers acting on stage. An eloquent example is in the prologue of Claudio Monteverdi's *Ritorno di Ulisse in patria* on Giacomo Badoaro's libretto (1640): here the allegorical figure precisely 'human fragility' («umana fragilità»), so that we have a body — and a voice — representing a non-body (an allegory) which, in turn allegorizes the fragile and transient physical condition of the human being. These kind of contradiction between bodily and non-corporeal elements is a central aspect of *The Flood*'s theatricality and music.

Having abandoned the hope of a collaboration with Eliot as a librettist, after the latter's eventual refusal, Stravinsky finally turned to Robert Craft. Although he had contributed to Stravinsky's activity in countless ways — as a ghost-writer, assistant, in-house critic, secretary, director, consultant — Craft had not yet made a concrete creative contribution to a work by Stravinsky. On this occasion, indeed, he had a decisive and multi-facetted role in the creation of the work in terms of both its overall structure and its musical-dramaturgical organization. Craft conceived the text of the libretto by putting together several passages from *Genesis*, the *Te Deum* and *Sanctus* hymns (for the choir of the angels which opens and close the opera), two English mystery plays from the York cycle (*The Creation and the Fall of Lucifer* and *The Fall of Man*), a third mystery play that is part of the Chester code (*Noah's Flood*), and several sources including Shakespeare and Dylan Thomas for Satan's arias[24]. For the text of the three plays, he drew on an edition by Arthur Cawley, entitled *Everyman and Medieval Miracle Plays*, which was most likely suggested to Stravinsky by Eliot at the time when his collaboration as librettist was still envisaged. Interestingly, in the introduction to the publication, Cawley focused on the difference between the genres of biblical representation (mystery play) and morality play:

---

[24].   Craft's typescript of the libretto, with Stravinsky's handwritten annotations and modifications, and a copy of Cawley's edition, with Craft's autograph annotations, are held at the Paul Sacher Stiftung in Basel (Igor Stravinsky Collection). Two pages of Craft's libretto are reproduced in facsimile in Dübgen 2012, pp. 84-85.

«Morality play does not dramatically represent people or episodes, but personifies good and evil, showing them in conflict»[25], adding a remark of some interest in the symbolic perspective of the work: each play is a complete narration in itself of a single phase of human history, but is at the same time a part for the whole, a synecdoche of the whole cycle of human history represented by the entire cycle of plays. The story represented thus symbolizes, in its very completeness, the eternal cosmic story.

Craft also suggested several aspects of the general outline of Stravinsky's score — the structure and subdivision into musical and dance numbers — as well as certain stylistic, technical, compositional, and instrumental choices. An important document testifying to Craft's role is the typescript that is transcribed in full in the first column of TABLE 1[26]. The text is undated but was probably written just before Stravinsky started working on the composition, about late January 1961. In it, Craft provided precise details about the overall structure of the work in terms of number, time (expressed in minutes) and type (narration, choreography, arias, melodrama, and so forth) of the various sections. The structure largely corresponds to the final form (second column of TABLE 1), although it is quite roughly sketched out.

As can be seen from TABLE 1, the result of this complex genesis was a relatively short work in which all the typical components of Stravinsky's musical theatre can be found: music, (also in the traditional operatic form of aria), choruses, melodrama, pure recitation, dance, mime. The dance-mime component, moreover, is subtly articulated: Balanchine provided moments of 'pure' group dance — «The Building of the Ark» and «The Flood» — and different kinds of gestures for Adam and Eve, Noah and his family, and for Lucifer/Satan. Even the music alone presents a great variety. Although almost all the pieces are based on the serial technique, very different styles and languages are used, from an almost diatonic one, reminiscent of various neoclassical models (*Te Deum*), to a strongly chromatic, rhythmically complex, and markedly gestural style, typical of Stravinsky's serial works from *Movements* onwards.

---

[25]. CAWLEY 1959, p. 5.

[26]. Paul Sacher Stiftung, Igor Stravinsky Collection. The text is also published, in Italian translation, in LOCANTO 2004, pp. 265-268.

Supernatural Beings, Human Bodies: *The Flood*

Table 1

Robert Craft's preliminary layout [transcription]	Strucutre Dance/pantomime/ special effects	Musical strucutre Vocal technique	Serial technique[*] Cadences
[f. 1] From: R. Craft *The Flood* (23 minutes) Notes: 1) *Prelude* – The representation of Chaos.	*Prelude* (Representation of Chaos) abstract visual art	[bb. 1-5] 'Chaos chords' (full orchestra)	Complete circle of fifth
		[b. 6] '*Jacob's Ladder*' (instrumental transition)	O^5 and R^5 superimposed $f_\sharp$ - $c_\sharp$
		[b. 7] Final chord (winds)	$d_\flat$ - $a_\flat$ - $e_\flat$ - $b_\flat$ - f - c
At the end a chorus of angels singing *Te Deum* in Latin (approx.: 2 minutes)	*Te Deum* Visual art (no dance): iconostasis with angels	[bb. 8-61] *Te Deum* (Choir SA)	[bb. 24-25, 35-36, and 44-45]: Hexachord I verticalized (repeated three times) $c_\sharp$ [b. 8] b - $f_\sharp$ - $c_\sharp$ [b. 59]
		[bb. 60-61] 'Divine approval' chords	Complete circle of fifths split into two chords
2) *Prologue* – Narration: (Very simple music: – 2 pianos, perhaps chords very empty-like Beginning of second part of *Perséphone* (approx. 3 minutes)	Narration (The Creation of the World). Special effects (abstract art)	[bb. 62-82] Voice-over	[bb. 62-67]: 12 verticals of the four-part serial array
	God's voice (The creation of the Man) Stylized pantomime	[bb. 83-115] Bass duet «A Skillful Beast»	$g_\sharp$ - $f_\sharp$ [b. 85] $c_\sharp$ - $g_\sharp$ - $d_\sharp$ [b. 115]
	Narration (The creation of Lucifer)	[Between bb. 115-116] Voice-over	
	God's voice Stylized pantomime (Lucifer)	[bb. 116-126] Bass duet «I Make Thee Master»	$c_\sharp$ - $d_\sharp$ [b. 117] $f_\sharp$ - $g_\sharp$ [b. 125]
	Narration (Lucifer's pride) Stylized pantomime (Lucifer)	[bb. 127-129] voice-over	Hexachords of the rotational array of O^a verticalized
	Lucifer's aria (The fall of Lucifer) Stylized pantomime	[bb. 130-151] Tenor *aria* «The Beams of My Bright» (Last five measures in *Sprechstimme*)	

309

	Narration (Satan's feelings of revenge) Special effects	[between bb. 151-152] (Voice-over)	
	Satan's aria Grotesque pantomime	[bb. 152-167] Tenor *aria* «God Made the World for Love»	$f♯$ - $c♮$ [b. 152] $g♯$ - $c♮$ [b. 166]
(Interlude) (camera: scene dissolves to Earth. Repeat half of music of *Prelude*. But perhaps in reverse form or different speed. (approx. 30 seconds)	*Melodrama* (Original Sin and Banishment from the Garden of Eden) Stylized pantomime (Adam and Eve)	[bb. 168-178] Voice-over only (Narrator); then voice-over with musical background (Narrator), Tenor (and a female voice for Eve)** *Sprechstimme*	Complete circle of fifths split into three chords [bb. 177-178]
		[b. 179] 'Jacob's Ladder'	O^5 and R^5 superimposed $f♯$ - $c♮$
3) *Dialogue*: God and Noah (perhaps two narrators' voices again or perhaps God; perhaps two basses like the Grand Inquisitor scene in Don Carlos (approx.: 3 minutes)	God's voice (bass duet) and Noah's voice (speaker) alternating (God reveals to Noah his plans) Masked pantomime	[bb. 180-247] Bass duet «I God, that all the world» (instrumental parts: Arpa, Piano, Gr. C., Vl. I and II, Vle) and Noah's speech alternating. Only Noah's last intervention is in *Sprechstimme*	The string parts are based on the verticals of the rotational arrays of hexachords R^a, R^b, I^b, R^a, $O^{b...}$ Two basses, arpa, piano (God's voice): $g♯$ [b. 181] $f♯$ - $c♮$ [b. 215] $d♯$ [b. 217] $f♯$ - $c♮$ [b. 221] $c♯$ - $g♯$ [b. 224] $c♯$ - $g♯$ [b. 233] $d♯$ [b. 235] $c♯$ - $g♯$ [b. 246]
4) *The Building of the Ark*: Perhaps the ark they actually build should look like a modern spaceship Ballet (this might be entirely percussion music, rhythmic variations with a mounting complexity — several pitches of drums, bongos — metals, chimes, bells, etc. though a purely abstract, not representational piece. (approx. 3 minutes)	«The Building of the Ark» Choreography	[bb. 248-334]	[248-250]: the piece begins with the verticalization of the Row in two chords, with pitches 1-7 and 8-12 respectively [bb. 289-293]: six verticals of the rotational array of the hexachord O^b [bb. 329-334]: verticals of the rotational array of the hexachords O^a and O^b interspersed

5. *The Catalogue of the Animals*: Noah's wife, his three sons and their wives; a fast tempo piece — one minute — the six solo voices, speaking or singing, should perhaps differ widely in pitch. (approx. 1/2 minutes)	«The Catalogue of the Animals» Special effects (animals) and Masked pantomime (men)	[bb. 335-370]. Speaker (Noah, then Narrator)	
(*The Comedy* of Noah's Wife — she is the last 'animal' to enter the Ark. Noah and Wife — bass and deep alto. This is the last part of the catalogue and should continue with the same music) (approx. 1 minute)	«The Comedy» (Noah and his wife) pantomime	[bb. 371-398]. *Sprechstimme* [Noah, Noah's Wife] and speech [The Sons of Noah, Noah and his Wife]	[375-379]: verticals of the rotational arrays of the hexachords IR^b and R^a
6. *The Flood*: Ballet. (This is the big piece of the whole work — but since nothing actually happens, no movement take place, the piece might have a stationary form — like the ostinato in Lulu or the 32 *passacaglia* variations where Wozzeck dreams but doesn't move. This piece is an ideal opportunity to record the music electronically, for one could 'mirror' each instrumental idea electronically. The storm is outside the Ark, so the music would come from 'outside' electronically at this point (more) [f. 2] The whole thing could be a huge ciaccona in cancrizans form: i.e. the form of the storm (approx. 7 minutes)	«The Flood» (Choreography)	[bb. 399-456]	[bb. 401-453]: verticalization of various serial segments‴
7. *The Covenant of the Rainbow*: Noah, narrator, Chorus. Some music as Prelude. Ends in Narrator quoting Bible and *Te Deum* in Heaven	«The Covenant of the Rainbow» God's voice (bass duet) and Noah's voice (speaker) (God's Covenant With Noah) Masked pantomime (Noah's family)	[bb. 457-489]. Bass duet «A Covenant, Noah» (instrumental parts: Fl. gr. I, Fl. alto, Arpa, Piano, Vle, Gr. C.) and Noah's *Sprechstimme*	[bb. 479-486]: verticals of the rotational arrays of the hexachords R^a and R^b $g_\sharp$ [b. 458] b - $f_\sharp$ - $c_\sharp$ - $g_\sharp$ - $d_\sharp$ [b. 477] (end of God's part)

	(The representation of Chaos) Almost dance (*pas de deux*) (Adam and Eve)	[bb. 490-495] 'Chaos chords' (full orchestra)	Verticalization of all of the 12-tone row Complete circle of fifth
		[b. 496] *'Jacob's Ladder'* [the same as bb. 1-6]	O^5 and R^5 superimposed $f_\sharp$ - $c_\sharp$
	Satan's aria Pantomime	[bb. 497-518] Tenor aria « The Forbidden Act»	
	Narration (God's blessing of Noah and his family) Visual art: iconostasis with angels	[bb. 519-525] Voice-over	
	Te Deum Visual art: iconostasis with angels Special effects (abstract images)	[bb. 526-579] The same as the first *Te Deum* (bb. 8-60) but with a final fade-out	
		[bb. 580-581] 'Divine approval chords' (in reverse order)	*Complete circle of fifths split into two chords*
		[b. 581] Last statement of the *'Jacob's Ladder'*	O^5 and R^5 superimposed $f_\sharp$ - $c_\sharp$

˙. On the terms 'verticals of the rotational array' and '12 verticals of the four-part serial array', see above and STRAUS 2001, pp. 152-182.

˙˙. In the score Eve's *Sprechstimme* part is given to the voice of the Narrator.

˙˙˙. This is the longest passage involving the use of verticals of rotational arrays in Stravinsky's serial compositions.

˙˙˙˙. See above for an illustration of the technique.

Once the structure of the work had been established, it had to be translated into a visual project well suited for television. This too was the result of a complex genesis, in which various individuals with different cultural and professional backgrounds intervened. According to Charles Joseph, Robert Craft should be named among them. Joseph argued that, in addition to devising the general outline of the opera and to suggesting many ideas about the visual component of the spectacle, Craft also had an influence over the purely technical decisions concerning television media, such as the shots and the sets. However, Craft's role in the visual aspects of *The Flood* deserves a few more words. Charles Joseph bases his hypothesis mainly on a typewritten account of a private meeting between Craft and Graff — who, in early 1959, had invited Stravinsky to compose *The Flood* for CBS — which took place in New York in the spring of 1960. Here Craft provided a detailed illustration of various aspects of the music, the libretto, and the scenario. According to Joseph, the account reveals that Craft also touched on «several technical matters that were absolutely critical, including the use and positioning of cameras»[27]. However, as far as I can see, in the copy held at the Jerome Robbins Dance Division at NYPL, although Craft occasionally hints at matters such as the «tempos of camera fade» or «timings of text», he mentions these aspects without ever getting to the heart of the technical matter. The text clearly shows that his references to the technical aspects of television production were designed merely to reassure the producer — quite understandably — that Stravinsky was aware of the problems of the medium, and that he intended «to avoid as many theatrical suggestions as possible [...] The entire work [will be] conceived in television terms. It will not be a theatre work televised».

The typescript transcribed in the first column of TABLE 1 shows that Craft's role chiefly concerned many musical-dramaturgical aspects. However, in the rare cases where he envisaged a visual equivalent to the music, he displayed a typically theatrical, and especially operatic, mindset. He suggested several famous operatic works, from Verdi to Berg, as possible musical-dramaturgical models to be employed in some scenes. For example, in the dialogue between God and Noah, he proposes using a bass duet, as in the famous Grand Inquisitor scene in Verdi's *Don Carlos*. He did not imagine making use of the possibilities of dissociation-recombination between sound and source provided by the electronic medium, as we can see in the final version of the *The Flood* (a duet of basses is associated with the voice of God; Noah express himself in simple speech). Elsewhere, he envisaged using musical palindromes or musical forms based on the *ostinato* technique in dramatically static scenes. There are illustrious precedents for similar solutions in musical theatre, namely Berg's *Wozzeck*, or the music for the interlude in the middle of the second act of *Lulu*. Craft's only reference to a technical aspect of television production — a transition — concerns the cross fade in the *Interlude* that leads from heaven to earth, where the *Melodrama* takes place.

Much more decisive than Craft's was Balanchine's contribution to the visual component of the work. Many visual aspects were envisaged by Stravinsky and Balanchine in several meetings between 14-16 March 1962, the day after the composer had completed the orchestral score, and on 11-12 April, just two months before the videotaping of the dance sections in New York. An account of these meetings was later published in the *Dialogues and a Diary* with the title 'Working Notes on *The Flood*' (hereafter cited as *Working Notes*)[28]. It consists of a sort of script with occasional observations on the music, the choreography, the gestures of the actors/dancers, the costumes, and the television direction, as well as various other considerations and comments. Here Stravinsky and Balanchine also envisaged many television realisations of their ideas. However, if we look at the definitive movie, we can see that their intentions, as expressed

---

[27]. JOSEPH 2001, pp. 150-151.
[28]. *DIALOGUES AND A DIARY*, pp. 82-98.

in this text, were only partially realized — and it could not have been otherwise, since many of their ideas did not adapt well to the television medium.

An even more important step toward the final visual conception of *The Flood* was taken during the television producing process, when Balanchine could work very closely with the television director Kirk Browning. Balanchine, in contrast to Stravinsky, had already gained experience of working in television[29]. According to Charles Joseph, despite his enthusiasm and personal efforts to supervise the dance segments, Balanchine was in the end dissatisfied with television's failure to transmit his choreographic ideas. In an interview with Bernard Taper entitled 'Television and Ballet' he stated, «I wanted to make choreography that was not too obtrusive — which did not interfere with the music. [...] I intended to make changes and improvement — but we got into the studio, the panic took over, and then suddenly it became impossible to do what needed to be done»[30]. However, Balanchine's dissatisfaction should not necessarily be taken at face value. Perhaps many of the negative views expressed by scholars about the choreography for *The Flood* seem more like an uncritical acceptance of Balanchine's judgment than an independent and objective interpretation.

Balanchine's collaboration with Browning is well documented. Balanchine's stance toward television was rather ambiguous: on the one hand, he was highly critical of television as a medium for representing dance; at the same time, however, he made a huge effort to work out methods that could overcome the limitations of television, and this is precisely what happened in *The Flood*. According to Brian Rose, «(t)hrough experiments and an open recognition of the medium's limits, [Balanchine and Browning] found a mutually agreeable approach to the tricky business of transferring large-scale ballet movement to the small screen»[31]. Charles Joseph quotes the critic Arthur Todd, who attended the videotaping of Balanchine's choreography, spending seventeen hours in the CBS Studio observing the choreographer working. Todd maintained that «(t)he choreographer's deep involvement was obvious, whether in studio rehearsal or during the taping with director Kirk Browning. Camera angles, placement and timing were all planned in sympathetic collaboration between choreographer and director»[32]. According to Joseph, «Todd spoke of Balanchine always having the camera in mind and by extension, of his concern for the viewer». In addition to this evidence, one can point to a 1992 interview with Browning by Brian Rose, in which the director clearly states that the decisions about the visual aspects of the work were not just his own but were taken collectively with Balanchine and the set-designer Rouben Ter-Arutunian[33].

---

[29]. For an overview of Balanchine's involvement with television, see JOSEPH 2002, pp. 281-282; JOSEPH 2001, p. 143.

[30]. BURDICK 1962, pp. 120-121; the passage is reprinted in TAPER 1996, p. 246.

[31]. ROSE 1992, p. 66.

[32]. 'What Went Wrong' (Interview to Balanchine by Arthur Todd), in: *Dance Magazine*, XXXVI (August 1962), p. 40, quoted in JOSEPH 2002, p. 408, fn. 13.

[33]. JOSEPH 2001, p. 287, fn. 9; ROSE 1992, pp. 92-93.

Balanchine and Browning's close collaboration is well documented by a large number of photographs that were taken during the preparation of the spectacle, now held at the New York Public Library (Ills. 3-4). Hundreds of shots show the choreographer discussing with the television director. Balanchine's gestures clearly show his intention to adapt his three-dimensional vision of the group of dancers and mimes to the vision of the space of the television screen.

Ills. 3-4: Balanchine and Kirk Browning during the videotaping of the choreography for «The Building of the Ark» from *The Flood* (NYPL, Jerome Robbins Dance Division).

Another important contribution was provided by the scenographer Rouben Ter-Arutunian. In a sense, he represented more the theatrical than the television side of the group: his activity and his training had taken place in the context of classical ballet. Since 1951, when he moved to New York from Germany (he was born in Georgia), he had been closely associated with George Balanchine and the New York City Ballet. However, since the mid 1950s he had begun a series of collaborations with television, and *The Flood* was just one of them. Ter-Arutunian contribution to the 1962 spectacle can be seen above in the surreal style of the masks, such those of Lucifer/Satan (ILL. 5) and the grotesque-looking masks of the human (Noah and his family), midway between ancient Assyrian sculpture and a typical representation of extra-terrestrial creatures, according to a stereotyped vision of their bodies (large heads with big dark eyes with no pupils) which was taking root in the collective imagination of mass media culture (ILL. 6)[34].

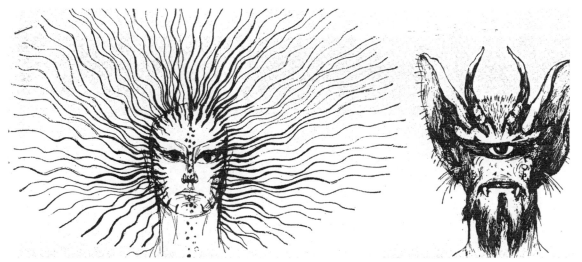

ILL. 5: Rouben Ter-Arutunian, preparatory drawings for Lucifers' and Satan's Masks (*Newsweek*, LIX/21 [21 May 1962], p. 53.)

Finally, the most important contribution to the visual aspects of *The Flood* came from Kirk Browning himself. His role in this respect has been largely underestimated, if not entirely neglected, by scholars[35]. This may be due to the normal assumption — or prejudice — that although in television productions many decisions lie with the director, these are purely technical decisions, which do not concern the artistic or aesthetic dimension of the work.

34. On Ter-Arutunian's account of his collaboration to *The Flood* see TER-ARUTUNIAN 1966.

35. JOSEPH 2001, p. 278, defines him cursorily as «an opera theatre experienced veteran during those still relatively experimental years of early television». DÜBGEN 2012 makes no reference at all to Browning in the whole of her monograph.

Ill. 6: Rouben Ter-Arutunian, preparatory drawing for Noah's Mask (NYPL, Jerome Robbins Dance Division).

Apart from the ideological implication of this assumption, *The Flood* is rather unusual also in this respect, since Browning — and Rouben Ter-Arutunian — did not limit themselves to negotiating their technical solutions with the ideas — largely theatrical in conception — that had been previously sketched out by Stravinsky, Balanchine and Craft, but also introduced many ideas of their own.

Browning had already widely experimented with the use of television as a medium to represent theatrical, musical and dance performances. According to Brian Rose, he had established himself as the country's most prolific and versatile television director in this field since the late 1940s. He was one of the key figures who ensured that cultural programming based on the traditional performing arts became one of the main attractions of American television. The television simulcasts of the celebrated Toscanini radio concerts with the NBC Symphony Orchestra were one of his most important productions. More interestingly for us, he was also the director of one of the first operas commissioned and conceived for television in the USA, the famous *Amahl and the Night Visitors*, with music by Gian Carlo Menotti[36]. He also directed numerous performances by the New York City Ballet. His association with Balanchine began with the 1956 NBC Opera Theatre production of *The Magic Flute*.

Between Theatre and Television: The Problem of 'Realism'

Given the complex genesis of the work we have just discussed, and the different conceptions and cultural backgrounds of the individuals involved in its creation, one may wonder if the best way to approach *The Flood* is to consider it as a theatrical work (an opera in the traditional sense) or as a true television spectacle. Is it, in other words, «an opera for television or a television opera»?[37]. If we accept the definition of 'television opera' as a work «which could not, under any circumstances be adapted for the stage»[38], we should conclude that *The Flood* does not belong entirely to this genre, since, shortly after its broadcast in June 1962, it was performed several times, under the direction and supervision of Stravinsky and Craft, in several European theatres, without requiring any substantial changes[39]. Also when Balanchine, with the help of Jacques D'Amboise, restaged the opera as part of the 1982 Stravinsky Festival at Lincoln Center he had to make very little structural changes.

Most scholars, in fact, tend to judge *The Flood* as being the result of an essentially theatrical conception which was entirely unsuitable for television. According to Stephen Walsh, for example, all of Stravinsky and Balanchine's ideas, as sketched out in the *Working Notes* «[...] would actually work well on a stage, where crudity of detail can be masked by lighting and distance», while, «the idea that they might be televisual presumably comes from some vague notion that in studio all things are possible and abstraction or surrealism are therefore appropriate genres. But this was to prove both technically and aesthetically a mistake»[40]. Walsh's allusion to «abstraction and surrealism» hits the mark, as we will see later. However, his statement that *The Flood*, in its final form, was unfit to the electronic medium is not entirely true and requires some refinement. The starting point in the creation of *The Flood* was, no doubt, a fundamentally theatrical conception on the part of Craft, Stravinsky and Balanchine. This is also evident from Stravinsky's own statements about the nature of the work. In a long passage

---

[36]. The work was commissioned by NBC and broadcast on television on 24 December 1951 from the NBC Opera Theatre in New York as the debut production of the most famous Anthology programme *Hallmark Hall of Fame*.

[37]. Barnes 2003, p. 2.

[38]. According to Jack Bornoff's definition (about Benjamin Britten's *Owen Wingrave*) quoted in *ibidem*.

[39]. Hamburg, Staatsoper, 30 April 1963. Same production: Zagreb Festival, Spring 1963; and Milan, Teatro alla Scala, Spring 1963.

[40]. Walsh 2006, p. 454.

of *Expositions and developments* dedicated to *The Flood* dating back to a few months before the *Working Notes*, when he had completed only the Prologue[41], both he and Craft still spoke of the work in purely theatrical terms:

> R[obert] C[raft]: To what extent do you visualize the staging of a theatrical work as you compose the music? For example [...] do you already entertain concrete ideas about its theatrical realization?
>
> I[gor] S[travinsky]: my first idea for *The Flood* [...] was a theatrical conception. My next preliminary notion was that *The Flood* should be a dance piece in character, a story told by dance as well as by narration. And, in fact, I have followed this idea: even the *Te Deum* is a dance piece, a fast-tempo dance chorale[42].

Later, as the TV premiere approached, Stravinsky began to shed a different light on the work, describing it as something genuinely conceived for the electronic medium. So, in the *Working Notes*, he claimed that he had not been interested in writing an 'opera' in the traditional (theatrical) sense; and that he had always had the needs of television in his mind[43]. He also recanted his own statements (quoted above) that they dated «[...] from the first stages of work», and maintained that he allowed them «to stand as they are only because they might give a peep into the preliminary machinations of an old theatre composer's garrulous mind»[44]. However, his main concern here was the question of theatrical time against television time, and not whether the overall conception of the work was a theatrical or TV-specific one:

> Television should someday succeed in sponsoring a new, in the sense of more concentrated, musico-dramatic form [...]. Visually it offers every advantage over stage opera, but the saving of musical time interests me more than anything visual. This new musical economy was the one specific of the medium guiding my conception of *The Flood*. Because the succession of visualizations can be instantaneous, the composer may dispense with the afflatus of overtures, connecting episodes, curtain music. I have used only one or two notes to punctuate each stage in The Creation, for example, and so far I have not been able to imagine the work on the operatic stage because the musical speed is so uniquely cinematographic[45].

---

[41]. According to Craft's own statement: *EXPOSITIONS AND DEVELOPMENTS*, p. 123. A detailed chronology of the composition process of *The Flood*, based on the autograph dates of the sketches, can be found in STRAVINSKY – CRAFT 1978, pp. 463.

[42]. *EXPOSITIONS AND DEVELOPMENTS*, p. 127.

[43]. «[*The Flood*] was commissioned for television after all, and I could not regard this commission cynically». *Ibidem*, p. 127. See Stravinsky's reference to his new «non-operatic musical thought» in the letter to Thomas S. Eliot dated 8 April 1959 in STRAVINSKY – CRAFT 1978, p. 540. See also *ibidem* the letter to Eliot dated 6 August 1962.

[44]. *EXPOSITIONS AND DEVELOPMENTS*, p. 127.

[45]. *DIALOGUES AND A DIARY*, p. 97.

In truth, the work *was* initially conceived by Stravinsky as theatrical piece, despite having been commissioned for television. Also Balanchine's description of the work, while stressing the difference from the ballet genre, was in accordance with an anti-realistic and theatrical conception:

> This is a miracle play more than a masque. As I see it, it's a church play or a choreographed oratorio. Most importantly it's not a ballet. The Flood could have been produced with actors speaking, or with singers and actors, or it could have been an opera. Our version is a musical composite. It's all done in gesture by dancers and objects[46].

Nevertheless, we cannot entirely dismiss the impact of television on the visual aspects of the 1962 production: the TV director Kirk Browning did his best to 'remediate' Stravinsky and Balanchine's 'theatrical' ideas to the codes and requirements of television. The process of adaptation to the new medium went through a series of stages. A comparison of the *Working Notes* with the final product throws much light on the way in which Browning (and Balanchine) intended to adapt their musical and choreographic choices to the television medium.

We must therefore distinguish two moments: the initial conception of the work, still essentially theatrical, by Craft, Stravinsky and Balanchine; and the subsequent transformation / adaptation of this original core of ideas by Kirk Browning (and partly by Ter-Arutunian). This process makes *The Flood* an interesting case from the perspective of this book, as two different ways of representing the body meet and coexist: the typically theatrical one, and the one typical of electronic media and television.

My proposal, then, is to consider the bodily and visual components of *The Flood* in the light of the mediatisation processes. I am using the term 'mediatisation' in the sense of Philip Auslander's influent book *Liveness*[47]: the condition taken on by a live performance in a 'mediatised' culture; a culture, that is, profoundly conditioned by the codes of the mass media. According to Auslander, a 'mediatised performance' is not merely a live performance that is circulated on television or in other forms based on the technologies of recording and reproduction, but the result of «a process whereby the traditional fine arts [...] come to consciousness of themselves as various media within a mediatic system»[48]. In another sense, since, according to Auslander, a live performance can even itself function as a kind of mass medium — in this sense, we can consider the transformation of a theatrical work into television

---

46. 'What Went Wrong' (Interview to Balanchine by Arthur Todd), in: *Dance Magazine*, XXXVI (August 1962), p. 40, quoted in JOSEPH 2001, p. 144.

47. AUSLANDER 2008.

48. JAMESON, Fredric. *Postmodernism or The Cultural Logic of Late Capitalism*, Durham, Duke University Press, 1991 (Post-Contemporary Interventions), p. 162, cit. in AUSLANDER 2008, p. 5.

form to be an example of re-mediation[49] — we could consider *The Flood* as a special case of 'remediation' in a televised form, of an originally theatrical spectacle. In this case I am using the term 'remediation' in the sense of Jay David Bolter and Richard Grusin's book *Remediation*: the incorporation or representation of one medium in another, or rather the use of some typical characteristics of one medium within another[50].

The effects of mediatisation in *The Flood* are most easily visible in the two big dance sections of the work («The Building of The Ark» and «The Flood») (Ill. 7). Balanchine conceived both choreographies with some shots already in mind. «The Building of The Ark», for example, is basically conceived for a single camera shooting technique. The vision is almost always frontal and oriented toward the viewer. The camera pans and dollies on the group of dancers slowly and almost imperceptibly, and only when necessary to encompass the whole group (which expands and shrinks continuously), but without using an excessively long shot. Only once in the sequence (at b. 304 of the score), in correspondence to the muted trumpets tremolo in flutter-tonguing, the camera enters the dancers' group in medium close-up and with a different angle[51]. Only occasionally during the sequence is the camera level slightly raised, to film the group of dancers from above. At first glance this may seem a rather traditional — in the theatrical sense — use of the camera. On the contrary, it was intended to produce some depth effects when used in combination with the group movements, which were designed by Balanchine precisely to this end. Toward the end of the sequence, for example, while the camera takes a medium shot of the group, some dancers move nearer to it. At b. 315 the camera starts zooming in and at b. 318 some dancers come in very close, with their backs to the camera, almost in the manner of an extreme close-up; all this produces intriguing perspective effects. Just a year before *The Flood*, the single-camera technique was employed to obtain depth effects by Birgit Cullberg in her ballet *The Wicked Queen* (Ill. 8). Cullberg was one of the most important pioneers in the field of television dance. She created many ballets for this medium[52]. It is very likely that Balanchine was aware of Cullberg's experiments with television. In 1960 her ballet *Lady from the Sea* had been premiered in New York by the American Ballet Theatre at the Metropolitan Opera House; and in 1961 *The Wicked Queen* won her the Prix Italia, a prestigious international competition dedicated specifically to radio and TV productions.

---

[49]. According to other scholars, theatre is never a 'medium' in the sense that «one can make a movie 'of' a play but not a play 'of' a movie». Susan Sontag cit. in Auslander 2008, p. 5. However, Auslander (*ibidem*, pp. 10-15) demonstrated that this is not entirely true: there have long been plays based on movies or television programs, and live performance can even function as a kind of mass medium.

[50]. Bolter – Grusin 1999.

[51]. Given the limited availability of the original video and the difficulty of establishing an exact starting point for the film, from now on the various points of the movie will be indicated according to the bar numbers of the musical score.

[52]. See Cullberg – ReutersWärd – Lauritzen 1987, p. 16.

ILL. 7: backstage at CBS Studios in New York: the New York City Ballet *corps* in the first sequence of « The Building of the Ark» from *The Flood* (*Life*, 8 June 1962, p. 96).

On other occasions Balanchine's ideas about the bodily movement of the dancers and mimes of *The Flood* were implemented by Browning according to a more radically different set of codes (that of television) than the typically theatrical ones devised by the choreographer in the *Working Notes*. Browning's solutions, entirely based on the possibilities and on the conventions of the electronic medium, could not even be imagined by Balanchine's still theatrical imagination; at the same time, however, they seem to 'contain' and subsume his ideas and his theatrical codes within the new medium, as is typical of remediation processes. A good example is offered in the *Catalogue of the Animals* scene. In the *Working Notes*, Stravinsky and Balanchine considered how to solve the problem of portraying the selection of the animals and their transportation on board the Ark by Noah's sons. They examined a series of possible solutions: taking photographs or making drawings of real animals, creating short animations, and framing a series of stylized representations of animals or parts of their bodies, showing skiagraphics, and so on:

Ill. 8: Birgit Cullberg in *The Wicked Queen* (1961).

I[gor] S[travinsky]: During the loading, Noah's sons stand by like longshoremen. Noah speaks slowly, and before the music begins, but the narrator reads his verse as fast as he is able. The narrator could have a comb-and-tissue-paper, or Jew's-harp, timbre and an American accent, like a square-dance caller or a tobacco auctioneer.

> G[eorge]. B[alanchine]: The animals could be shown skiagraphically, as ominously large background silhouettes, but this probably requires animation. Or toy animals and wooden miniatures could be shown looming towards the audience on three conveyor belts (left, right, centre, overhead); and if not toy animals, then photographs of real ones, or representative stylized parts, tusks, humps, splayed or padded feet, zebras' stripes, tails, manes, trunks, wings, though this, too, implies the participation of graphic arts. Rapid changes in camera angles might be exploited also, thus suddenly showing the animals from above or below, or about to tread on us full face. [...] Another notion to consider is that if the animals are miniatures, Noah's sons could stand by the conveyor belts, pick them up and throw them into the Ark — the surface of the screen, the audience's lap — like children heaping toys in a basket[53].

Clearly enough, these ideas were designed to create a situation that might appear, to some extent, representational but not realistic; in other words, anti-illusionistic and anti-realistic, in the sense discussed in the first chapter of this book. At first glance, given their allusions to the use of camera angle, they would also appear to transcend a theatrical approach and to be well suited to the potential of a television screen. However, Stravinsky and Balanchine were imagining a scene that took place in real time within a circumscribed space which, besides the use of miniatures, could even be a theatrical stage. Their ideas simply reflect a tradition of visual arts and twentieth-century theatre with a surrealist imprint, but they still don't make full use of the television's codes and conventions. Browning's solution, on the contrary, fully exploited the potential of video editing, using only the parts of Stravinsky and Balanchine's idea that served the purpose. Instead of moving on conveyor belts, the miniature animals are arranged in long rows on an illuminated plane from which they are shot in close-up and extreme close-up so that they appear to have the dimensions of real animals. The sudden changes of shot make them look as though they really are moving in procession. Noah's sons are filmed separately in a series of medium shots and medium close-ups. They are seated with their heads swivelling rapidly in all directions as if looking for something that we cannot see but that is clearly moving in front of them. They point to something, count on their fingers, and turn to each other as if to discuss something. They neither speak (the list of animals is rattled off by the speaker in the form of a melodrama) nor communicate through facial expressions since their faces are covered by the large masks designed by Ter-Arutunian (ILL. 9). No aspect of the set suggests that they are physically close to the toy animals (and indeed they are not). The idea that they are selecting and pointing out animals is conveyed by the editing, by means of which we occasionally see glimpses of the animals on the screen. Although the method employed is different, the core of the original idea by Balanchine and Stravinsky (the use of toy animals) is preserved and the end result, in anti-realistic theatrical terms, fulfills their aims.

---

[53]. *DIALOGUES AND A DIARY*, p. 95.

ILL. 9: backstage at CBS studios in New York. Noah and his family (members of the New York City ballet) during the taping of «The Comedy». Costumes and masks by Rouben Ter-Arutunian (*Saturday Review*, 16 June 1962, front cover).

These last examples show that *The Flood* was the result from a negotiation between two different artistic conventions: those belonging to a long tradition of anti-realistic musical theatre, of which Stravinsky had ben herald[54], and those typical of the new technologies of television based on video recording and editing. Television too had developed its own 'anti-realism', which, however, had emerged as a 'fantastic' version of the realistic conventions of cinema and television, thanks to the use of special effects. The question of realism/anti-realism in television and in television opera, however, must be articulated in more detail.

'Realism' is a cultural construction which depends essentially on conventions, in film and television as well as in other media[55]. Film, as a medium, is basically indifferent to both realism and anti-realism. It breaks through the boundaries that have been traditionally established by film theory between these two modalities of representation, for it «engenders a unique event of sight and sound that does not have to be perceived to be a real event or an illusion of such

---

[54]. See Chapter One.
[55]. FISKE – HARTLEY, 2003, pp. 127-135.

an event»[56]. However, in the American culture of the early Sixties, the idea of 'realism' was firmly associated with the conventions of Hollywood narrative cinema, which were based on principles of narrative continuity and temporal linearity, and on an idea of the film as a sketch of a diegetically closed world. Television had originally based its 'realism' more on theatrical conventions than on cinematic ones. In the early stages of its development, television technology was not yet able to accurately replicate the cinematic discourse, and therefore its resemblance to theatre was still quite evident. Things, however, changed when the technological equipment of television studios became more sophisticated[57]. Finally, by the early sixties, both the American television and cinema audiences were definitively oriented toward the 'realistic' show based on the codes and conventions of Hollywood narrative cinema.

The genre of television opera had followed a quite different path from television in general. According to Jennifer Barnes, the earliest television operas eschewed realism[58]; but this is true especially for the subjects — none of the first television operas did chose a contemporary subject, or one that included the elements of realism preferred by television — and of the music-dramaturgical forms, which were still largely drawn from the traditional typologies — arias, recitatives, *duetti*, ensembles, etc. — of opera, traditionally considered unsuitable for creating a sense of narrative continuity and verisimilitude. However, some elements of conventional 'realism' remained. First, the storyline was usually linear, simple, and direct. Secondly, the use of the camera and the montage tried to present the events in a straightforward, illusionistic, and realistic style. A look at Gian Carlo Menotti's *Amahl and the Night Visitors* would clearly show how this kind of 'realism' still characterizes the early 'popular' television operas. Things changed by the end of the 1950s, with the development of new technologies for recording images[59]. Although most of the interest of the recording technology was the possibility to easily achieve an 'instant replay', recording machines also transformed the production techniques and processes, by offering new possibilities to deal with performers, locations, and pre-recorded materials. These opportunities were suddenly exploited by television productions. In the genre of television opera, they encouraged an entirely different kind of visual style, which adopted many anti-realistic features[60]. By the early 1960s, many television operas had incorporated elements of fantasy, which were made possible by the special effects based on the technology of video reproduction and video editing. Many television opera — even those less tied to the

---

[56]. SEEL 2015.

[57]. AUSLANDER 2008, p. 20.

[58]. BARNES 2003, p. 8.

[59]. The first model of video recorder, the VR-1000 produced in 1956 by Ampex, was quickly adopted by the main American TV stations. In England, the BBC had developed since 1950 a video recording system called VERA. Later, in 1953, the RCA presented its own system, with longitudinal helical scanning. As the tape ran at 9m per second, a reel lasted from four to fifteen minutes at most. For this reason it was suddenly abandoned.

[60]. BARNES 2003, p. 9.

tradition of twentieth century avant-garde art and more inclined towards mass culture — like *Labyrinth* by Gian Carlo Menotti (NBC, 1963) and *Tobias and the Angel* by Arthur Bliss (BBC, 1960), were written, according to Jennifer Barnes, to display «the full range of the most recent television technology»[61]. In these works, «composers ignored television's preference for realism and instead concentrated on producing works that incorporated effects impossible to achieve on the stage»[62].

However, even these fantasy and fairy-tale elements obtained with special effects fell within an otherwise conventional narrative discourse based on the conventions of 'realistic' films. Indeed, anti-realism in cinema and television can affect various aspects and levels: the use of non-realistic forms of representation of reality (a purely stylistic-visual aspect); the use of non-linear narrative structures; a vision of the film itself as a sequence of sound and visual events that have little (or no) similarities with the ordinary experience of reality. In the abovementioned television operas of the early 1960s only the first of these levels was involved. Their underlying dramaturgical and narrative structure was still linked to theatrical models of a decidedly more 'realistic' matrix than those of Stravinsky's theatre. In *The Flood*, on the contrary, even the underlying narrative structure of Robert Craft's libretto, although basically linear, was rather fragmented and discontinuous, due to the combination of heterogeneous elements — the biblical story and the fragments of the morality plays. Stravinsky's theatrical aesthetics, in short, was at odds with both Hollywood realism and the 'fantastic' realism of many popular television operas of the day. Therefore, once Browning 'translated' this anti-realist theatrical conception into the specific television language by using special effects, in the eyes of American viewers of the 1960s the result looked much like a delirium of images and sounds. And this was probably another reason of the failure of *The Flood* as a television opera[63].

DIFFERENT STYLES, DIFFERENT BODIES

In *The Flood* each medium (sets and costumes, dance/mime, and music) is articulated in a variety of styles which correspond to the bodily /disembodied nature of the various characters and aspects of the opera. The first distinction that immediately stands out concerns the visual aspects (sets and costumes): the celestial sphere (God and all those things or characters that are or related to him, like the Angels) is represented in a purely abstract (non-representational), anti-realistic style. Special effects and totally abstract figures abound; human bodies and

---

[61]. *Ibidem.*

[62]. *Ibidem.*

[63]. DÜBGEN 2012, p. 109, speaks of «stilisierte Abstraktion». JOSEPH 2001, p. 132, recalls «the surrealistic sets, the abstractness of the dancing, the bizarre visual effects».

ILL. 10: backstage at CBS studios in New York: a cameraman moves in on Noah and his family (members of the New York City ballet) during the taping of «The Comedy» from *The Flood* (reproduced in DÜBGEN 2012, p. 101).

human gestures are entirely avoided. The human sphere, on the contrary, is associated with a representational — although non-realistic — visual and gestural style. To some extent, the two spheres also correspond to two parts of the opera: the former (divine) occupies the entire first part up to «The Building of the Ark», plus a scene in «The Covenant of the Rainbow»); the latter concerns all the human actions and events which take place in the second part of the opera: the building of the ark, The Catalogue of the Animals, and the argument between Noah and his wife («The Comedy»). The turning point between the two spheres occurs when God and Man meet again after the Original Sin: the dialogue between Noah and God before the construction of the Ark. In the *Working Notes* Balanchine and Stravinsky clearly recognized the 'transition' function of this central scene: «Up to this point», they maintained, «*The Flood* may seem to have been a spatial fantasy, a myth, a limbo of symbols. Now it is brought down to humanly tilled earth»[64]. To portray the passage from one sphere to another, Stravinsky and Balanchine imagined exploiting the effect created by the camera angle (ILL. 10). This is one of

---

[64]. *DIALOGUES AND A DIARY*, p. 94.

the few ideas of the *Working Notes* which seem to have been genuinely designed for television by Balanchine and Stravinsky themselves, also without Browning's intervention:

> G[eorge]. B[alanchine]: The God-Noah dialogue could be seen like a tennis game, back and forth from the earth-level view of Noah to the light of the iconostasis, which is the visual anchor throughout The Flood. Generally speaking, the audience's view up to this point has been from above, but we now see Noah from, as nearly as possible, his own position. I would like to elevate the dancers to audience eye level by means of a platform, not only because dancers should not be shown from above, but also because the audience should identify itself with the Noah family[65].

Browning and Ter-Arutunian were very careful to distinguish between the divine and human sphere by means of the opposition between abstract/representational to an even greater degree than Balanchine and Stravinsky had originally intended. God's interventions and the narration of the Genesis are always associated with 'abstract' images created with television special effects. A good example is the scene accompanying the narration of the Creation of the World (bb. 62-82). Here the TV director and the scenographer entirely avoided any simple figurative portrayal of the various elements of the created world named in the biblical narrative (the moon, the sea and the desert etc.) in favour of a series of superimposition and cross-fade effects[66]. The scene begins with the vision of the abstract representation of 'celestial effulgence', which Stravinsky and Balanchine had foreseen including midway through the preceding *Te Deum* (b. 46). Even in the narration of the creation of the «Living creatures that moveth» they only resorted to entirely abstract images. The idea of creatures beginning to reproduce and wander about the earth is conveyed with a series of images superimposed over extreme close-ups on dark objects moving on a light background. The images therefore do not represent the entities named in the account of Genesis uttered by the speaker; they are merely evoked in an entirely abstract manner.

From the point of view of choreography, Balanchine used a different method of characterization, which however corresponds to the abstract/representative dialectic of the TV scenery: the dichotomy between bodily movement and immobility. In Balanchine's aesthetics, in fact, a characterization based on different levels of 'abstraction' would not make much sense, since he never considered dance as an 'abstract' form of representation as opposed to 'realistic' gestures. Unlike visual art, dance could never be, for him, a truly non-representational art, even when used in those plotless choreographies which are often referred to as 'abstract dance'. In an essay entitled 'The Dance Element in Stravinsky's Music', he maintained that

---

65. *DIALOGUES AND A DIARY*, p. 94.

66. According to Browning, «Rouben [Ter-Arutunian] had some ideas about how to supply visual metaphors for the creation». Browning quoted in ROSE 1992, p. 92.

[n]o piece of music, no dance can in itself be abstract. You hear a physical sound, humanly organized, performed by people. Or you see moving before you, dancers of flesh and blood, in a living relation to each other. What you hear and see is completely real. But the after-image that remains with the observer, may have for him the quality of an abstraction. Stravinsky's music, through the force of its invention, leaves strong after-images. I myself think of Apollon as white music, in places as white-on-white. [...] For me the whiteness is something positive (it has in itself an essence) and at the same time abstract[67].

Nor did Balanchine resort to the dichotomy 'pure' dance *vs* pantomime. As can be seen from TABLE 1 (second column): in *The Flood* men express themselves both through pantomime (in the scene of the Catalogue of Animals and in «The Comedy») and through dance (in the «Building of the Ark» and «The Flood»). Mime is also used by Lucifer / Satan — and in different ways, as we shall see shortly. Adam and Eve, although they mostly use an essential and stylized form of mime, in the last scene they mention some dance steps.

Balanchine, therefore, resorted to a different opposition: that between immobility and movement: gesture, mime, dance, and so forth. Instead, he takes all of these modes of expression as different registers of a common tendency in Man towards bodily expression. This is very important from a musical standpoint, as we will see shortly.

Let us now consider the musical component. Stravinsky created a variety of musical idioms that would correspond to the opposite bodily natures and kinds of visual representations. He succeeded in this, essentially, in three ways:

1. by diversified vocal characterizations of the roles;
2. by a particular use of the diatonicism-chromaticism opposition[68];
3. by using different musical styles: from a strongly gestural and bodily one, to a 'disembodied' one.

From the first point of view (the diversified use of the voice), according to Stravinsky, one of his initial ideas for *The Flood* was that «the celestial should sing while the terrestrial should merely talk» — another aspect that shows the typically theatrical (operatic) mindset of Stravinsky's initial conception of the work[69]. Beyond its obvious symbolic meaning — song symbolizes a higher condition of being with respect to the simple spoken word —, this difference aims at creating a musical-vocal equivalent of the different visual styles. Stravinsky articulated this dichotomy in depth, differentiating each element (singing and speaking) in

---

[67]. BALANCHINE 2006, p. 141.

[68]. See my discussion above in Chapter One.

[69]. As Stravinsky himself admitted: see *EXPOSITIONS AND DEVELOPMENTS 1962*, p. 123.

several stylistic degrees and shades, suited to the different characters. So, God's singing voice is very different from that of Lucifer/Satan. Humans usually use a *Sprechstimme* technique (they do not « merely talk»), although sometimes their voice is very close to ordinary speech.

As for the chromatic/diatonic opposition, its use in *The Flood* requires detailed explanation. In Chapter Two we have seen that it had always been one of Stravinsky's chief methods of characterization for conflicting roles or dramatic circumstances; and that in the Russian theatrical tradition stemming from Glinka's *Ruslan and Lyudmila*, chromatic, and more in general non-diatonic, harmonies were conventionally associated with a magic, supernatural, fantastic, non-human, 'Orientalistic' sphere, as opposed to the simple, ordinary, natural, human, 'Occidental' (Russian) one, represented by diatonicism. We can grasp a convention of this kind, albeit each time with a different inflection, in every major work Stravinsky wrote for the theatre, from *The Firebird* to *The Rake's Progress*. In *The Flood*, however, these conventional meanings are literally reversed: the divine sphere, visually and musically 'disembodied', is associated with the presence, at strategic points — mainly cadences — of diatonic harmonies resulting from superimposed perfect fifths, which strongly attenuates the overall chromatic environment generated by the use of twelve-tone rows[70]. On the contrary, the human sphere is associated with a much more markedly chromatic harmony, in which no diatonic harmony appears at the cadence points, giving rise to an a-centric harmonic context ('atonal', in Stravinsky's sense of the word).

One may wonder why this reversal of the traditional meaning associations of chromatism and diatonicism. The explanation depends to a good extent on a symbolism associated with the musical structures of the work: «The real, created world is one of chromatic flux and movement», while «The world before time and when time again ceased is static, symmetrical, and, in a deep sense, diatonic», as Joseph Straus clearly summarized[71]. To better understand how this symbolism works, we can start noticing that Stravinsky put the complete circle of fifths at the very beginning of the work — and then again towards the end (bb. 490-495), just before Satan's last aria «The Forbidden Fruit» — to represent the primordial Chaos. Stravinsky's 'Chaos' has several precedents in the history of music, the most illustrious of which is the *Ouverture* of Haydn's *Creation*. However, while in the latter what is musically represented of Chaos is the idea of primordial disorder — through a complex mixture of different musical stylistics, and the juxtaposition of numerous motifs — Stravinsky's extremely concise representation of Chaos — just in two chords entrusted to a string tremolo — is anything but disordered, as can be seen on the first page of the short score (ILL. 11), where Stravinsky has shown (see his

---

70. See the last column in TABLE 1.

71. STRAUS 2001, p. 228. This and many other symbolic aspects of *The Flood* are also discussed at length in LOCANTO 2008.

lines) the structuring criterion[72]: the two string chords are respectively based on a complete circle of ascending fourths and descending fifths. Both circles start from *c*, and their 12 notes are coupled according to the pattern 1-3 /2-4 / 5-7 /6-8 / etc.

ILL. 11: Igor Stravinsky, first page of the short Score for *The Flood*. Paul Sacher Stiftung, Igor Stravinsky Collection. By kind permission.

To understand the symbolic logic underlying Stravinsky's use of the complete circle of fifth at the beginning of the score, we must consider that all the musical harmonies and scales, both diatonic and chromatic, can be obtained by the circle of fifths through a convenient rearrangement of some of its notes. Therefore, the complete circle can be understood as a 'primordial' and omni-comprehensive form, from which all the musical materials can be drawn, in the same way as in the neo-platonic Christian perspective God is seen as the origin from which all the created world is generated through a process of vertical descent towards ever-lower forms. Now, diatonic harmonies and scales can be simply obtained by selecting a segment of no

---

[72]. See for example BROWN 1989. According to a different interpretation, Haydn represented Chaos by continuously avoiding perfect cadences (see for example RIETHMÜLLER 1973). The use of tremolo characterizes at least another musical representation of chaos, that of Jean Fery's Rebel *Les elements* (1737). Another representation of the chaos preceding Haydn can be found in the Overture of Rameau's *Zaïs* (1748).

more than seven *consecutive* notes from the circle of fifths. Chromatic harmonies and scales, on the contrary, can be obtained by selecting *non-consecutive* notes of the circle of fifths, that is, by radically upsetting the order of its notes. A complete twelve-note row, finally, can be understood as a particular reordering of the notes of the complete circle of fifths: Each twelve-note row, in other words, corresponds to a *specific reordering* of the notes of the circle of fifths. The crucial word here is *order*: since the concept of 'order' in music implies 'time' and 'movement' as well (one thing coming *before* or *after* another *in time*), the change of the note order of the circle of fifths is considered a move from a still a-temporal and immobile dimension of God to the dimension of time and movement of the created world. To sum up:

• The complete circle of fifths represents the a-temporal and immobile dimension of God;

• Diatonic harmonies, which preserve the order of notes of the circle of fifths, represents something close to divinity and a-temporality;

• Chromatic harmonies (and twelve-tone rows), which continuously upsets the order of notes the circle of fifths, represents something distant form divinity and fully involved in time and bodily movement.

In addition to the initial and final Chaos chords, the complete circle of fifths reappears at bb. 60-61, immediately after the *Te Deum* and before the narration of Genesis. Here two chords, defined by Stravinsky in his *Working Notes* as «a kind of approval of what the chorus has been singin»[73], split the circle of fifths into two parts: g - d - a - e - b; and $f_\sharp$ - $c_\sharp$ - $g_\sharp$ - $d_\sharp$ - $a_\sharp$ - f - c. The same two chords reappear after the final recapitulation of the *Te Deum* (bb. 580-581) but with a different instrumentation and inverted order, so as to restore the circle of fifths ($f_\sharp$ - $c_\sharp$ - $g_\sharp$ - $d_\sharp$ - $a_\sharp$ - f - c; 2nd chord: g - d - a - e - b). In both cases, these are associated with an image that refers to the divine sphere: the fade-out from the angels singing the *Te Deum* (bb. 526-279) in the presence of God and an abstract figure (a light effect) representing the radiance of God. Another instance of the complete circle of fifths is at bb 177-178, in the scene of the Banishment from the Garden of Eden. Here the complete circle is split into three chords by fifths starting from the words «And God knew [...]». There is just a note (a) out of place:

1st chord: $f_\sharp$ - $c_\sharp$ - $g_\sharp$ - $d_\sharp$ - [a];

2nd + 3rd chords: f (=$e_\sharp$) - c - g - d - [a] - e - b

Stravinsky also find a way to obtain many diatonic harmonies based on the circle of fifths from the structure of the fundamental twelve-tone row of *The Flood*. The technique is shown by Stravinsky's holograph serial chart reproduced in Ex. 1[74]. The fundamental (Original) row begins on $c_\sharp$ and ends on $g_\sharp$, a perfect fourth down (or perfect fifth up). The following staves of the chart contain five derived serial forms, instead of the usual three. Each form is obtained from the previous one (not from the fundamental row, as is more common in twelve-tone

---

73. *DIALOGUES AND A DIARY*, p. 90.

74. Paul Sacher Stiftung, Igor Stravinsky Collection.

EX. 1: Igor Stravinsky, *The Flood*, serial chart (Paul Sacher Foundation, Igor Stravinsky Collection).

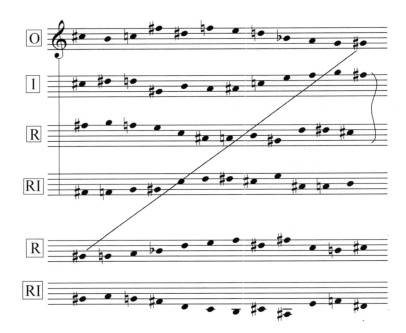

technique) by inverting its intervals or retrograding its notes[75]: the second row is the inversion (I) of the first (O); the third row is the retrograde (R) of the second (I); the fourth row (RI) is the inversion of the third (R). Then the fifth row is again the retrograde (R), but this time of the fundamental row (O) on the first stave (see the diagonal line traced by Stravinsky); finally, the sixth row (RI) is the inversion of the fifth (R). Now, given the interval of perfect fifth(/fourth) between the first and last note of each row, if we read in vertical the first and last column of the chart, we get respectively:

$c\sharp$ - $c\sharp$ - $f\sharp$ - $f\sharp$ - $g\sharp$ - $g\sharp$
... and
$g\sharp$ - $f\sharp$ - $c\sharp$ - b - $c\sharp$ - $d\sharp$

---

[75]. This is a quite unusual procedure in respect to both Viennese dodecaphony and Stravinsky's habits. Schoenberg and his pupils, in fact, usually followed a specific transformation succession: Original – Inversion (of the original) – Retrograde (of the Original) – Retrograde of the Inversion. Stravinsky normally used the following order, which he drew from Ernst Krenek's *Studies in Counterpoint Based on the Twelve-Tone Technique* (KRENEK 1940, p. 11): Original – Inversion (of the Original) – Retrograde (of the Original) – Inversion of the Retrograde. The difference lies in the fourth transformation (Retrograde of the Inversion for the Viennese, Inversion of the Retrograde for Stravinsky). The two orderings are identical in terms of inner interval structure but differ in transposition level. The technique adopted in *The Flood* is still different.

Ex. 2: Igor Stravinsky, *The Flood*, «A skillful beast» (Voice of God), bb. 85-90 [...] 110-115.

... that is (omitting the repeated notes) a diatonic collection made of a cycle of five notes (four consecutive fifths) from the circle of perfect fifths:

$b - f_\sharp - c_\sharp - g_\sharp - d_\sharp$

335

With the addition of one more note at both sides of the sequence — *e* and *a*♯ — this would be a simple B-major diatonic scale:

[*b*] - *c*♯ - *d*♯ - *e* - *f*♯ - *g*♯ - [*a*♯] - (*b*)

As can be seen from the last column of TABLE 1, the chord by fifths *b* - *f*♯ - *c*♯ - *g*♯ - *d*♯, or parts (or single notes) of it, can be found at the beginning and at the main cadences of many musical sections related to the divine sphere[76]. In particular, all the episodes in which we can hear the voice of God start and end with a chord (or a note) belonging to this collection. This is simply because these episodes make use a different combination of rows drawn from the serial chart of Ex. 1, which all begin and end with one of these five notes. Two rows are entrusted in linear form to the two bass voices; the third row is played by the accompanying instrumental part. Consider, for example, the first intervention of God's voice at b. 83, on the words «A skilful beast» (Ex. 2): the two bass voices use rows 5 and 6 (R and RI respectively) of the serial chart. The instrumental part uses row 4. In this way, at the beginning and end of the passage one obtains respectively *f*♯ - *g*♯ and *c*♯ - *g*♯ - *d*♯. Significantly, the whole group *b* - *f*♯ - *c*♯ - *g*♯ - *d*♯ appears on the last words pronounced by God at b 458, at the end of «The Covenant of the Rainbow».

The diatonic harmonies obtained by superimposing two rows of the six basic serial forms can also be found in the brief instrumental transition of harp and woodwinds that follows the representation of Chaos in b. 6 (Ex. 3, which recurs in three other places: b. 179, b. 496 and b. 581). Stravinsky called this transition 'Jacob's ladder', the connection between God and Earth on which Jacob sees angels passing in his dream at Bet-El (*Genesis*, 28, 12)[77]. In the visual counterpart it corresponds to a cross-fade from the image of the angels to an abstract figure on an empty background, symbolizing a transition towards the divine dimension. The overlapped serial forms with which it is built are O and R transposed down by a perfect fifth. The transposition has not prevented the two rows from producing at the end a vertical relation *c*♯ - *f*♯ that is part of the diatonic set *b* - *f*♯ - *c*♯ - *g*♯ - *d*♯.

Vice versa, in the part of the work concerned with human beings (the building of the ark, the argument between Noah and his wife in «The Comedy», The Flood) Stravinsky systematically avoids any clearly diatonic harmony, both in the middle and at the beginning/end of the phrases. The use of the twelve-tone series is now aimed at obtaining strongly chromatic lines (and not diatonic vertical aggregate). The rows are never superimposed; therefore, the fifths between the initial and final notes do not bring forth diatonic groups, as happens in the divine parts. The various forms of the row or their two halves (the two hexachords) are now used in a chiefly linear manner or according to the technique of the verticals of the rotational arrays

---

[76].   «[...] my plan of musical cadences [...] [is] particularly strong in this music; I felt the need for very definite musical punctuation marks. (The listener must have a sure sense of location — topographical location — in this work)». EXPOSITIONS AND DEVELOPMENTS, p. 124.

[77].   DIALOGUES AND A DIARY, p. 93.

Ex. 3: Igor Stravinsky, *The Flood*, 'Jacob's ladder', b. 6.

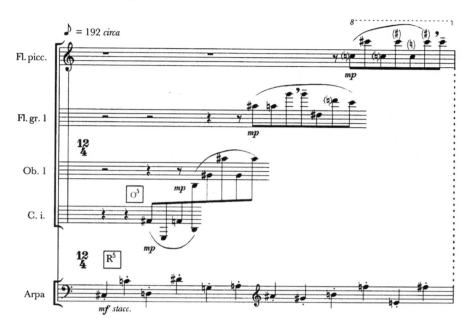

discussed in the previous chapters, which in this case produces strongly chromatic harmonies (the use of verticals is summarized in the last column of TABLE 1).

However, despite the distinctiveness of this symbolism, in my opinion the diatonic-chromatic opposition in *The Flood* concerns a purely *structural* level of musical construction that would not have many implications on the production of meaning and the construction of the staged body if it were not associated with other musical aspects. Also in this case, as in that of the *Firebird* discussed in the Chapter Two, we can see how the sole pitch structure (the chromatic / diatonic opposition) is an essential but not sufficient component to produce meaning and for the musical construction of the staged bodies. If considered as a separate and self-sufficient structural aspect, the diatonic-chromatic dialectic, and Stravinsky's symbolism of the circle of fifths would seem a purely music-analytical datum, whose meaningfulness (and whose perceptibility) would be difficult to prove. On the contrary, it makes much more sense to assume that the various bodily connotations (the immobility of the divine bodies; the movement of the bodies of living creatures) result from the combination of several musical elements.

This brings us to the last of the three abovementioned ways in which Stravinsky differentiates the various musical idioms of *The Flood*: through different types of musical gestural style, characterized by a complex of musical factors:

1) a-gestural (disembodied) style = vocal-polyphonic style, homophonic polyphony, sustained harmonies, stepwise movements in the polyphonic parts, regular and homogeneous rhythmic figures, clear underlying pulse.

2) gestural (embodied) style: instrumental writing, complex (not homophonic) polyphony, extremely varied rhythms (and polyphonic rhythm), broken melodic lines, wide intervallic leaps, sudden changes in dynamics.

The first style corresponds to that of many compositions from Stravinsky's neoclassical period in which the music expresses a sublimated, and almost incorporeal vision of the body; the second style is that typical of much post-Webernian serial music of the Fifties, including Stravinsky's own composition from *Movements* onwards, in which a strongly bodily and gestural character emerges again.

To sum up: each medium (images, dance/mime, music) is articulated on a similar dialectic opposition between two different styles:

	Divine sphere	Human sphere
Images (sets, special effects)	Abstract	Representational
Bodily movement (mime/dance)	Immobility	Movement
Harmony (music)	Diatonic	Chromatic
Musical style	Gestural	A-gestural

In the terms of Nicholas Cook's 'metaphor' theory of the musical multimedia, we could say that this formal resemblance between the various media allows for the transfer of an 'emergent meaning' (that is, a meaning which does not exist in each medium if considered alone, apart from the others) between them, so that they reinforce each other in the process of meaning production[78].

Stravinsky employs the chromatic-gestural style always in association with the visual aspects associated with the human sphere. In the music for «The Catalogue of the Animals» and «The Comedy» this connotation is particularly strong. Something similar could be also said of the music for the dance section of «The Building of the Ark», were chromatism and continuous unfolding of short musical gestures evoke the laborious and frenetic movement of the men and women in building the ship (Ex. 4). Robert Craft speaks of the 'onomatopoeic' quality of this piece: «The Flood's musical images», he maintains, «include felicitous variations on conventions» such as «[...] the onomatopoeic carpentering in "The Building of the Ark": different speeds and volumes of hammerings in percussion and trombones»[79]. «The Building of the Ark» is one of the most representative works of Stravinsky's late gestural style. The piece begins with a series of short gestures, much in the style of the *Variations for orchestra*, and then gradually creates a complex polyphony made of flutter-tonguing and tremolos. The latter is an important and recurring gesture in *The Flood:* since it is one of the most distinctive aspects of the Chaos chords, and of both the danced piece of the score («The Building of the Ark and The Flood»)[80].

---

78. Cook 1998, p. 70.
79. Craft 2006, p. 185.
80. See above Chapter One.

Ex. 4: Igor Stravinsky, *The Flood*, «The Building of the Ark», bb. 248-263. © Copyright 1962 by Boosey & Hawkes Music Publishers Ltd. By kind permission.

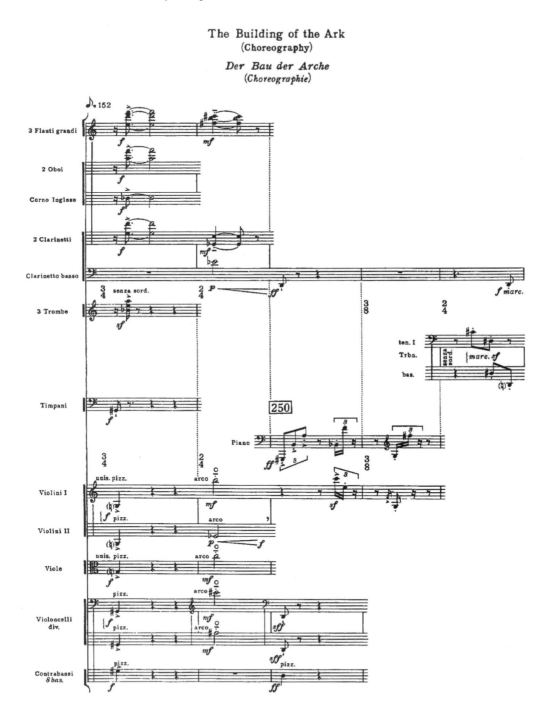

The only apparent exception to the 'rule' (gestural-chromatic style = human bodily movement) could be found in the narration of the Creation of the World, for which Stravinsky composed a highly chromatic-gestural music (Ex: 5), while Browning and Ter-Arutunian resorted to the entirely 'abstract', as we have seen before. The reason for this 'exception', however, becomes evident if we consider that chromatic-gestural musical style appears exactly in the point where the text of Genesis mentions for the first time the «moving creatures». To represent this hint at earthly life and to moving bodies within the biblical narration, the *Working Notes* recommended the use of figurative art (a series of images of the created world which, although strongly stylized and anti-realistic, were nevertheless figurative rather than abstract), and envisaged a little choreography at measure 68, precisely in correspondence to the words «living creatures that moveth»:

> I[gor] S[travinsky]: The Genesis recitative could be accompanied by a montage of pictures symbolizing the Creation. For instance, at the words 'Let the dry earth appear', we might see photographs of the moon, of the sea, of deserts. This is the place for animation and graphic arts [...] G[eorge]. B[alanchine] has an idea for a hand ballet of rubber sheets and plastic water bags manipulated to suggest shapes and forms. But we might also show structures of roots and bones, à la Tchelietchev, and of hands sprouting grass from the fingers. [...] The recitative becomes an *arioso* at measure 68. This should be danced by one or perhaps several people representing not humans, but non-associated movements, or explanatory movements. Or the flexing movements of any living creature's discovery of its body. This section should be thought of as a choreographic relief to the purely pictorial recitative[81].

In the final version of the opera, Stravinsky and Balanchine gave up the idea of the 'little choreography', and their suggestion to make use of figurative art and representational manner was intentionally avoided by Browning and Ter-Arutunian, whose visual realization of this scene was entirely 'abstract as we have seen before. The reason for this disagreement is very simple: while Stravinsky and Balanchine considered this part of the biblical narrative from the point of view of its *content* — the moving creatures and the created world — Browning and Ter-Arutunian considered it as being part of the divine sphere of the entire work, in which the focus is on the divine Creator, not on its creatures. They placed, in other words, more emphasis on the divine nature of the act of creation than on the result of the act itself. In the end, only Stravinsky's 'gestural' serial music remained true to the original idea for the Creation scene: that of representing the physical life and the movement of the created world, instead of the immobility of the divine sphere. Thus, the music for the Creation of the World is a classical 'exception that proves the rule'.

---

[81]. *DIALOGUES AND A DIARY*, p. 90.

Ex. 5: Igor Stravinsky, *The Flood*, «The Creation of the World», bb. 68-75. © Copyright 1962 by Boosey & Hawkes Music Publishers Ltd. By kind permission.

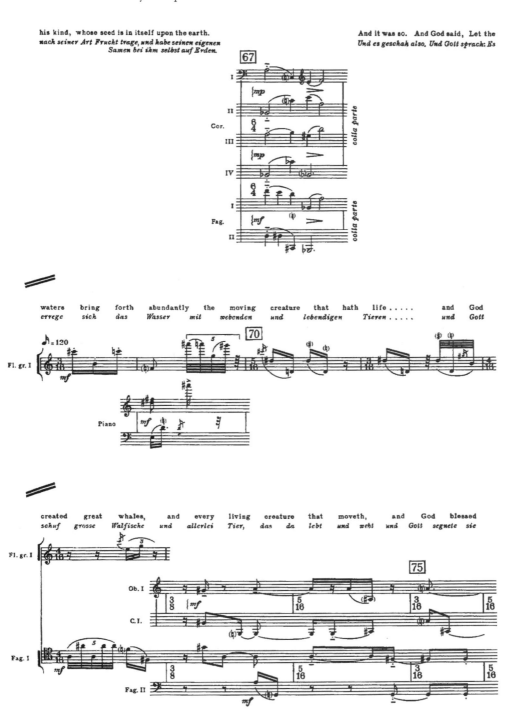

More difficult to understand in this symbolic logic is the musical representation of the Flood (Ex. 6), the central moment of the narrative and of the entire work. Stravinsky himself was not sure whether it should be ascribed to the divine sphere (from which the flood originates) or to the human one, in which the flood takes place. In *Expositions and Developments,* he said:

> I still have so few ideas for The Flood in its scenic form. Perhaps I will choose something 'realistic' and 'representational'; water is a real thing, after all, and so are earth, light, darkness, and animals. But 'realism' is also a question of style[82].

In the end, he seems to have opted for a representation of the Flood as an event that belongs to the earthly, human sphere: no clear diatonic harmonies can be found in the piece, nor in the cadential points: the serial technique used — the verticalization of serial segments: see TABLE 1, last column — tends to produce even more chromatic aggregates than the original twelve-tone row itself. Overall, the musical style looks quite gestural: apart from the static sustained chords, the instrumental parts create a continuous unfolding of short musical gestures. At the same time, however, the overall temporality of the piece is totally static. The harmony is immobilized in the continuous oscillation between the chord g - $g\sharp$ - a and c - d - $d\sharp$ - $f\sharp$. In the melodic part a sequence of even sixteenth notes (with metric changes) each time starting from the same pitch (a) is continuously repeated by the flute and violin parts in tremolo. The music, moreover, has a palindrome form: starting from the middle of the piece (b. 427), it goes backwards with the same notes in reverse order, as had been already suggested by Robert Craft in his typescript (see TABLE 1, first column):

> [...] since nothing actually happens, no movement take place, the piece might have a stationary form — like the ostinato in *Lulu* or the 32 passacaglia variations where Wozzeck dreams but doesn't move. This piece is an ideal opportunity to record the music electronically, for one could 'mirror' each instrumental idea electronically. The storm is outside the Ark, so the music would come from 'outside' electronically at this point.

Stravinsky seems to have understood the palindrome as a symbolic figure of an 'atemporal' condition. «This *La Mer*», he maintained, «has no '*de l'aube à midi*' but only a time experience of something that is terrible and that lasts»[83]. Thus his musical representation of the Flood seems to put together, inside each other, two musical aspects that in the overall symbolism of the work have opposite meanings: the chromatic-gestural style associated with human bodily movement, and a static overall harmony, which can be associated with the atemporal condition of the divine sphere. The latter seems to contain the former within itself, making it almost inaudible.

---

82. *EXPOSITIONS AND DEVELOPMENTS*, p. 126.
83. *DIALOGUES AND A DIARY* 1963, p. 96.

Ex. 6: Igor Stravinsky, *The Flood*, «The Flood» (Choreography), bb. 399-408. © Copyright 1962 by Boosey & Hawkes Music Publishers Ltd. By kind permission.

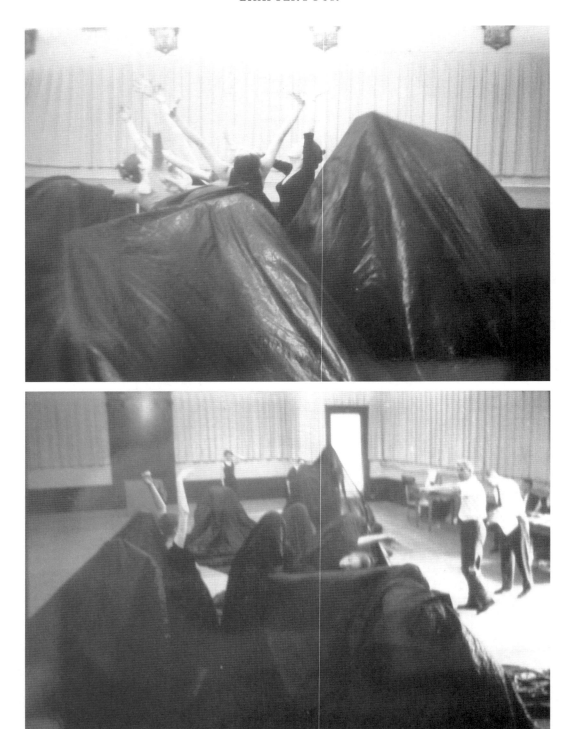

Ill. 12: Balanchine coaching the choreography of «The Flood» from *The Flood* (NYPL, Jerome Robbins Dance Division).

This interpretation is consistent with Balanchine's choreographic representation of the Flood. The TV set was entirely covered by black plastic sheeting, under which a group of male dancers moved on their knees, thus making the black surface go up and down, like waves. From time to time, some female dancers in large white robes appeared among the sheeting, performing running steps and waving their arms aloft. The men lifted and rotated the women while always remaining invisible under the sheeting, so that the women seem lifted by the force of the waves. The whole performance was shot by Browning from different angles and at different distances, from medium close-up to long shots, and then edited with fades, overlapping, and dissolves[84] (ILL. 12). In spite of its apparent representative intent, Balanchine's choreography is highly symbolic: in the same way as in Stravinsky's music a static musical element 'envelops', so to speak a music that is otherwise very dynamic and gestural, also in Balanchine's choreography an incorporeal matter (the black sheeting, under which the invisible bodies of men move) envelops the gesticulating bodies of women.

FROM HEAVEN TO EARTH

In *The Flood*, the visual, gestural and musical meaning associations discussed above are subtly articulated to describe the corporeal or incorporeal nature of the various characters. Let us begin with God, the incorporeal being *par excellence*. From the visual point of view, his voice is constantly associated with an abstract image obtained with special effects. The clearest example is a double ellipse with a series of concentric circles at the centre (vaguely recalling the form of an eye — which was also the logo of CBS) which accompanies the first utterance of the Voice (lines 62-82). The geometric figure is framed within an electronically superimposed image, like the beams of light that shine from the empty centre.

This style of visual representation corresponds to the strongly a-gestural style of the music. The 'voice without body' of God is conveyed by a bass duet with musical accompaniment. We have seen that the idea of intertwining two male voices to represent God's voice was suggested by Robert Craft, who had the Grand Inquisitor scene of Verdi's *Don Carlos* in his mind; however a very similar solution had been used by Stravinsky in the religious cantata *Babel* of 1944, where God's words (Genesis, 1-11, 1-9) are entrusted to a two-part male chorus[85]. Interestingly enough

---

84. «G[eorge] B[alanchine]: "I imagine a floor covered with a shiny bitumen-like material, a deliquescent black surface bubbling like an oil field. Underneath this black tent the male dancers bob up and down from their knees, here and there and all over the camera area, like furuncles. [...] The female dancers move among the mounting and bursting blobs of black. The men are the waves and the women the people drowning in them. The men fling and twirl the women, then swallow them in the folds of their black substance. The audience should feel that it is drowning"». *Ibidem*, p. 76.

85. ANDRIESSEN – SCHÖNBERGER 1989, p. 113, notice that «Stravinsky's God, generally, has a forked tongue». In Stravinsky's musical output the male duet — not associated with God — first appeared in *The*

Ex. 7: Igor Stravinsky, *The Flood*, symmetric inversion and motivic relationships in the voice of God, bb. 85-100.

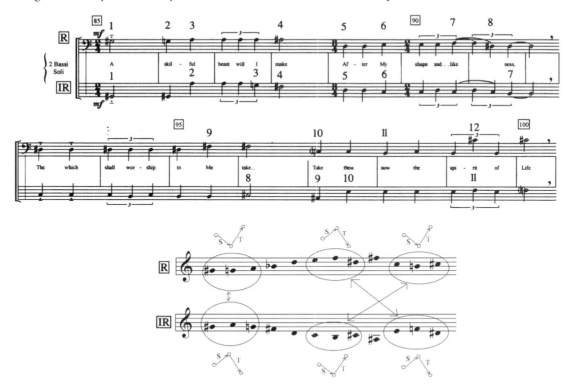

for us, on that occasion Stravinsky had rejected the music publisher's (Nathaniel Shilkret) suggestion to entrust God's voice to the narrator and to use the choir for the construction and destruction of the Tower of Babel[86]. On the contrary, he gave the narration to a speaker, and God's words to a men's choir, believing that spoken language was not suitable to express God's voice.

In *The Flood*, the two male voices are intertwined in an almost homophonic counterpoint, albeit with frequent displacements (see again Ex. 2). The vocal style vaguely resembles early vocal polyphony. Despite constant metric changes, the rhythm is set by a regular underlying pulse (quarter note)[87]. In the instrumental part, the bass drum provides an interrupted sixteenth-note rhythm. The closest example of this style in Stravinsky's work is, not surprisingly, a piece on liturgical text: *Introitus* (1965), in which a very similar combination of male voices and percussion (timpani and tam-tam instead of the bass drum of *The Flood*) is used.

All this brings about a sensation of cold abstractness and disembodiment, to which also contribute the geometric symmetry of the pitch structure, since in all the episodes the two bass

---

Nightingale and was later used in many other works such as *Renard*, *Œdipus Rex*, and *Threni*.

[86].   See WHITE 1979, p. 417.

[87].   On Stravinsky's use of a single-beat metric unit a structuring element see WALSH 2017.

voices are always based on two twelve-tone rows which are the inversion of each other, so as to bestow rigorous symmetry upon the structure. Ex. 7 shows the symmetrical relationships created between intervallic motives (tone-semitone) contained in the row. The monotony of this rigid structure is broken only by the colour of the instrumental parts, which changes at each episode, going from the dark colour of the cello and double bass (bb. 83-115, 116-126), to the metal of harp and piano (bb. 180-247) and to the ethereal sound of the violas and flutes (alto and regular) (bb. 457-489)[88].

Another entirely disembodied voice — but for completely different reasons and in a very different sense — is the male voice (of Lawrence Harvey) entrusted with the narration of the biblical tale — just like in *Babel*. It is a true voice-over, placed on an extradiegetic level from that of the *dramatis personae*. This 'epic' element brings *The Flood* closer to *L'Histoire du soldat* and *Œdipus Rex*, in which the strategy of off-stage narrations had been first experienced. However, in *Histoire du soldat* the voice of the narrator has a specific (notated) rhythm which is coordinated with that of the instrumental parts while in *Œdipus Rex* and *The Flood* the narrator expresses himself in ordinary spoken language. Julien Ségol has shown how the introduction of the 'speaker' — the term itself is evocative of the radio voice — in *Œdipus Rex* can be considered as an early sign of the impact of the mediatized radiophonic universe on Stravinsky's theatre, and that this phenomenon can be understood as a part of his broader tendency of depersonalizing and de-psychologizing the human voice as well as music in general[89]. From the perspective of this book, it could be added that this phenomenon also corresponds to the operation of neutralization and sublimation of the implied body of human voice (and of music as well). In *The Flood*, thus, we can see the culmination of this process of mediatization, which had already begun with the speaker of *Œdipus Rex*.

Stravinsky approaches the voice of the Narrator in *The Flood* in a similar way to *Œdipus Rex* also from the point of view of its coordination with the instrumental parts. Sometimes the narration takes place with no music at all (for instance, in the narration of The Creation of Lucifer), as is usually the case in *Œdipus Rex*; sometimes the voice is set against a musical background (see for example the narration of The Creation of the World) — this happens just once in the opera-oratorio, in the last intervention of the speaker, which unfolds against a percussion background. When narrating The Banishment from the Garden of Eden, the voice-over is perfectly synchronized with the two tension-laden chords in the brass section in b. 177, as instructed in the *Working Notes*[90]. Thus, Harvey's voice seems to be coming 'in and out' of

---

[88]. «I saw that God must always sing in the same manner, in the same tempo, and I decided to accompany Him by only bass instruments at first, until I saw that this could become monotonous». Expositions and Developments, p. 124.

[89]. Ségol 2014, pp. 377-378.

[90]. Dialogues and a Diary, pp. 92-93.

the musical narration, commenting and 'narrating', in its turn, the drama. From Stravinsky's essentially theatrical point of view, this would result in an effect of estrangement and, in this sense, anti-representational with respect to the dramatic dimension. However, due to the different conventions of the two media, the effect and the meanings of an off-stage narration in the theatre and of a television voice-over are quite different. the American audience of the 1960s might have perceived the narrator's voice in *The Flood* as a sort of documentary narration.

Even more imbued with diatonic elements is the *Te Deum*. Here the notes *b* - *f♯* - *c♯* (the first three notes of the referential *b* - *f♯* - *c♯* - *g♯* - *d♯* diatonic chord) can be found in many cadences (all three notes are exposed in vertical at b. 59], and melodic lines are directly derived from the 'Chaos chords'. Ex. 8, reproducing a serial sketch for the bars 8-15 of the piece[91]. The two upper staves (nos. 1 and 2) contain the first two phrases of the vocal part, respectively based on the twelve-tone rows contained in the second and fourth lines of the serial chart of Ex. 1 (row I on *c♯*; row RI on *f♯*). The lower staves (nos. 3, 4, and 5) show in sequence the genesis of the line of the horn accompanying the vocal part: the third staff contains the succession of the notes of the first 'Chaos' (see again ILL. 11): *c* - *b♭* - *f* - *e♭* - *a♭* - *g♭* [*f♯*] - *d♭* [*c♯*] - *e* - *b* - *d* - *a* - *g*. On the fourth stave the entire line is transposed from *c* to *c♯*, and finally, on the last one it is symmetrically reversed around *c♯*, ending on *f♯*. All this results in a strongly diatonic passage, in keeping with the incorporeal nature of angels and their proximity to God (according to Isaiah VI, 1-3).

Ex. 8: Igor Stravinsky, *The Flood*, sketch for the *Te Deum*, bb. 8-15 (Paul Sacher Stiftung, Igor Stravinsky Collection).

---

[91]. Paul Sacher Stiftung, Igor Stravinsky Collection. The sketch s transcribed and analyzed in detail in ROGERS 2004.

Some aspects of the visual representation of the Angels are not entirely consistent with the idea of immobility and incorporeality that, following the same logic, should be associated with their almost divine nature. The reason has not so much to do with theological issues (in both the Old and New Testament angels are represented as supernatural beings acting as intermediaries between God and men) but with the genesis of the work: Stravinsky had first planned to realize the *Te Deum* as a dance piece. Even in this original hypothesis, however, it was very clear to him that an essential feature of the representation of angels should have been their lack of motion, which corresponded to their incorporeality. The body of the dancers, covered by the great wings, and even their gender should have been only partially discernible. And although moving to some extent, they should never have performed dance movements that involve a large movement in space, such as jumps and running steps, as can be argued from his early description in *Expositions and Developments*:

> The Angels should be costumed to show their faces and their three tiers of folded wings (the Seraphim). The angels should bend, turn, sway to right and left, but never leave their places — certainly never run, jump, fly, or spread their wings. They must have sex, too, whatever theology may say: four men and four women. One does not see specific sexual characteristics, of course, but only differences in height; this is for choreographic reasons[92].

Rouben Ter-Arutunian drafted a scenic solution perfectly suited to Stravinsky's idea: in his drawings (ILL. 13) we can see three Seraphim covered by their large wings and enclosed in three niches within which they could have moved very little.

Later, for reasons we don't know — but probably to be more consistent with the overall symbolism of the work according to which only human bodies move and dance — Stravinsky and Balanchine discarded the idea of a dance piece, leaving the choreography only to the two main moments in the history of men («The Building of the Ark» and «The Flood»). In order to avoid, as much as possible, the use of artistic-figurative elements (according to the principle that God and the beings close to him are associated with non-representational symbols) they finally resorted to the idea of the Byzantine icon. As an art form that cannot simply be classified as figurative — given its strong stylization and its symbolic and transcendent meaning — the icon lent itself well to a representation of the angelic figures as divine creatures. Stravinsky and Balanchine imagined enclosing the icons of the Seraphim within a sort of iconostasis (the screen separating the sanctuary from the nave in Eastern Christian churches of Byzantine tradition).

> The angels are Seraphim, Russian-style, and we are aware of their wings rather than of bodies or faces. The camera pulls downward, and we discover that

---

92. *EXPOSITIONS AND DEVELOPMENTS*, p. 125.

ILL. 13: Rouben Ter-Arutunian, preparatory drawing for the Seraphims singing the *Te Deum* (NYPL, Jerome Robbins Dance Division).

they are framed like icons, and that together they form a triangular altar. I[gor] S[travinsky]: "This iconostasis should resemble a real Byzantine altar with the Chiasma or X symbol on top"[93].

Finally, the television set of the *Te Deum* was created by Ter-Arutunian in the form of a large triangular iconostasis with ten Seraphim painted on it, in a style vaguely resembling that of the Byzantine icons. In correspondence with the faces of the angels, there were holes through which masks with large eyes could be glimpsed. No performing body, therefore, could be seen.

The musical style of the *Te Deum* (Ex. 9) reflects the ambiguities of its genesis: the supernatural, bodyless nature of the Seraphim corresponds to some a-gestural aspects of the music, such as the continuous, almost mechanical oscillation of the whole tone between $c_\sharp$ and $d_\sharp$ in the upper vocal part at every new verse of the hymn delimited by the anaphora of the pronoun (« *Te* Deum Laudams [...] » / « *Te* aeternum Patrem [...] » / « *Tibi* omnes angeli [...] » / « *Tibi* Cherubim et Seraphim [...] ». Like many other disembodying aspects of Stravinsky's

---

93.   *DIALOGUES AND A DIARY*, p. 89. On Stravinsky's ties with the theology of icons and orthodox theology in general see PASTICCI 2014, pp. 32-38; see also PASTICCI 2012, p. 87.

Ex. 9: Igor Stravinsky, *The Flood*, *Te Deum*, bb. 8-26. © Copyright 1962 by Boosey & Hawkes Music Publishers Ltd. By kind permission.

music this is a stylistic hallmark of liturgical music: in each verse the oscillating whole tone $c\sharp$ - $d\sharp$ module is repeated as many times as is necessary to cover the length, each time different, of the lines of the hymn delimited by the anaphora, to then conclude each time with the same cadence d - $g\sharp$ - b - a). It is therefore an extensible musical form (also used in many other pieces by Stravinsky such as *Les Noces* and the *Mass*), adaptable to lines of unequal length, exactly as happens in Gregorian psalmody (not surprisingly, Stravinsky playfully said of his *Te Deum* that it was «not Gregorian but Igorian chant»)[94]. Other elements of the piece, however, such as the sudden appearance of the orchestral chords at the end of each cadence have a more markedly gestural and expressive character; and in the *Sanctus* final section (bb. 46-60) the syncopated rhythm clearly reveals Stravinsky's original intention to compose a dance piece. This distinctive melange of gestural and a-gestural, corporeal and incorporeal, immobilizing and dynamic elements lends itself perfectly to representing an angelic dance.

Let us now turn to Lucifer/Satan. His representation is one of the most complex. He is not a human being and as an angel (before the Fall) he is close to God and to the other angels singing the *Te Deum*. However, after the Fall he becomes the most distant being from God, while remaining an immortal being. This transformation is expressed by all artistic components. On a visual plan, the highly stylized sets and costume of Lucifer, who wears a white, shimmering mask with stylized rays and two big wings recalling those of the Byzantine iconostasis of the *Te Deum*, is changed into the black, grotesque-surreal mask of Satan (see again ILL. 5). Lucifer's essential and elegant movements of the wing became Satan's grotesque gesticulation (a sort of pantomime) of the harms in his aria «God Made the World for Love». All these visual aspects had been clearly envisaged by Stravinsky and Balanchine in the *Working Notes*:

> Photographically speaking, Satan is Lucifer's negative polarity. What was white becomes black, and the lips turn dark red. The mask shrinks to skull size and becomes a corruption of its former features. The wings grow hideously veined, like a bat[95].

Lucifer/Satan's voice (the only operatic voice in *The Flood*), too, undergoes a transformation. Lucifer's vocal style is that of «a high, slightly pederastic tenor»[96]; Satan's voice is a «sibilant sweet voice wholly different from the trumpeting Lucifer»[97]. Stravinsky's reference to specific gender connotations (as in the case of the Angels) clearly shows how the bodily aspects were important for his musical imagination. Lucifer/Satan's 'ambiguously gendered' and embodied voice is the opposite of God's male-gendered but strongly a-gestural bass

---

94. *Ibidem*.
95. *Ibidem*.
96. *EXPOSITIONS AND DEVELOPMENTS*, p. 124.
97. *DIALOGUES AND A DIARY*, p. 92.

Ex. 10: Igor Stravinsky, *The Flood*, aria (Lucifer) « The Beams of My Bright », bb. 130-145. © Copyright 1962 by Boosey & Hawkes Music Publishers Ltd. By kind permission.

duet. «The notion that God should be sung by two basses», Stravinsky maintained, «and Satan by a high, slightly pederastic tenor (at any rate, Satan is sexually less 'sure' than God) came to me somewhat later»[98]. As for the musical style, Lucifer's first aria «The Beams of My Bright» (Ex. 10), although largely chromatic, contains various diatonic references, consistent with the idea that Lucifer is still close to God and to the angels his peers. The brief aria stars from $c_\sharp$ (the first pitch of the Original twelve-tone row) and ends at b. 144 with the almost-diatonic melodic statement $f_\sharp$ - $g_\sharp$ - $b_\sharp$ - $a_\sharp$ - $c_\sharp$ (reordered as a segment of diatonic scale: $f_\sharp$ - $g_\sharp$ - $a_\sharp$ - $b_\sharp$ - $c_\sharp$) on the words «I will be highest of heaven». After the Fall, the music of Satan's arietta «God made the world for love» takes on a much more chromatic character, and a more intricate rhythm. This 'embodied' musical characterization is the opposite of God's disembodied voice: Satan, Stravinsky maintains, «walks on a carpet of complex and sophisticated music, unlike God, and his vanities are expressed, to a certain extent, by syncopation»[99].

The episode of the Fall of Lucifer shows another good example of Browning's typical remediation strategies. Once again, a typically theatrical conception — illustrated by the *Working Notes* — is at its base, but its television implementation is possible only thanks to special effects. It also shows how Stravinsky's musical gestural style evokes bodily movements even when these are no longer directly associated with music. Let us examine it in detail.

According to the *Working Notes*, starting with the words «Lucifer was vain» of the Narrator (b. 127), the dancer (Edward Villella) was to begin to move: he had to jump to a higher rock with each chord, miss the last one, and finally, just before his *arioso* begins, fall again at floor level, «dancing a lithe, athletic 'twist'»[100]. Stravinsky had conceived the music for this scene in a strongly gestural musical style: each 'jump' is musically represented by a typical two-chord gesture. In Chapters One and Two we have seen how this gesture is usually associated with a (visible or imaginary) bodily movement brusquely interrupted by such a jump-and-landing, a rise-and-drop, etc. Here the association with the jump is most typical. Moreover, on this occasion the harmony of the five gestures is structured in such a way as to create the sensation of a 'progression' between them, exactly as, in the visual counterpart, the leaps of Satan outline an ever-higher progression. The pitches of the five gestures are derived from the five lines of a transposition-rotation serial array as shown in Ex. 11: each time the note $c_\sharp$ — with which all five lines of the array start — is followed by a 5 note chord, with the remaining 5 notes of each the transposed line of the array (i.e. apart from the original, non-transposed one, on the first staff of the array), in reverse order (see encircled numbers 5, 4, 3, 2 and 1 in the musical example). In each chord the five notes are disposed in such a way that the upper note is each time higher, thus creating an ascending line a - $a_\sharp$ - c - d in the upper part of the overall harmonic

98. *EXPOSITIONS AND DEVELOPMENTS* 1962, p. 124.

99. *Ibidem*.

100. *DIALOGUES AND A DIARY*, p. 91..

passage. In this way the increasingly wide leaps between $c_\sharp$ and the upper note of the following chord create an overall musical gesture that evokes the image of higher and higher jumps, with $c_\sharp$ as their 'base'.

Ex. 11: Igor Stravinsky, *The Flood*, serial construction of the five 'jump' chords, bb. 127-129.

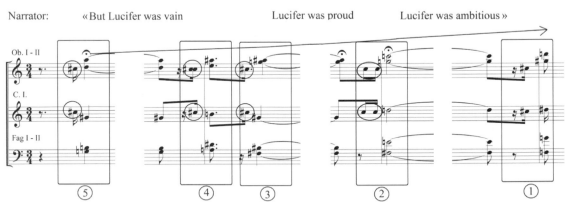

Browning implemented Stravinsky and Balanchine's idea in a much less 'theatrical' way, by using special effects and by avoiding the dancer having to actually jump. The whole sequence starts with the narration of the creation of Lucifer (between bb. 115 and 116). During the bass duet «I Make Thee Master» Lucifer stands in a wide shot with a low camera angle, so as to appear as a statuesque figure. In the following aria «The Beams of My Bright», his mask is filmed in close-up. The four chords that Stravinsky and Balanchine had planned to synchronize with the jumps are instead synchronized with the movements of his head. During the aria «The Beams of My Bright» Lucifer is filmed in medium close-up while opening and closing his wings proudly. His gestures are highly stylized and essential. With the last words of the aria («My power surpasses my peers, I will be highest of heaven»), we see Lucifer in a very wide shot, showing us that he is standing on a high pedestal. When the Fall occurs, Lucifer's voice is turned into a suffering *Sprechstimme*, which is synchronized with a close-up of a puff of smoke, which fills the screen. Then a negative polarity effect and a rotation of the camera gives the impression that Satan, now entirely encompassed in a wide shot, is falling down swirling in a void. At the end, when the camera stops rotating, the dancer lies down on the ground and shakes his legs in the manner of a grotesque pantomime. The idea of the rotating camera and of the negative effect had been foreseen by Stravinsky and Balanchine, whose description, however, is still linked to twentieth century theatrical and visual-artistic modernist traditions, more than to the linguistic codes of television:

> A short pause at the end of measure 151 will suffice for camera tricks to create sensations of pinwheeling, of falling, and turning upside down. If it were a Cocteau film, Satan would do a parachute jump, The Fall might also be symbolized pictorially, for example, by photographing the tracings on a plate when two atoms collide [...][101].

Even more distinct from the abstract and disembodied mode of representation of the voice of God is that used for human beings (Noah and his family), whose condition is furthest from divinity. They are dressed in long tunics that are not remotely realistic — there was no attempt to convey a sense of 'period costume' — and wore stylized masks with unnatural dimensions and a vaguely surreal appearance (see again ILL. 9)[102]. These costumes prevent the audience from seeing their bodily and facial expression, and they limit their movements, which are reduced to the gesticulations of the arms and some head movement (like in Stravinsky and Cocteau's ideal staging of *Œdipus Rex*). However, these bodily movements, together with the chromatic-gestural style of the music and the use of *Sprechstimme* technique give human characters a physicality and even a 'realism' diametrically opposed to the abstract and bodiless vision of God. They mix conventional elements drawn from different theatrical traditions. Some of them, such as the pleading hand gestures of Noah's sons in «The Comedy» (b. 383), recall the mimic code of classical ballet pantomimes. Others seem to derive from the conventions of dance — more than mime — in classical ballet, as can be seen, for example, when Noah's children forcibly pick their mother up and carry her onto the boat, making her first spin twice on her heels — a probable allusion to the partnering lift technique of classical ballet. Many gestures, like Noah's wife drinking from the bottle or her slapping her husband at the end of

---

[101]. *DIALOGUES AND A DIARY*, p. 91.

[102]. «I do not yet see how to costume him [Noah], except that I am sure he should have a beard, perhaps a terraced, Assyrian beard. For me, the Bible, like all myths, exceeds any limitation of period in a visual sense, and this is why I still have so few ideas for *The Flood* in its scenic form. Perhaps I will choose something 'realistic' and 'representational'». *Ibidem*, p. 126.

their quarrel, seem typically comedic. Balanchine was very careful in creating a kind of gestures that were very stylized (and in this sense anti-realistic) while looking quite similar to everyday gestures. In «The Comedy» , for example, Noah's wife is reluctant to follow her husband onto the Ark. Craft's text, drawn from the Chester mystery *Noah's Flood*, reads[103]:

Noah:	Wife, come in! Why stand'st thou there?
	It is time to go or drown, that I swear.
Noah's Wife:	I see no need, though thou stay all day and stare.
Noah (aside):	(Lord, that women be crabbed ay,
	And never are meek, that I may say,
	As is well seen by me today
	In witness of you each one.)
	Come in, wife, in twenty devils' way...
Noah's Wife:	I will not come in today,
	And I shall not drown.
	Row forth, Noah, "save thy life"
	But mind thee, find a new wife.

Balanchine's pantomime adds another comedic element to the scene: Noah's wife prefers to stay and drink rather than follow her husband[104]. This can be understood by the bottle (the only prop used in the whole scene) she holds in her hands and by the emphatic gestures of the arms and the torso, which reveal her inebriation. ILLS. 14-15 shows Balanchine teaching the dancer Joysanne Sidimus — at the time one of the members of Balanchine's New York City Ballet — how to perform the gesture of drinking). The result is at the same time stylized, grotesque, and 'realistic'.

«The Comedy» cannot be understood as a pantomime in the strict sense of the term, for the mimes are also given a reciting voice. Of course, this is not actually the voice of the performers but only that of the characters: the mimes limit themselves to follow with their gestures the sense of the words delivered by an actor reciting the text with a *Sprechstimme* technique, always against a musical background, that is in the form of a melodrama. Unlike theater, in which the origin of the voice from a different place in the stage than the one occupied by the mime (or from the orchestral pit) allows us to 'unmask' the technique of the dissociation of roles, thus increasing the anti-illusionistic effect, for the television viewer the voice usually seems to come from the same place occupied by the actors, thus being ideally associated with them. The use of

---

[103]. Craft's libretto reworks the original late medieval text in more regular strophic forms. The text of the mystery play here reads: «*Noah*: Wife, come in, why standest thou there? / Thou art ever forward, that I dare swear: / Come on God's half, time it were, / For fear lest that we drown».

[104]. «Noah's wife could be characterized as a Xantippe with a bottle. She has disregarded the Ark when it was building, and she is on her way to a pub when the flood begins». *DIALOGUES AND A DIARY*, p. 95.

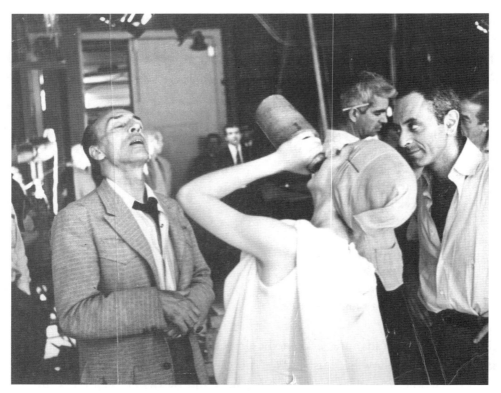

ILLS. 14-15: Balanchine coaching Joysanne Sidimus in the role of Noah's wife (mime) (Joysanne Sidimus private archive, by kind permission) (on the right in ILL. 14: Kirk Browning and Rouben Ter-Arutunian).

the mask, in this case, helps to create an 'illusionist' effect, since it prevents the audience from recognizing the dissociation of roles (the fact that it is not the actor/mime who speaks). On the contrary, in a theatrical work like *Renard*, the use of masks does not allow any illusionistic association of the voices to the characters, not only because they are singing (not speaking or using *Sprechstimme*) and because it is possible to notice their different origins in the stage space, but also because there is no relationship between voices and characters (the same character can be associated with different voices; in *Renard* even a polyphonic group of voices can be associated to a single animal/character). In *The Flood*, on the contrary the characters, mimes are always given the same male or female — according to their gender — voice. Paradoxically, therefore, the use of the mask in combination with the *Sprechgesang* achieves, on TV, a much more 'realistic' effect than in the theater.

Stravinsky's music (Ex. 12) contribute to this characterization by means of the gestural-chromatic style and through a particular use of *Sprechstimme* technique. The notated rhythm in the vocal part is shaped around the normal declamatory rhythm of theatrical delivery. There is nothing to indicate the melodic profile of the voice (as was the case in Schoenberg's *Pierrot Lunaire*) apart from the two levels: relatively higher (= a musical figure placed relatively higher with the stem pointing down) and relatively lower (= a musical figure placed relatively lower with the stem pointing up). Ultimately, here, the *Sprechstimme* appears quite like spoken drama. Something similar, but from the opposite side, happens in the narrating voice of The Catalogue of the Animals: while not a true *Sprechstimme* — it is simply entrusted to an actor's voice reciting over the musical background — it speaks in a very similar manner to a *Sprechstimme*. Its inflections emphasize the accents of the poetry, like a doggerel, and its falsetto sounds like a «comb-and-tissue-paper, or Jew's-harp, timbre». Stravinsky also suggested an «American accent» like that of «a square-dance caller or a tobacco auctioneer»[105].

All this gives all these mediatized voices a sort of realistic-grotesque character. Of course, it could hardly be said that the use of *sprechstimme* is an 'illusionistic' or 'realistic' expedient. Even Arnold Schoenberg, in his famous foreword to *Pierrot Lunaire*, maintained that the main purpose of this vocal technique was not to imitate natural or realistic language at all[106]. In *The Flood*, however, far from the expressionist climate of *Pierrot lunaire*, and in the mediatized form of television, *sprechstimme* takes on a very different meaning. Along with Balanchine's stylized 'realistic' gestures it provides the humans of *The Flood* with a 'body' (since the masks and the long tunics prevent us from actually seeing the performers' real bodies in their entirety). Paradoxically enough, thus, the 'human voices' mediated by television, along with Balanchine's 'human gestures' give the anti-realistic, surreal, and almost extra-terrestrial masked figures of *The Flood* a sense of 'realism' and embodiment.

---

105. *DIALOGUES AND A DIARY*, p. 95.

106. SCHOENBERG 1914, p. [1].

Ex. 12: Igor Stravinsky, *The Flood*, «The Comedy», bb. 371-378. © Copyright 1962 by Boosey & Hawkes Music Publishers Ltd. By kind permission.

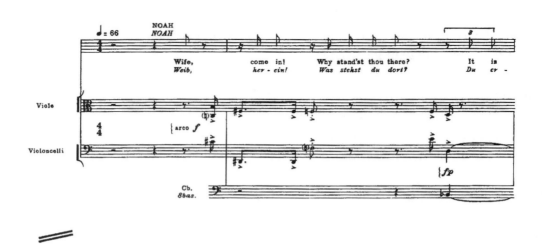

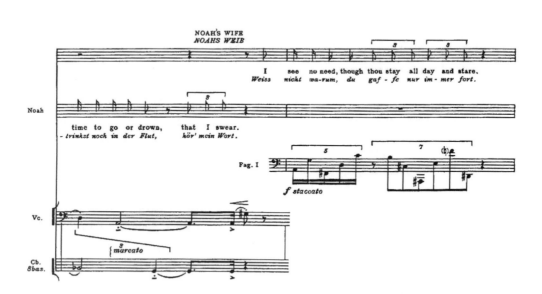

Finally, let us turn to the two characters whose bodies are the only human bodies — entirely visible throughout *The Flood*: Adam and Eve (Jack D'Amboise and Jillana). In the biblical and theological perspective of the libretto, their condition is not entirely human, at least until they commit the Original Sin. As such they are not subject to time (the corruption of their bodies). Therefore Ter-Arutunian and Balanchine conceived for them scenes, costumes and gestures diametrically opposed to those of the antediluvian men. While the latter have their bodies covered by long tunics and their faces hidden by large masks, the bodies of Jillana and D'Amboise are covered only by the classic pants and leotards of the dancers, which reveal all the anatomical features of the male and female body. While the gestures of mortal men tend to take on realistic traits typical of the comedic tradition, Adam and Eve's gestures always remain strongly stylized and 'abstract'.

The two ancestors of humanity first appear in the bass duet «A Skillful Beast» in which God creates Man. Here Balanchine establishes for them a series of static poses — more than gestures — shaped around memorable iconographic models from the artistic-visual tradition. Adam's head position and the inclination of his pelvis vaguely recall Michelangelo's *David*. The two figures stand still like statues, slowly and sinuously moving only their arms, until touching one another's index fingers as in Michelangelo's *Creation of Adam*. Balanchine's intention was, basically, to bestow a stylization upon the two characters, rendering them similar to a static two-dimensional image: a painting, a statue facing forward or a bas-relief. In this regard, in his *Working Notes*, he pointed out that using profile poses — a typical theatrical method of simulating statuary stances or 'animated bas-reliefs' (as in Nijinsky's *Faune*, for example) — would not have served the purpose. In fact, the expedient worked well on the stage, but not on the screen, where space is much more ambiguous and indefinite as far as proportions and depth are concerned. Balanchine, in fact, observed that «Profiles are unclear in TV and space is as undefined as soup»[107]. Browning achieved Balanchine's intent mainly by using a back-lighting effect, so as to make the two figures appear as silhouettes. Adam's bust, shot in medium close-up, first appears framed in luminous rays (a superimposed effect), where, due to a cross-fade, he takes the place previously occupied by the abstract image of God (the double helix). By doing so, the depth of the image practically vanishes. The camera follows Adam's hand moving leftward and then zooms in on it. After a medium close-up on Eve, the camera follows her hand moving rightwards towards Adam's and finally zooms in on their hands with the tips of their index fingers pointing at each other, as in Michelangelo' *Creation*.

During the scene of the Original Sin, Adam and Eve's gestures, as well as the whole scenery (the Tree of Knowledge appears as a bundle of tubes from which hang filaments similar to cascades of leaves), remain very stylized, particularly as a result of the backlighting that shows us only the profiles of the bodies. Their costumes and the details of the set are only visible in the

---

[107]. *Dialogues and a Diary*, p. 91.

backstage stills (ILL. 16). Adam and Eve appear in the same poses that they held during their previous scene (the creation of Man) but are now framed entirely in a medium shot together with the Tree and the Serpent, played by a mime wrapped in a costume «[which] must have an excremental shape»[108]. According to the *Working Notes*, after the Original Sin, Adam and Eve should have first been entangled in the branches of the Tree before taking their statuary pose, finally beginning to *walk* during the Banishment from the Garden of Eden[109]. All this was consistent with the general principal according to which divine and immortal beings (as Adam and Eve were before the Original Sin) are characterized by stylized gestures tending towards immobility, while mortals move, walk and gesture in a more 'realistic' manner. However, in the final version of the film, Adam and Eve do not walk after the Banishment but rather remain on the spot of the Original Sin, entangled in the coils of the Tree. Nevertheless, this allows Balanchine to illustrate the evolution (or 'involution', if seen from the theological point of view) of their gestures in an extremely subtle way, alluding to the conventions of classical ballet. Adam remains still until Eve, through a very slow gesture, moves her hands close to his mouth, symbolizing the offer of the Forbidden Fruit. Thereafter, the man loses his stillness and begins to move his arms and torso as well, creating a figure together with the woman's arms (and meanwhile the Tree clutches them). The meaning of this gesture is revealed only much later, at the end of the film, when Man and Woman reappear on the same spot of the Original Sin, giving us the sense that time, meanwhile, has not passed at all. The Tree has disappeared, and Satan has taken its place, in the shape of a bat, not unlike that which he appeared in during the aria, «God Made the World for Love». The two dancers now move as in a no-handed *lift* of a *pas de deux*. The woman, hanging from the neck of the man, who spreads his arms, performs a series of rotations of the legs without ever touching the ground with her feet. Her movements take place very slowly. In Balanchine's symbolic conception, the traditional gender construction associated with the *pas de deux*, where the *lift* represents the woman's dependence on the man, is subverted, the weights of the two bodies seemingly balanced against something external to them. Adam appears unnaturally unbalanced forward, almost at 45 degrees, perhaps thanks to a trick that is not visible in the film, or perhaps due to a raised angle of the camera, which in the meantime has begun to move over the heads of the two dancers. A mysterious force seems to be holding him up, preventing him from falling forward with the weight of the woman. Behind them, Satan follows closely, his arms wide open. The camera dollies towards the winged figure until the shot fades to the sole image of Satan singing the final aria, with its cynical prophecy: «The Forbidden Act Will forever Disobey».

---

[108]. *Ibidem*, p. 75.

[109]. «[...] they cover themselves with black leaves from the now blackened tree and *walk* in shame from Eden». *Ibidem*.

ILL. 16: backstage at CBS Studios in New York: Jacques d'Amboise and Jillana in the role of Adam and Eve in *The Flood* (*Life*, 8 June 1962, p. 95).

The fact that Adam and Eve begin to dance in a way that recalls certain conventions of classical ballet only after they have lost their condition of immortality demonstrates that in the symbolic structure of *The Flood*, the mortal condition of humans — and their bodily nature — is associated with the concept of *movement* as represented by dance and music. Ironically enough, Stravinsky decided not to provide any specific music for our ancestors, from whom, in a theological perspective, our bodily nature descends. Adam and Eve never sing, nor do they speak — apart from the very few words «Who is there?» addressed by Eve to the Serpent. They only appear during the music of God or that of the Devil. A curious circumstance for the only two entirely visible human bodies of *The Flood*. It is perhaps another 'theological' allusion to the perennially uncertain and divided condition of human being.

Bibliography

Abbreviations

Autobiography
Stravinsky, Igor. *Chroniques de ma vie*, 2 vols., Paris, Denoël et Steele, 1935; English translation: *An Autobiography*, New York, Simon and Schuster, 1936 (reprint New York, Norton, 1962).

Conversations
Stravinsky, Igor – Craft, Robert. *Conversations with Igor Stravinsky*, London, Faber and Faber, 1959; American edition: Garden City (NY), Doubleday 1959.

Dialogues and a Diary
Id. – Id. *Dialogues and a Diary*, Garden City (NY), Doubleday, 1963.

Expositions and Developments
Id. – Id. *Expositions and Developments*, London, Faber and Faber, 1962; American edition: Garden City (NY), Doubleday, 1962 (quotations are from the edition Berkeley-Los Angeles, University of California Press, 1981).

Memories and Commentaires
Id. – Id. *Memories and Commentaries*, Garden City (NY), Doubleday, 1960 (quotation are from the edition Berkeley-Los Angeles, University of California Press, 1981).

Poetics
Stravinsky, Igor. *Poetics of Music: In the Form of Six Lessons*, preface by George Sefereis, translated by Arthur Knodel and Ingolf Dahl, Cambridge (MA)-London, Harvard University Press, 1970.

SSC I-III
Stravinsky, Igor. *Selected Correspondence*, edited by Robert Craft, 3 vols., London-Boston, Faber and Faber, 1982-1985.

Themes and Episodes
Stravinsky, Igor – Craft, Robert. *Themes and Episodes*, New York, Knopf, 1967.

BIBLIOGRAPHY

BOOKS AND ARTICLES

ACOCELLA 2001
ACOCELLA, Joan. 'The Lost Nijinsky: Is it Possible to Reconstruct a Forgotten Ballet'?, in: *The New Yorker*, 7 May 2001, p. [3].

ACOCELLA – GARAFOLA 1991
André Levinson on Dance: Writings from Paris in the Twenties, edited by Joan Acocella and Lynn Garafola, Middletown (CT), Wesleyan University Press, 1991.

AGAWU 1991
AGAWU, Kofi V. *Playing with Signs: A Semiotic Interpretation of Classic Music*, Pricenton, Princeton University Press, 1991.

ALBRIGHT 1989
ALBRIGHT, Daniel. *Stravinsky: The Music Box and the Nightingale*, New York, Gordon & Breach, 1989.

ANDRIESSEN – SCHÖNBERGER 1983
ANDRIESSEN, Louis – SCHÖNBERGER, Elmer. *The Apollonian Clockwork: On Stravinsky*, Oxford-New York, Oxford University Press, 1983.

ANDRIESSEN – SCHÖNBERGER 1989
ID. – ID. *The Apollonian Clockwork: On Stravinsky*, translated by Jeff Hamburg, Oxford-New York, Oxford University Press, 1989.

ANTOKOLETZ 1984
ANTOKOLETZ, Elliott. T*he Music of Béla Bartók: A Study of Tonality and Progression in Twentieth-Century Music*, Berkeley-Los Angeles, University of California Press, 1984.

ANTOKOLETZ 1986
ID. 'Interval Cycles in Stravinsky's Early Ballets', in: *Journal of the American Musicological Society*, XXXIX/3 (1986), pp. 578-614.

AUSLANDER 2008
AUSLANDER, Philip. *Liveness: Performance in a Mediatized Culture*, London-New York, Routledge, [2]2008.

AUSTERN 1998
AUSTERN, Linda Phyllis. '«Forreine Conceites and Wandring Devises»: The Exotic, the Erotic, and the Feminine', in: *The Exotic in Western Music*, edited by Jonathan Bellman, Boston, Northesastern University Press, 1998, pp. 26-42.

BABBITT 1968
BABBITT, Milton. 'Remarks on the Recent Stravinsky', in: *Perspectives on Schoenberg and Stravinsky*, edited by Benjamin Boretz and Edward T. Cone, Princeton, Princeton University Press, 1968, pp. 165-185.

Bibliography

Babbitt 1986
Id. 'Order, Symmetry, and Centricity in Late Stravinsky', in: *Confronting Stravinsky*, edited by Jann Pasler, Berkeley-Los Angeles, University of California Press, 1986, pp. 247-261.

Babbitt 1987a
Id. 'Stravinsky's Verticals and Schoenberg's Diagonals', in: *Stravinsky Retrospectives*, edited by Ethan Haimo and Paul Johnson, Lincoln, University of Nebraska Press, 1987, pp. 15-35.

Babbitt 1987b
Id. *Words about Music*, edited by Stephen Dembski and Joseph N. Straus, Madison, University of Wisconsin 1987.

Babbitt 2003
Id. 'The Composer as a Specialist', in: *The Collected Essays of Milton Babbitt*, edited by Stephen Peles, Stephen Dembski, Andrew Mead and Joseph Straus, Princeton, Princeton University Press, 2003, pp. 48-54 [first published as 'Who Care if You Listen?', in: *High Fidelity*, viii/2 (1958), pp. 38-40].

Balanchine 2006
Balanchine, George. 'The Dance Element in Stravinsky's Music', in: *The Opera Quarterly*, xxii/1 (2006), pp. 138-143.

Banes 1998
Banes, Sally. *Dancing Women Female Bodies Onstage*, London-New York, Routledge, 1998.

Baranova Monighetti 2013
Baranova Monighetti, Tatiana. 'Stravinsky's Russian Library', in: *Stravinsky and His World*, edited by Tamara Levitz, Princeton, Princeton University Press, 2013, pp. 61-78.

Baranova Monighetti 2014
Ead. 'Working on *The Rite of Spring*: Stravinsky's Sketches for the Ballet at the Paul Sacher Stiftung', in: *Igor Stravinsky: Sounds and Gestures of Modernism*, edited by Massimiliano Locanto, Turnhout, Brepols, 2014 (Speculum Musicae, 25), pp. 101-136.

Barnes 2003
Barnes, Jennifer. *Television Opera: The Fall of Opera Commissioned for Television*, Woodbridge, Boydell Press, 2003.

Barsalou 2008
Barsalou, Lawrence W. 'Grunded Cognition', in: *Annual Review of Psychology*, lix (2008), pp. 617-645.

Beaumont 1935
Beaumont, Cyril W. *Michel Fokine and His Ballets*, London, Dance Horizons, 1935.

Beaumont 1937
Id. *The Complete Book of Ballets: A Guide to the Principal Ballets of the Nineteenth and Twentieth Centuries*, New York, Putnam, 1937.

BIBLIOGRAPHY

BEAUMONT 1981
ID. *Michel Fokine and His Ballets*, London, Dance Horizons, 1981.

BELLOW 2016
BELLOW, Juliet. *Modernism on Stage: The Ballets Russes and the Parisian Avant-Garde*, London-New York, Routledge, 2016.

BENNET – POESIO 2000
BENNETT, Toby – POESIO, Giannandrea. 'Mime in the Cecchetti «Method»', in: *Dance Research*, XVIII/1 (2000), pp. 31-43.

BENOIS 1910
BENOIS, Aleksandr. 'Chudožestvennije pis'ma: russkie spektakli', in: *Reč*, 18 July 1910.

BENOIS 1941
ID. *Reminiscences of the Russian Ballet*, translated by Mary Brimieva, London, G. P. Pumam's Sons, 1941.

BERGER 1963
BERGER, Arthur. 'Problems of Pitch Organization in Stravinsky's Diatonic Music', in: *Perspectives on Schoenberg and Stravinsky*, edited by Benjamin Boretz and Edward T. Cone, Princeton, Princeton University Press, pp. 123-155.

BERNSTEIN 1993
BERNSTEIN, David. W. 'Symmetry and Symmetrical Inversion in Turn-of-the-Century Theory and Practice', in: *Music Theory and the Exploration of the Past*, edited by Christopher Hatch and David W. Bernstein, Chicago-London, University of Chicago Press, pp. 377-407.

BLEEK 2013
BLEEK, Thobias. '«...de la musique sauvage avec tout le confort moderne!»: The Orchestral Design of *Le Sacre du Printemps*', in: DANUSER – ZIMMERMANN 2013, pp. 81-101.

BOLTER – GRUSIN 1999
BOLTER, Jay David – GRUSIN, Richard. *Remediation: Understanding New Media*, Cambridge (MA), MIT Press, 1999.

BORIO 2005
BORIO, Gianmario 'Aesthetic Experience Under the Aegis of Technology', in: *Musical Listening in the Age of Technological Reproduction*, edited by Gianmario Borio, London-New York, Routledge, 2005 (Musical Cultures of the Twentieth Century), pp. 3-22.

BOSS 1992
BOSS, Jack. 'Schoenberg's Op. 22 Radio Talk and Developing Variation in Atonal Music', in: *Music Theory Spectrum*, XIV/2 (1992), pp. 125-150.

Bibliography

Boss 1994
Id. 'Schoenberg on Ornamentation and Structural Levels', in: *Journal of Music Theory*, XXXVIII/II, pp. 187-216.

Boulez 1968
Boulez, Pierre. 'Stravinsky Remains', in: *Notes of an Apprenticeship*, translated by Herbert Weinstock, New York, Knopf, 1968, pp. 72-145.

Bowman 2004
Bowman, Wayne D. 'Cognition and the Body: Perspectives from Music Education, in Knowing Bodies, Moving Minds: Towards Embodied Teaching and Learning', edited by Liora Bresler, Dordrecht-London, Kluwer Academic, 2004, pp. 29-50.

Boykan 1963
Boykan, Martin. 'Neoclassicism in Late Stravinsky', in: *Perspectives of New Music*, I/2 (1963), pp. 155-169.

Braun 1988
Braun, Edward. *Meyerhold: A Revolution in Theatre*, London, Methuen Drama, 1988.

Braun – Pitches 2016
Meyerhold on Theatre. Fourth Edition, translated and edited with a critical commentary by Edward Braun, introduction by Jonathan Pitches, London, Bloomsbury, 2016.

Brody 1993
Brody, Martin. 'Music for the Masses. Milton Babbitt's Cold War Music Theory', in: *The Musical Quarterly*, LXXVII/ 2 (1993), pp. 161-192.

Brown 1989
Brown, A. Peter. 'Haydn's Chaos: Genesis and Genre', in: *The Musical Quarterly*, LXXIII/1 (1989), pp. 18-59.

Brown 1993
Tchaikovsky Remembered, edited by David Brown, London-Boston, Faber & Faber, 1993 [abridged English translation of *Vospominaniya o P. I. Chaykovskom*, Moscow, Gosudarstvennoye muzykal'noye izdatel'stvo, 1962].

Brown 2012
Brown, Adrienne. 'Analysis and Meaning', in: *Bewegungen zwischen Hören und Sehen. Denkbewegungen über Bewegungskünste*, edited by Stephanie Schroedter, Würzburg, Königshausen und Neumann, 2012, pp. 181-200.

Bryullova 1980
Bryullova, Alina Ivanovna. 'P. I. Tchaykovskiy', in: *Vospominaniya o P. I. Chaykovskom*, Moscow, Gosudarstvennoye muzykal'noye izdatel'stvo, 1962; reprint Leningrad, Muzika, 1980, pp. 106-119 [Bryullova's recollections written in 1929 from her first meetings with Tchaikovsky in the 1870s, up to his death in 1893].

Bibliography

Buchanan 2017
Buchanan, Melonie Annete. 'Maestro: Enrico Cecchetti and Diaghilev's Ballets Russes', in: *Dance Chronicle*, xc/2 (2017), pp. 165-191.

Buckle 1979
Buckle, Richard. *Diaghilev*, New York, Atheneum, 1979.

Buharaja 2018
Buharaja, Edmond. 'La formalizzazione sonora della «Danse Sacrale» del *Sacre du Printemps* di Stravinsky', in: *Analitica. Rivista online di Studi Musicali*, xi (2018), n.p.

Burdick 1962
Burdick, Eugene. *The Eighth Art: Twenty-Three Views of Television Today*, New York, Holt, Rinehart and Winston, 1962.

Caplin 1998
Caplin, William. *Classical Form: A Theory of Formal Functions for the Instrumental Music of Haydn, Mozart, and Beethoven*, Oxford-New York, Oxford University Press, 1998.

Caporaletti 2005
Caporaletti, Vincenzo. *I processi improvvisativi nella musica: un approccio globale*, Lucca, LIM, 2005.

Caporaletti 2014
Id. *Swing e Groove: sui fondamenti estetici delle musiche audiotattili*, Lucca, LIM, 2014.

Caporaletti 2019
Id. *Introduzione alla teoria delle musiche audiotattili. Un paradigma per il mondo contemporaneo*, Rome, Aracne, 2019.

Carpenter 1988
Carpenter, Ellon. *The Theory of Music in Russia and the Soviet Union, ca. 1650-1950*, Ph.D. Diss., Philadelphia (PA), University of Pennsylvania, 1988.

Carr 1993
Carr, Maureen. 'Le Carillon féerique, une clef disparue de l'*Oiseau de Feu*', in: *Analyse Musicale*, xxxii/3 (1993), pp. 40-53.

Carr 2014
Ead. *After the Rite: Stravinsky's Path to Neoclassicism*, Oxford, Oxford University Press, 2014.

Carruthers 1990
Carruthers, Mary J. *The Book of Memory: A Study of Memory in Medieval Culture*, Cambridge, Cambridge University Press, 1990.

Bibliography

CARTER 1997
CARTER, Chandler. 'Stravinsky's «Special Sense»: The Rhetorical Use of Tonality in *The Rake's Progress*', in: *Music Theory Spectrum*, XIX/1 (1997), pp. 55-80.

CAWLEY 1959
Everyman and Medieval Miracle Plays, edited by Arthur C. Cawley, New York, Dutton, 1959.

CHEMERO 2004
CHEMERO, Antony. *Radical Embodied Cognitive Science*, Cambridge (MA), MIT, 2004.

CHUA 2007
CHUA, Daniel K. L. 'Rioting with Stravinsky: A Particular Analysis of the Rite of Spring', in: *Music Analysis*, XXVI/1-2 (2007), pp. 59-109.

COLLECTION 1922
Collection des plus beaux numéros de «Comœdia illustré» et des programmes consacrés aux ballets et galas russes depuis le début à Paris, 1909-1921, edited by Maurice and Jacques de Brunoff, Paris, Maurice Brunoff, 1922 [available online: <gallica.bnf.fr>].

COMŒDIA 1910
Comœdia illustré: journal artistique bi-mensuel, II/18 (15 juin 1910) [available online: <gallica.bnf.fr>].

CONE 1962.
CONE, Edward T. 'Stravinsky: The Progress of a Method', in: *Perspectives of New Music*, I/1 (1962), pp. 18-26.

COOK 1998
COOK, Nicholas. *Analasyng Musical Multimedia*, Oxford, Clarendon Press, 1998.

COOK 2001
ID. 'Theorizing Musical Meaning', in: *Music Theory Spectrum*, XXIII/2 (2012), pp. 170-195.

COOK 2013
ID. *Beyond the Score: Music as Performance*, Oxford-New York, Oxford University Press, 2013.

COOK 2018
ID. *Music as Creative Practice*, Oxford-New York, Oxford University Press, 2018.

COOPER 1990
COOPER, Barry. *Beethoven and the Creative Process*, Oxford, Clarendon Press, 1990.

COWELL 1926
COWELL, Henry. 'The Process of Musical Creation', in: *American Journal of Psychology*, XXXVII/2 (1926), pp. 233-236.

BIBLIOGRAPHY

COX 2016
Cox, Arnie. *Music and Embodied Cognition: Listening, Moving, Feeling, and Thinking*, Bloomington-Indianapolis, Indiana University Press, 2016.

CRAFT 1967
CRAFT, Robert. *Bravo Stravinsky*, photographs by Arnold Newman, text by Robert Craft, foreward by Francis Steegmuller, Cleveland, World, 1967.

CRAFT 1972
ID. *Stravinsky: Chronicle of a Friendship, 1948-1971*, New York, Knopf, 1972.

CRAFT 1984
ID. *Present Perspectives*: *Critical Writings*, New York, Knopf, 1984.

CRAFT 1992
ID. *Igor Stravinsky: Glimpses of a Life*, London, Lime Tree, 1992.

CRAFT 2006
ID. *Down a Path of Wonder: Memoirs of Stravinsky, Schoenberg and Other Cultural Figures*, London, Naxos, 2006.

CROSS 1998
CROSS, Jonathan. *The Stravinsky Legacy*, Cambridge, Cambridge University Press, 1998.

CROSS 2003
ID. 'Stravinsky's Theatres', in: *The Cambridge Companion to Stravinsky*, edited by Jonathan Cross, Cambridge, Cambridge University Press, 2003, pp. 137-148.

CULLBERG – REUTERSWÄRD – LAURITZEN 1987
CULLBERG, Birgit – REUTERSWÄRD, Måns – LAURITZEN, Bertil. *Dance in New Dimension: Birgit Cullberg and the TV Ballet*, Stockholm, Proprius, 1987.

CYR 1982
CYR, Louis. '*Le Sacre du Printemps*, petite histoire d'une grande partition', in: *Stravinsky: Études et témoignages*, edited by François Lesure, Paris, Jean-Claude Lattes, 1982.

DAHLHAUS 1986
DAHLHAUS, Carl. 'Was heisst «entwickelnde Variation»?', in: *Bericht über den zweiten Kongress der Internationalen Schönberg-Gesellschaft*, edited by Rudolph Stephan and Sigrid Wiesmann, Vienna, Universal, 1986, pp. 280-285.

DAMASIO 1994
DAMASIO, Antonio R. *Descartes' Error: Emotion, Reason, and the Human Brain*, New York, Putnam, 1994.

Bibliography

Damasio 1999
Id. *The Feeling of What Happens: Body and Emotion in the Making of Consciousness*, New York, Harcourt Brace, 1999.

Damasio 2010
Id. *Self Comes to Mind: Constructing the Conscious Brain*, New York, Pantheon, 2010.

Damsholt 1999
Damsholt, Inger. *Choreomusical Discourse: The Relationship between Dance and Music*, unpublished Ph.D. Diss., Copenhagen, University of Copenhagen, 1999.

Danuser – Zimmermann 2013
Avatar of Modernity: «The Rite of Spring» Reconsidered, edited by Hermann Danuser and Heidy Zimmermann, London, Boosey & Hawkes, 2013.

Davis 2010
Davis, Mary E. *Ballets Russes Style: Diaghilev's Dancers and Paris Fashion*, London, Reaktion Books, 2010.

Dübgen 2012
Dübgen, Hannah. *Strawinsky im Kalten Krieg*, Kassel, Bärenreiter, 2012.

Dufour – Niccolai 2020
Dufour, Valérie – Niccolai, Michela. 'Des faiseurs de goût. Les Ballets russes et le renouveau de la critique chorégraphique en France. Le cas de *L'Oiseau de feu* (1910)', in: *La Critique musicale du XXe siècle*, edited by Timothée Picard, Rennes, Presses Universitaires de Rennes, 2020 (Hors collection), pp. 293-302.

Dyachkova 1973
I. F. Stravinskiy; Stat' i material'i, edited by Lyudmila Sergeyevna Dyachkova and Boris M. Yarustovsky, Moskow, Sovistsky Kompozitor, 1973.

Edgecombe 2006
Edgecombe, Rodney Stenning. 'Cesare Pugni, Marius Petipa and 19th-Century Ballet Music', in: *The Musical Times*, cxlvii/1895 (Summer 2006), pp. 39-48.

Egidio 2005
Egidio, Aurora. *Aleksandr Tairov e il Kamernyj Teatr di Mosca 1907-1922*, Rome, Bulzoni, 2005.

Eisenstein 2000
Eisenstein, Sergei Mikhailovich. *Mnemozina: Dokumenty i fakty iz istotii russkogo teatra XX veka. 2*, edited by Vladislav V. Ivanov, Moscow, Editorial URSS, 2000.

Eisenstein 2004
Id. *Quaderni teatrali e piani di regia (1919-1925)*, edited by Ornella Calvarese and Vladislav Ivanov, Soveria Mannelli (CZ), Rubbettino, 2004.

BIBLIOGRAPHY

EVANS 1933
EVANS, Edwin. *Stravinsky: «The Firebird» and «Petrushka»*, Oxford, Oxford University Press, 1933.

EWELL 2020
EWELL, Philip. 'On Rimsky-Korsakov's False (Hexatonic) Progressions Outside the Limits of a Tonality', in: *Music Theory Spectrum*, XLII/1 (2020), pp. 122-142.

EWEN 1936
Composers of Today, edited by David Ewen, New York, H. W. Wilson, 1936.

FARRELL 1990
FARRELL, Suzanne. *Holding On to the Air*, Gainesville, University Press of Florida, 1990.

FATYKHOVA-OKUNEVA 2008
FATYKHOVA-OKUNEVA, Elvira Anatolyevna. 'N. A. Rimskiy-Korsakov - prepodavatel' teorii muzyki (po uchenicheskim tetradyam A. K. Glazunova)', in: *Rimskiy-Korsakov*, St. Petersburg, Composer, 2008 (St. Petersburg Musical Archive, 7), pp. 170-192.

FISKE – HARTLEY 2003
FISKE, John – HARTLEY, John. *Reading Television*, with a new foreword by John Hartley, London-New York, Routledge, ²2003.

FLAMM 2013
FLAMM, Christoph. *Igor Strawinsky. «Der Feuervogel», «Petrushka», «Le Sacre du Printemps»*, Kassel, Bärenreiter, 2013.

FOKINE 1914
FOKINE, Michail. 'The New Russian Ballet, Conventions in Dancing. M. Fokine's Principles and Aims', [letter to the editor of *Times*, (London), 6 July 1914], reprint in *What Is Dance? Readings in Theory and Criticism*, edited by Roger Copeland and Marshall Cohen, Oxford-New York, Oxford University Press, 1983, pp. 257-261.

FOKINE 1961
ID. *Memoirs of a Ballet Master*, translated by Vitale Fokine, edited by Anatole Chujoy, London, Constable & Co., 1961.

FOKINE 1962
ID. *Protiv tečenija: vospominanija baletmejstera: stat'i, pis'ma*, Leningrad-Moskva, Iskusstvo, 1962.

FOKINE 1974
ID. *Gegen den Strom. Erinnerungen eines Ballettmeisters*, edited by Lydia Wolgina and Ulrich Pietzsch, Berlin, Henschel, 1974.

FOKINE – ARROWSMITH 2014
FOKINE, Isabelle – ARROWSMITH, Paul. 'The Work of Mikhail Fokine – Q&A with Isabelle Fokine',

BIBLIOGRAPHY

[interview by Paul Arrowsmith to Isabelle Fokin], in: *DanceTabs*, 24 July 2014, <https://dancetabs. com/2014/07/the-work-of-mikhail-fokine-qa-with-isabelle-fokine/>, accessed January 2022.

FORTE 1986
FORTE, Allen. 'Harmonic Syntax and Voice Leadding in Stravinsky's Early Music', in: *Confronting Stravinsky: Man, Musician and Modernist*, edited by Ian Pasler, Berkeley-Los Angeles, University of California Press, 1986, pp. 95-129.

FRAZZI 1930
FRAZZI, Vito. *Scale alternate per pianoforte*, Florence, Forlivesi, 1930.

FUCHS 1905
FUCHS, Georg. *Die Schaubühne der Zukunft*, Berlin, Schuster & Loeffler, 1905 (Das Theater. Eine Sammlung von Monographien, edited by Carl Hagemann, 15).

FUCHS 1909
ID. *Die Revolution des Theaters. Ergebuisse aus dem Münchener Künstler-Theater*, Munich, G. Müller, 1909.

GARAFOLA 2011
GARAFOLA, Lynn. 'The Legacies of the Ballets Russes', in: *Experiment*, no. 17 (2011), pp. 31-46.

GARCÍA-MÁRQUEZ 1990
GARCÍA-MÁRQUEZ, Vicente. *The Ballets Russes: Colonel de Basil's Ballets Russes de Monte Carlo, 1932-1952*, London, Knopf, 1990.

GILLAN 2013
GILLAN, Matt. '«Dancing Fingers»: Embodied Lineages in the Performance of Okinawan Classical Music', in: *Ethnomusicology*, LVII/3 (2013), pp. 367-395.

GODØY – LEMAN 2010
Musical Gestures: Sound, Movement, and Meaning, edited by Rolf Inge Godøy and Marc Leman, London-New York, Routledge, 2010.

GOLONKA – WILSON, 2013
GOLONKA, Sabrina – WILSON, Andrew D. 'Embodied Cognition Is Not What You Think It Is', in: *Frontiers in Psychology*, LVIII/4 (2013), <https://www.frontiersin.org/articles/10.3389/fpsyg.2013.00058/full>, accessed January 2022.

GOODY 1987
GOODY, Jack. *The Interface between the Written and the Oral*, Cambridge, Cambridge University Press, 1987.

GORMAN 1996
GORMAN, Paul. R. *Left Intellectuals & Popular Culture in Twentieth-Century America*, Chapel Hill (NC), University of North Carolina Press, 1996.

Bibliography

Griffiths 2005
Griffiths, Graham. 'Fingering as Compositional Process: Stravinsky's Sonata Sketchbook Revisited', in: *British Postgraduate Musicology Online*, May 2005, <http://britishpostgraduatemusicology.org/bpm7/griffiths.html>, accessed January 2022.

Griffiths 2013
Id. *Stravinsky's Piano: Genesis of a Musical Language*, Cambridge, Cambridge University Press, 2013.

Grigoriev 2009
Grigoriev, Serge. *The Diaghilev Ballet: 1909-1929*, London, Dance Books, 2009.

Gritten – King 2006
Music and Gesture, edited by Anthony Gritten and Elaine King, Aldershot, Ashgate, 2006.

Gritten – King 2011
New Perspectives on Music and Gesture, edited by Anthony Gritten and Elaine King, Farnham, Ashgate, 2011.

Guest 1980
Guest, Ivor. *The Romantic Ballet in Paris*, London, Dance Books, 1966, ²1980.

Haimo 1997
Haimo, Ethan. 'Developing Variation and Schoenberg's Serial Music', in: *Music Analysis*, xvi/3 (1997), pp. 349-365.

Hatten 1994
Hatten, Robert S. *Musical Meaning in Beethoven: Markedness, Correlation, and Interpretation*, Bloomington, University of Indiana Press, 1994.

Hatten 2003
Id. 'Thematic Gestures, Topics and Tropes', in: *Music Semiotics Revisited*, edited by Eero Tarasti, Helsinki, Hakapaino, 2003, pp. 80-91.

Hatten 2004
Id. *Interpreting Musical Gestures, Topics, and Tropes: Mozart, Beethoven, Schubert*, Bloomington, Indiana University Press, 2004.

Henley 1932
Henley, Homer. 'Music: The Anatomy of Dissonance', in: *Argonaut*, 27 May 1932, p. 10.

Hicks 1993
Hicks, Michael. 'Cowell's Clusters', in: *The Musical Quarterly*, lvii/3 (1993), pp. 428-458.

Bibliography

HODGINS 1992
HODGINS, Paul. *Relationships between Score and Choreography in Twentieth-Century Dance: Music, Movement, and Metaphor*, Lewiston (NY), Edwin Mellen Press, 1992.

HODSON 1996
HODSON, Millicent. *Nijinsky's Crime Against Grace: Reconstruction Score of the Original Choreography for «Le Sacre du Printemps»*, Stuyvesant (NY), Pendragon Press, 1996.

HODSON 2008
EAD. *Nijinsky's Bloomsbury Ballet: Reconstruction of the Dance and Design for «Jeux»*, Stuyvesant (NY), Pendragon Press, 2008.

HOGAN 1982
HOGAN, Catherine. '*Threni*: Stravinsky's «Debt» to Krenek', in: *Tempo*, no. 141 (1982), pp. 22-29.

HORLACKER 2011
HORLACHER, Gretchen. *Building Blocks: Repetition and Continuity in the Music of Stravinsky*, Oxford, Oxford University Press, 2011.

HUTCHINSON GUEST – JESCHKE 2010
Nijinsky's «Faune» Restored, edited by Ann Hutchinson Guest and Claudia Jeschke, Philadelphia, Gordon and Breach, 1991; reprint Binstead, Hampshire, Noverre Press, 2010.

JACKSON 1991
JACKSON, Berry. 'Diaghilev: Ligtining Designer', in: *Dance Chronicle*, no. 14 (1991), pp. 1-35.

JANS – HANDSCHIN 1989
Sammlung Igor Strawinsky: Musikmanuskripte, edited by Hans Jörg Jans and Lukas Handschin, Winterthur, Amadeus, 1989 (Inventories of the Paul Sacher Foundation, 5).

JEANNEROD 2002
JEANNEROD, Marc. *La Nature de l'esprit: Sciences cognitives et cerveau*, Paris, Jacob, 2002.

JEANNEROD 2006
ID. *Motor Cognition: What Actions Tell the Self*, Oxford-New York, Oxford University Press, 2006.

JENSENIUS *et al.* 2010
JENSENIUS, Alexander Refsum – WANDERLEY, Marcello M. – GODØY, Rolf Inge – LEMAN, Marc. 'Musical Gestures: Concepts and Methods in Research', in: GODØY – LEMAN 2010, pp. 12-34.

JERS 1986
JERS, Norbert. *Igor Stravinskys spate zwölf-ton Werke (1958-1966)*, Regensburg, Gustav Bosse, 1986.

Bibliography

Johnson 1987
Johnson, Paul. 'Cross-Collectional Techniques of Structure in Stravinsky's Centric Music', in: *Stravinsky Retrospectives*, edited by Ethan Haimo and Paul Johnson, Lincoln, University of Nebraska Press, 1987, pp. 55-75.

Jordan 2000
Jordan, Stephanie. *Moving Music: Dialogues with Music in Twentieth-Century Ballet*, London, Dance Books, 2000.

Jordan 2007
Ead. *Stravinsky Dances: Re-Visions across a Century*, London, Dance Books, 2007.

Jordan 2011
Ead. 'Choreomusical Conversations: Facing a Double Challenge', in: *Dance Research Journal*, XLIII/1 (2011), pp. 43-64.

Jordan 2013
Ead. '*Le Sacre du Printemps*: mito e tradizione nella musica e nella danza' in: Veroli-Vinay 2013, pp. 85-107.

Joseph 1974
Joseph, Charles. *A Study of Igor Stravinsky's Piano Compositions*, Ph.D. Diss., Cincinnati (OH), University of Cincinnati, 1974.

Joseph 1982
Id. 'Stravinsky Manuscripts in the Library of Congress and the Pierpont Morgan Library', in: *The Journal of Musicology*, I/3 (1982), pp. 327-337.

Joseph 1983
Id. *Stravinsky and the Piano*, Ann Arbor (MI), UMI Research Press, 1983.

Joseph 2001
Id. *Stravinsky Inside Out*, New Haven-London, Yale University Press, 2001.

Joseph 2002
Id. *Stravinsky and Balanchine: A Journey of Invention*, New Haven-London, Yale University Press, 2002.

Joseph 2011
Id. *Stravinsky's Ballets*, New Haven-London, Yale University Press, 2011.

Karsavina 1948
Karsavina, Tamara. 'A Recollection of Strawinsky', in: *Tempo*, n.s., no. 8 (Summer 1948), pp. 7-9.

Karsavina 1961
Ead. *Theatre Street: The Reminiscences of Tamara Karsavina*, New York, Duttom, 1961.

Bibliography

KERMAN 1980
KERMAN, Joseph. 'How We Got into Analysis, and How to Get Out', in: *Critical Inquiry*, VII/2 (1980), pp. 311-131.

KERMAN 1985
ID. *Contemplating Music. Challenges to Musicology*, Cambridge (MA), Harvard University Press, 1985 (reprint as *Musicology*, London, Fontana, 1985).

KIRSTEIN 1970
KIRSTEIN, Lincoln. *Movement and Metaphor: Four Centuries of Ballet*, New York, Praeger, 1970.

KOZAK 2020
KOZAK, Mariusz. *Enacting Musical Time: The Bodily Experience of New Music*, Oxford-New York, Oxford University Press, 2020.

KRAMER 1988
KRAMER, Jonathan. *The Time of Music*, New York, Schirmer Books, 1988.

KRENEK 1940
KRENEK, Ernst. *Studies in Counterpoint Based on the Twelve-Tone Technique*, New York, Schirmer, 1940.

LAKOFF 1993
LAKOFF, George. 'The Contemporary Theory of Metaphor', in: *Metaphor and Thought*, edited by Andrew Ortony, Cambridge, Cambridge University Press, 1993, pp. 202-251.

LAKOFF – JOHNSON 1980
LAKOFF, George – JOHNSON, Mark. *Metaphors We Live By*, Chicago, University of Chicago Press, 1980.

LAWSON 1957
LAWSON, Joan. *Mime: The Theory and Practice of Expressive Gesture, with a Description of Its Historical Development*, London, Pitman, 1957.

LE GUIN 2006
LE GUIN, Elisabeth. *Boccherini's Body: An Essay in Carnal Musicology*, Berkeley-Los Angeles, University of California Press, 2006.

LEMAN 2007
LEMAN, Marc. *Embodied Music Cognition and Mediation Technology*, Cambridge (MA), MIT, 2007.

LENORMAND 1915
LENORMAND, René. *Étude sur l'harmonie moderne*, Paris, Le Monde Musical, 1912; English translation *A Study of Modern Harmony*, Williams, London, 1915.

LETELLIER 2008
LETELLIER, Robert Ignatius. *The Ballets of Ludwig Minkus*, Cambridge, Cambridge Scholars Publishing, 2008.

BIBLIOGRAPHY

LETELLIER 2012

ID. *The Ballets of Alexander Glazunov, «Scenes de Ballet», «Raymonda» and «Les Saisons»*, Cambridge, Cambridge Scholars Publishing, 2012.

LEVITZ 2004

LEVITZ, Tamara, 'The Chosen One's Choice', in: *Beyond Structural Listening: Postmodern Modes of Hearing*, edited by Andrew Dell'Antonio, Berkeley-Los Angeles, University of California Press, 2004, pp. 70-108.

LEVITZ 2012

LEVITZ, Tamara. *Modernist Mysteries: Perséphone*, Oxford, Oxford University Press, 2012 (ACLS Humanities E-Book).

LEWIN 1962

LEWIN, David. 'A Theory of Segmental Association in Twelve-Tone Music', in: *Perspectives of New Music*, I/1 (1962), pp. 89-116.

LEWIN 1968

ID. 'Inversional Balance as an Organizing Principle in Schoenberg's Music and Thought', in: *Perspectives of New Music*, VI/2 (1968), pp. 1-21.

LIEVEN 1973

LIEVEN, Prince Peter. *The Birth of the Ballets-Russes*, London, Allen and Unwin, 1936; reprint edition, New York, Dover, 1973.

LOCANTO 2002

LOCANTO, Massimiliano. *Pensiero musicale e procedimenti costruttivi nell'ultimo Stravinsky*, Ph.D. Diss., Cremona, University of Pavia, 2002.

LOCANTO 2007

ID. 'Armonia come simmetria. Rapporti tra teoria musicale, tecnica compositiva e pensiero scientifico', in: *Storia dei Concetti Musicali: Armonia, Tempo*, edited by Carlo Gentili and Gianmario Borio, Rome, Carocci, 2007, pp. 199-246.

LOCANTO 2008

ID. 'Il «Diluvio» di Stravinsky tra simbolismo e tecnica seriale', in: *Drammaturgie musicali del Novecento: teorie e testi. Atti del Convegno internazionale di studi (Centro studi musicali Ferruccio Busoni, Empoli, Cenacolo del convento degli agostiniani, 14-16 ottobre 2004)*, edited by Marco Vincenzi, Lucca, LIM, 2008 (Quaderni di Musica/Realtà, 56), pp. 251-292.

LOCANTO 2009

ID. '«Composing with Intervals». Intervallic Syntax and Serial Technique in Late Stravinsky', in: *Music Analysis*, XXVIII/2 (2009), pp. 221-266.

Bɪʙʟɪᴏɢʀᴀᴘʜʏ

Lᴏᴄᴀɴᴛᴏ 2014

Iᴅ. 'Igor Stravinsky's *The Flood* in between Theatre and Television', in: *Igor Stravinsky: Sounds and Gestures of Modernism*, edited by Massimiliano Locanto, Turnhout, Brepols, 2014 (Speculum Musicae, 25), pp. 383-414.

Lᴏᴄᴀɴᴛᴏ 2018

Iᴅ. 'Choreomusichology beyond «Formalism»: A Gestural Analysis of *Variations for Orchestra* (Stravinsky-Balanchine, 1982)', in: *Music-Dance, Sound and Motion in Contemporary Discourse*, edited by Gianfranco Vinay and Patrizia Veroli, London-New York, Routledge, 2018, pp. 35-56.

Lᴏᴄᴀɴᴛᴏ 2021ᴀ

Iᴅ. 'Challenges to Realism and Traditions: Stravinsky's Modernist Theatre', in: *Stravinsky in Context*, editred by Graham Griffiths, Cambridge, Cambridge University Press, 2021, pp. 153-161.

Lᴏᴄᴀɴᴛᴏ 2021ʙ

Iᴅ. 'Film', in: *The Cambridge Stravinsky Encyclopedia*, edited by Edward Campbell and Peter O'Hagan, Cambridge, Cambridge University Press, 2021, pp. 154-158.

Lᴏᴘᴜᴋʜᴏᴠ 2002

Lᴏᴘᴜᴋʜᴏᴠ, Fedor. *Writings on Ballet and Music*, edited and with an introduction by Stephanie Jordan, translated by Dorinda Offord, Madison (WI), University of Wisconsin Press, 2002.

Mᴀᴇs 2002

Mᴀᴇs, Francis. *A History of Russian Music: From Kamarinskaya to Babi Yar*, Berkeley-Los Angeles, University of California Press, 2002.

Mᴀᴛᴛʜᴇᴡs 2006

Orchestration: An Anthology of Writings, edited by Paul Mathews, London-New York, Routledge, 2006.

Mᴀʏᴇʀ 1977

Mᴀʏᴇʀ, Charles S. 'The Influence of Leon Bakst on Choreography', in: *Dance Chronicle*, ɪ/2 (1977-1978), pp. 127-142.

McFᴀʀʟᴀɴᴅ 1994

McFᴀʀʟᴀɴᴅ, Mark. 'Leit-Harmony, or Stravinsky's Musical Characterization in *The Firebird*', in: *International Journal of Musicology*, ɪɪɪ (1994), pp. 203-233.

McFᴀʀʟᴀɴᴅ 2011

Iᴅ. 'Stravinsky and the Pianola: A Relationship Reconsidered', in: *Revue de musicologie*, xᴄᴠɪɪ/1 (2011), pp. 85-110.

McFᴀʀʟᴀɴᴅ 2014

Iᴅ. 'Stravinsky as Analyst: *The Firebird* and *Petrushka*', in: *Igor Stravinsky: Sounds and Gestures of Modernism*, edited by Massimiliano Locanto, Turnhout, Brepols, 2014 (Speculum Musicae, 25), pp. 157-173.

BIBLIOGRAPHY

MENARY 2013

MENARY, Richard. 'The Enculturated Hand', in: *The Hand, an Organ of the Mind: What the Manual Tells the Mental*, edited by Zdravko Radman, Cambridge (MA), MIT, 2013, pp. 349-367.

MENIN – SCHIAVIO 2013

MENIN, Damiano – SCHIAVIO, Andrea. 'Embodied Music Cognition and Mediation Technology: A Critical Review', in: *Psychology of Music*, XLI/6 (2013), pp. 804-814.

MERLEAU-PONTY 2012

MERLEAU-PONTY, Maurice. *Phenomenology of Perception*, London-New York, Routledge, 2012.

MEYER 2013

MEYER, Andreas. 'Disrupted Structures: Rhythm, Melody, Harmony', in: DANUSER – ZIMMERMANN 2013, pp. 103-129.

MILLING – LEY 2000

MILLING, Jane – LEY, Graham. *Modern Theories of Performance*: *From Stanislavski to Boal*, London, Palgrave Macmillan, 2000.

MINORS 2012

MINORS, Helena Julia. 'In Collaboration: Toward a Gesture Analysis of Music and Dance', in: *Bewegungen zwischen Hören und Sehen. Denkbewegungen über Bewegungskünste*, edited by Stephanie Schroedter, Würzburg, Königshausen und Neumann, 2012, pp. 163-179.

MORRIS 1988

MORRIS, Robert. 'Generalizing Rotational Arrays', in: *Journal of Music Theory*, XXXII/1 (1988), pp. 75-132.

MÜLLER 1984

MÜLLER, Alfred. 'Igor Strawinsky: Movements for Piano and Orchestra', in: *Melos*, XLVI/2 (1988), pp. 112-139.

NABOKOV 1949

NABOKOV, Nicolas. 'Christmas with Igor Stravinsky', in: *Igor Stravinsky*, edited by Edwin Corle, New York, Sloan & Pearce, pp. 123-168.

NEFF-CARR – HORLACHER 2017

The Rite of Spring at 100, foreword by Stephen Walsh, with John Reef, edited by Severine Neff, Maureen Carr and Gretchen Horlacher, Bloomington (IN), Indiana University Press, 2017.

NEIDHÖFER 1991

NEIDHÖFER, Christoph. 'Analysearbeit im Fach Komposition/Musiktheorie über die Movements for Piano and Orchestra von Igor Strawinsky', Ph.D. Diss., Basel, Musik Akademie der Stadt Basel, 1991.

BIBLIOGRAPHY

NEIDHÖFER 1999
ID. 'An Approach to Interrelating Counterpoint and Serialism in the Music of Igor Stravinsky, Focusing on the Principal Diatonic Works of His Transitional Period', Ph.D. Diss., Cambridge (MA), Harvard University 1999.

NOE 2009
NOE, Alva. *Out of Our Heads: Why You Are Not Your Brain, and Other Lessons from the Biology of Consciousness*, New York, Hill & Wang, 2009.

PASLER 1986
PASLER, Jann. 'Music and Spectacle in *Petrushka* and *The Rite of Spring*', in: *Confronting Stravinsky: Man, Musician and Modernist*, edited by Jann Pasler, Berkeley-Los Angeles, University of California Press, 1986, pp. 53-81.

PASTICCI 2012
EAD. *Sinfonia di Salmi: l'esperienza del sacro in Stravinskij*, Lucca, LIM, 2012.

PASTICCI 2014
PASTICCI, Susanna, 'Stravinsky and the Spiritual World of Orthodox Theology', in: *Igor Stravinsky: Sounds and Gestures of Modernism*, edited by Massimiliano Locanto, Turnhout, Brepols, 2014 (Speculum Musicae, 25), pp. 31-48.

PERLE 1955
PERLE, George. 'Symmetrical Formations in the String Quartets of Béla Bartók', in: *Music Review*, XVI (1995), pp. 300-312.

PERLE 1990
ID. *The Listening Composer*, Berkeley-Los Angeles, University of California Press, 1990.

PERLE 1991
ID. *Serial Composition and Atonality: An Introduction to the Music of Schoenberg, Berg, and Webern*, 6th revised edition, Berkeley-Los Angeles, University of California Press, 1991.

PHILLIPS 1984
PHILLIPS, Paul Schuyler. 'The Enigma of Variations: A Study of Stravinsky's Final Work for Orchestra', in: *Music Analysis*, III/1 (1984), pp. 69-89.

POESIO 1993
POESIO, Giannandrea. *The Language of Gesture in Italian Dance from Commedia dell'Arte to Blasis*, Ph.D. Diss., Guildford, University of Surrey, 1993.

POUSSEUR 1971
POUSSEUR, Henry. 'Stravinsky selon Webern selon Stravinsky', in: *Musique en jeu*, III/1-2 (1971), pp. 21-47, 107-126.

Bibliography

Pr. Off. 1910
Programme officiel de la saison russe à l'Opéra [25, 28 and 30 June 1910], Paris, [n.p], [1910] (Paris, BnF, Bibliothèque-musée de l'Opéra, RES-2248. Available at <gallica.bnf.fr>).

Prokhorov 2002
Prokhorov, Vadim. *Russian Folk Songs: Musical Genres and History*, Lanham (MD), The Scarecrow Press, 2002.

Ratner 1980
Ratner, Leonard G. *Classic Music: Expression, Form, and Style*, London, Schirmer, 1980.

Reyland – Thumpston 2018
Reyland, Nicholas – Thumpston, Rebecca. 'Introduction', in: *Music, Analysis, and the Body: Experiments, Explorations, and Embodiments*, edited by Nicholas Reyland and Thumpston Rebecca, Leuven-Paris-Bristol, Peeters, 2018, pp. 1-14.

Riethmüller 1973
Riethmüller, Albrecht. 'Die Vorstellung des Chaos in der Musik: Zu Haydns Oratorium *Die Schöpfung*', in: *Convivium Cosmologicum: Interdisziplinäre Studien. Helmut Hönl zum 70. Geburtstag*, edited by Anastasios Giannarás, Basel, Birkhäuser Verlag, 1973, pp. 185-195.

Rimsky-Korsakov 1877
Rimsky-Korsakov, Nikolay Andreyevich. *Sto russkikh narodni pesen*, St. Petersburg, Bessel, 1877.

Rimsky-Korsakov 1884-1885
Id. *Uchebnik garmonii*, St. Peterburg, 1884-1885.

Rimsky-Korsakov 1960
Id. *Polnoe sobranie sočinenij: literaturnye proizvedenija i perepiska. 4: Učebnik garmonii*, Moskow, Muzgiz, 1960.

Rimsky-Korsakov 1964
Id. *Principles of Orchestration*, edited by Maximilian Steinberg, translated by Edward Agate, New York, Dover, 1964.

Rimsky-Korsakov 2005
Id. *Practical Manual of Harmony*, translated from the 12th Russian edition by Joseph Achron, edited by Nicholas Hopkins, New York, Fischer, 2005.

Rogers 1968
Rogers, John. 'Some Properties of Non-duplicating Rotational Arrays', in: *Perspectives of New Music*, VII/1 (1968), pp. 80-102.

Bibliography

ROGERS 2004
ROGERS, Lynne. 'A Serial Passage of Diatonic Ancestry in Stravinsky's *The Flood*', in: *Journal of the Royal Musical Association*, CXXIX/2 (2004), pp. 220-239.

ROSE 1986
ROSE, Brian Geoffrey. *Television and the Performing Arts: A Handbook and Reference Guide to American Cultural Programming*, New York, Greenwood Press, 1986.

ROSE 1992
ID. *Televising the Performing Arts: Interviews with Merrill Brockway, Kirk Browning, and Roger Englander*, Westport, Greenwood Press, 1992.

ROWLANDS 1999
ROWLANDS, Mark. *The Body in Mind: Understanding Cognitive Processes*, Cambridge, Cambridge University Press, 1999.

ROWLANDS 2006
ID. *Body Language: Representation in Action*, Cambridge (MA), MIT, 2006.

RUST 1994
RUST, Douglas. 'Stravinsky's Twelve-Note Loom: Composition and Pre-composition in *Movements*', in: *Music Theory Spectrum*, XVI/1 (1994), pp. 62-76.

SAID 1978
SAID, Edward W. *Orientalism*, New York, Pantheon Books, 1978.

SANGUINETTI 1993
SANGUINETTI, Giorgio. 'Il primo studio teorico sulle scale octatoniche: le 'Scale alternate' di Vito Frazzi', in: *Studi Musicali*, XXII/2 (1993), pp. 411-446.

SAVENKO 1995
SAVENKO, Svetlana. '*L'Oiseau de feu*: zur Geschichte der ersten Fassung', in: *Mitteilungen der Paul Sacher Stiftung*, VIII (1995), pp. 31-35.

SCHAEFFNER 1924
SCHAEFFNER, André. 'Une nouvelle forme dramatique: Les chanteurs dans la «fosse»', in: *Revue musicale*, 1 November 1924, pp. 18-36 [also in ID. *Essais de musicologie et autres fantaisies*, Paris, Le Sycomore, 1980, pp. 297-316].

SCHEIJEN 2009
SCHEIJEN, Sjeng. *Diaghilev: A Life*, translated by Jane Hedley-Próle and S. J. Leinbach, Oxford, Oxford Universtity Press, 2009.

BIBLIOGRAPHY

SCHERLIESS 1993

SCHERLIESS, Volker. 'Zur Arbeitsweise Igor Strawinskys – dargestellt an den Symphonies d'instruments à vent', in: *Vom Einfall zum Kunstwerk: der Kompositionsprozess in der Musik des 20. Jahrhunderts*, edited by Hermann Danuser and Günter Katzenberger, Laaber, Laaber-Verlag, 1993.

SCHMIDT 2011

SCHMIDT, Lisa M. 'Sound Matters: Towards an Enactive Approach to Hearing Media', in: *The Soundtrack*, IV/1 (2011), pp. 33-42.

SCHOENBERG 1914

SCHOENBERG, Arnold. [Forward to:] *Pierrot Lunaire*, Op. 21, Vienna, Universal Edition, 1914.

SCHOENBERG 1995

ID. *The Musical Idea, and the Logic, Technique, and Art of Its Presentation*, edited and translated by Patricia Carpenter and Severine Neff, New York, Columbia University Press, 1995.

SCHOLL 1994

SCHOLL, Tim. *From Petipa to Balanchine: Classical Revival and the Modernization of Ballet*, London-New York, Routledge, 1994.

SCHOUVALOFF – BOROVSKY 1982

SCHOUVALOFF, Alexander – BOROVSKY, Victor. *Stravinsky on Stage*, London, Stainer & Bell, 1982.

SCHRÖDER 2018

SCHRÖDER, Julia H. 'Experimental Relations between Music and Dance since the 1950s: Sketch of a Typology', in: *Music-Dance, Sound and Motion in Contemporary Discourse*, edited by Gianfranco Vinay and Patrizia Veroli, London-New York, Routledge, 2018, pp. 141-156.

SEDLMEIER – WEIGELT – WALTHER 2011

SEDLMEIER, Peter – WEIGELT, Oliver – WALTHER, Eva. 'Music is in the Muscle: How Embodied Cognition May Influence Music Preference', in: *Music Perception*, XXVIII/3 (2011), p. 297.

SEEL 2015

SEEL, Martin. 'Realism and Anti-Realism in Film Theory', in: *Critical Horizons*, IX/2 (2015), pp. 157-176.

SÉGOL 2014

SÉGOL, Julien. 'Œdipus rex ou l'œuvre au neutre: un dispositif anti-fictionnel?', in: *Igor Stravinsky: Sounds and Gestures of Modernism*, edited by Massimiliano Locanto, Turnhout, Brepols, 2014 (Speculum Musicae, 25), pp. 363-381.

SHAPIRO 2011

SHAPIRO, Lawrence. *Embodied Cognition*, London-New York, Routledge, 2011.

Bibliography

Shepard 1984
Shepard, John. 'The Stravinsky Nachlass: A Provisional Checklist of Music Manuscripts', in: *Notes*, Second Series, XL/4 (June 1984), pp. 719-750.

Sichardt 1990
Sichardt, Martina. *Die Entstehung der Zwölftonmethode Arnold Schönbergs*, Mainz, Schott, 1990.

Siegel 2018
Siegel, Marcia B. 'Pavilion of Secrets', in: *The Sentient Archive: Bodies, Performance, and Memory*, edited by Bill Bissell and Linda Caruso Haviland, Middleton (CT), Wesleyan University Press, 2018, pp. 228-245.

Smart 2004
Smart, Mary Ann. *Mimomania: Music and Gesture in Nineteenth-Century Opera*, Berkeley-Los Angeles, University of California Press, 2004.

Smith 2000
Smith, Marian. *Ballet and Opera in the Age of Giselle*, Princeton, Princeton University Press, 2010.

Smyth 1997
Smyth, David H. 'Stravinsky at the Threshold: A Sketch Leaf for *Canticum sacrum*', in: *Mitteilungen der Paul Sacher Stiftung*, X (1997), pp. 21-26.

Smyth 1999
Id. 'Stravinsky's Second Crisis: Reading the Early Serial Sketches', in: *Perspectives of New Music*, XXXVII/2 (1999), pp. 117-146.

Smyth 2000
Id. 'Stravinsky as Serialist: The Sketches for *Threni*', in: *Music Theory Spectrum*, XXII/2 (2000), pp. 205-224.

Sorley Walker 1982
Sorley Walker, Kathrine. *De Basil's Ballets Russes*, London-New York, Hutchinson-Atheneum, 1982.

Souritz 1990
Souritz, Elizabeth. *Soviet Choreographers in the 1920s*, edited and translated by Sally Banes, with additional translation by Lynn Visson, Durham-London, Durham University Press, 1990.

Spies 1965a
Spies, Claudio. 'Some Notes on Stravinsky's *Abraham and Isaac*', in: *Perspectives of New Music*, III/2 (1965), pp. 186-209.

Spies 1965b
Id. 'Some Notes on Stravinsky's *Variations*', in: *Perspectives of New Music*, IV/1 (1965), pp. 62-74.

Bibliography

Spies 1967
Id. 'Some Notes on Stravinsky's *Requiem* Settings', in: *Perspectives of New Music*, v/2 (1967), pp. 98-123.

Steshko 2000
Steshko, Joni Lynn. *Stravinsky's «Firebird»: Genesis, Sources, and the Centrality of the 1919 Suite*, Ph.D. Diss., Berkeley-Los Angeles, University of California, 2000.

Straus 1990
Straus, Joseph N. *Introduction to Post-Tonal Theory*, Englewood Cliffs, Prentice-Hall, 1990.

Straus 1991
Id. 'The Progress of a Motive in Stravinsky's *The Rake's Progress*', in: *Journal of Musicology*, ix/2 (1991), pp. 165-185.

Straus 2001
Id. *Stravinsky's Late Music*, Cambridge, Cambridge University Press, 2001.

Stravinsky 1927
Stravinsky, Igor. *My Life and Music – «The Firebird» and «Petrushka»* [Annotations for AudioGraphic Music Rolls, unpublished typescript], Basel, Igor Stravinsky Collection, Paul Sacher Stiftung, microfilm 119.1-001627.

Stravinsky 1928
Id. *My Life and Music – «The Firebird»*, Notes for the Duo-art AudioGraphic roll of *The Firebird*, Aeolian Company LTD, London, rolls nos. D759 (oct. 1928), D761 (Jan. 1929), D763 (Jan. 1929), D765 (Mar. 1929), D767 (Mar. 1929), D769 (Mar. 1929).

Stravinsky 1969
Id. *«The Rite of Spring»: Sketches, 1911-1913*, London, Boosey & Hawkes, 1969.

Stravinsky 1985
Id. *«L'Oiseau de feu» fac-similé du manuscrit Saint-Petersbourg 1909-1910*, studies and commentaries by Louis Cyr, Jean-Jacques Eigeldinger and Pierre Wissmer, Geneva, Minkoff, 1985 [Deluxe full-color facsimile in the original folio format of the orchestral score of the complete ballet composed in St. Petersburg, 1909-1910. Published by the Conservatoire de Musique de Genève on the occasion of their 150th anniversary. Commentary in French and English].

Stravinsky 1996
Id. *L'Oiseau de feu / Жаръ-птица / The Firebird / Feuervogel*, critical edition by Herbert Schneider, London-Mainz, Eulenburg, 1996.

Stravinsky 2013a
Id. *«Le Sacre du Printemps»: Manuscript of the Version for Piano Four Hands: Facsimile*, edited by Felix Meyer, London, Boosey & Hawkes, 2013.

BIBLIOGRAPHY

STRAVINSKY 2013B
ID. «*The Rite of Spring*»: *Facsimile of the Autograph Full Score*, edited by Ulrich Mosch, London, Boosey & Hawkes, 2013.

STRAVINSKY – CRAFT 1978
STRAVINSKY, Vera – CRAFT, Robert. *Stravinsky in Pictures and Documents*, New York, Simon and Schuster, 1978.

SUDNOW 2001
SUDNOW, David. *Ways of the Hand: A Rewritten Account*, foreword by Hubert L. Dreyfus, Cambridge (MA), MIT Press, 2001.

SVETLOV 1911
SVETLOV, Valerian Yakovlevich. *Sovremennyy balet*, St. Petersburg, 1911 [French translation: *Le ballet contemporain*, edited by Léon Bakst, French translation by Michel-Dimitri Calvocoressi, Paris, De Brunoff, 1912].

SWAN 1973
SWAN, ALFRED J. *Russian Music and Its Sources in Chant and Folk Song*, New York, Norton, 1973.

TAPER 1996
TAPER, Bernard. *Balanchine: A Biography*, Berkeley-Los Angeles, University of California Press, 1996.

TAPER 1984
ID. *Balanchine: A Biography*, New York, Time Books, 1984.

TARUSKIN 1985
TARUSKIN, Richard. [Review of:] 'Igor Stravinsky. *L'Oiseau de Feu*. Fac-similé du manuscrit Saint-Pétersbourg, 1909-1910. Geneva: Éditions Minkoff, 1985', in: *Current Musicology*, no. 40 (September 1985), pp. 66-73.

TARUSKIN 1992
ID. "Entoiling the Falconet': Russian Musical Orientalism in Context', in: *Cambridge Opera Journal*, IV/3 (1992), pp. 253-280.

TARUSKIN 1993
ID. 'The Tradition Revisited: Stravinsky's *Requiem Canticles* as Russian Music', in: *Music Theory and the Exploration of the Past*, edited by Christopher Hatch and David W. Bernstein, Chicago, University of Chicago Press, pp. 525-550.

TARUSKIN 1996
ID. *Stravinsky and the Russian Traditions: A Biography of the Works through «Mavra»*, 2 vols., Berkeley-Los Angeles, University of California Press, 1996.

Bibliography

Taruskin 2010
Id. *Music in the Early Twentieth Century*, Oxford-New York, Oxford University Press, 2010 (The Oxford History of Western Music, 4).

Tchaikovsky 1957
Tchaikovsky, Pyotr Ilyich. *Rukovodstvo k prakticheskomu izucheniyu garmonii*, in: Id. *Polnoye sobraniye sochineniy. 3a*, edited by Vladimir Protopopov, Moscow, Gosudarstvennoe Muzikalnoye Izdatelstvo, 1957, pp. 1-162.

Ter-Arutunian 1966
Ter-Arutunian, Rouben. 'In Search of Design', in: *Dance Perspectives*, xxviii (1966), pp. 6-48.

Treitler 1959
Treitler, Leo. 'Harmonic Procedure in the Fourth Quartet of Béla Bartók', in: *Journal of Music Theory*, iii/2 (1959), pp. 292-298.

Tucker 1992
Tucker, Susannah. *Stravinsky and His Sketches: The Composition of Agon and Other Serial Works of the 1950s*, 2 vols., Ph.D. Diss., Oxford, Oxford University, 1992.

Tymoczko 2002
Tymoczko, Dmitri. 'Stravinsky and the Octatonic: A Reconsideration', in: *Music Theory Spectrum*, xxiv/1 (2002), pp. 68-102.

Van den Toorn 1983
Van den Toorn, Pieter C. *The Music of Igor Stravinsky*, New Haven (CT), Yale University Press, 1983.

Van den Toorn 1987
Id. *Stravinsky and the «Rite of Spring»: The Beginnings of a Musical Language*, Berkeley-Los Angeles, University of California Press, 1987.

Van den Toorn – McGinness 2012
Id. – McGinness, John. *Stravinsky and the Russian Period: Sound and Legacy of a Musical Idiom*, Cambridge, Cambridge University Press, 2012.

Van den Toorn – Tymoczko 2003
Id. – Tymoczko, Dmitri. 'Colloquy about «Stravinsky and the Octatonic: a Reconsideration»', in: *Music Theory Spectrum*, xxv/1 (2003), pp. 167-203.

Varunts 1997
Varunts, Viktor. *Igor Stravinskiy: Perepiska s russkimi korrespondentami. Materiali k biographi. 1*, Moskow, Sovietskij Kompozitor, 1997.

BIBLIOGRAPHY

VEROLI 2014

VEROLI, Patrizia. 'Un balletto "ritrovato"? La cosiddetta ricostruzione del *Sacre du Printemps* di Nižinsky (1987)', in: *Cento Primavere. Ferocità e feracità del «Sacre du Printemps»*, edited by Nicoletta Betta and Marida Rizzuti, Turin, Edizioni dell'Orso, 2014, pp. 39-62.

VEROLI – VINAY 2013

I Ballets Russes di Diaghilev tra storia e mito. 1, edited by Patrizia Veroli and Gianfranco Vinay, 2 vols., Rome, Accademia Nazionale di Santa Cecilia, 2013 (L'arte armonica. Serie IV: Iconografia e cataloghi, 5).

VINAY 1987

VINAY, Gianfranco. *Stravinsky neoclassico. L'invenzione della memoria nel '900 musicale*, Venice, Marsilio, 1987.

VINAY 1993

ID. 'Le geste ou le mot: Stravinsky ou le refus de la bigamie en musique', in: *Les Cahiers du CIREM*, special issue: *Musique et geste*, XXVI-XXVII (1993), pp. 91-96.

VINAY 2007

ID. 'Abbozzi della discordia: Gide, Stravinsky e *Perséphone*', in: *«Musica se extendit ad omia». Studi in onore di Alberto Basso in occasione del suo 75° compleanno*, edited by Rosy Moffa and Sabrina Saccomani, Lucca, LIM, 2007 (Collana dell'Istituto per i beni musicali in Piemonte), pp. 843-857.

WALDEN 1979

WALDEN, William. 'Stravinsky's Movements for Piano and Orchestra: The Relationship of Formal Structure, Serial Technique, and Orchestration', in: *Journal of the Canadian Association of University Schools of Music*, IX/1 (1979), pp. 73-95.

WALSH 1993

WALSH, Stephen. *Stravinsky: «Œdipus Rex»*, Cambridge, Cambridge University Press, 1993.

WALSH 1999

ID. *Stravinsky – A Creative Spring: Russia and France, 1882-1934*, Berkeley-Los Angeles, University of California Press, 1999.

WALSH 2006

ID. *Stravinsky – The Second Exile: France and America. 1934-1971*, London, Jonathan Cape, 2006.

WALSH 2017

ID. 'Dionysos Monometrikos', in: NEFF-CARR – HORLACHER 2017, pp. 402-416.

WHITE 1979

WHITE, Eric Walter. *Stravinsky: The Composer and His Works*, Berkeley-Los Angeles, University of California Press, 1966, ²1979.

Bibliography

WHITE 1997
ID. *Stravinsky: A Critical Survey, 1882-1946*, Minelola (NY), Dover, 1997.

WILEY 1984
WILEY, Roland John. 'The Symphonic Element in Nutcracker', in: *The Musical Times*, CXXV/1702 (1984), pp. 693-695.

WILEY 1985
ID. *Tchaikovsky's Ballets*, Oxford, Oxford University Press, 1985.

WILEY 1985
ID. *Tchaikowsky's Ballet: «Swan Lake», «Sleeping Beauty», «Nutcracker»*, Oxford, Clarendon Press, 1985.

ZBIKOWSKI 2002
ZBIKOWSKI, Lawrence M. *Conceptualizing Music: Cognitive Structure, Theory, and Analysis*, Oxford-New York, Oxford University Press, 2002.

ZBIKOWSKI 2011
ID. 'Musical Gesture and Musical Grammar. A Cognitive Approach', in: GRITTEN – KING 2011, pp. 83-98.

ZIEHN 1976
ZIEHN, Bernhard. *Canonical Studies: A New Technique in Composition*, Milwaukee-Berlin, A. Kaun-Richard Kaun, 1912; reprint *Canonic Studies*, edited by Ronald Stevenson, London, Kahn & Averill, 1976.

INDEX OF NAMES

A

ADAM, Adolphe 112

ADAMS, Diana 37

ADORNO, Theodor Wiesengrund 302

AFANASEYEV, Aleksandr 64, 185

AGAWU, Kofi 1, 87

ALBRIGHT, Daniel 19

ANANIASHVILI, Nina 55

ANGIOLINI, Gasparo 106

APPIA, Adolphe 5-6

ARCHER, Kenneth 47, 49, 55

ARDOLINO, Emile 30

ARENSKY, Anton 65

ASHTON, Frederick 52

AUDEN, Wystan Hugh 19, 306

AUSLANDER, Philip 320

B

BABBITT, Milton 255, 259, 304

BACH, Johann Sebastian 265

BADOARO, Giacomo 307

BAKST, Léon 12, 45, 55, 63-64, 81, 113, 179-180

BALAKIREV, Mily Alekseyevich 185, 191

BALANCHINE, George 28-31, 35, 37, 42-43, 50-51, 59, 115, 299, 301-303, 305, 308, 313-318, 320-322, 324, 328-330, 340, 345, 349, 355-357, 359, 361-362

BANES, Sally 181-182, 184, 187

BARANOVA MONIGHETTI, Tatiana x, 244

BARNES, Jennifer 301, 326-327

BARON, Auguste 109

BARTHOLONI, Jean 71

BARTÓK, Béla 221, 261-262

BEAUMONT, Cyril 89-90, 100, 107, 165

BEETHOVEN, Ludwig van 197, 208, 211

BENJAMIN, Leanne 53, 183

BENOIS, Alexandre 6, 10-11, 14-15, 17, 20-21, 60, 64-65, 69, 89, 117, 178, 184, 192

BERG, Alban 221, 260-262, 297, 313

BERGER, Arthur 230, 237

BERIOSOVA, Svetlana 52

BILIBIN, Ivan 51, 117, 185

BLASIS, Carlo 108

BLEEK, Thobias 217

BLISS, Arthur 327

BLOCK, Aleksandr 13

BLUM, René 50

BOCCHERINI, Luigi vii

BOLM, Adolph 45, 51

BOLTER, Jay David 321

BONONCINI, Giovanni Maria 224

BORIO, Gianmario x

BORNOFF, Jack 318

BOSS, Jack 260-261

BOULEZ, Pierre 251

BRAHMS, Johannes 160, 217

BRECHT, Bertolt 17

BRENTANO, Franz 201
BRITTEN, Benjamin 318
BROOK, Peter 5
BROWNING, Kirk 305, 314-317, 320, 322, 324, 329, 340, 345, 354-355
BRUN, Dominique 49
BRYULLOV, Vladimir Aleksandrovich 84
BRYULLOVA, Alina 84
BRYUSOV, Valéry 6
BUCHANAN, Melonie Annete 111
BUCKLE, Richard 59, 184
BULGAKOV, Alexey 50, 111
BUONARROTI, Michelangelo 361
BUSONI, Ferruccio 6, 224
BYRON, George Gordon, Lord 21

C

CABOT, Sebastian 301
CAPLIN, William 85
CAPORALETTI, Vincenzo 202-203
CARR, Maureen x, 126
CASELLA, Alfredo 13
CAWLEY, Arthur 307
CECCHETTI, Enrico 106, 111, 185
CERCHIAI, Luca x
CHAGALL, Marc 51
CHECCACCI, Federica x
CHERUBINI, Luigi 87
CHOPIN, Fryderyk 65
CHOUQUET, Gustave 108
COCTEAU, Jean 356
COLEMAN, Emily 304
CONSOLO, Ernesto 231, 233
COOK, Nicholas 24-25, 209, 338
COOPER, Barry 209
COPE, Jonathan 53, 114, 183
COPEAU, Jacques 5-6
CORALLI, Jean 87
CORAZZA, Elia Andrea 30
COWELL, Henry 195-196, 206, 273
CRAFT, Robert 63, 71, 75, 197-198, 207, 210, 212, 218, 220, 254-255, 259, 272-274, 296, 299,

301, 304-305, 307-308, 312-313, 317-320, 327, 338, 342, 345, 357
CRAIG, Edward Gordon 5-6
CULLBERG, Birgit 321
CYR, Louis 63, 67, 70-71, 74, 117
CZERNY, Carl 220
CZINNER, Paul 53

D

D'AMBOISE, Jacques [Joseph Jacques Ahearn] 299, 301, 318, 361
DANILOVA, Alexandra 54-55
DAVIS, Mary E. 181
DE BASIL, Wassily [Vassily Grigorievich Voskresensky] 50, 57
DENHAM, Serge 50
DENIS, Ruth St. [Ruthie Dennis] 29
DIAGHILEV, Serge [Sergey Pavlovich] 6, 7, 10-13, 18, 48-54, 57, 59, 64-66, 69-71, 81, 89-90, 94, 99, 101, 116, 120-121, 178, 183-184, 186-187, 192
DIDELOT, Charles-Louis 59, 82
DOLIN, Anton 48
DREW, David 53
DREYFUS, Hubert 225
DRIGO, Riccardo 66, 83
DRUPSTEEN, Jaap 300
DÜBGEN, Hannah 300
DUFOUR, Valérie x
DUNCAN, Isadora 46, 90, 190
DUVERNOY, Alphonse 83, 88

E

EHRENBERG, Vladimir 14
EISENSTEIN, Sergei 94-95
ELIOT, Thomas S. 305-307, 319
EVAN, Edwin 126, 174-175, 178
EWELL, Philip 227

F

FARRELL, Suzanne 28, 30, 35-37, 42-43
FATYKHOVA-OKUNEVA, Elmira 230
FERY, Jean 332

FLAMM, Christoph 68-69, 117-118
FOKINA, Vera 50
FOKINE, Isabelle 55-57, 109, 114, 117
FOKINE, Michail viii, 45-46, 50-51, 53-61, 63-65, 67-69, 71, 73-75, 81-82, 89-91, 93-95, 97-101, 104-110, 113-114, 116-117, 120-121, 124-125, 144, 165, 181-183, 185-189, 192-193
FOKINE, Vitale 46
FONTEYN, Margot 52, 182
FORCE, David x
FORTE, Allen 24
FRANCO, Susanne x
FRAZZI, Vito 231
FUCHS, Georg 5-13

G

GIDE, André 17, 19
GLAZUNOV, Aleksandr Konstantinovich 59, 65-66, 82, 120, 230
GLINKA, Mikhail Ivanovich 121, 173, 178, 186, 331
GOLOVIN, Aleksandr 45, 51, 54-55, 63-64, 69, 124, 179
GONCHAROVA, Natalia 51-52
GORSKY, Aleksandr 90
GOZZI, Carlo 17
GRAFF, Robert 254, 301-302, 306
GREENBERG, Clement 302
GRIEG, Edvard 65
GRIFFITHS, Graham x, 198-199, 207, 215-216, 219-220, 226
GRIGORIEV, Serge 50, 52-53, 101, 104
GROSS-HUGO, Valentine 49
GRUSIN, Richard 321
GUEST, Ann Hutchinson 49

H

HALÉVY, Fromental 87
HARCOURT-SMITH, Simon 304-305
HARRISON, Jay S. 254
HARVEY, Lawrence 301, 347
HATTEN, Robert 1, 26-28, 35-36, 87
HAVELOCK, Eric 208

HAYDN, Franz Joseph 331-332
HODGINS, Paul 28-29
HODSON, Millicent 47, 49, 55
HOGARTH, William 21
HUSSERL, Edmund 200-201
HUXLEY, Aldous 303

I

IASTREBTSEV, Vasily 231
IELLATCHITCH-STRAVINSKY, Marie x
ILLIANO, Roberto x
ISHERWOOD, Christopher 303
IUZHIN, Vladimir Vasilyevich 70
IVANOV, Lev 84

J

JAQUES-DALCROZE, Émile 29, 49
JESCHKE, Claudia 49
JILLANA [Jill Zimmerman] 301, 361
JOHNSON, Mark 26-27, 31, 200
JORDAN, Stephanie x, 26, 37-38, 45, 49, 51, 72-73
JOSEPH, Charles 71, 74, 82, 198, 219-220, 300, 303-304, 312, 314
JURGENSON, Pyotr 71, 74-75, 77, 102, 187

K

KAISER, Georg 5
KALLMAN, Chester 19
KARSAVINA, Tamara 45, 50, 52, 90-91, 101, 103, 181-185, 187
KAWAKAMI, Otojirō 8-9
KELLER, Maurice 65
KERMAN, Joseph 24
KINBERG, Judy 30
KIRSTEIN, Lincoln 192, 303
KOCHNO, Boris 21, 184
KOENIG, Wolf 301
KONRADI, Herman 84
KONRADI, Nikolay 84
KRAMER, Jonathan 35
KRENEK, Ernst 39, 259, 296, 334
KRIEG, Kaitlyn x

Kroitor, Roman 301
Kubrick, Stanley 306
Kuchka, Mighty 13
Kuralt, Charles 301

L

Lakoff, George 26-27, 31, 200
Leacock, Richard 301
Le Guin, Elizabeth vii
Leman, Marc 199, 201-202
Lenormand, René 222
Levinson, André 95, 107, 189
Liebermann, Rolf 301
Liepa, Andris 55-56
Liepa, Ekaterina 55
Liepa, Maris 55
Lieven, Peter, Prince 118
Liszt, Franz 231
Littmann, Max 12
Locanto, Giulio x
Lopokova, Lydia 50, 184
Lopukhov, Fedor 51, 54-55, 72-73, 89, 104
Lyadov, Anatoly 65-66
Lyon, Robert 175

M

Macdonald, Dwight 302
MacGibbon, Ross 55
Maeterlinck, Maurice 11
Mahler, Gustav 217
Malipiero, Francesco 6, 13
Markova, Alicia 51
Marschner, Heinrich 87
Mason, Monica 53
Massine, Léonide 47-50, 114
Matthew, Paul 218
McFarland, Mark 126, 129, 140, 175-177
McLuhan, Marshall 217
Méhul, Étienne-Nicolas 87
Menary, Richard 203-205, 220
Menotti, Gian Carlo 318, 326-327
Merleau-Ponty, Maurice 200-201, 225

Meyer, Felix 74, 198, 206, 216
Meyerbeer, Giacomo 14, 87
Meyerhold, Vsevolod 5-6, 8-11, 13, 17
Minkus, Ludwig 66, 83, 87-89
Minsky, Nikolai 15
Mitusov, Stepan 14
Monelle, Raymond 87
Monteverdi, Claudio 307
Moore, John x
Morabito, Fulvia x
Mosch, Ulrich 216, 248
Musorgsky [Mussorgsky; Moussorgsky],
    Modest Petrovich 65, 118, 186

N

Nabokov, Nicholas 255
Newman, Arnold 272-274
Nezhny, Anatoly 55
Nezhny, Anna 55
Niccolai, Michela x
Nicholas, Larraine 45
Nijinska, Bronislava 49
Nijinsky, Vaslav 12, 47-50, 60-61, 184-185, 192
Nikitina, Varvara 185
Noverre, Jean-Georges 59, 82, 106-107

O

Oettingen, Arthur von 222
Ong, Walter 208
Oppenheim, David 301

P

Pasler, Jann 3
Pasticci, Susanna x
Pavlova, Anna 105, 184, 187
Perle, George 233, 261
Perrot, Jules 87
Petipa, Marius 12, 59, 66, 82, 84, 86, 120, 185
Philipp, Isidor 219
Pierné, Gabriel 50, 64, 104
Pirandello, Luigi 5, 17
Pizzetti, Ildebrando 231

INDEX OF NAMES

PONOMARE, Vladimir 55
POWELL, Michael 305
PUGNI, Cesare 66, 83, 86, 89, 120
PUSHKIN, Aleksandr 21

R

RAKSIN, David 302
RAMBERT, Marie 49
RAMEAU, Jean-Philippe 332
RAMUZ, Charles-Ferdinand 17
RATNER, Leonard G. 1, 87
RATZ, Erwin 85
RAVEL, Maurice 98, 217, 245
REMIZOV, Aleksey 64, 187
REYLAND, Nicholas 25
RIMSKY-KORSAKOV, Andrey Nikolayevich 6-7, 10
RIMSKY-KORSAKOV, Nikolay Andreyevich 6, 11, 65,
    69, 91-93, 98, 118, 121, 124-125, 130, 143,
    148, 165, 173, 181, 185-186, 190-191, 196,
    215, 218-219, 226-231, 234, 237
ROERICH, Nikolay Konstantinovich 47, 104
ROSE, Brian 314, 317
ROWLAND, Mark 201, 203
RUBINSTEIN, Anton 91
RUBINSTEIN, Artur 197
RUST, Douglas 285, 293

S

SAID, Edward 179
SAINT-LÉON, Arthur 120
SALA, Massimiliano x
SAVENKO, Svetlana 67
SAWYER, Elisabeth 29
SCHAEFFNER, André 20
SCHILDER, Paul 201
SCHNEIDER, Herbert 63
SCHOENBERG, Arnold 85, 160, 213, 219, 221, 255,
    259-262, 297, 334, 359
SCHOLL, Tim 11-12, 95
SCHUMANN, Robert 65
SCRIABIN, Aleksandr 102, 221
SECHTER, Simon 224

SÉGOL, Julien 347
SEREBRIAKOVA, Yana 55
SHAKESPEARE, William 307
SHAWN, Ted 29
SHILKRET, Nathaniel 346
SICHARDT, Martina 260
SIDIMUS, Joysanne x, 357
SIEGEL, Marcia B. 54, 56, 182-183
SMIRNOV, Dmitrij 101
SMITH, Marian 61, 88, 108, 112
SOMES, Michael 52, 182
SONTAG, Susan 321
SPOHR, Louis 87
STANISLAVSKY, Konstantin 6, 11, 95
STEINBERG, Maximilian 218
STELLETSKY, Dmitry 64
STEPANOV, Vladimir 49
STRAUS, Joseph 1-2, 256, 258, 268, 274, 288, 331
STRAUSS, Richard 160
STRAVINSKY, Catherine 71
STRAVINSKY, Fyodor 7
STRAVINSKY, Soulima 198, 220
STRICK, Joseph 304
STRUVE, Nikolai von 208
SUDNOW, David 225-226, 230

T

TAGLIONI, Filippo 112
TAIROV, Aleksandr 9
TALLCHIEF, Marie 51
TANEYEV, Sergey 65
TAPER, Bernard 314
TARUSKIN, Richard 13, 17-19, 59, 64, 67, 81, 92-93,
    95, 101, 121, 124, 126, 129, 144, 165, 185-186,
    227, 230-231, 234, 240
TCHAIKOVSKY, Modest Il'yich 84
TCHAIKOVSKY, Pyotr Il'yich 59, 61, 72, 82-84, 89, 98,
    227
TCHEREPNIN, Nikolay 64-66
TCHERNICHEVA, Lubov 52-53
TECK, Katherine 29
TER-ARUTUNIAN, Rouben 305, 314, 316-317, 320,

324, 329, 340, 349-350, 361
THOMAS, Dylan 305-307
THUMPSTON, Rebecca 25
TIMOFEYEV, Grigory Nikolayevich 207
TODD, Arthur 314, 320
TREITLER, Leo 261
TUČA, Michail 165, 191
TUCKER, Susannah 265, 278
TZAEVICH, Ivan 68

V

VALOIS, Ninette de 51
VAN DEN TOORN, Pieter 175, 230, 239
VERDI, Giuseppe 14, 313, 345
VEROLI, Patrizia x, 49
VIGANÒ, Salvatore 106
VILLELLA, Edward 301, 354
VINAY, Gianfranco x, 18
VISHNEVA, Diana 55
VSEVOLOZHSKY, Ivan 89

W

WAGNER, Richard 6, 11, 14-15, 87-88, 95, 144, 157,
        160
WALSH, Stephen 7, 100, 124, 318
WEBER, Carl Maria von 87
WEBERN, Anton 221, 260-262, 297
WEILL, Kurt 5
WHITE, Walter 253
WILEY, Roland 61, 72-73, 84, 89

Y

YACCO, Sada 8-9
YAKOVLEV, Andrei 55

Z

ZBIKOWSKI, Lawrence 200
ZIEHN, Bernhard 224
ZIMMERMANN, Heidy x